Dragon KING

RULER OF THE REALM

C.C. RAE

Calypso Books®

**DRAGON KING
RULER OF THE REALM**

This is a work of fiction. All the characters, names, incidents, organizations, and dialog in this novel are either the products of the author's imagination or are used fictitiously.

Calypso Books titles may be ordered through booksellers or at www.ccrae.com

ISBN: 978-0-578-58623-6 (hc)
ISBN: 978-0-578-58621-2 (sc)
ISBN: 978-0-578-58622-9 (e)

A pulse of light rolled out from the origin of the unwavering light beam, overtaking the city in a flash, enveloping them where they stood for a blinding moment. Seconds later a warm, tingling breeze rolled through Atrium, rushing up the slope of the hill and washing over them.

Nicole turned to him, "What was that?" Her voice was quietand hoarse and her face pinched with concern.

"I—uh …" His thoughts lurched back to Venarius at the bottom of the hill—but when Raiden looked again, he could not find the man where he had been standing only moments ago. "I don't know," he said, dragging his gaze back to her. The weight of fear resisted the lightness of relief in his chest—she was alive, they'd overcome the Council, proved his visions wrong; and yet, there was still Venarius. His gaze fell from her face, following her troubled eyes—she was looking at his chest with a curious expression.

She raised her hand and lifted a crystal key that was hanging from a cord around his neck, turning it between her fingers before her quizzical eyes. But he was distracted by the key hanging around *her* neck, and lifted the dark crystal cluster that had been carved into a key. Her gaze flicked between what lie in her hand and what lie in his.

Then she looked up at him, her eyes wide with dreadful realization.

"Oh no," she murmured.

Raiden swallowed the lump in his throat, and they looked to the column of light, still reaching up into the night, beckoning them toward the heart of Veil.

The Hidden Magic Series

Hidden Magic

Lost Prophecy

Dragon King

Read the comic on WEBTOON
HMHS

Acknowledgments

This book would not have been possible without my friend and editor Karmen Leggett. Thank you, Ms. Leggett. You were the toughest teacher I had in my entire academic career and, to this day, you help me strive to be a better writer. Thank you for your generous dedication of so much time and care to this literary child of mine. Most of all, thank you for your endless encouragement, your constructive criticism, your love, and your support.

To my students,
There will be bad days, but there will
always be people who care.
Thanks for all the good days in Room 202.
Love, Ms. Rae

☙

To my readers,
Thank you for taking this journey
with Nicole, Raiden and Gordan.
Please know that this is
not the end of their story,
but we are embarking on the
darkest chapter.
This book is about trauma,
and the struggle to heal,
but as always we
will face it
together.

N
W E
S
Navn
Pharos
Taroth
Besina
Wayward
Sea
Witch
Haven
Atrium
Candhrid
Cantis

Orodon
Coron
sor
Elysian
Sea
Meridian
idlands
ol
Hypatia
Eanna
Avalon
Sea
Tine
Avalon

Gordan's thoughts roiled in a storm of worry around Nicole, and he did his best to believe he had done the right thing, leaving her there on that beach. He wanted to turn around and go back to her the entire return trip to the wastelands, but he told himself that was selfish—that wanting to be with his friend didn't matter more than her safety. He was conspicuous—even in human form, people would recognize his eyes as clearly as they'd spot a dragon in the skies. He told himself that it was wrong to think she couldn't reach the city and find Raiden on her own, yet his heart kept straining to turn around.

He left her on the shore just after sunrise, and it took him until sundown to reach the wastelands. The prospect of returning to the dragon haven in the middle of the mountains made him feel heavier than the mental acrobatics it took to leave Nicole alone. The ruins scattered at the edge of the plains at the feet of the mountain range was as far as he cared to go. There was nothing for him among his kind, so he curled up and slept among the pillars of a broken temple.

He spent each day since his return to the wastelands watching the horizon even though he knew it would take her time to get to

Atrium, and time to find Raiden before the Council could find her. His anxiety festered, but it was too late now. If he went back, he would have to find her, or do what he hated most and step into the ether, hoping that when he emerged, he wouldn't be jeopardizing her safety. His fears of putting her at risk smothered his thoughts of being by her side. Instead he had to believe that she found Raiden, that they were biding their time to find a way out of the city, and that they would materialize out of the winds together.

The only way he could tolerate the waiting was to point his gaze in her direction, an effort to peer through that immense space between them and catch an impossible glimpse to see they were all right and on their way.

All there was for him to see day after day was the parched blue sky hanging over the crumbling graveyard of the old world, fragments and ruins from every corner of the world left behind. He lay atop the ridges at the edge of the mountains where he could watch the plains and the horizon, his long body draped over the rocks like a miserable cast-out hide. To pass the time, he flicked his tail against the rocks. Every now and then he let out a fiery sigh into the bitter breeze. Once each day, he stretched his wings out over the emptiness to spend some time in the company of the blistering cold winds that hissed to him *Nicole and Raiden will not come.*

This was not so different from his life before the tower, before them. He had grown accustomed to that solitude once before and with each day that passed, he attempted to sidle back into that bitterly familiar place. Still, it was difficult to sink into his old life while keeping his eyes on the horizon in case the winds were wrong.

The sea was a thread-thin ribbon of blue to make the pale sky jealous. His keen eyes could just reach the ocean on clear days, but the island of Cantis and the mainland far beyond were as imaginary to him as the old world was to all of Veil. Six days passed since he left Nicole on the beach of the mainland. What he would have given for Raiden's gift of the Sight, to know if Nicole was in his future, no matter how distant.

For six days he questioned his choice to let her go alone. For five days, he watched the horizon lie straight and steadfast, a staring contest he was doomed to lose. The horizon never blinked, no matter how harsh the gritty winds or how blinding the sun. At night the flat blue wall at the end of the world as he knew it transformed into an infinite strait of stars, and strange lights drifted out of the ruins after sunset to hang in the air.

Gordan didn't really know what the lights were. They retreated into the ruins at dawn and every dusk they emerged like fireflies, perhaps lingering traces of the magic that made this realm, whisking the people and pieces of the old world to their new safe haven. Maybe they were wisps of that long-lost wild magic from the beginning of everything, primordial phantoms of change in the night.

It was in that vividly bright darkness on the sixth night that the horizon finally broke under his gaze and blinked. A razor-sharp column of light erupted out of the distance, slicing straight up through the stars, beyond the edge of the wastelands, beyond the Wayward Sea, beyond Cantis even.

When a ripple of hazy light rolled across the distance and washed over him, his heart seized on this strange phenomenon and believed it could only be a sign of one thing—Nicole. Somehow, he knew this beacon led to her, but its unwavering presence struck him with a sour note of dread. The stunning stream of light was a rift in the sky like daylight slipping through the crack in a door left ajar into a dark room.

He jumped up from the rocks, expecting that door of the night sky to swing open and let the light flood the whole world—but the brilliant white thread remained constant, taut and straight in the sky, concealing its meaning in silence. His heart twisted with the uncertainty. Was that light her triumph or her end?

He could not stay in the wastelands watching that beacon. The hole left by his friend's absence was as significant as the one left by the loss of his only love to Death long ago. He and Nicole were two creatures of the same substance, not blood or bone or parentage, but that deeper immaterial matter of a person. Of all the other dragons in his brood there was no doubt shared lineage, the same sire or dam or even both, but he never knew true kinship until Nicole. He would gladly face the pending death sentence waiting for him on the mainland to find out what happened to her rather than spend millennia never knowing.

He heaved a tremendous sigh into the night, and leapt off the ridge into the air, keeping the beacon in his sight. As each hour of his long journey passed, he stared it down, but it did not fade, flicker or waver—not even when dawn threw its pale blue blanket over the stars. The sun rose to the east and beside it the column of light stood, a white line straining to shine through the coming brightness of the day.

The light of day spread and the shining beacon grew fainter in the blue sky. At last the horizon could no longer taunt him. Instead it recoiled, rolling backward to keep its distance as he advanced eastward.

The wastelands were shrinking behind him by the time the last star disappeared into the daylight. The time that passed watching the ocean below him was more frustrating than lying on the rocks and watching the horizon. Even though every minute brought him closer to the mainland, each minute would slip by no faster than the last and every hour slogged along slowly, weighed down by his worries.

He saw Cantis float toward him across the ocean, and he watched it pass beneath him like the sad debris of a shipwreck drifting on the currents. He wondered if anyone would ever return to that island to revive it, but who could ever see that cemetery as a place to live? Once Cantis was behind him and only half his journey to the coast remained, he felt lonelier than before. He could not stop himself from thinking of the last time he made this crossing, carrying someone no less dear than his own heart, her voice in his ear and her arms around his neck.

This time he had nothing but the roaring wind to fill his ears —it spoke only of storms, storms of the sea crashing against the land and storms of men converging on each other. The winds knew the world better than the sun, for the sun knew not what transpired during her nightly absences. But Gordan didn't want to hear about storms, he wanted to hear about Nicole. He supposed he had to be grateful that all the blustering air currents wanted to whistle into his head today was nonsense about change. The worlds were always changing and so the winds were the ancient senile soothsayers rambling on as always until their wisdom turned to predictable nonsense.

Gordan took a deep breath, tasting the salt in the air and heaving his anxieties out of his chest for a brief respite until more seeped out of his heart, an endless cycle. The sight of the mainland on the ocean twisted and pulled his stomach between relief and fear. *Maybe she'll be there, standing on the beach right where I left her*, his heart mused in its pained delirium. But as he glided down close enough to the water to feel an invigorating spray against his face and the beach rushed forward to meet him, there was nothing but silent sands and shushing waves reminding him to be quiet, stay hidden. *You aren't welcome here*, the waves hissed at him as he looked up and down the shoreline for a sign he would not find.

He had a choice to make, transform on the beach and travel slow and as well-concealed as he could, or keep flying and let himself be seen. He didn't want to trade any more time for safety, so he kept his wings stretched wide and gave a few strong thrusts to climb back into the sky as the beach rushed by beneath him. Gliding over the trees—a sea of shriveled brown hands reaching into the air with waiting claws—his gaze swept back and forth, his mind returned to the dangers of a lost time in the old world when men through savagery against anything unlike themselves hunted dragons to prove they were brave and to prove their god was true.

A vivid island of green seized his attention. He could not pull his gaze away, and although he knew he should keep flying, something about that peculiar patch of summer in a brown winter quilt whispered *Nicole* to him. As he drew nearer, he spotted the modest cottage and before he even touched the ground, he felt her all around this place.

He landed in the soft grass of the small clearing around the house. Until that moment, he hadn't noticed the girl, perhaps because she hadn't moved, or hadn't screamed as he approached. As he regarded her, gazing wide-eyed back at him, he could be sure she had indeed seen him, thus, her composure baffled him. She sat perched on an old thick-woven basket, half buckled under her weight.

The urgency drumming in his chest pushed him to speak to the girl, but he knew it would be an easier transaction if he looked a little more human. So, he begrudgingly summoned up the magic he needed to condense himself into the shape of a man, remembering to conjure up some pants in the process, which—in his haste—resulted in a replica of the first garment to come to his mind: the pair of loose plaid trousers he had seen Nicole's brother Mitchell wearing their first morning together in Tucson.

To Gordan's surprise, as he settled into his small human frame and crossed the grass between himself and the house, he spotted a smile on the girl's face. The place radiated with Nicole's presence. The breeze that slipped out from the rustling trees, the earth beneath his feet, even the very stones of the cottage before him hummed with Nicole.

"She's not here," the girl said dragging his attention back to her—cloud of tight black curl around her kind dark face.

"I beg your pardon?"

"She left days ago," the girl continued.

The door of the cottage opened and a tall willowy woman stepped outside, not seeing Gordan at first. "Fen, who are you talking—oh," she gave a tiny start at the sight of him. Was it the grayish skin that glistened ever so minutely like scales? Perhaps the violet eyes and sharp narrow pupils?

"I told him Nicole is already gone," Fen said.

"How could you possibly know I am looking for Nicole?" Gordan finally took command of his voice.

"Isn't everyone?" Fen asked with a short laugh.

The woman interjected, "she carried Dragon's Breath with her for one thing… and Nicole is the kind to befriend a dragon, isn't she?" She chuckled. "Not to mention anyone wearing that, well," she gestured toward the garment on his lower half to conclude—it certainly had the odd look of the old world.

Gordan was far less interested in her summations and more concerned with the confirmation that Nicole had been here. "How long ago did she leave?"

"Three days," the woman answered with concern weighing down her words.

Fen frowned.

"Is there any chance you know what that light means?" Gordan pressed further, turning his gaze toward the white line of light, faint to the northwest but ever steadfast.

"Some travelers popped through Witch Haven this morning and said the light is coming from the old palace. I don't put much stock in gossip, though," the woman said with a shrug.

"They're saying the keys have been claimed," Fen added.

"They can't possibly know that," the woman said.

"I'm not saying it's a fact, but it sounds possible, doesn't it?"

"I suppose." The woman wrung her hands, fingers stained green—*she's a floramor*, Gordan realized. He could feel their worry knotting in the air, but he had to detach himself from this oasis of Nicole's presence and people who loved her. They had no more information for him. He turned away, supposing his departure would be rather appreciated.

"Are you going after Nicole?" the girl called after him when he was several paces away.

He answered over his shoulder. "Yes."

"When you find her, will you tell her we miss her?"

Gordan could feel Fen's sadness reaching through the breeze, straining across the distance. The woman stood beside Fen looking at him with a similar plea in her eyes, her mouth pressed into a firm worried line. How like Nicole—he smiled to himself.

"I will," he replied.

Fen straightened up a little with cheer and smiled at him. Before he turned away, Gordan spotted a third figure, a smaller girl, standing just enough in the threshold to peer around the doorframe at him. A pale face framed by straight black hair. Her dark eyes glinted with depth beyond her years and they bored into him hopefully. He turned away from the little family and, he hoped, toward Nicole.

Nicole wrenched herself out of the Council's great hall, snapping her eyes open with relief to find she was back in Raiden's apartment. She wasn't holding his sword, her body was her own—yet she couldn't help feeling suspicious of the peaceful silence around her as her heart continued to race. *Where is he?*

Now that she was awake, she remembered how she had ended up here, balled up on the small couch in a cradle of cushions. She wasn't sure how long she had slept. Her body still ached, drained and battered by her abuse of that inner power last night. Her mind was filled with anxious static, glad to be awake despite her lingering exhaustion.

She reminded herself what was real. Last night she reclaimed her body from the Council, and she killed them, but she lost herself somewhere dark. Had she really won, when they succeeded in pushing her to be exactly what they insisted she was? When she dragged herself back from that black pit inside her, Raiden was there. The courts were destroyed, the great hall in her nightmare was no more. A blinding beacon erupted into the sky and a wave of light washed over the city.

Dropping her gaze, she saw the key hanging from her neck. A

dark purple cluster of quartz carved into a rough key. *I guess that was real too.* She vaguely remembered trying to navigate their way through the rubble of the courts when her body gave up completely. The last thing she remembered was the firm warmth of Raiden's arms, but where was he now?

Her straining bladder pushed her off the couch cushions. She unfolded her stiff legs and set her feet on the floor, then she heaved her weight up and stood for a swaying second before shuffling across the living room and through the kitchen to the bathroom. Once she plopped down onto the toilet, she sagged, relief streaming beneath her. Her mind cleared just a little, making room for her senses again. A cut in her sleeve caught her attention. There was an angry red scratch across the inside of her forearm, stinging with freshness. She stared at it, not recalling the cause, then decided it must just be another of her many scrapes and bruises from last night.

She realized Gim was draped over her collarbones, curled around her neck in his favorite spot, but she didn't know when he had emerged from his hiding place. The thought of Gordan struck her heart, a cold note of sadness ringing through her chest as she ran her fingertips along the warm scaly back of the little golden serpent that clung to her.

At the sink the faucet turned with a tiny high squeak and cold water gurgled over her hands. She cupped them together and, when they were full, dropped her face in. The icy splash cut through the slick layer of oil on her skin and pried her sleep-heavy eyes right open. After burying her face into a towel for a minute longer than was necessary, she wandered back out of the bathroom. In Raiden's room the bed was empty, so she turned toward the living room, her heart thudding faster in distress.

When she stepped into the kitchen, she noticed a figure sitting slumped over the table in slumber. For a split-second Nicole thought it was Raiden, but the head of blond-grey hair pulled back into a ponytail corrected her. It was his father. She had not noticed him on her way to the bathroom. Why wouldn't he have gone to sleep in the bedroom—unless he had been keeping watch over her when he succumbed to sleep.

What's he keeping watch over, she wondered. The unstable fera that might lose control again? The weapon that needed to be kept out of the wrong hands? Or—she looked down at the key hanging from a long cord—could this key be exactly what she feared it was?

A story of an abandoned palace in the heart of Veil crept out of her memory. Raiden told her about the people who erected it as monument to their hopes and dreams for this new realm. However, they couldn't agree who would hold the keys and so the palace and the power of their unity, suddenly broken, forced them out and sealed the palace shut. If the key around her neck and the one around Raiden's were those keys, then that would make them…she didn't even want to think the word. She just wanted to know where Raiden was.

She sighed, pacing quietly in the living room, not wanting to wake Raiden's father.

"Everything all right?" A groggy voice asked from the kitchen.

Nicole saw him sitting up, rubbing his eyes.

His question summoned up bile in her throat, and she had to swallow it back. *All right? How many people died last night because of me? I killed every last member of the Council. Venarius and his organization are still out there—who knows where. I don't know where Raiden is. I have the key to the whole fucking realm hanging from my neck and I don't want it!*

"Where's Raiden?" she asked, avoiding his question.

"He said he would be back soon," he said, looking up at the clock on the wall.

Nicole looked to the clock as well, almost seven in the morning.

"They're just working on getting the court's lower levels cleared, the seers are still down there."

"What?" Nicole balked, a sucker punch of guilt and horror hitting her stomach. She realized her shoes weren't on her feet. The toes of her boots peaked out at her from beside the end of the couch.

She snatched a boot and shoved the corresponding foot down its throat.

"It's fine, they'll have them out soon."

Nicole yanked the second boot on. "I should be there to help," she grumbled through her teeth and stormed toward the door. *I made that mess after all. I trapped those people down there when I brought the Courts down on top of them.* As a final impulse she took the key off and tossed it across the room onto the couch.

"Wait—uh—"

Nicole did not wait. She wrenched the door open and stepped outside into the biting morning air. She shut the door behind her. It was a relief to escape the thick warm comfort of the apartment. She set her thoughts on Raiden and slipped into the air before his father could follow her out the door.

The sudden solid contact with stone beneath her feet jarred her a little as she appeared beside Raiden. He jerked his gaze toward her with surprise and she wondered if his turquoise eyes would ever stop being so startling to her.

He opened his mouth to say something, closed it, and then began again. "Sleep all right?" He moved his hand toward hers.

She was relieved to see him. He had changed out of the bloodied clothes she had cut to tatters last night. The evidence was gone, but she was reluctant to touch him after what she'd done. "Not really. I want to help," she said, turning her attention to finding her way to where the seers were trapped.

They stood in a vast pit of stone, some crumbled piles of block, some whole walls still intact and leaning in precarious angles around them.

"I think we're almost there," he said, no doubt seeing the guilt on her face. "You didn't put them down there, Nicole. It's not your fault. We'll get them out."

Nicole didn't want to have this conversation now. All the guilt in her heart made it feel like lead and words wouldn't change that. Only making things right could.

"You can't get in through the ether?"

"Even in ruins the spells barring the ether are causing us trouble. We can get past some walls, and others we can't, especially down in the low levels," Raiden explained. "We have to move it all out of the way."

She nodded, looking down at the terrain as she made her way deeper into the destruction toward the sounds of grunts and shifting stone. The gritty shuffles of Raiden's steps followed close behind her as she descended into the hole that was once the Council's court building. They navigated down the mounds of crumpled stone, and Nicole eyed broken sections of staircase lying around, the steps leading in bizarre directions like she had fallen into a war-torn M.C. Escher scene.

Some of the stones around them pulsed with a faint light as they passed, and Nicole realized she was walking through the ruins of corridors she had traversed during her brief out-of-body experience the night before.

"It's a little different than I remember it," she mumbled.

"Once we get the seers out, we can get away from this place," Raiden said, his words saturated with optimism and distain.

"And go where exactly?" She wondered, noticing the key bouncing against her abdomen with every step. She halted, frozen in shock, there it was hanging from her neck again. *Really?!* She took a deep breath and kept moving.

Raiden was silent, glancing toward the sky for just a moment. Nicole looked up, and saw the column of light still reaching endlessly upward. She had hoped that beacon would be gone today. Raiden looked ready to say something—but Loak appeared from behind a leaning wall, bear-hugging a massive stone block to his bare chest—his white shirt tucked behind him into his belt.

"Look who it is," Loak said, carrying the stone over to a pile and releasing it. The stone hit another with a great crack that slapped her eardrums.

Nicole hoped her cringe passed as a smile. She didn't know how else to greet the giant man whom she only met informally the night before when he scooped her off that table to whisk her away from her impending execution. To him she had been unconscious, but she had been eerily aware of everything happening around her and to her.

"Where'd Leone get to," Loak wondered.

"Oh, I left him back at the apartment," she said, hiking her thumb back behind her.

"How did the search go, Raiden?" Loak inquired further.

Raiden exchanged an uncomfortable look with him. "There was no trace of him or anyone else back in the rebel's hideout."

"Trust me. He's long gone," Loak assured him with a shake of his head.

"For now," Raiden said.

Nicole's stomach squirmed, she knew they were talking about the leader of Dawn. "Venarius?" she asked.

Raiden hesitated. but Loak answered. "It turns out he was behind the rebels."

"Excuse me," another voice barged in and Andrus appeared. "He was behind *Eulina*. The rebels were a movement with a cause before he showed up." He eased himself down onto the pile of stones and sighed like it was his blue velvet couch back at the rebel base. "Fera, good to see you. How's the shoulder?" He asked with forced nonchalance.

She appreciated the completely unveiled attempt at throwing her a lifeline to escape the conversation, but from the corner of her eye, she could see a sour expression pass over Raiden's face at the mention of her shoulder. He hadn't been the one to hurt her, but their unfortunate encounter played out as it did thanks to Raiden's altered memory.

"It's fine, Andrus," she answered, tracing a small circle in the air with her left elbow. Her shoulder was still stiff, but then every part of her ached today, the physical fatigue that came after magic-over-load, which she was becoming rather accustomed to now. "How's it going in there?"

"It's stuffy. Progress is slow but we're almost in," he said, heaving himself up off the rocks that grumbled and shifted with his departure.

Nicole followed Andrus, relieved to leave Loak and Raiden's conversation behind. She didn't want to talk about where her enemies might be lurking, or what they were going to do about Raiden's and her apparent inheritance of the entire realm. As far as she understood, under the Council's leadership the realm was still divided up into states that had been the old kingdoms. *Veil will just revert back to the old kingdoms,* she hoped even though she knew better. There were some states without their royal families that relied on the Council's leadership.

Andrus led her into the corridor, mostly intact and almost precisely how she remembered it aside from the occasional ceiling stone out of its place. Daylight couldn't reach them. The stones all around them glowed with their presence, but the light flickered, foreboding the eventual failure of whatever magic was at work. The feeble light mirrored the waning life of this dying building. They turned a corner and ventured maybe a hundred feet into the enclosed corridor before coming to a doorway blocked by a section of collapsed wall.

Caeruleus was there clearing stones out of the path of the door. His uniform jacket was gone, his white sleeves rolled up and his slate grey trousers were covered in dust. It was clear that a lot of work had already been done from the mounds of debris lining the walls. A particularly large stone barely budged an inch at Caeruleus' effort bracing his back against it and pushing with his legs.

Nicole couldn't stop her gaze from zeroing in on the patch concealing his lost right eye—*the last time we were together he thought I was unconscious,* she thought grimly about her out-of-body observance of his and Loak's rescue attempt. It was a strange sensation to look at him knowing what he had done for her, after she had marred him irreparably. He only glanced at her for a moment and looked away too fast for her to read the emotion in his eye. He continued his efforts like she wasn't there as she took position beside him,   placing her hands against the smooth side of the stone and pushing.   Together they slid the stone aside several feet.

"That's good," Caeruleus declared, breathing heavily as he straightened up, his gaze carefully avoiding hers.

Just last night he'd risked his life to help her, when he didn't know her, despite all he'd been told about her, and now he was doing his best to ignore her. She wondered if he was scared of her, or if he hated her—she couldn't blame him if he did, though.

"This looks like it could come all the way down at any moment," Andrus said, regarding the portion of wall leaning across the corridor and against the door.

"Let's see if we can get the door open at all," Caeruleus suggested. "Carefully," he added, acknowledging Andrus' concern with a nod.

Andrus knocked on the door with the polite cadence of a solicitor. "Would anyone in there like to get the hell out?"

A jumble of muffled voices answered in the affirmative through the thick door.

Caeruleus took the door handle and opened the door. It swung outward but only a few disappointing inches before meeting the obstruction of the fallen wall.

"No one is fitting through that," Andrus said.

"Oh, really?" Caeruleus huffed.

Nicole rolled her eyes and stepped between them, reaching for the door. The power in her core was not so eager to rise to the surface, her body still worn and weak, but she dragged it out and pushed it through her hand, into the door handle. The door creaked, wood grains swelling with light for a moment. Andrus and Caeruleus cringed, leaning away.

Nicole pulled on the handle. The lower half of the door split and opened like a Dutch door.

"Well, there you go," Andrus said.

Caeruleus ducked into the chamber. "Is anyone hurt?"

Nicole swallowed a lump. Then one by one people filed out, stooping to get through the squat doorway.

"Just follow the corridor that way," Andrus ushered with a wave.

The seers were a mixed assembly, all ages, from white-haired elders shuffling along in a permanently stooped posture to children as young as ten snapping upright and breaking into a grateful march down the corridor. So, the Council had never stopped tracking down seers. She wondered how long those youngsters had been in the courts, how desperately had their families tried to hide them and their unfortunate gift only to fail?

Nicole looked into every face and—except for the youngest seers whose eyes were still clear—she saw clouded eyes. Some eyes looked back at her through a slight haze, a faint mist across their vision, others couldn't possibly see her at all through the thick milky fog in their blinking gazes. Those who could see her looked at her with profound recognition. The youngsters gave her sly smiles, their gazes bright with knowing. The older seers who could still look at her and see her face gave her looks ranging from gracious relief to troubled pity.

She wanted to ask them who they were, how long they'd been here, where would they go now, were their families out there waiting for them? The thought of counting them was lost in the crowd of her unspoken questions, but given the several minutes that passed as seers wandered to freedom, the number could be no less than a hundred, perhaps closer to two hundred. Caeruleus emerged.

"That's all of them," he announced.

"Great," Andrus clapped his hands together. "Job done!"

But as the guys turned to follow the seers, Nicole turned the opposite way, moving beneath the leaning wall and deeper down the corridor. She wanted to check another chamber. It was uncanny to travel down this passage with a body, to feel her progress in every step. When she came to the next tall door, she reached out and instead of passing right through it, she took hold of the handle and pulled. At first the door wouldn't shift. Her body was so achy that every movement came with an angry twinge, but she couldn't bring herself to summon up magic again. She latched onto the door handle with both hands, braced one foot on the wall beside the door, and pulled again.

The hinges whined and the door moaned, scraping across the floor as it opened a few feet. A gaping black maw greeted her. Before she could think about lighting her way, the column of darkness rushed forward, enveloping her in a black flapping cloud. A chorus of caws sounded through the passageway as the ravens from the record hall spilled out the open door and surged toward their freedom.

Nicole sagged with relief that the sudden onslaught of shadows was merely an aviary exodus. She peered into the blackness of the unlit hall beyond the open door and considered letting this minor obstacle deter her. But when she looked down the hall with the thought of going back, she spotted some of the debris along the way—broken pieces of the stones from the walls and ceiling, still glowing in response to her proximity. She snatched a baseball-sized lump of rock that glowed even brighter in her hand like a falling star a child believed could be caught.

Holding the stone out at arm's length, she stepped through the doorway. The stone chased back the darkness enough for her to see a few feet around her. The last time she crossed this vast hall it was bright, the regiment of bookshelves stood tall and straight in their lines. But today she would not enjoy a simple stroll down the avenue between rows of shelves to the other end of the long chamber. The shelves were toppled, their books and scrolls littered the floor.

❧

Venarius stepped lightly through the rubble littering the floors of the remaining lower level of the courts. He wore a satisfied smile. He had planned to bring down the Council from their high hill himself, but his victory had been achieved by-proxy thanks to his creation. Watching from the streets below as the courts crumbled had been such a thrill that even now, hours later, the thought of his creation's glorious power gave him chills. He wished he had been inside to see it all firsthand.

With the Council gone he didn't have to worry about the annihilation of his hard work any longer, and he was eager to usher

18

his creation back to the purpose he had laid out for her long ago. He stopped a moment at the doorway into the hall of records, following the faint echoes of her footsteps into the shadowy hall.

❧

Raiden watched, his heart heavy, as the seers file out of the tunnels and into the daylight. A part of him felt like he might see his mother among them—safe all this time, locked away with all the others, like his father had been—but, of course, she wasn't there. The seers young and old passed him, feeling familiar. Even though he knew he'd never seen any of their faces before, he felt like he had.

"Can we go home now?" One girl asked, her soft hand clinging to the wrinkled brown fingers of a milky-eyed woman who smiled.

"Yes, Dear, we can go home."

The girl looked up at him and he looked away, not wanting her to spot the Sight in his eyes.

Andrus and Caeruleus emerged from the buried passages without Nicole.

"Caeruleus, where's Nicole?" he asked.

Caeruleus looked around. "Still back there, I guess."

Raiden huffed in frustration and brushed past him and into the stone corridor. None of it was familiar to him, so he listened for footsteps, unable to shake the fear that there might be someone else down here besides Nicole and him. Loyal court agents could have been trapped in the lower levels too. He passed doors that were blocked and eventually came to one large door split in half, the lower half open.

"Nicole?" He ducked through the low door and stepped into the chamber.

It was quiet and the stones in the ceiling glowed with a feeble white light—the courts spells dying, but enough that he could see the room. Concentric rings of chairs faced the center of the room where a massive crystal ball sat fractured on the floor. Even broken, just glancing at the crystal ball hit him with the Sight. He looked away, cringing at the disjointed cacophony of a fractured future. He could grasp nothing from the flashes but sound and nausea. The

Sight burned and pounded in his head.

Finally, the Sight receded and he turned toward the door. His foot grazed something and he looked down to see a small crystal ball, still spinning and rolling in a little circle. Unlike the great broken crystal behind him, this one didn't pull him into the Sight. He bent over and plucked it off the floor. This time the Sight was a warm pulse in his head, a slight pressure, and the crystal in his hand clouded with shadow. Then within the little sphere he saw Nicole walking through a dark room.

He closed his hand around the crystal, blocking its images from his eyes, and he pushed the Sight back without struggle. The crystal seemed to make the Sight entirely new and tame. He tightened his grip on the smooth sphere, telling himself he should leave it, but he slipped it into his pocket before he ducked back through the doorway.

❧

The sounds of Nicole's careful steps to avoid fallen books echoed around the hall. Whispers of shifting stone and tiny fragments dropping from the ceiling answered her shuffling feet in an unintelligible conversation. She climbed and stumbled over the downed shelves in her path, her left hand devoted to holding her light. The distance across the hall felt endless with nothing but darkness beyond her small field of light. The door at the other end had to be a figment of her imagination dreamed up in the delirium of her harrowing night. There was nothing here but the edge of reality and the void beyond. But after what felt like half an hour the curtain of shadows slid aside and the light from the broken stone in her hand reached the door.

Last night she had passed right through the door. It could have been locked for all she knew, but if it had been it didn't matter now. The door was still in its frame, but just barely, looking like it had been struck from the other side, its iron hinges torn from the frame and the wood was even split in places. She managed to squeeze her body through the gap between the doorframe and the failed hinges on the door's edge.

One of the many pillars from the chamber lay toppled around the door. Her stomach clenched with dread as she climbed over the stone disks, the separated vertebrae of a great buckled spine. Streams of white daylight spilled down from fractures in the ceiling above. What had seemed an endless expanse of darkness existing in another plane of existence last night, now proved to be a rather ordinary crumbled chamber, much smaller than she would have expected. The illusion of infinity was shattered—the room was finite—a sad cavity buried in earth-bound ruins.

Her heart dropped cold and hard into her stomach. Where there should have been a large book upon a pedestal, there was now a small mountain of crumpled pillars. That strange tome and the echoing voices within—the pages she had hoped held more answers, other prophecies, or perhaps just other possibilities—were crushed and buried.

"Nicole?"

A voice called, stretched thin by the cold empty chamber between them. Her name slipped through the door behind her. It was Raiden. She knew that wary tenor of concern, even distant and echoing. Nicole sighed and shimmied back through the sliver of space between the door and the threshold.

"I'm here," she answered without raising her voice. Her words still managed to fill the hall of toppled bookcases. She thought she heard him sigh when she answered him, but the sound just as easily could have been the shuffle of her feet as she made her way back across the mess of bookcases and scattered records. Atop one mound of fallen records the stone slipped from her sweaty grip and it fell, knocking and clattering down into the tangle of broken wood shelves and crevices between books until it tumbled out of sight and its light was gone. Across the hall Raiden held out his hand and a shining orb hovered over his palm, casting a radius of light through the shadows, illuminating her way.

"What were you doing in here?" he asked as she scrambled down the last bookcase.

"I was here last night, kind of. I wasn't sure if it was real or just a dream.”

“And?”

“It wasn’t a dream,” she said. “And I’ve seen enough of this place.”

“Let’s get out of here then,” he suggested, turning toward the door and raising his hand in an invitation for her to lead the way.

Venarius stood in the darkness of the records hall, listening to the pair of footsteps bid him farewell and fade away.

“Nicole,” he said—his creation named for victory, *how fitting*.

The key hanging from her neck felt heavier the more she thought about it. Raiden and she emerged from the tunnel through the remnants of the Council into the open air. They were greeted by the stream of light shining steadfastly into the sky.

"Go on," Caeruleus said, shooing a raven off of his shoulder. The large black bird hopped away from him and swooped over to a pile of stone not three feet way where it perched and clicked its beak.

"I think we can safely say the courts are empty," Raiden said as he and Nicole joined the others. "Now what do we make of that," he wondered, nodding toward the light in the sky, a distant celestial scepter standing on its own with unwavering authority.

"Only one way to know for certain," Loak offered, pulling his shirt back on.

They stood in the crater that remained of the courts, Nicole, Raiden, Caeruleus, Loak, and Andrus. She squirmed in her skin, loitering here made her uneasy. It wasn't even standing in her own destruction that made her uncomfortable, or the fact that she had killed the entire Council here and their remains were somewhere in this rubble. This place was where she had hurt Raiden, and she couldn't stop seeing what she did to him. She didn't want to be here any longer. Her attempt to inch her way to the edge of their cluster and creep away failed; the guys managed to encircle her in a haphazard sort of security detail—accidental or intentional, she couldn't be sure.

"How do we get there?" Raiden wondered, standing behind her. "We're all too exhausted to make the shift through the ether. And to be honest, after last night, I don't particularly trust that the ether is safe."

"Even with the central line buried under the courts, the vox network should still function," Loak said. "We might be able to contact the Council's nearest ship."

Nicole's stomach clenched with hunger churning deep into her core that let out an aggressive grumble. Surprise flushed her face as everyone looked to her.

Andrus let out a laugh. "I'm with you. Food first, plans later." He broke away from their formation and Nicole jumped gratefully into step behind him to escape the circle.

"I won't turn down something to eat," Loak agreed, following behind them.

They climbed out of the pit of ruins in relative silence, listening to the sounds of the city around them. Since the destruction Nicole caused in the middle of the night, Atrium had been shaken awake and unable to sleep. When they reached the edge of the hole and descended the hill toward the streets below, people were gathered around the hill gawking up at the courts, now just a broken empty shell. Others were staring up at the beacon—the thick gray sky she had come to know in Atrium was clear and blue today.

As they passed these people on the streets, Nicole stole glances at their faces. Some studied the beacon with puzzled expressions, others with mild wonder, and some faces were masks of worry.

Only the few people who had been there to witness the keys appear around Nicole and Raiden's necks knew what the beacon was heralding. Nicole lifted the key and tucked it into her collar, letting it fall to the end of its cord and hang beneath her shirt.

She saw Andrus watching her with repressed amusement on his face.

"Not ready to be called 'Your Highness' yet?"

"Just call me Nicole—not your highness *or* fera—thank you," she grumbled.

Andrus laughed. "As you command," he answered.

She glared at him, but Caeruleus' voice behind them stole her attention.

"How soon can you be here?"

Nicole glanced over her shoulder to see him wearing his agent mask, that silver segmented face shield with orange eyes. Then Raiden strode up beside her and she dropped her gaze to the street while she folded her arms across her chest, hugging herself against her shame as they walked.

"Great," Caeruleus said and pulled the mask off his face.

They zig-zagged their way along six short blocks and ended up on a familiar street where food vendors and eateries competed to fill the air with enticing aromas. The haze of savory spice and syrupy sweetness overwhelmed her nose and rushed into her brain. Her head spun amid confused cravings, her mouth watered, her stomach twisted and growled with impatience.

In less than ten minutes they were seated around a table with food in their hands and eating with intense focus. Despite the chaos of the night before and the demolition of the realm's government, the bustle of Mat Street seemed unaffected. The conversation around them, however, buzzed with the fate of the Council and Atrium.

"… suppose my brother can move to the city without any trouble now…"

"… seems a bit ominous to me…"

"… is it a coincidence that it showed up last night after the Council fell to the rebels?"

"Oh, the rebels aren't responsible for the Courts, I can tell you that."

"How would you know that?"

"My neighbor was there—oh yes—said there was a fera in the city. Wager you anything it was the fera that did it. It's just like the old stories, isn't it? Destruction like that."

Nicole didn't even flinch at the suggestion of her role in last night's events. She wasn't under any illusion it was going to remain a secret. She wasn't sure if she was becoming numb to what she'd done or if she was just too hungry to care about anything but her food.

"… I want to see for myself what that light is all about. It's to the northeast and we all know what's out there."

"Nonsense, it's nothin' to do with that old palace."

"Oh—been there, have you? I don't trust gossip, only way to know is to see."

No one stopped chewing, but they all looked up at one another, gazes shifting to Nicole and Raiden as they listened to strangers' chatter. Raiden looked to her and she looked at him, the key still hanging from his neck out in the open. He moved like a street magician as he scooped the key into his palm and made it disappear beneath his shirt like she'd already done.

There was an unspoken understanding not to say anything, even indirectly, about the fate of the realm now dangling from Nicole and Raiden's necks. It was suddenly comical, the two of them sitting there in the middle of the bustling food district having a meal while Atrium tried to comprehend the severity of the last nights events— a chicken that hadn't quite yet realized its head had been cut off, a little frantic, oblivious to its own demise.

Nicole chanted to herself to the cadence of her chewing—*no, no, no, no*. This wasn't the plan. She was supposed to come to Atrium to get Raiden. They were supposed to leave Atrium with lives that belonged solely to *them*. She promised Gordan that they would meet him in the Wastelands. After that there was no plan other than to figure out what to do with themselves and their freedom. But now there was a shackle around her neck, pulling her deeper into Veil, further from Gordan, further from freedom than she could even fathom. *I can't be in charge of an entire realm.*

She forced the wad of food down her throat, only half chewed and too dry. She couldn't taste it anymore. Her stomach was subdued at least. A black blur swooped in and landed with a little thud on the table beside Caeruleus. It tilted its head at him and let out a loud caw in his face.

"Get out of here," Caeruleus grumbled, yanking a piece off his sticky pastry and lobbing it several tables away. The raven scrambled after its prize. Loak stood up, wandered over to a vendor and returned minutes later with something wrapped up snugly in brown paper.

"Shall we?" Loak prodded the rest of them out of their seated stupors.

Nicole got up and followed in a daze. As they walked down streets she vaguely recognized, she let Raiden take her hand and that contact burned her conscience. When she looked down at her hand in his, all she could think about was the sword in hers and what she had done to him. At last they arrived at Raiden's apartment and when everyone filed in through the door, she managed to slip away from his grip.

The small apartment felt even smaller with five bodies milling about the living room and kitchen. Loak had to dip his head slightly to one side to avoid the ceiling as he crossed the room and passed the parcel of food to Raiden's father, still sitting at the kitchen table where she left him, the picture frame containing the photograph of him and his late wife sitting in front of him.

"Much obliged," Leone said in earnest as he unwrapped the food, his eyes red.

Loak clapped him on the shoulder and pulled the other chair away from the kitchen table to sit down. At last he could hold his head up straight.

Once they were all inside with the door shut, Caeruleus began. "I was able to reach Captain Rhee on the Tempest. They weren't far from Atrium and are heading this way as we speak. She said they could be here in little more than an hour."

Nicole's heart hammered. An hour? And that conversation was

at least twenty minutes ago now. *The only place I want to go is home.* She drifted across the room and sank onto the couch. Andrus flopped back unceremoniously onto the cushions on the other end and looked ready to fall asleep. He dropped his head back, the scars riddling his face and neck made brown constellations on his skin. Nicole tried to focus on the conversation in the room.

"Say we get there and find out what we all suspect is true, then what? Even if these are the keys to the palace, what is that even worth?" Raiden said.

"With the Council gone the states will more than likely revert back to the old kingdoms. The Council allowed the surviving monarchs to represent the royal states because they were familiar, trusted. We all know they'll happily resume control. This realm is going right back to where it was before the dragon wars," Caeruleus insisted.

"Don't underestimate the power of an old hope," Leone warned. "There are a lot of people in Veil who still believe the day will come, and they're right to believe it."

"The whole realm can see that beacon," Loak said. "It's only a matter of time before people realize what's going on and it reaches every corner of Veil."

"But Caeruleus has a point," Raiden said. "What are the chances that the people of the royal states even care? Their kingdoms are what they know, there's a reason the Council maintained the borders."

"Even so, there are the open states that relied on the Council far more for stability," Loak added.

"Aside from that, at the very least it means we now have a stronghold," Loak offered. "You still have enemies. Without the Council around I think we will see members of Dawn come out of hiding."

"I'm not so sure a palace emitting a beacon is the best place to hide from anyone," Caeruleus suggested.

"It doesn't matter if your enemies know where you are as long as they can't get to you," Loak countered.

"No one has been able to get into that palace in all the centuries since the doors shut. I'd say that's a safe place to be, regardless of any expectations that might come with it," Leone added in agreement with Loak.

Nicole waited for Raiden's response, for his refusal, reluctance even, but he just nodded. She could see he was exhausted and anxious, but his complacence stoked the growing resistance in her heart. She didn't want a big shiny palace and a realm full of people to worry about. She just wanted to get the hell away from this city, this realm, and the stranger she had become here. Her mind dragged her back to last night, an anchor pulling her down into that dark place, too deep to hear the conversation in the room with any clarity.

Loak's voice became a heavy muffled baritone, Caeruleus and Raiden's voices distant tenors in the background of her memory where she was in the Council's great hall. She remembered every second, and despite the pain of her anger and magic ripping through her, she had relished ending their lives. They hadn't just tried to kill her, they toyed with her, tortured her, forced her into a sick game, to play the cat while Raiden was the mouse. She knew she shouldn't think back on her own brutality with so much satisfaction, shouldn't find peace in that place, but she did. That was the first and last time she had been in complete control of her life, and she felt the need to savor that memory, take a gasping breath of air from that fleeting freedom before she was dragged into a new unknown.

Reluctantly, she pulled her mind back to Raiden's apartment. The food in her belly seemed to finally assist her, the ache in her muscles was finally dissipating.

"I suggest we be there to meet Captain Rhee when the Tempest arrives," Caeruleus said, his voice became clear in Nicole's consciousness again.

"Agreed," Raiden said, "I think we should leave Atrium as soon as possible, but I'd like to stop and see a friend first."

"We can meet you at the hill," Loak suggested.

Nicole thought Andrus had dozed off, but he opened his eyes, lifted his head from the couch and stood up as if on cue. She suspected he had been conscious and listening to the whole conversation.

"I've got some affairs to set straight myself," Andrus said. "I'll catch up with you." He gave Nicole a discrete nod and followed the others as they filed out the door, leaving Nicole and Raiden alone in the apartment sooner than she anticipated.

The door was shut and the room fell quiet before she could utter a single word.

Raiden looked at her and she looked back at him. The silence was taut between them. Nicole turned away from the dilemma by crossing the living room and grabbing her bag from the back of the kitchen chair.

"Look at that," she said, swinging the bag onto her shoulder, "I'm already packed." Her attempt at a lighthearted quip fell horribly flat and instead imbued the air with her melancholy.

Raiden's expression stiffened into what looked like the effort to resist a frown and perhaps an attempt to smile.

"Let's go see Tovar," he answered. The only things he gathered before they left the apartment were the sword with its silver-winged hilt and the picture of his parents from the kitchen table.

⁓

Gordan left the house behind, continuing for a time on human legs, covering a minuscule distance at an unbearably slow pace compared to flying, but as constraining as the human form was, he was surprised to find he felt pleased by the familiarity of it now. Perhaps he felt closer to Nicole this way. All the time he had enjoyed in her company he had been confined to his human form. It was not so distasteful to him now, but it surely would not get him to Nicole anytime soon.

He took in a deep breath. As he released it, he let his human body untwist and expand into his true shape, wings stretched and ready to fly. On four legs he broke into a gallop down the dirt road leading away from the little house until a break in the canopies overhead allowed him to leap back into the sky.

Nicole hid her hands inside her short maroon cloak, but Raiden hooked his long arm around her shoulders instead. She shrank beneath his arm, the weight of every cut she inflicted upon him last night pressed down on her through that contact. She had hurt him and she felt like she had no right to enjoy the comfort and the warmth of his arms.

She felt like she was trapped in a riddle. He wanted to follow the beacon and keep her safe, but she just wanted to run in the opposite direction, far from all she had done, from what she'd become. *There's no such thing as a safe place anymore*, she thought. He wanted to keep her safe in his arms, but *he* wasn't safe so long as he was with her.

It occurred to Nicole as she listened to the chatter of conversation on the streets and drifting out of windows, that many people had no idea the Council was gone.

"…no there's just a big hole where the courts used to be, saw it with my own eyes…"

"But if the rebels won wouldn't they be in the streets saying so?"

"Don't know…"

"…suppose they're hunkered down somewhere, eh?"

"It's been hours since the courts fell."

"Mum, what happens without the Council?" A little girl asked, tugging on a fist-full of her mother's loose trousers as they passed Nicole and Raiden in the opposite direction.

Nicole glanced at the black-haired girl with dark brown eyes and remarkably long lashes that nearly grazed her eyebrows. She looked about six, and Nicole thought about her nieces, safe and sound at home, far away in another realm asking their parents, *where's Nikki, when is she coming back?*

"I don't know, Love," the mother answered with dazed uncertainty.

In Nicole's imagination the mother's voice became her sister Francis answering Ashley and Ryleigh.

They arrived at the shop. The walk was short, a left turn, a couple blocks, a right turn. Nicole recognized the door, the sign, TOVAR'S CHARMS & TRINKETS. She'd been here before. The door was shut, locked. A card that said CLOSED sat tucked into the corner of the display window and there were only shadows inside, but Raiden still knocked.

Enough time went by to convince her Tovar wasn't inside, but Raiden waited and so she waited, still caught in his arm. At last the lock clicked and the door opened. Tovar appeared, deep lines of worry and exhaustion on his face until he recognized who was standing at his door. His eyes brightened and the friendly visage Nicole remembered from her first encounter with the shop owner appeared.

Tovar sagged with relief in his doorway and jumped back, waving them inside. "Come in, please. I'm so glad you're both—last night—I thought—" he stammered, trying to dance away from that fatalistic train of thought.

"We all did," Nicole said, unafraid of it. Everyone had been right to think the worst, they were just lucky to have been wrong. She felt Raiden's arm slacken and she stepped away, taking a sweeping look around the shop to mask her desire for distance as simple curiosity.

Tovar shut the door. The lights remained off and the shop was dim. Shadows hung like curtains from the ceiling between the rows of shelves.

"What happened last night?" Tovar asked Raiden.

Nicole listened while she browsed without any interest, glancing at the items on the shelves while she listened. There was much about last night's events that she didn't know. Raiden left her at the apartment and never came back. When Tovar showed up at the door, she knew something was very wrong, but she still had no idea what had happened between the time she watched Raiden walk out the door and when she saw him again in the Council's vast chamber.

"They cast a redirection spell on the shop, when I tried to get home, I ended up in a locked cell."

Nicole felt her chest grow tight, expanding with phantom anxiety coming back to haunt her. *Because of me,* she thought. She tried to focus on contents of the shelves while she listened to Raiden's story. She could feel the panic of last night scratching lightly at her heart, trying to creep back in because last night wasn't the end of this. It was the end of the Council, but Venarius would come again and next time he might not just put Raiden in a cell.

"There was someone in the cell with me. An apprentice alchemist, I didn't get a name but their teacher apparently studied under the Alchemist Hessian. Venarius supposedly needs this apprentice to translate Hessian's journal for him."

"To what end?" Tovar wondered.

"The apprentice said Hessian had worked with a necromancer on his life's pursuit to create a manmade soul."

Tovar's voice took on a softened tone of wonder. "An alchemist and a necromancer…"

Tovar trailed off into a silence that sounded sinister to Nicole, this combination was obviously not a good one.

"And not just any necromancer, Venarius, the founder of Dawn. It would seem his great grandson has dusted off the family legacy."

"So then, how does Hessian and the secrets in his journal play into all this," Tovar's question hung in the air unanswered, and Nicole looked up to see Raiden's expression pinch into a frown. Tovar managed to divine the answer from the silence. "The fera?"

Raiden nodded with a sigh. "The apprentice claims they were created by Hessian and Venarius and that's why Venarius wants the notes in the journal," Raiden answered.

"He wants to create more of them," Tovar said.

"I think he's desperate," Raiden continued. "Caeruleus found the Council's records on all the past encounters with the fera. It would seem Hessian betrayed his partner and went to the Council with information and the journal as well. It was listed in the case index of documents; only it was missing when Caeruleus looked for it."

"That is troubling," Tovar said. "Someone in the Courts had to be working with Dawn. What else was there in the Council's records?"

Nicole watched Raiden hesitate and look her way. The look in his eyes told her what Caeruleus found was worse than they had suspected.

"Sooner or later I'll need to know," she said.

He answered her with a sad smile and continued. "There were accounts of every fera sighting, the old Council propaganda, and their agents' confrontations with the fera. Every single mission to apprehend the fera ended the worst possible way. Every fera the Council found was provoked into a fit of destruction, which they didn't survive. The thing is, they were children. Only one of the original fera seemed to evade the Council and presumably escaped to the other realm."

"And the soul remained there," Tovar added.

Nicole stepped behind a shelf to escape whatever poignant looks might have come her way and to hide her dismay. They had been children. One got away and lived an entire life in hiding—so that was the fera before her. It was a surreal thought, a past life, were they the same person or two different people? Was it like waking up with amnesia and living an entirely different life than before, a blank slate? Or could she reach that life, peel back the shreds of herself and find that person there inside her? To think she'd spent an entire lifetime running already. She needed to know if that had been the fera's whole life, if the fera had died in hiding even after escaping to the old world?

"But how did you escape the cell?" Tovar asked.

"I found the loophole in the seal on the door. It prevented just about every means of getting it open, destroying it, or getting through it. But they didn't think to cover rudimentary tactics. I pulled the pins from the hinges."

Nicole went on pacing between the shelves as she listened.

"On my way out, I happened to overhear the rebel leader and Venarius speaking. They got a report that Nicole was in the courts. He told her to send the rebels and…well, ultimately, she did as she was told. I got out of there as quickly as I could and made it back to the apartment."

Tovar pondered this for a moment, scratching the grey stubble on his chin. "I don't suppose he had any other choice. Without the translation of the Hessian journal, he couldn't afford to let her die when she's the only *fera* left."

Again, Nicole took a step to place a vase in between her and their gazes until the weight of the word *fera* dissipated from the air and Raiden continued.

"By the time I reached the courts, the rebels were rushing in. They thought they were fighting for their revolution, but Venarius was pulling the strings, and he was trying to get to Nicole before the Council could…" She was in his line of sight this time, standing in the center aisle of the store just a few feet away. Raiden looked to Nicole, hesitant to say it.

"Execute me," she finished, shifting her eyes to Tovar and feeling suddenly annoyed by the delicate treatment. She let out a huff, dispelling the heat building inside her.

Raiden winced and it occurred to her that maybe he couldn't say it because the thought of her death and how narrowly it had been avoided pained *him*. Her irritation cooled into guilt. From this point she more or less knew the rest of the story, so she sulked into the next aisle.

"Once I was inside, everything moved so quickly it's almost a blur," Raiden continued, and Nicole felt her body tense as his story drew closer to the carnage. What had their encounter in the Council's chamber been like through his eyes? "We only made it out alive because of Nicole, and thankfully the Council is dead."

Nicole sagged, uncertain if she was relieved or disappointed in his hasty summary of the end of it. She turned an ear down toward her shoulder and her neck answered with a tense crack.

"Well," Tovar said with a sigh, "that does make the future uncertain now doesn't it? The Council is gone and that beacon in the sky…"

"About that," Raiden said and Nicole grew uncomfortably warm. She felt like her skin was shrinking, and the key was growing, pulling the chord into the back of her neck.

Tovar tilted his head with interest.

"There's something else," Raiden said, hooking the chord around his neck with his finger to pull the key out from beneath his shirt.

Tovar's eyes went wide. There was no delay in understanding. Nicole squirmed. She felt like a kid on one of those old game shows. *Welcome to Legends of the Lost Realm, complete all the challenges, face the hunter, save your friend, best the Council's agent, make it through the maze of Atrium City, find Raiden, take back control of your body before the timer runs out.* She did it. She won, but for all that the prize ended up being something she absolutely did not want. All that was missing was the theatrical disembodied voice. *Congratulations, Nicole Jameson, for killing every last member of Veil's government! You've won a brand-new palace, complete with royal duties and all the hopes and expectations of an entire realm!*

"I—I can't believe this—one of the keys of sovereignty right here in my—"

"Two," Raiden corrected.

"I beg your pardon."

"*We* have both keys," Raiden explained.

The last thing she wanted to do was show off her key to double Tovar's delight, but just hearing the news compounded his exhilaration.

"This is incredible, Raiden!" Tovar exclaimed, his voice still soft somehow. Years fell away from Tovar's face, his eyes wide and bright with excitement, his open-mouthed smile framing the elation of re-kindled hopes and shattered disbelief.

"Tovar, there's no telling what this all means yet—"

"Nonsense, it means exactly what it means, *two keys, two kings to lead the realm.*"

Tovar sounded like he was reciting a nursery rhyme. Nicole felt slightly nauseated, so she forced her attention onto the shelf full of small desk clocks, quill pens and candelabras as she tried not to add her breakfast to the assortment.

"We aren't exactly prepared to go announcing it to everyone just yet," Raiden said, attempting to quell Tovar's enthusiasm.

"Of course," some severity returned to Tovar's voice.

"But we are expecting a ship that will take us to the palace. We need to see if this is all really happening. Will—would you be opposed to joining us? It's just—we could use all the allies we have with us given the circumstances. Dawn and Venarius are still out there, and these keys, whatever this comes to…"

"Certainly," Tovar said. "Yes, of course," he added with a fervent nod. "Let me just gather up a few things." He hurried to the back of the shop, rummaged beneath the counter, turned to the back wall and opened a door that had been perfectly unnoticeable.

With Tovar out of sight in his back room, Nicole drifted back toward Raiden where he stood near the shop door.

"It's easy to forget how much catching up we have to do," Nicole muttered. "A lot can happen in a week."

Raiden sighed and opened his mouth to say something, but Tovar hurried back, his shoes thumping against the wood floor.

"I've got my essentials," he said, lifting the suitcase he had in each hand, both slender and light given the ease with which he moved them. They looked like they could barely hold a couple short stacks of folded clothes.

Nicole wondered what his essentials were.

"I suppose we should be off to meet the others at the hill," Raiden said. "What about the shop, Tovar?"

"I'll lock it up, it will be fine."

When Raiden gave him a skeptical look Tovar added, "I'm not worried, just simple charms and trinkets, nothing valuable enough to mourn the loss of if someone even managed to get in," he said with a shrug. "Shall we?"

Nicole took the opportunity to be the first out the door in a dazed pace—still trying to believe she would wake up from all this. Raiden followed, leaving Tovar to secure the shop and catch up with a brisk pace. They walked down Rood until they came to Emerald Street, which led directly to the hill at the center of the city.

A shadow passed over them and Nicole looked up to see the belly of a manta ray. It took a moment for Nicole's mind understand the shape—it was a ship—flying rigidly through the air rather than flapping gently as the sea creature would have. Its surface was glossy and grey against the blue-sky overhead.

"I believe that's our ride," Raiden said, optimism straining in his voice.

She watched it solemnly as it passed.

They had a clear view of the aircraft as it swooped down over the hill, a single stalk extended from the underside of the ship's landing gear that opened like a telescope and four toes unfurled at the end like a bird's food as it touched the ground. Nicole tilted her head, bemused by the metallic manta balancing on a single leg, flamingo-style.

Residents of Atrium pointed and eyed the ship, some came hurrying onto Emerald street to get a look at it. It was one of the Council's ships after all. Nicole could see the questions in their eager gazes. Was this the Council returning? Would they finally have answers about the destruction of the courts? If the rebels were victorious, why had they all made themselves scarce? But if this wasn't the Council, who was in charge? What would happen to Atrium and to Veil?

Nicole wanted to hide from all those eyes and their worries. She could only be grateful that she walked through these people's gazes unregistered, just another person on the streets. They did not look to her with their questions, not yet at least.

When they reached the road that encircled the hill where the ship stood on its single leg, Nicole spotted a door at the bottom of the ship's stalk and their party was gathered around it. A couple new faces were there—two women, one short, the other a towering figure like Loak. There was a raven on Caeruleus' shoulder, again, and his pale olive face was heavy with exhaustion and defeat—he had apparently resigned himself to the bird's presence.

"Raiden," Caeruleus called with a wave. She watched his gaze avoid hers yet again. "Perfect timing. We—"

"I have to interrupt you boys," said the shorter woman with just a few inches of disheveled straight black hair. "We're going to find ourselves swarmed by a lot of interested people, and it won't take long before their curiosity turns into panic when they realize the Council isn't here and we didn't come with answers."

Nicole looked around and saw the people wandering over, their steps still slow and tentative.

"Agree with you there, Cap," Loak grumbled.

"If you're coming, then get in," the captain ordered, giving a tense look around at her passengers and the onlookers migrating toward the ship. The captain made an abrupt about face and stepped through the door at the base of the ship's single leg. Loak ducked in after her and pressed himself as far to the back of the space as he could. Everyone filed in, filling up the cylindrical compartment. The available space disappeared quickly as everyone stepped inside—Caeruleus, Leone, Tovar, Raiden, Nicole, Andrus, and the dark-skinned woman who was surely a head taller than Raiden.

The door slid shut. Nicole found herself standing front to front with Raiden. With Andrus's back against hers and what amounted to virtually no wiggle room, her chest was pressed against Raiden's ribs as hard as any desperate embrace they had shared in the past, but she did not feel comforted by that firm contact. She didn't bother to peel her cheek off his sternum to attempt an uncomfortable look up at him. Thankfully, about when everyone started squirming, the door opened again.

Nicole hadn't even noticed any movement, not the slightest fraction of G-force pushing her weight into her feet, no lurching of the circular elevator when it stopped. The two people behind her jumped out and she whirled around to escape after them. Everyone stepped out of the elevator with a grateful sigh.

"Here we are," the Captain said as she stepped out last. "Pep, let's get off the ground."

"Yes, Captain," answered the woman who stood dwarfing Andrus. She didn't salute but there was deference in her firm nod as she moved at a brisk pace for another door.

Nicole got only a brief look at Pep as she left. Her skin was a deep violet, almost black. Pep had vivid golden eyes the same as Loak's that peered out from her face like the yellow centers of midnight colored pansies. She had to be seven feet tall. The only person taller than her was Loak, but not by much. She wore the same sunset orange jumpsuit as the captain although where the captain had room in her loose pants, Pep filled out her suit with abundant curves as snuggly as everyone had fit into the elevator. Pep took long strides and disappeared through the doorway.

"Now then," Captain Rhee sighed. She took a few steps into the group and stopped beside Nicole. She was a few inches shorter than Nicole and Andrus, which probably made her about five-three, the shortest among them. "This is the cargo hold, nothing more to say about it, let's move this get-together to the deck."

The vast space around them drew Nicole's eyes upward to the ceiling high overhead. Structural beams along the walls from ceiling to floor gave the cargo hold a distinct feeling of being inside the ribcage of a massive metal beast, much the way the insides of gargantuan animals were portrayed when her favorite cartoon characters were swallowed by a monster, no internal organs, just a great empty space lined with rib bones.

Captain Rhee turned on her heel, the sole of her boot squeaking, and she marched toward the same door through which Pep had departed. Nicole followed, gravitating toward Rhee, or perhaps slightly repelled by everyone else.

Beyond the cargo hold was a short passageway to another door. Rhee stopped at this door, waved her hand over a sphere imbedded in the wall beside it, and the door slid open. "Straight ahead," the captain said, standing post at the door and ushering everyone through it. The ship gave a little shudder and Nicole imagined the manta ray lifting its flamingo leg off the ground.

They moved through the second doorway into a wider corridor, the walls smooth and silver, curved slightly like they were bulging outward, straining to contain the brightness from the band of white light running along the ceiling.

Captain Rhee waited for everyone to pass through the second door into the corridor and shut the door behind them.

"For our late arrivals, I'm Min Rhee, Captain of the Tempest. Welcome to the deck. Stone, if that bird shits anywhere you're cleaning it up. The rest of you, I don't know."

Caeruleus stepped easily into the task of introductions. "This is Loak Clyson the Council's most senior agent."

"I've heard the name," Rhee said with a respectful nod.

Caeruleus continued, "and Leone Cael—"

"*Former* agent and convicted traitor," Leone chimed cheerfully.

Nicole stole a glance at Raiden and caught the brief moment that his brows synched together. She couldn't imagine what his father's presence was doing to him.

"This is Andrus, one of the rebels," Caeruleus continued. "Raiden Cael and Nicole. She…uh, removed the Council from power last night."

"That's one way to put it," Andrus murmured.

Nicole had to swallow back the thick film of discomfort in her throat.

"I see," Captain Rhee said with stiff nod. "We had no information. Our last orders from the Council after we brought you back to the courts were to return to business as usual. I can't say what that means now with the Council gone…but I guess we can start with this favor of yours. Where are we headed?"

"Toward the beacon," Caeruleus said.

"I didn't sign on for some great quest here. Do you know something about that light that I don't?"

"Raiden," Caeruleus deferred to him with a glance.

Raiden moved to pull the key out from beneath his shirt and Nicole sighed, doing the same. When both keys dangled in clear view, Captain Rhee's eyes went wide.

"Are those what I think they are?"

"That's what we'd like to know," Raiden explained. "We're pretty certain the beacon is coming from the old palace."

"Sard the stars," Rhee murmured. "All right then, to the midlands." She turned to march down the corridor but stopped and turned back around. "Make yourselves comfortable. Ladders to the upper deck and the sleeping quarters if anyone needs some rest are here in this corridor," she said, gesturing with a sweep of her arm at the shiny walls.

Nicole eyed the sleek walls and only now noticed that there were several archways along the corridor.

"I'll be in the bridge with Pep, anyone is welcome to accompany us." Captain Rhee resumed her march toward the bridge at the opposite end of the corridor.

Loak and Leone followed her.

"I've got to get myself some sleep," Andrus muttered. He stepped up to one of the arches on the wall. When he was close enough to breathe on it, what had been a solid metallic panel shifted into a haze of silver mist. He stepped through it and it solidified behind him.

Curiosity stirred Nicole out of her lassitude and she followed, stepping up to the wall, watching the panel quiver into a shiny smoke screen. Reflexively she closed her eyes as she walked through it. On the other side she found herself in a coffin-sized cylinder with nowhere to go and a ladder inches from her face. She stepped onto the bottom rung and took hold of the cold metal. She looked up, expecting to see Andrus's feet not far above her. They were not. Before she could climb, the ladder slid upward, fast enough to feel her organs being pushed toward her feet for a split second.

❧

Raiden instinctively fell into step to follow Captain Rhee down the corridor, but when he glanced over his shoulder and did not see Nicole doing the same, he lurched to a sudden halt. He filled his lungs and let them deflate in a sigh.

"Are you prepared for this?" Caeruleus asked despite his earlier skepticism. He stood in the hall just a few strides ahead of Raiden.

"What choice do I have?" Raiden shrugged. Life had never stopped to ask him *are you ready for what comes next?* Not when his father never came home, not when he was made an orphan and left to survive in a dead city, and not when the Sight showed him the first friend he'd known after a decade of solitude being torn away from him just like everyone else in his life had been ripped away— he sank for a moment and had to shake the memory from his head.

"Can *she* handle this right now?"

Raiden felt a surge of irritation toward his friend, to tell Caeruleus that the answer to his question lay under the patch on his face, that the Council knew the answer too and he might as well ask them, but he couldn't move that distain past his lips. He knew he shouldn't be angry at Caeruleus. They had been as good as brothers once. Caeruleus had done the right thing last night—he chose an innocent life over the Council. The source of Raiden's anger was just…everything. He couldn't figure out what to do with his frustration, his uncertainty, his hatred for what still loomed over Nicole's and his head. He took a deep breath and huffed, knowing it was better to turn and walk away than lash out at his friend. He made his way to the archways leading to the upper deck.

Gordan's conviction to fly straight to Nicole no matter who might see him wavered when he spotted the village. He wasn't far from the home of Nicole's friends. If his memory of Candhrid from before the wars was accurate, this village was called Witch Haven. He veered south and gave the village a wide circuitous berth. He had the distinct feeling that people all over the mainland would be casting their curious eyes toward the beacon to the northeast, and so he stayed low and flew over the dense forest where there were sure to be no roads, travelers, or farms.

The slender pillar of light, pale as a daytime moon in the blue sky, beckoned him to Atrium. At least Gordan thought this until he could see the walls of the city in the distance and realize that the beacon was farther still beyond that—much farther. Maybe the rumor that family heard—that the light was coming from the old palace—was true after all. His suspicion that the light had something to do with Nicole now didn't seem so likely. A storm of foreboding gathered in his chest, churning with his uncertainty and the string of unusual circumstances that followed. There were no guards at the gate; this Gordan could see from a long way off. In light of this, Gordan felt safe enough to land right outside the wall where he transformed once again into his human form, conjuring the same soft trousers as before without a thought.

The wall was high but not too high for him. He sprang off the ground and scaled the wall with the ease of a house cat in a garden. At the top he looked out across the city. He'd never laid eyes on it before, but he knew there was something terribly wrong when his gaze fell upon the hill at the center of the great compass. Ruins toppled into a crater. This could not be the great court of the Council. His heart struck his sternum with nauseating dread; it knew what his mind cringed away from—something happened here and it involved Nicole.

Below him just inside the wall, a wide street followed the curve of the city's outer limit. What might have allowed four wagons to pass abreast comfortably was half-choked by the stands and tents of merchants and market-goers, but the noise and bustle Gordan would have expected from such a scene was missing. Boisterous bartering had been replaced by the quiet din of murmurs, the hushed exchange of rumors instead of goods and money, and the trade of anxious inquiries and hearsay rather than prices and offers. The collective unease pervading the air hit Gordan like a swelling current, deceptively gentle at first then gradually overwhelming him. The wave of the city's nervous energy very nearly pushed him off the wall.

He leaned into it and stepped off the wall, dropping with a soft thud between the stones and a canvas-lined stall. What he needed was a cloak. Gordan thought of the last time he wore one, he couldn't say when it was exactly, but if he was going to conjure a cloak that wouldn't dissolve in a matter of an hour, he needed the details, not just the length, and color; he needed to have the substance of the thing in mind—the weight of it, the course fibers, the smell even. He went into his memory for a cloak and the most vivid recollection he had was from centuries ago, before Veil. He remembered wearing the hood pulled down over his face as he walked the wet winding streets of a village, keeping his head down so humans would not see his uncanny eyes and expose him for the vile thing he was to them. He remembered the weight of the thick mud clinging to the hem, the musty smell of the fabric.

The cloak appeared around his shoulders; even the mud was there. Possessed by the fears of his past, he adjusted the hood and tugged it down so that his eyes were shielded from outside gazes. Fully cloaked, the only part of him that could be seen was his bare feet. With long anxious strides and an eager tempo pounding in his chest, he slipped among the stands and into the mass of people. *Get to the center of the city*, that was his only thought. He navigated a maze of streets and buildings with his eyes downcast at the cobblestone. He maneuvered through the ebb and flow of pedestrians by the sight of legs from the knees down. But he was forced to look up frequently to choose his path, stealing looks as quickly as he could, hoping no one would catch his eyes.

His sense of direction was acute; with every turn he made, he still knew precisely in which direction the hill at the center of the city was. He listened to the conversation around him as he went, trying to piece together the events of the previous night. Whatever happened to the courts happened in the middle of the night. That much he picked up easily from the fragments of chatter.

"…died in the attack last night. Avora told me. She looked a wreck."

"I can't believe they were with the rebellion and we didn't know…"

Pain and awe in strangers' voices prickled Gordan's senses. It was difficult to keep track of his own feelings while so many others churned around him.

"… the posters of that young lady, that was the fera, wager my life."

Posters? Gordan searched discretely for them until he was startled by the sight of Nicole's face looking back at him from a white page upon a wall at the mouth of an alley. He studied the fierce, slightly blurred, expression. His hands reached for the poster before he thought better of it—*I might draw attention.* He pulled the poster down anyway and folded it, tucking it into his waistband.

"Don't believe everything you hear from some kid claiming they were with the rebels when it all happened…"

Some conflict between the Council and the rebels came to a head last night, but where did Nicole fit into it? Her plan was to find Raiden and get out. Would she join a group of rebels seeking strength in numbers?

"…you think that's the Council?"

"Certainly didn't stay long. If they were alive, they'd want to rub it in the rebels' faces, wouldn't they? Make sure everyone knows they're still in charge."

"So, you think they're dead."

"Why else would one of their ships come and go so fast?"

"Well, if the rebels won, how come *they* aren't celebrating in the streets?"

"Simple. They lost too."

"You're craftin' nonsense, you old fool."

"No matter. You can be sure things'll get messy when everyone figures out what's what. No Council, no agents, no order…"

Gordan was forced to turn away from those voices as he stair-stepped and zig-zagged his way to the remains of Nicole's enemy… former enemy.

"…where do you think they're headed? No Council anymore. What the limbs doin' without the head?"

"Sure looks like they're flying straight for that light out there."

"I wonder what it is."

"What's it matter?"

The urge to look up toward that mysterious beacon lifted Gordan's chin, but he caught a glimpse of a young girl's inquisitive stare and jerked his eyes back down. He didn't suppose he was in much danger, she was too young to know what dragon eyes looked like. He cursed himself for letting the mood of passing strangers seep into his mind and sway his actions. Confusion, curiosity, wonder, anxiety, uncertainty of all the people in Atrium was smothering his own thoughts and instincts. But at last he came upon rubble in the street, and the sight of it dredged up his fear like heaving up a buried anchor.

He peaked out from under the edge of his hood, across the road that encircled the hill. Toppled pillars and great shattered sheets of stone littered the slope. A pair of children scrambled up a slab of stone to slide back down on scraps of wood. Gordan turned his head when they came into his hooded view; he caught only a glimpse of their grey coats and a brief flash of one's curly blond head and the other's long dark hair swinging free.

"Where's that ship going?"

"Is the Council coming back?

"Will school be closed since there are no leaders anymore?"

They climbed back up to the top of their slide, clattering cheerfully through the remains of the realm's government.

"Get back here, you two," a father demanded in a stern yet calm tone. "I don't care if the dragons fill the sky and bring back the fires of war, you'll still be going to school."

The little ones let out groans of disappointment, slipped back down the sleek stone, and trudged across the road to their father's side. Gordan watched the small feet shuffle along behind a larger pair of briskly stepping shoes.

It wasn't until they were gone that he noticed his breathing, more forceful than usual, his skin crawled beneath the heavy cloak because the air here below the hill was different— a familiar charge of energy. Dread slithered through his innards, a slimy worm of nausea squirming past his liver and around his stomach. He made his way up the hill, all the while fighting back the swelling vertigo. He could feel Nicole all around him, like she was hanging in the air, dripping down the ruins, seeping out of the cracks of broken stones. It was so unbearably…wrong—not the warm hum he knew. He had known people's presence to linger like a scent, like residual warmth, faint and fading, but not like this. This summoned up the horror of battlefields, young men, their bodies in pieces, scattered, but not quite dead. The horror of feeling the presence of a single soul in shards, some of it flickering with fear behind him, more of it twitching with anger in front of him, this disjointed sensation multiplied a dozen times over. Bile rising in Gordan's throat forced him to shove that memory away. A soul was not meant to be torn, scraps strewn about, like cheap fodder for a hungry world.

Gordan reached the top and looked down at the shallow pit of destruction. He grew dizzy gazing into the overwhelming devastation, not to the structure that once stood here, but to the soul he could feel on every fragment of stone around him.

"What happened?" he whispered to Nicole because he felt like she was here listening, his eyes searching as though he might spot her somewhere in the wreckage, or worse, pieces of her.

The sounds of the world around him were as dull and muffled as if he were underwater, and he was in a way, submerged in a flood of grief. Nicole could give him no answers, her tattered presence couldn't tell him whether or not she found Raiden, or how she ended up here in the house of her enemy before it all came down. As always, her mind remained a mystery to him while he swam in a turbulent sea of her agony in this place. He could not cover his ears or close his eyes to escape the torture all around him—and it was laced with a rage that made him shudder.

He swallowed hard, unable to admit that she was gone. Was all that was left of her the hatred clinging to broken marble, the terror writhing in these nooks and crannies, her fiery hope and passion reduced to ashes, all but washed away by a tide of anguish? That was not the Nicole he had come to know and yet that was undoubtedly what remained of her here. This place did not smell like victory. His head shook, his body trembled with the effort to deny the evidence, but reason was cold and unyielding. His eyes burned.

Gordan felt himself gasping under the weight of sorrow, and he couldn't be sure if it was Nicole's or his own anymore. He pulled back his hood, shed the weight of the cloak, but felt no better exposed to the crisp cool air. This phantasm of her final moments, the residual pain radiating from the rubble, an eerily prolonged echo of her heart's final cry, screaming at him, it plunged him into a place so dark he couldn't be sure he was still standing in the ruins, couldn't trust that the sky was still above him. He left Nicole on the coast to travel alone, thinking she was safer without a companion that would condemn her, and this is where she ended up. *We should have gone after Raiden the moment the Council summoned him,* Gordan scolded himself bitterly. He had convinced Nicole that Raiden would be fine, that going after him was suicide, that she was more important to keep safe than Raiden. *I let them break us apart, and then I struck the second blow.*

Raiden, he thought, forcing his mind away from the past he could not change, to something that could be done, someone to find. Had Nicole reunited with him or not? If he was alive, where would he be? If Raiden survived Nicole's fate, where would he go? He supposed Raiden would do as Gordan himself felt inclined to do—first, he would punish whom he could for the loss of his kin, if he could, but the Council had already met the fate they deserved. In Gordan's mind that left only one action, the most difficult—and not because it required a portal to the other realm—telling Nicole's family what happened. He was certain Raiden would take on this mission, that is, if he was even alive. Gordan hoped Raiden was not so unlucky as that, to be left behind after losing the only person he cared about; in that fate he and Gordan were alike.

Gordan bowed his head in acceptance of the tragic purpose life had thrown at his feet to find a way to the other realm. Nicole's family was there, clinging desperately to the hope that she would return. He would take up this grim task as his penance for letting Nicole walk away from that beach alone, to snuff out their hope, to break their hearts because was there anything crueler than letting them go on hoping for something that would never come?

The site of Nicole's last moments was a pool of thick black sludge, clinging to his legs, pulling him deeper. The longer he stood there the more firmly stuck he felt—slipping into numbness. For a few uncertain minutes he thought he might prefer to stay in that dark numb place, because it was almost peaceful.

He plucked the folded poster from his waistband and opened it to take his last look at his friend and it wasn't even the Nicole he knew, the vividly kind young woman who had looked at him with compassion when he didn't deserve it. He let the poster fall. Convincing his legs to move was a tremendous feat of will, but the further he got from the ruins, the easier it was to move away. The numbness retreated. He trudged through the receding agony, stumbled around the stones tricking his senses into expecting her sudden appearance, and slipped down the slope of the hill.

Onlookers gawking at the destruction watched him as he reached the street below, not wearing his cloak any longer or keeping his head down. He marched forward, putting distance between the fragments of Nicole and him, his eyes straight ahead. He ignored the muttered words of disquieted people as he passed. Someone gasped. Another shouted, "Dragon!" He rolled his shoulders, releasing the tension in his vertebrae and he transformed to a chorus of screams.

☙

The ladder stopped and a floor slid across the opening below Nicole, closing the tube with the abruptness of a guillotine. She hopped off the ladder and through an identical archway into a not-so-identical corridor. To her right, instead of the tunnel-view toward the front of the ship, the corridor opened up into a great glass dome. To the left the corridor appeared to reach down the length of the ship with several doors on each side, the sleeping quarters Captain Rhee had mentioned. The doors to unclaimed rooms were open. She caught the last glimpse of Andrus's back as he trudged through the nearest open archway and disappeared. The door closed.

Nicole didn't feel like sleeping although her body was heavy. Mostly she felt…nothing, not even the soreness from earlier. The ache in her limbs had dispersed, but she still felt like someone had stuffed her with lead pellets. She didn't want to close her eyes while the buzzing swarm of terrible thoughts and memories occupied her head, so she turned toward the distraction of the viewing deck to drown those thoughts in the sky.

They were above Atrium and a clear sky nearly surrounded her. By stepping closer to the domed glass, the sky wrapped around her, and she felt like she would be swallowed up by blue eternity. Her eyes went warm and when she blinked an inexplicable tear fell, with nothing but unbroken empty sky in her eyes she hadn't noticed her vision blur with moisture. She wiped her cheek and looked at her fingers, perplexed by the shine of the tear.

What am I supposed to do now? She peered into the blue—both a wall and a void—until her eyes hurt, her head ached—*what am I supposed to do now?*—the question was a sharp rock rattling around inside her tender mind.

"Nicole," a gentle voice slipped into her crushing silence. His footsteps approached, heels striking the floor like timid knocking at the wall she was trying to put back up. *Can I come in,* the cadence of his steps asked.

She acknowledged him with barely a hum. The ship dipped slightly to the right and a faint vertical line of light glided across her view until it stopped in the center of the glass and the ship leveled out. A scream expanded in her chest, but by the time it left her lungs and traveled up her airway, it was reduced to a long sigh.

Nicole could almost hear the reassurances forming in Raiden's mouth.

"What's it like," she wanted to spare him from empty promises and outright lies for her sake, "knowing who you would have been if things had been different—if you hadn't known me?"

He stopped and stood beside her. "It's maddening to remember. No matter how briefly, I was someone who didn't know you, and I can't make that person go away. He's just sitting there in the back of my head and I hate him."

He looked straight ahead at the beacon for a long time, and Nicole didn't know what to say anymore.

"I tried to preserve you," he said. "I let myself remember pieces of that night in the castle, that you stopped Moira and saved my life. I hoped—when I didn't remember everything we had been through and how I felt about you—that gratitude for your help would mean something to me. I still feel like it should have worked," he said with a bitter chuckle. "But without you all I had was how much I hated the Council, though; and subverting their agenda was my goal, but ultimately Caeruleus mattered more. I didn't like what they wanted to do to you, and it was easy to give you the benefit of the doubt because you had given me a second chance at life, but I eventually let myself believe what everyone else did, that the fera was dangerous, so that I could justify helping Caeruleus."

"He's your best friend, Raiden. After what I did to him of course you felt differently about me," she spoke softly, wishing she could take that weight off Raiden's shoulders. *Is this all there is between us now—guilt?*

He spit out an ironic laugh. "Before I wiped my memories, I gave Caeruleus those clothes hoping you would recognize them. It was the only way I could convince him not to go after you the day we found the portal in Cantis. I knew full well what fate I might be condemning him to, betraying him like that. I could only hope he wouldn't push you that far. But without my memories…" He shook his head.

Without me, she amended silently.

"I was willing to help the Council accomplish their goals, *knowing* it was all so wrong, but it didn't matter so long as it kept Caeruleus alive. And I hate knowing that I made those decisions because now that I remember everything, it feels like the worst kind of betrayal of what I promised to do. I don't like who I became, and I cannot separate myself from that person now even though I have my memory back."

Raiden's shame enveloped her, seeping into every crack in her, threatening to wash her away. His guilt was her guilt, and it all amalgamated into something too beastly for either of them to take on alone. Were they two people who loved each other, or just two people so entangled in each other's problems and guilt over the choices they'd made that they couldn't get away from each other? She wished she could untangle it all and free him from it. She stepped away from him, up to the glass until she could place her hand against it, then his arms closed around her from behind. His chin came to rest atop her head. When she closed her eyes, she saw him baring one of many strikes of his own sword. She wanted to pull away, but his arms were secure around her. She was trapped. Did he notice the way she tensed?

"We found him, in Cantis, Caeruleus and I found that man—"

She could hear the last two words catch in his throat, the ones he couldn't bring himself to say.

"The one I killed," she didn't ask. She knew.

"I went to leave that letter. I brought Caeruleus as a cover. The portal opened when we were there."

She let out a quiet empty laugh. "And I had no idea you were so close." She tried not to let her mind wander down the path of if she'd known—she'd have been through that portal in an instant and maybe they wouldn't be standing here. Maybe they'd be with Gordan instead of on their way to something far worse than facing the Council—useless painful thoughts.

"I should have told Caeruleus everything. I should have trusted him."

"You don't know that things would have turned out any better if you had. We can't change any of it. You made the choices you thought were best. None of them were easy. You don't have to make it all more painful in retrospect. We'll just go crazy doing that."

Raiden lifted his cheek off her head and released her, turning her gently to look at her, his blue green eyes hard as turquoise stones peering at her from beneath his deep auburn hair.

"I kept Caeruleus from going through that portal because I knew he *would* find you. I told myself that I needed to keep you safe, give you the time you needed to close the portal and get away—"

"I understand, Raiden, you don't need to—"

"Yes, I do," he insisted. "I knew you didn't need protection from Caeruleus. I was protecting him from you. I didn't want him to confront you because I feared he could end up like that man. Even before I got rid of my memories of who you are, I believed you were capable of becoming the fera the Council said you were."

She sighed, too numb to be surprised or hurt by his confession. "Well, it turns out I am. I tried my level best to kill Caeruleus, and the Council pushed me until I became exactly what they said I was. You want to protect the people you love, Raiden. That's always been who you are. You altered your memories, but who you are didn't change." *They changed me.*

His heavy brows pressed down, but his eyes went from stone to those familiar pools, Caribbean waters in the sun. She knew she couldn't assuage his guilt any more than he could ease hers. *Are we turning into some human chimera fused by grief and shame?* They couldn't fix the past, so what could they do?

"The worst of it is…when I walked into that room last night, I had given up on fighting what the Sight had showed me. I'm ashamed of that."

"Well," she said, searching for an avenue away from last night. "No offense, but none of your visions have come true."

He smiled, releasing a soft genuine laugh, bringing her back to the start of all this when her enemies were still waiting in the wings for her, back when everything still seemed like a dream instead of a nightmare, when she saw no harm in letting down her guard, when there was no harm in letting herself go along with a pleasant dream because she was sure she would wake up. It would all fade into the muck of a groggy mind, and she would be safe inside her walls again. But in truth the dream was real and what she used to call her life had faded into a surreal haze with each passing day.

She was awake, like some poor participant of a stage hypnosis show coming to at the snap of the hypnotist's fingers to find she'd done something utterly embarrassing—she had taken down one of her walls and let someone in. Mere days ago, she had been avoiding the notion that Raiden was anything more than a dear friend who needed someone to look out for him and who didn't deserve to be dragged down by her problems even while she traversed an unknown realm and risked capture by her enemies to get to him. Now here she was, wide awake, willing to admit that she'd let Raiden into her heart—only to realize that all she had to share with him now was blackened rubble and smoldering ashes.

He sagged where he stood, dropping his face into his hands and rubbing his eyes. "We haven't even had the chance to catch up properly," he pushed his hair back—it fell back over his eyes. "How long has it been?"

Nicole went through the days in her head. It had been Friday—she thought—when the Council took Raiden. She and Gordan drove to Ventura, then Saturday they went to Tucson. Sunday had been their only day of peace with Mitchell. Monday Caeruleus found her on campus and lost his eye, that day she and Gordan returned to Yuma where she opened a portal to Veil. They flew through the night and made it to the mainland the next day. Gordan returned to the wastelands. Nicole walked for a day and slept in a tangle of two oak trees. She walked for another day and slept among some massive stones. The next day bandits chased her into an orchard that belonged to Keren and the girls—she spent that day recovering from a fever. She spent a second day with them only to be found by Caeruleus *again*. She left Keren and the girls on the third day and made it to Atrium. She spent that night in an inn where Caeruleus and Raiden—who did not remember knowing her—found her. The rebels intervened. The sun rose on her second day in Atrium in search of Raiden and that day she found him. That night—last night—everything went horribly wrong.

"Ten days, I think," she answered, folding her arms against herself.

He exhaled a sound of disgust, or disbelief. The jumbled murmur of conversation tumbled into the quiet of the observation deck as Loak, Leone, Tovar, Caeruleus, and the raven, still on his shoulder, all wandered from the corridor behind them toward Raiden and Nicole. Her body tensed at their approach.

"Quite the view," Leone remarked, taking in the blue expanse from one side of the massive window to the other. "Better than the one from the bridge." He spoke almost to himself, with a wistful tone.

"The Captain says we should be there in a few hours," Loak

reported, he stood the furthest from the window. "I think I'll get some sleep myself." He turned back toward the corridor and wandered into an open room.

"*You* should get some sleep, Raiden," Caeruleus said. His concern was obvious to Nicole. He turned and marched away to claim a bed.

Nicole remembered that Raiden had been up all night since delivering her to the apartment.

"It can take weeks to fully recover from overusing vigil's brew," Tovar said and Nicole looked to Raiden. "A few hours' sleep will do you some good," he added as he turned to go as well.

She had gotten used to the dark circles under his eyes. They had been there since she found him, but they didn't belong there. Even when she first met him, with his propensity to avoid sleep when he could in order to evade the Sight, the skin below his eyes had never been so dark, almost like bruises. The longer she studied his face the more exhausted he looked to her.

"All right," he consented as he moved his feet and made for the sleeping quarters. He kept his eyes on the floor ahead of him as he passed his father like the man wasn't even there. Nicole suspected that Leone being the only one left was what really chased Raiden toward a bed.

"No sleep for you?" Nicole asked after they both watched Raiden disappear through the doorway at the very end of the corridor.

"No," he said, finally looking at her and giving her a sad smile. "I think I'll stay right here. I haven't seen the sky in far too long."

She felt her face crumple, her heart aching for him as much as for her own family, waiting in the other realm—her realm, or could she call it that anymore? Did a fera belong in that realm? Could the old world still be a part of her new life? What about her family, back home wondering if they would ever see her again? Nicole dropped her gaze to the floor, not knowing what she could possibly say. Leone faced the glass and peered out into the blue. She turned and followed Raiden.

The door of the room was still open and Raiden was inside, pacing. Nicole stepped over the threshold and looked back to see a lever on the wall beside the doorway. The lever was almost vertical, leaning away from the doorway. She took hold of it and turned it toward the door, it moved a quarter turn and stopped. The door slid closed with a whoosh and a soft thud.

"So," she said. "Vigil's brew?"

"I may have used it a few more times than I should have," he admitted with a shrug. "It keeps you awake, but when it wears off… stars—exhaustion hits you with a vengeance."

"Is that what happened when I found you? You were crashing from that potion?"

The chagrin that stretched his mouth into a tight close-lipped smile answered her question. She thought back to yesterday, bumping into a man staggering down the street only to realize it was Raiden. He looked right at her but didn't seem to see her. He appeared to surface from a dream and was barely able to stay on his feet. They made it back to his apartment and she managed to get him onto the bed. He slept for a few hours, but then—well, he hadn't slept since.

She let her exasperation escape her chest and crossed the cramped room, took him by the arm and led him two measly steps to the bed, clearly intended for one body. She stepped out of her own boots along the way while pulling both her bag and her cloak off over her head to let them drop into a heap on the floor. Raiden sank onto the edge of the bed, removed his boots and the rumpled unbuttoned uniform jacket. He tossed it across the room where it landed in a slate-grey wad atop her cloak and bag.

Ten days ago, when they had been alone in a room, they had been different people, eager hands searching for ways past clothing and urgent lips locked together. That Nicole seemed like a stranger to her now. Despite those memories the notion of kissing and petting felt foreign to her again like it always had before she met Raiden. Now here they were, alone in a room together, and she was afraid of his clothing coming off, afraid of seeing the marks she had left on him with his own sword. Thankfully, this time, shedding clothing was just a chore, and he didn't remove anything else.

Raiden slumped back onto the mattress, lying awkwardly on the edge, one foot still on the floor like she had seen her brother do to keep the bed from spinning when he partied a little too hard. She climbed over Raiden and took the narrow space between him and the wall, settling onto her stomach and folding her arms under her torso. Gim wriggled around her neck and she slipped into slumber before she even realized how tired she still was.

Raiden heard the ticking of a massive clock that sounded like it was hanging over his face. Confused, he moved his head in a feeble attempt to shake it out of his ears. It went away. He relaxed and tried to sink back into the black mire of his mind, but the sound struck again, a steady knocking. This time he made sense of it, knuckles bouncing against the door.

He coaxed his eyes open, greeted by a bleak grey ceiling that numbed his brain for a moment. A third round of knocking reclaimed his focus. He blinked, sat up, one foot already on the floor. He heaved his weight off the bed. His head felt too heavy atop his neck and his body swayed over his feet, searching for that sweet spot of balance. He felt worse after getting a few hours of sorely-needed-sleep than he had before admitting how badly he needed it. He lumbered to the door, grabbed the lever and turned it a quarter turn to the right. The door slid aside. Caeruleus, his eye patch lost in the disheveled black waves of his hair and for a moment he looked as though he wasn't missing an eye.

"We're almost there," Caeruleus said with a glance into the room.

Raiden couldn't stop his eyes from following his friend's gaze. He looked over his shoulder at Nicole, prone, arms folded beneath her chest, chin tucked in against her shoulder, and the side of her face mostly hidden by a tangle of brown curls. By the time Raiden turned his eyes back to Caeruleus, he was walking away down the corridor.

Raiden shrugged away from the doorway and dragged his feet back across the room to sink onto the narrow mattress once again. He lay down facing Nicole and saw her eyes were open looking at him through soft brown spirals.

"Hey," he said.

"Hi," her voice was small.

"Sounds like we're almost there," he murmured.

She closed her eyes and pushed out a little huff through her nose. He reached over to move those few rogue curls away from her face, noticing a sliver of red on her cheek, a scratch. His vision was a little fuzzy with exhaustion, but he was sure it hadn't been there earlier. Then a golden lizard popped out from the crook of her neck. Before he could pull his hand away, the dragon in miniature crawled onto his hand and scrambled up his arm. It scurried over his shoulder as he sat up and tried to catch it. It circled his torso a few times, evading his hand. The inspection lasted about five seconds before the dragon's breath ran down his other arm, across the bed and back to Nicole.

"I forgot all about that."

"His name is Gim," she said, sitting up. Gim moved up her arm, a glistening blur, and returned to her neck where it curled around her. "He actually saved my ass on our way to Atrium," she said, laughing almost privately.

"From what?"

"A tree, of all things," she chuckled.

He frowned while her eyes were down. "From a tree?" He stood up and Nicole crawled off the bed.

"We slept in this massive tree one night and it tried to close up around me. Gim woke me up," she explained as she pulled on a boot.

Raiden was hit with a strange mix of relief and concern, annoyance and blinding anger. It wasn't that he doubted her ability to take on the entire world by herself if she had to, he just hated the thought of her facing it alone, he hated the reason she had been on her own, and the reason they were still running to find a place safe enough to hide.

"You don't have to feel bad about every little thing that happened just because you weren't there," she said, pulling on her other boot and straightening up.

He sighed. "It's not about what happened," he confessed, feeling a decade of terrified, agonizing solitude welling up in him. Those buried feelings were unearthing themselves these days—the price he had to pay for feeling nothing all those years, perhaps. He thought about the night before, walking into the Council's great hall sure that they weren't going to get out of it alive. He didn't walk in there to protect her, to rescue her. He didn't want her to have to face the fate he saw in his terrible visions alone. And he didn't want to be left behind without her. "No one should have to face the world alone. I have. I don't want that for you."

Raiden watched Nicole's expression soften, then darken with some unknown pain. "I wasn't alone the whole time," she said. "I had Gordan, he kept me steady, but we agreed that he shouldn't come with me on the mainland. I didn't want to put him in danger. He didn't want to put *me* in danger, but he didn't want me to be alone either, so he left me Gim." She dropped her gaze to the floor, but he caught the glisten of wet eyes and his heart panged with gratitude for the dragon he had hated.

He sighed. This was all wrong. They were heading in the wrong direction. He had his family back but she didn't have hers, and he was pulling her further from them in this desperate bid to keep her safe—but how could Venarius overcome a palace that had kept everyone out for centuries? How else could they go up against some-one like him?

"Ray," Caeruleus called, his voice strained with urgency and disbelief. "You two need to see this."

Nicole started and hurried out the door. He lurched to follow, socks slipping on the floor. As he turned into the corridor his feet flailed out from beneath him and his hand hit the floor to keep him upright. At the other end of the ship everyone gathered at the massive domed window. He ran the length of the corridor and slid to a halt beside Nicole at the window, nearly slamming into the glass.

The ship was flying low and the grassy earth below them pitched and undulated like the waves of an emerald sea. Hills, they were sailing over the hills of the midlands and out ahead of them stood the monument Raiden had only ever seen as illustrations in books.

At a distance it looked like a lone mountain, jutting sharp and incongruous from the soft rolling ocean of green mounds. Illustrations could not prepare the eye for the gleam of it, great veins of exposed crystal ran through the stone walls, shining in the sunlight. Raiden was so captivated by the palace that he didn't immediately notice what had sparked that incredulous tone in Caeruleus' voice.

Surrounding the palace was a dark mass, a strange stain on the bright green carpet draped over the hills. The ship swooped in closer and his eyes picked out familiar shapes and patterns from the strange formation. People. Not just people, a veritable camp. An impromptu city had sprung up, tents, caravans, wagons, and throngs of people. He stared in awe and saw people springing out of thin air on the fringes of this massive gathering.

"We aren't the only ones looking for answers," Loak muttered into the glass.

Raiden tried to fathom how quickly the news would spread as more and more people realized the mysterious light was emanating from the old palace. Of course, they would flock here to see for themselves. And if these people were here, did that mean they were eager to embrace that feeble hope the realm had almost given up on?

"We'll be on the ground in two minutes," Captain Rhee's voice buzzed through the air of the upper deck, breaking everyone but Nicole out of their group trance at the window.

Tovar, Caeruleus, Loak, and his father all turned away from the window, sharing their poignant looks with Raiden while he watched Nicole linger, peering through the glass, her face a stiff mask concealing her thoughts. The ship swooped around the palace as Rhee sought the ideal place to set down.

"Nicole?"

She didn't answer. A spasm of concern pinched his face, but he knew he needed to put his shoes on. They would be on the ground all too soon. He left her at the window, glancing back twice to see she was still there as he shuffled briskly down the corridor back to the room.

Nicole stared out the window with eyes locked open, but the scene was a blur, a watery haze hitting her retina, creeping into her mind and merging with the deep bruise-blue storm clouds roiling there. *There are people down there...hundreds—thousands—of people.* She barely noticed the soft jostling and final lurch of the ship landing, taking position over the ground and finally sinking onto its single leg because she was dizzy with the panic in her head and swaying with the nausea churning in her belly.

She wanted to disappear, willing her form to slip into the air and escape. Instead, she felt suffocated by the weight of her own body like she'd been shrink-wrapped. A logical thought sprouted in her mind, *there's something about this ship that's stopping me,* some spell or ward to prevent exit—or entry—through the ether, she supposed.

"Nicole?" Raiden's voice startled her out of her frantic concentration.

She whirled around, away from the window.

"We should get down there," he said gently, and she knew he could see the terror written across her face, *I'm not ready* as clearly as red paint.

"Right," she consented stiffly. If she was going to get the hell out of this, she needed to get off the ship first. *Maybe we can give the keys back*, she thought. The bloody thing had refused to be left behind in Raiden's apartment that morning, but maybe it could be left here, maybe they could put them back and walk away.

Raiden had her cloak over his arm. He passed it to her.

"Thank you," she said, taking it and shaking the garment inside out so that the deep crimson fabric was inside and the course grey fabric, like the crackling static on a television screen, was turned out. She didn't want to stand out any more than she had to now. She wanted to disappear into that fabric, that world of static. She pulled the cloak on and commanded her legs into a march beside Raiden to the ladders. It was like walking through a dream—everything somehow crisp and detailed in the moment and yet a fuzzy impression once it was behind her—down the ladders to the lower deck, everyone gathering outside the bridge to meet the Captain who opted to join them on their visit to the palace. *I want to see this for myself*, Rhee's far away voice drifted into Nicole's mind.

Nicole was numb, sinking so deep into her thoughts that the physical world could not penetrate her awareness. She was a sleepwalker following a herd, down the corridor, into the massive empty cargo bay where their footsteps sprang outward into the open space and bounced around them making them sound like an army rather than a small group of seven. They all crammed into the elevator that lowered them through the ship's landing stalk and deposited them onto the ground. Nicole didn't feel any different being pressed from all sides by other people because that was precisely how she had been feeling since waking up to a world where a key to the realm was really hanging from her neck.

This is ridiculous, she rambled to herself incredulously. *Sovereignty can't just fall from the sky, materialize around your neck on a wave of light and give you a job you don't want. What kind of system for establishing authority is that?* If she had been having this inner dialog out loud, she would be shouting, her voice cracking, as everyone stepped out of the elevator and onto the squishy grass-covered earth. *I'm not doing this.*

The ship sat perched on a hill behind the palace, too steep for people to gather and set up their camps. It was the kind of hill Nicole would have conquered as a child, reaching the top breathless but victorious only to lie down and roll to the bottom in a dizzying exhilarating rush. But she tromped down the slope like everyone else, their steps falling heavily as they leaned back to fight gravity's alluring tug.

The mountainous palace sat in a sort of shallow valley at the bottom of the several surrounding hills, a great gem nestled in the soft depression of a plush earthen pillow. As they hiked around the base of the palace Nicole pulled her hood up and refused to look up at it. She watched her feet in the grass and tried to keep her breathing slow as the distant roar of a crowd reached them. Her heart thudded faster as the crowd grew louder. Hundreds of voices conversing—excited and confounded by the arrival of one of the Council's ships—hit Nicole like an ocean wave, scrubbing away the clarity of her thoughts, words she was trying to write in the sand. They reached the fringes of the crowd, which had an air of an unruly spontaneous festival. Voices cried out to them.

"Did the Council send you?"

"Where is the Council?"

She was vaguely aware of Raiden's hand around hers. Nicole poured her mind into that contact, attempting to escape the voices from the crowd hitting her by counting the calluses on Raiden's palm against hers. Her hand was slick with anxiety, easily able to slip free of his grip. But the tension in his hand was familiar. *He doesn't like crowds*, she remembered, feeling his eagerness to get through the masses in his quick pace. She squeezed his hand sympathetically. *He panics around this many people and the noise*—she recalled the first time she saw it, when he walked into the crowd of students at her high school. He had needed her hand then and he needed it now, so she let him lead her through the crowd while she kept her head down, her hood blocking out everything but her feet, Raiden's legs and their joined hands between them. There was a crisp chill in the air, enough to turn her breaths into little white puffs despite the sun shining unhindered overhead.

"The doors won't open."

"They're still sealed."

"We've already tried."

Countless voices called to them from nearby and deep in the crowd.

Her heart seized at the sight of stone-hewn steps suddenly at her feet. Her legs were still on auto, her hand latched to Raiden's, and up she went before she could think of saying she would rather not. She had to drag her eyes up from the ground, and by the time she managed it, they were almost to the top of what seemed only half a staircase, a far more welcoming entrance than the ungodly height of the courts atop the hill in Atrium. The doors were massive but somehow still modest compared to the Council's ornate doors.

If I walk up to those doors and they open for us does that mean I'm agreeing to this? Am I signing some sort of contract if I step inside this place? Her heart raced so furiously she imagined the thumping blood in her head as a fist knocking against those tremendous doors. *Maybe they won't open*, she thought desperately as they reached the top step and approached the doors. On cue to crush her feeble hope and smother her in the sickening fear she'd been harboring all morning, the doors split apart.

The light of the beacon surged through the narrow opening. When the flash hit them, everyone raised their hands to shield their eyes and braced themselves, but the flood of light—although it seemed to crash through the doors with physical force—was merely light. The palace sighed—a wave of warmth and a surge of air met their faces—it had been waiting for them with bated breath. A hush fell over the humming crowd below as suddenly as the doors opened. The light died and the air went cold again. There was dead silence as the doors opened the rest of the way, slow and heavy, hinges moaning with a yawn that had been building for centuries.

A great collective murmur rose up behind them from the gathered people. Nicole looked up, there was no more beacon reaching into the sky. She dropped her gaze to the open doors. Contrary to what might have been suggested by the shining beam of light bursting from within the grand structure, through the gaping doorway, the entranceway was dim—a mouth of shadows.

A clatter of shoes upon stone surged behind them. Nicole and everyone around her turned to see a wave of people washing up the steps, questions pouring from their mouths in an indiscernible cacophony.

"You might want to pull those keys out," Loak leaned down behind them and rumbled low between Nicole and Raiden's ears.

This was apparently the clearest answer to the flood of questions. Nicole found the chord against her neck, hooked her finger around it and pulled until the key emerged from beneath her shirt and cloak. She glanced at Raiden, seeing his own key now against his chest. His gleamed, white and made of crystal that almost glowed. Hers was a dark purple amethyst.

The nearest eyes fell on the keys and those who understood passed the news back, and it moved through the crowed.

"The keys!"

"They have the keys!"

"The keys have found their kings!"

"The keys have been claimed!"

Strangers lunged forward to take Nicole and Raiden's hands; words she couldn't quite keep up with tumbled from their mouths and she could only grasp some here or there, like *honor, unbelievable, at last!* Then people around them began to disappear, she imagined them slipping through the ether back to their homes, to the bustling streets of their towns to deliver the news. Bouquets of flowers large and small materialized in people's hands and were thrust into Nicole and Raiden's arms. The encampment below became a roar of excitement, cheers, singing, laughter, applause, and the people's stillness broke into a mess of movement, some rushing back to their tents, their caravans, still more people disappeared on the breeze, swept away like dandelion seeds and swallowed up by the sky.

A loud caw from behind her crashed through her mind and she jumped, realizing Caeruleus was beside her. The raven on his shoulder puffed up and cawed again. Nicole looked at it. The raven turned its head to peer at her with one black eye, taking her in carefully with a curious gaze that seemed to be looking past her face. Then it snapped its beak in a triplet of clicks.

"Should we wander in, see what's inside?" She wasn't sure who said it. Tovar? Leone?

"I suppose so," Raiden said, she recognized his voice mostly from its proximity to her right ear, but she could tell even he was as stunned by all this as she was mortified, his words sluggish with trepidation.

They crept through the doorway. Nicole couldn't help looking up at it as they passed from the sunshine into the musty dimness. As soon as she and Raiden stepped over the threshold, the doors slammed shut behind them—Tovar and Captain Rhee bringing up the rear were shoved inside—stirring the air with a forceful gust and bone-shaking boom that startled her and the bouquets dropped from her arms, flowers scattering at her feet. They were closed up in dusty grey silence. The exuberance outside murmured through the doors as a distant muffled roar.

"Welcome home," someone murmured and a couple anxious chuckles bubbled through the group's collective tension.

The raven sprang off Caeruleus' shoulder and into the enormous entranceway, the rustle of flapping wings echoing and fading. The vastness of the castle's interior was palpable—the silence felt fragile—stretched thin to fill the emptiness. The height of the ceiling dwarfed them like Jack in the house of the giant. It didn't press on Nicole with an overwhelming grandeur and expectation that she had anticipated. The space felt timid to her, shut up and veiled in its shadows, swathed in the dust of centuries past, like a drawn-out silence between two strangers. It was relief from the noise outside.

Then conversation broke the silence, a stone plunking into placid water.

"This could turn into chaos in a real hurry," Loak's low voice commanded attention even when he was muttering.

"That's more of a crowd than I expected," Caeruleus confessed.

"There's sure to be more as the word spreads," Leone added.

"Not everyone is necessarily going to be happy about this," Captain Rhee said. "The royal states liked things precisely as they were with the Council, I can tell you that. I doubt they'll be eager to hand their authority to a dusty old prophecy."

"Without the Council, power would naturally return to the state leaders," Tovar agreed. "How receptive they will be to honoring the old pact of Veil's first denizens may rely heavily on the overall consensus of their people."

"Let's not get ahead of ourselves," Leone suggested. "The important thing is there are people out there right now who sounded more than eager to call themselves subjects of the keys. At least to everyone out there celebrating, you two are the kings they've been waiting for."

"A word of advice," Rhee offered. "Don't let them see you don't know what you're doing," she said with a chuckle.

"Hey," Raiden's voice sounded gently in her ear. "Are you all right? Still with me?"

Nicole blinked. Had he noticed her gaze boring into the floor? Maybe he picked up on her breaths turning short and quick. The soothing silence of the palace disintegrated into the percussive jumble of voices, multiplied in echo by the cavernous ceiling. She managed to pull her heavy stare away from the floor and look up at Raiden.

Why did he have to look at her like that? His eyes earnest with his desire to be beside her. He had looked at her with that same gaze even while she swung his sword at him. How could he still look at her like that?

"I need a little time to think," her words tumbled out of her mouth in a mumble. "I went from an execution to a coronation in a matter of hours. I—I just need—" her voice failed her and her eyes fell away from his bright understanding gaze and onto a corridor, an escape route. "I won't be gone long," she insisted hastily, her stride tense as she held back the urge to run until she was out of sight. Her hand closed around the key.

She didn't glance back.

Seven

Someone asked, "Where's she going?" but Nicole was already around the corner and a long corridor stretched out before her.

The urge to run pulled at her, stretching her legs to their full stride, pushing as hard as her lungs and heart would allow. She pulled the key off her neck and dropped it. A tiny *ting* rang out as it hit the stone floor. *I can't be here anymore.* The corridor was long— it flickered. A familiar set of ornate doors appeared ahead of her— the Council waiting behind them. *No—not here!*—her magic swelled with the furious pounding of her heart until it rolled through her. *Anywhere but here*, she pleaded and then she wasn't.

The sudden shift of through the ether derailed her. The dim hall erupted with sunlight. The walls sliding past her fractured into dark pillars—trees whipping by her. Hard polished stone turned into spongy grassy earth under her feet. Her stride faltered between the imperative to run and the reeling shock of change. That split second of slack confusion in her muscles turned into a stumble and she fell. Her body came to a stop and she felt every part of her sag against the earth, yet her head insisted she was still moving, spinning. The sky looked down at her and her eyes swam in it.

The hissing of a breeze through canopies filled the air. She rolled over onto her stomach. Then she dragged her legs up under her torso, the ground still wobbling, or maybe she was. She pushed herself up onto her hands and knees, and spotted it—that damn key swinging like a pendulum from her neck. She groaned as she sat up, but when she looked ahead, her heart grew a little lighter. A short laugh slipped past her mouth at the sight of Keren's cottage. With giddy drive she picked herself up and stumbled forward into a jog. She hit the door. It was unlocked and she practically fell over the threshold when it opened.

She was halfway across the living room when the door to the kitchen was yanked open, but the look of concern on Keren's face broke into one of delightful shock, eyes wide and mouth opening into a smile. The girls were on her heels, peering around her through the kitchen door.

"Nicole," they chorused.

"Hi," she said, breathless.

Asi and Fen pushed past Keren and captured Nicole in a dual embrace. Nicole was a little surprised at the intensity of their joy and her own. For only spending two days with them they still felt like family.

"There were some terrible rumors in town today," Fen said into Nicole's collarbone.

"People were saying the fera destroyed the courts," Asi murmured into her back.

Nicole cleared her throat. "I did do that," she confessed. The girls released her to step back and stare, eyes wide with admiration and she wasn't sure she deserved it.

"We were starting to worry," Keren admitted. "You have a knack for timing though, I must say. With that light in the sky, a dragon showing up here this morning, and the rumors in town—"

"Dragon?! Gordan was *here*?" Her heart pitched forward against her sternum.

"He was," Keren said. "Looking for you."

Nicole let out a pathetic hybrid of a whimper and a groan. "Did he head for Atrium?" She asked, her heart accelerating into frenzy so soon after regaining a calm beat. "He's going to get himself killed, that son of a—"

"Well yes, but the whole village of Witch Haven saw him fly over earlier, and he was heading west again. Had to be him, I can't imagine *two* dragons would suddenly be crazy enough to return to the mainland on the same day."

"That—he's gonna—why would he—" bursts of incoherent frustration and concern grumbled out of her throat.

"All right," Keren soothed, closing her green-stained fingers around Nicole's hand to pull her out of her downward spiral. "There's nothing between Witch Haven and the coast, and no one blood thirsty enough to kill a dragon could have been prepared for him anyway. He's far out to sea and well out of sight by now. I'm sure he's perfectly fine," she insisted.

Nicole squirmed a little with the urge to protest even though what Keren said was completely reasonable. *He's not all right*, she thought with a dreadful certainty that she didn't understand and didn't like. Flying over Veil in plain sight was so blatantly dangerous and only days ago he wouldn't risk it. She feared he would only do something like that if he no longer cared about his safety. Her face pinched in her attempt to find comfort in Keren's logic, fighting back the dread persisting in her chest.

"Are you hurt?" Fen asked, taking her right hand from Keren to examine it. Nicole realized she was looking at the strange scar that started between the base of her index and middle fingers, an erratic red path like a thin creeping vine traveling over the back of her hand to her wrist and up her arm and not quite concealed by the white fabric of her sleeve. Fen's deep brown eyes followed the lines, faint through the fabric, up her forearm, snaking and fracturing its way toward her elbow, until her cloak hindered the examination any further.

"A few marks maybe, and a bruise here and there, but I should be all right," she tried to prop her words up with confidence and hide the underlying confession in her head, *I don't feel all right*. But she shoved her honesty back beneath little truths and optimistic statements.

"We're so glad you're here in one piece," Keren assured her.

She almost laughed to herself, *one piece…sure.*

"What happened in Atrium?" Asi asked.

"Did you find him?" Fen demanded.

Raiden, she thought, and a jolt of guilt hit her. "Yes," she said, sadness softening her voice. "I found him. And he's all right. Even our friend, the agent with one eye, is all right."

The girls' faces puckered with distaste.

"Why would we care?" Fen countered.

"It turns out he's Raiden's childhood friend. And…for all the trouble he caused," she said, thinking of Gordan with a sharp pang, "he risked everything to help me last night. Even if it was for Raiden's sake, he betrayed the Council at a terrible price. He lost his eye following their orders, but he lost his wings to help me."

She didn't feel the need to tell them about the gruesome repercussions of Caeruleus breaking his oath to the Council, the wings they'd given him turning into torturous writhing growths, deforming and withering until Loak severed the cancerous things from his back and cauterized the amputations. A tiny involuntary shudder moved through her body like it was trying to pull her mind back to the here and now and shake off the memory.

"I have to thank you," she said, forging ahead forcefully to leave the events of last night behind her. "For all you've done for me, hiding me, both here and in Atrium—the cloak, the money. I wouldn't have made it to Raiden without you."

"Why isn't he with you?" Asi asked.

"He, uh…well, I left him with his friends. They've got some things to take care of, and I was anxious to let you know I'm okay." She looked down guiltily for the little lie. She had ended up here quite by accident, in her panic to be anywhere but the palace. No doubt the cottage had come to mind because it felt safe, like home. She loved these three people, undoubtedly. But no matter how small the lie, it felt shameful to her.

When she glanced around the room to keep her guilty gaze from meeting their eyes, she noticed her large camping backpack sitting beside the fireplace, her hiking boots sitting beside it. Her heart gave a little leap of hope at the sight of them like these relics from her old life might somehow be hiding spare pieces of her.

"Do you mind if I change clothes, I've been in these for days," she said, her voice stuck in a monotone daze. Maybe she could put herself back together.

"Of course," Keren said, sounding scandalized that Nicole should even ask such a thing. "Take some time to wash up, feel human again. After what you've been through…" Keren didn't finish her voice shrinking with uncertainty. "Are you hungry?" She asked instead.

Nicole's stomach seemed to wake up at the sound of the question. Hours had passed since she had eaten breakfast in Atrium, and it hadn't stayed with her long. "Actually, yes."

"Right then. You go clean up. There's a loaf of bread about to come out of the oven and fresh eggs gathered this morning."

Nicole nodded, feeling like she was being pulled too tight in every direction, between Raiden and Gordan, being with Keren and the girls and going back to her own family, between safety and insecurity, relief and worry, a conflagration of anger and thick smothering uncertainty. She felt too hollow to withstand it. She was no anchor; she was a beat-up porcelain doll drawn and quartered by the world, fractured and creaking against the strain of too many sharp strings.

When she closed herself in the bathroom, she shut everything out, put the cacophony of conflicting thoughts in her head on mute, and enjoyed the glorious isolation. She stepped out of her boots, pulled off her cloak, peeled off her shirt, shimmied out of her pants, removed the key from her neck and dropped it in the pile with the rest of it, glaring at it for a moment—shedding everything until she was nothing but bare skin exposed to the chill in the air. She shivered. She made herself stand there, uncomfortable in her own vulnerability. The musty smell of oils from her skin, the grime of days without a shower, and the sour notes of long dried perspiration wrinkled her nose.

She stepped gratefully into the stream of hot water, burning away the layer of filth and pain clinging to her. For several long minutes she just stood beneath the near-scalding rain, hissing and gurgling out of the spout over her head. She let it pummel her shoulders. She dropped her head back and let it crash into her face and against her chest, her arms folded firmly against her breasts. When she managed to pry her arms away from her body, she found the bottle hand-labeled *Madam Lock's Silken Cleanser*. She poured a single glug onto her scalp and scrubbed. The steam-filled bathroom ignited with lavender and rose. The perfume saturated her brain for a dizzying moment as she grabbed the bar of soap. It smelled of lemon and ginger—a relief from the floral assault—and she rubbed it vigorously against her arms, into the grown-out hair of her underarms, over every inch of skin like she could wash away everything that happened since she last stood in this bathroom.

After standing under the water several minutes longer than it took for the last suds to slide away into the drain, she finally turned the water off. The silence was sudden. Her eardrums pounded in the absence of the roaring cascade. The bathroom was an open cavern for the heavy drips of water plunking into the drain. Steam lingered in the air as she dried off and realized she'd left her backpack downstairs. She was relieved at least that the key hadn't reappeared around her neck, and she supposed she wasn't far enough away from it for it to jump back to her.

She squeezed the towel around her hair and dried herself off before wrapping the towel around her body and rolling the top down a couple times so it would stay put. Then she scooped up her pile of clothes and shoes, tucking it all into one arm before she stepped out into the hall to make her way downstairs.

Although the air was cold relative to the humid bathroom and prickled her skin with goose bumps, the decent to the living room was enticing with the warm aroma of yeast in the air, bread hot out of the oven. The living room was empty and she heard the gentle indiscernible murmurs of Keren and the girls conversing in the kitchen.

She let the wad of clothes drop to the floor beside her bag as she bent over it and plunged inside to dig out some clothes. Her dad's brown leather jacket rolled up tight came out first. Then she pulled out a few articles of clothing, thick black compression leggings, a grey T-shirt, a sock, her red hoodie, a sports bra, a thong. With mostly everything she needed to assemble the old Nicole, she set to work putting that girl together piece by piece, thong, bra, leggings, shirt, hoodie, sock—she only had one.

She shoved her hand deeper into her bag to find a second sock and as her hand fished through folds and jumbles of fabric it found the hard, slender object that she knew immediately to be her cell phone. She pulled it from the depths of the bag out of habit and curiosity. Maybe she was summoning up shreds of the old Nicole after all. She set the phone down and dove back in for a sock and finally came up with one, it was brown and the one already on her foot was beige but it hardly mattered to her. She pulled it on and shoved her feet into her fleece-lined boots, yanked the laces and tied them with a double knot.

The cell phone sat on the floor, screen down, and she eyed it, tempted to check it despite how stupid that seemed to her. But the ghost of a girl in the back of her head kept insisting she pick it up.

"Oh fine," she muttered, snatching the phone up to turn it over. The screen lit up, filled with message notifications.

She unlocked her phone; the battery was down to two percent. Without a second thought she unlocked her phone. There were two missed calls and voicemails from her dad. She listened to the first one...

"Hey, Babygirl. Just wanted to hear your voice. Call me back and let me know you're all right...okay?" Her dad's voice burned her eyes and she couldn't bring herself to listen to the other message, but there were a dozen or so unread text messages.

From Roxanne:

Marco

Marco

> Marco?
> Where are you Polo?
> Nicole?
> Please answer

From Mitch:

> Where the hell are you??
> Campus is chaos right now. Some huge fight? GUNS?!
> Please tell me you're okay
> NICOLE so help me if you don't answer
> Dad called
> What am I supposed to tell him?
> Goddamnit Nicole

The hunger in her belly turned to sour nausea, and she had to swallow back the thick shame in her throat. Some of the texts were received while she was in Veil—*how is that even possible*—she should answer. She tapped the reply box and began an answer to her brother: *I'm okay! I'm coming home!*—but the screen went black—it was dead. She let out a little groan.

"Oh, here you are," Asi's voice lit up the dark silence in the room.

Nicole looked up to see Asi stroll out of the kitchen, the scent of hot bread wafted after her. Keren was right behind her.

"Feel any better?"

Nicole felt stuck under that question because she *had* felt better after her shower, but now she didn't. "A little," she said, settling on a half lie.

Asi wandered over and swooped in on the pile of Nicole's dirty clothes.

"You don't have to do that," she said.

"I have laundry this week," Asi answered with a matter-of-fact shrug, her short black hair swinging.

"Bread needs a little longer to cool," Fen said as she emerged from the kitchen.

"And what's your plan now that you're free?" Keren wondered.

Nicole felt crushed by this question too. *Am I?* "Well, you see,

there's still—"

"Nicole," Asi said, lifting the key from the wad of clothes. "What's this?" It hung in the silence like an accusation.

Nicole sighed. "My new problem," she muttered under her breath.

"What?" Fen cocked her head.

"It's one of the keys to the realm," Nicole said. "Do you want it?"

"That's a laugh," Keren said, chuckling, but then she saw the stony gloom on Nicole's face as she begrudgingly took the key and put it back around her neck. "You're not joking."

"I wish I was—I kind of left Raiden to deal with it for now. I'm sorry to do this to you, but I really have to go."

"You just got here," Fen said.

Nicole pressed her lips together and looked both the girls in the eyes. "I left my family without explanation. They don't know what happened to me. I've been gone for days, for all they know I'm never coming back. And Gordan's out there too, alone. I don't know what to make of his recklessness today…but I really need to make sure he's all right."

The girls' sad frowns lifted with understanding.

"How long ago was it you all saw Gordan fly over Witch Haven?" Nicole asked Keren.

"We were in town about three hours ago?"

Fen confirmed with a nod.

Nicole pulled on her father's fleece-lined leather jacket and tucked her phone into the inner pocket, snapping the button closed. She zipped the jacket halfway closed and looked up, catching the downturned expressions of Asi and Fen directed at her.

"You'll see me again soon, I promise."

"Be safe," Keren implored.

"I will," she promised feebly.

Nicole gave Asi and Fen a quick hug each and turned to march out the front door, her anxiety pushing her into the run. This time she knew to expect the jarring shift in her surroundings as she strode into the ether with purpose. She knew the dense packed soil of the orchard was going to become deep golden sand. She expected the pungent salty smell of sea air to bulldoze over the rich earthy scent of the orchard. Her momentum slowed to a stop at the water's edge.

This was where she last saw Gordan. She hadn't come here expecting to catch a glimpse of him out over the horizon. She knew he was long gone and out of sight, but the thought of crossing the ocean between the mainland and Cantis summoned up cold anxiety from her belly. The dangers lurking in the sea made her question the power that she had been too busy to doubt until now. She didn't know how far it was, but she had met the creatures haunting those waters and that was one reunion she definitely didn't want.

I've shifted from Ventura, California to Tucson, Arizona. She reminded herself. *With a passenger,* she added, arguing away the shiver of insecurity and the memory of icy water gurgling in her ears. *Fuck those mermaids, I'm going home.*

Gordan landed on the shore of Cantis. He couldn't keep flying at that desperate draining pace any longer. After hours in the sky, beating his wings furiously and straining his aching heart to get away from Atrium as fast as he could, he was exhausted, both physically and mentally.

The stones grumbled and clattered under his weight as he trudged halfway up the beach before collapsing into a heap of sorrow. He could go no further, so he sank into the bed of smooth icy stones, unable to deny his body rest any longer. Sleep did not come to relieve him, but his heart eased and his heaving breaths slowed. He recovered enough to fold his fatigued wings against his back and pick himself up. It took him longer than usual to tear his thoughts away from the agonies in his head and concentrate on his form enough to change it once more into the shape of a man, but at last he straightened up on two legs, regaining the balance of his gangly stature to stumble his way up the stony beach and shuffle into the city of Cantis.

He drifted through the streets, back to the modest two-story house hiding among the taller buildings like a child in a crowd. Being here again he could almost see Nicole at the door. There was a faint charge in the air as he neared the front step, a familiar spark, the spell Nicole had placed on the door to keep out unwanted visitors. His hand closed around the knob, eager to touch a trace of her, and warmth rolled through him.

The doorknob turned and the door opened for him, the maker of this spell did not consider him an intruder. He walked through the house, tracing his steps from the last time and conjuring a phantasm of Nicole from his memory; she was just a cold shadow that detached from his imagination, her footsteps made no sound and the memory faded. Their time here had been so short, there wasn't much of her here really. But perhaps there was another place he might find a trace of her still lingering, a place where he could get closer to her memory.

❦

Nicole's feet hit the wood of the dock and she staggered forward, half embracing her momentum and half fueled by a flare of fear to get the hell off that untrustworthy pier. The sun had dipped to a late afternoon slant, veiled by a salty grey marine haze in the air.

When she reached the beach, she relaxed and looked around. The crescent-shaped bay was empty and quiet, the water barely lapping at the shoreline. To her left a rocky peninsula curled out like a protective arm, near enough that the jagged rocks and few trees were high over her head. To her right in the distance at the opposite end of the curved shore, the cliffs of Cantis jutted out into the water far enough away to look miniature. Ahead of her the empty city of Cantis waited for her—for anyone really—exactly how she and Gordan left it. Beyond the city was the forest and on the other side of that a silent crumbling castle, home only to memories now. What happened there had been nightmarish to the girl she used to be—but now she almost felt nostalgic for those child's-play horrors.

She took a deep breath and marched toward the city. When she wandered into the deserted streets, this time they felt different to her. To be fair the streets were precisely the same, just as desolate, just as silent, but they didn't unsettle her now like they had the first time she walked through them, or the second time for that matter. Now they felt familiar, not from a sense of knowing which way she was going, but because she felt a sense of belonging here, like she was the missing figure from this solemn painting. She pressed on, trying not to think any more of empty things when she should be thinking about finding her friend.

Gordan has to be here. Of course, she didn't *know* this for certain. She felt it. He hated the wastelands. So, if he didn't go back to the wastelands, then *maybe* he was here. She tromped through a thin layer of new snow in the street with a resolute cadence, following her memory—sometimes just guessing and hoping it was a faint wisp of recollection instead—back to Raiden's childhood home. To her surprise as she looked down at her feet, she spotted a set of footprints in the thin snow. She let them guide her.

When she turned yet another corner onto what finally felt like a familiar street, a figure in the distance made her heart leap with violent joy. But Gordan's name stuck in her throat, and she went cold in an instant, realizing the person standing in the middle of the street was not Gordan at all. He looked like a kid, so pale he almost disappeared into the snow-dusted city. In fact, he did disappear. She stood there a moment, blinking, feeling foolish before she continued down the street, anxiously looking up from the footprints to check around her as she went.

She took in everything with more scrutiny as she walked at a brisk pace, shrugging against the cold. At last she spotted it, the only single-family dwelling on the street flanked by three and four-storied apartment buildings, a little yard bordered by a wooden fence and flanked by shop fronts. It was so comically incongruent, she found herself wishing she knew how it came to be like this. She supposed she could ask Leone someday. If anyone knew, he would.

The footsteps led right to the front door. She stopped at the gate—it was only as tall as her thigh—and stepped over it. As she lifted her other leg over, suddenly the pale stranger was standing beside her in the street. Startled, she jerked herself back, her heel caught the gate and she fell, landing hard on her butt. He was a young, barely a teenager, and not pale because he was fair and lightly dressed, but because he was ghost-like, white-washed and insubstantial. His eyes were piercing; they alone seemed almost solid, white stones, unblinking.

"You can see me," he said, his surprise weighed down by a drowsy tone. "You're different than before, the music has changed. Your melody is…broken."

Nicole stood up, brushing the snow off her hands and pants. The eerie pale boy didn't move, just looked at her like he was distracted by something. He turned his head a little like he was listening for something.

"I'm sorry, do I know you?" she asked.

His eyes shifted back to hers. "Of course, you do. You must know Death to see it," he said. "But how well do you know Death? I hear a dissonant chord in your song now, I think you know it better than most. Even better than Raiden."

Nicole swallowed hard, unsettled. Her skin prickled with goose bumps at the sound of Raiden's name, and she shuddered against the cold. This strange boy's gaze made her stomach churn and the sour taste of bile hit her molars.

"What do you want?"

"The music," he said, closing his eyes. "Just to listen to it. I've never heard anything like yours before." He stood there motionless, looking like he was luxuriating in the silence, hearing music she could not. "Is Raiden dead? Could that be why your song is so disjointed?"

Her body tensed. "No, he's fine," she answered tersely.

"Do tell him Amarth says 'hello' when you see him. This place has been even bleaker without his song around."

As Nicole backed up until she was at the front door of Raiden's house, she wondered—did Raiden have to live with this creep around his entire time alone on the island? At least now he was free of this place, and he had his best friend and his father back.

The knob turned in her hand. Her heart thudding in her throat, eager to get inside even if it had to leave her body on the front step.

Once the door was open, she ducked inside, whirled around and shut it, relieved to get away from Amarth.

She peaked out the front window. He was still standing outside the gate, eyes open again and looking directly at her through the clouded glass, but he did not follow her. Although her heart was drumming with adrenaline, Amarth clearly wasn't after her, he was just *strange*. She watched him as he watched her, unwilling to step away from the window while he was out there. *You must know Death to see it—he's dead then, a ghost?* Then finally he turned and walked down the street, fading into the air after several steps. She wasn't sure if seeing him disappear made her feel better or worse. But he was gone at least, or seemed to be, so she turned away from the window.

"Gordan," she called into the house.

Nothing. Silence. Thumping—someone upstairs? No, it was in her chest, her heartbeat. Creaking—the floorboards under her feet as she shifted her weight anxiously.

"Gordan?"

She ventured deeper into the dark interior of the house, heading for a partial staircase which she could barely make out through the faint grey light that managed to slip in from outside. The lower half of the staircase was gone. The silence of the house felt like lead in her gut, and she struggled to defy gravity even for a short hop. Her feet barely made it to the first viable step. She latched onto the remnant of the railing, which creaked and halfway snapped as she pulled herself up the last several steps.

"Gordan," she called one last time even though her heart had already hit bottom.

At the landing the door to Raiden's childhood bedroom on the right was still closed as she had left it. The door to the left into Raiden's sanctuary was open, but she could already see there was no one inside it. *His footsteps led to the door, though.* She wandered into the room to confirm her disappointment. The first time she had been here with Raiden—when he was still a stranger whom she half expected to vanish the next time she woke up—was the night she found out about the Council and their expectation that Raiden would *escort* her to Atrium for them.

It had been the same day she found that shift token which led her to—the memory struck her with such intensity that she gasped and realized where Gordan was. The force of her epiphany and the rush of adrenaline opened the reservoir of power insider her. That familiar crackling heat surged through her, swept her up in a current, and she cut through the ether between Raiden's room and the tower like lightning through a storm. Her boots hit the floor of the tower so hard her legs buckled under her. She scrambled back onto her feet, realizing she was on the upper level.

The last time she was here it had been so dark, the middle of the night. Now grey daylight glowed dimly overhead, the roof of the tower gone. There was a thin layer of flakey frost on the stone floor. Nicole didn't pause or even slow to take in the tower. Once her gaze found the dark square mouth to the stairs leading down, she sprinted for it.

"Gordan?" She called before she took the first step down.

The heavy thuds of her boots on the stone steps drowned out any answer that may have come. The drumming of her feet echoed, and her heart mirrored their rhythm. Her gasping breaths rasped in her ears. She couldn't see. The feeble daylight didn't make it more than a few feet down the stairs. *Light,* she thought explosively and several specks of light appeared like fireflies blinking out of the darkness, swelling into baseball-sized bubbles.

Illumination spilled into the lower chamber, washing away the darkness like grime and revealing a tall figure shuffling like a sleep-walker across the open room. A pained sound—half laugh, half sob—broke free from her lips and she jumped the last two steps.

He was moving toward her when she slammed into him. He was sturdier than his slender frame suggested, but she supposed that had to be because he was a creature the size of a pick-up truck condensed into a man-sized form.

"You scared me, you know! Flying over the mainland—what the hell were you thinking—and what are you *doing* down here?"

His arms closed around her feebly for a brief moment and then fell to his sides.

"Gordan," she said, perplexed by his silence. She released him. "Come on, let's go."

He shook his head. "Go where? You're not real," he said, looking her in the eye. "I went to Atrium and all I found were shreds of you."

There were trails of tears on his cheeks. *Shreds of me? Does he think I'm...dead?* The thought struck her with a pang of sadness. She swallowed hard, his words echoing through her. She wasn't surprised to hear that the hollowness and the missing pieces inside her were palpable to him. That was his gift as an empath.

"That doesn't mean I'm not real, Gordan," she insisted, both to him and herself.

"Listen to me...talking to myself." He leaned against the wall, his eyelids blinked slow and heavy above dark circles, the weight of exhaustion sagging his tall slender build. "You're only a memory, a dream," he said, sinking down to the floor.

The floor tilted a little under her and her head went hot. She wanted to refute him, but how did *she* know she wasn't a phantasm of the past? Her enemies had scrubbed away the person she thought she was, exposing some raw, angry and scared creature. The Council called her fera and now the people of Veil called her king. She needed to know what she was supposed to call herself. She wondered if the name *Nicole* belonged to her anymore because it felt like an old sun-bleached label cracking into pieces and peeling off in the heat of a summer afternoon.

Nicole knew full well she had broken little by little along the way. She had felt herself crack a little when she jabbed a scalpel into the neck of a retreating enemy, bathing her in arterial blood and a dark satisfaction. She fractured further when she tried to kill Caeruleus the day he showed up in Raiden's clothes to bring her back to Veil. And she demolished what was left—*in case of emergency break glass*—because the girl she had been was standing in the way of their last resort, the rage that finally burned through the Council's control of her body. She had been willing to destroy every last piece of who she used to be to watch the Council and their courts burn.

There had been no blackout, no surrender to some hidden brute driven only by survival. She saw every moment of it through clear steady eyes, remembered each death with cold lucidity. The teenage girl she had been was an unfortunate but necessary casualty, collateral damage in the fight to keep her loved ones safe, to survive even if it meant being someone broken and empty and unknown when she staggered away as the victor. The person she was now did not look back at what she'd done with guilt or even somber acceptance of self-defense. The person she was now found an odd peace in that memory, the comfort of control, the gratification of justice. She didn't know much else about this new mostly empty Nicole today, but she knew she was real.

"I most certainly am *not* a dream," she growled at Gordan. "This is a damn nightmare. Now get up. We're leaving," her command echoed through the tower. She thought she heard the stones in the walls tremble.

Something in her voice, perhaps, stirred his attention. He looked up at her. He blinked.

"Nicole?"

He was on his feet before her sarcasm could escape her lips. He locked his arms fiercely around her. In her shock all she could do was blink.

He murmured, "How are you—In Atrium—I saw—I *felt* you…everywhere, like you shattered."

"I guess I did," she mumbled into his chest, trapped, and let out a humorless laugh. "But I *am* here."

Gordan opened his arms and stepped back.

"Raiden?" he asked and she saw deep concern in his eyes.

"He's fine, and it turns out so is his father."

The several floating spheres of light drifted around the room and one passed by, igniting the surprise in Gordan's violet eyes. In the shifting of the light Nicole finally noticed that Gordan was bare skin above the waist and wearing a familiar pair of plaid pajama pants just like the ones her brother Mitchell had.

"What are you wearing?" She laughed, the sound bounced around the chamber.

Gordan looked down. "It was the first garment that came to mind," he explained defensively.

"Okay," she chuckled. "Let's get out of here."

Gordan looked around like he was seeing where they were for the first time. "Yes, please."

☙

Nicole sat in the center of the bed, her legs folded, ankles crossed in front of her like her arms crossed against her chest guarding her from the chill in the room of Raiden's house. Her lights milled about close to the ceiling, throwing slowly drifting shadows here and there among the piles of books.

Gordan sat on the chair that belonged to the mostly buried desk, facing Nicole and leaning his chest against the back of the chair, arms resting along the top. His story had been short, a lonely return to the wastelands, wallowing in a muck of uncertainty and anticipation as he waited day after day, watching the horizon until the beacon appeared and the restless need to know Nicole's fate dragged him off his belly and into the sky again. He felt Nicole languish during his account of the destruction he found in Atrium and the discovery of her fate, how certain he had been that she was gone.

"I'm so sorry I put you through that," she said, shaking her head.

"Tell me what happened," he implored.

Her story chased away the melancholic afternoon light and darkness crowded in at the window to hear her recount the days since saying goodbye to him on the shore of the mainland. Gordan savored the sound of her voice, hoarser than before, grating against the silken silence of the room, a rougher, slightly deeper timbre than he had known during those days in the other realm.

As he listened, he could feel the abrasive affect the last several days had on her—he could hear it in her voice, feel it in the chilly room. He could see the exhaustion in the curve of her spine and her shoulders sagging forward where she sat. Despite the subtle rasp, her voice still rose and fell through octaves of emotion as she told her tale.

Now and then she would rake her curls back, and he'd hear her fingernails scraping along her scalp as the short wild brown curtain slid away from her face. Gordan caught a glimpse of her jaw line, a brief flash of her neck where a peculiar red pattern crossed her skin like the branches of lightning. When he watched her right hand more carefully, following its near constant movements throughout her story, he spotted the same erratic red lines.

This new addition wasn't the only difference from the Nicole he had last seen. She was missing about half the length of her hair, the shorn ends hanging just below her jaw. And perhaps it was the darkness outside and the moving lights above, but her eyes seemed darker, exhausted, and sad. Still, the most drastic change in her lay deeper than strange scars and altered features.

He felt that change in the tower—it was how he mistook her for a mere shadow of herself. There was less of her. Before she had an aura that used to fill any space to bursting, and now there was a gaping hole in her presence that pulled hungrily at the world, yearning to fill itself.

She slowed as the story came to her final encounter with the Council. Her words were timid steps through broken glass, quiet, halting here and there as she picked her way through the horror of being trapped in her own body while the Council moved her like a puppet, and Raiden refused to defend himself. As she relived it, he felt every pang, ache, fracture and break in his own heart. Now he understood the remnants of her that he had found back in Atrium.

"There's still something I don't understand," Gordan said. "I thought that beacon was linked to you somehow. What do you know of it?"

"I wish I could say nothing," she grumbled, and she pulled a chord around her neck until a key emerged from her clothes. She held it out toward him so that he could see the deep purple crystal key against the pale calloused skin of her palm.

"A key," he observed. "And the light?"

"When it appeared so did this, and so did another key…around Raiden's neck. The light was coming from the old palace and when we got there, it went out."

Gordan's mind seized on the equation. Not just a key, *two* keys. He knew the history of Veil, the songs, the prophecy.

"You and Raiden," he said, plunging into the shock of understanding. Peace would welcome chaos, the prophecy said. Oracles were a different kind of seer, with keener eyes. They always got to the substance of a thing, ignoring the shell of it, the details, the people living it—not by choice or some malicious drive to conceal the answers from those who sought them. He had known only one oracle in his lifetime, but he understood they saw the depths of the world, past the facade of time, into the core of existence; the same way he couldn't help seeing deeper into people and often forgot to notice the details on the surface. He always supposed the difference between oracles and other seers was not the Sight, but the soul, an ability to feel more deeply, to comprehend the gravity a single life could have in the world—much like people without the Sight, everyone has eyes but not everyone cares to really *see* with them.

"I couldn't stay there," she said. "There were thousands of people outside the palace, everyone wanting to know about the light, what it meant, and when we got there, the doors opened for us. I dealt with the Council, but I still feel like a passenger in my own body again, watching as someone else pull the strings." She shuddered, remembering what the Council had made her do to Raiden. "I can't go through what's left of my life all tied up in everyone else's expectations, pretending to be someone I don't want to be. I can't be the ruler they want."

"Did you tell Raiden this?"

Nicole cringed. "More or less? I told him I needed a little time and that I wouldn't be gone long."

He could feel her guilt welling up in the room.

"We hardly had a moment to ourselves," she said. "Everyone was so eager to find out about the keys and that damn beacon. The

91

ship showed up and it was time to go, then introductions, and sleep that Raiden needed more than anything. Before you know it, we're inside the palace, and I'm a goddamn ruler and no one asked me if I wanted any of it. I had to get out of there."

"I understand," Gordan said. "But what about Raiden? I'm sure by now he's realized that you needed more than a few minutes."

Nicole's face crumpled into a grimace, and she dropped her head back like she was washing her face in a downpour of shame, then she slumped forward into the bed, burying her face in the cold bedspread with a groan. "I'm the worst," she mumbled into the fabric.

"You're not. Raiden will understand."

"I can't go back," her words were muffled in the mattress, and then she lifted herself back up. "My family needs to know I'm okay."

"I agree, but you're *Raiden's* family and you just disappeared. He needs to know you're okay too."

"He's got Caeruleus and his *father*. They're more family than I am."

"They don't change the fact that Raiden needs *you*."

"Why should he? Just because I'm the first friend he made after losing everyone in his life? He's got them back now. I'm just someone he's known for a week."

"You're more than that, Nicole, and you know it. What does a week have to do with anything? You let me into your heart without knowing me. Love is not measured in time. I observed the two of you enough to understand that Raiden needs your spirit in his life."

"What if I don't have that anymore?" she snapped. Gordan felt the shadows in the room flinch. "What good am I to him when I'm not the same person? They pushed until I became exactly what I didn't want to be. They burned everything I thought I was."

"You're here. That's what matters," he said insisted. "You're alive."

"I'm not so sure," she muttered.

"What are you sure of then," he asked.

Several long seconds of silence passed.

"I'm not who I was," she said. "I'm not the person Raiden thinks he loves. I'm not the person my family said goodbye to…and that scares me because I'm not sure I want to be that person again even if I could. I just don't know who that makes me now. Or if the people I love will love the person I'm becoming."

Gordan studied the rhythm of her heart, he could feel it pulsing in the air—guilt, shame, sadness, and confusion.

"They will still love you. It doesn't matter that you've changed," he insisted. "Parts of who you were might be gone, but you're still Nicole. I know because you came to find me just like you promised. You pulled me out of that cell for a second time. You still love fiercely, care deeply even through your own pain. You try to heal others no matter how broken you feel. You're not all gone, the parts of you that matter most are still here."

A weak smile pulled at her lips, but she kept her eyes on the blanket, some doubt that she didn't want to utter seeping through her silence.

"Believe me," he implored. "I see you more clearly than you see yourself."

She pushed out a feeble laugh despite the weight of everything pressing down on her. He knew she was still in there, at least, under all her uncertainty, all her wounds…the ones he could see and the ones he could feel.

Nine

Nicole sighed. "We've got to get home."

Gordan smiled at her. He smiled more now, and every time he did, she felt a little warmer in the cold.

"Let's go home, then," Gordan said. This rustled her gloom with a surge of sentiment.

"Isn't it next to impossible to open a portal?" Nicole asked. "There has to be magic on the other side, and I'm not there."

"Difficult, but not impossible, not for you. That hunter managed to open one, didn't he? He couldn't have come through the one we barely managed to get back through. That night with Moira it closed right behind us. And he certainly didn't come through the one in your brother's bedroom before we closed it. He must have arrived after we left Yuma. If there were enough traces of your magic lingering around for him to get through then, maybe there is enough for you to do it now."

"So, we're just going to wander around this island attempting to open portals and hoping we find the right spot closest to my leftover magic that may or may not be hanging around in Yuma."

"Precisely."

"Great." She climbed off the bed.

"Oh, you mean now," Gordan realized with a light matter-of-fact tone.

Nicole took one last look around Raiden's sanctuary. The house was filled with cold nostalgia, like the air around a loved one's grave, conjuring up memories devoid of their warmth. Gordan followed her out of the room. They made their way through the house. Nicole opened the front door just a crack and scanned the street, moonlight lit the snow-frosted city outside and cast everything in a soft blue glow. There were old dark storefronts and the unlit lamp-posts, some still standing straight and some leaning or toppled, but there was no movement, no human shapes waiting.

"Is something wrong?" Gordan asked.

She knew better than to lie to him. If he asked *is something wrong*, it was because he sensed her unease in her hesitation. "There was a…boy out there earlier. He was pale and—I don't know—unsettling. He acted like he knew me and kept talking about music and death."

"A death keeper," Gordan said with a nod. "They tend to linger in places like this."

"Like ghosts?"

"Ghost is one name for them. They are souls that choose to remain in Death rather than live again," Gordan explained. "They aren't threatening by nature, not usually anyway, but they couldn't hurt you if they wanted to. They exist in Death, but sometimes you can see them if you yourself have come to know Death."

"Oh," she said.

"You needn't worry about it. I can see them, and so can Raiden."

That did make her feel a little better. Not being alone, having friends who have stood in the same dark room and seen the same phantoms as her, offered a chilly kind of comfort. She opened the door and they stepped outside into the icy moonlight.

〜

In the realm known as *the old world* by people in Veil, a house lay quiet—not dead silent like those in Cantis, just the dark sleepy kind of peace ready to break with the opening of a door and the flicking of light switches. In this house a large shaggy black dog sighed, dozing on the rug by the front door, waiting for it to open again. Instead, the air rippled and swirled in the yellow light falling from the single bulb above the door.

"I think it worked that time," a voice said, muffled and little warbled.

The black dog lifted its head, suddenly stricken with vigilance, but the tingle in the air was warm and familiar. Nicole seemed to step through the wood of the front door.

The dog sprang to its feet, invigorated and elated.

"Bandit," Nicole sang as the dog lunged at her, throwing front paws up onto her chest and standing on hind legs. Bandit pushed her back a step, and she dipped back into the portal for a moment. A pair of hands braced her and eased her forward. Bandit dropped back to all fours, barking, whining, jumping, and wagging. Gordan emerged through the portal after her, stepping into the jubilation of her one-dog welcoming party.

She looked around, realizing the portal was up against the front door. Anyone heading for the door would end up in Veil instead. "Oops," she said through a laugh as Bandit jumped up again, assaulting her with affection.

"Yes, I missed you too," she answered Bandit's joyous panting and patted his side with several thuds. "Let's close this portal," she said.

"There doesn't appear to be anyone here," Gordan remarked, looking around at the darkness beyond the entranceway.

"Dad must be out, I guess its dinner time," she muttered, concentrating on finding the edges of the portal. The icy night air of Cantis wafting into the much warmer house gave her a clear idea. She let her magic seep out like feelers. She raised her hands to the edges of the portal, the opening was a cold prickle against her fingertips and around it the barrier felt like thick humid air. It was like pulling closed curtains made of fog; the barrier wasn't substantial anymore now that she was back in the old world. She was struck with how easy it was to part the barrier with all her magic in the air, like turning a heavy velvet stage curtain into a mist. It was no wonder she could see through it when she was home in her realm.

Is this still my realm? She looked around the dark house. *Is this still my home?* There remained one enemy out there looking for her, and he had who-knew-how-many people at his disposal. He sent the hunter who almost abducted Roxanne. He had a whole rebel movement serving him unbeknownst to even them. Nicole shuttered to think how many people served Venarius outside of Atrium, and nothing was stopping them from finding her here except a barrier that amounted to little more than a smokescreen.

"Shall we wait for your father to return?" Gordan wondered.

"No, I think I know where he is, and I'm hungry," Nicole said, looking at Gordan and realizing he couldn't go out bare-chested and wearing pajama pants. "Here," she said, sliding open the door to the coat closet and pulling out one of her dad's hooded sweaters. She tossed it at Gordan and grabbed her dad's plaster-splattered work boots from beside the front door. "Put those on. Let's go."

The truck was exactly where she left it, parked in the driveway. The old white truck was dull and slightly orange in the lazy glow of the neighborhood streetlights. For a strange moment she felt like she was someone else, a high school girl who had a friend to meet for last-minute plans, whose only worry lurking in the back of her mind was a hefty essay she kept putting off as the deadline drew nearer.

That life was gone, that girl was gone. Nicole watched Gordan—wearing his sweater and unlaced boots—stroll around the truck to the passenger side with a comfortable gait. He moved like he belonged, and in the dark no one would notice he had the slightest unearthly look about him, a skin tone that wasn't quite human, eyes that certainly were not.

The night was cold. *Is it still January?* She wondered as she caught the handle of the driver's side door and lifted. The door opened, unlocked, and she remembered parking it in the driveway, thinking there was an intruder waiting for her inside her house. *I guess I forgot to lock it.*

Gordan opened his door and they both dropped themselves onto the dusty bench seat. Nicole's hand suddenly felt wrong—empty—*keys*. With a rush of heat that flickered through her flesh like contact with a hot iron, sudden and brief, a wad of keys at the end of a lanyard appeared in her hand.

Everything about settling into the truck was oddly comforting, shutting the light metal door which clanged harshly in the night, pulling the belt across her chest and lap, and the sharp click of the buckle, her muscle memory guiding the key into the ignition in the dark, the rasping chug of the engine as it turned over and settled into its rumbling idle, shaking them in their seats. This was her security blanket, wrapping around her and shutting out her troubles, drowning out her doubts and fears in the rattling of the cabin, and the gentle roll backwards out of the driveway. The effort to turn the manual steering wheel awakened the muscles of her arms and back, and the roar of four old cylinders revved as she shifted into first gear and drove away from the house.

The vibration of the engine hummed through her cells like a thousand tuning rods clashing as they turned onto 16th street. She felt strange, like her body was set to an eerie frequency that linked her to the past—déjà vu in reverse, and she was sharing her skin with a ghost of the girl who used to wear these clothes, drive this truck and call this desert town home. She knew at least twelve years of these streets' history—she could remember going to the video rental place when she was little before it closed down and turned into a shoe outlet, and she could tell you the colors that the corner donut shop had been for a decade before they painted it fresh—but now she felt like a visitor. *Is it because I feel like I can't stay—do I want to stay?*

It was a slow creeping dread she had come to know after discovering the power inside her—after learning that she was a disruption to the peace between Veil and the old world, a separation so successful that one realm had completely forgotten that the other was anything more than time tattered stories and myths—that despite living her whole life in the old world, she no longer belonged. This world felt safe, she knew the rules here, but her presence threatened the protective isolation of Veil and the safety of anyone who stood in the path of her enemies who were all too willing to follow her home.

But what if I didn't have enemies? The idea struck her, an abrupt clumsy clamor of hope. *What if we end this thing with Venarius and I'm free to just live my damn life?* With no one coming to threaten her family in order to get to her, she could call this realm home again if she wanted. Secrecy be damned. Let the old world know magic again. Why should she care if she shattered other people's realities? Why should she feel obligated to hide just to keep the peace? But there was still Veil. There was the key hanging around her neck, the weight of it just heavy enough that she couldn't forget it for long.

They cruised over the 16th Street bridge that crossed the East Main Canal, that serpentine waterway drifting lazily through town, and the truck rumbled up the hill onto the mesa.

❧

Nicole pulled into the parking lot beside a small building with an illuminated bottle cap reading A&R GRILL. As she suspected and hoped, she spotted her father's large white four-door pick-up, which dwarfed her dear old beater when she pulled in next to it. She turned the key and the rumbling stopped dead, leaving them in a briefly dizzying stillness.

Gordan broke the silence. "Are we going inside?"

Nicole blinked, realizing that she'd lost herself in the sudden quiet, stalled without even a thought in her mind, starring ahead through the windshield, and she couldn't be sure if it had been a few seconds or a few minutes since she shut off the engine.

"Yeah," she answered, pulling her mind out of its stasis. Her hand found the door handle and pulled while her mind floated listlessly along, Ophelia drifting down the river. The door swung open and a brisk gust from the night barged into the cab, disrupting the relative comfort of the still air. The cold slithered through her clothes, past her unzipped jacket, through the fabric clinging to her

99

legs, raising goose bumps on every inch of her skin as she got out of the truck and Gordan did the same. Vehicles motoring down Fourth Avenue shushed past them on their way across the little parking lot, along the narrow sidewalk past the windows of A&R to the front door.

Through the large street-facing windows Nicole saw into the bar, mostly empty tables, and even caught a glimpse of a familiar middle-aged man with black hair going grey sitting at the high top. Her heart gave an anxious thump. She pulled open the heavy glass door, and Gordan walked in behind her like a shadow. Her dad was seated at the bar, wearing jeans and a blue hoodie—his back to the door when they stepped inside. The waitress set his plate of tacos in front of him. He didn't turn around at the ring of the bell over the door, but the server looked up with a warm smile and called a welcome to them.

"I'll be right with you," she said.

Nicole stood there as the door swung shut behind Gordan, trying to find the words to announce herself to her oblivious father when she noticed the waitress had placed a burger beside her dad's plate where no one was sitting. Then someone caught her attention from directly across from the entrance in the little nook where the bathroom doors were hiding just out of sight. Her brother emerged from the bathroom—forest green beanie on his head, denim sleeves folded up on his forearms—and stopped at the sight of her.

Mitchell stared for a moment, tensed with an expression of shock that she had imagined and expected back when she tried to explain the sudden presence of magic and portals in their lives. His slack face twisted into a tight frown and he stormed across the room looking furious. Despite his hardened eyes, he clapped his arms around her.

"Where the *hell* have you been?" His voice trembled a little despite the stern tone.

"I'm sorry," she apologized into his chest, her words muffled against him as the buttons of his shirt pressed into her cheek.

Mitchell's harsh voice drew their dad's attention. Nicole saw him glance their way and lurch off his stool so fast he knocked it over with a short moan of the legs against the floor and a loud wooden *whack*. Michael had his arms around the two of them in seconds and together they crushed her in the warm weight of surprise and relief.

Her brother and father's joint embrace lasted what felt like ages, their arms laden with regret for taking their last hugs for granted and reluctance to ever let her go again.

Nicole had never been so unsure of what she could believe anymore. In the arms of these people who had always been there, the constants in her fluctuating existence, she sank into doubt like quicksand, struggling against it and only sinking deeper. What was real anymore? How could two of the most reliable presences of her eighteen years seem so surreal to her now? How could their crushing embrace, so insistent and undeniable to her senses, feel so utterly impossible? Her eyes burned, she wanted to cry, feeling like she'd lost them even though they were right here, and she couldn't understand why. Perhaps she was feeling her own absence in their arms, a surrogate mourner for their loss because she had returned but the Nicole they knew had not.

They released her and the suffocating sadness ebbed.

"You've been gone five days," Mitchell accused with an incredulous growl.

"I know," she said, shrinking where she stood, thoroughly chastised.

"Gordan," Michael said. "Good to see you."

"Yeah, thanks for bringing her back," Mitchell said with a disparaging look at her.

"Actually, she brought me back," Gordan said.

Nicole caught a tiny wrinkle form on her brother's forehead before he smiled.

"Well, what are we doing? Come, sit down," Michael insisted, waving toward a high table and hurrying back to the bar first to right the toppled stool, then to move his and Mitchell's plates from high top to table top.

The waitress appeared with a couple ice waters as Nicole and Gordan took the seats beside each other. Mitchell and her dad settled into the seats across the table.

"Good to see you back, Nicole. Turkey sandwich?" she asked Nicole with a knowing smile on her mouth. She was the usual hostess-slash-server, and she'd heard Nicole's family order their favorites countless times in the last few years.

"You got me," Nicole confirmed.

"And for you?" she turned her dark brown eyes to Gordan.

"I'll have the same as her," he said, nodding toward Nicole.

"Perfect, I'll be back."

Mitchell watched her go and once she was far enough away for his liking, he whipped his attention back to Nicole.

"What happened?" he demanded. "On campus. I heard there was some insane commotion. Everyone said there was a shooting, the wildcat statue was knocked down. What in the hell happened?"

"Easy Mitch," Michael urged.

"One of the Council's men showed up," Nicole answered. "So being discrete wasn't really a priority. I—uh—needed a little assistance from the wildcat."

"Wait, you threw the statue at him?" Mitchell asked, his eyes alight with that same fervor usually there when they dissected their favorite movies.

"Technically it pounced on him," she explained.

"You brought it to life?" Mitchell's volume erupted past the acceptable limit of a discrete conversation. "You brought a statue to *life* and I missed it?"

"The *chef* can hear you," their dad warned.

"The guy had some sort of gun with him. He shot Gordan."

Gordan cleared his throat. "It grazed me, only paralyzed my leg for an hour or two."

"Yeah, but when he lost an eye, he bailed, so we got the hell out of there. We went back to the apartment, but I couldn't let them bring that kind of threat here again—first Roxie and then that— you could have easily been mixed up in that incident Mitch. I didn't have any other choice but to take the fight to them."

Her dad sighed uncomfortably. Mitchell frowned.

"The Council is gone, by the way," for their sake she jumped to the end, which was so far from the end of it.

"Gone?" Michael said and Nicole wasn't sure if she heard doubt in his voice, or he was looking for the comfort of clarity.

"They're dead. All of them," she replied with swift cold words, bracing herself for shock or even horror on their faces, but to her surprise her brother and father both sagged in their seats, their stiff furrowed expressions went soft. She had expected dismay, but they only looked relieved—they didn't know the details, after all, whose hands were stained and how.

"Good," Mitchell said, finally picking up his burger and sinking his teeth into it.

Michael cleared his throat. "Let's keep the discussion of who's dead down to hushed tones," he murmured.

"We could be talking about a television series for all anyone knows," Mitchell said, chuckling around the food in his mouth.

"Well, how about we save the rest of it for when we're at home," he added. "Where we can enjoy the story openly." There was a lightness of amusement lurking in between his words, and Mitchell smiled across the table as he chewed.

The smile pulling at her mouth was bittersweet.

"Here we go, you two," the waitress announced the arrival of their food, swooping in with a plate in each hand and placed identical sandwiches in front of Nicole and Gordan.

"Thank you," Nicole said and Gordan nodded in agreement beside her.

"Anything else I can get you guys? Another IPA?" she asked Michael.

"Sure, why not," he said with a boyish shrug.

"Coming right up."

"Wait, what about Ray?" Mitchell asked.

The question halted the first bite of her sandwich. "Oh," she said, pulling the warm food away from her mouth while the sticky sweet smell of the balsamic glaze teased her. "I found him. He's fine." She brought her sandwich back to her mouth.

"But why isn't he here?"

She pulled the sandwich away again, her stomach clenching angrily with impatience. "Because he's in Veil. It's a long story. Can I eat first?" she asked with an exacerbated sigh.

"Yeah, yeah, fine," Mitch muttered, stuffing a few fries into his mouth.

Nicole noticed Gordan was quiet, already intent on his sandwich, which was half gone. She indulged in a silent chuckle and bit into hers, happy to lose her thoughts to the satisfaction of the first warm bite of turkey, cranberry and balsamic tang.

Ten

Nicole stood in her room. It was exactly how she had left it, naturally, from the torn and abandoned school backpack left outside the closet to the articles of clothes thrown over the wooden rungs of her loft bed and the open door of her old reclaimed wardrobe. The strange thing was, despite knowing every detail like she'd been there only yesterday, it had an uncanny air, like a room that wasn't hers, leaving her uncertain what she could touch or where she should sit.

She felt like a voyeur who knew too many things about the person who lived here. Like the necklace lying in a tiny gold pile on her dresser, a small wishbone on a delicate chain, which she'd only worn a couple times before she realized she didn't like how fragile it felt—she worried about breaking it.

"This is more difficult than I expected," Gordan remarked behind her in the doorway. "I thought you would feel more like yourself once you were here—more comfortable."

"It's not that I'm *un*comfortable. It just feels more like a museum than my home," she said, catching her reflection in the mirror of the open wardrobe door. There was a tired girl in the glass looking back at her. She was wearing Nicole's clothes, but her gaze was harder and her mouth set a little deeper in the corners, her curls shorter, the end of an angry red scar peeking out from beneath the collar of her shirt. In only ten days she somehow looked years older.

With uncanny certainty she looked at the doppelganger knowing Nicole was not there, but if Nicole was gone who was this changeling left in her place? The fera before her came to mind, tapping politely, a past life she thought she didn't know. She felt bad that she didn't know the name of the last fera, but she felt closer to that life now than the one she'd lived in this room for eighteen years. How could the pieces that were left of her keep that angry soul sealed in its silent tomb? *Not again*, it glowered, smoldering with outrage. This presence was familiar, and she knew it had been there for days, peaking through the cracks and emerging last night when she tore herself free from the Council.

She deserved to chase down the life she wanted, one where the person in the mirror wasn't a stranger to her. Part of her felt like she owed it to the fera before her, like it was her chance too. *End this,* the fera encouraged. She agreed. The fera before her had been someone's prey for a lifetime. So, in *this* life, maybe it was time to be the hunter.

"Nicole? Are you all right?"

Gordan's voice broke her trance. She blinked. The person in the mirror was her, not the fera from another life with her face, just Nicole, looking more tired than the last time she'd been in this room. She had the sense that she'd lurched to a sudden stop, her head still swaying. Everything was too quiet.

"I feel anxious here," she admitted.

"Why?"

"Because it's quiet and peace is so...breakable. It doesn't last."

"I wouldn't say—"

Bandit barked downstairs and there came the sound of a knock against glass, someone at the backdoor. The rhythm was urgent. There was the distant metallic scraping of the deadbolt sliding aside, and the knob turning. Then the door whined open.

"Raiden," her dad's voice greeted—like he wasn't expecting him so soon but wasn't surprised by his arrival either.

"Is she here?" Raiden blurted. He sounded short-of-breath. Her heart clenched.

Nicole's heart lurched and she looked at Gordan who looked back with a silent *told-you-so* on his mouth.

"What do you mean 'is she here?'" They heard Mitchell ask with convincing incredulity. "Shouldn't she be with you?"

Nicole sighed and hurried past Gordan into the hall.

"That's not funny, Mitch," she called on her way down the hall. She stopped on the landing to add, "That's just mean."

Raiden spotted her from where he stood at the backdoor below, and his body sagged drastically; he looked close to buckling under his relief.

"It was a little funny," Mitchell muttered.

Nicole made her way down the stairs, the rhythm of her feet like a heartbeat, and Raiden met her at the bottom step, arms eager to close around her.

"You scared me for a bit there."

"I did say I would be back," she reminded him. "I wasn't going to disappear forever."

"Things haven't been going the way we planned," he said, releasing her from his arms. He looked up past Nicole to the landing atop the stairs. "Gordan," he said. "I'm glad you're here."

"Likewise," Gordan answered.

Nicole heard the note of surprise in Gordan's voice, and she felt sure that he was attempting to reconcile Raiden's previous sentiments toward him with this new reaction, just as she was.

"Why isn't the whole crew with you?" Nicole wondered.

"Caeruleus and Loak are waiting back in Cantis," Raiden admitted.

"Oh."

"Who?" Michael asked, suspicion in his voice at the sound of names he didn't know.

"Friends," Raiden explained. "I grew up with Caeruleus, and Loak was my father's good friend."

"Is," Nicole corrected.

"*Is* my father's good friend," Raiden said.

"And they're waiting back in Cantis because?" Mitchell pressed.

Nicole and Raiden looked at each other, stuck in silence while they both searched for the right words and hoped the other would be the one to answer first. Her dad eyed them, no doubt suspecting the complexity of the answer in their hesitation.

"Maybe it's about time for that long story," Michael suggested.

❧

Relieved to have the shoes off his feet, Gordan sat soaking up the silence in the living room from his place at one end of the L-shaped couch. Nicole sat snug in the corner of the couch with her legs crossed in front of her, which meant her left knee was in Raiden's lap beside her, and he rested his arm on her leg, soothing his anxiety with that contact. But she comforted herself with her arms crossed firmly against her body while she pressed herself back into the couch cushions. Gordan could feel that while Raiden wanted her closer, she was keeping herself away as discretely as she could.

Mitchell sat on the other end of the couch, his back braced against the arm so that he could face Nicole and Raiden. Michael stood, occasionally pacing the living room while he listened to the story with severe interest. Nicole and Raiden pieced it all together, her days and his; taking turns to craft the entire tale for them, leaving out the more distressing details of their confrontation with the Council.

Gordan watched Mitchell's face pinch and felt a little suspicion in the air. Perhaps he didn't trust this sanitized details of this story. Gordan could read Nicole's soul like a book, but after eighteen years together, Mitchell seemed to read his sister just as well.

The reveal of the keys to the palace waiting for them back in Veil weighed the silence down like a massive iron anchor sinking further into the depths of uncertainty. No one quite knew how to break the expanding silence. Even Gordan didn't believe it yet, and he heard this news hours ago.

"That's…" Mitchell made the first attempt to break the silence.

"That's got to make me royalty by relation, right?"

Laughter bubbled up through the heavy silence, first from Nicole, then Michael and Raiden.

"I'm serious," Mitchell insisted without so much as a smile. "That makes me a prince or something. I'm pretty sure that's how it works, brother to the queen is a prince."

"I think that only applies if Dad was royalty—"

"Nope. I'm going to insist you call me Prince Mitchell now," he demanded.

"Fine," Nicole agreed, laughing quietly. "Then Bandit might as well be a prince too."

At the sound of his name, the shaggy black dog flopped against the carpet and got up, wagging his way to Nicole to insert a smiling, mouth-breathing head into her lap.

"He sure is moving a lot faster with you back home," her father remarked.

"I told you he was bummed with her gone," Mitchell said.

"Hold on," Nicole said, looking up at her brother. "What day is it? Should you even be here, Mitch?"

"It's Friday," he answered. "But my sister disappeared and I spent two days in my apartment hoping she'd turn up and trying to figure out how to tell dad when she didn't. I came home on Wednesday to tell him, and wouldn't you know it, he had a tough time with that, so school didn't seem all that pressing."

Despite his light tone, the mingling of Mitchell's anger, grief and relief permeated the air in the room; it infected everyone like a sickness and Nicole darkened with painful guilt that hit Gordan as a wave of nausea.

"And I'm a prince now, so I can do whatever the hell I want, can't I?" Mitchell added, breaking the spell of sadness on the room.

"So, in other words, business as usual," Michael said, crossing his arms and twisting his mouth.

Nicole laughed and Mitchell scowled back at her, but Gordan didn't feel any real vitriol in the air.

"What *is* business as usual now? I mean, where do you even

start?"

Nicole tensed. Her smile fell.

Gordan dared to insert himself into the conversation for the first time since the lot of them sat down. "More importantly," he spoke easily, because to him—and to everyone in this room who cared about Nicole—it was the most pressing matter. "There is the matter of Venarius. He is still out there. We know he still has plans for Nicole. He went to great lengths in Atrium and failed to reach her. That won't be the end of it.

"The man kept me locked up for a decade for purposes still unknown. He is patient. He is persistent. He is far more worrisome that the Council ever was. He could very well have even more power in Veil than the Council had, especially now that they are gone."

Gordan felt Nicole's tension ease from across the couch. Venarius was, apparently, less troubling to her than her new status and authority as royalty. Nicole gave him a grateful look, her hands absently stroking Bandit's head in her lap.

"He's right," Raiden agreed. "I wish I could say we have a plan to deal with Venarius, but we don't."

"What if we look for him?" Nicole suggested, so readily that Gordan suspected the idea had been there waiting.

"Look for him?" Michael repeated with skeptical discomfort in his voice.

"Yes. We already know he's looking for me. He's going to come sooner or later. What if we lured him out?"

"How exactly?" Mitchell asked.

"We can't avoid this key thing, can we? So, what if the whole realm knew that the new queen was the fera? Chum the waters and wait for him to show up," she said.

"That makes you the chum," Mitchell pointed out.

"Obviously," she said.

Gordan felt Raiden's silence smoldering with concern and fear. In fact, every man in the room seemed to be boiling with the same turmoil, churning around Nicole. She was the center of a maelstrom and this family was poised to tear apart anyone who dared attempt to reach her. To Gordan's relief the dog's persistently happy glow disturbed the thick atmosphere of the room. The building storm of worry was dizzying—he'd never experienced his own emotions echoed so many times over in other hearts, pounding in furious unison.

"It'll work," Nicole said with grim confidence.

"We know—that's why we're so quiet," Mitchell muttered.

"We just have to be prepared, and what better way than with a royal entourage?" She shrugged.

"Loak already has plans for recruiting guards," Raiden said almost reluctantly, glancing at Nicole. Gordan was glad to see that Raiden seemed to understand how troubled Nicole was by this future as monarchs looming over them.

"Does this Venarius person know where you are now?" Michael wondered, his forehead deeply furrowed with concern.

Raiden answered before Nicole could shrug. "I doubt it. After the Council fell, he disappeared. He missed his opportunity to get Nicole, and I looked everywhere for him. The rebel hideout was completely abandoned. If he has heard of the keys and the new kings by now, I'm almost certain he can't know that it has anything to do with Nicole, not yet—"

"Always assume he knows," Gordan interrupted, immediately feeling the sting of his cold remark in the room, toppling the small shelter of comfort Raiden was attempting to build around them. "That's the only way you can be prepared for him."

"All right, then," Michael said, sounding like he'd forced down a mouthful of something foul. "We will assume there's a chance that strangers might show up. Nevertheless, you're all staying here tonight. Understood?"

Gordan caught the little smile that broke Nicole's solemn mask.

"You got it, Dad," she said.

"I should let Caeruleus and Loak know," Raiden added, getting up from the couch and striding resolutely to the back door.

Nicole looked to be completely oblivious, turning her full attention to Bandit, placing her hands on each side of the dog's face and shaking his head gently, to which the dog threw its open jaws back and forth in playful ferocity.

Gordan realized that this time in Nicole's home was going to be far shorter than he'd hoped. If playing royalty to find Venarius was the plan, then she wouldn't be coming to the wastelands with him, or staying here at home either where he would happily stay with her. He sank into disappointment and immediately scolded himself. How could he even think for a moment that his sadness was as important as ending this? He reminded himself that he'd gotten more than he could have asked for: Nicole was alive, she would be surrounded by allies. So, he would have to wait a little longer for her to claim her freedom; just this morning he had faced a world without her in it.

He didn't want to worry about tomorrow—about saying good-bye or wondering how long he would have to wait before he could see his family again—but he could smell it on the horizon and feel dawn's imminent approach like an impending war. The sun would return and this plan to lure their enemy out of the shadows would have to begin.

☙

Raiden jumped through the portal into Nicole's backyard, landing squarely on the cool deck bordering the pool. Nicole stood waiting for him, her arms folded against the cold, shifting her weight between the toes and heels of her boots in the growing grass.

"Did you know to jump when you first got here?" she wondered.

"No," he said. "Loak caught me before I ended up in the water." There was a smile in his voice and she wondered if he was remembering the same incident she was.

She watched him cross the yard and stood there silently.

"How are they doing over there?"

"Cold and a little grumpy about having to guard the portal all night, but I can't quite bring myself to feel guilty about it. I missed this place more than I realized," he said with a smile and a shrug.

Nicole sighed, her shame ready to burst out of her chest. "I'm sorry I disappeared on you like that. That was a shit move."

Raiden frowned. "Don't be. I should have realized we needed to come back. After everything you just endured with the Council—I'm the one who should be apologizing. I let my concern for your safety chase me down a path I don't want any more than you do. I couldn't ignore the opportunity these keys might be to face what we know is coming."

"Fine, we're both jerks," she said, managing a bitter laugh.

He smiled. Now that they were off that runaway train—even if it was just for a night—she could breathe, she could think, she could remember the heartrending moment when Raiden slipped out of her hands ten days ago, and she thought she might never get him back. How much she missed him, how badly she needed to know that he was okay, how much she wanted to hug him again—that desire pained her now after what she put him through. She was still reluctant to touch him, but she needed to synch her arms around him.

She stepped toward him, banishing the space between them. He didn't say anything. They sank into the stillness and peace that had evaded them for what seemed like months, knowing that it was doomed to be brief. Nicole's arms tightened around him, her muscles trembling with effort and shaking with the cold memory from the Council's great hall.

"I wasn't running away from you, it was everything else," she mumbled into his heart, crushing him with all her strength. "There's been so much in the way."

"I know."

"I didn't think I was going to find you," she admitted.

"You did, though. It seems you're getting quite good at it," he said with a chuckle.

She turned her face and pressed her cheek against him. "Stop getting into trouble, would you," she said.

"Stop causing trouble, then," he teased.

Her laughter doubled as jovial sobs. "You're the one who stole from a madwoman."

"I'm glad I did, that stupid decision led me right to you."

"And me to Gordan. I guess stupid decisions are the best kind for the three of us," she said, bemused by this return of lighthearted conversation.

"Speak for yourselves. I don't make stupid decisions," a voice said in the dark.

Nicole snickered. "Gordan, quit being a creeper."

There came a soft thud from the shadows beyond the light of the patio and then Gordan appeared, barefoot but still wearing Mitchell's pajama pants and her dad's hooded sweatshirt. Nicole looked down and realized they were knee deep in growing grass. She detached herself from Raiden, and they both pulled their legs free.

"I could almost believe the last ten days never happened," Gordan said with a subtle smile betraying the imitation of his old cold tone.

Raiden extended his hand to Gordan, and Nicole watched them shake hands with a smile hidden casually behind her fingers. She even saw the hint of surprise on Gordan's face. She could only guess at Raiden's sentiments but Gordan could surely feel them loud and clear. Their unspoken reconciliation made her almost giddy. She loved them both so much, and now she had them back. She'd be damned if she ever let either one of them go again.

"Did you *ever* think the three of us would end up living in a palace," she said.

"The three of us?" Gordan gave her a look of confusion.

"Yes, the three of us. What did you think was going to happen—that I was going to wave goodbye as you flew off to the wastelands again?"

"Well…" that was exactly what he had thought.

"Don't be ridiculous."

"You want to bring a dragon into the palace of the keys? I'm hardly the one being ridiculous here," Gordan countered, looking to Raiden for agreement.

"It's ours now. We can bring anyone we want into the palace,"

Raiden said with a shrug.

Gordan just shook his head like an adult arguing with children.

"You three having a party out here?" Mitchell called from the backdoor.

"No, we were just coming inside," Nicole said, turning Gordan around by his shoulder and pushing him toward the door while she grabbed Raiden's hand and pulled him along with them.

"Are…those my pajamas?" Mitchell asked with a slight smile, only now noticing the flannel pants Gordan wore as he stepped inside the house.

Raiden's heart sank a little when Nicole said goodnight and pulled her hand from his to disappear into her room, but he figured she was better off in her own bed because he had noticed her tense in his arms several times since last night. He was leery about letting his guard down to sleep anyway, and he considered keeping watch all night.

Venarius already sent someone to Cantis looking for Nicole, but did he have any idea what happened to that man? Did Venarius know his hunter made it to the old world and found her greatest weakness: her home, her family and friends? Maybe he didn't. The hunter didn't make it back to Veil alive, and Caeruleus brought the body back to Atrium. Raiden shook his head, he couldn't trust the peaceful quiet of the house or the night outside—even with Caeruleus and Loak guarding the portal from back in Cantis.

Raiden pushed his hair out of his face with both hands and sighed. He was drained and could probably fall asleep standing up—certainly no good as a line of defense against Venarius. He wiped the anxious sweat from his palms against his jacket and felt a hard mass inside his pocket—the crystal ball from the seers' chamber back in the courts.

His hand disappeared into his pocket and came back out with the crystal ball almost with a mind of its own, or perhaps the Sight could take control of more than his eyes. He only wanted to see through the night, into the morning, to know they would be all right and give him the peace of mind to shut his tired eyes.

The Sight pounded in his head and the crystal clouded as he looked into it with the portal on his mind. Then he saw the pool lit by the streetlight in the night, the night passed without so much as a ripple over the water where the portal waited unseen. The sky lightened and the streetlight went out. He pulled his gaze from the crystal, relieved and feeling heavier with exhaustion. Knowing he could let himself sleep suddenly made it hard to stay awake. He shrugged off his jacket and fell onto the bed without a care about his boots or anything else. Everything would be all right, at least for tonight.

Nicole was hesitant to close her eyes, even in the familiar comfort of her own bed, knowing that Raiden was safe and that Gordan was on the roof outside her window where he insisted he was most comfortable. Her first dark dream on Raiden's couch in Atrium had not seemed worth concern after what she had endured the night before. The second time—dozing in the sleeping quarters of the Tempest—left her with a tiny nagging concern that the strange sharp darkness would be waiting for her this time. She tried to convince herself that even the worst nightmares couldn't hurt her, but waking up twice from that place with new marks on her body, whispered to her with sinister certainty that she was very wrong. She knew she wasn't imagining it, the scratch on her cheek had definitely not been there when she closed her eyes in the sleeping quarters on the Tempest. But what could she do? She needed sleep.

She shut her eyes with resolute acceptance even if it meant waking up with a scratch or two. Still, before the soft support of her mattress beneath her could melt away into unconsciousness, she couldn't help thinking that if whatever was lurking in the darkness of her mind could leave scratches on her body then it could probably do much worse.

Gordan felt oddly elated to be lying upon the roof outside Nicole's window again, the hard-undulating surface of the roof tiles against his back. It was the welcome serenity of the familiar. He was at ease here in a way he had never been anywhere else in either realm. He was home, the first he had ever known, and yet Nicole did not sink into the peaceful slumber that awaited him in his contentment. Some trouble deep in her heart was immune to the safety of her home and the comfort of her bed—it pained him. He might have dozed off along with Nicole had her thick creeping anguish not wafted out the open window from her room.

His contentment drained from him as he lay there, growing tense, reluctant to even let himself sleep knowing such a cloud was churning in her dreams. He tried not to worry, hushing his instinctual concern. He couldn't save her from bad dreams. She was safe in her bed with both Raiden and himself nearby should something real come for her in the night. Despite the taste of her nightmare hanging in the air, he coaxed himself to sleep.

It was still dark when he snapped upright, awakened by a spasm of pain in the air around him, raking against his skin like a cold blade. He was on his feet and through the window before he could fully shake the daze of sleep from his mind. All at once his bare feet landed on the soft carpet of Nicole's room, a thump broke the silence and the thick scent of blood hit his nose—Nicole's *and* his own. Nicole hissed, awake, inhaling through her teeth.

"Nicole," he said.

"Gordan?" she answered, leaning to look over the edge of her bed, groggy and rubbing her head.

Even through the shadows he could see the gash on her hand and the blood trailing down her forearm, dripping off her elbow. "You're bleeding," he said softly.

He watched her strain to see through the dark with sleep lingering in her eyes, blinking as she looked at her hand, and then she rolled away from the edge of the bed to wrestle off her sleep shirt, elbowing the ceiling in the process. When she climbed down the foot end of her bed the shirt was wrapped around her hand.

As his adrenaline waned, Gordan felt the hot sting of a wound on his own hand, warm blood welling from his skin. He watched Nicole shuffle from the room, mostly bare skin in only a bra and shorts, shirt twisted around her hand. He looked down at his hand more closely, trying to understand when he managed to get this same wound, but his stomach went heavy with suspicion that this might be the dangerous side of his empathetic gift and his deep connection to Nicole. Whatever cut her had cut him too.

Nicole hurried down the hall and into the bathroom, shutting the door before she flicked the switch on the wall and the light that hit her eyes mercilessly. She unwrapped her hand, peeling away the shirt, sticky with blood. In the glaring bathroom light, the red of her blood was disturbingly vivid against her pallid skin. She looked up at herself in the mirror and saw someone who looked ill, pale, heavy, drained, and weak.

She placed her right hand over the bleeding cut on her left hand, it went from her pinky knuckle to the base of her thumb. Pulling a small stream of magic from her core was like tugging on a spool of thread. She stitched her skin back together with that warm electric hum and when she removed her hand, the skin was unbroken and only a faint pink scar remained. There was still blood all over her hands and arm. She sighed, nudging the faucet on with her clean elbow and shoving her hands into the hissing cascade of cold water, wishing she could wash away the dream from her mind as easily as the blood from her skin.

Why? she wondered as she scrubbed. Back in the courts she had pulled herself out of that pitch-black hole, clawed her way back to the light, to Raiden and Gordan and her family. Why, then, did she feel like she was still there? Why was that pit waiting for her every time she closed her eyes, tearing at her? *I'm not there anymore. I'm safe. I have my family. I'm home. So why...?*

She moved her forearm under the running water and rubbed

away the evidence of her wound. She wanted to believe this was still part of the dream because she wanted to stay in the world where she knew the rules—where dreams couldn't hurt you and nightmares disappeared once you opened your eyes. But those rules were broken when portals opened and magic stirred in her veins. The soft fibers of the bath mat squished under her toes. The noise of the water was magnified inside the bathroom and flooded her ears. The florescent lights overhead were scathingly bright. Her senses were overwhelmed; it was very real.

She snatched up the bloody shirt, twisting it into a wad that hid the red stains on the inside, and flicked the light off before she opened the door. Complete and utter blackness eclipsed her eyes. She had to find the doorknob blind and shuffle cautiously into the hall. Holding her breath, she paused, listening for disturbances from her brother's or Raiden's rooms. Nothing. For a heartbeat or two she considered turning toward Raiden's room, but she didn't want to wake him. Sleep was far too precious to take from him right now—even for haunting dreams that inflicted wounds, so she crept back to her room and closed the door. There was only a dim light from the neighborhood street lamps outside slipping through the window, casting Gordan in total shadow where he stood in the center of the room, right where had she left him.

"What was that?" he asked, hushed.

"Just a nightmare I guess," she murmured evasively, not wanting to tell him where sleep was taking her, even though he knew she'd been bleeding.

"No," Gordan said and exhaled a tiny flame into his hand with a huff and held it up in front of him. The orange light bloomed in the room, and he held it next to his other hand, revealing an identical gash on the back of his hand. "It wasn't *just* a nightmare."

Her stomach dropped. It looked deep, but his skin also looked thicker than hers, and for the first time in the firelight she really saw the tiny scales of his not-so-human skin. His wound was bleeding, but not as much as hers had.

"I—" she was stunned, how could Gordan have a wound like

hers; it was *her* darkness inside *her* head. "I don't know what it was," she breathed. "Here." She stepped forward, taking his hand. She pressed her palm against the wound and drew out another thread of magic. His skin grew warmer beneath her hand as the wound closed and healed.

"Thank you," he said as she removed her hand and wiped away the remaining blood with her wadded-up sleep shirt.

"I'm so sorry," she whispered

"Has this happened before?"

"It was just a scratch last time."

"So, it's getting worse," Gordan said, his violet eyes wide with dismay.

She didn't know how to respond. A shiver snaked through her; she blamed the chill of a winter night in her room while she stood there in a sports bra and a pair of old boxers. She glanced out the window—still dark, but what did that matter? She sure as hell wasn't going back to sleep.

Shaking her head, she sighed and foraged around her room for clothes, leggings, a shirt—any shirt—underwear from her dresser drawer. Gordan stood there still holding the small flame in his hand, a yellow flower trembling in the darkness throwing its light on his frown and her anxious movements. His gaze never felt charged to her, it was neutral, and she knew his eyes did not linger on what he might see as she peeled off what she had been sleeping in and slipped into a clean thong and bra, yanked the shirt on, shimmied into her leggings, wobbled on one leg as she shoved feet into socks and stepped into her grey chucks.

It wasn't until she found herself struggling to tie the laces of her shoes that she realized her hands were shaking. Her fingers fumbled through their task and she stood up, trying not to let the tremble of her fear and uncertainty show, but all she had to do was glance at him—she knew he could feel it, see it in her eyes. The firelight flashed in his violet gaze, mirroring her gloom for a moment before he sighed. He closed his hand, crushing the flame and snuffing out the light.

She was blind again and didn't see his embrace coming. His arms caught her in surprise and relief.

"We can figure this out," he assured her.

She didn't want to let her doubt escape her lips, so she said nothing until he let her go. She stepped back.

"I'll be out in the shop," she murmured. "Will you do me a favor?"

"What?"

"Don't tell Raiden."

She could *feel* Gordan's disparaging look.

"If it doesn't stop, I'll tell him," she insisted to placate his disapproval.

"Fine."

☙

Gordan reclined on the slope of the roof once again, listening to the metal clangs coming from within the shop where the white light inside beamed through the one window, and Nicole's uneasy aura could not be dulled to his senses even by walls. Behind him the rest of the house remained silent and peaceful, Raiden and Mitchell oblivious to this strange new foe lurking in Nicole's dreams.

He watched the distant glow of dawn creep toward them in the east. His senses tuned on Raiden—lost deep in slumber—body and soul weighed down by the events since his unwilling departure to Atrium. Gordan could feel that weight buried in Raiden's unconsciousness—it was lead in his mind, a pervasive tension in his chest, and Gordan thought of a storm cloud, dark and laden with water the moment before its torrential downpour finally falls. At least for Raiden, sleep offered him some degree of healing. Raiden would awaken rested and lighter until a new day's worries latched on and added their weight once again. For Raiden, like anyone, sleep was palliative. For Nicole it had become dangerous.

Gordan ruminated over what he did know. Two nights ago, she faced the Council and despite her victory, she staggered away from that fight wounded. How could he help her overcome something hiding inside her, threatening to rip and tear her slowly into even smaller pieces when he could not see it, could not be with her when she faced it?

He exhaled his distress into the cold morning air and watched the white puff disappear like a will-o'-the-wisp. The new scar on his hand whispered a warning to him—one that echoed the death keeper he had met in Cantis. *Are you willing to follow her still, with such a path before her?*

☙

Raiden awoke puzzled by a dream, or was it a vision? He sat up, groggy and confused. Lingering in his mind was something fuzzy and unclear with pieces of such vivid focus that he suspected the Sight had been slipping in and out of a strange dreamscape conjured from memories.

Somewhere in that bizarre melding of golems and a cramped closet turned coffin, of Nicole slipping off a broken bridge before he could reach her and him running lost through endless corridors in the Courts unable to find his way to the Council's chamber where Nicole faced them alone, there had been uncannily clear moments that overwhelmed his senses and convinced him that he was *there*—some grand spacious hallway filling with smoke, the dark shapes of dragons hissing and snarling, spitting flames through the acrid cloud, the floor trembling underfoot—a great mansion falling to ruin as the earth opened like a terrible mouth—then a fleeting glimpse of Nicole, her hands and forearms riddled with bleeding cuts. It was this last image that startled him out of unconsciousness.

Unhindered daylight set the south-facing windowpane aglow. He swung his feet onto the floor, his movements still slow and heavy although his heart pounded eagerly as he wandered down the hall to Nicole's room. The room was dimmer than his. Her window looked to the west. Before he made it three steps beyond the doorway, Gordan's voice drifted in through the open window like a lazy breeze.

"She's down in the shop," he said.

"Oh," Raiden answered, relieved and feeling foolish for his worry. Of course, she was fine. When would he stop letting every little dream and vision make his gullible heart tremble in fear?

He turned to leave the room but hesitated.

"Gordan?"

A few seconds went by and Raiden thought Gordan was no longer outside the window, but then he answered, "Yes?"

Raiden wanted to ask him about the dragons back in the wastelands, he wanted to know what the sentiments of the exiled were after all this time. He wanted to know if that surge of dragons had been vision or dream. But he didn't want to poison the air with mistrust when he was so grateful toward Gordan.

"I'm glad you were here for her—that you *are* here."

There was another long silence.

"My presence might be more trouble than help over there," Gordan warned.

Raiden let out a soft laugh. "I'd still rather have you on our side."

"That might make you the most foolish king in Veil's history."

"Maybe," Raiden agreed easily, but Nicole needed the people she loved. Any trouble Gordan caused couldn't outweigh the benefit of having him around.

He left the room, stopping in the bathroom to relieve the pressure in his bladder. When he turned on the faucet, he couldn't help noticing a few drops and smears of blood around the sink. His face pinched with concern and he returned to his room to change out of his Atrium clothes.

As he passed Mitchell's room, he glanced in to see his bed was empty, nothing but a disturbed sheet and blanket piled onto the mattress. He wasn't really surprised to realize that he had slept so long. At least his mind was clearer today. He was surprised to notice the bag he had packed still sitting beside the door where he left it.

As he pulled some clean clothes from the bag, he wondered if the lingering effects of the vigil's brew might be the cause of the unnaturally vivid dreams, maybe it wasn't the Sight at all, just remnants of the brew's magic-induced clarity bubbling up in his dreams. Pulling on the pair of jeans and the maroon sweater was a welcome change from the uniform he had been wearing. He felt more like the person he wanted to be in these clothes.

He felt so at ease as he descended the stairs, he could almost forget he'd even been gone, but he couldn't forget that they would be leaving all too soon to return to Veil. In the kitchen Michael looked up from his coffee.

"Morning, Raiden."

"Good morning."

"Mitch and Nicole are out in the shop," he said.

Raiden caught a glimpse at the time from the clock on the stove. It was half past ten in the morning. He'd slept a whole turn of the clock.

"Here," Michael said.

Raiden saw he was holding out a mug of coffee.

"You look like you could use it," Michael said with a chuckle.

"Thank you." Raiden took the mug, supposing he had stared at the clock longer than he needed to.

With coffee in hand, Raiden made his way across the living room, out the back door, and across the backyard to the shop. The door was open and he could hear Nicole and Mitchell inside. When he walked through the door, there they were. Nicole was lying on a bench holding a metal bar laden with a metal disk on each side over her, which she then lowered to lightly touch her chest before pushing it back up.

He watched. The curves of her shoulders and arms had always seemed slender and unassuming to him until now, but he realized her comparative size to her father, brother and himself were misleading. Mitchell stood behind her head, his hands hovering at the ready. She lowered the bar again and pushed it back up a little slower this time. Mitchell watched the bar rise.

"One more—"

Her head gave the slightest shake of doubt.

"Try," Mitchell insisted.

She inhaled and lowered the bar until it grazed her shirt. She exhaled and pushed the bar back up, shaky this time. It halted halfway.

"Come on," Mitchell said.

But her pause stretched on for a long second, and Mitchell latched onto the bar before it sank back down. With his assistance she pushed it back up and onto a rack that propped it up over the bench. She sat up, looking agitated.

"I wasn't going to get that one, Mitch," she said.

"You gave up. You had it," Mitchell said as he walked around the bench; then he glanced over his shoulder and spotted Raiden standing in the doorway. He turned to face Raiden. "Look who it is. Sleeping Beauty finally arrives."

Just behind him Nicole, with a sheen of sweat and a frown on her face, pressed her lips together into a disparaging line. She lifted her foot off the floor and pushed at the back of Mitchell's knee—his leg buckled but he kept himself from falling completely to the floor.

"Hey!" Mitchell protested.

"Good morning," she said to Raiden, ignoring her brother's hyperbolic outrage and offering a smile that looked strained to him. "Did you sleep all right?"

Raiden smiled, glad to see her. His eyes fell to her bare arms, no wounds. The red branching scar that traveled up the length of her right arm had faded to a shade of dark pink overnight. She was healing fast. *Scars fade*, he thought. "Yes," he answered, eager to forget the unsettling dreams. "I did."

She must have seen his eyes lingering and her hand moved to her arm self-consciously as though she could cover the entirety of the mark with just her palm.

"I didn't realize how strong you are," he said, nodding toward the bar, wanting to bury thoughts of the scar.

"Yeah, strong girls can hide in plain sight," Mitchell said laughing.

"Putting on muscle is harder for women," she said indignantly.

"At first glance they *seem* non-threatening, but when they *flex*." Mitchell tapped her shoulder with the back of his hand. "Go on, do it."

Nicole rolled her eyes, raised her elbows and curled her fists toward her shoulders; the curves of her arms grew pronounced, her biceps grew as she flexed, but Mitchell lunged in front of her, flexing his much larger arms, one bent and the other pointing toward the ceiling crying, "Uh oh, that's a total eclipse."

Nicole dropped her arms and swatted him.

He laughed. "Don't sweat it, Nikki, your lady muscles are still impressive. But let's face it, I'm—"

"An asshole?"

Mitchell's laughter roared, and he caught her in his arms, lifting her off her feet. "I missed you, shrimp."

Raiden wished this didn't have to end, being home with Nicole and her family. But they had to go back to Veil. They had to prepare themselves for Venarius. They didn't have time to worry about dreams and what may or may not have been visions. *The future changes*, he had to keep telling himself that.

❦

Nicole was at a loss for what to pack. Any other day she would throw her usual clothes in a bag and be done with it, but suddenly the fact that she was going to Veil to pretend to be a queen had her looking at her wardrobe of denim, workout clothes, and hoodies in dismay.

"Hey," Mitchell said from her doorway.

"Hey," she said, still staring at her empty bag on the floor.

"How is Roxy doing?"

Nicole looked up. "She's good. She was really freaked out by my radio-silence, of course, but I convinced her everything's pretty much all right now. She knows I'm going to be in Veil a lot, but I didn't have the heart to tell her what's still going on."

"Good call," Mitchell nodded. "Was…her brother there by any chance?"

Nicole smiled. "No, he wasn't."

"Too bad he's in Phoenix and not Tucson. I don't know why I never dated either of them," he mused.

"Because Justin is straight and Roxy is asexual," Nicole reminded him.

"Oh, right. Alas, I'm a sexual being."

Nicole rolled her eyes with a snort.

"Having trouble packing?"

"No."

"Your bag is empty."

"I haven't started yet."

"I'm sure you have something queenly to wear in here," Mitchell said, marching into her room and pulling open the doors of her old refurbished wardrobe. He rummaged through the hanging garments from one end to the other.

"Hey," he said, pulling a hoodie on a hanger out. "I never see you wear this."

"Yeah, it's too…fashion-y," she said, waving her hand at the pullover hoodie from their mom's favorite athletic line. The hood was big and the sleeves slightly bell-shaped. "And pink."

"It's *mauve,* you heathen," Mitchell said, feigning outrage.

She laughed. "Fine, it's too mauve for me."

"Put it on. Let me see."

She sighed, unzipped her red hoodie and shrugged it off, took the sweater from Mitchell, and pulled it on.

"Yes," he sang. "It works." He reached forward and pulled her hood up. "You look like Robin Hood meets teen witch."

"Oh perfect," she said sarcastically.

"Every queen has got to have a look—Queen of Leggings and Sweaters, but I'm sure we can get you some corsets once you're over there."

"I'll pass. Wait, we?"

"Yeah, I'm coming with you."

"You are?"

"Of course, I am," Mitchell's tone dropped to a more serious octave. "You're my sister. You were only gone five days and that was torture, not knowing. Who knows how long you'll be gone, and I'm not going back to school to sit in lecture halls while you look for some psychopath that's threatening this family. That's my business too."

"Can't argue with that," she admitted. She would feel the same way if the roles were reversed; she'd never let Mitchell face something like this without standing beside him.

"And, really, I couldn't *possibly* miss your first royal ball," he said, pressing his hands in prayer against his lips.

"There will not be any balls," she insisted.

"Oh," he laughed, hooking an arm around her and giving her an affectionate shake. "There will be balls, little sister. Mark my words."

The portal waited over the water of the pool in the backyard, its presence discernible by the gentle swirling of the water below it just a step away from the edge of the cool deck where the shallow end of the pool sloped into the deep end.

Nicole eyed the portal, a subtle shimmer and wobble in the air. As she thought of stepping out over the water, she couldn't help recalling a time when she'd done just that and stepped onto solid ice, back when discovering what she was had been all magic tricks and wonder, before the truth bulldozed through her life.

Everyone was outside, Gordan, Raiden, Mitchell, her dad and Bandit—those departing and those bidding them farewell. They had already done two practice runs of the whole affair inside the house, embraces, handshakes, *I-love-yous* and *be-safes*, but Nicole could feel a third-round building now as they stood at the pool's edge with nothing left to do but leave.

"We'll close the portal once we're through," Nicole reminded her dad. "I'll figure out a way to visit," she said quietly to him, not really wanting Raiden to hear. The less people knew of her sneaking back home the safer her father would be…she hoped.

"All right," he said. "Be careful," he added.

130

"I will," she replied dutifully, reminded of the first time he let her drive to Tucson by herself to visit Mitchell, double and triple checking that she was thinking about all the things that could go wrong—like he was—do you have extra water in case you break down, do you remember how to change a tire, do you have your pepper spray?

"Everyone ready to do this?" Mitchell asked masking what sounded like nerves with his usual gusto as he stepped up beside them.

She glanced at their dad, wondering if this was news to him too, but by his placid expression she guessed Mitchell had already discussed this with him and had his approval if not his encouragement.

"I guess that means we're ready," she said.

With his packed bag on his back, Raiden stepped off the edge of the pool first, disappearing from sight as surely as he had stepped through a curtain.

"Wow," Mitchell muttered. "So, it's as easy as that."

"Easy as that," she confirmed with a nod.

Gordan gave her an apprehensive smile, looking as unlike the Gordan she first met as he could—wearing a white cable-knit turtleneck, jeans and well-worn lace-up leather boots. Mitchell had dressed him this time. Gordan took a deep breath and followed Raiden, pausing a moment before he slipped through the unseen seam in the fabric of the old world.

"Your turn," she said, patting his backpack.

"Right," he said, adjusting his beanie and tugging on the grey coat he wore over his hoodie. "Okay."

"You have until three before I push," she warned.

"All right," he grumbled and took a huge step out over the water with his eyes closed. Mitchell vanished into the air.

"Bye Dad," she said one last time. *One of these days saying good-bye isn't going to feel like it actually could be the last one,* she hoped.

"Bye baby girl," he said with one last fierce hug. His embrace lingered, his arms trembling and she could feel his fear; her eyes burned with it. When he finally let her go, she blinked back tears and knelt down in front of Bandit.

"See ya, Buddy," she cooed and hugged him, burying her face in his shaggy black neck for a moment while he stood there oblivious with his open-mouthed smile, mouth-breathing happily.

She stood up and swung her bag onto her back. Michael squeezed her hand once more before she hopped out into the portal like she'd skipped off the cool deck a thousand times before growing up, leaping into the air on hot sunny days. Instead of dropping into a loud crash and rush of gurgling water, she felt the charge of magic prickle her skin, a threshold of thick air rolling over her.

❧

Gordan stood a few steps from the portal waiting for Nicole. She emerged from the air like a sudden apparition, nearly running into Mitchell who was still standing there marveling at his new surroundings. He watched her shudder as the cold hit her, hunching down into her large jacket, pulling the big metal zipper up a little higher. Winter in Cantis was much colder than winter in Yuma. She took a deep breath—a little flurry of dirt behind her hinted at the closing of the portal as swift and easy as shutting a door. He smiled a moment at her, abandoning the cumbersome words of spells with ease like shrugging off the unneeded weight of a heavy cloak.

They were standing in the debris of an old store front that looked as though it had suffered an explosion; most of the front wall scattered at the edge of the street. Nicole paused to take in the scene around her feet with a grim mask before stepping into the street beside him. Rubble grumbled under her steps.

She let out a little white huff and gave Gordan a tiny smile. Raiden's two associates—whom Gordan knew to be Loak from Raiden's greeting and Caeruleus from their confrontation and Tucson—eyed him with cold glances from the middle of the street. He looked to Nicole who spotted their chilly demeanor. Her jaw clenched. Raiden proceeded awkwardly into introductions.

"Loak, Caeruleus," he said, clearing his throat to get their attention when they didn't pull their glares away from Gordan. "This is Nicole's brother Mitchell."

Mitchell finally pulled himself out of his bewildered daze to step forward and greet them.

"Hey," he said, his eyes widened as he took in Loak's incredible height.

Loak shook Mitchell's hand. "Good to meet you, Mitchell."

"Er, Mitch," he said. "Nice to meet you too."

Then Mitchell glanced at Caeruleus and a dark expression crossed Mitchell's face so swiftly that Gordan might have doubted it if it weren't for the little burst of loathing that seeped into the air. Caeruleus stopped cold before he could raise his hand in due course, and Mitchell reverted back to his usual easy countenance, turning away from him decidedly as though Caeruleus didn't even exist.

"So," Mitch said, taking a grand look around. "Is that your wonderful castle?" He nodded toward the partially crumbled edifice atop the mountain in the distance to the northwest.

"No," Raiden answered.

"The palace is on the mainland," Loak said, hitching a thumb over his shoulder.

"Right," Mitchell replied. "How do we get there?"

"Your favorite way to travel," Nicole said on the verge of a grin.

"Aw, no, are you kidding?" he moaned. "I thought you guys have a flying ship something-or-other."

"We do," Raiden said. "Sort of, but that's not how we got here."

"This was a private trip, no one outside the palace knows that the kings aren't *inside* the palace right now," Loak explained.

"Fine," he sighed. "Let's get this over with," he grumbled, taking Nicole's hand like a teen disgusted by being chaperoned. Then Nicole held her hand out to Gordan.

"Ready?" she asked.

"I beg your pardon," Loak said.

"Now just a minute," Caeruleus started, but Mitchell threw such a venomous look at Caeruleus that his dispute fell silent.

"I know you are the one with the key here," Loak said, straining for a reasonable tone to mask the rigid discomfort in his stance. "But bringing a dragon back to the mainland isn't exactly going to be the best foundation for your reputation as a ruler of Veil."

Nicole look a long, slow breath and a swell of outrage from her heart gave Gordan a tiny thrill. She might not be a dragon, but he was sure she was about to breath fire.

"Let me make this clear," she said, keeping her voice level. "I'm not here to be a monarch. I'm not here to rule, or *craft a reputation* that makes everyone happy. I'm here to find Venarius. That's it. And I'm going to do that with my *family* with me. Gordan is a dragon, you can get the fuck over it and so can everyone else," she said. Gordan could feel her pulse quicken with the rush of her anger and heat radiated off her. He stole a glance at Raiden's expression and saw the corners of his mouth twitch with a smile.

Loak towered like a monolith in stark silence, and his mask of composure didn't flinch save for his eyebrows lifting. "All right then," he said.

"Raiden?" Caeruleus said, ignoring Mitchell's scowl.

"Like Nicole said, he's family," Raiden answered.

Caeruleus just blinked at him.

Gordan felt Nicole's tension break.

"Gordan," Nicole insisted once more, holding out her hand, and he took it, feeling her pulse through her palm. She tightened her hand around his.

Nicole slipped into the ether, holding fiercely to her brother and Gordan, focusing hard on them, imagining all three of them standing in the entranceway of the palace—the only part of the palace she could clearly summon from her memory. As she strained to keep their three forms together across the distance, she felt the key beneath her clothes grow hot against her skin. The key tugged hard against its chord, yanking the three of them forward into the solid world, hard stone beneath their feet, walls reaching overhead and arching high above them toward a great crystal oculus in the ceiling. It was remarkably clear for a skylight that had been neglected for centuries. Nicole suspected magic at work in the way the sunlight shimmered as it fell through the crystal pane.

They were obviously in the palace, but this room was one Nicole had not seen during her first brief visit. She, Mitchell, and Gordan all rotated where they stood, taking in the magnitude of the vast sleepy chamber. Aside from the glistening skylight overhead, there were no windows. They stood in the column of light, peering into the dim veil of shadow beyond.

Nicole stopped when her gaze fell on two distinctive shapes—thrones formed from solid crystal, one bright and the other dark just like the two keys. Raiden and Caeruleus stepped out of the ether together, arriving beside them. From the look of confusion on Raiden's face, Nicole supposed he hadn't been aiming for this room either. He looked to her with a flicker of apprehension in his eyes. She wondered if he was finally feeling as hijacked as she was now. The keys seemed to have wills of their own, a need to return home.

A few minutes later Loak's voice burst into the silence, his naturally booming baritone amplified by the sprawling expanse of the throne room.

"There you are," he said. "I couldn't shift inside. Landed at the bottom of the front steps. Seems your keys do more than make this place light up and open the front doors."

"The thrones must be an anchor for them," Raiden added. "Like they're jump tokens."

"We've got a lot to learn about this place. Oh, and Tovar caught me on my way here. He wanted to speak to you," he said.

Nicole felt sure he meant Raiden and not her.

"Caeruleus, we're going to put up enrollment lists for recruits around the camp. Tovar charmed some paper for us, no fake names. Care to join me?"

Caeruleus agreed without a word, stepping into a brisk pace across the room to join Loak and together they departed through the towering archway. As Mitchell gawked at the ceiling, Gordan's eyes took in his amazement and Nicole caught a tiny smile on his mouth.

"Who's Tovar again?" Mitchell asked.

"The friend who helped me back in Atrium," Raiden said. They all drifted toward the doorway, leaving the thrones to sit empty behind them.

"The guy who erased your memories?" Mitchell confirmed with a mildly disapproving tone. "You're sure you got them all back, right?"

Raiden's stride faltered for a step. "Yes, of course."

Nicole prodded Gordan with her elbow, hoping to break his silence. "Hey," she prompted. "Something wrong?"

"I don't think you realize what we're going to be dealing with here," he murmured between them as their slow pace put distance between Raiden and Mitchell.

"But if you don't remember something, how do you know you're missing that memory?" Mitchell persisted.

Nicole lowered her voice and muttered to Gordan. "Honestly, people's comfort zones are the least of our problems."

"Offended leaders and disgusted subjects aren't all that's at risk here. You could start another war, Nicole. At best Veil is still dominated by the same sentiments toward dragons that they had at the end of the war, and they greet me with a mob and an execution. At worst you divide this realm into people willing to forgive and those who refuse to, leading countless people right back into conflict."

Nicole listened, what did she know of it, after all? In the severity of his quiet voice, she could hear his anxiety and concern for the lives of people he didn't know—even those who despised him.

"You know I don't want that. I don't think it will go that far. We won't be here that long, just until Venarius comes creeping out of his hole with his next plan. We take care of him, then we go home. Then we're free."

"You really think it will be that easy?"

"No. I don't think it will be easy at all, but I don't think he'll pass up an opportunity after missing out the last time. I expect him to show up at every turn and take every chance there is," she said.

They trailed behind Raiden and Mitchell through the corridors.

"I don't think we'll have to wait long for him to show up. The challenge is going to be beating him at his own game, and I'm hoping we will be prepared."

"To do what, exactly?" Gordan asked.

Nicole sighed. "Do you think it's safe to take a man like him alive?"

"No."

She let her silence say the rest.

"Venarius isn't your only problem," Gordan said in a whisper this time, and she knew he meant the nightmare and the wounds.

"I know," she assured him.

Raiden lead them down a corridor and up a staircase to where the ceilings weren't quite so high and the doors were narrower. All of the doors were closed except one, and Raiden knocked once as he stepped into the threshold.

"Ah, Raiden," Tovar said without looking up from his task. "Good." He was bustling around, organizing a baffling amount of stuff: boxes, bottles, books, jars. Nicole couldn't fathom where it had all come from when he had left the city with only two slender suitcases. Then she realized she was still thinking like someone from the old world. Of course, all this had been in those cases.

Tovar stopped and looked up at them, suddenly realizing there were more visitors than just Raiden. "I see you found Nicole and there are new faces with you," he remarked at Mitchell's presence, and then when he saw Gordan his posture stiffened upright. Tovar's friendly lined face fell slack.

Raiden took advantage of Tovar's stunned silence. "This is Mitchell, Nicole's brother," he said, and then turned. "And Gordan."

"My other brother," Nicole said, concealing her preparation to pounce behind a composed smile.

Tovar reclaimed his pleasant expression.

"Of course," he cleared his throat. "Please forgive me. I wasn't expecting—I've never met—" Tovar stepped forward and extended his hand to Gordan who took it. Tovar gave Gordan's arm a good shake. "Gordan," he said. "Welcome." Then he turned to Mitchell. "Mitchell was it?" he asked, offering his hand.

"Mitch," he answered, shaking Tovar's hand.

"What did you want to talk about?" Raiden asked.

"Yes. Right," Tovar shook his head and patted his chest as though searching for the missing thought in a pocket. "We have people lining up to see the kings, formally. I think we should prepare to let them in, but the place is a bit of a dustbin. We should consider hiring staff, not just royal guards, and get this place cleaned up."

"Uh," Nicole's brain was sluggish. "We don't have a way to *pay* staff...do we?"

"No, not exactly," Tovar admitted. "But there are staff quarters down with the kitchens, and that's something. Plenty of people will work for a place in the household until we can come up with money to pay them wages. A safe place to sleep and food to eat holds a lot of value during uncertain times."

"Sounds fair for now," Raiden said.

"Wonderful," Tovar said.

"I think I'm going to wander and get to know this place a little better," Nicole said, eager to get away from the details of turning an empty palace into a fully functioning royal household. *This isn't going to be my life*, she insisted, *I'm just a visitor.*

"Oh," Mitchell perked up with interest. "Can we claim rooms?"

"I don't see why not," Nicole said as she turned out the door, trying her damnedest not to run out of the room. As she wandered down the corridor with Gordan and Mitchell, she felt herself slipping into the wonder of the palace. She refused to let duties and expectations weigh on her. She'd made her decision. She wasn't here to fill that role. *I'm not going to live another damn day trapped in a life I don't want.* She just wanted the chance to marvel at this world. The kid who had dreamt of castles and mysteries within them wanted to race down these grand halls, open every last door, and find all the secrets hiding in these quiet towering walls.

"Let's get lost in here," Mitchell said excitedly.

She laughed, the kid in her bubbling out. "We could play the ultimate game of hide and seek."

"It would go on for days," Mitchell added.

"Well, we've got to enjoy this place while we can, won't have it to ourselves for long," Nicole said. "Soon we'll have *staff.*"

"Yeah, that's going to be a little weird."

"Think of it like living in a hotel," she shrugged.

"You know, numbering the rooms might help a lot," Mitchell laughed, opening a tall door and peering inside. The room was empty.

All of the rooms were empty. Aside from the two ostentatious seats in the throne room, there wasn't a single piece of furniture anywhere. Naturally, they wouldn't have furnished the whole place before all hell broke loose over the question, *who's going to lead us?* Then again, maybe they really broke into factions arguing about what color drapes to put in the rooms. Nicole snickered to herself.

"What?" Gordan asked.

"Nothing," she insisted.

The second floor had several rooms, and some were a branching network of even more rooms within, but it wasn't until they found their way up to the third and fourth floors that they discovered smaller rooms with their own washrooms and toilet closets. They had found the bedroom suites, more modest ones on the third floor, larger more spacious suites on the fourth with little entrance halls into the bed chambers, dark windowless closets the size of her bedroom back home in Yuma, and much too large wash rooms.

"Now this is more like it, but I bet there are even better rooms on the next floor," Mitchell said when he spotted the next staircase, rubbing his hands together with a zealous nod.

"Who needs bigger rooms than these," Nicole wondered she and Gordan followed Mitchell up to the next floor.

"These rooms would most likely be for your court. I suppose there will be even larger suites for important guests, and larger ones still for you and Raiden," Gordan offered with matter-of-fact disinterest.

Nicole and Mitchell slowed to gawk at him.

"What?" Gordan kept walking. "Did you think I've never been in a palace before?"

"Well…kinda," Mitchell said.

"I found you in a dungeon, Gordan," Nicole said. "And you haven't exactly mentioned all the royal friends you've had over the centuries."

Gordan released a quiet laugh.

"I merely spent a short time in a royal court. It was a long time ago. I wouldn't say I have ever enjoyed the friendship of any royalty, in this realm or the other."

"All right, fine," Mitchell said. "Here we go," he announced excitedly as they came upon the stairs.

They indeed found more exquisite suites on the fifth floor, there were fewer seeing as each one was so expansive, only six. The three of them wandered through the empty rooms—rooms upon rooms that seemed like they would change around them and trap them in an alternate dimension of endless chambers.

"Are these big enough for you, *Prince* Mitchell?" Nicole demanded as they walked down the corridor outside the sprawling chambers.

"They were…acceptable," he said, putting on a pompous air as they encountered another set of stairs, wide and curving upward. "But we don't know what's up here yet."

On the sixth floor there were even fewer doors, only two it seemed.

"Hey," Mitchell said, ahead of them down the hall. Mitchell stood in front of a door looking perplexed. "It won't open."

"Are you pushing when you should be pulling?"

"Ha ha, no, really. It won't open."

Nicole and Gordan stopped in front of the door. It was the first one in this corridor and there looked to be one at the other end. In the wall around the door veins of amethyst curled and spiraled out into the smooth stone.

"This must be my room," she said, taking a cue from the key hanging around her neck. She stepped forward and took the twisted handle.

"What makes you think—"

The large door opened easily for her. She turned back to her brother and swung her key. "It's color coded," she grinned and wandered in.

"Of course," he said, stepping into the massive chamber. "You get the biggest room."

"Hey, you want to be a king? Be my guest," she said, holding her key up to him with a bitter laugh.

"Nah, purple isn't my color. Thanks."

She sighed, shrugging her bag off her back and letting it drop to the floor. Mitchell shed his backpack as well.

"So, I guess we're all sleeping on luxurious royal floors tonight," Mitchell said, looking around, appraising the cold stone's potential.

Nicole gave Gordan an expectant look, knowing precisely where her brother was headed.

"Oh, *wait a minute*," he said with mock epiphany, "You could do a little hocus pocus and whip up some beds for us, right?"

"Oh absolutely, I'm sure we could fashion you a hammock or something," she said.

"Come on, Nikki," he groaned.

She sighed. "All right," she said and looked up into the vaulted ceiling before she closed her eyes and thought of a pillow, a great big plush pillow the size of a king-sized bed. Then a pair of hands grabbed her by the shoulders and yanked her back before a massive thump hit her ears. She opened her eyes to see Gordan had pulled her out from under her creation.

"Holy shit," Mitchell cried through a roar of laughter, leaping into the air and belly flopping onto the pillow. His body sank into the burnt orange fabric with deep cranberry stripes and his howl of delight was muffled into almost nothing.

"You've been practicing," Gordan said with a note of approval.

"Oh, you know," she shrugged. "Conjuring food, growing houses, little things." She could laugh at herself now. Her magic was second nature when she embraced it. It was no wonder she struggled to control a force she had been afraid of, trying to keep it in for fear of affecting the fragile world around her. In a weird way she was lucky to have her enemies dragging her out of her sheltered hiding place, forcing her to fight. If she had gained this new power and tried to live a life back home in Yuma, keeping it inside so she could continue being a part of a magicless world, how long would she have lasted before she broke?

Mitchell sat up for air, taking an amused gasp. "Will you make one for me? But something less hideous, maybe green."

Nicole forced a smile at her brother and batted her eyelashes at him with sarcastic sweetness while she crafted a large emerald green pillow as big as a double bed and conjured it out of the air over her brother's head. He looked up and then he ducked. The green mass landed on him, sandwiching him between the cushions.

"Hey, come on!" his outrage was smothered. The green pillow twitched and lurched as he wrestled himself out from underneath it. "Very funny," he said, panting as he emerged. Although he tried to sound annoyed, there was a smile in the corner of his mouth. "I take issue with this unfair advantage of yours."

"You had an unfair advantage over me pretty much my whole life," she reminded him, conjuring a yellow tasseled throw pillow over his head. "If you've got a problem with payback then maybe you should hit the spell books." She let the pillow fall. He dodged, laughing, and ran for the door. She thought up an army of cushions and in seconds they were sailing at him from every direction, glancing off his shoulder, hitting him square in the butt, falling onto his head until he escaped into the safety of the hallway outside and the room was littered with pillows, a battle field of sleep-over legends.

Nicole and Gordan followed into the hall where Mitchell stood catching his breath.

"*Prince* Mitchell, Slayer of Pillows in retreat," Nicole teased.

"We will do battle again, sister," he promised in his best dramatic voice. "Your reign of terror will end."

They broke down into laughter.

"Okay, come on," Mitchell said, waving them down the hall and marching ahead.

"I'm pretty sure that room is only going to open for Raiden," Nicole said. The door down the hall was framed in a starburst of white crystal like the key around Raiden's neck.

Mitchell sighed. "I guess a regular old enormous room will have to do."

Nicole laughed. "What about you Gordan? Enormous room or somewhat-less enormous room?"

"You can't sleep at the foot of Nikki's bed forever," Mitchell teased.

"He doesn't sleep at the foot of my bed."

"Have you even seen him sleep?"

"I…" Nicole wasn't sure now. "I think so."

"I sleep," Gordan insisted.

"Well then, let's get you a room," Mitchell said, hooking his arm around Gordan's and marching on, ahead of them there was an identical wide curving staircase leading down to the fifth floor like the one at the opposite end of the hallway that had brought them up. She watched their backs as they went, appreciating the sight—this was why she didn't want him going back to the wastelands. She didn't want him to be alone anymore.

Thirteen

Nicole took one last long look up at the door to Raiden's room, feeling her mind slow with the stunning beauty of this dim sleepy palace. She wished it could stay this way; she dreaded the thought of it bustling with staff, royal guards pacing the halls and standing at the doors. When she turned to follow Mitchell and Gordan, a deep shadow in her periphery seized her attention. There was an archway back in the center of the corridor on the other side of the hall from the two grand doors of the royal bedrooms. Had it been there before?

She wandered over and peered into the shadows, it seemed to be a simple passageway, but Mitchell and Gordan hadn't noticed it at all.

"Huh?" She took a few curious steps forward. Then her foot slipped on a sleek sloped floor. She leaned back as she fell. The passage was steep and down she went, sliding. Her heels didn't catch on anything, and she couldn't stop herself with her hands. She couldn't see anything. The passage turned this way and that until it rounded a corner and there was an archway of light ahead, rushing toward her. Before she knew it, she slid out through another archway, across an empty corridor and into the wall.

She inhaled through her teeth, picking herself up. But when she looked across the hall there was no archway there. She frowned, crossed the hall and placed her hand against the wall. Nothing but solid stone. When she straightened up she looked left and right, not sure which corridor she was in or which way to go. Studying the hall, high ceilings, a tunnel of stone that looked identical in both directions, she suddenly found herself in a different corridor—the long avenue to the Council's ornate doors stood before her and her heart raced. Heart racing, she looked over her shoulder, then back again—the doors to the Council's chamber were no longer there. Then someone appeared around the corner.

"I was just on my way to find you," Raiden said.

"Here I am," she said with a strained smile, hoping he didn't hear the tremble in her voice.

"Learn all this place's secrets yet?" He asked.

"Not quite," she said, pushing out a weak laugh. "I think that could take a while."

"Where are Gordan and Mitchell?"

"I don't really know," she confessed. "I kind of ended up here by accident. What floor are we on?"

"The second floor, I just left Tovar's study around the corner. How is it you got here by accident?"

"Right," she said, wishing the hall looked more familiar, but then again it was only her first time seeing anything beyond the entryway. "I should find Mitch and Gordan," she said, turning toward what she thought was the way to the stairs. "There was an archway on the sixth floor, and I don't think it was there until I walked past it. Mitchell and Gordan didn't seem to see it at all. It was this short little passageway that just dropped out under my feet, I never would have expected an escape slide in a place like this."

"Physical passages are safer than magical ones and are easier to hide," he said.

They made their way up through the third and fourth floor. Before they could reach the staircase up to the fifth, Mitchell and Gordan arrived at the bottom and spotted Nicole with Raiden.

"There you are," Mitchell said with noticeable exasperation.

"Where did you go?" Gordan wondered.

"Just to the second floor to get Raiden," she said with a shrug, deciding not to tease Mitchell with secret passages that might only open for the keys.

Mitchell shrugged it off. "Since you're here, your *highnesses*," he said with an exaggerated bow. "I was thinking I should have a title, or duty, or something… Maybe leading your personal guard—you know, whip your last line of defense into shape."

"You'll have to take that up with Loak, he's already set himself to the task of recruiting and training troops. I'm not sure how far they've gotten, but you have my approval at least. Tovar has concerned himself with the matter of hiring staff. He wants to let people in soon since they are out there waiting, Loak wants to wait until the palace is 'better secured' which will take time. His standards are not easily met."

"Doesn't sound like a bad thing to me," Mitchell said. "We're talking about your safety, after all. Who's to say that Venarius guy doesn't hobble right in disguised as an old hag and walk right up to Nicole?"

"I'm in no hurry to start *receiving subjects*," she said. "And we are by *no* means ready to take on Venarius."

"I think you might find that you're better prepared than you think, at least while you're in the palace," Gordan said. "There is quite a lot of magic here."

Mitchell and Raiden both looked at Nicole.

"I mean other than Nicole," Gordan added, noticing their attention. "This place stayed sealed for centuries, impenetrable to anyone trying to claim the keys by force. We already know it keeps anyone but Nicole and Raiden from entering through the ether. I'm willing to bet there are more protective enchantments here that we know nothing about yet."

"Tovar can help us answer that question," Raiden suggested. "And Loak will have a better idea of how to secure this place if we can clearly define the enchantments around here."

"I would like to assist in that effort, I am not a spell worker, but I can lend impeccable senses to the task," Gordan said.

"And I'd like to chat with Loak," Mitchell added. "If you can lead the way."

"Certainly," Raiden agreed.

They all turned and then stopped, looking back at Nicole who stood there ready to watch them go.

"Go on, then. You don't need me," she said, flicking her hand through the air.

She watched them all hesitate a moment, and she held back a smile while they each struggled with the idea of letting her out of their sight. She knew what her brother was thinking; he'd miss out on exploring the palace. The look in Raiden's eyes reflected a sad pang in her chest—he had had enough of being apart. Gordan wore the look of a tortured child, and she couldn't help but question his desire to go on a group search for the enchantments in the walls when he disliked groups and when most of the people here were leery of his presence. But the moment of reluctance passed, and the three of them were on their way.

Nicole turned the opposite direction, growing leery of the corridor ahead of her.

☙

Gordan took one more glance back to see Nicole shrinking down the hallway. He would have liked to drift through empty halls with her, but he had ulterior motives. He wanted to observe these people, Tovar, Caeruleus, Loak, and see what he could glean from them.

The last time he had been in their company, he had been preoccupied with Nicole and Raiden; it was more comfortable to hide in the shelter of people who cared for him and block out those who wore their disproval and distain on their faces. But he had to put these people's opinions of dragons aside. Just because they might not like his presence in this palace didn't mean they couldn't be trustworthy allies to Nicole. Raiden, after all, had openly disapproved of Gordan's presence when they first met, but Gordan trusted Raiden's character long before Raiden returned that trust.

He wanted the chance to form his own opinions of these people who would be close to Nicole. As of now he couldn't say that he would be willing to leave Nicole alone with anyone but her brother or Raiden.

"Raiden," Gordan broke the silence of the three of them walking down the fourth-floor corridor. "Do you mind if I ask how much you know about your friends?"

Raiden did not answer for several paces. "No, I don't mind."

"Loak," Gordan prompted.

"From my time in the courts, I gathered that Loak had a seemingly spotless record with the Council. He trained their agents after all. Although he was my father's partner, and it is hard to believe his treason didn't tarnish Loak's reputation in some way. I don't know why they arrested my father, or how Loak avoided incrimination. But whatever the circumstances, my father doesn't seem to doubt their friendship after all these years."

"What about Tovar," Gordan said.

"I've only known him a couple weeks now, but he was willing to risk more than he should have for a stranger. He was helping the rebel efforts—which is most likely the reason he agreed to help someone openly opposing the Council—he's an incredible spell worker. Part of me thinks he helped me just because he liked the challenge my requests presented him. He ran a simple charm shop, but he clearly has the talent for difficult work and enjoys it—the kind you couldn't do in the city without being registered and watched closely by the Council."

"I see."

"And Caeruleus," Gordan pressed.

Raiden stayed quiet as the air grew tense. Mitchell wore his disapproval of Caeruleus on his face.

"I realize it's hard to forgive his loyalty to the Council," Raiden said defensively. Gordan felt Raiden's heart beat harder with defiance. "But try to understand his motivations. We both lost everyone we knew in Cantis. You can't reason a man out of his pain. I blamed the Council—they had taken my father first and failed to protect Cantis—but Caeruleus blamed Dawn. He believed the only worthwhile means to bring them to justice was to contribute to the Council's efforts. He believed Dawn was in Cantis to find the fera all along, and at the time I couldn't tell him they had wiped out Cantis to hide a dragon. I didn't want to let on about any more than I had to. If I had explained, he would have asked a lot of questions. He would have checked the tower, found no dragon at all and then you would have been a part of the equation. I couldn't let the Council know about you, Nicole needed an ally they didn't know about."

"That's understandable," Gordan said.

"So, you didn't trust him," Mitchell said.

"I should have. We grew up together," Raiden continued. "I knew him better than anyone. I should have trusted him from the start in Atrium. I allowed him to be deceived by the Council. It's my fault he ever went after Nicole, my secrets did that."

"People change Ray, you knew a kid. You don't know this guy any better than you know Tovar," Mitchell suggested. Gordan felt Mitchell's cold dislike in the air.

"In that case I don't know you any better than I know either of them," Raiden countered. "If you're counting days."

Mitchell blustered. "I'm Nicole's brother, there's no question where my loyalties lie."

"Well, Caeruleus is *my* brother," Raiden countered. There was fire in his voice. "And he broke his oath to the Council to help Nicole, remember? He threw his lot in with us once he realized what was really happening. That should be proof enough of where *his* loyalties lie."

"The guy was willing to abduct an innocent person," Mitchell said. "No matter what the circumstances, that says a lot about a man."

"I'm guilty of the same offense," Raiden said with a heavy heart. "Without my memories I put my friend before what was right. I helped Caeruleus, hoping to keep him alive, because loving people clouds your judgment. If you can forgive *me* for doing something so abominable, why not Caeruleus?"

Mitchell recoiled into silence, stewing in disgust and annoyance. Gordan frowned. He hoped Raiden was right. Surely the trials of Atrium City proved that their allies were indeed allies. Still, he needed to observe these people himself. Tovar seemed the one to start with; he had not been averse to the presence of a dragon. From their handshake alone, Gordan had only sensed cordiality and curiosity from the man.

They passed the remainder of the trip to Tovar's workroom in silence, Mitchell still churning with anger and chagrin, and Raiden frowning under his own cloud of discontent. When they reached the door, it was still open. Raiden knocked on the threshold.

"Back so soon?" Tovar looked up.

"We're on our way to find Loak, but Gordan had a thought about our efforts to secure the palace," Raiden said.

"Let's hear it," Tovar said, waving them all in.

"I've noticed quite a lot of enchantments are in these walls. It seems to me that there could be protections and barriers we don't know about. Identifying them would allow us to better assess our needs and efforts toward keeping Venarius out," Gordan explained. He tried not to let his interest in Tovar show. He let his eyes drift around the workshop now and then, but kept his attention wholly on the aura Tovar exuded and the deeper glimpses he got from brief eye contact.

"You're absolutely right," Tovar said, nodding. "We know that quite a powerful magic has kept this place sealed for centuries, and we saw for our own eyes the link between the keys and the palace is more than symbolic."

What struck Gordan immediately was the earnestness in Tovar's eyes. He did not shy away from eye contact, and he was invigorated by the discussion of magical study.

"Loak found out this morning that he couldn't shift inside, but Nicole and I could," Raiden added.

"The keys, of course," Tovar said. "Yes, I should think the builders laid quite a few enchantments in these walls."

"I have felt them here and there; however, I don't have the learning in spell-craft to identify their functions. I can only lend my senses to the efforts," Gordan said, drawing Tovar's gaze back to his so that he could get a deeper look.

"Perfect. I know Raiden to have a rather irksome ability for finding hidden spells as well," Tovar said with a chuckle. "Let me track down some of my tools—still a bit disorganized here—just a few tricks to help us work things out, and I will meet you down in the entranceway. Seems the right place to start, those doors kept the whole realm out for centuries after all."

"All right," Raiden agreed.

Gordan nodded, still considering Tovar as they left his workroom and made their way down the corridor. The man was warm, particularly toward Raiden. Lurking beneath it, though, all Gordan found was a deep sadness tucked safely away. Not buried and ignored, but quiet and peaceful, the kind of sadness one has lived side-by-side with for almost a lifetime, greeted every day and embraced, carefully preserved because at its core is something too precious to let fade. Tovar didn't seem far beyond his middle years, and yet he was alone. Raiden hadn't mentioned a family. Mitchell walked beside Gordan to his right and Raiden to his left. He felt rather like a mother keeping her quarreling sons apart.

Mitchell was still agitated, although now he seemed to have acquired a note of embarrassment, but he didn't show it in the slightest. Mitchell's expression remained firmly neutral. Raiden stewed in his preferred poison of worry, which Gordan had come to know all too well in his short time with Raiden. His proclivity toward over-thinking his troubles had cost Gordan more than one night's sleep during his first several days in the old world with Nicole.

"You're just going to work yourself into an anxious frenzy and end up turning to the Sight, which we both know makes this worse," Gordan said.

Raiden gave him a startled look that quickly turned to chagrin. His cinnamon complexion mostly camouflaged the rush of blood to his cheeks, but Gordan felt Raiden's pulse spike and his eyes betrayed him.

"You're right," Raiden said with a frustrated sigh.

"Taking on any enemy is best done with all your focus on the here and now."

"But," Mitchell chimed in with unusual reluctance. "Getting a glimpse of what Venarius might throw at us…couldn't that be an advantage?"

"Perhaps," Gordan conceded. "Assuming he sees something useful, it would only mean an upper hand in that particular situation. What about the plans he does not see? Thinking we know what is to come could ultimately blind us to other tactics, lure us into foolish confidence. Preparations in response to a vision could very well change the circumstances entirely and lead to different outcomes for which you aren't prepared, all because you're expecting what Raiden has Seen. And I can assure you, Venarius will be preparing multiple plans. He will have a plan for every opportunity. He has resources all throughout this realm."

"It sounds like you're saying there's no way we can beat this guy," Mitchell said.

"I am merely saying the Sight is not the answer," Gordan rephrased. "Raiden knows well enough how glimpses of potential futures affect our actions."

"What do you mean?" Mitchell wondered.

"When I first met Nicole, I saw her execution," Raiden explained. "I didn't know it at the time. I saw these flashes of her… dying, watching her slip into oblivion."

"Jeezus, Ray, why didn't you tell me?"

"Can you honestly say you would have slept at night with that knowledge…even if it was only a possibility?" Raiden countered. "Because I couldn't, and the more I didn't want to see it the more I kept seeing it. The more I use the Sight, the harder it is to keep it at bay."

"But things turned out differently with the Council," Mitchell said.

"That's right. On our trip to Cantis, I saw her dead beneath a kelpie and that turned out differently too, but not because of anything I did to change it. That's Gordan's point, the knowledge is not always helpful. The future is always changing, but seeing it does something to you. The kelpie proved to me that a horrible vision could be wrong, but the pain of that vision, of Nicole's demise in the Courts, didn't go away just because I knew it might *not* happen. Knowing that the worst is possible is nothing like seeing it happen right before your eyes, hearing it, feeling it."

"And letting anxiety about the future smother everything else in your life is a swift journey to madness," Gordan added. "Do yourself—and Nicole *and me*—a favor, Raiden," he said, looking Raiden hard in the eye. "Don't go down that road."

"I won't," Raiden insisted, putting his hands up in surrender.

They made it to the first floor where Loak's distinctly deep voice could be heard rolling through the halls.

"Don't you think we're rushing?" a familiar tenor hit Gordan's ear. Caeruleus.

"No," Loak said. "The ones who are here now, before anyone knows who the kings are, have the mind to serve. You don't want the ones who come crawling in after the news spreads that one of the keys is in the fera's hand. Those will be the ones you can't trust. Venarius will know as soon as the people meet her; we need to recruit before that happens."

"That doesn't automatically make them trustworthy," Caeruleus scoffed.

"No, it just means they are less likely to be moles."

"Who's to say Dawn isn't out there among the crowds now? They despise the palace and the prophecy; they want to destroy this realm and go back to the old world. Why wouldn't they be curious? Why wouldn't they be the first to line up among the recruits to get inside and bring us down?"

"Maybe this place has the solution," Raiden suggested as they approached.

Loak and Caeruleus turned. Gordan caught Caeruleus

clenching his jaw as he kept his gaze away from them. There was a faint buzz of anxiety in the air and Gordan was a little surprised. He expected hostility in the air, not insecurity, shame and...jealousy. Mistrust rolled off Mitchell and Gordan knew that was for Caeruleus alone.

"What's that supposed to mean?" Loak wondered.

"There's a lot of magic in these walls. It has kept out intruders without fail for centuries. You need a key to get through the ether into this place."

"So...what, you think you can use this palace as a sieve to catch untrustworthy recruits and identify the worthy ones?" Caeruleus asked.

"To an extent," Raiden said with a shrug. "We still have to decipher all the enchantments to know for sure. Maybe the magic is just everything that kept this place sealed off until the keys found keepers. But from what we know already, there is sophisticated magic here—almost like this place is alive. Stars in the bloody sky, it *sent* the keys to us. It's got to be capable of keeping out the dishonest and dangerous."

"That would certainly make this job a lot less maddening. When you have to suspect everyone, it's impossible to trust anyone," Loak grumbled, shaking his head.

"We should ask Captain Rhee to stick around," Caeruleus said. "We could use a leader like her, and having a ship at our disposal doesn't hurt either."

"Not a bad idea," Loak said, "if you think you can convince her and if you can do that before she leaves."

"What?" Caeruleus balked.

"She disappeared back to her ship a while ago, could be long gone already," Loak said with a shrug.

Caeruleus let out a groan and trudged into a jog toward the two great doors, taking the subtle haze of annoyance with him. He pushed one open and slipped outside. Gordan felt tension in the air go slack, and Mitchell cooled a little beside him. It was a relief to feel the air clear as he tried to read Loak more closely; too many people and clashing emotions could make deciphering individuals an impossible task. People don't keep their energies neatly to themselves. Energy spreads out and mingles; people affect each other, and so the more people around, the harder it would be to read them. Gordan's best opportunity to get to know everyone would be before they were all surrounded by palace staff and visiting subjects.

"What are your plans for the recruits, Loak?" Raiden wondered.

Loak exuded a towering air of confident contentment. But when Loak's occasional glance passed over him, Gordan noticed the slightest ripple of distrust in the air.

"Well, we'll have to see how many we have. We'd like to have enough for a royal guard dedicated to your safety and a separate regiment for the town," Loak explained.

"Town? What town?" Raiden asked.

"You've got yourself a nice little settlement forming out there, Raiden. There's already a paved road leading right up to the palace steps. I believe I heard the people calling it Keystone."

Gordan felt Raiden's heart quicken, an animal in a trap, suffice to assume the gravity of this life he had hastily embraced for its safety and resources was finally closing in on him. He was a king now, and he was finally realizing how ill prepared he was for it.

"We practically have everyone here," Tovar's voice turned everyone's attention down the corridor.

Tovar had a bag hanging from his shoulder, the contents of which clinked and rattled, containing glass containers and other odd tools. Gordan had never spent time as an apprentice to any kind of teacher. He mastered transformation younger than most dragons and picked up a few necessities along the way, like conjuring clothes—poorly for many years until he got much better at it. It was clear that Tovar lived a life devoted to an intimate knowledge of the arts.

With Tovar's arrival to their cluster, the distant moan of a door in the entranceway went unnoticed by everyone but Gordan who glanced back to see a middle-aged man who bore a striking resemblance to Raiden but with brown eyes, fair skin and blonde hair. His footsteps finally caught Loak's attention.

"Got those enrollment lists up around our budding town out there," Leone said, finally seizing Raiden's attention.

A battering ram of sorrow crashed into Gordan's chest. There was a spark of joy there, but it was smothered by a tide of devastation. Gordan fought back the urge to gasp and fold himself over. He knew the soul-crushing sensation all too well——it was exactly how he had felt thinking he'd lost Nicole. He had to steady himself, so he grabbed Mitchell's forearm for support and threw an amazed look at Raiden who stood there like a stone despite being the source of this anguish. Raiden's forehead puckered with effort to appear unscathed by his father's presence. From the corner of his eye Gordan caught Mitchell's concerned glance.

Worse still was the second wave of torment coming from Leone. It was a dizzying mix of pride and relief, grief and regret, terrible sinking shame, and loss—the only note that harmonized with Raiden in their dissonant clash of pain that overwhelmed Gordan.

"Are we ready to find out these walls' secrets?" Tovar asked.

"Of course," Raiden said.

"Leone," Loak clapped him on the back. "Let's leave them to it. Never was good at this sort of thing."

"Right," Leone agreed and the two of them set off down the corridor together at a leisurely pace.

Raiden watched them go and Gordan watched Raiden, his rigid posture relaxing little by little as they went. Then he finally glanced at Gordan, still gripping Mitchell's arm and fighting the urge to buckle even as the devastation receded.

"Are you all right, Gordan?" he asked.

Gordan glared at him. "I could ask you the same question," he growled quietly between them.

Raiden's eyes went wide for a brief moment, glistening with moisture and guilt. He blinked and barely shook his head so that Gordan couldn't be sure he was answering or just composing himself.

"Well then, shall we get started?" Tovar inquired.

Mitchell spoke up. "Er, I don't think I can really help with this sort of thing. I think I'll—"

"Nonsense," Tovar said. "Another set of eyes is never a bad thing. You may learn a thing or two, never know when those hidden talents show up."

Mitchell allowed a sheepish grin to creep across his face. "Sure, why not."

Gordan realized his hand was still caught on Mitchell's arm, so he uncurled his fingers carefully as though he could release him without Mitchell noticing. But Mitchell looked at him and offered a gentle smile.

"Better now?" he whispered.

"Yes," he answered. Raiden escaped into conversation with Tovar, distracting himself from the anguish awakened by his father. Gordan could breathe again.

Nicole discovered new staircases on the fourth floor, which they had missed by getting caught-up in Mitchell's hunt for better and better rooms.

There was something soothing about wandering through the sleepy passages of the palace alone. In the space all to herself, she could parse out her thoughts and feelings twisting themselves into knots inside her. In the silence she was free to wander. She didn't have to pretend to be okay.

She explored the tower absently. The staircases that spiraled higher and higher captivated her less by the empty palace than by the strange sense of company she had the deeper into the silence she went. It was much that same sensation she had felt back home looking into the mirror and knowing that the fera before her was somehow present—her tomb disturbed, her silence broken, her anger stirred.

Nicole wasn't sure…could a past life really dig its way out of its resting place? She wondered if she should tell anyone that the previous fera seemed to be with her now. But what did that even mean? Perhaps it was just her mind conjuring up something—anything—to fill a void.

Nicole let out a laugh that shuffled around the silent stone chamber and came back to her sounding more uncertain than amused. Still, she couldn't help wondering if a past life could move in and take the reins. *No,* she insisted. *We're the same soul, aren't we? She's not an intruder trying to take control.* Nicole thought back to the Council and shuddered, her skin crawling with the memory of their presence inside her. She couldn't deny that it was strange to be alone with the distinct feeling that she wasn't alone—like the fera before her was watching her struggle sympathetically.

Nicole stopped at the sound of voices.

"Can he be trusted, though?"

"Raiden trusts him," Loak's low voice answered.

In their silence she supposed they were talking about Gordan and she clenched her teeth together. At least they could give him the benefit of the doubt.

Loak's baritone continued. "When are you going to tell him?"

Nicole looked around trying to determine where they were before realizing they were coming up the stairs below her in the tower.

"I don't know how—or if I can even do that to him." It was Raiden's father.

"He is no stranger to tough decisions *or* mistakes. Just ask him about Atrium," Loak said. Their voices grew closer, clearer through the echoes. "He understands doing whatever it takes to keep the people he loves safe. He would have ended up in the cell next to yours trying to help Caeruleus."

A pang of sadness struck her. Raiden had risked his freedom for Caeruleus, trying to keep him alive because she really was as dangerous as everyone said she was. It was only because he fell for her that he refused to believe it, and without that confounding irrational emotion he had seen her for what she was.

"I still can't believe this is where we ended up, after everything we went through."

Loak let out a low rumbling chuckle. "You spend years trying to keep your family away from this mess, and your boy falls in love with the fera. He's gotten us in deeper than you ever did."

Nicole felt her face burn with embarrassment and shame.

Leone answered with a warm laugh that had an undertone of sadness to it. "I guess he managed to end up like me after all."

The sudden halt of their laughter made Nicole's stomach twist.

"Ever think of just going home? Take Raiden back to live with the rest of the celengels? My sources tell me Nicole was quite the flyer in Atrium. She'll fit right in on Terra Celestia—maybe they'll make an exception for her. Venarius can't get to her there—problem solved."

Raiden's dad is a celengel? Then that means Raiden—

"You know they won't. She doesn't have wings. They want nothing to do with earthborn."

"Then there's no avoiding this. We both know Venarius will go through anyone and everyone he has to in order to get what he wants."

"And I will happily stand in his way, Loak. I didn't deserve this chance, but I have it thanks to her."

Nicole flared with heat. It struck her now, hearing them talk about her, she was the problem. Her allies were only here for Raiden, to keep her weight from dragging him down. She thought of Caeruleus, his avoidance of her. He had acted for Raiden's sake, but why would his sentiments about her change suddenly? She was still the fera, who was friends with a dragon, put his friend at risk and had taken his eye.

"Serves me right for letting a bloody bird drag me into something that had nothing to do with me," Loak said.

"The mountains are right where you left them, my friend," Leone laughed.

"And they'll be there when this is over," he replied.

Nicole finally dared to peer over the railing of the spiraling staircase, but she didn't spot them below. The cadence of their boots against the stone floors gradually waned into silence and when she heard their voices again, they were faint and jumbled by echo in the tower corridors. She straightened up and sighed, glad they were gone, but troubled by their conversation repeating in her head. There was nowhere to run from this.

A shadow swooped into her vision, jarring her out of her spiraling thoughts as it landed on the railing—the raven. It cawed at her.

"You again," she said, offering a sad smile. "Do *you* like it here?"

It cawed.

"At least someone should…"

❧

Raiden felt a little better with every protective spell they uncovered. The vast majority of them appeared to be concentrated around the threshold of the main doors—although Tovar said that while the spells were anchored to the entranceway, they spread through the palace like roots. Raiden, Tovar, Mitchell and Gordan had walked over the threshold, out of the palace doors and back in enough times to look like a troop of fools, but they managed to determine that the palace itself provided a formidable line of defense, especially at its threshold.

"Now let's see what happens if I try to enter in disguise," Tovar said, hurrying back out the doors. He paused with his back to them, waved his hand over his face and head, and then turned to them as a completely different person. His mostly grey hair turned jet black. His warm lined face was smooth with youth, one eye a piercing stony blue and the other covered by an eye patch virtually lost behind the wavy black hair around his face. Tovar had made himself into Caeruleus.

Raiden laughed. Mitchell scoffed beside him.

"How did I do?" Tovar asked with a grin on Caeruleus' face.

Before Raiden could answer, the real Caeruleus approached the steps and made his way up to the palace entrance.

"We're about to see, I suppose," Raiden chuckled.

Tovar turned a curious glance back at Caeruleus who slowed at the sight of his double as he reached the top of the steps.

Caeruleus came to stand beside Tovar. At first glance they seemed to be the same man except for their vastly different attire,

Caeruleus still in his Atrium uniform and Tovar in the far less stately trousers and tunic beneath a course coat with several pockets around the waist for tools. With the two Caeruleuses side by side, the minute differences became clear. Tovar was missing the thin white scar just above the eyebrow of Caeruleus' surviving eye, a mark Raiden had given him when they found his father's sword as boys. They had taken turns fighting off invisible monsters, and when Raiden's mother caught them, Raiden's startled swing nicked Caeruleus. They had been in terrible trouble, but joked about him almost losing his eye. It happened just weeks before Caeruleus' father moved them to the mainland, he recalled. The nostalgic smile on Raiden's mouth fell flat, remembering his friend's departure.

"What's going on?" Caeruleus wondered, his expression unsettled and confused.

"We're testing the palace's defenses against deceit," Tovar explained. "Shall we?"

"All right then," Caeruleus agreed and they both stepped through the doorway.

Unremarkably, Caeruleus crossed the threshold without incident, but his doppelganger's face melted like a mask of wax too close to a fireplace and revealed Tovar, whose hand immediately moved up to his nose to investigate.

"As I thought," Tovar announced. "It seems this place has quite the arsenal of wards against deception. We cannot conceal weapons, pass through unseen, and disguises can't even make it through the doors."

Raiden watched his friend slink away from Tovar and stand beside him. He glanced at Caeruleus, realizing how much catching up they still hadn't done, and suddenly he felt heavy. Lost time was a dark moon eclipsing every relationship he had. How could he begin to reclaim them? Caeruleus, Nicole, his father, he had them all back and yet he felt far from them. He had kept so much from Caeruleus—even failed to trust him and now there was an uncomfortable barrier between them. Nicole seemed lost and he wasn't sure how to lead her back. His father was a stranger with the likeness of a memory; there was far more about the man Raiden didn't know than he could say he did.

"Wait," Mitchell said, pulling Raiden out of his reverie. "Gordan, aren't you sort of disguised?" Mitchell nodded toward Gordan. "How come you didn't get turned into your natural state?"

"This may not be my natural born appearance, but this is as much who I am as my other form," Gordan said. "There's no disguise to be unraveled."

"Oh," Mitchell uttered.

"It's really more a change of shape than identity," Raiden offered. "Like a different set of clothes."

"These wards are clearly more sophisticated than just foiling disguises. Let's try another experiment and see if the palace can discern motive," Tovar suggested.

"'Discern motive'?" Mitchell repeated skeptically.

"Yes," Tovar said, steering Mitchell by the shoulders, guiding him over the threshold and leaving him outside the doorway. "Your goal is Raiden's key."

From the corner of his eye, Raiden saw Caeruleus turn to face the door and cross his arms to watch.

"You want me to take it?"

"I want you to try," Tovar clarified.

Raiden held his arms out in welcome. Mitchell shrugged and strode toward him, but he didn't make it through the doors. The air of the threshold stopped him like a pane of glass, and Mitchell hit it face first, cursing and bending forward to place his forehead in his hand. Raiden caught Caeruleus fighting a grin.

"Marvelous," Tovar chuckled.

"Yeah," Mitchell agreed sarcastically, rubbing his forehead.

"Now see if you can go back inside," Tovar insisted.

Mitchell huffed and stepped forward again, but this time he crossed the threshold unimpeded.

"There, you see," Tovar said excitedly. "Lesson learned, you had no desire to try taking the key again and the palace let you in."

"That's all fine and well," Caeruleus said. "But what about

people who are already inside. If the wards can be tricked so easily by changing your mind, can't someone get inside and *then* decide to take the key?"

Caeruleus turned to Raiden and reached for the key hanging from Raiden's neck, but before he could lay a finger on it, Caeruleus was knocked back and slid across the floor right out the entranceway by an invisible force. Mitchell howled with laughter, which filled the high-arched ceiling of the entranceway with a chorus of echoes.

Tovar blinked, watching expectantly as Caeruleus slid to a stop at his feet. "Ah, but you see, you cannot have the intention of taking the key and mask it by merely thinking you will not take it because if you know you will change your mind then the intention is still there. But even accounting for someone who has no intention to steal the key when they enter and then decides to betray the king after they're inside, well, we've seen how that would go."

"Right," Caeruleus said as he heaved himself back onto his feet. "So, we've established Raiden and Nicole are perfectly safe as long as they're inside the palace."

Mitchell's laughter waned into stifled snickering as Caeruleus marched back inside. Tovar followed him.

"True, the palace itself should be the perfect tool for recruiting; however, just because someone has no intention of posing a threat does not make them loyal. That much will still be up to us to determine," Tovar said.

"Men and women don't show up loyal," Caeruleus said. "That's something you earn. I better go talk to Loak. Captain Rhee agreed to stay for a few days."

"I'll join you. He wandered off with my father," Raiden said, falling into step beside him. "There's no telling where they are."

As Raiden and Caeruleus passed the others, Raiden couldn't help but notice the gaze Gordan cast at Caeruleus. What could Gordan sense from his friend that Raiden could not?

"I think there could be more to find. We haven't accounted for nearly all the purposes the amount of spell work here suggests. Shall we continue?" Tovar asked Mitchell and Gordan.

"Certainly," Gordan answered.

"I'm not playing guinea pig anymore," Mitchell muttered.

Their voices went faint behind Raiden as he and Caeruleus walked in silence into the palace corridors. For three floors and many hallways they both attempted and failed to break the wordless wall between them. Raiden couldn't decide where to begin, an apology or his deep gratitude, and beside him Caeruleus would glance at him, looking ready to speak only to seal his lips shut and look ahead once more.

"I made a mess of things," Raiden sent the words stumbling from his mouth. "You lost your eye because I kept secrets. I didn't trust you with the truth, and I set you up for potentially far worse than losing your eye in my bid to keep her safe."

Caeruleus inhaled sharply and sighed.

Raiden continued. "I'm sorry…I know those words are meager and saying them every day for the rest of my life wouldn't amount to what my actions cost you."

"Once is plenty, Raiden," Caeruleus insisted. "The last time I spoke to you before that night, you were *helping* me track her down in the city. Next thing I know she knocks down the doors into the Council's chamber demanding to know where you were."

Raiden couldn't quell the smile that tugged at his mouth. She was willing to face anything, run straight into the fire, for him.

"She wouldn't even attack me," Caeruleus continued. "She tried to talk to me and I was bound by orders. I couldn't disobey my blood contract, Ray, even though I wanted to. Her willingness to get caught for you was all I had to go on. It didn't make sense for her to lie about knowing you when her life was on the line, so I believed her, but I was confused. I didn't wholly believe it until you showed up in the courts—I just had to see the look on your face when you saw her. But, I'm still in the dark here. Fill me in."

"I altered my own memory," Raiden said, the words weighing him down. "I told you that Nicole had saved my life back in Cantis, that much was true, but I left out everything that happened before that."

"So, when you helped me find her that night," Caeruleus wondered.

"I didn't know that I knew her. I kept her a secret from myself to keep her safe from the Council. I only let myself remember that we crossed paths the night Moira almost killed me, that she saved me. I hoped that would salvage some of my loyalty to her."

"But," Caeruleus frowned, "you didn't help her. You helped me instead."

"You're my best friend, Ruleus. I knew that what the Council wanted to do to her was wrong, but I wasn't going to let you die on their mission. The only way to do that was to help you."

Caeruleus was silent for many steps.

"You'd already lost your eye following their orders," Raiden continued. "And the worst part is that I was partly responsible at the time, I just didn't know at the time."

"How was my eye your fault?"

"I gave you those clothes."

"Right," Caeruleus said with a shrug, not understanding the significance.

"I gave them to you before I altered my memory. I knew she would recognize them. I wanted to give her a head start if you managed to track her down."

Caeruleus chuckled and Raiden looked at him with dismay to hear him laugh.

"Knowing now what the Council did to the fera—what they had planned for her—I can't blame you in the least for what you did," Caeruleus said. "Sure, I probably would have thought differently if you had told me from the start that you loved her. I would have thought you were insane, or had a death wish, and I still somewhat think that, but we can't help whom we love, can we? I convinced you to do so many stupid things when we were kids. What made you think I wouldn't have gone along with you this time?"

"Nine years, Caeruleus. I was stuck in Cantis alone. I had no way of knowing how nine years on the mainland with your father might have changed you, and I didn't have the time to find out. I knew only one thing—that you chose to join the Council. I was stuck in the courts; the Council had eyes and ears everywhere. I wish I had done things differently. Even knowing the Council could have listened to every word, I wish I had told you everything."

"Tell me now, then," Caeruleus said.

They made their way up the flight of stairs to the fourth floor, and Raiden led Caeruleus through the memories he had kept from his friend and eventually from himself. As he traced his steps through his past for Caeruleus, Mitchell's troubling challenge crept back into his mind. What if his memories hadn't all been restored? Tovar had warned him that there was potential that memories could be affected, damaged, by the process, but Raiden had been so desperate and resolute in his decision that the risk to his memories couldn't outweigh the benefit of protecting Nicole.

"You weren't wrong to do it," Caeruleus admitted. "I saw the Council resort to taking what they needed from people's minds, criminals and their own agents alike. *Anything for the good of the realm*, they'd say. They didn't trust you, Raiden. They thought Nicole might have enthralled you with some spell—not far off, ay? But if they had known how you felt about her, known everything you told me, they would have chosen very different tactics. They'd have used you as bait long before the rebels got to you."

"That doesn't make me feel any better about it," Raiden confessed.

"It should. I get it, Ray. Really, I do. I wasn't there for you, but she was. I can see why you're willing to risk so much for her. You made the decisions you thought were right. You didn't make a mess of things, this was a mess to begin with. There's not going to be a clean way out of this thing with Venarius either. I can't hold any choice you made against you. As for her part I can't even hold it against Nicole. What's done is done. I just ask that you don't keep me in the dark anymore."

Caeruleus' forgiveness pained Raiden more than it soothed him. "I'll make that promise," he said.

They reached the fourth-floor corridor and looked from one abandoned end to the other.

"How in the stars are we supposed to find people in this bloody place?" Caeruleus muttered.

"I wish I knew," Raiden said with a heavy exhalation, anxiety creeping in as he realized he had no idea where Nicole was or if she was even in the palace still.

Nicole knew she was still inside the palace, though she couldn't say where and knew that remembering the way back was out of the question. She wandered her way up to a tower, and she would have to hope she could wander her way back to a part of the castle that she knew. But for now, at least she was happy to see what was at the top of this tower. The staircase was narrow and turned tightly in a cramped coil of steps, nothing like the vast open spiral of the grand east tower she'd left behind earlier.

These steps kept coming like she was on a twisting conveyor belt, and as her legs protested, she grew more determined to get to the top. What could the craftsmen of this monument to peace and safety from persecution have intended for the highest room in the tallest tower? There weren't any windows, but veins of crystal in the stone let light through the walls as she went, lighting the staircase with a soft glow. When the endless twisting incline and the burn in her legs became hypnotic, she came to the landing where the ceiling was too low for her to stand up straight. In the ceiling there was a round door.

"Someone messed up here," she muttered.

Nicole crouched and placed herself beneath the door. She

pushed with her hands, but it didn't budge. So, she lay down on her back and kicked it with both feet. The door opened with a bang. She stood up straight with a triumphant sigh but immediately cringed at the rank, musty smell that hit her. She found herself in a filthy circular chamber. Wind blustered around the room, coming from one of the four windows standing open. The floor was coated in dirt, leaves, and most notably a combination of bird shit and dark matted lumps—owl pellets, she realized when she looked up and saw several round faces of barn owls peering down at her from the ornately carved arches in the ceiling.

"Hey," she said.

They blinked at her.

"You lot have some pretty nice digs up here," she said, nodding. It was as beautiful as any other room in the castle she had seen— naturally, aside from who-knew-how-many decades of windblown debris and owl droppings carpeting the floor—the four windows were as tall as her, pointed at the tops, and grimy so that the daylight was hazy and dull in the room. She cringed against the smell, even with fresh air moving across her face it was hard to ignore.

"Mind if I clean up a bit?" She asked, looking up at the round faces and blinking eyes, which she took for consent. "Great."

Pinching her nose shut, she took a deep breath and let all the built-up tension from the last two days roll through her. The air churned with heat and every last speck of filth joined the growing spinning mass in the center of the room. Then the smelly dust devil spun right out the open window.

"Oh, I hope that doesn't hit anyone," she said, cringing at the thought.

The owls overhead flapped and rustled, puffing up and shaking out their feathers. One of them sprang up and bounded on four legs to the other side of the beam, revealing a cat's form beneath its owl head and wings. She marveled open-mouthed for a moment, not owls, little griffins.

"Sorry," she cooed, beaming at them. She took a tiny sniff and smelled nothing but the fresh air from outside, grass and a distant note of pollen.

Then the floor caught her eye. No longer buried beneath a layer of bird poop and regurgitated wads of fur and rodent bones, an intricate design of crystal in dizzying fractals lay imbedded in the stone floor.

"Wow," she breathed in awe, studying the floor as she made her way to the center of the mesmerizing design. "Pretty fancy for an attic," she said.

At the center of the room was a circle of stone about the size of a manhole cover with a set of concentric crystal circles that formed something like an eye. She stepped onto it. When she looked up, she saw that the four windows and stone walls were no more, there was no wall, or rather, the windows had opened up until the wall was nothing but window and the ceiling seemed to float overhead.

In her surprise she jumped back away from the center of the room and in a blink the walls and windows were as they had been before.

"What the hell?"

She stepped back onto the stone center of the floor and once again the windows spread until there was only glass between the floor and the ceiling. Nicole turned on the stone spot in the center of the room and when she stopped to look out the window, the land before her rushed in her direction. She lurched off the spot again, laughing.

"It's a telescope," she realized. "This whole damn room is a telescope."

She stepped back into the center of the floor and looked ahead, watching the land of Veil rush toward her as her gaze soared over the rolling grasslands, then a sprawling forest, past a great maze of mountains and canyons, and on across high plains smattered with towns that came to an abrupt halt at the sea where a sprawling city crowded around a white castle that stood perched on the end of a cliff-lined peninsula. She didn't know which direction she was looking, but she could surmise that this was one of the thriving royal states she'd heard about.

What she wanted to see was Keren's orchard, just to check on the girls. The only problem was she didn't know which direction they were located. Nor did she know which direction she was facing. Pulling her gaze away from the distant coastline to the floor beneath her feet was disorienting, but her vision righted and she stepped off the eye.

Studying the room more carefully, her eyes followed the point of one window up to the ceiling. The griffins were settled back in, some sleeping, and few still watching. Then she noticed that there were four intricately carved arches above her crossing each other in the center of the ceiling, like a compass. Then she spotted them, the curling letters N, E, S and W carved into the arches where the ceiling met the wall.

"I think they're somewhere to the Southwest?" she murmured. She knew Keren's orchard was not far from the coast and that when she and Gordan had flown from Cantis to the mainland, their journey had been eastward. "Let's see." She found the south and west markers on the arches, and lined her gaze up with the un-marked arch between the two before stepping back onto the eye in the center of the floor.

This time she noticed that when she cast her eyes at the horizon, she rushed forward, but when a familiar circular city moved toward her and she focused on it, the forward rush of her vision slowed to a halt, placing Atrium before her. Her mouth twitched with a scowl at the sight of the rubble in the center of the city; then she lifted her gaze and on it went beyond Atrium, over a sprawling expanse of forest, past the town of Witch Haven, and across more bristly bare treetops until she spotted an eruption of green leaves in the canopies—Keren's orchard.

In the small clearing inside the fruit trees, Keren and the girls' comfortable cottage sat peacefully, the garden atop the roof, vibrant and near overflowing. Nicole's vantage from above reminded her how far away she really was, and she felt more sad than relieved to see Asi step through the front door as she released her fox from the house to bound and roll in the grass outside.

Nicole sighed and stepped off the eye once more, turning toward the round door in the floor across the room. She dropped to the landing below—the doorway at her hips when she stood—and grabbed the iron handle of the circular door. With one last look at the owls in the arches above, she ducked down and pulled the door closed.

When she reached the bottom of the telescope tower, she huffed. She couldn't possibly remember the way back. She had turned too many corners, climbed too many staircases. Then she looked down at her key, closed her hand around it and dematerialized into the air. The key pulled her like a magnet drawn to the throne room, she turned around, face-first into someone's chest. She looked up.

"Raiden."

"Hi," he laughed.

"Did you just…"

"Caeruleus and I split up looking for Loak. I got a little turned around, so I took the easy way back."

She smiled, looking around. "We need a map of this place."

"I just hope we find Caeruleus and the others before they starve," he muttered.

She forced a laugh but her heart dropped as her gaze swept the grand space around them—polished floor beneath their feet, the double doors behind Raiden. Her heart rate quickened and room grew darker.

"Were you lost too?" he asked, smiling.

She took a deep breath, forcing her attention back to him. "Yeah," she admitted, catching his eye as his smile fell into a straight sad line for a moment. Everything flickered—they were in the Courts, Raiden riddled with wounds and frown of resignation on his face—then they were in the bright throne room once more. She had to get out of this room—get Raiden out. "Hey," she said, fighting to keep her breathing slow and steady. "Since no one knows where we are," she continued, taking his hand in both of hers tentatively, her heart hammering anxiously at the contact. "They won't know we *aren't* here in the castle."

"What do you mean?"

She had to get out of that room, but she wanted him to see the good things that happened while he was gone, maybe knowing that she hadn't been entirely alone would ease his guilt. She let the trembling desire to be back at Keren's orchard filled her chest and she let it out, exhaling as the magic swept them up, prickling her skin with goose bumps before they dissolved into the ether.

"Oh," Raiden said when their feet hit solid grassy earth. "That's what you mean."

They were standing before the cottage in Keren's orchard. She took a deep shaking breath, hoping Raiden didn't notice, and let it out. Her heart eased to the sound of trees rustling gently in the sunshine.

Asi was still outside, and she started at the sight of them. "Fen! Keren!" she shouted into the house.

"They really want to meet you," Nicole murmured to Raiden as Asi rushed across the grass to greet Nicole with a hug.

Fen ran out the front door. "Nicole's back," she called over her shoulder as she jumped into Nicole's arms for a hug.

"Girls, this is Raiden," Nicole said, glancing at him to see a broad smile on his face.

"This is a pleasant surprise. Nice to meet you," he said.

"I'm Asi," she said with a shy wave.

"Fen," said Fen, smiling.

Keren appeared in the doorway. "So, this is your Raiden," she said with a sly smile.

"I am," he answered.

Nicole's face went hot and she fought the grin trying to twist her mouth. *My Raiden?*

"Nice to finally meet you," Keren said.

Asi and Fen beamed, sharing a furtive look, before chiming in.

"You look just like the picture," Asi remarked.

"I knew she'd find you," Fen said.

"She's quite good at that," he said to Fen.

"Well, come inside," Keren said, waving them all toward the door. "Put Gim in the fireplace and let's have something to eat."

Nicole took Raiden's hand, and her heart surged into an anxious crescendo. Raiden loved her, she knew that, and it terrified her more than Venarius. She'd been so afraid of losing him that she forgot how scared she was of loving someone. Now here she was, unable to deny it or escape it. This was like holding something delicate. It was beautiful and she adored it, but she was scared of ruining it. She was unbearably aware that he could and no doubt would get hurt again because of her. He would be better off without her, but she would be even more broken without him.

They followed Keren and the girls inside and from the corner of her eye, Nicole watched Raiden look around wearing a subtle smile.

"Nicole," Asi burst with some fervent thought. "Did you find your friend? The dragon." Asi plopped down in the large brown chair beside the fireplace.

"Yes, I did," Nicole said as she coaxed Gim off her neck and into her hand to deliver him to the fireplace where a small fire smoldered. She turned away from the hearth to see Raiden sink into a spot on the couch beneath the window.

"Where is he now?" Fen wondered, perching beside Asi on the arm of the chair.

"We left him back at the palace with my brother and the others. They don't know we snuck away," she said, placing her finger against her guilty grimace as she crossed the room and sat beside Raiden.

A light scratching at the front door prompted Keren to open it. An orange blur shot into the living room before leaping into Asi's lap with a chatter of affection.

"What's it like at the palace?" Asi leaned forward into her question, squishing Shio a little beneath her torso.

"It's...empty," Nicole chuckled. "But I don't think that will be the case for much longer, unfortunately."

"It looks like we will have staff and guards soon," Raiden explained. "This business of being kings is strange for all of us, especially as we don't really know how willing the realm is to accept the sudden emergence of the keys. There's already a camp of thousands outside the palace, and it looks like they're settling in to stay."

"To think," Keren chuckled. "The sick girl we found turned out to be a fugitive and ended up royalty."

"Whoa, I'm not royalty," Nicole said, putting her hands up. "This is just temporary. I'm only wearing this key as long as it takes to lure Venarius out into the open so that we can end this." She was adamant, even though the key seemed magically linked to her and removing it didn't seem likely.

"Venarius?" Fen frowned with confusion.

"The leader of Dawn," Raiden explained and when he was met with silence and nonplussed expressions from Keren and Fen, he continued. "They are a long-standing syndicate of magic that believes Veil is exile not a sanctuary," Raiden said.

"I can't say I've heard of them," Keren admitted, "even in all my years traveling. I suppose the work of a floramor just doesn't lead one into those circles."

"I've heard of them," Asi said with distaste.

"How?" Fen wondered.

"My father is a part of Dawn. That's all I know really, I overheard him speaking to a man who wanted someone's memory erased and they mentioned Dawn."

Fen's face pinched. "What does that Venarius guy want?" she asked Nicole.

Nicole glanced at Raiden.

"Dawn's founder of the same name apparently helped create the fera and so his grandson thinks Nicole belongs to him," Raiden explained, his discomfort plain on his face. "The Council wanted to destroy the fera, but the first Venarius had some plan for them."

"And maybe even Gordan," Nicole added. "They had him locked up for a decade, and we still don't know why."

"Well, I suppose it's some relief to know he's not trying to *kill* you," Keren said.

"Most likely just anyone who gets in his way," Nicole amended. "Which is precisely what everyone I love wants to do," she muttered.

Keren and Fen exchanged hard glances of concern, and Asi dropped her chin to her chest, frowning down at Shio in her lap. The fox was oblivious to the tense conversation, purring and trilling at Asi's scratches.

"He's not going to have an easy time getting to you," Raiden said, so softly that she was sure his words were meant only for her, but his murmur was the only sound in the room, and she suspected everyone heard him. She wasn't here to entice them into the fight. She just wanted to see them before things got too complicated, and she wanted them to meet Raiden. She didn't want to risk Venarius finding out about them, visiting this time could have been a mistake for all she knew.

"I wish I could stay," Nicole confessed, covering her gloom with a smile. "I wanted to come see you at least."

"We should probably get back soon. We certainly don't want anyone back there realizing we've disappeared," Raiden said, giving Nicole a nudge.

"Can I come with you?" Fen asked, hopping off the arm of the chair.

Nicole went cold. Raiden took her hand without so much as glancing at her.

"The palace is quite possibly the safest place in the realm," he offered, and she eased a little at his effort to assuage her panic.

"Is that true?" Nicole asked.

"While you were getting yourself lost in the palace, Tovar, Mitchell, Gordan and I were deciphering the palace's defenses. It's a fortress, there's a reason no one ever managed to break in to take the keys in all these centuries."

"Well—"

Fen cut Nicole off. "Does that mean I can go?"

"Who am I to tell you what you can and can't do," she answered. Fen was seventeen, back home she could be a senior in high school just like Nicole, and what did that matter? When had life ever cared how old they were? *We're both just kids, and we're both adults*, she thought. Just because she was afraid of what could happen to Fen being close to her, just because there was a key around her neck did that mean Nicole had any right to authority over her? And as Raiden said, the palace was possibly the safest place in the realm, maybe she should bring them all with her.

Fen looked to Keren who put her hands up. "It's your decision. I do think your talents are wasted here."

Fen jumped with a tiny cry of delight trapped behind her lips and rushed across the room and up the stairs.

"What about you?" Keren asked, turning to Asi.

Asi looked down at Shio in her lap. "I should probably stay here with Shio," she said, lifting her head to smile, but her mouth was strained with disappointment. "Besides, I can't leave you all alone," she said to Keren.

"Nonsense," Keren scoffed. "Don't you worry about me. I have Ferdie and the trees."

"But Shio…"

"There aren't any rules against animals in the palace," Nicole said. "My brother is there after all."

Asi giggled.

"You can come home whenever you want," Keren added.

Asi lit up, scooped the fox up into her arms and hurried up the stairs calling, "Fen, I'm coming too!"

"Are you sure you're all right with this," Keren asked.

"I don't know. I want them wherever they will be the safest. I'm just not sure where that is anymore," she confessed, feeling dangerous with all the power humming inside her and helpless at the same time because deep down she knew that there was no such thing as a safe place in this or any world.

⁙

Not long after the girls finished packing their things and they all had a small lunch, the obligation to return to the palace pressed on Nicole and Raiden.

"What do you say, girls? Ready to go?" Nicole asked, setting down her empty teacup.

"Yes," they chorused.

Everyone filed out the kitchen door into the living room.

"Don't forget your bag this time, Nicole," Keren said, snagging her camping backpack by the strap and handing it over to Nicole.

"Right, thank you," she said, leaning toward the fireplace. "Come on, Gim." She held out her hand. A little tongue of fire sprang out of the embers and onto her palm. Gim crawled up her arm and she turned to hold her hand out to Fen.

"Have you ever shifted before?" Nicole asked her.

"No," Fen said, bouncing eagerly.

Nicole looked to Asi, clinging to Shio who squirmed against his entrapment. "Hold your stuff tight, Fen," Asi warned.

"All right," Nicole said.

"Be safe," Keren said.

Nicole's smile faltered and she glanced at Raiden who tried to bolster her spirits with a smile of his own. How could he do that? After all that he lost, all those years alone sustained by buried pain and revenge, after what she had put him through, how could he smile like that at her? Her eyes burned with the question, and she dropped her gaze before it went watery.

"Let's go," she said, ignoring the pang in her heart.

Asi and Fen looked up at the ceiling of the throne room with mouths open in awe.

"I've never seen a room so big," Fen said.

Nicole thought she saw a brief pucker of aversion pass over Asi's face when she did not offer the same sentiment as her sister.

"It's definitely a lot to take in," Raiden said.

"Do you want to have a look around, find a room?"

"Yes," Fen and Asi agreed in exuberant unison.

Nicole's surroundings faded into insignificance and she grew increasingly aware of Raiden walking beside her to the point that she burned with agitation at his proximity. He remained quiet while they led the girls up through the second and third floors to the fourth where they had their choice of suites so large that they were delighted to share one as it was more space than Keren's entire cottage and the barn included.

After conjuring them enough pillows to fill a bedchamber into which Shio promptly disappeared, Nicole left them to get settled.

"If you go wandering around and get lost, I can't guarantee you will be found," Nicole warned. "Have fun."

The girls laughed.

She and Raiden walked through the chambers of Fen and Asi's suite and back out to the corridor of the fourth floor.

"You get a room all to yourself, you know," she said.

His hand closed around hers. "Lead the way."

They made their way to the sixth floor. Nicole was disconcertingly aware of her heartbeat against her ribs and her hand sweating in his. When they arrived at the tall door surrounded by the white starburst of quartz, Nicole pulled her hand sheepishly from Raiden's grasp and held her hands up.

"Here we are," she said. "All yours."

The door opened for Raiden and they stepped into a vast chamber that was identical to the extravagantly empty chamber just down the hall behind the door that would only open for Nicole.

"Stars," Raiden said. "It's…too much space for one person."

"Yeah," she agreed feebly.

Raiden sighed. "Will you talk to me? We've hardly had the chance to be alone and I'm afraid this might be one of the last opportunities we really get before this all…" he trailed off and let the thought die in silence.

Nicole took a deep breath and looked at him. He stood before her with a pained understanding on his face, identical to the expression he wore only two nights ago in the Council's chamber as he stood there, unflinching, taking every strike of his sword in her hands. She felt her stony mask crumple and a sob slipped past her lips. He had known precisely what was happening. He had walked into that chamber, not to go down fighting her fate but to join her in it. If he hadn't been there, she might not have wrenched herself free from the Council's grasp because she had come to terms with that fate for herself until he decided to follow.

And just when she thought it was over, everything continued to spin on out of her control. The horror of very nearly ending his life with her own hands hadn't left her; it slithered around her every time she looked at him, held his hand, let his arms close around her, and she didn't know how long she could live with it.

Raiden had his arms around her before she could navigate

through her thoughts and find what to say, how to explain herself and how horrible she'd been the last two days, pulling away from him, disappearing on him. She was lost. It was so much harder to admit she loved him now because her heart was crowded by fear, guilt, anger, despair, and her love for him was floundering in those dark waters. She crossed her arms behind him and held on, crushing him in the last two weeks' pent-up need to know he was okay when they were apart.

"I hurt you," she said, "and I can't stop seeing it."

"I'm all right now," he assured her.

If she hadn't found him in Atrium, he would be a different person now—better off not knowing her. If she hadn't found him in Atrium, perhaps this would all be over. The Council would have been victorious. She would be gone. There would be no fera left for Venarius' plans. Raiden would be free to move on, never even knowing he had lost her.

"I don't want to hurt you again," she said.

"You won't."

"Being with me puts you in danger."

"I don't know if you've noticed, but you're the one who has kept me alive more than once. I feel pretty safe with you."

She wanted to laugh but a sob came out, muffled into his chest. *Don't let go*, she felt the fera in the back of her mind implore her with a sadness that burned Nicole's eyes. Nicole realized with sharp pang in her heart that the fera had spent her life alone, created without a family, running, hiding, trusting no one. How else had she managed to evade capture for an entire lifetime? She let no one share her life or the dangers that came with being what she was. *The fera before me never knew this*—a family, a safe haven in someone's arms, people who loved her. Did she finally get to know it through Nicole?

Nicole needed them, Raiden, Gordan, Mitchell, Keren, Fen, Asi, people who knew what was coming for her and chose to stand beside her anyway. She wouldn't be alive today without them, and she knew she couldn't finish this without them. *They're going to get hurt*, she thought, arguing with herself.

"Will you promise me something?" Raiden asked after a long silence.

"What?"

"Whatever happens—" his pause shuddered in his chest. "Please don't try to face Venarius on your own."

She was quiet. She didn't want to make that promise. He finally pulled away from their embrace and looked at her expectantly, imploring her with his ocean eyes.

"All right," she said. "I promise." She watched the tension in Raiden's shoulders break with relief, but her promise seemed to take the weight from Raiden and bestow it on her in turn.

He looked at her and she could only bare his eyes for so long in silence.

"What?"

"I'm just studying you," he said.

"Oh." She fidgeted self-consciously.

"I forgot the details of your face for a while, and I'm not sure I got them all back," he explained. "Like this freckle," he said brushing her cheekbone just under her eye with his thumb, but he didn't lower his hand. "And how much your eyes look like honey." He raised his other hand and held her face there, looking at her seriously until her composure broke into a laugh. Then he lowered his head and she expected a kiss, but he pressed his forehead to hers instead and she felt relieved.

"It would be foolish of me to ask you if you're okay," he murmured. "I know you're not. After everything…I don't expect you to be."

Nicole fought the stinging tears behind her closed eyes. Raiden knew what it was like to be shattered. He knew gathering up the pieces took time. Relief expanded in her chest and escaped as a quiet sob. She wanted to explain what was inside her but she wasn't sure she could.

"I can't put things back the way they were. Everything may be different but I still want to be with you. That's not going to change," he declared.

She gave a tiny nod, her voice trapped in her constricting throat.

"Well," he said, lifting his head and then pecking her lips with a kiss so brief she almost missed it. "Do you want to hide here for a while?"

A smile broke through her gloom for a moment. She nodded, her gaze falling to the floor. He wrapped his arms around her and straightened up, lifting her off the floor. She folded her arms behind his neck and rested her head, letting herself believe that nothing bad existed outside this embrace—that she didn't live in a world where her enemies had crawled through her body and hurt someone she loved. After what seemed too long for them to be missing, but not nearly enough time to ease her heart, she sighed.

"We wouldn't want to cause a panic," she said regretfully.

"Right," he answered—setting her down.

❧

Gordan dreaded the arrival of staff and guards as he and Mitchell left Tovar in his workroom muttering happily about the spells that made this palace a perfect safe haven. Hiring would be easy, recruiting would be swift, and before they knew it, this place would be bustling with people. Wouldn't those people be surprised— appalled even—to find that a dragon was a part of the monarchs' inner circle? No, Gordan was not looking forward to that.

"Tovar seems like a cool guy," Mitchell mused. "Think he might teach me a thing or two hundred about magic?"

"You should have asked him," Gordan answered.

They walked and the silence made the corridor seem even longer.

"Is something wrong?" Mitchell asked. "You look…" he furrowed his brow in imitation.

Gordan realized how tightly clenched his forehead was with unease and forced it to relax. "Just a little anxious about being here, in the middle of the mainland, around so many people who hate me."

Mitchell's hand clapped down on his shoulder and took him by surprise.

"Things change Gordan," Mitchell lowered his voice. "How long has it been? Aren't we talking several generations ago now?"

"Hate is pervasive, easily spread and difficult to weed out," Gordan said. "It's true that over a century has passed, but of the dragons that obeyed the Dragon King, followed him, killed for him, those who were not killed in the end of the wars live in exile to this day. It is no simple matter: the dragons followed their king willingly and they deserve exile, but they were encouraged by lies and enticed by promises. Their king fostered hate among the dragons upon our long history of alienation."

"Alienation? Even by the magical world?" Mitchell asked.

"As the old world changed, we were among the first targeted and hunted by the new holy men, but our fellow creatures of magic kept their heads down; they blended in as long as they could; they hid more easily than we could. They watched dragons fall victim to the sport of slaughter, demonstrations of a new god's divine power over imaginary evil.

"When at last we found our way past the borders of the old world and into this safe haven on the edge of existence, we kept to ourselves more so than ever. As the rest of them retreated into this realm, we could not bear to live among those who had watched us die for the glory of men's gods. The Dragon King exploited that divide. He cultivated a loathing so deep that he stirred even indifferent souls into mindlessly angry legions."

"Jeez," Mitchell breathed. "That's...some complicated bad blood."

Gordan agreed in silence. They walked on, their footsteps falling in unison.

"Were you among them?" Mitchell asked.

"Hmm?" Gordan's mind had already drifted away, back to worries.

"During the wars, were you among the Dragon King's legions? Did you have a hand in the conquest and the killing?"

Gordan could feel Mitchell's apprehension once the question

was in the air between them. Mitchell was afraid of his reaction and perhaps the answer, but Gordan couldn't hold it against him for wondering.

"I was not among those legions, no. But I played my part in it, we all did. Even those who stood by in silence deserve their exile," Gordan said, and he relished the pulse of relief from Mitchell. He thought Mitchell might ask what part he had played, and Gordan tensed in anticipation, but to his relief Mitchell did not ask.

"Well, people have to move on at some point, and I can guarantee you Nicole will go Medusa on anyone who dares to even look at you the wrong way," Mitchell said, chuckling. "We were so protective of her, and I guess she learned that. You couldn't tell her it was a brother's job to be protective and a sister's job to be protected. She knew we needed someone looking out for us too and she was right. Everyone needs that. She's always been fiercely protective—of dad, Tony, me, her friends."

"That is precisely the first thing about Nicole that I learned," Gordan said, chuckling fondly.

"She came to my rescue more than once, like when I dated my first boyfriend publicly after only dating girls," Mitchell said. He paused to let out a silent laugh. "It's funny how people just can't wrap their heads around someone liking men *and* women. People sure as hell understand finding more than one ethnicity or body type attractive—how different is it really?"

"What happened? What did Nicole do?" Gordan watched Mitchell, as captivated by Mitchell's emotions as he was to hear stories about Nicole before he knew her.

"Eh, one of the girls I dated got really hostile about '*being used*' to hide that I was into guys. She made a big scene about it. Nicole put her in her place right there in the hallway at school, and no one said a word about me coming out as bi after that. What she said to Loak earlier today—" Mitchell snickered and Gordan smiled, half infected by Mitchell's amusement. "—yeah, it happened a lot like that," he said.

But Mitchell's humor grew thin and transparent. Gordan

glanced at Mitchell, his face baring a wistful half smile. Mitchell teased Nicole and her nature irritated him for the very reason he was here in another realm with them, she had a way of storming right into trouble because she was focused on others. But beneath Mitchell's annoyance he hid his adoration for his sister and a phantom of pain.

Then Mitchell's delicate mask of amusement cracked. "I wouldn't be here without her," he said quietly. "You'd think people have better things to do than tell you that you don't exist, that you can't feel what you feel, that you're either confused or greedy—it's bullshit. But when you hear it enough, you can start to believe it. When you're invalidated enough, you give up on your own right to exist, and just...don't want to anymore. But Nicole...she wouldn't tolerate it, not what people said and not me giving into it."

Gordan's heart turned to a knot as Mitchell pushed out a laugh and looked ahead. The facade was gone. The air around Mitchell trembled.

"You're more frightened than you let on," Gordan remarked quietly. "There's nothing wrong with that."

Mitchell shook his head, "This is your world, Gordan." He stopped a moment to look at him. "You can't imagine how terrifying this is. When you and Nicole disappeared on me...Look—I've seen some incredible things in a short amount of time, portals, giant fiery monsters, and the things Nicole is capable of doing with hardly a thought—it's not as though dad and I didn't have all the proof we needed to believe it, but..."

"You didn't believe it was real," Gordan supposed.

"No. All the worst of it was hiding a world away, he said, walking again. "I thought I believed it, I really did, until you two were gone, and all I had were the crazy stories about what happened on campus. When you didn't come back, it was the worst feeling I've felt in my life, worse than Mom leaving. I finally fucking believed it, and it hit Dad harder than it hit me. I think he really thought this was all a dream; he kept shoving it all back and shrugging it off until Nicole came home covered in blood and left him in Ventura. Then he comes home and I'm there waiting to tell him what happened." Mitchell sighed. "I'm glad Nicole wasn't around to see it. He was so sick when it sank in. He didn't eat for a couple days. I only managed to convince him to shower, get dressed, and leave the house for dinner the night you two came back…don't tell Nicole."

"I'm sorry," Gordan said.

"Don't be. It wasn't your fault we didn't take it seriously until she was gone, and it sure as hell isn't your fault that things are the way they are. I'm just glad you both came back."

Being included in Mitchell's relief made Gordan's heart sputter briefly.

"Will your father be all right with the two of you here?"

"Hard to say. The man is great at keeping his troubles to himself, Nicole learned from the best. He sure seemed to feel better knowing we'd be here together—look out for each other, that's the rule in this family."

Gordan nodded in agreement. The two of them had managed to wander up to the third floor and on to the fourth when a door opened ahead of them. Two familiar young ladies stepped out into the hall and froze at the sight of Gordan and Mitchell.

"It's you! Hello again," the younger girl said, her dark eyes aimed at Gordan.

"Are you Nicole's brother?" the older girl asked Mitchell.

"Yeah," Mitchell said, glancing at Gordan in confusion. "Who are you?"

"Fen."

"Asi."

Delight and gratitude burst in Mitchell's chest like fireworks as his face lit up with recognition at their names.

"I just have one question," Mitchell said. "Can I hug you?"

The girls looked at each other, confusion-creased foreheads above their smiles, but they nodded nonetheless.

"Why not?" Fen answered and Mitchell threw his arms around them both, lifting them off their feet before setting them down.

"Thank you," he said with soft severity. "Which one of you erased Caeruleus' memory?"

Asi's face went pink. "I did."

"Bravo, kid," he said. "So, you're the potion guru," he directed at Fen.

Fen stammered through her embarrassment but Gordan sensed her swelling of pride. "Oh, not really, no, I—"

"She can brew anything," Asi insisted, cutting Fen off.

"I suppose it's foolish to ask how you got here," Gordan offered. "Do you know where Nicole disappeared to?"

The girls shook their heads.

"She and Raiden went somewhere together," Fen said with a shrug.

"In that case maybe we shouldn't bother looking for them," Mitchell said, then his head lurched forward like he'd been struck from behind. "Hey!" He whirled around but there was no one behind them. Down the hall Nicole and Raiden reached the bottom of the stairs.

"What was that for?" he demanded.

"Luck," Nicole said. "I see you've met Mitch," she said to the girls. She wore a smile on her face but the air around her was bleak.

Then from the furthest end of the hall a muffled jumble of voices preceded the opening of a door and Loak, Leone and Caeruleus emerged from the stairwell of the eastern tower.

"Look who it is," Loak's voice barreled down the corridor.

"We found Caeruleus, lost as a kitten," Leone chuckled.

"You two were as lost as I was," Caeruleus muttered. "Who are they?"

Fen and Asi made valiant efforts to contain their laughter, but couldn't keep from smiling.

"Friends I met on my way to Atrium," Nicole said easily, camouflaging her amusement more successfully than the girls. "This is Fen and Asi."

Caeruleus shifted his eye from Mitchell, to Nicole and the girls. Gordan felt his confusion, but didn't suspect anyone but Raiden would be willing to fill him in on his lost memory of confronting the family that had been harboring Nicole.

"There you are," Tovar's voice called from the other end of the hallway.

Gordan and Mitchell turned around to see him marching vigorously to reach them. "Thank the stars for seeking spells. Wonderful, practically everyone is here. The subjects outside have been putting together a celebration all day. I can't see any reason to squash their enthusiasm, we have to eat, after all. I do think we should bring the festivities into the palace since Nicole and Raiden are safest inside."

"Someone will have to go tell our friends on board the Tempest," Loak said.

"Sounds great, I'm starving," Mitchell said.

Fen and Asi lit up and beamed at each other.

There was too much excitement mingling with hunger and nerves amongst everyone for Gordan to single out Nicole, but he didn't need the clarity of his empathic sense to recognize her discomfort as he watched her shrink where she stood. Without so much as looking at her, Raiden seemed to detect what Gordan could see quite plainly because his hand closed around hers.

❧

Nicole avoided going downstairs to the unfurling festivities as long as she could, or as long as Fen and Asi would allow after they took their time deciding the best clothes they had for a celebration. Nicole had only a bag of sweaters, leggings and jeans from home, and of course, her packed bag that she retrieved from Keren's house. All the stuff she had brought with her when she set out from home to end things with the Council, her clothes, a few books, and the red and grey cloak that Keren and the girls purchased for her was clean and folded at the top of the bag. She wore the nicest article of clothing she had, the mauve sweater, over her leggings and hiking boots.

Nicole watched from the pillow pile as the girls dressed. Fen put on a shin-length skirt of vibrant green and yellow and a simple yet impeccably made white tunic that was loose and hung to her hips. She added a red sash around her waist. Asi pulled out two garments in the same pale green cloth, a pair of soft pants and long tunic almost to her knees but slit up the sides to her waist. Nicole let their giddy ritual distract her, but when they were ready to go downstairs to catch the preparations, she wanted to dive into the small mountain of pillows and bury herself.

"Nicole," Asi asked, the lightness in her voice gone. "Are you really okay?"

Fen looked to her with the same concern echoing Asi silently on her pinched face. Nicole tried to smile and knew she was failing.

"I…don't know what to say. Sometimes I do feel okay, when I'm with the people I love I can forget what happened and I'm myself again, I can laugh." She shrugged.

"But other times?" Fen sank down into the pillows beside her.

"Other times I feel like I'm still there, like the Council is still inside me and my skin crawls and I don't want to be in my own body anymore," she explained, hearing the tremble in her voice.

Asi looked to Fen then Nicole and sat down to sandwich Nicole between them.

Nicole took a deep breath. "And now I have to play King on top of trying to fix this mess I made of everyone's lives." *And fix myself,* she thought. She knew she couldn't expect anyone else to do it.

"You didn't make a mess of our lives," Asi insisted. "You made ours better. Don't forget that."

"Yeah," Fen agreed. "No one should have to carry so much on their shoulders, but at least you're not alone and you don't have to do it all at once."

"And we can help," Asi added. "How can we help?"

Nicole smiled and it felt real. "Enjoy the party tonight. Have as much fun as you can so that I can feel like *something* good has come out of this insanity."

"I think we can do that," Fen said.

Asi nodded in agreement.

"I suppose we should get down there," Nicole muttered unenthusiastically.

"Come on," Asi insisted, pulling Nicole to her feet.

"You just have to be there, eat, smile, and meet people—no problem," Fen said.

"Sure, that's easy," Nicole agreed facetiously.

Asi and Fen escorted her downstairs, Asi holding her hand like the flight-risk she was.

"Wait, where's your key?" Fen asked.

Nicole sighed and pulled it out from inside the mauve sweater. It was the only way people would be able to recognize her, perhaps a handful of people got a look at her face yesterday, but it was the key they would all be looking for tonight.

As they descended the stairs to the first floor, they passed Gordan sitting in thought upon the steps.

"Hey," Nicole said. She knew exactly why he was hiding here, he didn't want to be among the people any more than she did.

He stood, his expression furrowed.

"You don't have to," she offered quietly. "Probably better if you don't. I'll be fine."

His face softened.

It wasn't the best place to introduce him, in a hall filled with people whose exuberant celebration could be swiftly turned to outrage by the wrong spark. For his sake—for his safety—Nicole wouldn't drag him into throngs of people. She slipped her arms around him for a brief hug.

"I don't want to do this," she whispered desperately into his chest. She would rather walk into that hall to face Venarius than hundreds of people—*subjects*—who thought she could…what? What did these people think she and Raiden would change?

Gordan returned the embrace and answered in her ear. "Stay for an hour. They just want to see you."

She pulled away, nodding. "Wish me luck."

Gordan offered her a sad smile and watched her go.

Asi grabbed her hand again and away to the grand entranceway they went. What they found was a hodgepodge family gathering amplified by one hundred. People bustled around the entranceway and into the throne room where all the doors were open and an avenue of tables had sprung up, each one different like they had been conjured by many different people all at once—some basic wooden tables all angles and no fuss, some carved tables all curves and elegance. Strangers heaved large platters onto the tabletops. She spotted Loak easily delivering a massive plate in each hand laden with a whole pig and some bird that was much too large to be a turkey, setting them down at the centers of different tables along the way.

Nicole, Asi, and Fen wandered along the causeway of food—a table filled with meat, a table piled with breads, a table buried under great bowls and pots of soups and stews, one laden with fruit, another with cheese—following it through the entranceway and into vast throne room where the last several tables were almost over-flowing with pies, tarts, pastries, and more sweet confections than Nicole could name. But the best of all were the two towering cakes, each sitting upon a throne at the head of the last table, dessert royalty.

"Raiden had them do that," a familiar voice said in her ear as Mitchell snuck up behind her.

She smiled; they couldn't sit on the thrones if the cakes already were—a perfect avoidance maneuver. She could almost enjoy his little joke. There was something undeniably endearing about the affair, a humble patchwork celebration that made up for its lack of extravagance with its diversity and abundance. The warm informal-ity of it eclipsed the grandeur of the setting. The ornately carved ceilings' silent pleas for pomp and circumstance were drown out by common reveling without exhausting formalities and customs. But the spacious entrance-way soon filled with bodies and noise.

Nicole drifted through the night clinging to Raiden's hand in the flood of subjects, a blur of smiling faces, an indistinct jumble of greetings and congratulations, thanks and blessings. She knew he needed her hand to steady himself against his unsettling anxiety in crowds as much as she needed his to anchor her down and keep her from running away.

The flurry of tantalizing scents was dizzying, the roar of jubilation deafening. She was in constant motion, pulled on by Raiden, bumped, jostled, tapped, her free hand shaken vigorously time and again. Occasionally Raiden stole discrete embraces, turning to her as though to say something quietly between them, but really, he just needed a moment to shake the memories from his head, and she reminded him where he was by simply saying, "I'm here."

They crossed paths with Mitchell several times, always with a different food in his hand, enjoying himself immensely. Then Andrus was there, crossing their path.

"Where have *you* been?" Nicole wondered, a little aghast that she'd forgotten all about him and realized she hadn't even seen him since yesterday.

"I've been hanging out on the Tempest with Rhee and Pep, they need a medic on board anyway. Rhee booted the last guy for some incident with Caeruleus, and it's a lot cozier than a creepy empty palace," he chuckled. "But this I can get used to," he said, toasting them by lifting a wooden goblet with a short stem, sloshing some of the foamy beer over the side.

☙

Venarius stood outside the palace among the overflow of celebration that spilled out the doors of the palace and down the steps to the street of the blooming town. Looking up at the open doors and the light pouring out over the joyous fools who probably believed the light from this old palace meant something, Venarius scoffed—such a childish notion—a withered dream revived, a better future in this exile.

They're still trapped by the idea that this realm is our home. How perfect that one of those kings was indeed the key to something greater for the people of Veil. *She's the key to unlock our chains, we will leave this prison.* He made his way up the steps and through the doors, curious to see her up close, watch her, know her.

Nicole had a sneaking suspicion that Raiden's navigation through the crowds had something to do with avoiding his father as she could never quite get more than a glimpse of him here and there. They stayed inside the palace, but the people came and went along the train of tables and outside the doors where the festivities spilled down the palace steps and onward through the town below them. Fen and Asi disappeared into the excitement, but found Raiden and her now and then. Nicole could have begrudgingly endured this the entire night attached to Raiden if not for Tovar tracking them down with an anxious frown on his face.

"Raiden, an emissary from Taroth insists on a brief audience with you," Tovar said, looking flustered.

"That's fine, I suppose," Raiden agreed and Nicole wondered if he just wanted the excuse to escape the crowded hall. He made his way through the crowds, Nicole's hand still fused to his.

"Um," Tovar began uncomfortably. "He expressly said he only wanted to speak to you, Raiden."

Raiden stopped. "Why?"

"That's how they do things in Taroth," Tovar said, rather like someone talking about a neighbor they abhorred but trying to sound tolerant.

"I don't care. Go talk to him," Nicole shrugged. She wasn't about to complain since emissaries, ambassadors, and diplomacy were the last things she wanted anything to do with now or ever, that was way too deep into this charade for her liking.

Raiden scowled and sighed. "Fine."

She watched Raiden and Tovar disappear into the crowd. Detached from him she felt adrift, uneasy, overwhelmed by everything around her. She was so relieved to catch her brother in passing that she grabbed his hand, a child again seeking her big brother's protection.

"Mitch!" she cried, only partly because she had to raise her voice above the noise.

"Hey, there you are," he said, the familiar loose lilt of inebriation in his voice. "Where's Ray?"

"He went somewhere with—"

"Don't worry, we'll find him," Mitchell insisted.

Nicole sighed and let her brother go on his intoxicated quest without bothering to explain to him that she wasn't *looking* for Raiden, she was looking for someone to keep her steady.

"Never mind," she muttered, slipping through the crowd, nodding to joyous waves, smiling at people's shouts, and shaking hands that were thrust at her as she went until she reached the fringes of the party and lurched into the cool quiet air of empty corridors, away from foolishly hopeful people throwing blind praise at someone they didn't even know just because of a stupid key hanging from her neck.

They didn't know who she was or what she had done—she was no one and had done nothing to deserve their adoration. She pitied them for how desperate they were for change, how starved they were for something better than what they had, and that they thought she could fix this realm when she was still trying to mend herself.

☙

Tovar led Raiden into a small private chamber off the throne room that he hadn't known was there. Inside a man in multiple layers of fine white clothing stood waiting with rigid formality that made Raiden straighten his spine in a similar fashion.

"Good evening," the man said, with an almost imperceptible bow and a pompous pursed mouth.

Aside from the key hanging from his neck, Raiden knew he didn't look the part of a king. In fact, of the two of them, the emissary from Taroth looked more like royalty.

Raiden didn't want to talk to the man, but still he reciprocated his greeting hoping he didn't sound snide. "Good evening."

"King Heimskur of Taroth hoped to be the first to send his sincerest congratulations and hopes that you and your queen will accept his invitation to be his honored guests in Taroth."

Raiden clenched his teeth. He'd rather be suffocating in the crowd than talking to this man.

"Thank your king for his sentiments and his invitation. Good night," Raiden said, turning away and catching the flabbergasted look on the emissary's face as he went.

As he passed Tovar, Raiden was sure he was suppressing a laugh. Behind him Tovar bid the emissary good night and followed Raiden back out to the revelry. He stopped to scan the sea of faces for Nicole.

"Nicely done," Tovar said, stopping beside him and holding back a chuckle.

"I know that wasn't exactly the best way to start a relationship with one of the royal states," Raiden said with disinterest, more concerned with finding Nicole.

"With Taroth I honestly can't think of a better way to have handled that," Tovar chuckled.

"Fen!" Raiden called when he spotted her and Asi scurrying away from the dessert tables with glistening pastries in hand. "Have you seen Nicole?"

Fen shook her head and spoke in Asi's ear, then Asi shook her head. The girls shrugged at him. He sighed and kept searching, skirting the crowd as best he could.

"Hey!" Mitchell called, waving at him.

"Mitch, where's Nicole?"

"She's around," he said, swiveling his head pointedly before turning back to Raiden. "She's here somewhere, I just saw her. She's lookin' for you."

Raiden frowned, casting another scouring gaze across the faces in the hall, but wherever a head of dark curls caught his eye, the individual was *not* Nicole.

Nicole closed the door to her room, relieved that no one else could open it. It was dark and the single orb of light hovering at her shoulder did little to penetrate the dense shadows of such a vast chamber, but it was enough light for her to find her way across the room still riddled with cushions to the large pillows where she threw herself down. It was bliss, her flesh and bones sinking heavily into silent stillness while her thoughts dissolved into exhaustion.

Yet another huddle of subjects offering their hands to shake caught Raiden in his search for Nicole. They raised goblets into the air. His smile was strained and he swallowed back his unease as his heart rate quickened and a chill hit him despite the sweat clinging to his skin. Once he was free to press on, he let his smile fall. Somewhere in the room a scream of laughter cut through the low rumble of noise, and he couldn't shake the dread creeping in or the sounds of shouts and terrible shrieks that the walls of his home in Cantis could not keep out. His breaths grew short and fast and the darkness of his time locked in the hall closet crept in at the edges of his vision.

Then a hand dropped onto his shoulder, clamping down and steadying him with its firm weight. Startled, he turned his head to see his father.

"Come on," he said, barely audible, and guided Raiden out of the joyous throng before he could even steady his mind enough to protest.

Leone escorted Raiden to the chilly corridor beyond the celebration where they stopped below the stairs leading up to the second floor.

"Are you all right?"

"I'm fine," Raiden insisted even though he wasn't. "I don't do well in crowds." He kept his eyes down, rubbing his face a moment and pushing his fingers back through his hair.

"You seemed to handle it fairly well earlier—"

"I had Nicole with me," Raiden explained, pinching the bridge of his nose still trying to shake off his memories of that horrible night in Cantis. "Have you seen her?"

"I saw her head this way not too long ago. She might be upstairs."

Raiden sighed, relieved to know which way she'd gone at least. His heart rate slowed, easing into the surreal moment standing in the dark, which might have perpetuated his anxiety if not for the presence of his father—an anachronism breaking the illusion. Leone was a figure from faded memories and old photographs, brief flashes of nostalgia and sad dreams of a different life. His father had not existed for so long that his presence was now surreal and disquieting.

A tiny sound escaped his father's lips, but he refrained from whatever he was about to say.

Raiden supposed this was bizarre for him too. How many years had he been gone, living in a cell dreaming of his family? Was it sixteen years now? The son Leone remembered was with his wife—gone. Before him was a man he didn't know with the same name he had given his child twenty-two years ago.

"You know, I spent every day wishing I had been there," Leone said.

"So did Mother," Raiden admitted heavily.

"What happened? I hate to ask you to relive it, but I need to know," his father implored.

"What did Loak tell you?"

"Just what the Council announced—that the entire city was lost and Dawn was to blame. They used the story to rekindle the waning support of the realm for a time."

"Strange they knew to find me there when they wanted a convenient pawn," Raiden muttered.

"That would be thanks to the seers. The Council has had them searching for the fera for decades, and with her ending up in Cantis, there was little chance you *wouldn't* have crossed her path."

Raiden considered this for several slow moments, his mind sluggish with fatigue.

"How long did they know Nicole was coming?" Raiden wondered—had they known when he was still a boy alone in Cantis?

"Caeruleus might have the answer to that. Loak was not privy to the machinations of the Council with regards to the fera. *He* didn't even know you were alive until you arrived in Atrium. I thought I died when he told me."

"The Council told *us* you died on assignment," Raiden said.

"I'm sure your mother knew that was a lie."

"She never told me. She let me believe it."

"She was protecting you."

"Well, no one was there to protect her. They sent golems; I can only imagine how many to be honest because I didn't see most of it from inside the hall closet. She sealed me in. I don't know where she got the money for a spell like that, but she pushed me in and I had to listen to the screams of an entire city. I had to listen to her die while nothing could touch me. I was stuck in there for hours after it ended until the spell wore off. And then I was alone...for nine years."

"I'm sorry," his father whispered. He sounded defeated.

"I know." There was no harsher punishment for his mistakes and his absence than losing his family. Hearing the story had to be as torturous to him as it was for Raiden to tell it. Perhaps that pain of knowing what happened was his father's attempt at penance.

"How," Leone paused to swallow back his grief, "how did you manage nine years by yourself?"

"I stopped feeling. I read books. I figured out how to get by, fishing, scavenging in the city, foraging in the woods. I thought of nothing but survival and justice for Mother. Then I found Nicole," Raiden said. Just saying her name lifted his heart out of the muck of those memories.

"Right. You were looking for her in there. I'll let you get back to that," Leone said, clearing his throat.

"Thank you," Raiden muttered, turning toward the stairs.

"Raiden?"

"What?" He stopped to glance back over his shoulder.

"If you don't want me around, I'll go."

Raiden took a deep breath. His head was oddly light and his vision fuzzy. His heart felt like it had been wrung out, clenched and aching. His body was twice as heavy as usual, just standing there on the stairs was a precarious balancing act.

"Stay," he said, thinking of his mother and closing his eyes against the sudden burn. She would have wanted—with all her heart—for them to find each other. "You've been gone long enough."

&

Nicole was asleep and in the same darkness she had found herself the night before. It was a nebulous place, the unknown pressing in around her, but it was familiar to her too. The ground beneath her was firm and smooth. Her footsteps echoed coldly, and she felt sure she was standing on a polished marble floor. She didn't *like* being there, but in all honesty, she couldn't say it was worse than the real world. Awake, even with everyone she loved around her, she was stuck in a life she didn't want, trying to figure out how the hell she was supposed to win the freedom to walk away from it and toward one she wanted.

It was hard to say if she was moving forward or just going nowhere. She thought she was walking, but there was no way to know.

It was just her, the darkness, and the urgency of searching, the anxiety of missing something, the dread of knowing she might never find it even if she searched for a lifetime. She tried countless times to cast some light around her, but she apparently had no magic in *this* place.

❧

Gordan wandered through the castle, content in the dark corridors lit only by the moon and starlight coming through windows. He could see well enough—the shadows were not so dark to him. The jubilant noise of the celebration was all but a whisper, so faint he could convince himself he was only imagining it, a memory haunting him and coaxing him to get as far from the festivities as possible.

Then something in the air changed, creeping through his peace and casting a disturbing chill upon his solitude in the empty corridor. This odd energy in the air perplexed him. He could not decipher the tenuous aura, a frequency of unease and isolation, but he knew without a doubt that it was Nicole's.

Turning back the way he'd come, Gordan's light steps turned into a hard, resolute march, back through the corridors following the eerie tremble in the air to Nicole, or rather to the closed door of the grand chamber which opened only to her key. At first he wasn't sure what to do. She was asleep, that he could sense through the door, but his mounting concern pushed him to wake her. Then came the sensation of sinking, loathing, sorrow, the nausea of despair, and he could no longer let her remain undisturbed.

He threw his fist against the door several times.

"Nicole," he called.

He pounded the door, his heart echoing the frantic cacophony. He heard a gasp from within and felt the rhythm of her heart lurch into a frenzy of adrenaline. Moments later the door opened and her face appeared, eyelids heavy and lips pressed into a straight line.

"Gordan? What happened?"

His own heart, tight with apprehension, eased to see her there, relieved to catch no scent of blood in the air. The dark cloud was gone and nothing but the harmless shroud of night and her groggy confusion hung in the air.

"Nothing," he said and felt a current of worry roll up behind him—it was Raiden, he was looking for her too. "Just trying to find you."

"Oh," she said, opening the door entirely. "I couldn't take any more of it down there."

"I can't blame you," Gordan said, and he heard Raiden's footsteps announcing his arrival behind him. "Raiden," he said, turning to him. "Enjoy the party?"

"More or less until I met the emissary from Taroth." The little bubble of light at Raiden's shoulder drifted toward his face when he stopped, and he waved it away, cringing against the light in his eyes. The light scattered for a second, and reformed, floating up and out of the way to linger in the doorway over their heads.

"Pleasant guy, was he?" Nicole asked sarcastically, her eyes fixed on the light.

"About as self-important as you would expect a king to be," Raiden said.

Gordan could taste the disgust in the air. "Taroth hasn't changed much then."

"Now there's an idea," Nicole said,

Raiden and Gordan both looked at her.

"What?" Gordan asked.

"Sending emissaries," she said. "Why don't we ask Captain Rhee if she and Pep can take Caeruleus and Andrus around Veil on our behalf, diplomatic bullshit, but mostly making sure the news of the fera with the key gets out everywhere—you know, extend our invitation to Venarius wherever he may be lurking."

Gordan looked at Raiden who looked back at him.

"Why Caeruleus and Andrus?" Raiden asked.

"One of the Council's agents and one of the rebels, someone from each side of the Atrium conflict," she said with a shrug. "Also, Caeruleus is probably the best at that formal stuff after all his time with the Council, and Andrus—well, he'll probably tell people about me being the fera without us even asking him."

Gordan chuckled to himself, *a shame she doesn't want to be a king.*

They made Nicole's chamber their hiding place, all of them slumped on the massive cushion as time crawled secretly around them until Gordan could feel the distant drone of a thousand revel-drunk psyches disperse several floors beneath them.

"I believe the celebration has finally reached its end," Gordan said.

Raiden had fallen asleep an hour ago as they lay there talking, musing about a world that had never been torn apart, where Veil had never existed and its people were never isolated. Would they have survived if they fought for their rightful place in the world back then? Or would the world look exactly as the old world looked today, magicless and choking on its own poisons?

"I better go find Mitchell and peel him off the floor," she said, rolling off the pillow and lumbering to her feet.

"I'll come," Gordan said, sitting up and springing into a light pace behind her.

They both glanced back at Raiden.

"He's out cold," she murmured, the corners of her mouth twitched with a fleeting smile.

"That kind of exhaustion takes a lot of sleep to recover from," Gordan said. "I suspect he hasn't had much genuine rest in a very long time."

He turned away and left Raiden to the depths of that restorative slumber and caught up with Nicole. He could *feel* her frowning.

"We've really done a number on ourselves, haven't we?" Nicole said, so softly the sound was almost lost in the echo of her footsteps as they stepped out into the hall. "He's been through hell, and I just brought more of the same into his life. He deserves peace."

Gordan didn't know what to say, or what she needed to hear, so he matched her pace and walked beside her with his senses tuned to her psyche, putting out twisting tendrils into the air around her as though in her silence she was searching for some answer beyond herself.

They made their way back downstairs to the main corridor that was the palace entranceway and avenue into the throne room. The last remaining revelers staggered out the palace doors with arms around more sober companions who kept their path straight and their balance more or less steady.

Asi and Fen came dancing in through great doorway, taking turns spinning and dipping each other now and then, their swaying gaits heavy with exhaustion but their moods light, almost intoxicated, with delight.

"Nicole," they sang together and broke out laughing at their unintended harmony.

"Hi, girls," Nicole said. "Have a good time?"

"Yes," Fen answered on an exhalation of satisfaction.

"There was music outside," Asi said. "I can't remember the last time I danced at a party. I don't think I ever have actually." She laughed, unperturbed by her revelation.

"We're looking for Mitchell," Nicole said.

"Is that him?" Fen said, pointing.

Gordan's gaze followed the direction of Fen's finger to a pair of denim-clad legs that could be seen dangling off a table. Nicole marched along the row of tables, stopped beside the legs, lifted an arm and pulled. Mitchell sat up smiling, his beanie askew.

"Hey," he said, looking ready to tip back.

Gordan made his way to Nicole's side while Asi and Fen trailed behind him.

"Come on, Mitch," Nicole said, taking his arm to pull him off the table.

"Let me," Gordan insisted. Nicole was strong, but Mitchell was still much taller than she was.

"All right—but, just so you know, he gets pretty silly when he's drunk," she said.

"Gordan," Mitchell said cheerfully and somewhat surprised as if he'd just realized whom he had been looking at.

Gordan was hit by a wave of unfiltered and dizzying enthusiasm, and *he* almost staggered under the influence of Mitchell's ine-briation. Mitchell threw his arm around Gordan's shoulders and hopped off the table. They were just about the same height, but now Gordan noted how much broader Mitchell's shoulders were than his own as he draped Mitchell's muscled arm around his neck.

"Alas," Mitchell crowed up toward the ceiling. "The party must end." Gordan steadied him with an arm around Mitchell's back.

A pair of stifled giggles came from Asi and Fen as Gordan escorted Mitchell out of the throne room.

They stopped at Fen and Asi's room.

"Good night," Asi said drowsily.

"See you tomorrow," Fen waved.

"Where are they going?" Mitchell wondered when they disappeared and closed the door.

"To bed, Mitch. It's late," Nicole said.

"Oh," he said. "Where are *we* going?"

"To bed," Gordan said.

Mitchell leaned away from Gordan to look at him, and Gordan had to hold tight to his arm and waist so that he didn't tip himself right over. "You and me?"

Nicole snickered.

"You—you're going to bed," Gordan clarified.

"What about you?" Mitchell asked.

"Uh," Gordan wasn't sure how to answer.

"He's got important things to do," Nicole said easily.

"Oh, right. Dragons do important stuff."

Nicole tried to smother another laugh that came out her nose instead.

Onward they trudged, Gordan shouldering the unsteady weight of Mitchell whose haze of intoxicated amusement was infectious, a sickness that was hard for him to resist in such close proximity. He was relieved to finally reach the top of the stairs and Nicole's chamber was in sight.

Raiden was precisely where they had left him, asleep on the massive pillow, arm thrown over his eyes and his mouth open, his breathing rasping in the back of his throat.

"Here we are," Gordan said, presenting Mitchell with the green pillow Nicole had dropped upon him earlier that day.

Mitchell cast a swaying gaze at the pillow and then back at Gordan.

"Thank you, sir," Mitchell said, sliding his arm off Gordan's shoulders and rocking forward.

Gordan thought he lost his balance until Mitchell's mouth met his in an abrupt kiss. It was so brief that he was stunned and stood there frozen as Mitchell spread his arms wide and flopped back onto the pillow announcing, "Good night!"

Nicole let out a breathy laugh. "I warned you."

Gordan stood there dumbfounded as his blood raced through him like a brush fire. Mitchell was already unconscious—his contagious intoxication nullified in slumber—but there was still a giddy heat lingering in Gordan's chest.

☙

Gordan knew Nicole was gone before he even opened his eyes the next morning. He sat up and glanced across the large striped orange and burgundy pillow to see she wasn't there. Raiden was still right where he'd fallen asleep, now curled on his side. Mitchell lay sprawled prone on the edge of his pillow with his face hanging partly off and a hand planted on the stone floor beside a half-drained bottle of water that could only have been put there by Nicole.

Gordan looked around, but her presence felt far too distant for her to be wandering the royal suite, stone walls, stone floor, stone buttresses, all swirls and striations in shades of grey and veins of quartz. The only color in the room came from the conjured cushions scattered about the floor, vivid eruptions of incongruity, shocking and pleasing to the eye.

A deep breath drew Gordan's attention to Raiden who rolled onto his back and sat up looking wholly confused. He looked around, spotted Gordan, and tilted his head.

"What?" Gordan asked.

"Nothing," Raiden answered, but Gordan could feel a pang of unease ringing faintly in the silence of the room.

He supposed it was just Nicole's absence that, whenever inexplicable, stirred anxiety in Raiden's heart. Venarius and his motives lurking out in the world hung heavily on all of them, Raiden especially—he had come so close to the man and had seen the treacherous lengths Venarius had gone to in order to secure the fera for his plans.

"She's still in the palace," Gordan offered—high above them it would seem. He supposed she was wandering again, somewhere in the towers.

Raiden sagged a little. In the palace Venarius couldn't get to her—that was enough to ease his fears. He heaved himself off the pillow and lumbered past Gordan.

"Excuse me," he said, wandering deeper into Nicole's chambers, muttering that this place was far too big and that the bathrooms were too far away.

Gordan realized that morning was the tipping point; everything surged forward with building momentum. He kept a steady focus on Nicole's distant presence while he observed the orchestrations of the others. Raiden delivered Nicole's idea to the others, and it wasn't mid-day before Caeruleus and Andrus were aboard the Tempest on their way with Rhee and Pep.

The palace silence dissolved into the growing bustle of Loak and Leone recruiting guards, Tovar hiring staff and awakening the sleeping corridors into a humming household for the first time. As the number of inhabitants in the palace increased, Gordan disappeared upstairs, first to check on Mitchell.

The door to Nicole's chamber was open just as he and Raiden had left it, but when he walked in, Mitchell was *not* where he'd left him. The emerald green pillow was empty.

Gordan stood there puzzled and not a moment later Mitchell came dragging his feet from the depths of the chamber where the bathroom was hidden away. Mitchell let out a sound halfway between a grunt and a mumble that might have been words.

"Hey, Gordan," he managed to say more clearly. Head-pounding misery and nausea radiated off him. Gordan leaned away. "Must have been a hell of a party, huh?" He chuckled, sinking onto the pillow before snatching up his water bottle.

"You don't remember?"

"That was no ordinary booze," he said, shaking his head. "I didn't drink more than I normally would, a couple beers, no big deal—but goddamn." He tipped the bottle up and guzzled the last of the water.

"It was, indeed, an interesting night," Gordan said.

"Where is everyone?"

"Downstairs mostly, I was about to look for Nicole myself."

"Good luck. I think I'll stay here," Mitchell said, easing back down onto the pillow with a heavy sigh.

"There should be food downstairs somewhere; there was quite a bit remaining from last night," Gordan suggested as he made his way back to the door.

Mitchell groaned.

Gordan wandered for almost an hour, following Nicole's presence like a thread, only this thread could go through walls and he could not, so several times he would end up closer to her but at a dead end which meant doubling back and trying another route until at last he was marching up the spiraling steps of a tower and *knew* Nicole was above him.

He reached the top of the stairs and shouldered open the round door above him to find a circular chamber filled with light and Nicole.

"Hey," she said, sitting against the wall with an owl griffin in her lap and another sitting beside her. "I knew you'd find my hiding place eventually."

"Not a bad hiding place," he said, hopping up into the room and closing the door.

"How's Mitch?"

"Alive."

"Good enough," she said, a shred of a smile in the corner of her mouth.

"How are you?" Gordan asked.

"Me? I didn't think you had to ask."

"I don't," he said. He could plainly feel her brooding uncertainty and distress echoing in her heart, but only she could explain it. "I want you to tell me about it."

"I'm not sure what to say," she said, dropping her gaze down to the small griffin purring under her hand in her lap.

"Well then," Gordan said with a sigh. "I'll join you in silence." He walked across the room and sat down beside her. From the other side of Nicole, the second owl regarded him for a couple slow blinks.

That tower room became his haven as the highest reaches of the palace were rarely even thought about by the relatively small company that inhabited the place, even including the staff that moved into their quarters that day. Gordan hid in the tower more than either of them in the days that followed, and only Nicole knew to find him there.

But Nicole could not always be found in the tower when Gordan looked, and he soon realized she was disappearing from the palace altogether. Each morning Nicole and Raiden were caught up receiving the onslaught of gifts arriving to the palace, furniture, tapestries, horses, food.

Nicole begrudgingly welcomed visitors alongside Raiden although no one would have known by her demeanor what Gordan could feel in the air. Although Gordan kept his distance from visiting subjects, he could feel Nicole's cloud of writhing distress each time she left the throne room. And Raiden reluctantly gave Nicole her space, keeping himself busy in the company of Tovar and his father as they assisted in the training of the guard—or Tovar to check in on the coordination of staff, visitors, gifts, and more. Most of the gifts Raiden wanted doled out as payment to the staff.

Gordan recognized the same tactic Raiden had used during his solitude in Cantis—productive distraction, a near obsessive pursuit of progress to smother his fears. Nicole was always on his mind and Gordan knew this because whenever they crossed paths Raiden would ask him, "Have you seen her?"

To which Gordan learned to answer, "She's in her usual hiding place." It wasn't a lie, after all Gordan had no doubt she found a place to hide so far from the palace that Gordan could detect no trace of her. But Raiden would smile weakly—undoubtably thinking she *was* somewhere in the palace—and return to his distraction. Nicole always turned up for dinner after all, to spend time in the kitchens with Raiden and then bring food up to Gordan in the tower.

After the fourth day placating Raiden's anxiety, Gordan grew too guilty to let it continue. He supposed she was disappearing to Keren's orchard, but leaving the palace was a risk she shouldn't be taking alone.

⁊

The tower wasn't far enough away from everything for Nicole—the tower was still part of the palace after all, and in the palace she was a king. Looking out over the land of Veil wasn't much of an escape, it only reminded her of all the people looking to her to save the realm—that is, except Cantis. It was silent, empty, devoid of expectation. It was the perfect place to hide. There was nothing stopping her from slipping through the ether and leaving the palace, and there was comfort in the familiarity of Raiden's house. She could breathe easier. She didn't have to smile for anyone's benefit, didn't have to hear about the goings-on of the palace or get dragged into another round of formal audiences bearing gifts.

We've brought you a tapestry of Veil, your highnesses.
Please accept our finest stallion, my king.
The finest silk in the entire realm for you, your majesty.

She huffed because she'd have to go back. She always had to go back. But while she was in Cantis, she took solace in no one knowing where she was as she sat on Raiden's bed and puzzled over the conundrum of putting herself back together with pieces missing. She couldn't *think* in the palace, not about anything other than the expectations hanging from her neck.

She hadn't intended to stay long when she first slipped away to

Cantis. At first she told herself she just needed a few minutes to herself. Time among Raiden's books tempted her—it was a room full of doors, each offering her escape—in a strange way it was like getting to know the real Raiden. The urge to go home to Yuma was ever present, but she didn't want to leave a portal out in the open, unprotected. Her the third day hiding in Raiden's room she opened one of his countless books to find spells on portals and doorways. If she could safely hide a portal home, then she could spare her father the torment of waiting who-knew-how-long to know his child was alive and well.

This project was a perfect distraction from everything she left behind in the palace—a door that would take her from Raiden's house back home to hers in Yuma. She set out to use the same solution Raiden had employed to keep his safe haven out of reach from the few other scavenging survivors lurking in their holes. Nicole wondered where they might be whenever she wandered Cantis when she felt stir-crazy. Sometimes she hiked the forest, sometimes she ran the maze of the city first until she was lost and then until she found her way back to Raiden's house. She never caught any sign of anyone else, not a shadow behind a grimy window, nor a sound of movement inside the solemn buildings. Were they still lurking in somewhere, scratching through debris for what they could use? Did they know the island was safe now, that Moira was gone and they could come out to live better lives out in the sun?

She knew who would have the answer, and he was always around. She got used to him, his sudden appearances, his unblinking gaze shifting to her, the way he would fade out of sight, but his presence lingered in the air like when you know someone is watching you.

"Amarth," she said. "I know you're here somewhere."

No answer came. She asked anyway.

"Are the other survivors still around?"

"Of course," the soft monotone emerged from the silence.

"I mean are they alive," she said.

"Oh—then no."

"Do you know what happened to them?"

"One killed the other over some squabble and jumped off the cliffs himself years later."

"Oh," she said, her spine sagging in disappointment as she looked out over an empty broken city from where she sat upon one of the taller roofs. It didn't have to stay this way, the debris could be cleared, its destruction rebuilt. It could be alive again, not the same, but alive. *I can do it,* she thought, *I'll fix things*. Her lungs swelled with possibility and then deflated abruptly with the return of the nagging imperative that she needed to get back to the palace before anyone worried.

She scooped the key hanging from her neck into her hand and scowled down at it. Using it as a facade to search for Venarius was one thing, but what about when the search was over, what about after the fight when—hopefully—Venarius was no more. She pulled the key off, squeezed it in her hand, pulled her arm back angrily and hurled it out across the rooftops. It sailed through the air, glinting in the light as it fell too far off for her to even hear the crystal hit stone. Then she dropped her gaze and there it was, hanging against her belly unceremoniously.

She dropped her head back in frustration at the thought of returning. It wasn't just that she wanted to be away from the palace, from the reverent and eager looks, from the *your-highness*es and bows, the royal audiences and gifts. She wanted to stay where Gordan wouldn't have to bear her psyche, a mix of melancholy and the creeping madness of a trapped animal. She tried to spare him as much as herself. When she was stuck in the palace her mood was turbulent. She was easily agitated, confused, startled and prone to unsettling flashbacks of the courts when she walked the tall corridors or crossed the polished floor of the throne room.

She looked around, feeling safe in the silence of Cantis and annoyed by it. Part of her hoped that if she sat out in the open long enough, Venarius would find her and she could face him. She imagined getting to confront him without putting the people she loved in harm's way. They would be safe no matter the outcome.

Something nudged her back and she jumped, lurching forward and slipping down the slope of the roof at her feet. She slowed to a stop, her feet dislodging old brittle shingles along the way before they caught the gutter. An animal cry from above her turned her panic to confusion though her heart was still reeling. She looked up to see a ruffle of feathers and wide blinking eyes peering back at her.

"You!" she said, her surprise erupting into dumbfounded laughter as she scrambled back up the slant of the roof. The young griffin, its fluff had given way to an awkward long-limbed adolescence in the weeks since they first met.

When she reached the top of the slope and straightened up on the flat rooftop, she was shocked to see he had grown to nearly twice his previous size. Before the griffin had been the size of Bandit. She had scooped it up so easily into her arms, all feathers and fur. Now it practically matched *her* in size.

It lunged at her, letting out little shrieks. She knew she couldn't be mistaken, it remembered her. It occurred to her that it might be unwise to pat and ruffle a creature with a set of massive talons scraping against the roof in its excitement, but she fell into the habit of greeting a dog.

"Have you been living here?" She wondered, glad to know there was some life around after all and that whatever curse seemed to claim this island was not unbreakable. The sun fell slowly toward the sea, toward the wastelands in the west, reminding her with a blinding stare how long she had been gone—too long, a couple hours with her dad and Bandit, then a little too much time lost in thought while she stalled here. She had to get back.

"I'm so sorry, buddy, but I've got to go. I'll be back," she promised. The griffin just blinked at her, oblivious, then burst into motion, bounding around the roof once more. She took advantage of its distracted excitement and slipped through the space between the rooftop and Raiden's room of books, feeling like a cruel kid pretending to throw a ball for a dog.

Trudging into the hallway, she sighed. Across from her stood the door to Raiden's childhood bedroom, shut and silent, but now that doorway led back home to Yuma, opening to the hallway outside *her* childhood bedroom. It had been a complicated code to crack even with the spell Raiden had used right there in the book for her. The feat required an opening in the barrier, which she could do, but her link home was nebulous, depending on where home in the old world was relative to Cantis. She solved the problem with shift-token magic, first opening a portal where she could, switching the door knob from Raiden's door with the door knob from her door, then closing that portal and returning to Raiden's house where she was sure her stupid idea would fail. But she used the portal spell from the book while turning the knob and activating the shift token. She was so shocked when it worked that even through the portal her scream of triumph had startled her father as he stood in the kitchen with his coffee.

Naturally, the doorway between the palace and Raiden's house had been no trouble at all, requiring only a new door conjured at the end of the hall that led to nowhere, a door in her chamber, and the same spell that Raiden had used in his house, turning an unassuming closet door into the passage to his room upstairs. She marched down the hall to the new door, wrenched it open in annoyance and stepped back into her chamber in the palace.

❧

Gordan knew the moment Nicole returned. Following the unique frequency of her psyche through the palace, Gordan passed a female staff member in the hall. The woman glanced up in passing, timid but at least she wasn't horrified by him. To Tovar's credit, he had managed to find people who were generally tolerant of the idea that there was a dragon living in the palace. Most of them didn't lay eyes on Gordan for several days, and when they finally did, he was most often in Nicole's company or Mitchell's or Raiden's. Some of the staff members were reluctant at first, keeping their wary eyes on him longer than normal, veering slightly farther away from him in passing. But most of them exuded a little apprehension and curiosity, which was far better than the disgust and suspicion he expected. He still avoided almost everyone in the palace, but he could walk the palace corridors almost comfortably.

His senses led him to the royal chambers where he found Nicole stepping into the hall and closing her door—she kept it closed these days.

"Where are you going?" he demanded.

"Down to the kitchen for some food?"

"I mean when you leave the palace," he said.

She shushed him, looking down the hall both ways, for Raiden no doubt.

"Well?"

Nicole opened the door to her rooms and pulled him inside. In the last four days she had nearly filled the room with hanging fabric, great swaths draping from ceiling to wall, hanging straight down like pillars and turning the space into a forest of colored cloth— gifts from subjects *for fine gowns*, but Nicole put it to a far more practical use. "It was too empty in here," she said flippantly as they walked through the fabric.

She led him weaving through the room, brushing aside curtains of silk and brocade as she went until they reached the wall, and she pulled aside yet another sheet of cloth, vivid red and turquoise. There was a plain arched door, rather ordinary, drab wood, not the kind of door found anywhere in this extravagant place.

"This one is to Keren's cottage." She let the curtain fall and turned to make her way a few paces through the tangle of textiles and pulled aside another to expose a different door. "This one goes to Raiden's house in Cantis—I got the idea from him actually. I found the spell he used in one of the books and figured why not? No one can get in here but me, and I left a seal on the house in Cantis."

Gordan listened, undeniably impressed but far more concerned about her leaving the safety of the palace so much. She was concealing her wounds and troubles with a swell of pride for her hidden doors and some fresh delight that she was keeping in the front of her mind, draped over her heart like the pretty fabrics hanging in the room around them, hiding what Nicole didn't want others to see.

"It's not as though I'm out there looking for Venarius on my own," she muttered as he scrutinized her. "I just go there to be alone. I run, I read Raiden's books about magic theory—maybe I'll find the answer to beating Venarius—and I now I can go home to visit dad. No one even knows I'm leaving the palace."

"Except me," he reminded her.

"You know it would only worry Raiden—I just need to get away from this place to keep my sanity," she said, a tremble in her voice.

There it was—the facade fell away—her wounds were as raw as ever. *She's never going to heal in this place,* he understood that. He could feel all the cracks in her heart and he wanted to hug her, to hold her together.

"It worries *me* knowing you're out there alone, and I don't like letting Raiden believe you're safe in the palace when I know you aren't…but I care about your sanity too." He sighed.

"You're not going to scold me for keeping secrets?"

"You scold yourself enough, don't you think?"

Her face pinched with uncertainty and a draft of guilt stirred the atmosphere in the room.

"I just want you to spend less time alone," he confessed. "And if you would permit me to be a little selfish, I miss you. If you must leave the safety of the palace, would you bring me with you?"

She smiled at him, but her face was still scrunched with sadness.

Gordan enjoyed their time in Cantis, as much as he could enjoy watching his friend busy herself to ignore what was eating at her—exerting herself to the point of exhaustion, whether physically or magically. He did enjoy being away from the palace as much as she did, away from the haze of so many psyches living together. At least he could keep an eye on her, but he was lying whenever he agreed with how much she didn't want to go back. As good as trips home with Mitchell and time in Cantis mending its destruction was for her, Gordan was always relieved when they walked back through the door and returned to the security of the palace.

In the ten days since Gordan insisted Nicole stop sneaking away alone, he had expected Raiden to notice their absence and investigate without Gordan having to give away Nicole's secret himself— but Raiden was just as willfully distracted as Nicole.

A knock at the door seized their attention only moments after they walked back into her chamber. Nicole took a deep breath and marched toward the door, swatting aside fabric as she went. Gordan trailed behind, wondering if maybe Raiden had finally come looking for them. She let that breath out slowly before she opened the door to a young woman who couldn't be much older than

Nicole.

"Your Highness, the king asked me to let you know that the Tempest has returned," the woman said with a serious nod.

"Could you call me anything but 'Your Highness'?" Nicole asked and Gordan could feel her straining for politeness.

The woman looked startled and then flattered. "Of course, er, my lady," she stammered.

"Thank you."

The woman blinked patiently at Nicole.

"Um...Gordan and I will be down shortly," Nicole said.

She smiled and dipped in brief curtsey before whirling around and bustling away.

Nicole sagged and dropped her head back with a sigh. "All right, let's go."

"Must I?" He teased, dreading that world as much as she did.

But Nicole turned to him with sincerity in her eyes. "Please."

"I was only joking."

Her attempt at a smile was heartbreaking. Gordan took her hand and felt her dismay ebb a little. He knew what was so disconcerting to her. The return of Caeruleus and Andrus from their tour as emissaries meant that the bait had been cast; it marked the start of their hunt for the man stalking her. Next, they would venture out of the safety this palace provided, like wandering blind into the dark to find a monster before it could find her—and no doubt the monster could see in the dark.

They closed the door to Nicole's chamber behind them and made their way downstairs, a journey that felt endless in the long tall hallways. Nicole held Gordan's hand and walked so close that she was pressed against his arm at first. But as they neared the first floor, she bolstered herself and released his hand. Her heart let out a spasm of anxiety like someone flinging away her lifeline. She didn't want everyone to see the fear he had felt in the hard, clammy grip of her hand. She straightened herself up as much as she could when she marched into the throne room where everyone was gathered.

"There you are," Mitchell said, jumping between them to clap

Nicole on the back and hook an arm around Gordan.

"Here I am," she said with lackluster enthusiasm.

"Come on, it sounds like we're invited to a lot of parties," he added, steering Nicole and Gordan into the group with an arm around each of them.

Gordan had to crane his neck forward to see around Mitchell and catch Nicole's cringe. When forced into groups he relied far more on her expressions to read her as he was still overwhelmed by multiple clashing auras.

Nicole was a little relieved to be caught in her brother's arm as they crossed the absurd expanse of the throne room to where everyone was gathered. Captain Rhee and Pep looked only mildly interested and she supposed they already knew all the news Caeruleus and Andrus had to deliver. Loak and Leone both stood with crossed arms like stern parents waiting for unfortunate news. Raiden was sitting on the step below the thrones, elbows on his knees and his chin resting on his hands, wearing the subtle frown he always seemed to sport lately, but when he saw her, he perked up, sending her a small smile. He only ever wore his borrowed old-world clothes these days and so looked as out of place as she, Mitchell and Gordan always did—tourists in another realm.

She thought she was the last one there, but noticed Tovar was missing and then heard the sound of footsteps hurrying behind them.

"Goodness," Tovar said on a heavy breath. "My apologies, lost in the workroom as usual."

"You're right on time, Tovar," Raiden assured him.

"What's the word?" Loak asked.

"Well, you have a lot of invitations," Caeruleus said.

"And one interesting request," Andrus added.

"Request?" Nicole couldn't fathom the notion.

"The king of Orodon has a bit of a problem that's keeping his people from the mines. Orodon's livelihood relies on the ore and minerals they mine. Unfortunately, they haven't been able to go into their mines since just before winter set in."

"What's keeping them from the mines?" Raiden asked.

"A manticore moved in," Andrus said. "Caused a lot of trouble before the winter. The problem is their mines are almost all connected, and the thing uses them like a cozy little sanctuary."

"The king was particularly interested in Nicole's assistance," Caeruleus added.

Nicole could almost laugh. Spreading the word about her being the fera worked a little too well. *Send a monster in to fight a monster, that's what they're thinking.*

"I'm sorry," Mitchell said, raising a hand like a student. "I feel like I should know what a manticore is."

"It's a flying nightmare," Andrus said. "Lion's body, man's face, lots of teeth, and a stinging tail. Deadly from all sides, and if that wasn't enough, the sound of its roar temporarily paralyzes you."

With a sarcastic retort, Mitchell asked "And we should get involved because?"

"They would make a great ally," Leone insisted. "They were one of the last holdouts in the Dragon Wars. Their king died fighting alongside his people."

"That's right," Loak agreed. "His daughter took up her father's mantel after the wars ended and was supportive of the Council uniting the realm. Her grandson is king now."

"I'll agree to all the trustworthy allies we can get," Raiden said. He looked to Nicole. As did everyone else, and she realized they were waiting for her agreement.

"They need help," she said. "That seems like reason enough."

"Wherever we go, we must keep in mind the potential for encountering Venarius," Tovar said.

"Dawn has never had a strong presence in Orodon," Loak said, sounding a little defensive.

"I dare say it's the least likely place we'd find him," Leone agreed.

"But what about the rest of the invitations? Are we ready to venture forth where the risk is higher?" Tovar asked.

"I would say our royal guard is as prepared as they can be," Loak answered. "But honestly, I think we all know that with Venarius it will come down to those of us closest to Nicole."

"I meant are we mentally prepared to set out on this mission, to lure out and apprehend the leader of Dawn," Tovar said.

Nicole studied the faces around her, the silence that followed clearly weighed heavily on Mitchell and Raiden and, she noted with some surprise, Leone.

"I'm ready," she said, smothering her anxiety in defiance.

Raiden looked at her, his eyes unreadable turquoise stones.

"Well then," Tovar said. "Perhaps we should set out on a tour of the realm."

"The Prince of Nol *insisted* you come to his birthday celebration. And the Queen of Eanna has said you are welcome any time, but hopes you can visit Eanna during their vernal festival," Caeruleus said.

"When is the Prince's birthday?" Tovar asked.

"The fourteenth of Martius," Caeruleus said.

"And the vernal festival is the first ten days of Aprilis," Tovar said, his brow furrowed in thought.

Nicole raised a finger, *Maritus and Aprilis?* "You use the Julian Calendar?"

"More or less," Tovar said. "The separation from the old world had a peculiar effect on time for us here. Our days are longer as you know, twenty-six hours. But a year in Veil is still the same length as a year in the old world, from solstice to solstice. We had to adapt the calendar a little. Our year begins on the winter solstice, there are twenty-eight days in every month except for a twenty-ninth day in December. The Romans' calendar was the most well-known and it was easiest to keep with a few adjustments."

"Uh," Nicole's head was spinning a little trying to keep up with Tovar's flash lesson on calendars. "So what day is today then?"

"The twenty-fifth of Februarius if I'm not mistaken," Tovar replied.

February twenty-fifth, she thought, *and back home it's the fifteenth.*

"That gives us less than a month to deal with the manticore in Orodon," Leone said.

"We can get you there quickly," Rhee offered. "But we can only take so many on the Tempest—certainly not a whole royal entourage."

"A small party then," Tovar said.

"Where Nicole goes, I go," Raiden said.

"Ditto," Mitchell said.

"I'll go," Caeruleus said.

"You'll want Loak there with you," Leone said. "Nothing like a couple locals on your side to make a good impression with the king."

Loak chuckled. "It would be nice to be home."

Nicole turned to Gordan who gave her a sad frown. "I don't think it would be a good idea," he said.

"He's right. That's an issue that requires more time and delicacy than we can afford right now. If we're going to handle a manticore, best to do it without that particular tension in the air between you and the king of Orodon," Leone said.

Gordan nodded in agreement. Her heart sank further.

"All right, so that's five of you," Rhee confirmed.

"How many of the guard can we bring?" Leone asked.

Rhee hummed skeptically. "Ten, maybe fifteen if everyone gets cozy in the sleeping quarters. It's an overnight flight, and I can't have anyone sleeping in the cargo hold."

"That will work." Leone nodded.

"Leone and I can see to the preparations for the tour to Nol and Eanna. We can pass through Meridian on our way to Nol if they will allow us."

"We didn't stop in Meridian, that's a tricky one," Caeruleus admitted. "They aren't exactly welcoming. Not even the Council ever had influence there. They've been independent since the beginning."

"Can't land anywhere in that forest anyway," Rhee added.

"I guess we'll see how welcoming they are to travelers with the keys to the realm," Loak said.

"If they aren't too keen about us passing through to Nol we can always go around. It would only add a few days to the journey," Tovar said. "And we can get to Eanna by boat instead. It's a short trip across the Avalon Sea."

"How were things in the open states, Caeruleus?" Loak asked with a stiffness that suggested he was anticipating the worst.

"They're trying to go about their business like the Council isn't gone, just to keep order, but there's no one above them to pass any bigger problems or to pay their salaries. With the fall of the courts in Atrium, the lesser courts in the states aren't getting paid. Some have left because of no income; some have stayed to keep the peace. It's shaky at best right now. It looks like the people amassing around the palace are mostly from Dusor to the north of us and a substantial number from Atrium. The city feels slightly unhinged, but it's not complete chaos by any means. A lot of the surviving rebels have stepped in to keep the peace without the Council and their agents. Most people just want to go about their lives."

"It could definitely be worse," Loak agreed.

"But it looks like Taroth has decided to lend its 'assistance' to the state of Navn in this time of disorder. The king sent several advisors to Navn's lesser court and even graciously provided some of his own royal guard to help keep the peace," Caeruleus said, his tone steeped in sarcasm.

"Of course, he did," Leone said with a scoff.

"Besina seems to be doing fine, of course they've always managed well enough without much involvement from the Council anyway."

"Sounds like you might want to take up the king of Taroth's invitation to visit," Tovar said.

Nicole wanted to bow out, *not my job, not my problem*. What did it matter if some pompous king occupied the open state next door? But then she reminded herself this was just a part of the game, play the role to lure Venarius out into the open. When she glanced at Raiden, she noticed the crease of concern on his brow, but was he worried about Manticores, matters of the states, or Venarius?

"We just might," Raiden said. "Honestly, if I had to pick a place for Venarius to be hiding, it would be Taroth."

"The Council suspected the root of Dawn to be buried in Taroth as well," Loak added. "They were never able to weed it out though, not without breaking their illusion of unity."

"Well the illusion of unity isn't a problem anymore, is it?" Andrus chuckled.

Nicole lost focus, her mind slipping into the mottled echoes of everyone's words around the gaping throne room until talk of Taroth and its subtle conquest tactics melted into a distant dream-like muffle of voices. *Just have to play along until we get him*, she thought. *Just have to deal with a manticore, that's got to be far easier than the Council, certainly less horrible than a royal birthday party.* She cringed, sensing formal gowns in her future. She shuddered.

"Hey, you hungry?" Mitchell said in her ear.

"Yeah," she said.

He nodded and jumped into the conversation. "So, when do we leave for the manticore hunt?"

She cringed at the word *hunt*.

"Pep and I need to do some maintenance on the Tempest, and she needs a rest to replenish her central power," Rhee said. "We should only need a day."

"That's settled then," Raiden said, standing up with an air of finality. "One venture at a time. Taroth and Navn will have to wait."

"Of course, of course," Tovar agreed. "We'll concern ourselves with the journey to Nol and Eanna, and be ready to depart when you return."

"Thank you, Tovar."

Nicole was relieved to see Raiden looked as tired of this conversation as she was. Loak Caeruleus and Leone hardly seemed to notice Raiden drift away from them as they discussed the Council's previous dealing with Taroth.

"Captain Rhee," Tovar inquired, "might I ask you about the rest of the Council's alatus fleet?"

"Sure," Rhee answered.

Mitchell seized the opportunity and broke away from the cluster as Raiden reached Nicole's side. With Raiden and Gordan flanking her, the three of them followed Mitchell who set a course for the kitchens.

The warm glowing kitchens was the only good place inside the palace. Even with the growing number of staff, she liked being in the kitchens. She and Raiden had taken up the role of cooks after the left-overs from their royal welcome celebration disappeared, and that had happened more quickly than they expected with a growing guard and incoming staff to feed. They had kitchen duty to themselves for a couple days before Tovar found a few cooks to join them.

The kitchen remained the place where they were treated like anyone else, possibly because the cooks had no idea who they were for several days since they both rarely wore their keys in plain sight. Raiden wore his clothes from the old world, jeans and sweaters, just like Nicole—they didn't look like kings in the least. The cooks were mostly lost in their work, too busy to spare much attention to the people who whisked food away to the mess hall. Nicole and Raiden were just two more faces from the palace who showed up to help. When the cooks finally realized they were the kings none of them let on. They continued greeting Nicole and Raiden with informal nods and calling them simply by name, no *highness* or *majesty*.

Nicole was always glad to be in the kitchen; it was the only place she and Raiden were ever together just as themselves anymore without their roles as rulers or preparations for enemies hanging around them like vultures. She preferred the warm crackling music of the kitchens, ovens roaring softly, pots clanging occasionally, and the quiet presence of the other cooks—her safety net for being with him. If they were completely alone together, she couldn't avoid the sickening anxiety she had about touching him. But in the quiet company of the oven fires and other cooks, she could relax, enjoy an hour or two near him, sharing the silent communication of glances and little smiles while they willfully ignored the world outside the kitchens.

Neither one of them wanted to poison the comfortable air.

Raiden knew talk of his time preparing for Venarius with Tovar and Loak's growing ranks would bury Nicole's smile in a tomb of dark rumination. Nicole couldn't tell him that she spent her time out in the unprotected silence of Cantis to get away, or that she still went to sleep and woke up with wounds—what could he do about that anyway, besides worry. *I'll figure out how to make it stop,* she told herself every morning. She just needed to get past it—fix the broken record of her mind, skipping on a loop of that night in the courts—accept that she couldn't change what happened. *I beat them. They got what they deserved. The memories will fade,* she insisted to herself. She just needed to wait it out. She avoided her unhelpful memories to prepare for the next fight. She trained her body at home in Yuma when she took Mitchell home to visit their dad. She trained her magic in Cantis under the watchful eye of Gordan. But she couldn't tell Raiden she was leaving the palace while he grew more and more anxious about the very thought every day. So, their unspoken agreement not to mention Venarius or their efforts to prepare for him remained unbroken, at least in the kitchens.

Stepping into the kitchens lifted the weight a little, and she inhaled gratefully as they arrived.

"Hey Amin," Mitchell acknowledged as he strode into the kitchen first.

Amin glanced up from kneading, powdery smears of flour on his dark face. He smiled—that was his only greeting—he never said a word to Nicole or anyone since she'd met him.

"Welcome back," said Tierney, the freckled woman with kind brown eyes and hair contained in a green cotton cap.

"Wait a minute," Mitchell said. "There are four of you now."

"Impressive," muttered Arin as she heaved a tray of baked bread from the red mouth of the oven and nudging the door shut as she turned. The woman looked so much like her brother Amin with their identical caps hiding their hair that Nicole would have mixed the two of them up often if not for Arin's septum ring, her fierce bright black eyes, and her quick tongue.

The new cook was another woman, wearing a green cotton cap

like the other three cooks. She was busy chopping vegetables so deftly that her knife made an impressive rhythm against the cutting board.

"Gwyn joined us yesterday," Tierney said.

The fourth cook looked up and smiled. "Hello," she said, blinking back moisture in her pale blue eyes after turning an onion into a mound of tiny pieces. Then her face turned to slack surprise. "Raiden?"

Nicole turned a curious look to him only to see dismay on his face. He shook it off quickly. They knew each other, Nicole could see that much, but why the passing dread in his eyes? She couldn't help but feel like the spell of the kitchen had been broken, there was tension in his posture.

"What brings you here?" Raiden asked.

"When we heard about the keys and the budding city by the palace, I thought it sounded like a great new start. My brother disagreed. So, he stayed in Atrium, and here I am," she explained.

"You came all this way to be a cook in the palace?" Mitchell wondered.

"Well, no. I came hoping to apprentice with a wand maker. No surprise, none would have me," she chuckled. "Since I couldn't find an apprenticeship, I had to find work and lodgings *somewhere*. Someone mentioned to me that the palace was still taking on staff, so here I am. Why are *you* here?"

"We, uh, happen to be stuck with the keys," Raiden answered.

"The keys?" She looked between Nicole and Raiden. "Then— that means *you're* the fera?"

Nicole was startled by Gwyn's fervent attention.

"That's what everyone is saying," Gwyn added, cringing at her own outburst.

"They're not wrong," Nicole said, her body as tense as Raiden's. "But I generally go by Nicole, not 'the fera.'"

"Oh stars, of course, I'm sorry," Gwyn stammered, her pale complexion going pink.

"Here to make some dinner, Love?" Tierney asked, rescuing

Gwyn.

"And to escape the 'your majesties' of course," Nicole added with a chuckle—it was a sad sound. "Any dough for me?"

"None that's ready," Arin answered. "It's all baked. But lucky for you, we already made it your way."

"'Your way'?" Mitchell asked.

"I taught them how to make Dad's Stromboli," she said, smiling. "Can you all take a break for dinner?"

"Gladly," Arin said. Amin nodded in agreement, gathering up the supple dough into a smooth ball and placing it into a bowl. He tossed a towel over the bowl and left it to rise.

"We've just put the other loaves and the pies in, plenty of time for a break," Tierney agreed. "The soup can wait, Gwyn, have something to eat."

Gwyn put her knife back down shyly, chagrin still clinging to her face. The lot of them gathered around one of the empty tables where Arin sliced a couple loaves that disappeared into everyone's hands in a matter of minutes.

Compelled to soothe Gwyn's embarrassment, Nicole sat next to her.

"So, I'm curious about wand making," she said and Gwyn looked up, her eyes brightened. "Why wands?"

"It's a fascinating art," Gwyn said. "I never really had much interest in the family business—making pies—but I couldn't find a wand maker apprenticeship in Atrium and, well, it's always the same story. There aren't many wand makers, and they stick with their tired old traditions—no women. I actually taught myself how to make them, but no one would buy what I made, and I had to settle for working at the pie shop."

"I'm not from Veil, so don't know much about wands," Nicole confessed. "Just that they help you focus your magic I guess?"

"Yes," Gwyn said, excitement building in her voice. "Wands are an incredible tool, although they have been regarded more as a fashion of late, and I believe that they can be improved... unfortunately, I don't have anyone to work with for feedback on what I've made."

"You mean you need people to test them out?" Mitchell leaned into their conversation eagerly from across the table.

"Well, yes, tradition has always been to make wands and find the right fit for customers, see what wand best compliments their unique strengths. That's one reason why it's such a difficult business to start. To have a wide variety of wands for customers you need a lot of materials, and that takes a lot of money. I've made maybe ten wands in the last two years with what I have been able to afford. But I believe wands could be custom made specifically for an intended user. I've done some research into it, trying to understand what makes materials right for different people, but I've only collected information on around thirty people and their wands. There so much more research to do."

"I'll volunteer for research," Mitchell said. "Fen is teaching me about potions, and Nicole has tried to teach me some little spells, maybe a wand will help me out."

"Every person I can match with a wand helps, assuming one of my wands is a fit for you of course, but I need a larger pool of study, more people and the wands that they matched with. Some people bond with crystal wands over wands of wood for instance. See, what I theorize is that wands help people balance themselves and their power which allows them to achieve greater feats and more focused performance. Some bond with very neutral wands, and I suspect it is because they are inherently steady and neutral themselves, but others are…I guess you could stay charged with different influences in their substance, both physical and spiritual, which bond with wands that have a complementary energy, the sort of opposite to balance them. Understanding the bond between user and wand would allow for crafting wands perfectly tuned for an individual, but the masters laugh at the idea. It's not how they do things, too much trouble. They slap together countless combinations and sift through them to find one that works for each customer. It's true that it's more time efficient in the long run, but I want to *understand* the link between a person and a wand."

"Wow," Nicole said, nodding. "I can only imagine how frustrating that has been, carrying around a passion like that and having your way blocked by men who just don't like change. I see why you wanted an apprenticeship, but screw the *masters*. Sounds to me like you could change the world of wand-making."

"Thank you," Gwyn said.

"Make her the official royal wand maker and people will be lining up for her work," Mitchell mumbled through his food.

Gwyn's eyes went wide.

Nicole looked to Mitchell, "That's actually a great idea."

He scoffed. "Obviously."

Nicole laughed. "What do you think?" she asked Gwyn.

"I—I would be beyond grateful," Gwyn said.

Nicole glanced up at Gordan, watching her with a quiet smile, and then noticed Raiden, looking troubled again.

"Well, look at you, not two whole days in the kitchen and you've been promoted," Tierney chuckled.

Gwyn blushed again and dropped her head to bite into her food.

Nicole did the same, tearing into the large heel of the loaf in her hand, pleasantly surprised by the punch of aromatic spices, cardamom, ginger, cumin and coriander, cloves and cinnamon, a marriage of flavors she knew from Indian curries. Inside the bread there were thick chunks of chicken.

"Do you like it?" Arin asked.

Nicole, caught with her mouth full, could only answer with a hearty nod. "I like it even better than how I make it," she confessed once she forced back her mouthful.

Arin straightened up with a tiny satisfied smirk on her mouth and elbowed Amin. "Thank you," she said.

"So, any developments?" Tierney wondered with a sheepish expression.

"You won't have as many to cook for very soon," Nicole said with a shrug.

"How's that?"

"Nicole, Raiden and I are going on a trip to Orodon," Mitchell said. "Loak and Caeruleus and some guards too. When we get back, we're all going on a royal tour of Veil."

Nicole glanced again at Gordan, observing in silence, always doing his best to disappear when he was caught among a group of people. His eyes darted away from the gazes of others, except hers. He looked her in the eye. There was a question on his face and she understood that '*what's going on*' look.

Her eyes darted to Raiden once more, suspicious that his sudden consternation was perplexing Gordan, and perhaps her own confusion over the matter wasn't helping. The three of them were a terrible knot of crossed psyches in the silence—Nicole suddenly realized everyone had gone quiet, preoccupied by their food.

Then Raiden inhaled sharply, standing up. "Excuse me," he said. His words came out in a rush as he left.

As Raiden disappeared from the kitchen Nicole pulled her concerned eyes from his back and looked to Gordan. He raised his eyebrows, looking away and dipping his head down as though he did not see her gaze, but he touched his finger to the middle of his forehead—no one else seemed to notice, but she knew he meant it was the Sight. Gordan could pick up on Raiden's visions, then.

"I've been trying to learn a few things from Tovar, but its harder than it seems," Mitchell said, still locked in conversation with Gwyn.

"I'd like to help if I could," she said.

"Think one of your wands might be a good fit?" Mitchell suggested.

"That's a start. If you match with any of mine, at least you could improve your spell work," she said to him.

Nicole listened halfheartedly, her mind trailing after Raiden, the urge to follow him smothering her appetite.

"What about Nicole, if a wand would help me, it would help her too, right? She's almost as new to this as I am," he laughed.

"I doubt any of my wands would hold up for a fera. We could try though," Gwyn offered with a nervous edge to her voice. Nicole remembered the sad make-shift wand—a mere stick—bursting into sparks and splinters what felt like ages ago. Gwyn was probably imagining a similar fate befalling her creations.

Nicole set her food down, ready to follow Raiden.

"We can dig out my wands later," Gwyn said to Mitchell, "after I—"

"Nonsense," Tierney said. "That soup isn't important. Go on, you're the royal wand maker now, aren't you?" Tierney chortled and took a bite of her food.

Gwyn jumped up, swiping the cloth cap off her head, eager to be freed from the kitchen. Nicole froze at the sight of Gwyn's hair as the long silver ponytail unfurled and swung behind her neck. That silver hair made her heart sink in an instant of understanding and, naturally, Gordan's gaze found hers. The only answer she could give him was an uncertain frown as she got up and hurried after Raiden.

He wasn't far ahead. She could hear his footsteps echoing in the hallway as she ran up the stairs. At the top she saw him halfway down the corridor. She ran at an easy lope and caught him by the hand, her heart clenching a little.

"Hey," she said breathily, she knew he wasn't okay so she wouldn't ask. "What did you see?"

He sighed. "It was too chaotic to decipher," he admitted, turning to her. "It wasn't anything good though, noise and smoke." He closed his eyes and shook his head. "I deny the Sight and so I can't control it, but I can't keep it out entirely, and it drives me mad to get these fragments when the stakes are as high as they are. They could be some clue we need, and I can't help wanting to know." He took a deep breath. "But I can't have it both ways, I just..." His voice shook with frustration.

Her first instinct was to wrap her arms around his ribcage and rest her cheek against his chest. She didn't know any better way to remind him that what mattered was the here and now even though it scared her a little. Horrible memories tried to crowd into their embrace.

"It's one possibility you're seeing, that's all," she said into his shirt. "There are at least a hundred awful possibilities for us. Hell, my mind seems to do nothing but craft new ones every night. Who cares which *one* the Sight brings you on any given day?"

His arms closed around her and his chest heaved with a chuckle. "Are you trying to cheer me up with even more doom?"

"If it works," she said. "I like to think there are just as many possibilities that turn out all right. The ones we're afraid of are just easier to see. Maybe that's why the Sight seems to bring you the bad ones."

"The possibilities the Sight brings are so tangible that they feel like they have more weight than other possibilities," he said.

"Like having Gwyn around feels like she's more likely to be in your future now?" she supposed.

She listened to a sigh deflate his lungs.

"Hey. Remember that last terrible vision that kept bothering you?"

"I wish I could forget."

"What happened in that vision again?" she asked, feigning ignorance.

He huffed. "You were executed," he said uncomfortably.

"And did that happen?"

"No."

"Exactly," she said.

Raiden was silent. His arms tightened around her for a moment then he leaned back, lifting her chin with his curled finger and placing a kiss on her lips. Her heart raced, reminding herself that she was just as guilty of forgetting about what she had here and now. Being here with Raiden now was her sweet tiny victory over the Council's plans for her and that terrible vision. The soft warm contact of his lips against hers was broken as she was yanked from Raiden's arms and into a vision.

The Sight seized Raiden with a vengeance, wrenching him away from that gentle moment into another place, somewhere far from the palace, but not far from Nicole. He knew this place. He could not mistake it especially as it crumbled around them. They were in the Council's great hall again, Nicole at the center of that deep green marble floor as it fractured and split apart, but this was the *past.* An all too familiar wave of crackling heat pulsed through the crumbling chamber, crashing through him. The rumble of the shaking stones, the deafening crack of marble breaking, and Nicole's chilling scream filled his ears. The vividness of visions was nothing new to him, but he was unnerved by the completeness of this memory—then he was seized again by the invisible hand of the Sight, pulled deeper, into another vision that was strangely similar to the first.

Salty air flooded his nose. Before him was someone else, a woman, her tanned face lined with years of sorrow and twisted into a curious expression, something like bittersweet relief as the walls of the modest shack buckled around her and the ground split under her feet. Water rushed in, churned around his ankles; he looked up, realizing that they were surrounded by the sea.

Then the vision stopped and his mind slammed back into his body, back into the present, where Nicole had pulled away from him, blinking with wide stunned eyes. Her breaths were shallow and quick, then she took one deep breath. He understood her expression. She hadn't expected to ever live that moment in the courts again, feel the pain of it. He remembered the first time she accidently shared one of his visions, experienced her own execution, and the look on her face had crushed him.

"I—" he searched for words, his breaths quick and halting. "I don't know what that was." The first vision had definitely been a memory, but the second…

"I think it was the past," she said, barely more than a whisper. "My past."

"But the elderly woman—" he shook his head, confused. Then he recalled the sea surging in around them.

"No, that was me—or, it was the fera before me," she said, her voice bemused but certain.

"Then that was the Candhrid peninsula sinking," he said, understanding the waves rushing in on them.

"Have you ever seen the past like that before?" Nicole wondered.

"No," he said.

They stood there in silence, still wrapping their minds around what they'd just Seen and gradually the shock of it subsided. The uncanny realness of the visions faded with each passing second—the smell of the ocean cleared from his nose, and Nicole rubbed her arms, chasing away the phantom fire of her magic still lingering in her skin—until they were memories again.

"That was so weird," she muttered. "Seeing your dad there."

"What?"

"Your dad was there with me—I mean with the fera before me."

He realized he must have been seeing the second vision through the eyes of someone who had been there—his father. He shook his head. He needed to know why the past was reaching out to them. How much more did they not know?

"Come on." Raiden took Nicole by the hand and led her at an anxious pace down the corridor.

The rhythm of their footsteps was urgent and as they passed two members of staff who hastily curtsied. Raiden noticed them cast anxious looks at each other, but he said nothing. Nicole said nothing. He could walk no faster without breaking into a run, and Nicole shifted into a jog every few strides to keep up.

He marched right back to the throne room where his father, Loak and Caeruleus were still huddled together, keeping their voices low enough not to echo.

"I need to talk to you," Raiden said when he was only halfway across the room, his voice filling the space.

The three of them turned.

"Who?" Loak asked.

"My father," he said, finally reaching them. "Were you there when the fera sank the Candhrid peninsula?"

Surprise contorted all three of their faces.

"How could you possibly know that?" Caeruleus wondered.

"I—yes, I was," Leone answered. "I was sent after her."

"We both were," Loak corrected him. "And your father was arrested for treason a few years later in part because of that mission," Loak said, folding his arms.

"I was arrested for more than that," Leone muttered.

"Because you failed to bring her in?" Raiden pressed.

Loak spit out a laugh.

"Because I opened the portal for her," his father said.

Nicole's grip synched tighter around his hand.

"You should have told me what you were doing," Loak muttered.

"That's the only reason you weren't arrested too."

Raiden stood there, sinking into this knowledge, clutching Nicole's hand. His father had to have known the risk, he knew he would get caught yet he helped the fera escape anyway. He put that stranger before himself and his wife. Raiden considered the alternate path and a sense of vertigo crept in as he imagined a world where the fera had gone to the courts never to come out, never to be born again in the old world as a girl named Nicole—in that world his father would have never been arrested, he would have come home to his wife and son.

"Raiden?" Nicole's voice was quiet. He squeezed her hand.

He could see it all, both the clear unchangeable paths of the past, and the ones that could have been taken—the individual threads that made an intricate illusion of fate, that what lay ahead was as immutable as what was behind them. Suddenly it all seemed to unravel, there was no fate, only choices and possibilities as Nicole said, and he had been the one tying himself up in the threads he feared the most. Today was crafted by innumerable threads, the choices made not only by Nicole and him, but also his father, Caeruleus, Venarius, the Council, Moira, and countless others. No one could craft their fate alone, a single thread in an immense design, but the more people they had on their side, the more power they would have. The more people Venarius controlled and called his allies, the more power he had to create the future he wanted.

This was the game then—whoever pulled the most threads, would have the most influence on the outcome.

"Son?"

Hearing that from his father jarred Raiden from his thoughts and, surprisingly, steadied him a little.

"Sorry," Raiden said. "I'm trying to take it all in."

"How did you find out?" his father wondered.

Raiden looked to Nicole and she cringed a little. "A vision," he said.

"Of the *past*?"

"It was a shared vision," he explained. "I think it must have something to do with our minds being in the past when the Sight crept in. First we Saw what happened in the courts and then—" he looked to Nicole.

"Then back to almost the same event, the destruction, only I was the fera before me, and I saw you there," Nicole explained, looking at his father.

Leone frowned, lost in thought or memories for a moment. "I suppose I hadn't stopped to think you and I had met before," Leone said with a soft laugh.

"I should thank you, for her and for me," Nicole said, the slight tremble in her voice didn't convey the force of her gratitude and sympathy which Raiden could feel in the grip of her hand as she laced her fingers through his. He felt what she couldn't say—that she understood what had been sacrificed for her, that words weren't enough.

Raiden closed his eyes for just a moment. He and his father had had the same opportunity, the same choice to help an innocent stranger because it was right even if it cost them their freedom, their family and friends. When Raiden didn't remember Nicole, he chose Caeruleus even though he knew the fera didn't deserve any of it. His father had chosen to help the fera. In all the years Raiden thought he knew the kind of man his father had been and the choices he made, for all Raiden's efforts *not* to be like his father and thinking he would be a better man than him, it turned out Raiden was indeed nothing like him, but his father was the better man after all.

Perhaps that was how it ought to be. If this all came down to a choice between beating Venarius and what was right, then Raiden knew at least he could make that choice. He could do whatever it would take to keep Nicole safe, to keep all the people he loved safe. He refused to let her down again—to lose her or anyone else he loved. He would hand this realm to the Dragon King to end Venarius if he had to.

"We'll get him," his father said and Raiden opened his eyes. "We'll finish this."

"It's been a long time coming," Loak said.

"We do have a manticore to take care of first," Caeruleus reminded them. "One challenge at a time."

"We may not have the luxury of facing one problem at a time," Nicole said, and regretted it when all eyes fell on her, especially Caeruleus' stony blue stare.

"She's right," Loak said with a nod.

She never wanted to disappear more, drawing attention back to the fact that she was blood in the water drawing sharks, putting everyone in danger. Raiden brought her hand in his up to his heart, pulling her a little closer.

Nineteen

When Leone, Caeruleus, and Loak finally gave in to their hunger pangs and went in search of food, it was hours past sunset. Nicole hadn't found her appetite since leaving the kitchens, but knew she needed something and not eating was the first clue to everyone around her that something was off.

The kitchens were quiet, Tierney and the others had already cleaned up and gone to bed, but a couple loaves were left for them. Nicole dutifully took a piece of the loaf, as did Raiden, but he didn't sit down.

He nodded his head toward the door and she followed, glad to be alone with him instead of sitting there among Leone, Loak and Caeruleus, in particular, who only ever seemed to have disapproval in his eye if he even looked at her.

"Goodnight," he said to his father and the others.

They mumbled and nodded, raising their food in a farewell salute.

Nicole and Raiden ate their food in silence and were finished before they reached the second-floor corridor.

She brushed the remaining crumbs from her fingers and let them fall shamelessly to the floor. "I have no business being royalty,"

240

she said quietly and laughed bitterly—what choice did she have?

"I wish I knew how to get away from the keys when this is finished," Raiden said.

That was only a problem she'd have to deal with if she survived the confrontation with Venarius, but she knew better than to joke about that with him, regardless of how valid it was.

"Me too," she admitted. "I can't tell you how many times I've already tried to get rid of it but it always comes back."

They fell into silence again until the third-floor corridor. Still nagging at her was the guilt of learning that Raiden's father had ensured the freedom of the fera before her. She thought her legacy of causing pain couldn't get any worse, and now this. She couldn't quite swallow the fact that in some horrible tangled way, Raiden's family had been broken for her sake and his mother's life traded for a stranger's. No doubt he saw that connection as well, but did he see her differently now? *Is that all I really do in this world, destroy things?*

The doors to the Council's chambers flashed before her in the corridor. She closed her eyes, shaking them away. "What we saw in that vision," she said, trying keep herself in the palace beside Raiden.

"Hmm."

"I mean, what we know about your dad and—" her voice got caught in her throat, and she realized just how scared she was that he might forever see her as the reason his mother was gone. She wasn't ready for him to walk away from her, not when she hadn't figured out how to get close to him again, how to be okay in his arms, how to tell him she needed him to stay while she picked up her pieces.

Raiden stopped and his hand caught hers. She dared to open her eyes. The doors were gone. He turned her to face him as his blue-green eyes searched hers. His beautiful face went blurry. The hallways were lit and she couldn't hide.

"Hey," he said.

She dropped her gaze to the floor and he raised it back up, cradling her jaw in his hands.

"What is it?"

"If your dad hadn't helped the fera—"

"No," he said. "Don't go to that place. If my father hadn't done what he did, I don't know if my mother would still be here, maybe he wouldn't be here either, but I *know* you wouldn't be here..."

She nodded her head in his hands, but she couldn't help thinking she might prefer that. *I wouldn't be the fera. I wouldn't be a killer. I wouldn't be putting so many people I love at risk. I wouldn't feel so lost. I wouldn't be a goddamn queen.*

"With me," he added.

Her eyes burned and she closed them. *I wouldn't have him. I wouldn't have Gordan. Or Keren, Fen and Asi.* A laugh and a sob both escaped at once. She opened her eyes.

"Don't think for a second I'd ever wish my father had chosen differently, all right?"

Her face pinched with the urge to cry because for a moment she wished Leone *had* made the other choice. He sighed and lowered his forehead to hers. His fingers slipped down her arms to her hands and laced themselves in hers.

For that moment she felt a peace she hadn't felt in a long time until from the corner of her eye, she saw someone try to hurry past them. She lifted her head and saw the young man, a member of the staff, give an awkward bow as he went.

"Please excuse my intrusion, your majesties," he stammered and hurried off down the hall.

Nicole huffed, dropped her head back in exasperation.

Raiden smiled and pulled her onward. They made their way up to their rooms where her door opened and Fen and Asi emerged.

"Hi, Nicole. Hi, Raiden," Fen said.

"We were just—" Asi saw Nicole's eyes widen. "—looking for you."

"You found me," Nicole said.

Fen smiled. "Yes, uh..."

"But it can wait until tomorrow. I'm tired," Asi said, a little too triumphantly.

"Right. Me too," Fen agreed and they hurried down the hall.

"Goodnight," Nicole called.

"Goodnight," they sang back and disappeared down the stairs snickering.

Nicole took a deep breath. She avoided this, arriving at their rooms together. It hadn't been hard the last twelve days with Raiden so involved with training the guards or strategizing with Tovar after dinner, he would be so tired he'd fall asleep early, and she would disappear after dinner lurk around the castle until it was late so that she wouldn't have to make some excuse to be alone. She didn't want to let on that she didn't even sleep in her room most nights, where she'd slip into that dark place and wake up with bleeding cuts.

"Why do I miss you so much when we see each other every day?" Raiden asked.

"Because we spend most of our time together pretending to be people we aren't," she said, ashamed for avoiding him as much as she avoided the palace and her memories.

"Can we change that?" The crease in his brow over his pleading eyes crushed her heart.

She knew he could see her hesitation before her answer. "Of course we can. Uh, my room is a bit of a mess though."

He nodded and they wandered to the door down the hall, he opened it, and she realized she hadn't seen inside it since the first time. There was a grand wooden bed, so massive that it had to be twice as long and twice as wide as a king-sized bed, and several of the rugs that had been given to them as gifts were spread haphazardly around the floor, overlapping and adding warmth to the stone room.

"Nice digs," she said, skipping into a run and throwing herself onto the bed where she rolled into the center. "But is the bed big enough?"

Raiden stepped up onto the foot of the bed, walked across it and fell down beside her.

"This whole place is too big," he said, looking up at the ceiling. "Why does anyone need this much room?"

"It's probably a more appropriate size for Gordan," Nicole said.

"I don't think the staff could handle him roaming the corridors like that."

She laughed, imagining Gordan on a stroll through a palace in his massive winged form, the true dragon, tail swinging behind him. The staff would probably throw themselves against the walls of the corridors.

He sighed. "I missed that."

"What?"

"Your laugh," he said.

She turned her head toward him, and he turned his gaze to hers.

"Do you know what else I miss?"

"What?" She searched his eyes for the answer while her heart pounded with anticipation, afraid of visions.

The inches between them disappeared and he kissed her. It sent her heart reeling, but she fell into the moment, not the past, not some terrible future, just the sweet pleasant warmth of his lips pressed against hers and the conspicuous absence of the electricity which his kiss had once sparked in her.

His kiss lingered but he did not lean in any deeper. He inhaled as though he was breathing her in and then he pulled away. Relief rushed in with his departure, and she could feel her face buckling under sadness and confusion. She loved him, but she could not find the fire that used to seize her at his touch. If anything, she loved him more now than she did then, but her body didn't quite feel like hers anymore, and all she found in it now was reluctance and un-certainty.

"We'll figure this out," he said, and she supposed he had read something different on her face: worry maybe. He meant the man-ticore, navigating the royal affairs ahead of them and Venarius… but she was most troubled by herself because how could they possibly succeed in any of these things when she hadn't figured out how to fix herself yet?

She said nothing. She allowed him to gather her close to him and they stayed like that, listening to the sound of their breathing in the vast silence hanging over them. She waited, content in his quiet company, until at last Raiden fell asleep.

Nicole felt his embrace slacken and his breathing grow slower. Once she was satisfied his slumber was deep enough, she removed herself from his arms carefully and crept away from the silken bed. The great doors of their chambers could be opened by anyone from the inside. She let herself out of his room, but did not turn toward her bedroom. Instead she fell into the route she knew best through the passages of the palace.

It was a long silent walk broken up by the gradual climb to the highest room in the palace by way of five different stairways—not including the two staircases she had to take down to the fourth floor before making her way back up. He wouldn't be anywhere else— she was absolutely sure of few things these days, but where she could find Gordan was, without a doubt, one of those things.

When she pushed open the door and stood up into the room, he was sitting in the open window, one leg hanging out and swinging, while the little owl griffins came and went, one plunging out into the night as another swooped in and settled on Gordan's lap.

"Hey," she said, a little surprised by how heartbroken the word sounded. Seeing him here in their spot reminded her that she would have to leave him here when they went to Orodon.

"You will be fine without me," he said, still looking out the window into the night.

She was not as confident. "Yeah," she said, dutifully, because she would *have* to be.

But this time Gordan rolled his distant gaze back into the tower and pointed it at her, staring her down with unconvinced violet eyes.

"What?" she asked, defensively.

"Why don't you tell Raiden? I'm not the only one here for you."

"He already worries so much about everything else," she said. "I don't want to add something as silly as—"

"Don't do that," Gordan said. "Don't reduce what's torturing you."

She sighed. "You know the Sight drives him crazy, always tempting him, fanning the flames of everything he dreads, and then with Gwyn showing up…"

"The silver haired woman in his visions," Gordan said.

"It shook him and the Sight found its way in. I'm doing my best here," she said, "to help him believe in better possibilities than the ones he fears and the ones he's seen. Telling him how empty I feel…well, it doesn't offer a lot of hope for overcoming everything in front of us, does it? I don't want to put that weight on the fragile hope he does have."

"And what makes you think that hope is so fragile?"

"We're both barely keeping it together."

"When Venarius comes, it won't be your guards or your allies or your strategy that keeps you safe. It will come down to your will, as it has time and again. You may not feel strong right now, but suffering alone isn't going to make you any stronger. Letting others be there for you will."

"You know, sometimes I don't want your dragon-empath wisdom," she muttered, trudging across the room and plopping down beside the window.

"That's when you need it the most," he said sardonically, looking back out across the dark sea of rolling hills around the palace.

She huffed. "We saw the past," she said. "After we left the kitchens. Raiden was so flustered by the Sight and…I don't know, somehow we ended up in a memory instead of the future."

"We?"

"It happened once before, I shared a vision with Raiden when we kissed, and I saw my execution—kind of ruined the mood. But this time we were back in the courts when it was crumbling, and then back in Candhrid when it was sinking."

"Candhrid when it was sinking?" he repeated, looking to her utterly mystified.

"It was a memory from the fera before me," she said. "When she escaped Veil to the old world. I didn't just see it, I *lived* it, Gordan."

"Past lives *are* memories in a way, they're usually buried far too deep to find is all."

"It seems like mine is clawing its way out," she muttered.

"Because of one vision?"

"It's not just that vision," she admitted. "I've sort of noticed her presence lurking in my head and my heart sometimes."

"For how long?" He sounded concerned.

"Since Atrium," she said. "Why? Is that a bad thing?"

"I couldn't say," he answered, sounding troubled. "Most people's past lives are just whispers, undercurrents that influence them in imperceptible ways. It isn't uncommon for people to grow close to their past lives, and coincidental similarities between their current life and a past life can make them remember. Most often in dreams and so they are usually written off as dreams. You do have the unique problem of inheriting your past-life's enemies, that would explain uncovering memories…" He trailed off in a way she didn't like.

"But?"

"But for that past life to feel like a presence, like a separate entity? I can't say what that means."

"What? Do you think she'll try to take control?" Nicole tried to laugh but the joke fell like lead.

"It's certainly a possibility."

Nicole's heart gave an anxious thud against her sternum but she shook her head. "I don't think so. She doesn't feel like an intruder. She feels like a conscience, like memories and their lingering emotions. She's sad and she's angry, but I don't think she would want to live through this again. She already is—*I am*. If she's separate it's because she's a piece of me, and I'm in pieces days. I just have to put myself back together."

"Are you trying?"

"What?"

"Are you trying to put yourself back together?" Gordan wondered.

She flinched. She couldn't honestly answer *yes*. Mostly, still didn't know how. She had spent how many days in Cantis trying to prove to herself she was capable of more than destruction...capable of healing with every broken building she mended until her body burned with magical fatigue. Not even putting her body through her old tried-and-true rituals with weights got her any closer. Making he body stronger wasn't the answer, but—like with practing her magic until she was on fire—it never failed to chase away that phantom sensation of the Council in her veins.

"What are you waiting for?"

She took a deep breath. "I don't know how."

"Start with what you do know then," he said.

"You know your cryptic Zen bullshit gets annoying," she grumbled.

He laughed; the sound made her smile and reminded her of what Raiden had said to her. *I missed that…your laugh.* Even just a brief flash of joy from someone she loved was radiant. The darker the shadows around her, the brighter even the smallest spark seemed, and any amount of light was a relief. But that spark flitted away as she and Gordan fell into silence.

"Are you going to sleep up here again?" Gordan asked, a disapproving yet concerned slant on his brow. That was his way of disparaging her for not telling Raiden. At first, she'd been worried that whatever was lurking in the darkness behind her closed eyes might reach out to Raiden like it had Gordan that night they were home in Yuma. But they discovered in the following days that it only affected Gordan, so long as he was close enough to sense Nicole. Through that empathic link her demons could touch him, wound him, even when she was in her room and he was far away in the tower. One bad night, however, Nicole cried out when her dreams inflicted a deep gash across her leg, waking Raiden even through the walls of their separate chambers. After that, she took to sleeping in the tower with Gordan. It made sense, seeing as he ended up with the same wounds, and she could heal them easily enough.

Nicole, indeed, had every intention of sleeping up in the tower tonight when she left Raiden asleep on his bed, but she didn't want to admit that to Gordan now after the look he had given her.

"Last night wasn't so bad," she said. "I think I'll be fine in my room tonight actually." Even though he knew full well that last night had been as bad as any of them. His disapproval collapsed into concern.

"You never know, I could wake up without a scratch tomorrow," she said—*or not at all*—she thought grimly and forced a smile for Gordan.

He gave her a skeptical scowl, no doubt sensing her silent fatalistic thought.

"See you tomorrow," she said, pivoting on her heel with a wave.

"Have you *attempted* to fight this thing?" Gordan asked.

Nicole stopped and frowned down at the doorway at her feet.

"How do I fight something in my head, something I can't see or feel until it's tearing me apart?"

Silence—as she suspected, he couldn't answer her question.

"Goodnight, Gordan," she said softly, sorry that she could not ensure he would sleep well or that the invisible clawed hands in her head wouldn't awake him. That guilt cut her deeper than the darkness in her sleep, and he wondered why she couldn't tell Raiden.

She sulked back through the corridors and stairways to her room, her head tired and heavy but troubled by the thought of sleep. She approached Raiden's door, still barely ajar as she'd left it, in case she changed her mind. She considered going back into his room, she stopped, took the handle, closed his door and continued on to her own.

Her door opened to her weak pull on the handle and she trudged inside, pulling the door shut behind her. Shuffling through the hanging fabric, she reached her large pillow-bed and let out an exasperated huff. Going to sleep meant hurting Gordan. Then she thought of the other doors and heaved herself off the cushion. It didn't seem right to startle Keren by sneaking in to sleep on the couch in the middle of the night. Instead, Nicole made her way through the forest of cloth to the door that lead to Raiden's house in Cantis. Though her room was completely private, she opened the door carefully and slipped through, feeling like she might be seen sneaking out.

Arriving through the doorway at the end of the hall, she closed the door and tip toed—even though there was no one to wake— down the hall, into the room where Raiden used to spend endless hours reading, and threw herself down onto the cold bed surrounded by the shadowy mounds of books. This was where Raiden slept when he was alone all those years. The bed was comforting because in a strange way she felt close to Raiden while she lay in it. She conjured a large warm blanket, curled up beneath it and let herself sink, hoping for a better night or at least that she was far enough away from Gordan that her wounds would not reach him tonight. He deserved a break from all this—a sound night's sleep.

∞

Gordan sat by the window gazing lazily out into the night. The air around him grew quieter as Nicole drifted farther away, the cacophony of her psyche burdened by guilt, worry, anger, love, fear, confusion loneliness, and shame blurred together into an indistinct troubled haze with the distance. When her presence was suddenly gone, he started upright, tearing his eyes away from the peaceful night and toward the door in the tower floor. The owl griffin in his lap jumped up and sulked away.

"Nicole," he growled, sighing with annoyance. Had she gone to Keren's or perhaps home to Yuma? He wondered if he should fly halfway across Veil to see if she was hiding in the little orchard cottage. If she wasn't then he would have to fly all the way to Cantis, and she would probably wake up and sneak back into the palace before he could reach Raiden's house. Unless, of course, he could get into her room, in which case it was a mere stroll through a few doors to find her.

Gordan got up, his heart rate steadily quickening anxiously as he made his way through the palace. He hoped desperately that her door would be open, but he wasn't surprised to find it shut tight.

Knowing Nicole, she was more likely to crawl into a hole to be alone than turn to a safe haven that would elicit a concerned interrogation from either Keren or her father. Gordan let out a grumbling huff, leaned his back against the door and slid down to the floor to wait out the night.

౭

Nicole started awake, tangled in her blanket. She sat up, dropped her chin and pulled down the neck of her ripped shirt, straining her eyes down to see the angry red line spanning her chest. It was not the open bloody wound of a merciless strike, but the path of a slow deliberate scratch from something heavy and sharp. But the scratch wasn't what yanked her back to consciousness.

There came a distant pounding that perplexed her. Someone knocking on the front door downstairs? No, it couldn't be. Then it occurred to her that the sound was coming through the door at the end of the hall, from her room back in the palace. Wrestling the blanket off, she jumped off the bed, her shoes were still on her feet, and she hurried down the hall, following the faint cadence to the door that took her back to the palace. When she opened it, the pounding was suddenly so much closer and distinctly impatient. She shut the door to Raiden's house and hurried across her massive room, through silk and chiffon pillars billowing from the brief draft from Cantis, to the towering doorway.

She pushed the door open to find Gordan standing there with such a look of fiery annoyance that she recoiled.

"Why would you do that—where *were* you, I was—what if—"

"Gordan, look at me. I'm fine," she said, shushing him and looking down the hall anxiously.

"I had no way to know that," he said.

The pained expression on his face made her heart heavy. "I'm sorry. I just thought it would be better if you didn't have to be hurt every night too."

"Wondering if you were going to come back was worse," he said with a sigh. "It's not your responsibility to protect me from my gift. It's the only reason you're not enduring this alone."

"Okay," she sighed. "I get it. I really am sorry."

"I know you are, but you don't have to feel guilty about how others are affected by your troubles. For once stop putting everyone else first."

"Hey," someone called.

Nicole and Gordan looked to see Mitchell down the hall, hurrying toward them and still panting.

"Glad you're awake."

"I'm surprised *you're* awake, and doing cardio no less," Nicole said.

"Ha ha," he said. "I didn't go to sleep. Gwyn and I were up all night talking about wands and pouring over some books Tovar let her borrow. This stuff is really interesting, and we had an idea."

"Okay," Nicole said slowly, nodding.

"Well, come on," Mitchell said with a sigh.

"Oh, an idea that involves me," she said, stepping out her door and into the hall.

"No, I just thought I'd run up five flights of stairs and down one hundred-meter hallways to tell you we had an idea and be on my way," he grumbled as he made his way back toward the stairs and she followed.

Gordan did not follow. He watched Mitchell and Nicole turn onto the stairs and disappear. He turned back toward Raiden's room, walked resolutely to his door and knocked.

"Raiden?"

He heard a deep breath stir the fog of slumber within, the whisper of limbs dragging against fabric. Gordan knocked again.

"Raiden, can I speak with you?"

☙

"You want to make me a custom wand," Nicole clarified. "In a day?"

"Well no, it will take longer," Mitchell said, clearly disappointed. "But it's not a wand—well it is—and a sword at the same time. We're applying wand lore to a different design."

"Okay…why?"

"One, because a sword is way fucking cooler than a wand. Two, it's bigger. Gwyn was saying that part of the problem with wands not being able to withstand large amounts of power could be that there's simply not enough material to conduct and withstand the energy. So, I said why not make something bigger and she suggested a staff, which I guess some pretty powerful wizards have needed throughout history, but I suggested a sword. I mean, it's a great tool in its own right."

She laughed. "A tool."

"Okay, weapon," he said.

"Because this is war," she said, wishing it could be as much of a joke as she made it sound.

"You're damn right it's war."

"What do you need me for exactly?" She wondered, yawning.

"I want you to test my wands for the sake of study," Gwyn said.

"I'm going to ruin them all."

"For science, Nikki," Mitchell insisted.

"You mean magic."

"Same thing."

⁂

Raiden sighed, pinching the bridge of his nose. "I knew she's been keeping something a secret. I've been so distracted lately and figured she'd tell me eventually."

"I believe she will. I just think you needed to know sooner," Gordan said.

"How bad are they?"

"Some nights just scratches, other nights they're…well, they can be quite bad. She can heal them when she wakes, but all she's mending is a physical symptom. This goes far deeper."

Raiden's forehead puckered. "What do we do?"

"Be here for her," Gordan said. "That's all we can do."

"We have been here. I've been here, and she hasn't even told me that sleeping is causing her bodily harm. You've known about this, and she still tries to hide it. How is that helpful?"

A pulse of anguish hit Gordan, disrupting his thought. Raiden was hurt that Gordan knew this secret, yet he hadn't been trusted with it.

"The only reason I know is because my sense links me to the emotions and psyches of those around me. If I hadn't been there and she didn't see that it affects me too, I don't know that she would have told me either."

"I just don't understand keeping it a secret," Raiden said, dropping his head back and pushing his fingers through his hair. "She knows I understand. I know what she went through in Atrium."

"It's not just about knowing what happened," Gordan said. "She used to be so sure of herself, and she doesn't like admitting that she isn't anymore. I suspect she's ashamed by it. She thinks she should have pulled herself together by now and the longer she feels broken the more ashamed she feels."

A churning cloud of frustration and bitter sorrow spread through the room, chased by the heat of anger.

"I know it's frustrating—"

"If not for the Council and Venarius—"

"This is where we are, Raiden. The damage is done. Don't get caught up in who is to blame. Getting rid of her enemies won't fix this."

Raiden took a deep breath; his anger sulked away, leaving him with the far less satisfying company of his fears and melancholy.

"It's not easy knowing someone you love is in pain when you can't take that pain away," Gordan said, straining to keep his voice steady under the weight of his own *and* Raiden's emotions. He gladly bore those wounds with Nicole because what else could he do. He could not banish that pain, but he could at least stand beside her and share it.

"What if we could take that pain away?" Raiden asked.

"If you have learned nothing from your meddling in your own memories, then I cannot hope to convince you of how terrible that notion is."

"Fine. You're right," Raiden sighed.

"Just be there, Raiden, because I can't be there when you're both away in Orodon."

"I will," he said, his quiet words were heavy with sincerity.

❦

"Are you sure about this, Gwyn?" Nicole asked, looking at the three wands lined up on the table before her. "I mean, these are your best ones—"

"They are the stronger ones of what I have made, but not the best. I want to see how they react to you. What I can learn from these tests is far more valuable than the wands themselves."

"All right," she said, picking the wand to the right first. She fell back on her old practice charm—*ilumina*—and found that the wand pulled her magic down her arm like a magnet, jumping through the wand with a pulse. To her surprise the wand grew warm but did not tremble or creek. A glimmer of energy flourished from the tip of the wand and there was her tried and true orb of light.

"Oh, it worked," she said with a laugh.

"Sure," Gwyn said. "It could probably withstand small charms for some time. But try something bigger."

"Bigger?" Nicole wracked her brain for a task that fit the bill and decided on something that had to be near impossible—conjuring Raiden's letter that had slipped away into the ocean. Surely it was lost to the waves, pulled into countless pieces. How much magic would it take to gather its scattered molecules, or perhaps to reach through time to find it intact—would she pull it from her own past self's hands, change events somehow? That seemed big enough.

She pointed the wand at the table where she wanted Raiden's letter to appear and let her magic out. The wand drew it in, pulling it through her arm, filling with the buzzing heat until the silver bands glowed red hot and the polished black wood split along the grains and bulged like a swollen finger around rings until it burst with a crack. The silver bands scattered across floor, bouncing and tinkling as the splintered remains of the wand fell to the table.

"That's what I thought," Gwyn said with a studious nod. "The core was completely overwhelmed, it ignited. There's nothing left of it," she remarked, pinching some of debris between her fingers.

"What does that mean?" Mitchell asked.

"The core bears the brunt of the energy, and if it can't withstand the magic, then it is prone to combust. That just means the wand wasn't up to the task of channeling what Nicole can really do."

"What kind of core was that?" Nicole asked.

"That was my unicorn blood core. It's pretty hard to come by as they only really trust other animals, and the fey who refuse to harvest it unless they encounter the beasts wounded."

"Blood," Nicole cringed. "Why blood?"

"Most magic comes from within living things. Our bodies are what magic uses as a conduit. Wand making is essentially an art to craft something that acts like a living body, housing and channeling magic. The blood of magical creatures is some of the most common cores, but wand makers also use sap from certain magical plants."

"What's this one," Nicole wondered as she picked up the next wand.

"That's ironwood and leviathan blood," Gwyn said.

She could see the wood grain, but this wand felt twice as heavy as the first wand, its weight more like metal. It was a dark grey wood and its polish made it seem all the more metallic. Set into the iron-wood was a single line of copper twisting around like the stripe of a candy cane from end to end.

"Okay then, Leviathan," Nicole murmured and she tried once again to retrieve Raiden's letter from somewhere in the universe. The wand grew warm and then hot, but it did not fracture like the last one. With the wand pointed at the table, she expected it to break as she thought hard about that piece of paper filled with Raiden's handwriting. The wand grew hotter still, the copper burned her fingers, but she refused to drop it, she was used to that burn now. The air rippled like water and a soggy lump of pulp appeared on the table.

"What the hell is that?" Mitchell sneered.

Nicole laughed. "It *was* a letter Raiden left me in Cantis. I lost it in the ocean. I wasn't sure what I'd get if I tried to conjure it."

"That's some kind of success…I guess," he muttered.

"But the wand survived," Nicole added.

"Well, it didn't break," Gwyn said. "The core could still be burned up. Try something else."

Nicole shrugged and pointed the wand at her sad lump of wet paper to turn it back into a crisp dry sheet of parchment. The wand burned again, hissing, and a tongue of smoke twisted into the air from the tip of it.

"See, it's already burned up," Gwyn said.

"That was closer," Mitchell said.

"It was," Gwyn agreed. "But not by much."

"What's the last one?" Nicole picked it up, and it felt almost weightless, reminding her of Raiden's sword.

"That's hemel wood and phoenix blood. Just cast as much as you can," Gwyn said.

Nicole looked down at the wand that seemed so delicate it couldn't possibly hold up to a single spell, but if a phoenix could emerge from its own ashes as flesh and blood anew, then maybe this wand could withstand her fire longer than the others. She pointed the pale wand at the wad of soggy paper on the table. Her magic jumped through the weightless wood like it was her own finger and leapt from the tip as a sharp thread of light. The lumpy mass seemed to turn to liquid, spreading out into a flat rectangular puddle and then into a sheet of dry parchment. It was blank, a failure to retrieve Raiden's words, washed away in the sea.

"Keep going," Gwyn implored her.

Nicole shook off her disappointment and in quick succession she conjured anything that came to her mind, flicking the wand at the table each time—her favorite book, a cup of coffee which Mitch swiped so she conjured another.

She summoned Raiden's sword, his mother's old leather journal—she had been meaning to give it to him and kept managing to forget since misplacing it. Gim appeared on the table in a flurry of embers and jumped at his sudden change of scenery before spotting Nicole and scurrying onto the wand and up her arm. The wand seemed to hold up, each item came exactly as she willed it, but when she stopped—distracted by Gim—she could see the pale wood had darkened to a singed shade of black. Its fate, if she kept on using it, was apparent. She set it down on the table.

"That's interesting, the core holding out while the shaft of the wand burns," Gwyn said, picking up the wand to look at it more closely, the brittle burned wand cracked in her hands.

Nicole picked up the blank sheet of paper, regarding it a moment before folding it in quarters as she had once found it and tucking it into her pocket. She grabbed Raiden's sword, swung it onto her shoulder, and picked up her coffee cup to take a satisfying sip.

"Thank you, this has been very helpful," Gwyn said, looking up from the burnt wand.

"Good, I'm glad. I'd hate to ruin your hard work for nothing," Nicole said, taking the journal from the table as well and tucking it under her arm.

"I am very excited about this project. Your brother has been most encouraging. He's got the mind of a wand maker."

Mitchell beamed over his coffee.

"I only wish I could send you to Orodon with this great sword, sadly it's just an idea," Gwyn laughed.

"For now," Mitchell added.

"I'll need to find a sword smith to help me with this. Crafting wands is nothing like swords. I just worry about finding someone willing to work with unusual materials."

"I'm sure you'll find someone," Nicole said.

"What about Raiden's sword?" Mitchell asked. "Isn't that kinda special?"

"Yeah," Nicole said. "It was his father's though, so Leone could probably tell you more about it."

Mitchell nodded. "Where's he usually lurking?"

She shrugged. "With Loak?" She didn't really know where in the palace they had claimed rooms. Relieved they were done with her, she turned and wandered out of the room, clutching her coffee close as Gim crawled around her neck and shoulders.

Gwyn's new work shop was set up in a chamber just down the hall from Tovar's study on the second floor, so she set out to return Raiden's sword to him. Gim scurried down her arm to perch on her hand clutching the handle of her mug.

"Hey you," she said. Gim blew a little flurry of flames at her coffee. "How sweet." She chuckled, sipping her once-again-hot coffee. "How do you like the ovens in the kitchen, huh?"

Gim looked at her and spit a tiny flame—an answer she took to be generally positive for the little golden salamander. Coffee cut through the taste of sleep in her mouth and warmed her belly, but she was still slow and tired, shuffling along the corridors in a near trance until Gordan appeared, turning into the corridor just ahead of her. He wore a familiar look on his face that told her he had been on his way to find her.

"Hey," she said.

"Hey," he answered.

They met in the middle of the hallway.

"What's all this?" His eyes moved from coffee, to Gim, to journal, to sword, then to her.

"I did some speed conjuring to put a wand to the test," she said.

"Were you heading back to your room?" He asked.

"Why—you trying to keep an eye on me now?"

"Naturally."

"Well, I'm on my way to Raiden's room, actually. I've got to return something I stole and give him this," she said, plucking the journal out from under her arm with her free hand. "Then I suppose I have to pack for this manticore expedition."

"I can help you with that."

"I thought you said you'd never encountered a manticore before?"

"I haven't, but I can help you pack."

She chuckled. He smiled. They made their way toward the stairs.

Twenty

Raiden paced his room as he considered Nicole's dreams. There was a solution he knew of that might allow him to help her—an herb his mother used for him long ago. He paced to the door, hoping that Tovar would have what he needed. He tried to remember the last time his mother had used the herb. She always had some on hand as it had many uses to aid in sleep—but most significant to him was that when two people slept with the herb between them, they would share their dreams. He wasn't going to let Nicole face these nightmares alone now that he knew what was happening. He pushed his door open only to see Nicole hop backwards, Gordan standing beside her.

"Hi," Nicole said.

"Hi," he repeated. He was anxious to get to Tovar's study, but he always wanted every second with her that he could get as they seemed few and far between lately.

"Were you going somewhere?" she wondered.

"Nowhere more important than you," he shrugged, stepping back so that she and Gordan could come into the room.

She blushed yet eyed him suspiciously.

"I stole your sword—for wand-testing purposes." She swung it

off her shoulder and held it out.

He smiled, taking the sword from her. "How did that go?" He crossed the room to hang the sword on the corner of the bed frame.

"I ruined them all," she said with a chipper nod.

"Oh." He could feel his face wavering between a frown and confusion. He looked to Gordan who shrugged, unable to communicate any clues he might have.

"Oh, stop sharing concerned looks," she said. "I'm good at destroying things, I've accepted it."

Gordan folded his arms and frowned.

She shrugged. "Luckily, I didn't destroy this," she said, holding up the journal. "I meant to give it to you, but I kind of misplaced it."

"What is it?" He took hold of the soft leather; he'd never seen it before.

"I found that under your bed in Cantis, ages ago, when we went for the books. I spotted it under there—you know—when I found the shift token."

"That I remember," he said, chuckling.

"I thought it was your mother's at first," she said, "until I learned about the oracle Althea Divale. I thought maybe your mother was named after her."

Raiden opened the journal and read the name written across the first page. "My mother's name was Vervain."

"Oh," Nicole said. "Did she ever mention being related to the Divale family?"

"No. She did speak of them now and then, but she never talked about her family either. I can't imagine any other reason for her having something like this though. Althea Divale's personal journal?"

"I was so sure it was your mother's," Nicole said with quiet disappointment.

"Why?"

"She wrote about this vision of her future son, and I swear the boy she described is you," Nicole said.

Raiden opened the journal to the middle and was greeted by the chaotic tangle of writing. "We had to hide the fact that we were seers. The Council would have brought us both to the courts. Divale being the most distinguished name among seers in Veil, it would have been too much of a risk to keep the name or even speak of our linage if that were the case."

"Raiden, a descendant of the oracle Althea Divale," Gordan mused with an impressed nod.

"Maybe," he said with a shrug.

"Either way, that definitely belonged to your mother, so it's yours," Nicole said.

Raiden closed the journal. His doubts shrinking the longer he held it in his hands and the more he considered the circumstances of this object being in his home. It might have remained lost beneath that bed forever if not for Nicole. She had managed to find and give him a link to his mother's family. "Thank you."

Nicole smiled but the light in her eyes faded and the corners of her smile dropped a little; her joy had been real but fleeting and she strained to keep it on her face. She was hiding from him in plain sight. With renewed determination to see Tovar, he slipped the journal into the lining of his jacket where the weight of it sat comfortably against his ribs.

"I have to see Loak about who he has selected to come with us," he lied. "He always gets started early. Forgive me?"

He glanced at Gordan, who cast a quiet reproachful look at him.

"Of course," she said. "See you later?"

With a pang of bittersweet relief, he smiled, and trapped her face in his hands just long enough to plant a swift kiss on her lips. "Yes. See you later."

He concealed the urgency in his stride until he was out the door and out of sight where he could move down the stairs doubly fast.

As he made his way toward Tovar's study down the second-floor hallway, he stopped abruptly, surprised to see Mitchell step out of a door—still wearing yesterday's clothes—and into his path.

"Mitchell," he said.

"Hey, Ray. Where are you headed?"

"Tovar's—why are you…?" Raiden pointed to the room behind Mitchell.

"Oh, Tovar set Gwyn up in there to work on her wands. When are we leaving?"

"I'm not sure. I suppose Captain Rhee will let us know. Best to be ready soon," he said.

"Sure thing—hey, do you know where I'd find your dad?"

"He'll be with Loak and the guards having breakfast about now I would think," Raiden said, confused. "Why are you looking for him?"

Mitchell was already making his break down the hall toward the kitchens. "I've got to ask him about that sword of his, er—yours, for research," he said over his shoulder.

"All right then," Raiden said to himself.

"He might be more excited about this project than even I am," Gwyn said from the doorway.

Raiden swallowed back the discomfort in his throat, telling himself he didn't have to worry about his visions of the silver-haired woman even though he still did. "I'm glad you finally have the opportunity to pursue your dream," he said.

"Me too," she said. "I was so sure it wasn't going to happen when I took the job in the kitchens." She let out a laugh. "I thought, 'here we go again, back to the ovens. I guess I'm just not meant for anything else.' Now here I am with exactly what I wanted."

"You never can tell how things are going to turn out," Raiden said, hoping fiercely that was true because his fear of what he'd seen in the future refused to be banished completely.

"And what about you?" Gwyn asked.

"Pardon?"

"What do you want, Raiden? Because I don't think you want to be a king."

"No," he agreed easily. "I want to stop living in the past and worrying about the future, I just want to be with Nicole and the family we've made but without enemies constantly coming for us."

Gwyn's face pinched and she was quiet for a moment. "I hope I can contribute to achieving that," she said with a tiny hopeful smile.

"Thank you. We need all the help we can get," he said. "Speaking of which, I have to see Tovar about something. Please excuse me, Gwyn."

"Bye, Raiden."

He was relieved to step into his dutiful march as Gwyn turned back into her work room. It was a short trip to Tovar's door, and he knocked impatiently.

"I'm coming, Raiden," Tovar's muffled voice answered.

The door opened.

"How did you know it was me?"

"The anxious knock," Tovar said.

"Oh."

"Come in. What can I do for you?"

"I need an herb if you have it. Juno's Tears?"

"As a matter of fact, I do," Tovar said, turning to his large cabinet of drawers and small cupboards.

He plucked open the door to one of the cabinets and scanned the bottles and jars of dried plants, some whole and others ground into fine powders, but he didn't find what he wanted. He opened the cabinet door beside the first and looked, then shook his head.

"No, no, over here," he muttered to himself, moving over to the drawers and pulling them open one after another to peek inside until at last he said, "Ah, here it is. As you well know, some herbs have to be fresh, so I keep these drawers enchanted for such plants." From the small drawer he pulled a hearty little green sprig of leaves and cone shaped clusters of tiny blue flowers that looked as fresh as anything newly cut. "Juno's Tears," Tovar said, holding it out to Raiden.

He sagged with relief and took the herb. "Thank you."

"That has a lot of interesting uses, inducing visions chief among them. Popular herb among the seers although I think they often referred to it by another name."

"Vervain," Raiden said.

"Yes, that's it. What did you have in mind for that?"

"It's for Nicole," he said. "To help her sleep."

"I see, troubles with nightmares," Tovar said and sounded almost sad. "Sorry to hear that. Juno's Tears should do the trick, though."

"I hope so," Raiden said, tucking it into his jacket along with the journal.

❧

Not long past noon Captain Rhee announced that they could leave in a matter of a few hours, so everyone who was going had better pack and be on board before then. Along with Raiden, Loak, Nicole, Caeruleus and Mitchell, they were going with five of the new royal guard.

Nicole stayed with Gordan in the tower as long as she could before she had to meet the others at the Tempest.

She folded her arms and sighed. "Can't we just put an eyepatch on you and trade you for Caeruleus? Would anyone really know?"

Gordan chuckled.

She scrunched up her face. "He hates me. This is going to be an uncomfortable trip."

"He's jealous of you," Gordan explained matter-of-factly.

"Jealous?"

Gordan nodded. "Ashamed too. I imagine he doesn't know how to interact with you." He shrugged.

Nicole groaned. "This is worse."

Gordan chuckled. "You'll be fine."

Her heart gave a sickening thud. "Yeah," she agreed half-heartedly.

"Just promise me you'll be safe. Don't do anything risky. There's a solution and I know you'll find it," Gordan said when it was time for her to force herself through the door of the tower even though she wasn't ready.

"I promise. I don't want to kill this thing just because it's dangerous, but I have a feeling that's the solution Orodon is expecting from me. I'm the fera after all, what else do I do better than de-stroy and kill my enemies?"

Gordan frowned at her. "*So* much more," he said, imploring her to believe him with the force of his pained violet eyes.

She smiled and opened her arms to him. Her took her invitation and hugged her.

"Stay out of trouble," she said.

"I'll stay in the tower," he said and released her.

"Well then, wish me luck."

"Good luck."

☙

Nicole and Raiden were the last to board the Tempest. Raiden stood outside the ship where it waited, perched atop the hill behind the palace. The sea of grass rippled almost like water in the breeze. When she arrived at last, he offered her his hand, which she took, and they stepped into the elevator in the ship's solitary leg. Rhee stood waiting above in the cargo hold when they reached the top.

"Is that everyone who's coming?"

"Yes," Raiden answered.

"Good. Let's get the hell off the ground," Rhee said as she turned on her heel. Nicole and Raiden followed her from the cargo hold. "I wager we can be there tomorrow morning for breakfast in Orodon."

But Nicole's stomach twisted with nausea with the idea of tomorrow pressing on her. They stepped into the corridor leading to the bridge where the five guards were standing, each one against the wall between the doorways looking far more rigid and alert than Nicole thought they had any need to be while they were all safe on the Tempest. She hadn't encountered Loak's recruits yet as the palace basically protected itself, so he and Leone had been training them for nearly two weeks. She was a little surprised to see they were all wearing the same simple dark green jackets embroidered with a pair of mirrored upright keys.

"Pep, we're off," Rhee announced as she marched toward the bridge.

Nicole watched the eyes of the guards as Rhee passed them, but their gazes were locked straight ahead. What the training for royal guards entailed she had no idea—marching, staring exercises? Whatever the methods, less than two weeks had clearly been enough to master a cohesive presence of vigilance, but what about going up against a manticore, or the cunning schemes of someone like Venarius? Could anyone be prepared for that?

She tried not to think of the manticore, so instead she thought of Gordan, which wasn't much of a relief, just a change in worry. It was no secret that he lived in the palace, and that sort of thing surely spread quickly. Would the palace spells protect him, keep out an angry mob after a dragon, or did those spells only really protect the keys?

"What is it?" Raiden asked.

Nicole looked down the line of guards. How was she supposed to act around them? Like they weren't there? They were pretending to ignore her and Raiden, masks of focus pointing at the wall across the way, but acting like human beings weren't standing right there listening didn't sit well with her.

"I'm worried about leaving Gordan," she finally confessed, begrudgingly accepting the strangeness of being ignored *and* listened to.

"He has been on his own before, you know," Raiden teased.

She let out a single breathy laugh. "I'm serious. Do we know if the defenses keep out everyone trying to hurt *anyone* inside the palace? How do we know they don't just protect us? We don't know *where* Venarius is—he might still need Gordan, what if leaving him alone is a mistake?"

His expression hardened with solemnity. "Listen to me. Gordan will be so safe in that palace that he'll be bored out of his mind until we get back."

Nicole took a deep breath and let out a growling sigh, turning into Raiden and dropping her forehead against his chest. "This is gonna to be a long trip," she groaned into his sternum.

Nicole could tell they were in the air from the gentle dipping of the ship as it turned and righted on its course toward Orodon. She glanced down the hallway toward the bridge and was perplexed for a moment by one of the guards. She hadn't really met any of them yet, and for a moment Nicole thought her friend Roxanne was standing there.

Though she knew it was impossible, Nicole couldn't shake her surprise. From her golden hair, and bright sky-blue eyes to her fair complexion and button nose, this guard could be Roxanne's double, or at the very least a long-lost sister. As she studied the woman's face, Nicole noticed the guard's stern composure had crumpled into a pale mask of ill discomfort with the movement of the ship. Nicole stepped away from Raiden and approached the guard, a woman in her twenties.

"What's your name?" Nicole asked.

The guard jerked her eyes to Nicole who could see her face wavering between nauseated misery and surprise. "Lyana," she said.

"You might not feel as sick if you look out a window," Nicole said, nodding toward the archways leading to the upper deck.

Lyana glanced at her fellow guards to each side of her as if looking for permission or refusal, they exchanged shifting glances before locking their eyes forward again, determined to maintain their conspicuous invisibility. Reluctantly, Lyana stepped away from the wall and followed Nicole.

She guided Lyana to the ladder then went up after her, Raiden following close behind. When they stepped into the corridor of the upper deck, Nicole spotted Mitchell, Loak and Caeruleus at the great domed window, Loak standing between the two like a wall between enemy camps.

Nicole walked beside Lyana whose pace shrank to an apprehensive creep as she neared Loak and the window. Nicole wondered if she was anxious about being out of line.

"There you are," Mitchell said, noticing their approach.

Loak looked their way.

"Lyana," Loak greeted with raised brows.

"Sir," she said, cringing.

"She was looking sick," Nicole said. "Looking out the window helps."

"I see," Loak said.

"Thank you, your highness," Lyana said quietly.

Nicole's face pinched. "Please, call me Nicole," she implored. "I beg you."

Lyana smiled and nodded, her expression still a little miserable. Then, taking a deep breath and letting it out carefully she turned to stare out the window. Nicole stood there between Raiden and Lyana, Mitchell beside her and Loak towering on the other end of their line, all of them gazing out the window. Captain Rhee—or perhaps Pep—flew relatively low as the emerald plains undulated below the Tempest. Large curling clouds hung lazily in the sky, a herd of fluffy white cattle grazing in the blue, and the ship soared through them.

❧

The flight went peacefully for the remainder of the day and on into the night. Raiden observed with mild amusement as Nicole and Mitchell coaxed the rest of the guards out of their dutiful rigor, despite the tight-mouthed sideways glances of Loak who had spent the better part of a week instilling the decorum and diligence of their rank and duty into them. But he had placed Nicole and Raiden's authority above his own and so when she requested casual familiarity almost all of them obliged.

Only one of them, a man named Bode, could not be persuaded to join the rest of the party when Nicole requested. He would take no invitation to relax, sit, or talk with the rest of them and instead just stood nearby like a guard, perhaps slightly less rigid than before. Gregor, Sage, and Netti all eased away from their stiffness.

Raiden anxiously awaited the time when everyone would retreat to the sleeping quarters and thought about the herb hiding patiently in his jacket. His mother had been the one to teach him about Juno's Tears because of its connection to the Sight, protection and sleep— the ability to share dreams was only one of many uses. When he was small the Sight troubled him most in his sleep. He couldn't say what the visions had been after so long, but he did remember they were as good as nightmares to a child.

I don't like where I go when I'm sleeping, he remembered saying to her, he couldn't have been more than six or seven.

Well then, love, I'll go with you next time, she said.

She would be there with him in his dreams when the Sight tore his child fantasies to shreds and brought him visions. His mother didn't make them go away, but her presence was a comfort, and he could think of them as silly nightmares again and forget them when the sun rose.

He didn't know what was waiting for Nicole in her sleeping mind, or if there was any way he could help her fight it, but he could be there at least. He supposed someone would cave and be the first to head to the sleeping quarters.

They were all still gathered at the long table in the mess room for dinner. Raiden sat contentedly with Caeruleus to his left, beside him sat Loak and next to him at the very end of the table sat Andrus, the Tempest's new resident medic. Nicole sat close on his right and Mitchell beside her, while Lyana, Netti, Sage, and Gregor all sat on the other side of the table. The Tempest was only equipped with a conjuring soup pot that provided the same pork and potato soup every meal which saved Captain Rhee from needing a cook on board. To the pot's credit, the soup was good and hot.

Their dinner conversation had stretched on long after everyone's soup bowl was empty. Raiden was pleased to see Nicole engaging the guards so earnestly, and yet he noticed that she skillfully avoided Gregor and Netti's bright-eyed interest in being a fera by soliciting them for information about themselves. Her interest in conversation was camouflage.

Mitchell, however, made up for her evasive tactics and shared his best stories about how she revealed her magic to him when she shifted Gordan and him around Tucson, and his favorite story about how she brought a statue of a wildcat to life—which he lamented not seeing for himself—and the stories of chaos that ensued on campus.

Raiden tensed and caught the cold look Caeruleus gave him before he cast a side-eyed glance toward Mitchell. But Mitchell didn't go any further into the story, didn't mention the Council's man sent after Nicole at all; in fact, anyone listening would think that the incident with the statue happened as a complete accident or a prank. The way Mitchell told the story, no one would have known the circumstances were as deadly serious as they had truly been.

From the corner of his eye, Raiden watched Caeruleus sag with relief and drop his gaze to the table. He wished he had Gordan's ability to feel his friend's guarded emotions in that moment.

Across from Caeruleus Netti yawned, shielding her open mouth and hook nose with her olive brown hand; thick black brows pressed down over her squinted eyes. It was infectious. Gregor yawned, and then Raiden couldn't stop himself from doing the same.

"We should get some sleep," Caeruleus said, standing up.

Netti nodded.

Mitchell was the first to stand, reaching for the stack of four bowls from Lyana, Gregor, Sage and Netti. He stacked his, Nicole's and Raiden's then held his hand out to Caeruleus blinked with surprise as he handed over his bowl. The stack of bowls, spoon handles sticking out like silver tongues, grew to an impressive lopsided column with all ten bowls leaning against his chest as he hauled them away to the small kitchen at the back of the mess room.

One by one they all heaved themselves off the benches, bidding goodnight and wandering off to the ladders until Nicole, Raiden and Caeruleus were left at the table while Mitchell rinsed bowls in the sink. He could feel Nicole fidget uncomfortably before she got up and wandered over to her brother, any conversation between them drown out in the rushing water.

"He acted like it didn't even happen," Caeruleus muttered.

"I think that's how he moves past things," Raiden offered quietly as he stood up. "Selective focus and humor."

Caeruleus nodded, standing up.

The water turned off and the mess room fell silent.

"Well, sure you could do it like that," Mitchell said and Nicole laughed.

"You'd still be washing dishes otherwise," she said, patting him on the back.

They strode back across the room, and Raiden saw the same look of discomfort on Caeruleus' face that he would wear when his father entered the room or even came up in conversation when they were kids—discomfort, shame, and anxiety.

"Jeez, I'm beat," Mitchell said.

"You stayed up all night last night," Nicole reminded him.

"Oh yeah," Mitchell said chuckling. "I'm gone, you guys. See you tomorrow." Mitchell walked out into the corridor, slouched in exhaustion.

Nicole could not compose the confused expression of guilt and sadness weighing down her attempt at a smile when she looked at Caeruleus, but his blue gaze was on the floor. Raiden spotted it.

"I guess we should go up too," Raiden said.

Nicole kept her mouth shut, frowning to herself as she turned away from Caeruleus and led the way to the ladders. The ship was silent save for the low hum of its engines and their footsteps. They reached the upper deck which had grown dimmer than it was earlier, the lights of the viewing deck and the corridor to the sleeping quarters were a soft half-lit glow as though to tell them it was time for them to head to their beds like everyone else.

The three of them walked in an uncomfortable silence until Caeruleus turned to his room and said, "Until tomorrow, then."

"Goodnight," Raiden said.

Nicole opened her mouth but turned to the opposite door without a word and said nothing until he was inside and the door to their small room was closed behind him.

"Does he hate me?"

"Of course not. I can't really speak for him, but I know he doesn't hate you."

"How could he not? He lost an eye and his wings because of

me."

"No—because of the Council and the choices he made. We certainly both contributed to the outcome, but he doesn't blame you for defending yourself."

Nicole gave him a skeptical grimace, then rolled her head and sighed.

"I think the loss of his eye still stings a bit," Raiden admitted. "It's always going to be there, but it's not directed at you."

"I hope you're right," she said. "He just never says a word to me."

"So, say something to him. After everything he did for the Council, I'm guessing he doesn't know what to say," Raiden suggested sympathetically, remembering the guilt he had felt by the mere idea that the Council asked him to carry out those same orders, and that, for a time, Nicole believed he might.

Nicole finally smiled a little.

"We should get some sleep," Raiden pressed.

She heaved an exhale of exasperation from her chest and sat down on the bed with a defeated thud. "I don't know if I can."

"Why not?" His heart gave a hard nudge against his ribs, hoping she was going to tell him about the danger lurking in her dreams.

"I'm too anxious to sleep," she said, her eyes peering at the floor. "It's not just the manticore. I'm not royalty. I don't know how to do this, and we're meeting an actual king tomorrow. I don't know how to process this."

"He's just a person who leads his people. He asked for your help, he's going to be grateful—"

"That's what worries me—what if I can't deliver? If it comes down to killing this creature, I don't think I can do that."

"I know," he said, sitting beside her and reaching into his jacket for the journal. She didn't need to fixate on her worries. She needed a break from the pressure, a change of subject. "Do you want to tell me about Althea?"

"Sure," she said, her body releasing its tension, her shoulders dropped a little, her rigid spine relaxed.

They piled the bed's blanket and pillow, along with a few more conjured by Nicole, against the wall at the head of the bed and settled back against it all. The bed wasn't very wide, so they were pressed close together against the corner, Nicole with her head perched on his shoulder as she told him about the journal and how Althea's words had kept her company on her trek through Candhrid.

"You know she talks about how her visions are so intense they seem to take her into the moments she's Seeing," Nicole said.

"Like mine."

"It sounded to me like that's unusual for a seer."

"Well, she was an Oracle…" he said, unsure if he liked the implication of that fact.

"That would explain why she had a vision in here—its written on different pages, like it came to her in pieces—it was about the keys and the courts falling."

"What?"

"Here," Nicole said, taking the journal and flipping through the pages in search of the ones where dark erratic writing stood out in the tangle of quick but elegant handwriting. She stuck her fingers in between the pages as she found each part.

"Okay, here it is," she said, turning between the sections she had pinched between her fingers to put it together in order. "*Those who seek to save us will set loose children of discord and destruction. Among them they have but one fate and will break down the walls that seclude us. The pillars upon the hill will fall before dawn when chaos finds peace and peace embraces chaos. Two opposed in harmony will forge the key and unlock our chains.*"

"That's definitely a prophecy," Raiden said.

"I heard it in the courts too. There was this massive book…it got buried in the destruction."

Raiden thought for a moment. "Is that what you were looking for?"

She gave him a sheepish look. "I wanted to know what else might be in there…for a little guidance."

"Prophecies are more like riddles than guidance," he said with a chuckle.

"This one seems pretty clear," she said and yawned. "*Children of discord and destruction* are the fera and *the pillars upon the hill will fall before dawn* is the courts."

"All right, but *when chaos finds peace and peace embraces chaos?* And what about *two opposed in harmony will forge the key and unlock our chains?* That's one key, not two, so can that be about the keys of the realm?"

Nicole's face rumpled with the effort to decipher the meaning.

"See? Prophecies will only drive you crazy even worse than regular old visions."

"I guess you're right," she said with another yawn.

"Let's see what else she left us," he said, sneaking a glance down at Nicole.

"Yeah," she answered, nodding her head against his shoulder with her eyes shut.

Raiden flipped through pages of the journal for passages clear enough that he could read.

"…there's a storm coming. I wish I knew when, it is impossible to help anyone prepare when perhaps the storm will come in a day, in a week, or even a decade. Too many seers have made themselves a pariah sharing every ill-fated vision only to cause consternation when the calamity does not occur. People do not much like being stirred into fear…" The legibility was lost after that.

He flipped through several more pages for another clear passage.

"…strange to know my son so well when I have yet to even love a man. Some days I think I never will, but I so look forward to the days with my child."

The whisper of Nicole's breathing against his shoulder drew his gaze down once more. Her face was slack and peaceful. He sighed. She was asleep. He was relieved and worried, relieved she would get some sleep after all, worried for what that sleep might bring her. All he could do was close his eyes and hope the Juno's Tears—inside his jacket beneath his left arm and Nicole—would do its job and take him to her wherever she was in her slumber.

❧

Nicole walked through grey painted halls, an industrial multicolored carpet that blurred into a drab blue beneath her feet. She knew herself to be at school, although she knew there were no hallways at Cibola High School that went on endlessly with hundreds of classroom doors pressed in together only feet apart, too many doors to choose from, and she knew she had to find the right one. But the hall grew dim, the florescent lights above flickered, only half as bright, then the hall went dark, pitch black, and she was back in the void.

She turned to her right, knowing the doors had been just a few steps away, but she walked on for ten, fifteen, twenty steps into the black. Her high school was gone. She knew she was back in that infinitely inescapable version of the Council's chamber where something unseen stalked her. She took a steadying breath, standing there defiantly, refusing to run from it or toward it—wherever her foe may be.

"Strange place," Raiden's voice said beside her.

Her startled gaze lurched around and there he was standing in a pillar of light like that old tome of prophecies deep in the Courts. He was all that existed in the darkness.

"What are you doing here?" She asked, feeling stupid. It was a dream, at least she thought this place was still her dream, and she *had* fallen asleep to the sound of Raiden's voice.

"Just standing here, I suppose, same as you." He said with a shrug.

"Oh." She nodded.

"As long as we're here," he said, offering his hand.

She took it and held fast, afraid he would disappear into the dark like everything else, afraid whatever lurked there would take him, hurt him instead of her. Then she shook her head and caught him in her arms, so grateful not to be alone in this place. The world around them was still an impenetrable inky black fog, there was certainly still something out there, but she wasn't alone. His arms closed around her.

"Don't disappear," she said.

"I won't."

❧

A sudden jostle shook Raiden awake. The small grey room had never looked so good after the bleak darkness of Nicole's dream. He was appalled now to know how she'd been spending every moment of sleep since that night in the courts. He felt Nicole lift her head off his shoulder.

"I think we landed," he said.

She looked up at him groggy, confusion passing across her face, her forehead crumpled over her eyes.

"What is it?"

Her eyes shut. "Nothing."

"Did you sleep all right?"

"I did," she said with a note of surprise in her voice.

"Well then, we better put on our coats."

She turned her face into him again and mumbled something he couldn't decipher.

"What's that?"

"Nothing," she said, lifting her head and scowling as she crawled off the bed and went to the small trunk which Tovar had given to her, much more spacious inside than it appeared. He had given Raiden one just like it.

She bent over her trunk and dug through its contents until she found a sweater, which she pulled over her head. Then she fished out her large brown leather jacket and tossed it onto the bed. She produced a pair of long socks that she pulled over the pair already on her feet before stepping into her lace-up boots.

"Ready," she said gloomily. "I'm going to the wash room real quick." She opened the door and trudged out.

He smiled to himself and opened his own trunk to get himself some more layers. When Nicole didn't wander back into the room after several minutes, he ventured out and caught sight of her down the corridor, standing at the vast viewing window taking in the white world outside lit by the sun just rising over an eastern ridge.

Raiden joined her, silent awe pressing on them both to see the white robed peaks encircling them, a ring of ancient wise men cloaked in winter.

"Welcome to Coron," a velvety voice said behind them.

They turned to see Pep looking wistfully out at the mountains.

"Are you from here?" Raiden wondered.

"Not Coron, I'm from a village in a low valley south of here. But I have family here," she said, her mouth curling. "We should get everyone up," she added, nodding toward the corridor of doors.

❧

By 'everyone' Pep meant Caeruleus, Mitchell and the guards because Loak had been up for more than an hour and was keeping Captain Rhee company at the helm. Bode came out of his room looking like he'd been sitting there waiting for orders since he woke up. Sage, Gregor, Lyana and Netti all emerged ready and dressed. Mitchell didn't even answer the first time Nicole knocked, so she knocked again as Raiden went to Caeruleus' door.

"Mitch, we're here," she said, pounding a little louder this time.

A faint grumble came from within. She knocked a third time until the door finally slid open and Mitchell stood there looking half dead and annoyed.

"Good morning to you too, sunshine," she chuckled. "Time to meet royalty."

"Ugh," he said, letting his head fall to the side and turning back into his room dramatically, grumbling, "Why so early?"

In less than fifteen minutes everyone was standing in the cargo hold ready to descend. Loak went down with their five guards. While the rest of them waited for the elevator to return, Captain Rhee bid them farewell.

"I'll see you lot after I get myself some sleep," she said.

The door opened for them. Nicole, Raiden, Mitchell, Caeruleus and Pep stepped inside the elevator to descend.

"Sleep well," Nicole said.

"Thanks—careful out there," Rhee said gently to her as the door closed.

Nicole frowned. She hadn't yet considered how dangerous it was just to be outside here in Coron. When the door opened for them at the bottom, the morning light reflecting white off the snow hit their eyes. They stepped out into the biting cold air, blind for a few steps. Nicole expected to see no one, that they would be hurrying from the Tempest to get inside somewhere.

But a sudden burst of sound slammed into her, applause and cheers. The overwhelming whiteness receded, and her eyes adjusted to see they had emerged into the middle of a central clearing before a magnificent lodge of stone and wood, a small castle really, that exuded an aura of warmth and comfort. All around the Tempest people were gathered—not a space between shoulders to be seen—a crowd of black faces in a white world. A man with a massive silver fur draped over his shoulders flanked by several others in short cloaks and fur boots wrapped in strips of leather, the king, to be sure, emerged.

"Welcome," he boomed, spreading his arms wide.

As they drew nearer, it was no surprise to see that they were all incredibly tall like Loak and Pep. Here in Coron, it would seem, Loak was not remarkably tall at all. Seven feet was a comfortably average height.

"We're so glad you've come, Kings Nicole and Raiden," he said, stooping to shake Nicole's hand and then Raiden's. "I'm King Eisen. Please, come inside. My home is your home."

He was warm and jovial, but Nicole detected urgency in his voice. He turned back toward the grand lodge and everyone around him followed suit, Pep, Loak, the guards, Caeruleus and Raiden. Nicole and Mitchell exchanged a quick glance and lurched into a jog to catch up and keep up with the incredible strides of King Eisen and his people. The roar of the crowd hushed, replaced by a softer surge of hundreds of feet tromping through the night's fresh powder.

Nicole took one last sweeping look at the peaks surrounding Coron and the clear sky beyond them, half expecting to catch some dark shadow gliding in the distance, but there was only the whisper of a breeze, the icy chill, and the peaceful silence of the mountains. Once they were inside, the monstrous wooden doors were shut behind them, swinging slowly but closing with a deep resounding thud.

Ease fell over the entire party and the tension in everyone's posture slackened.

"I apologize for the hasty greeting," King Eisen said. "It is best to keep indoors. The manticore does not hunt in Coron, but its roar does carry through the mountains often enough. You can imagine the nuisance that alone can be—but forget that for now. We have cast sound-proof spells on our homes. Let us celebrate your arrival properly."

The entrance of the grand castle was impressive—wood beams crossed high above in overlapping patterns that were dizzying to look at. There weren't many windows and so the vast room was dark from the rich brown wood and the shadows filling the space between the beams. The room was lit by conjured lights floating above in the rafters like giant fireflies, and three great fires in the fireplaces—yawning stone mouths as tall as King Eisen—one on each wall.

"My treasures," King Eisen boomed in greeting at the approach of two young women wearing skirts that brushed their fur boots and long vests of the same dark silver fur as their father's pelt belted at their waists. "Come meet our honored guests." They came to stand beside their father, the taller of the two had pale gold eyes that glinted like jewelry. The shorter woman's stare was a piercing dark gold like polished tiger's eye stones.

They both inclined a slow nod toward Nicole and Raiden.

"This is Priseil," King Eisen said looking to his taller daughter on his left. Then he turned to the daughter on his right, "And this is Sigrid."

"Welcome to Coron," said Priseil.

"We're glad you have come," Sigrid said, her attention shifting immediately from Nicole and Raiden to someone beside them.

Nicole followed her gaze to Pep who stepped forward.

Sigrid opened her arms. "Penelopeia," she intoned with affection as Pep caught her face, placing a lingering kiss on her lips.

Nicole's face flushed watching their intimate moment and felt the corners of her mouth curling into a smile. She glanced at Raiden who shared a small envious look with her.

"Go, Pep!" Mitchell cheered quietly beside Nicole.

King Eisen laughed. "Lovers' greetings cannot wait. Come, let us all break fast as family." The hall filled with a cheer of concurrence.

Food was brought in by a team from the kitchens, and everyone took a seat at the large tables around the hall. What was a bar-height table and chair to Nicole was perfectly standard to the people of Orodon. Nicole's feet dangled above the floor, yet their feet were planted firmly on the ground.

Baskets of eggs were placed upon the table as were pots of porridge and platters of cooked meats. Nicole watched as Eisen and his daughters pulled ladles of thick barley porridge from the pots and into their bowls. They grabbed eggs which Nicole was surprised to see were, in fact, raw as they cracked them on the rims of their bowls and opened them into their piping hot porridge, mixing in the raw egg.

Nicole, Raiden and Mitchell all followed the lead of the Orodon royal family, breaking raw eggs into their steaming porridge. Small pots of honey and jams floated along the tables, which fought Nicole's grasp to keep going. When she plucked blackberry jam from the air, it drifted along again the moment she let it go. Pitchers of some warm drink were passed down the table from King Eisen to Priseil, to Nicole.

When she tipped the pitcher over her glass, a thick milk poured out. It was warm and fragrant with cinnamon and cardamom. Nicole passed the pitcher to Raiden then picked up her glass to smell what reminded her of horchata only it smelled more of oats than rice. After taking a curious sip she decided it was spiced oat milk. Nicole stole glances at Sigrid on the other side of King Eisen and Pep beside her who seldom seemed to look away from each other or the little boy sitting in Sigrid's lap eating from her bowl. She felt a pang of sadness for the distance she had created between Raiden and her.

The grand hall seemed full to bursting with warmth and mirth. But her eyes drifted from the faces of people enjoying their food and company to the far wall opposite her where there hung a gargantuan painting clad in a golden frame above the entrance.

The imagery was vivid and large enough for her to see all too clearly even from across the hall. A king of Orodon in the middle of a fray between his men and dragons, a modest band of gold around his head, he was wounded and bloody, staving off the gaping jaws of a dragon with a fierce grip on its fangs. The king's death made glorious and triumphant. She sighed, reminded why Gordan wasn't here.

"Nicole," Eisen's voice startled her. "This young man who looks like you, he is your brother?"

"Yes," she said. "My older brother Mitchell."

"Call me, Mitch," he said, leaning closer from where he sat between Raiden and her.

"And your emissary, Caeruleus, has come with you," he remarked.

"Well," Nicole said, looking past Mitchell and Raiden to Caeruleus who was busy eating and speaking to Raiden. "He is more than an emissary, he's Raiden's brother." She took a bite of her food.

Eisen scrutinized the two of them for a moment, no doubt noting their lack of familial resemblance. "I see—brothers of the heart. And how have you been adjusting to life as a king?"

Nicole almost choked on her mouthful of porridge. "It's certainly not the job I wanted," she said, trying to smile. "Or that I am at all qualified for, but you can't exactly argue with a key."

Eisen erupted with laughter and Nicole grinned timidly.

"I was quite relieved to hear one of the keys was in the hands of a woman," Priseil said. "And the fera no less. I think the key chose well—a woman whose strength demands respect. We heard you destroyed the courts in Atrium singlehandedly."

Nicole's smile turned to a cringe, *no doubt thanks to Andrus*, she thought. "That's…true," she said, unsure how to react.

"You will find nothing but admiration here in Coron, I assure you," Priseil said, turning her pale gold irises to Nicole with a smile.

"Oh," Nicole's face went warm with chagrin. "Thank you."

Mitchell nudged her with his elbow and smiled, that *see-you're-worried-for-nothing* look he loved to give her.

Breakfast lasted until everyone at the tables had leaned back against their chairs in defeat, only then were the pots and pitchers hauled off, the baskets of eggs and dirty bowls whisked away.

A wide man that made Loak look like a delicate creature approached their table, his face stern but he didn't utter a word, only bowed his head in deference to his king.

King Eisen stood and sighed. "This is Borh, my captain. I hope you will forgive me for hurrying into unpleasant matters."

Borh nodded to Nicole and Raiden.

♋

Nicole, Raiden, Mitchell, Caeruleus, and Loak were accompanied to a more private room with King Eisen, his daughters, and Borh. The room was spacious enough to comfortably fit them all with enough room around the table in the center of the room and a fireplace in one corner.

There was a wide low-backed chair draped in pelts on which King Eisen sat, resting his chin in his hand and letting the jovial warmth drain from his expression. The welcome mask fell and his dark face furrowed with concern, his dark yellow eyes burning with worry.

Raiden could see Nicole's body tense as they gathered around the table. A large map was laid out before them showing the mountain ranges of Orodon, the city of Coron and all the other villages tucked into the mountains and valleys around it. Scattered around the map were thick red X marks.

"These are all the villages that are affected by the manticore," Borh said. "Because the sound carries so far, we can only suppose a general area at the center as its most likely location."

"The paralysis hits no matter how faint the sound is, and the effect lingers for almost four hours. Complete paralysis for at least an hour I would say," Priseil added.

Eisen, Sigrid and Borh nodded in agreement.

"How frequently does it happen?" Loak asked.

"Several times a day, even sometimes at night, it would seem the beast knows well enough to use its voice against us. We have tried to deduce its schedule and determine its active hours and when it sleeps. But the times are not consistent enough to approach it safely even if we knew where it was. We do not want to risk lives if we can help it. Unfortunately, we've lost four of our comrades, purely by coming upon the beast by accident," Borh explained.

"We've sent out parties throughout the mountains in hopes of sightings that will point us in the direction of which mountain the manticore has inhabited," Sigrid added. "But so many of the mines are interconnected that it could be using them extensively. It has had a whole winter to learn them," Sigrid added.

"That is a problem," Loak muttered.

"Have you already tried sound muting spells against it?" Raiden wondered.

"They might work if we could cast one big enough to fill the entirety of the mines. But as it stands, the risk is still too high. We wouldn't know if the spell has reached the beast."

"I doubt that would be a problem for Nicole," Mitchell said.

"But there's no telling whether or not the manticore is even in the mines when we cast any spell. It could be gone when we do and return with the full use of its voice. Even in the lucky chance that we could silence it, it takes precious time to find the beast and then subdue it."

"And spells wear off," Caeruleus said.

"Precisely. Four families have already lost loved ones, we are reluctant to try again without a far more secure strategy. Silencing spells, sleeping spells…they are still risky without knowing that they have worked," King Eisen said.

Raiden's gaze drilled into the map, running over each red X, searching the illustrated peaks and valleys for the answer they needed. He looked to Nicole. She was frowning at the map, her eyes focused, then she looked up at him.

"This wouldn't be a problem if we were deaf," Nicole said, then turned to her brother. Mitchell's face lit up, but everyone else in the room was silent, exchanging blank looks stuck in the uncertainty between reactions.

"We could cast a temporary spell," Raiden said, looking at Loak.

Beside Raiden Caeruleus shook his head a little in disbelief. "That's—"

For a fraction of a second Raiden expected doubt.

"—brilliant," Caeruleus said.

"At this point *hearing* is your biggest problem," Mitchell said, sounding on the verge of laughter.

"But it replaces one problem with another," Borh said. "Telepathic bonds are more trouble than they are worth when you try to link too many people. In high stress situations you do not want to be sharing one linked mind."

"Mitch can teach everyone sign," Nicole said with a tiny shrug. Mitchell nodded.

"Sign?" Sigrid asked.

"Sign Language," Mitchell said. "Words made by your hands. It shouldn't be too hard to teach you the basics, just what we'll need to get through the mission."

"Without having to worry about paralysis, we just have to outnumber it and have a solid strategy," Caeruleus said.

"This can work," Priseil said.

"I have no doubt," Sigrid agreed.

They spent the next hour discussing the possible strategies for taking on the manticore: how to track it down and how to lure it out of the mines. They had no idea how a manticore would behave when its adversaries turned out to be immune to its roar. Perhaps it would flee when confronted by able-bodied foes.

"If it were to run, can't we just chase it somewhere remote?" Nicole asked. "Being unaffected by the paralysis allows us to treat it like any other animal, albeit still a dangerous one, but if it lived somewhere else before it showed up here, why can't we relocate it?"

"That's certainly a far more difficult solution than destroying the beast. There's no guarantee it wouldn't come back," Borh said.

"There's no guarantee a different manticore couldn't show up some day," Nicole said, folding her arms. "Should we set out to kill them all?" In the corner the flames swelled inside the mouth of the fireplace.

Raiden tensed, catching the glance Mitchell gave him with wide eyes.

Borh scoffed. "Of course not, just the one that's a problem. May I remind you it has already taken four of our own."

"Killing it won't bring them back. Is this about retribution or the safety of your people? If we can reclaim your mines without turning into monsters who slaughter a creature just trying to exist in this world like any of us are, then shouldn't we try? Maybe it's not possible, maybe we have no choice but to kill it, fine. But I refuse to partake if that is the only option."

Borh looked ready to say something until Sigrid spoke. "We are not bloodthirsty people," she said with assertive calm. "Humane removal of the creature should be our goal if at all possible, and it should be far more plausible without the threat of paralysis. We have the time and wherewithal to prepare ourselves."

"Perhaps we should take some time to wind down, let our guests settle in for their stay, and we can return to this matter with lighter minds," Priseil suggested.

"Splendid idea," King Eisen said, rising from his seat.

Borh grumbled in agreement.

Raiden could breathe a little easier as Nicole's irritated posture slackened and her arms fell to her sides once more. He took her hand and the hard line of her mouth softened.

They followed Sigrid and Priseil out of the room.

"You'll all be staying in the East Wing," Priseil explained as she led them back to the grand hall first and then to the eastern wing of the castle.

Raiden caught Nicole looking pointedly at the wall above the entrance to the grand hall—a towering painting hanging over the doors and reaching up toward the ceiling, almost filling the wall in its entirety if not for the doors and the windows on either side. In fact, everyone seemed to notice it now without the distraction of food and conversation. They all slowed as they passed, taking in the scene of the king fighting, wounded and bloodied, atop the body of a dead dragon while staving off the jaws of another with his bare hands.

"That's King Torvald. Thanks to him Orodon is the only kingdom that didn't fall to the dragons," Sigrid said, her voice brimming with admiration.

Raiden could see Nicole's thoughts churning behind the mournful expression on her face as she looked upon the painting. No one could blame the people of Orodon for their fear and hatred of the dragons that had waged a brutal and fiery conquest against the realm.

Could dragons like Gordan ever redeem themselves after what the Dragon King had wrought? If Nicole and Mitchell could forgive Caeruleus after being loyal and misled by the Council, surely there was a way to heal the damage done by the dragon wars. He had no doubt Nicole was turning this question over and over in her mind.

Perhaps it was Gordan waiting back at the palace weighing on everyone's mind that kept all of them—even Loak—from finding anything to say to Sigrid until she had her fill of admiring her great-great-great grandfather and continued on to the wide staircase waiting for them to the left of the entrance.

Sigrid led them past several doors. "Your guards have already been shown to their rooms, here," she said gesturing to the doors. Given how few paces were between each door they were each given small private rooms not far from the top of the stairs. She turned the corner and proceeded down a much longer hall with fewer doors.

"Is this where all the visiting royalty stays?" Mitchell joked.

"I suppose. You're the first royal visitors to Coron since we rebuilt after the wars," Sigrid said lightly. "They're all the same really. One for each of you," she said turning back to them. Her eyes shifted down a moment and then back up, spying Nicole's hand in Raiden's. "Or to share, of course," she added with a curled mouth and a pleased look. "I'll leave you to—"

Red lights appeared in the roof beams overhead like a sudden swarm of angry light bugs, pulsing in warning.

"What's that about?" Nicole asked.

"It's an alert that the manticore can be heard at the moment. They'll flash until the last of the echoes die so that we know when the air is clear," Sigrid said. "It will probably roar again, when it's out and about. It tends to do that. We know it's intelligent enough to know the effect it has and use it to hunt. Paralyze everything on the mountain and then track down its prey."

"At least you've learned its patterns to an extent," Loak offered. "The system you have in place seems to work well."

"Well enough to get by for now, but we cannot mine with it here. Our stored resources will eventually run out, and we will have nothing to sell or trade. The manticore affects the bulk of our mines right now, not just the tunnels that it's chosen to dwell in but even the other mines—" she paused, watching the lights fluctuate like a beating heart. They stopped. "We cannot sound-proof whole mountains, the minerals and magic within them interfere too much. Forgive me, we were taking some time free of this topic to clear our heads. Please, make yourselves at home. Priseil and I can show you around Coron this afternoon."

Sigrid glanced down at Raiden and Nicole's clasped hands and smiled as she left.

"No pressure," Mitchell said under his breath.

"I suppose I'll take this one," Loak said, turning to the closest door and leaving the rest of them in the hall.

Raiden, Nicole, Mitchell and Caeruleus stood looking down the hall at the other doors. Caeruleus took the room across from Loak's.

"I wonder what the view is like in here," Mitchell said pressing his lips together and disappearing into the next door down from Caeruleus.

"Should we take the two at the end of the hall?" Raiden asked, looking to her.

She looked ahead at the two doors across from each other, then at him. "Why? We only need one," she said.

"All right," he said, so pleased his face went hot and his heart skipped. "I suppose one room is enough space."

She shook her head. "Two weeks in a palace and you're already spoiled," she said, starting down the hall, pulling him along because he wasn't about to let her hand go.

They stepped into their room. The bed was wide enough for three people to sleep comfortably, it was small compared to the one in his chamber back at the palace, but utterly expansive after the tiny single person mattress aboard the Tempest.

"Bed seems a little small," Raiden said.

A quiet laugh escaped her but her smile fell.

"That idea you and Mitchell came up with," he said, thinking he knew what she needed to hear.

She pulled her hand from his. "Ah ah," she said, wagging her finger. "This is time away from the strategy room." She walked into the edge of the bed and turned, falling onto her back.

"Right," he nodded and stepped toward the bed to let himself fall beside her. He let the silence press on them for a moment before breaking it. "What do you suppose Gordan is doing?"

She inhaled and sighed. "He'll be in the tower, as usual," she said wistfully, her gaze peering into the wood beams crossing above her.

∾

Gordan wandered as far as he could in the circular confines of the tower, strolling when he was confident nothing would go wrong, pacing when he worried about not being there with them, occasionally pausing in the center of the room and gazing lazily across Veil into the mountains of Orodon.

The tower allowed him to watch the Tempest land in the city of Coron like he was there. The telescope eyes of the tower had no limit it would seem. He watched Nicole, Raiden and Mitchell disembark from the ship and disappear into the king's castle. Standing on the eye in the center of the room made it seem like he was close enough to say their names and see their heads turn to answer him, but the disconnect of distance was undeniable as he watched the crowds of people clapping and howling when there was nothing but the silence of the tower in his ears.

Soon he anchored himself on the eye and watched the skies over Orodon, searching for the manticore. When he spotted its dark shape gliding through the snowy peaks, his jaw clenched. It opened its mouth, but the roar was mute, just a gaping maw, rows of teeth, set into a contorted face halfway between a large cat and a man.

Gordan shuddered to know that whoever heard that soundless roar was paralyzed now. He scanned the mountains until he found the Tempest again, resting in the center of Coron. There didn't appear to be anyone outside, and he hoped they were all safe from the sound indoors. When he tried to relocate the manticore he could find it nowhere. At least it had no interest in the city seeing as he couldn't spot it anywhere overhead. Still, he spent the morning and afternoon looking for it—he had nothing better to do.

He didn't see people out in the open again all morning until several people emerged from the castle, marched to the Tempest and returned to the castle lugging chests and bags. Gordan lost interest in their faces once he saw they weren't Nicole or Mitchell or Raiden. So, he went back to keeping watch for the manticore, a help to no one as a look-out halfway across the mainland, but at last a party emerged from the castle and this time he spotted Nicole, brown curls crowding her face beneath a dark, fur-lined hood.

Nicole spoke to Raiden and then Loak, who pointed toward

Gordan in the tower. She turned and waved, throwing her arm in as large an arc as she could, smiling like she could see him as clearly as he saw her. Mitchell spoke to her. She answered and he turned to wave as well. Gordan smiled.

Twenty-two

"Who are you waving at?" Mitchell asked, his breath came out in white puffs in the afternoon mountain air.

"Gordan," Nicole said.

"Oh," Mitchell waved too. "Can he see us?"

"I don't know," she admitted. "But it felt good to wave to him anyway." She dropped her arm.

"Who is Gordan?" Priseil asked her, looking to the west curiously.

"My best friend back at the palace—he couldn't come," Nicole said.

"Wasn't Sigrid coming with us?" Raiden asked.

"She wanted some more time alone with Penelopeia," Priseil said, a smile pulling at her mouth. "Loak and I will show you around Coron."

"And you're certain it's safe?" Caeruleus asked, glancing at Raiden.

"There's always a risk that we could hear the manticore, twice is the most we usually hear it so our odds are pretty good now after the second time today. Even if we were to be so unfortunate, we just fall in the snow and they'll come get us after the sound dies."

"That's reassuring," Caeruleus muttered.

"Still we should get moving," Priseil added.

"Are there remedies to the paralysis?" Caeruleus asked.

"Oh, yes. We used up our stores of ingredients for that potion weeks ago, and we are awaiting a delivery of the herbs we need from Eanna. Queen Belen graciously agreed to send us as much as she could. For now, we can only wait out the paralysis," she said, leading them away from the castle and across the open square at the center of Coron.

The snow was nearly a foot thick and in the middle of the square it was fresh and undisturbed by the morning gathering to welcome their arrival. Nicole couldn't help smiling at the novelty of it, picking up her feet in a high marching tromp, creating a satisfying crunch of each step.

"Hey," Mitchell said beside her. "How hard would it be to make a sound bubble for this whole place? Like what they have for the buildings but…bigger?"

"I don't know," she answered. It would certainly make daily life that much easier for the people of Coron, but when Priseil heard Mitchell's question and turned a desperately hopeful look toward her, Nicole worried she couldn't deliver. "No reason not to try, I guess," she said, hoping to coax her confidence back out.

Someone placed his hand on her arm. She turned to see past her hood—it was Raiden. He looked at her like he could hear her self-doubt as surly as Gordan would have felt it. And then suddenly she was annoyed with herself— even angry—*of course I can do this. I can do more than just destroy things.*

Nicole took a deep breath, wondering if this would be easier with a spell, but they were already here and everyone was watching. She closed her eyes because she didn't want to see everyone else's on her. It was so quiet in the square with everyone waiting anxiously.

"Mitch," she said, keeping her eyes closed. "Sing something."

He chuckled, "Okay." Then he began, "*Bicycle, Bicycle, Bicycle. I want to ride my bicycle…*"

Nicole laughed, held her gloved hands in front her, and thought about putting a bubble around herself. "I want to hear myself, I want to hear myself," she whispered as she let her magic out, repeating those words until she could no longer hear Mitchell. She opened her eyes to see his mouth moving and he tipped his head this way and that as he sang.

"It worked," Raiden said beside her. When she looked to him, she realized there was a shimmer in the air between them and everyone else, confused looks on Caeruleus and Priseil's faces as they listened to Mitchell sing.

With another deep breath she let more magic out until her body burned and funneled it through her arms, moving her hands apart and pushing against the tiny sound-proof space around Raiden and her. The spell expanded past Priseil who was suddenly unable to hear Mitchell.

"It's working," she cried excitedly.

Nicole cringed, pushing the spell past Mitchell, still singing, "*I don't believe in Peter Pan, Frankenstein or Superman...*"

She could feel the fire in her bones, in her eyes, so she closed them and pushed harder until her ears rang, and she couldn't hear Mitchell anymore. She knew her hands were shaking furiously with the effort, and they felt like they would shatter.

"Nicole, stop," Raiden said, his voice thin and distant to her ringing ears.

Her vision went black for a moment, not an unconscious darkness, a memory—of darkness and ringing in her ears, the Council before her, faces contorted and panicked, no trace of that cold superior composure as one of their own sat impaled to his chair. And then the world was white again. The ringing quieted and the heat subsided. She blinked, looking down at her naked hands.

"Jeez Nikki, you burned your gloves clean off," Mitchell said, his voice lacking the humor she knew he was trying for.

"I—oh—I didn't realize it would take so much effort," she said and looked up at Raiden to see worry still clinging to his face.

He shook his head. "You never cease to amaze me," he murmured.

"Nicole," Priseil cried, lunging at her and catching her in her arms. She lifted Nicole off her feet like a child in an adult's embrace. "You are incredible!"

"Thank you," Nicole said sheepishly as Priseil spun her around and set her back down.

"No, thank *you*. Look," she insisted, pointing to the edge of the spell, a shimmer in the air that glowed more brightly where it touched the snow, creating a line. "You've sheltered the whole square and then some."

"Nicely done," Caeruleus said.

"We have to go tell Father and Sigrid," Priseil said, turning toward the castle and loping toward the doors.

It was impossible for any of them but Loak to keep up with the length of her strides, but they followed.

"This certainly makes getting around Coron less troublesome until we sort this all out," Raiden said.

Nicole's head was spinning as they stepped through the snow toward the castle, her skin still tingling, giddy from her triumph and a little dizzy from the expenditure of magic. A laugh expanded in her chest and she almost let it out when a low heavy crunch of snow from behind them made her turn.

The air whooshed from her lungs at the sight of massive lion-like beast an arm's length away. It looked her dead in the eyes. Her heart stopped. Before she could open her mouth, it opened its jaws and a deafening roar hit her ears like a dissonant blast from countless horns. Her body went numb and slack. The world tilted back. The sky fell across her vision, and she heard herself hit the snow with a muffled crunch as the brassy roar echoed in the air.

She knew this feeling—a body she couldn't move while death loomed over her. Her heart went careening back to Atrium, to the cold hard floor of the courts beneath her and the Council looking down at her. Had anyone inside the castle seen? Would they come to help or would they watch the manticore feed?

The crunching of the beast's steps approaching through the snow hastened her breathing into short panicked gasps. She heard the beast snort, could see it investigating her, raising its head to sniff the air and lower it back to her.

No. This isn't how it ends. Then the manticore turned its head to—what? Someone else in the snow—who had been right beside her?—*Raiden, Mitchell?* Her heartbeat turned to a hum of panic and fear and anger, then came the surge of fire from deep in her core. It rushed through her and suddenly the numbness turned to the pins-and-needles-pain of sleeping limbs, but she could move enough to roll herself over and raise her hand toward the beast.

She let out another wave, feeling like she'd crumple into ash as it rolled through her. The energy tore at her veins, down her arm, and through her hand. The pulse rolled through the air. She wasn't quite sure what she'd done. All she knew was how terrified she was and she let her magic out. Then to her shock, the manticore turned and fled like *it* was scared.

Nicole sagged, propping herself up in the snow despite the half-numb pain shooting through her arm and watching the manticore beat its black wings to escape the snow-clad earth. All she could hear was her heart pounding and her gasping breaths in her head. Her body felt like lead laced with a million needles.

She tried to get up and fell onto her belly instead. *I'm moving,* she told herself as she panted. *I shouldn't be moving and I'm moving.* Her magic had partly cleansed the paralysis. *Come on, come back,* she thought, reaching into that deep place once more. Gently this time, she let her magic spread through her, not a swath of fire but a tide of warm soothing water that washed away the pain of her deadened limbs until at last she could move them. At last her arms could bare the weight and she pushed herself up.

༄

Gordan stood in the center of the tower, trying to catch his breath, his hands in his hair, nails biting into his scalp as he tried to calm himself—the manticore was gone, and he watched as Nicole picked herself up from the snow—*she's all right,* he thought, his breaths short and quick.

He pulled his trembling hands away from his head and looked

at them, realizing they were too large for human hands and scaled, claws in place of nails, half-way transformed in his panic. He willed them back to the shape of delicate human hands and pushed them back into his hair, appreciating with a wry twitch of his mouth that this was what Raiden did when he was stressed.

He took steadying breaths. "She's all right. They're all okay," he said on each exhale. It had happened so fast, in the span of mere seconds the manticore was there. He should have been watching the sky instead of Nicole.

He let out a bitter laugh, *and what would I have done from here?* Gordan sighed, relieved to see Nicole helping Raiden to his feet. He threw his arms around her tightly, and Gordan felt a pang of sadness that he could not do the same. He dropped his head into his hands and rubbed his face slowly.

Whatever spell Nicole had cast in Coron was as good as baiting the manticore. She filled the valley with magic, and like any other creature it couldn't help being drawn to it. He dropped his hands, and the tension in his shoulders went slack when he saw Nicole helping Mitchell sit up.

I should be there, he thought and then begrudgingly recognized that he would have been just as paralyzed as everyone else and absolutely no help, just as he was standing in the tower watching from afar. He needed to step off that eye and herd his thoughts elsewhere for a while. The owls watched him walk to the open window and sit down.

☙

Raiden rolled Caeruleus over—like Mitchell and him, Caeruleus had collapsed face down in the snow. Nicole hurried over, dropped beside Caeruleus and placed her hand on his chest. After several seconds Caeruleus groaned and sat up on his own.

"Where is it?" he asked.

"Gone," Nicole said.

"I didn't see a single thing," Raiden admitted. "I heard it and next thing I knew I was face down in the snow."

Caeruleus nodded and so did Mitchell.

"Maybe we should get inside," Mitchell said, offering his hand to Caeruleus as Raiden stood up.

Nicole gasped. "Priseil." She jumped up and looked toward the castle, lurching into a run.

Priseil was slumped against the closed doors. From across the square Raiden could see Nicole take Priseil's hands and hold them close to her. After several moments Priseil lifted her head away from the door.

"Oh stars," she breathed. "I thought we were safe—I don't think I've ever heard it so loud—your spell…"

"It was inside the spell with us," Nicole said with a cringe.

Priseil stood up. "Everyone inside." She opened one of the doors, and they filed in before she shut it hard with a comforting, resonating thud. Then they all relaxed.

"At first I thought the spell backfired," Mitchell said.

"I cast it to keep sound out, it's not a force field," Nicole muttered.

"It's not your fault," Raiden said.

"I think it is. I think all that magic attracted it."

"You mean it was drawn to you?" Priseil asked.

"It's happened with animals before."

"And plants," Mitchell added.

"But if the manticore was in the square, if it was that close— what happened?" Priseil frowned.

"I didn't see anything," Caeruleus said. "I heard it and then I was face down in the snow. I was confused then intensely afraid."

"Yeah," Mitchell said. "Same."

"I heard something hit the snow behind us," Nicole explained. "I turned in time to see it before it roared and I collapsed. It just seemed curious to be honest, it came close enough that I could see it from where I fell. When it turned to Raiden, I was so scared. I just let my magic out and it ran."

"Maybe you filled the air with your own fear and made it feel what you were feeling. Why else would it run scared from defense-less people?" Raiden mused.

"Lucky for us," Priseil said. "But does this mean with you here the manticore might take an interest in Coron?"

"It could," Nicole admitted and her chest went heavy with guilt. "My spell out there might be more trouble than its worth. If the manticore keeps coming around because of me, then I have a better idea to keep your people safe."

❦

Gordan couldn't keep himself from watching Orodon for long. He returned to the center of the room, his desire to watch was stronger than the torture of his inability to be there. It was a relief to see Nicole appear outside once more. He scanned the sky anxiously, but it was clear. When he dared to turn his eyes back to Nicole, he saw she was unraveling the spell she had cast not two hours past.

Once her spell was no more, she returned to the castle, pausing to look in his direction before she disappeared through the doors. Her expression was drastically changed from the smiling face she had cast his way earlier, a frown carved deep into her visage—regret, guilt—a triumph turned sour far too quickly.

Over the next few days he spent most of his time keeping watch over the skies above Nicole. He saw people emerge from the castle now and then and soon there were lamp posts standing all around Coron that flashed violently red in response to the manticore's roar in the air.

The near deserted scene of Coron changed almost overnight. People were out and about, and when the red lights flashed, they all looked to sky. Then gradually Gordan noticed a change in people's behavior. They moved their hands more when speaking to each other, only he realized no one speaking at all—they were talking solely with their hands, making shapes one after another slowly and methodically.

When he caught sight of Nicole and Mitchell and saw the comfortable movements of their hands, he knew precisely who was behind this new custom in Coron. It looked like they had a solution after all, they eliminated the manticore's advantage by giving up their hearing. He smiled, proud and brimming with questions he couldn't ask. How were they inducing deafness? How did Nicole and Mitchell know this hand language? What was their plan for the manticore now? The people could live their lives, but the beast had claimed some of their mines, and there was certainly no way the king would give those up. Deafness did not remove all the dangers of taking on a manticore.

A knock at the tower door perplexed Gordan for a moment and he stepped off the eye, steadying himself for the dizzy transition of his gaze from Orodon to the room around him. All the people who would be looking for him were in Orodon. He bent down at the door and opened it to see Asi crouched below. She stood up, smiling.

"Hello," he said.

"Nicole said you might not come out. It's been four days you know," she said, looking around the tower.

"I am aware," he answered, hearing the consternation in his own voice.

"Well, they said they hadn't seen you in the kitchens at all, so I brought you something in case you're hungry," she said, crouching again, disappearing for a moment before standing back up into the doorway with a plate piled with cooked and cured meats, and some fruit.

"Thank you." He took the plate and she smiled at him again. Conversation with Raiden, Mitchell and Nicole had become easy. Conversation with other people was not. Since Asi wasn't leaving, he turned to the only thing he knew about her. "You can erase memories, isn't that right?"

The corners of her mouth dropped a little, but her smile didn't shrink entirely away. "I *take* memories," she said. "You can't really erase them. They have to go somewhere. You can bury them, like what Raiden did, and you forget, but they're still there somewhere."

"I see." Then that was the reason for the deep caverns of sorrow in her, but those shadowy depths were peaceful beneath her bright aura. He had spent so long alone before Nicole that he'd forgotten what a challenge it was to live around others. When he could not help but feel what those around him felt, he could sometimes lose track of his own emotions in the flood of others'.

"Is it confusing, having other people's memories mingling with your own?"

"No, not at all," she laughed. "Not because they aren't mine. Once I take a memory from someone it becomes mine like any memory. But I've never taken more than a few days' worth of time from someone. They do become my experiences in a way, but they don't confuse my identity or the memories I have made because they are just pieces. I think it would be different if I took someone's entire life of memories, then it might be hard to know the difference between them and me."

Whatever memories Asi carried with her, other people's pain or tragedies, they seemed to be the substance from which her gentle mirth grew. Nicole's sorrows, on the other hand, were sinkholes lurking beneath her path.

"Thank you. For the food and for something new to ponder."

"Of course. Uh, when should I come back?"

"I'm sorry?"

"With more food. Every four days can't be enough," she said, laughing.

"Nonsense, you're no one's servant. I will come down and eat."

"Great. I'll see you then," she said with a nod and disappeared through the doorway calling, "Goodbye Gordan."

❧

Nicole realized she had the wrong room when she stepped through the doorway to find Caeruleus reading in the small library. He looked up from his book from the wide chair beside the fireplace.

"Oh, hi," she said, caught by his attention before she could duck out of the room.

"Hello," he answered and she struggled to read his soft flat voice—was it sadness she heard, discomfort, dislike? She thought of what Raiden said, *talk to him.*

"I was just looking for Mitchell," she said, immediately feeling foolish for offering unsolicited information.

"I haven't seen him," he said, looking at her and blinking his eye.

"I'm pretty sure he's with Raiden somewhere," she muttered mostly to herself.

"Can't you move through the ether? You're good at it, like Raiden."

Nicole heard a trace of envy in his voice and remembered what Gordan had said. *Is he really jealous and ashamed?* It sure felt like he hated her…but she knew Gordan wasn't wrong about these things.

"I could, but he might be on the toilet, and I doubt either of us would appreciate that," she said, cringing toward the ceiling at the idea.

She was relieved to see Caeruleus smile a little, but it seemed weighed down by something.

"Do you not like ether shifting? Mitch hates it." She shrugged.

He looked at her with dazed confusion on his face, then understanding hit. "I've never been good at it."

"Oh."

"Raiden always excelled at it. I was so jealous of him when we were kids," he said, an affectionate curl in the corner of his mouth. "He tried his best to teach me, but I could never get any farther than across a room, or as far as I could see really."

"But in Tucson I saw you—" she stopped herself, cringing. *Why did you have to bring that up?*

"Right," he said, seemingly unphased by their arrival at the incident that robbed him of an eye. "I used a shift token to get back to the portal that day."

Her chest went tight and words rolled up her throat before she could quell the guilt. "I'm sorry about your eye."

Caeruleus actually laughed. "Thank you, but to be fair, I deserved it."

The deep blue gaze of his one eye was piercing.

"No, you didn't. You were being used. The Council—"

"It's kind of you to try to absolve my actions—but I knew what I was doing. I could have questioned the Council sooner. The only reason I defied them at all was because of Raiden. First, they were trying to blame him, and when you showed up looking for him, it was clear there was something between you. It's the same reason you're sorry for what you did, right—because of Raiden, because he cares about me? If it had been any other agent's eye would you feel bad about it?"

Nicole opened her mouth but didn't immediately have an answer. The truth was she wouldn't feel bad about any other agent's eye. She sighed. "Of course, I feel bad because your Raiden's friend. He talked about you so much I felt like *I knew you*. You matter to him, so you matter to me. It seems like all I'm good at anymore is hurting people," she hesitated.

"Honestly, I figured you hated me after what I did. Your brother sure does."

"Mitch is protective of me like Raiden is of you," Nicole offered. "He might be a jerk sometimes but he doesn't hate you…I certainly don't hate you. I was a little worried that you might hate me because of your eye and your wings…maybe even because of the danger I put Raiden in."

"I can't hate you for my eye, *or* my wings—those things...flying was amazing, but they granted the Council control of me through the oath I swore. I couldn't disobey their direct orders. When you came to the Council's chamber that night, I wasn't entirely in control of myself anymore."

Nicole shuddered, knowing the feeling.

Caeruleus continued, "I do worry about Raiden…and maybe I've been jealous that you got to be there for him when I should have been—but I've been gone for a decade, and I'm glad he found someone. You know, I wouldn't have him back at all if not for you." Caeruleus shrugged.

Nicole's face went hot, Caeruleus was the second person to say that.

Mitchell marched into the room. He pulled his flat hand away from his head almost like a salute and then moved his fist down in a spiral—*hi Nikki*—wearing the leather cuff that made him deaf so long as he had it on. They all wore their deaf charms more often for the practice. He stopped and looked at Caeruleus whose posture went tense. She was ready to smack Mitchell so that he would be nice when he raised his hand in another *hello* to Caeruleus.

"Hi," he answered, looking a little stunned and then remembering to sign instead.

Nicole sighed. She pointed to herself, cupped her hand in front of her face like a C, traced a couple circles around her nose, and pointed at him—*I was looking for you.* She pulled her brows down, crossed her fingers in the R sign and placed them across her chest below her collar bone, then shook her index finger—*where is Raiden?*

Mitchell shrugged.

"Caeruleus, when was the last time you saw Raiden?" she asked, turning to Caeruleus.

"I think after breakfast. He was with King Eisen."

Mitchell leaned into Nicole's line of sight, put his left palm up, put his middle finger to the butt of his hand and dragged it to his fingertips like he was striking a match—*RUDE.* She'd broken the cardinal rule of inclusion with a deaf person present. She rolled her eyes and summoned his cuff into her hand.

"Come on, we're practicing," he said, his smile undermining the carefully-composed hurt tone.

"You're just trying to be annoying, come on. Let's go find Raiden."

"Okay," he said, his tone relaxing. "Later Caeruleus," he added over his shoulder.

~

Gordan's impatience for Nicole's return was thin by the end of the second week. He wanted to know if Nicole was sleeping all right and if the wounds were still as bad as ever. Sleeping without incident should have been a relief to him, yet waking up without bleeding was strangely unsettling to him. He needed to know what they were planning inside the castle where the tower's sight could not reach them. He'd grown so antsy watching the manticore prowl the skies around Coron every day since the incident in the square that Asi took notice and came to check on him if he didn't appear in the kitchens to eat with her and Fen every day.

When he saw a gathering of people in the square at the first light of morning, he leaned into the scene, urging the tower's sight closer until he could see Nicole's face peaking out from her hood, and Mitchell's when he turned to talk to someone. Gordan counted heads, those of the shorter forms and the much taller ones. Nicole, Mitchell, Raiden with his sword on his back, Caeruleus with a crossbow in hand, the five guards, Loak, the King of Orodon, two women who flanked him, and ten more.

Gordan's heart lurched with the realization that this was it, the hunting party. They made their way onto the Tempest, having to divide into several smaller groups to take the elevator up. The ridiculously slow process drove him mad. He knew this wasn't going to be a swift endeavor—they didn't know where the manticore was. Not even he had managed to figure that out after two weeks of stalking its movements in the skies from across the mainland. It was impossible to see precisely where in the mountains it made its den.

He struggled to reclaim his patience as the Tempest departed from Coron and carried the hunting party a relatively short distance to a ridge only two peaks away, but it would have taken a party an entire day or more to reach on foot. Gordan hadn't spent much time traveling on foot in human form, and he supposed that guess to be generous for most humans although maybe not the people of Orodon, who tread easily through the deeper snow. The snow was deep enough, in fact, that the Tempest did not land, it opened its cargo door and the hunting party jumped down to land safely in the bed of white powder waiting for them. Then the ship left them.

Naturally, the king of Orodon's men led the way, setting the pace and creating a path through the snow that allowed Nicole and Raiden's shorter half of the party to follow without trouble. They hiked like this for an hour, occasionally stopped and moved their hands in sign to one another, pointing in one direction and then another. Gordan wished he understood the shapes and movements more intimately, but he supposed they were deciding which tunnels to search.

"That can't be their plan," he muttered. If they went into the tunnels—even protected from the manticore's roar—they could easily be cornered. Of course, they had Nicole, but her abilities were rather unpredictable of late. Gordan knew her well enough that her plan didn't involve killing the beast, but she hadn't been herself in weeks and she was not infallible.

The exchange was short and to his surprise Nicole assumed the front of the group. It made little sense to him at first as she struggled through the knee-deep snow until the snow melted all around her and the cold brown earth turned green. She marched, leaving a swath of Spring behind her as the rest of the party followed. Every head moved constantly to scan the mountain and the sky.

The Manticore had been drawn to her once, and they had every reason to believe it would be again. Five minutes passed. Gordan spotted it an agonizing minute before the first arm raised to point from within the group. He could see it open its jaws once, twice, but the party was unphased, and the manticore swooped down on them. From where Gordan stood all he could see was disorder. The manticore hit the ground almost landing in the middle of them and they scattered to avoid the reach of its barbed tail, swinging back and forth. Nicole got closer.

"What are you doing?" Gordan demanded under his breath.

Two nearby bodies sagged.

Paralysis? Had they been struck by the barbs? But then the manticore stumbled, struggling to hold its weight up, its leather wings, flopping lethargically but failing awkwardly as it sank to the ground. Gordan let out a laugh. She put it to sleep.

Caeruleus raised his crossbow and fired into the air, the arrow soared and then erupted in a red flash. Not a minute later the Tempest swooped over a nearby peak and approached their location.

They're planning to move it, he realized on the verge of laughter. Of course, Nicole convinced them to relocate it. It was a hundred times more dangerous than killing it right there. He wanted to scold her and hug her at the same time. But excited movement in the hunting party made Gordan's heart twinge with unease.

Some of the king's men threw their arms up in celebration, howling into the air. Gordan saw them pluck leather cuffs from their wrists. The tallest figure put up a stern hand, it wasn't time to celebrate yet, but the jubilant spirit could not be quelled even by their king's hand. The king removed his cuff and spoke, scolding his men into silence.

One of his men stepped forward, a hunting knife in hand, he snarled, pointing his blade at the manticore. Nicole stepped in front of him and one of her guards, a woman, lunged forward to stand beside her. Gordan could see Nicole was practically snarling as she spoke, raising her hand to the Tempest. The man with the knife barked back, pointing at the sleeping beast.

The King of Orodon spoke, then one of his daughters stepped forward and stood beside Nicole. The man sneered and put his knife away. Gordan eased in unison with Nicole until he glanced up and saw a familiar shape gliding over the mountain on leathery black wings.

∾

Nicole relaxed to see Borh's knife return to its sheath. She glanced toward the Tempest as it approached, and then Borh barreled between Priseil and her, shoving her to the ground and burying his knife into the manticore's neck with both hands and dragging it through fur and flesh, opening a bleeding maw that spilled steaming red onto the glistening new growth of wild flowers.

She screamed, only able to feel the angry grating sound in her throat with the silencing cuff still on her arm. Then half the party collapsed, King Eisen, Borh and most of his men. In a frenzy of movement, she saw another manticore hit the ground. It lunged for them, catching Priseil's arm in its jaws before throwing its head and tearing her limb away as easily as plucking a flower petal. Priseil's arm flew into the air among a spray of red glistening in the daylight and she staggered into Sigrid's arms, clutching her bleeding shoulder.

Nicole scanned the chaos frantically for Mitchell and Raiden as Lyana hit her at a run, pushing her aside as the manticore lunged again. Lyana fell beneath it. Rows of blood-stained teeth sank into her thigh and pulled away, leaving a gaping red crater in her leg. Nicole scrambled to her where she lay there shaking, her face white as the snow and her eyes wide. For a moment Nicole saw Roxanne's wide eyes. *'I've got you'* came out of her mouth but neither she nor Lyana could hear those flimsy words. Nothing could comfort the pallid horror on her face. In a panic she thought of a belt and it appeared around Lyana's thigh above the wound. Her hands fumbled to synch it tight. Then as suddenly as the manticore was there, another massive form erupted from nowhere, crashing out of ether and into the manticore, a familiar blur of scales. *Gordan?!*

She tried to stand Lyana up, to get her away from the fight. She saw Gregor trying to pull one of King Eisen's paralyzed men away from getting trampled only to be struck by the manticore's spiny tail in the chest and drop. Raiden and Caeruleus appeared beside them each taking one of the fallen bodies and shifting through the ether away from the fight. Nicole searched frantically for Mitchell, then Lyana's hand gripped her arm fiercely as the wrestling beasts tumbled toward them and Gordan's tail swung, swatting them clean off the ridge. Nicole held onto Lyana.

Fly, she thought. But she was lead. They were falling. She tried to pull them into the ether but couldn't think of where to go. All she could think was the manticore's blood spilling across the ground at Borh's feet, the look of horror and shock on Lyana's face—her leg torn apart—*she's bleeding out.* And Priseil's arm. *Will Gordan be all right? Where was Mitchell*—she hadn't seen him anywhere—*oh god where is he?* What if she lost them both? She couldn't tear her thoughts away from the deepening pit of dread, could not unravel her magic knotted tight in shock inside her. Then her world went black before she felt herself hit the ground.

☙

She was in darkness, alone, dazed, unsure if this was the darkness she knew well or the one you don't return from after falling off a mountain and forgetting how to fly. The answer found her, slicing through her doubt and her skin. *You're still here, you get to live with the fact that you failed. You messed it all up. You may have lost Mitchell, even Gordan, because you couldn't just kill it like they wanted. You had to make it about you, about being better than the Council. Well great job.*

She was vaguely aware of each cut as she waded back toward consciousness. *Wake up,* she thought. *Stop this—wake up.* But she was numb, and she couldn't move. Then something shook her hard, jarring her awake. Her eyes snapped open to Gordan's face. His mouth moved but she heard nothing through the thick magical silence in her ears.

She sat up, achy and slow, wedged deep into snow, no wonder she couldn't move. When she reached for the leather cuff, she saw the blood all over her thick coat. The snow all around her was red with blood and she thought of Lyana. She pulled the cuff off and sound hit her ears with a startling pop.

"Say something, Nicole," Gordan spoke, his voice soft and steady, but his face pinched with concern.

"You're here," was all she could think to say.

He smiled. "Yes, I'm here, and you're bleeding, quite a lot."

"Me?"

She looked down, and virtually hidden by the vibrant red stains on her clothes were cuts in the garment. That awareness finally broke the spell of numbness, awakening the pain in the wounds beneath. She could feel them everywhere, on her legs, her arms, her chest.

Lightheaded, she closed her eyes and coaxed her magic out if its hiding place. As it spread through her, she could feel each wound heal, the pain receded, torn flesh prickled and went warm, almost hot. The snow around them melted and they sank several feet until they reached solid ground and stood in an ankle-deep puddle at the bottom of a narrow valley. Twenty feet away the second manticore lay dead on the ground, its leathery wings had been torn off its back and Nicole realized that they must have tumbled right off the mountain too.

"You had me scared for a moment there," he said, his voice drawing her eyes away from the casualty.

"I scared—?" She swatted him. "*You* scared *me*."

"I'm all right. Not a scratch on me."

She sighed and threw her arms around him, squeezing as hard as she could.

"That hurts," he grunted.

She let go, startled, and looked at him more closely.

"You're stronger than you look, for a human," he said.

He claimed there wasn't a scratch on him, but there looked to be a bruise already forming under his eye, and he wasn't standing as straight as normal. His torso tilted to the left just enough to notice, like he was pressing his arm into his ribs for support.

"Sorry."

"I should be sorry, for knocking you off a mountain," he said. Then he frowned. "I thought you could fly."

"So did I," she said. "I don't even remember hitting the snow—wait, where is Lyana? She fell with me—she was—" *She's bleeding out! How could she be gone?*

Gordan looked around. "There," he said. Pointing to the edge of the melted snow stained red and depressed like someone had crawled through it.

"Lyana," Nicole called, pushing into the snow and letting out a little magic to part the way, following the red stains that trailed to the entrance of a mine.

"How did she even make it this far?" Gordan asked, his voice low with astonishment.

The abundance of red snow turned to pink patches and there was hardly a trail when they reached the mouth of the mine.

"Lyana," she called again, marching into the dim tunnel as she summoned a light into her hand. "She must still have her cuff on."

"Nicole," Gordan said, doubt heavy in his tone.

"Gordan, I *froze* up there," she said, words trembling with anguish. "She saved me. If she dies it's my fault."

"She can't be much farther," he said, attempting a hopeful lilt.

The sound of shuffling from the shadows beyond her light made her heart lurch. "Did you hear that?"

"I did."

Nicole hurried forward only to find the tunnel branched into three directions. "Oh no."

"There," Gordan pointed. "Blood." There was a red smear on a stone jutting out of the entrance to the tunnel on the right.

Nicole hurried ahead into the right-hand tunnel noticing a pale green glow blossom in a vein of tiny crystals. She stopped, put her hand against the stone and pushed her magic into the rock. The crystal vein lit up as her magic spread, and Nicole could feel every tunnel in the mountain. They branched and turned and crossed in such a maze it was dizzying. Yanking her hand away steadied her, and the tunnel ahead was lit with the green glow. Not far ahead as the tunnel curved, she saw the dark silhouette of a woman. She dropped the light from her hand and ran.

"Nicole," Gordan snapped at her. "Wait."

Nicole reached her, heart pounding with relief and heaving labored breaths in the thin cold air. Lyana stood there dazed, swaying like she was about to tip over. The belt was still synched around her upper thigh, but the cuff was not on her wrist.

"Lyana," she said.

"Nicole stop—she's dead," Gordan said, and she could hear the labor in his voice as he struggled to move quickly through the tunnel.

"But she's—" Nicole's eyes moved from the tourniquet up to Lyana's blank stare. Her face was slack and below her chin a long dark wound like a black smile across her neck, the green light casting a sickly shine on Lyana's blood-drained pallor.

Nicole's heart clenched. Lyana was dead, but her arm moved inhumanly fast and her hand sticky with blood snatched at Nicole's wrist, catching her thick sleeve in a fierce grip.

"He's here," Gordan panted.

She pulled, yanked and twisted but could not wrench her sleeve from Lyana's hand. Panicked, she threw her arms up and wrestled free from the heavy coat in Lyana's grip. Lyana dropped it and lunged again.

Gordan's hands caught Nicole and he yanked her aside, losing his balance and toppling into her, pushing her into the rough stone wall as Lyana sailed past them and staggered.

Gordan leaned on her, straightening up and turning himself to face Lyana. He wobbled. Nicole locked her arms around him and held him steady. Then the tunnel erupted in yellow-orange light and heat as Gordan spit fire from his human-shaped mouth. Lyana didn't react to the flames and would have kept coming if they hadn't blackened her form and reduced her to ash before she had taken three steps. The fire stopped. The tunnel went green and quiet again. The crystal light seemed dark after the wave of fire.

"Even the dead can be summoned," Gordan said gasping. "If she had gotten a hold of you, he could have summoned you both. He would have had you."

Nicole buried her face in Gordan's back, her eyes burning. "She was alive," she said through gritted teeth. "She would have survived—but he—" Nicole's mind raced. Venarius had to be in these tunnels. The burn of angry tears in her spread like a brush fire, and she wanted to find that son-of-a-bitch.

Gordan turned around and nearly sagged against her as he put his arms around her. "Please don't," he said softly and her fury cooled. This was not the time to confront Venarius; she couldn't leave Gordan hurt like this. He wouldn't forgive her for trying to face Venarius alone, and she wouldn't forgive herself if something happened to him because she tried.

"Come on," she said, holding his arm around her and turning toward the way out. "You're hurt, you liar."

He chuckled, a warm breathy sound in her ear. She could see the white light of day reaching feebly into the tunnel ahead of them, and a sobering fear of Venarius reclaimed her heart. She leapt into the ether holding fast to Gordan and daylight blinded them when they emerged outside the mines.

"Gordan! Nicole!" the distant voice was panicked, and its echo gave it an unstable edge—Mitchell.

"We should get back up there before Mitchell loses his mind," Gordan said.

She looked up at the steep walls around them, they were in a stone funnel. She closed her eyes again and set her heart on Raiden and Mitchell far above them on the ridge. They fell out of the ether, less gracefully this time, stumbling onto the ridge. Nicole barely regained her balance before the weight of a grown man hit her, nearly knocking her down if it wasn't for his arms clamping around her and holding her up.

"You scared me half to death," Mitchell said.

"Mitchell—careful, Gordan's hurt," she could barely eek the words out of her lungs.

"Oh jeez," he said, letting her go and turning to Gordan.

"A few bruised ribs is all," Gordan said.

Mitchell frowned at him and took his other arm, relieving Nicole of Gordan's weight so that he didn't have to stoop to lean on her.

"Thank you," Gordan murmured. Nicole's gaze found Raiden as he marched across the blood-soaked ground into her arms, his posture heavy with relief.

"Where's Priseil?" she asked into his chest.

"We got everyone onto the Tempest. Captain Rhee took them back to Coron. Priseil will live. If they can find her arm there's a chance to mend it."

Nicole looked around, there was no sign of the dead manticore except for the blood and what looked like a mound of ash soaking into congealing puddles and swirling in the breeze.

"You cremated it?"

"I thought that was best, bad enough how this all turned out, it didn't need to be made into a trophy too."

A surge of adoration for him washed her words away, so she pressed her face against his chest once more and held him a little tighter.

"We lost Gregor…and we couldn't find Lyana," he said.

"She was with me," she said.

"Was?"

"We have company," Gordan said, his voice still a little strained.

"You mean Venarius?" Mitchell asked, standing beside Gordan.

"Let's get back to Coron," Raiden said.

"All of us?" Caeruleus asked.

Gordan looked at Nicole with the same question in his eyes.

"All of us," Raiden said.

Fen and Asi leaned in with hungry gazes as Nicole paused, impatience practically jumped off them in sparks and Gordan listened.

"What did they do when you arrived?" Asi asked, looking to Nicole and then Gordan.

"Nothing," Gordan said. "The people of Orodon have an intense code of honor. Seeing as I saved their king, and his daughters…"

"Did they find Priseil's arm?" Fen demanded.

"They did, sort of—something else found it first." Nicole said.

"Oh no—what?" Asi shrieked.

"Turns out the two manticore's were rearing cubs in Orodon. The king's men brought back the two cubs for Priseil to kill in retribution for…ruining her arm."

The girls' faces twisted in disgust.

"Did she?"

This was Gordan's favorite part of the story because Nicole lit up. Admiration welled up around her and she smiled.

"She refused," Nicole said, savoring the words. "They were so pissed at their captain for what he pulled. Not that they didn't want to kill the manticore, they sure wanted to, but they had agreed we would try my plan and only destroy it if we had to. King Eisen gave his word and Borh disobeyed, that was beyond disgraceful to them."

"Ugh, *he* should have lost his arm," Fen muttered.

"Oh, he lost something far worse," Gordan said. "He was stripped of his title, his standing, and forced to leave Coron in disgrace. I doubt there will be anywhere in Orodon he can hide from his shame for that transgression against the king."

"Good," Asi said.

"What happened to Priseil and the cubs then?" Fen wondered.

"Nicole made her a wooden arm and enchanted it, almost as good as flesh and bone, she just can't feel anything with it," Gordan said.

"And she adopted the cubs, can you believe it?" Nicole said cheerfully.

"That's wonderful," Asi cried.

"But won't they still be a problem?" Fen asked.

"At this point they can only growl and make cute noises," Nicole said, chuckling. "Which makes your hands tingle a little like they fell asleep, but nothing serious. King Eisen really didn't like the idea, but he couldn't say no to Priseil after she lost her arm and lectured him about senseless violence. It sure sounded like this had been boiling in her heart for a long time."

"Wow," Asi said. "I wish I could meet her."

"You will, she and Sigrid said they would come visit us sometime."

"Are we really leaving for Nol in two days?" Fen asked.

"I think so. Tovar has been managing those plans."

"You're coming, right, Gordan?"

"Whenever Nicole goes somewhere without me bad things tend to happen. I'm not letting her out of my sight again," he said.

Nicole laughed.

"Are you still hurt, Gordan?" Asi asked with a troubled brow.

"Not at all. I heal quickly."

Nicole nudged him.

"And had Nicole's help," he added.

"Nikki," Mitchell's shout reached them before he appeared in the doorway. "Hey, come see what Gwyn has been working on while we were away." As soon as he appeared, he disappeared to make his way to Gwyn's workroom.

Nicole looked to Fen and Asi apologetically.

"That's okay. We should go home and see Keren anyway since we're going on a royal visit to Nol and Eanna as part of the queen's court," Fen said, elevating her voice with feigned importance.

Asi giggled.

"Give Keren a hug for me," Nicole said, unfolding her legs and climbing off the oversized pillow. Gordan followed, still trying to understand the subtle changes in her after two days with her in Orodon and the return home. Since his spontaneous arrival in Orodon, he couldn't seem to get a moment alone with her, so he settled for staying close enough to inspect the fluctuations in her.

"Find any answers yet?" she asked as they walked down the hall.

He pulled himself from his puzzled focus. "I beg your pardon?"

"I thought you might be having more luck than me. You'd think between the two of us we could actually figure me out," she muttered, laughing to herself.

"How have you been sleeping?" he asked.

"Surprisingly, all right," she said and laughed. "I still don't trust it."

"You should. There's nothing wrong with doing better."

"Isn't there—if I'm only okay because of you or Raiden? Am I really any better if I'm still not okay when I'm all alone?" Her voice sank into a hushed tone between them.

"Yes, you are," Gordan put his hand on Nicole's shoulder and turned her so that she had to look him in the eyes. "When you put a bandage on a wound, it doesn't mean the wound is gone, it just means you're all right enough to keep going while you heal. Naturally, you'll still think about it, there's still pain beneath the bandage, but eventually you trust it enough to go about your life, the pain lessens, you let yourself forget it's there, and in time the wound heals. Let the people you love be your bandage."

Nicole smiled, but closed her eyes like she was fighting back tears. She let out a string of quite sobs that also sounded like laughter and her gratitude possessed him—he wanted nothing more than to close his arms around her, but she beat him to it.

"Where the hell did you two go?" Mitchell's voice called from down the hallway, long out of sight and only now realizing they we no longer behind him.

"Wanna mess with Mitch?" Nicole whispered.

"How?"

"Ever heard of a piggy back ride?" she asked.

"A what?"

"You'll see," she said, moving behind him and jumping onto his back, wrapping her arms around his shoulders and throwing her legs around his waist. "Let's go."

"This is ridiculous," he said, hooking his arms under her legs to keep her up. It made sense to have her on his back when he was in his other form, however, like this—well, it was such an absurd way to get around that he couldn't help laughing.

She snickered into his shoulder, and Mitchell appeared around the corner.

Mitchell stopped and gasped, such a look of outrage and betrayal that Gordan would have believed it to be real if he wasn't getting an entirely different energy from him.

"Nicole, how could you? You're supposed to be *my* backpack."

"But Gordan's never had one," she said.

"I'm not so sure that I need one," Gordan said, confused.

"See? He doesn't need one," Mitchell agreed.

"What's wrong, don't you *trust* him with your backpack?"

Gordan smiled, catching on to their game, then frowned at Mitchell. "You don't trust me?"

Mitchell's feigned outrage melted and his cheeks flushed. Gordan felt Mitchell's heart sputter, a fluttering in the air that made his own heart clench a little.

"Sure, I trust you," he said, turning away abruptly. "When you put it like that," he muttered. "Come on, Gwyn is waiting for us, you know."

Nicole laughed through her teeth into Gordan's shoulder and whispered, "I knew it. I fucking knew it."

"Knew what?" Gordan's eyes followed Mitchell.

"He likes you. Come on, you of all people should be able to tell that. Can't you?"

"I—well," his throat tightened and he tried to swallow the words stuck there. He was so concerned about Nicole and tended to focus on her over anyone else, and, of course, he felt Mitchell's warmth and affection when he was with them—but just now Gordan definitely felt…something familiar that he hadn't felt for someone else in centuries.

"I thought so," she said brimming with satisfaction and he wondered if sometimes she was reading his mind.

❧

Nicole couldn't deny that she was interested by what Gwyn had worked on while they were in Orodon, but her attention kept sliding away for brief moments from the materials on Gwyn's work table to her brother and Gordan beside each other. Nicole tried to follow the account of all Gwyn had learned from Leone about celengel swords and the incredibly light metal they forged called taivallion, but she couldn't help notice Gordan glance at Mitchell while her brother was so focused on what Gwyn had to say that she suspected him to be trying a little too hard not to look at Gordan.

"I managed to get my hands on this, thanks to Tovar," she said, pointing to a rock no shorter than her forearm. It was irregular, dark greenish-brown, almost grey in some places, but light refracted off planes of vivid color in the rock—violet, aquamarine, orange. "This is harder to come by than its sister the moonstone."

"What is it?" Nicole asked.

"Black moonstone," Gordan answered.

"Precisely," Gwyn said. "Moonstone has been a popular material in wand making for its powers of protection from bodily harm, balance and clarity—its magic projects outward, like moonlight.

However, black moonstone's powers mirror the concealed aspect of the moon. It bolsters psychic strength and intuition, protecting the internal self—our emotions, our energy, and our mind."

"You want to make a sword out of this?" Nicole asked and spotted her brother taking a quick glance at Gordan.

"Not entirely, it will be the hilt and the core, and the blade will function as the shell. It's a wand in function and a sword in shape."

"I've already designed the blade and everything," Mitchell said with a grin.

"Oh, can I see it?"

"And ruin the reveal? Not a chance."

"Fine. So—what—you just brought me here to tease me?"

"Not at all," Gwyn said. "We're still missing some of the materials we need."

Gwyn gathered her long silver hair in her hands and pulled it over her shoulder where she twisted it nervously.

"And those materials are?"

"Blood for the core," Gwyn answered plainly.

"And your first-born child," Mitchell added.

Gwyn turned to him with a perplexed look.

Mitchell shrugged, wearing a tiny devious grin of satisfaction.

"We don't have time to wait for that ingredient," Gwyn said. "So just your blood will have to do."

Mitchell dropped his head back, laughing silently.

"All right, and what are the other materials you still need?"

"Well, we still need to figure out what to use for the blade. Leone said it could take weeks just to find Terra Celestia, and he didn't sound confident that they would be interested in sharing their secret for making taivallion. The metals in the wands you tried couldn't stand the heat your magic creates."

"You could use doragonian steel," Gordan said. "It's not weightless like the celengel's taivallion, but it is immutable to magic which can move through it but not affect it. It's forged in dragon fire. I wager it can withstand Nicole's magic."

Mitchell's eyes went wide and he turned to Gordan. "Yes! *That.*

Where do we get it?"

"It sounds promising," Gwyn said.

"All I need to make it is plumbago and wolframite; I believe King Eisen can provide us with those."

"You know how to make this metal?" Gwyn asked, her words suddenly exhilarated.

"If I haven't forgotten," Gordan said with a wistful smile.

"How long will it take?" Mitchell asked.

"Once I have the materials it should take three days at most."

"I would only need the blade and then I could assemble it from there," Gwyn said.

"Putting this all together will require some alchemy, will it not?"

"That's right."

"Then you'll need to be able to heat the steel in order to transmute it. I could stay behind, or you could use dragon's breath if Nicole wouldn't mind you borrowing Gim." Gordan looked to her.

"I don't mind."

"Great—it sounds like we're going back to Orodon then," Mitchell said. "Pep will be glad to make another trip, I'm sure. And Rhee prefers to be in the air anyway, so everyone wins."

"Hold up. Not quite everyone," Nicole grumbled. "You get to go on a sword-making quest, and I have to go on a royal road trip to the Prince of Nol's *birthday party?*"

"You're not leaving for two days. If we leave tomorrow and follow when we're done, we'll only be a few days behind you. I wouldn't miss your first royal ball for anything." He elbowed her.

She sighed. "Then we better go home and see Dad if you're taking off tomorrow."

❧

Gordan walked Mitchell and Nicole back to her chamber so that they could visit their father and went looking for Raiden. He wasn't in his room, which he tried first despite suspecting he would be with Caeruleus or Loak, but he eventually found him in Tovar's workroom. He did not want to intrude, so he waited in the hall.

"Everything is ready to go, but I would advise you get to know each other before we leave."

"Yes, all right. Thank you again, Tovar." Raiden stepped into the hallway, looking down at a sprig of tiny purple flowers between his fingers. When he spotted Gordan, he smiled.

"Walk with me?" Gordan asked.

"Certainly."

"Who is it Tovar wants you to meet?"

Raiden looked at him with faint confusion before saying, "Oh. The horses. He suggested Nicole and I get familiar with them before we leave."

"I see…is that Juno's Tears?"

Raiden twirled the sprig of flowers once. "It is."

"You aren't using it to have visions, are you?"

"No," he sounded startled. "Actually—" Raiden rubbed the back of his neck. "I've been using it to share dreams with Nicole. It's something my mother did when I was a child, when I had nightmares."

"I see."

"I haven't seen her wake up with a single wound since we left for Orodon."

Gordan frowned, deciding not to tell Raiden that Nicole's monster managed to get to her in broad daylight back on the mountain.

"I'm glad to hear that," he said, the truth weighing his voice down to a soft tone. "Sounds like that's what she has needed, and she knows it, which makes it all the more difficult for her. She is so used to feeling strongest on her own."

"I know the feeling. I convinced myself I was better off alone after all those years in Cantis—mostly because I had no choice. I thought not having anyone for so long meant I didn't need anyone anymore, like it was some advantage." Raiden laughed. "And then Nicole brought it all down around me."

"It would seem she has a remarkable ability to find and rescue the lonely," Gordan said. "I suppose in some way that's the fera in her. Perhaps independence is in her nature in part because her past life was one of forced solitude, so she feels the need to save others from being alone."

Raiden nodded, losing himself to some thought that chilled the air with dread.

"Tovar sent letters accepting the Prince of Nol and Queen of Eanna's invitations. It's been announced, by now most of Veil knows we're making formal royal visits," Raiden said.

"And so Venarius knows without a doubt."

"The moment we walk out of this palace—"

"Don't focus on the unknown. Focus on Nicole, keep her close."

"I don't like the prospect of being out there without you and Mitchell around. You two distract her from all this at least, and now we're going out there. He'll be waiting."

"Travel through Meridian to get to Nol, the fey might be difficult at times, but I can guarantee you Venarius has no supporters among them, nor do they tolerate the likes of Dawn to set foot in their forests. It will be the safest route. Mitchell and I will meet you along the way. You won't be more than three days without us."

"I'm worried about *you*," he said.

"We'll be perfectly fine. Unfortunately, the danger follows *her*."

They walked in silence for almost a whole corridor.

"Do the dragons hate us here on the mainland?" Raiden wondered.

Gordan's heart sank. "I wish I could say 'no', but it is not as simple as 'yes' either."

"Do you think the dragon king would ever try again if he learned that Veil is divided once again?"

"No," he said easily. "But why do you ask?"

"Weeks ago, I wasn't sure if it was a dream or a vision—I saw dragons in these halls. I suppose I have been worried the fall of the Council might set certain things in motion again and we'd be at the center of it this time."

"While the dragons don't all have the warmest sentiments toward the mainland, I can assure you they won't follow their king into conquest again. They do not have the numbers they once had, nor are they united like they were then. You can hardly call their king a king anymore."

Raiden's anxiety dissipated, but Gordan grew troubled by the notion. They were on the fifth floor when they heard a scream from above. They lurched forward in unison, running for the stairs as indiscernible shouts followed.

"Mitch! Help me!"

The door to Nicole's chamber was open. Gordan rushed in beside Raiden and couldn't believe the cause of the commotion. An adolescent griffin bounding through the room, pouncing on pillows, tangled in swaths of fabric now torn from the ceiling. The forest of textiles was sparser than usual.

"Come on, you—stop," Nicole pleaded, trying to catch the train of fabric trailing after the griffin as Mitchell jumped in front of it. The griffin slid to a stop, and Nicole grabbed a fist-full of cloth.

"Is that—how did it even *get* here?" Raiden balked.

"Don't you know about the door?" Gordan asked.

Raiden looked to him. "What door?"

Gordan looked to Nicole, surprised she hadn't told him yet.

She sighed. "I made a door to your house in Cantis."

"And…" Mitchell said.

"And a portal doorway from your house to Yuma so we could visit Dad."

"What's all the noise about in here?" asked Fen as she and Asi stepped through the door. "Keren almost didn't let us come back."

"And a door to Keren's place," Nicole added sheepishly.

"Is that a griffin?" Asi asked.

"He's my friend, but I haven't been to Cantis for two weeks. I didn't think he'd hang around. He must have found a way inside the house."

Raiden's silence churned with amazement, annoyance, admiration and a little lingering fear. "Sounds like he was determined to find you."

"Yeah, he burst through that door and I thought she was a

goner," Mitchell said, laughing, but there was an edge of real concern still clinging to his voice. The surprise had shaken Mitchell, just as screams had terrified Gordan and Raiden; they were all still trying to shake themselves free of the misunderstanding.

"I, uh, better go check on Dad in case he heard any of that—make sure he's not having a panic attack or something." Mitchell turned toward the two doors and slipped through the one to the left.

Gordan looked back at Nicole who sighed. The griffin lurched forward again, yanking Nicole with him, and she fell into the pillow and piles of fabric, utter exasperation on her face but a tiny smirk on her mouth nonetheless.

❧

Raiden watched with a smile on his face as Nicole explained to Gordan how to properly roll down a grassy hill and then demonstrated, the griffin chasing after her and Gordan following on foot down the slope. Mitchell laughed beside him as they stood at the top of the hill. Nicole's laughter from the bottom was so much like her brother's laughter.

"How do you make her laugh so much?" Raiden wondered.

"I don't know, Ray, we grew up together," he said, shrugging.

"I'm glad you came with us, Mitch. She needs that, and I worry that she'll be miserable without you the next several days."

"She's got you," he said, nudging his shoulder. "It's all this king stuff that makes her miserable and it's all to find that bastard Venarius—it's a shit sandwich and she's in the middle. I'm not the only one who can distract her."

"I feel like I remind her about it all more than I distract her," Raiden confessed.

"Do something about it, then. Help her escape. Get her away from this palace and all the royal bullshit. When was the last time you went on a date?"

"A date?"

"Good lord, Ray, really? A date—just the two of you, together, getting to know each other, enjoying yourselves."

Raiden tried to think of a time that fit that description. "I guess when we were back in Yuma casting spells in the yard."

"You mean because the Council abducted you?"

"Well, yeah, we haven't really had any time to ourselves since then."

"Take some time, then. You're about to leave on this royal tour, and you won't get the chance to be alone surrounded by an entourage. She needs a break from kings and enemies, and you do too."

Mitchell was right, but Raiden was anxious walking the hills in the shade of the palace even knowing Nicole had him, Gordan and Mitchell nearby, not to mention Sage, Netti and his father keeping close watch. The idea of Nicole and him being away from the palace just the two of them felt like too much risk.

"Venarius isn't *every*where, and there's got to be somewhere you can go for an hour or two. You can come and go from the palace after all. Who would even know you've left or where you're going? I think her sanity…and your relationship. It's worth the risk, isn't it?"

"I don't know," Raiden said.

Mitchell shrugged again. "Just my two cents. Take it or leave it."

Twenty-four

When it turned out that Captain Rhee wanted to leave before sundown, Gordan felt Nicole grow gloomier by the hour until he and Mitchell were side by side in the ship's elevator. They waved goodbye to her and Raiden before the door closed, and they ascended to the Tempest.

Gordan let out a sigh, pained by the look on her face and the fear in her heart. His broken promise not to let her out of his sight again growing heavy in his heart. He tried to assure himself that a few days wouldn't be a problem. The first part of Nicole and Raiden's trip would be dull and safe on the wide-open midlands and in the shelter of the Meridian forest.

"You nervous?" Mitchell asked.

Gordan cast a slanted glance at him, unsure how he felt about being read so accurately. "After all that has happened, leaving her does not sit well with me."

"Don't think I can keep you safe, huh?"

Gordan chuckled and detected the distinct frequency of worry from Mitchell. "You're very good at acting unperturbed."

"Yes, well, admitting how much it scares me to leave her wouldn't have made you smile like that." His expression changed, showing the anxiety he had tried to hide, but there was still a slight curl to his lips and pinkness in his cheeks. Gordan looked away hoping the sudden rush of heat through his body would cool.

The elevator door opened, releasing them to the cargo hold where Pep stood waiting for them.

"Welcome back," she said with a subtle smile.

"Don't you look pleased to see us," Mitchell said, summoning that sly humor of his once more as he stepped out of the elevator.

She rolled her eyes. "I'm *pleased* to be on our way to Orodon again," she said, then turned a kind look to Gordan.

He was affronted by a tide of gratitude in the air before Pep turned and marched out of the cargo hold. He and Mitchell trailed behind as she made her way to the bridge to join Captain Rhee.

"I'm so used to dislike and distrust that it's strange to receive anything different," Gordan said.

"You saved her wife and family," Mitchell said. "And really there's no reason not to like you."

Gordan looked at him.

Mitchell tried to maintain his casual denial of the uncomfortable truth, but his face broke into a cringe under Gordan's gaze. "Well, except for war crimes committed by your kind," he added, cleared his throat, and stepped into the ladder inlet to ascend to the upper deck.

Gordan shook his head fondly and followed.

Nicole watched the Tempest disappear into the darkening curtain of night hanging in the eastern sky and turned to hug Raiden, trying not to worry. They would be safer on their own than with her for several days, and for that she was relieved—even a little jealous— but she couldn't fend off the dread of watching them go, wondering if it would be the last time she saw them or if Venarius would find a way to her first. There was no telling what opportunity Venarius would take to get to her. After Orodon she couldn't be sure he didn't have a hand in everything that might be happening in all of Veil. She couldn't shake the idea even when logic insisted that the manticores had been troubling Orodon longer than she'd even known she was the fera.

Still, Venarius had found her high in the Orodon mountains, and he would come for her again and again until he had her, or until she killed him.

"Hey," Raiden said. "Do you want to get out of here for a little while?"

She looked up at him questioningly, but he simply took her by the hand and led her back to the palace. They walked and she studied him, suddenly more sociable than usual as they made their way through the palace. Raiden was apparently determined to stop and have a brief word with everyone they encountered about the preparations for the trip to Nol and Eanna. Nicole held his hand, along for the ride, still mystified by his question and the lack of further explanation as they made their way up to their rooms. Asi and Fen returned from their visit with Keren when he and Nicole arrived to her room.

"Are you two going down to dinner?" he wondered.

"We had dinner with Keren, but Tierney always has something good for dessert," Fen said, with a grin to Asi who nodded.

"Aren't you going to dinner?" Asi asked as they turned to the door.

"We've had our fill already, we're just going to have a quiet evening to ourselves tonight," he said easily.

Fen smiled.

"Okay, good night, then," Asi said.

"Good night, girls," Nicole said, her tone wistful with confusion.

They left and Raiden shut the door soundly behind them.

"What was that all about?" Nicole asked.

"So, everyone thinks we're here and knows why we aren't downstairs for dinner," he explained. "Where would you like to go?"

"Go?"

"To get away for a bit, you and me, on a date."

A bemused smile spread across her face. *A date*, she laughed.

She looked to the doors to Cantis and the orchard. "I know," she said, taking his hand and stepping toward the door to Keren's place. She knocked twice and opened the door.

They walked into Keren's living room and Keren emerged from the kitchen.

"This is a surprise," Keren said.

"We're just on our way to Witch Haven," Nicole said. "I wanted to say hi first."

"It's good to see you, but if you hang around here, you won't get to Witch Haven for hours."

Nicole smiled. "We'll see you later, Keren."

"Good evening, you two," she said, waving them off and turning back to the kitchen.

Nicole pulled Raiden through the ether, and they arrived on the main cobblestone road through the town of Witch Haven.

"Here we are," she said.

"I'm curious. Why here?" Raiden asked.

"It seemed like a really nice little town when I was here last time, but I didn't really get to see it. And there's someplace I want to show you."

"All right," he said.

They walked. The sun set. The street lamps lit themselves. No one on the street gave them any more than a cursory glance in passing. Walking through Witch Haven gave Nicole the sense of walking through an amusement park, the concept of which she had to explain to Raiden. Soon she was mortifying him with stories of the Yuma County Fair, of inescapable crowds stirring up the dirt underfoot, of the racket of mechanical rides, of everything lit up and adding its own melody to the carnival cacophony.

"I don't think you would like it," she said.

"Like it? I don't know if I would survive it," he said.

She laughed. "There are places to get away from the noise and the crowds," she said. "Like the small animal barn, you can see the rabbits and chickens. And there are the exhibition halls full of art and quilts and other pretty silent things."

"In that case maybe I would survive," he said.

"There it is," she said, pointing up at the hill as they approached the other end of town.

"That's what you want to show me?" he asked, looking up at the house on the hill.

"It's the Divale Manor," she said.

Raiden's face changed to quizzical interest, and he held tight to her hand as they marched up the hill to get a closer look. The house was dark and the lights of Witch Haven did little to illuminate the structure across the distance. He conjured an orb of light as they neared the front gate. She watched him look up at the many dark windows and then down to the plaque that read DIVALE MANOR. He placed his hand on it, and she wondered if she made the wrong choice for their date. Was showing him his family home and legacy too much?

"This is incredible," he said softly.

She let out a little sigh of relief. "I thought so too."

"My mother used to tell me that the past is more important than the future," he said, looking up at the house. "Because the past gives us the tools to craft our futures."

Nicole nodded, she couldn't disagree with that. "When we first met, you said you hadn't really thought about it because you were so focused on Moira, and you weren't even sure if you'd get a future."

He turned his gaze away from the house to look at her, his *ilumina* charm glinting in his eyes.

"Do you think about it now—the kind of future you want? Not what the Sight tries to show you, what *you* want to do with your life."

His smile hit her heart and it sputtered with a giddy warmth she hadn't felt in a while.

"I want to live a life that could fill a room with books. I want to see every corner of this realm *and* the old world. And family. I lost that for a while and you gave it back to me, in more ways than one." He looked back up at the house.

She looked to the house as well, a part of Raiden's history he never had the chance to know. In one of the first-story windows a pair of cat eyes reflected Raiden's light as they peered through the pane.

"What about you?" he asked. "Surely, you had plans before that portal opened. What about now?"

"I still want to go to school," she said. "I hadn't really decided yet, I was thinking about psychology and anthropology, eventually doing a year or two abroad. Maybe I still can," she said with feeble optimism, sure her GPA would be sunk disappearing the last semester of her senior year. But she supposed in a world where portals and Raiden were possible, her going to college was too.

"You will. And we can go to that county fair too," he said.

She laughed, imagining him and Gordan at the fairgrounds with Mitchell and even Asi and Fen. "I'll take you to the fair, but I think I better get you some headphones."

"Headphones," he said, clearly not knowing what they were.

A snicker escaped through her nose, holding her hand out to pull her cell phone and headphones through the ether from her room back home. She put the earpieces over his ears, flicked the on switch, and opened up her favorite playlist. He held the headphones curiously, and then his eyes widened a little as a smile caught one corner of his mouth.

That's what I want, she thought. She didn't want to be the cause of worry and furrowed brows on the faces of everyone she loved anymore. That was the future she was trying to make.

❧

Gordan had only managed to pull his short boots off—he rather despised them—when Mitchell arrived barefoot to his room.

"Hey," Mitchell greeted from the doorway, hands buried in the pouch of his dark blue hoodie.

"I thought you were going to sleep," Gordan said.

"I was," Mitchell explained, stepping into his room, "but then I thought how often do I get you to myself?"

Gordan wasn't sure how to respond. The answer was *hardly ever*, but Mitchell knew this.

"Is it weird to live like this—with humans—all the time now? I mean, Nicole found you in your natural form, right?" Mitchell fell back onto Gordan's narrow bed.

"That's true, but I have lived in this form often throughout my life. It has its functional advantages, like with metal working. These hands are just, superior for that work." Gordan said, turning his hands over, comparing the calloused and creased palms to the finer skin stretched over tendons and veins.

"Do a lot of you guys hang out looking like humans or no?" Mitchell wondered.

"Many are comfortable enough to spend time like this now and then. We use it when it's helpful. But some dragons spurn taking this form…I suppose mostly out of bitterness toward what the humans of the old world did to us, and those magic-folk who could hide in plain sight and turned a blind eye."

"Oh, they hate looking like the enemy," Mitchell said.

"Yes."

"What form do you like better?"

"This one," Gordan said easily, surprising himself by how readily that answer came when he'd always thought of the human form as cramped and used to consider himself happiest when alone in the sky. "After the time I lived in this form in my past, I grew to despise it. I forged weapons for the dragons, weapons used in the wars, and I'm not proud of that. But strangely enough, the longer I was with Nicole, the more comfortable this form became, and now I'm rather fond of it."

"Huh, I'm kind of fond of it too," Mitchell said.

Gordan looked at him, but Mitchell averted his eyes toward the ceiling, half a smile on his face. His heart pounded with suspicion as he felt a flutter of giddy exhilaration in the air between them.

"But, I like your other form too," Mitchell said. He sat up and turned his eyes directly to Gordan's. "You know, you don't have to stand on the other side of the room." He slid to the foot of the bed and leaned against the wall, the length of his legs humiliated the width of the mattress.

Gordan looked around. The room was tiny, and even standing on the other side of it, he wasn't far away, but Mitchell's disappointment with the distance pulled at the corners of Gordan's mouth. Two steps and he was at the bed, where he sat down at the head of the mattress facing Mitchell and leaning against the perpendicular wall.

"What's it like living with the dragons?" Mitchell asked.

"You mean in the wastelands?"

"No, what is it like with a bunch of you together. Are dragons social creatures? Do you have parties, form bands and make music, flirt and go on dates, or just—you know—hang out in caves and hiss at each other?"

Gordan failed so miserably at holding in his laughter that it sputtered forcefully past his lips. "I wish I could say the latter wasn't the more accurate guess."

"What—really?" Mitchell chuckled.

Gordan nodded, his laughter compounded by Mitchell's.

❧

A thud against his door yanked Gordan from sleep.

"We're here," Pep said from outside his room.

He opened his eyes, realizing he was curled on his side toward the head of the bed and below him Mitchell was curled on his side in the space between Gordan and the wall, the top of his head pressed against his sternum, their legs in a tangle. Gordan knew they hadn't been asleep long, having talked most of the night. He felt like he'd only just closed his eyes—they ached with fatigue. Gordan removed his arm from where it was hanging over Mitchell's shoulder.

"Mitchell."

Gordan extricated his legs and climbed off the bed. Mitchell didn't stir, his brown hair just long enough to flop over his forehead but not hide his eyes. Gordan stopped his hand from its curious desire to move Mitchell's hair. Instead, he found his shoes by the door where he had left them and put them on, unsure what to make of this growing familiarity between Mitchell and him. He knew what he hoped it was, but just the idea of feeling that for someone again scared him.

A long inhale from the bed drew his gaze back to Mitchell whose arm swept across the mattress before he opened his eyes.

"We're here," Gordan said.

"Great," Mitchell said, his voice hoarse and unenthused.

⁕

"Certainly, we can get you what you need," Priseil said.

"For bringing Penelopeia back so soon, you can have the whole mine," Sigrid said as she carefully laced her fingers together with Pep's.

Priseil smiled. "We can have you on your way tomorrow."

"Thank you," Gordan said.

"How's life with your new arm?" Mitchell asked.

"I still don't know my own strength with it," she said with a chuckle. "But I am adjusting. Sometimes I forget it is not my flesh and bone because there are times when I feel it, it will hurt or itch."

"Phantom pains," Mitchell said.

"Yes," Priseil nodded.

"Where is King Eisen?" Gordan wondered, somewhat relieved that he had not been here to welcome them and anxious that he might appear at any moment—his gratitude for Gordan's intervention on the mountain was too much for him.

"Oh, he's out with the cubs," Priseil said.

"The cubs?" Mitchell asked. "You mean the manticores?"

"Yes," she said laughing. "Seeing him take such a liking to them has been quite the surprise to us as well."

"She's jealous," Sigrid said. "*They* took a greater liking to father than her."

Priseil sighed. "They ate *my* arm—they *should* like me best."

The sisters laughed and Gordan felt Mitchell's reluctance as he joined them.

"You don't have any hard feelings about your arm at all?" Mitchell wondered.

Priseil's smile fell. "Of course, I do," she said solemnly. "But not toward the manticores. I cannot fault them for their nature. Borh, on the other hand, will live in disgrace for the rest of his life."

"Noted," Mitchell said.

"And how is Nicole?" Priseil asked.

"She and Raiden are getting ready to travel to Nol. We will be meeting them along the way after we return," Gordan explained.

"I see, in that case we could have you on your way before sundown," Priseil said.

Sigrid and Pep frowned to each other and turned away, murmuring.

⌘

"Do you think we'll catch them before they leave?" Mitchell wondered as the two of them watched a troop of Orodon's royal guard cart the materials they needed and then some up the wide ramp into the Tempest's cargo hold.

"I suppose if we get out of here by sundown and they don't leave too early tomorrow," Gordan said.

"Gentlemen," Priseil said, trailed by Pep, and they were both wearing satisfied smiles. "We've just spoken with Captain Rhee about a change of plans."

Mitchell looked to Gordan with a questioning gaze and then back to the women.

"I won't be flying with Captain Rhee any longer," Pep said. "I'm staying here in Coron."

"Captain Rhee has agreed to take me on as her new second-in-command," Priseil said.

"That's great," Mitchell said.

"Thank you again," Pep said to Priseil. "I have to tell Sigrid. Be safe." She lifted Priseil's hand and kissed it quickly before disappearing inside the castle.

"So, you're just going to up and leave?" Mitchell wondered. "Aren't you in line for the throne around here?"

"Sigrid will inherit the throne, and now she'll have her queen beside her. I would rather see Veil and find out what is truly happening in the other states."

"Then you've joined the right team," Mitchell said. "Do you need to pack?"

"Already done. I'm ready to leave," she said.

"Then let's get on that ship and tell Rhee," Mitchell said.

Nicole shuffled out of her cavernous bathroom in her boxers and sports bra, still thinking of the few lovely hours away from the palace the night before. She made her way through the hanging fabric to find the griffin sprawled across the bed-sized pillow. She shook her head, not about to share a bed with all those talons, no matter how sweet and affectionate the creature was.

I guess I have to name him now, she thought as she wandered into Raiden's room where he was repacking his trunk. She knew she should be doing so too, but being back in the palace had her floundering in her anxiety again, troubled by venturing out in the open with all the eyes of the realm including Venarius' upon them—which bled into Gordan and Mitchell's absence. She worried about them too. On top of that, she was exhausted but unnerved by the prospect of going to sleep.

That dark place had seized her in broad daylight, caught her in the midst of an adrenaline-stricken free-fall as far from sleep as someone could be—after more than two weeks without wounds. She suspected Raiden's presence had everything to do with it, but now she wondered if it had been a fluke and if he could keep her nightmares at bay indefinitely.

"Hey," she said.

He looked up from rummaging and smiled. It was baffling to her how his smile could strike her heart like a dart every time.

"Hey."

"Are you having a disagreement with your clothes," she said, nodding toward the mess. Garments were thrown over the open trunk lid, on the bed, and over his shoulder.

Raiden huffed. "From what Caeruleus tells me about Nol, I don't think I have anything suitable, so I suppose I'm just bringing it all."

She shrugged. "Let's wear jeans and tell everyone it's the highest fashion in the old world." She yawned.

He chuckled, pulled jeans off his shoulder and dropped them into the trunk. He pulled a watch from his pocket and checked it. "It's later than I thought."

"It feels pretty late," she said, another yawn stealing her voice. Nicole crawled across the vast mattress and sidled under the sprawling blanket.

"I thought you liked yours better."

"There's a griffin hogging it now," she said.

Raiden gathered the clothes off the bed and tossed them carelessly into the trunk. Raiden closed his trunk and shed his clothes down to his boxer briefs and the tee shirt he had on beneath the knit sweater. Her heart sputtered anxiously, and she realized she was relieved he shed nothing more. She dreaded seeing the marks she had left on him.

"Are you tempted to use the Sight," she wondered as he settled in beside her.

"Every day."

"Does it still catch you while you sleep?"

"Not lately—no. I dream of you mostly."

She let out a tired laugh.

"What's funny about that?"

"Just how sweet and corny you sound. You've been in my dreams too actually."

"Have I?"

"I wish I could say they were good dreams," she said. "But you're there, so they aren't bad like when you aren't."

"Then I'm glad to be there even if they aren't the best dreams."

"Maybe there are no more good dreams," she said, slipping halfway into sleep on a current of worry.

"Sure, there are."

"It feels like there's nothing but the bad left for us…we *know* it'll keep getting worse before it's over."

"That's true, it will, but not tonight."

Not tonight. She held on to his words and let herself sink back into the dark of her unconscious.

❦

The atmosphere in the Tempest was quiet and mostly content as they flew. Gordan hadn't expected the trip to be so pleasant, but he hadn't felt any animosity at all since he stepped aboard this ship. Priseil laced the air with little bursts of exhilaration as she piloted from behind the sweeping curved control panel. Hovering between Captain Rhee and her a replica of the Tempest composed of light, flying nowhere gently over the control panel.

"Don't you two want to get some sleep? It's late," Captain Rhee said from her seat beside the helm, slouching comfortably as Priseil concentrated on the night out ahead of them.

"Yeah. I guess we should," Mitchell said, rubbing the back of his neck and Gordan felt a spasm of giddy anxiety in the air.

"Makes the trip much faster," Rhee said with a chuckle.

"It was an honor to witness your first flight, Priseil. Goodnight, Captain," Gordan said as they left the bridge.

"Do you remember yours?" Mitchell asked as they walked down the corridor. "Your first flight?"

"Oh yes, it's not something you ever forget—"

The corridor pitched, throwing them against the wall before they slid back across the floor the other way. They fought to regain their footing. Gordan pulled Mitchell upright and steadied him on his feet.

"Captain?!" Mitchell called, running back to the bridge while Gordan kept at his heels.

Captain Rhee was at the helm now, and Priseil clung to her chair.

"We have a visitor," she said through her teeth.

They could see another form of light beside the miniature of the Tempest, a vessel shaped like a spearhead that darted ahead and veered into their path. It was barely visible in the night outside as the captain evaded, turning the Tempest hard, knocking Mitchell into Gordan and nearly off their feet again. Gordan had seen this ship before, many of its kind, shooting across the Wastelands.

"*Bloody*—strap yourselves down," Captain Rhee said through gritted teeth.

"What is that?"

"It's one of the Council's. They had a fleet of dozens, and there's no telling where they ended up after Atrium went dark—or who it is."

"What the hell do we do?"

"I fly. You hold on."

"Can't we shoot at it?"

"No. We're an *envoy*—that's an *enforcer*," she spoke through gritted teeth. "This was built to transport. *That* was built to deal with dragons."

"Meaning?"

"They have fire power and we don't."

"What *do* we have?" Priseil asked.

"If they manage to board, we have weapons inside," Rhee said. "And a dragon."

Three racing hearts surging with adrenaline and panic was almost nauseating to Gordan—he turned and staggered from the bridge, clearing his head with the distance and marching down the corridor toward the cargo hold.

"Gordan," Mitchell called from the bridge.

Their materials from Orodon were strapped down and secure— a relief to see. He didn't want to risk their supplies. He crossed the cargo hold, searching for a lever or something that might open the door, but a spear broke through the door and opened into a vicious hook, locking itself in before the Tempest jolted and the cargo door bent, its hinges moaning terribly. The cargo hold went red and a flood of light came with a blaring warning as the wind howled in duet.

"What are you doing?" Mitchell shouted in his ear.

"We can't do anything from in here," Gordan yelled over the wailing alarm.

"Didn't you hear what Rhee said?" Mitchell's hand caught his.

"That thing was designed to kill dragons." Red light flared in Mitchell's frantic eyes.

"I'll be right back," Gordan said, squeezing his hand for a moment before slipping his hand away and turning to the open cargo door. He ran to the edge and dove into the night.

The rush of falling was the spark to ignite him, and the heat of transformation rolled through him—he caught the metal cable and let his wings spread wide, sails in the wind that sent him sliding to the enforcer. His hands transformed into talons as they burned with friction. In seconds he was under the belly of the enemy ship.

He knew this enemy, impervious to fire, defensive spells on the outside, grappling hooks designed to pierce dragon hides and not let go. But the hook came from a small hatch toward the middle of the ship's belly and the enforcer's line locked to the Tempest was also a line direct to the inside.

It was a tight fit, but Gordan pulled his long slender mostly human form inside, cramped, dark and sharp around him.

This is going hurt, he reminded himself with a pang of anxious nausea in his stomach, realizing he'd been wrong to think he'd never have to do this again. He transformed in full, letting his form grow, bending metal, breaking framework and integral bindings until he'd reached his true size and shape, bursting through the top of the ship. The enforcer tilted, dipped and dropped. Gordan pulled himself free from the falling vessel and caught the cable in his talons before it snapped free from the underside of the plummeting ship.

"Gordan," Mitchell's shout was nearly drowned out in the wind and the wailing of the alarms.

He sighed, his wings were bruised, one possibly broken. Transforming back was his best way to immobilize them and let them heal. Clinging to the cable he suffered the pain of condensing himself once again, but once it was done the ache of his broken wing was a little quieter. The pain didn't make it easy to scale the cable trailing in the wind behind the Tempest. His shifting shoulder blades aggravated the pain in his wings as he climbed. When he hauled himself over the broken door, Mitchell was there to help him to his feet. The alarm went silent, but the wind still whipped at them in the red lights of the cargo hold.

"I can't believe you just did that," Mitchell said. "How did you even know it would work?"

"I've done it before," Gordan said, wincing at the aches in his back.

Mitchell shook his head and hugged him.

Gordan let out an involuntary cry and Mitchell jumped back.

"Oh—I'm sorry," Mitchell said, his face twisted with concern.

Gordan could feel Mitchell's agony—the turbulence of relief and panic mixing in the air. "My wings are a little worse for wear," he explained. "But I really am all right. I should be like new in a week."

Mitchell let out a groan of frustration and took Gordan's face in his hands. Gordan was stunned by how swiftly Mitchell's lips met his and how long they lingered before he pulled his hands away slowly, his fingertips brushed Gordan's jaw as they went. The reluctance in that release sent a shiver of delight down Gordan's spine.

"You had me scared to death," Mitchell said, clearing his throat as chagrin crept into his settling adrenaline.

Gordan cleared his throat. "Yes, well, if you had known it wasn't a huge risk, you might not have kissed me like that," he said, unable to keep the smile from his face.

"Oh—my heart," Mitchell said, playfully aghast. "Dragons *can* flirt."

"Are you two all right?" Priseil asked breathlessly as she arrived in the cargo hold.

"Yes, we're fine," Gordan said.

"Priseil, what's our status?" Captain Rhee's voice asked over the sound system.

"Come on," Priseil said.

Mitchell looked at Gordan and offered his hand. Gordan could only keep half of his smile down as he took Mitchell's hand. They returned to the bridge where Captain Rhee was rooted in her seat, hands gripping the U-shaped helm.

"How bad is it?" Rhee asked.

"The door is badly damaged, but still there at least."

The captain sighed. "We can still fly, but not as fast with our rear end hanging open, but we'll make it back…So, what in the infinite skies did you two pull back there?"

"Gordan took it down all by himself," Mitchell said.

Gordan was almost too distracted by the contact of their hands to explain. "A fleet of them arrived in the wastelands about twenty years ago. I believe the Council wanted to be the ones to finish the war for good. As it happened, we managed to find a way to victory—though not without losing many."

"Jeez. They tried to exterminate you?" Mitchell muttered, disgust in his voice as his hand closed a little tighter around Gordan's.

"Well, that would explain why no one heard about it," Captain Rhee said, staring out the window. "They were desperate to convince the people they were doing it all right. Must have kept that one to themselves until they were sure they could announce their success. When it failed, they acted like it never happened."

Mitchell scoffed. "Yeah, it doesn't sound so great to your people that their leaders got their asses handed to them by their enemy."

"No doubt it would have destroyed the already fragile unity they were trying to maintain," Rhee added.

"Perhaps that's why they were so desperate to preserve their success in wiping out the fera years ago. They knew Nicole would have undone the only victory they had to boast about—and she did," Gordan said.

From the corner of his eye Gordan, caught sight of Mitchell's jaw clenching. Then he glanced at Priseil, concealing a smile in the corner of her mouth as her gaze fell upon Gordan and Mitchell's joined hands.

Rhee shook her head. "Unity is a noble concept and all—everyone knows Veil needed it during the dragon wars—but forcing drastically different people together doesn't always work."

"They couldn't effectively lead this realm as one people, though,"

Priseil said. "Some of the kingdoms were so set in their ways there was just no having cooperation if the Council tried to change the laws in their regions. To keep peace and power, they *had* to defer to the original kingdoms, establish the royal states and allow the surviving royal families to act as leaders 'under' them."

"But it's safe to say our visit tonight wasn't anything to do with the Council," Mitchell said.

"No, my guess is the ship, maybe even the crew, was bought," Rhee said.

"Who else but Venarius," Gordan said.

"Did he think Nicole was here?" Mitchell wondered.

"Perhaps—although, I have a hard time believing he would take such a blatantly offensive approach at that to get to Nicole." Gordan's face pinched into a frown. Maybe Venarius knew exactly who was on this ship.

"So—what then—playing a head game?"

"Or trying to get rid of her inner circle," Priseil suggested.

Gordan looked to Mitchell who glanced back with troubled eyes.

❧

Nicole checked inside her trunk for the second time and a pair of massive paws hit the lid, slamming it shut.

"Finnegan!" She pushed the griffin off the trunk and opened the lid again, but could not find any glint of gold.

"Come on, Gim. I have to bring you to Gwyn before I leave," she said as she picked up the pack Keren had given her and checked in there. "Ah ha! Found you."

Gim leapt out of the bag, seizing Finnegan's interest, and something flitted out along with him. As Gim scurried up her arm, Finnegan rushed over in an attempt to catch him.

"No," she said sternly and Finnegan sat down. Gim disappeared into her hair, hanging around her shoulders again now, and she bent over to pluck the picture of Raiden off the floor. She smiled and tucked it into her pocket.

"All right, I guess it's time to go. Come on, Finn."

Finnegan bounded after her as she made her way for the door. She stopped abruptly when Raiden appeared, and then Finnegan slid into her, knocking her against him.

Raiden propped her up on her feet.

"Thank you."

"Let's hope he settles down before he doubles in size," Raiden said.

Nicole chuckled nervously. *Doubles?!*

Raiden smiled, trying to coax one from her. She managed half.

"Ready?" he asked.

Her answer was a resounding *no* drumming in her chest, but the only way to find Venarius was to leave the palace and let him find her. She thought of all the people trapped in this deadly game—people she loved and virtual strangers willing to put their lives on the line for her—and a flood of anger burned away her reluctance.

"Absolutely."

☙

They traveled south through the midlands, skirting the hills like flowing water in a serpentine path toward Meridian, the forest territory of the fey, not quite a kingdom, never a state governed by the Council.

Raiden could not quite settle into the tranquility of the journey, the grass rippling like waves on the undulating earth around them, the ease of their path through the hills on horseback and by caravan. They had agreed this was the way they'd make their journey, partly because it was a custom of the kingdoms that diplomatic visitors cross each other's boarders and countries out of respect, but mostly because their mission was to create ample opportunity for Venarius to make a move. And so, Raiden couldn't help looking at every hill as though the enemy were behind it. He listened to the wind in the grass anxiously, wondering if it was masking the sound of something more important.

Their horses, like most of anything they had acquired, had been gifts from the people of Veil, mostly from the people of Dusor known for its extensive farmlands. The horses, naturally, were dray horses, large sturdy animals bred for farm labor—certainly not the swift elegant horses of royalty, but Nicole's blue roan mare— Imber—was so remarkably unperturbed by Finnegan bounding around, that her patience and unshakable calm could only be described as regal.

Raiden's dun stallion—Apellon—snorted often at the griffin and was inclined to drift away from the exuberant young Finnegan, consequently putting Raiden farther from Nicole than he wanted to be. By midafternoon Finnegan's energy was spent, and he had curled up atop the caravan that followed behind Nicole; thus, Raiden was finally able to ride closely beside her.

He was relieved to see Nicole looked far more at ease than he felt. She would sometimes lean forward to lay across Imber's withers and stroke her neck, or she would tip her head back into the wind and smile, but whenever she looked his way, he knew she could see his disquieted nerves all over his face and her contentment would shift to mirror his frown before he could compose a smile for her.

Their company was small for a royal entourage—Nicole, Raiden, Leone, Loak, Asi, Fen, Caeruleus and Tovar were outnumbered by the guards three times over. When the sun dipped closer to the horizon, tents for the guards went up around the five caravans. They were quite spacious inside thanks to expansion spells and, really, they only needed two—one for Leone, Loak, Caeruleus and Tovar, and one for Nicole, Raiden, Asi and Fen. The other three caravans were merely decoys with travel supplies and traps for anyone not authorized by the spells to enter.

"So, we'll get to the river by tomorrow?" Nicole asked, her back to him as she brushed Imber. They stood between the two horses, backs to each other as they dragged the brushes against the sweaty withers. His progress was slow as he stopped often to peek over his shoulder at her.

"According to Tovar," Raiden said, watching Nicole reach as far as she could to brush her horse's back. Her feet stuck to the ground—it occurred to him that he hadn't seen her fly, or even so much as drift off the ground, since Atrium.

"How do we know if we're even welcome in Meridian?" She hopped to brush a little higher and landed on her feet again.

"I suppose we find out when we get there. The fey are never shy about driving unwanted visitors from their forest."

"I'm sure they'll be thrilled to receive the fera and all the trouble that tends to follow," she muttered.

Raiden huffed and turned to her. "They should be," he said, hooking his arms around her from behind and tucking his head into the crook of her neck. "Everything about you is worth every bit of trouble."

She laughed sardonically and said, "Yeah, okay."

The doubt in her voice pained him, despite her laughter. "I'm sorry, I can't release you until you believe me," he said, hugging her tighter. How could she not after everything they'd been through already? He wouldn't erase a single moment of his life with her in it, not even the worst parts.

"Raiden," she said, chuckling. "Come on."

He leaned on her more heavily and felt her sag under his weight. "Raiden."

He let out an exaggerated sigh and let his entire weight hang on her until she sank to the grass, trapped beneath him.

"Okay, I believe you," she cried through laughter.

"Really?"

"Yes," she said, snickering.

"Good," he said, getting up and pulling her to her feet.

She tried to scowl at him over the smile on her face.

"I'll remind you—" He took her chin between his thumb and index finger and kissed her. "—in case you forget."

Her cheeks flushed and she scrunched her lips together, crinkling her nose, fighting a smile as she turned back to Imber and resumed brushing. He half turned to Apellon, watching her a moment longer to see her float a few inches off the ground as she reached to brush Imber's back. With a smile on his face, he turned back to Apellon and spotted Asi and Fen poorly concealed by one of the wagons not far away, watching with grins on their faces.

⌘

"With so many of the palace residents gone with Nicole and Raiden, Tierney has given us half the kitchen for you to work," Gwyn explained.

"We're a whole day behind schedule," Mitchell said with a sigh.

"We could be a lot worse than a day behind schedule," Gordan reminded him.

"But we're not, we're fine, *and* we're a day behind schedule, which means Nicole is going to ask why."

"And?"

"Oh, you want to tell her that no one she loves is safe anymore, that we narrowly escaped an attempt by Venarius to get to her, and send her spiraling into anxiety?"

"You would lie to her about what happened?"

Mitchell's annoyance turned the air bitter. "No—I just don't think we need to tell her."

"I don't agree," Gordan said gently.

"This is killing her, you don't think I see it on her face every day? Telling her what happened last night will only make her feel even worse. I don't want to do that to her, why would you?"

Gordan took a steadying breath, resisting the influence of Mitchell's anger on his heart.

"Would you appreciate finding out that Venarius almost got to Nicole while we weren't there and she kept it from you?"

Mitchell frowned, his anger simmering back into irritation.

"That's what I thought. Now, if I get started tonight, I should be finished two days from now," Gordan said. "Gwyn, do you have a spare hair band?"

"Of course," she said, chuckling, pulling one from her apron pocket.

Gordan took it, thanked her, gathered his hair up atop his head, pulled it through that band a couple times and left it in a sloppy top knot where it would stay out of his way. Mitchell's scowl seemed to soften with mild surprise and his face flushed.

"What?" Gordan asked, puzzled by Mitchell's agitation. He couldn't quite understand the sudden flutter of attraction contending with Mitchell's bitter annoyance at their disagreement.

"Nothing," he said, shaking his head. "Never seen you put your hair up."

"Oh," Gordan tried not to smile—*something as small as that?* "It's a nuisance when forging."

"Do you need an extra pair of hands while you work?" Gwyn asked.

"No, I have everything I need, thank you."

"All right, I'll leave you to it and see to the rest of our materials in the work room," Gwyn said, waving as she left the kitchens.

"You're going to be up all night," Mitchell said, looking around the dark kitchens lit only by the glow from the single oven ready for Gordan to turn it into a forge.

"It will pass quickly enough…I used to enjoy this work."

"Right—so you don't need any company."

Gordan smiled. "No, but I would like some."

ٮ

The canopies of the ironwood trees of Meridian watched from over the top of the hills as the party traveled the second day to the edge of the midlands and reached the Jormungandr River a couple hours before sunset. It was too late to cross, so the guards set up their tents and those of them who had the last shift on the ten guards' horses stripped the saddles and brushed them down.

"I can't get over how big they are," Nicole said, captivated by the forest across the river. "They're like the giant redwoods."

"This is the first time I've seen them myself," Raiden said.

"They are a highly prized resource in this realm," Tovar said, leading one of the wagon horses over to the others for grazing outside the ring of tents around the wagons. "They're called ironwood for good reason."

"How can anyone even cut one down if they're like iron? Doesn't that keep them safe?"

"Actually, they are like any other tree. Ironwoods can be burned and they can be cut. It is after the wood is cut and dries that it hardens to its iron-like strength—the magical properties of their sap are the key to this transformation, which is to say the sap alone is even more precious than the wood."

"It's easy to guess why the fey don't like outsiders," Nicole muttered.

"Indeed. Unfortunately, since the beginning of Veil's kingdoms, there have been campaigns to harvest ironwood from Meridian and wars fought over ironwood. But during the dragon wars a great deal of the forest on the northern edge of Meridian bordered by Dusor and along the southern edge above Nol was burned quite completely. The fey, naturally, abandoned those areas and the new growth in those territories are uninhabited—and so provides a source of the wood for harvest that does not affect the homes of the fey. Please excuse me, we've got to get dinner going." With that, Tovar returned to the wagons.

She didn't have any argument left, but that explanation still didn't sit well with Nicole as she slid the saddle off Imber's back. The swooping movement of something in the sky caught her attention, and she looked up to see Leone swinging out of his horizontal position to land gracefully on his feet. He spent both days of their journey in the sky, keeping an eye out. She looked to Raiden and caught him watching his father as his golden wings turned to shimmering forms of light and retreated into his back.

"At what point did you realize the Council didn't give you your wings?" She wondered as she set the saddle down on the post beside Imber.

Raiden thought a moment. "When I saw Caeruleus receive his. At that ceremony I understood how The Council used a combination of blood-binding and alchemy to achieve the transformation—there was no way my wings had been their doing."

"You know I've only really seen them once," she added.

"Honestly, I forget they're there most of the time," he said.

"Good evening you two," Leone said as he strode toward them. "There's no one out here for miles but us."

"Thank you, Dad," Raiden said, and Nicole almost balked in surprise to hear Raiden call him that instead of *father*.

"Leone," Nicole said.

"Yes?"

"Did Raiden always have his wings?"

Leone laughed. "Naturally—he was born with them."

Nicole covered her mouth and Raiden gave her a perplexed look. "Baby Raiden had wings," she said from behind her fingers.

"He learned how to put them away before he was three, but he just loved to whip them out and startle people."

Nicole bit her lips together. "I almost can't stand how cute that is."

"Sure, cute until he started flying at age four, breaking nearly everything in the house. He'd jump off the highest places he could find wherever we went."

Nicole's laughter escaped through her nose, and Raiden looked at her with embarrassed confusion.

"Don't you remember?" she asked.

"I…thought I dreamt it all. I couldn't get them back."

Leone nodded, wearing a frown.

"The older I got and the fuzzier my memories became, it was easy to think of them as dreams."

Leone sighed. "That can happen—it has happened to many a celengel—self-doubt, forgetting how to be free. It happened to me."

"How did you get them back?" Nicole asked.

"Ah, well, soul-searching didn't do me any good, so I had to rely on the old fool-proof cure—falling. Your wings come right back. That's how I met Loak, actually, I found the highest cliff in Orodon, and he tried his damnedest to stop me from throwing myself off of it," Leone said, chuckling.

Nicole and Raiden shared a look of surprise that was shattered by laughter.

"And when did you finally find them again?" Leone wondered.

"Not long after meeting Nicole," Raiden said, casting a little smile at her. "Falling did the trick for me too."

"Oh," Leone said, concern creasing his forehead.

"Yeah, lucky for us both it's the fool-proof cure," Nicole said.

"I see."

Nicole thought a glow of pride lit Leone's face for a moment.

"I suppose I'll let you two finish tending to your horses and go help with…something," Leone said, a smile pushing up one side of his mouth.

"If I didn't know any better, I would say things don't seem as tense between you and your dad," Nicole said.

"I resented him for so much I didn't understand and, honestly, I'm grateful I was wrong. It doesn't undo the pain, or his absence, but…it's a relief to forgive him. Granted it's still a little strange after thinking he was dead for so long. We can't exactly pick up where we left off."

"What matters is you have him back," she offered. "And I'm glad, because I want to hear *all* the stories about baby Raiden."

Raiden laughed, pulling his saddle off Apellon.

They led Apellon and Imber away from camp to the river to drink.

"I bet Caeruleus has some good stories about you too," Nicole mused. "He already told me how hard you tried to teach him how to ether shift."

"Did he? So, you two finally found a chance to talk."

"Mhm."

The horses drank. Nicole and Raiden stood on the riverbank, looking up at the towering trees, the sun setting to their right, painting the sky in vivid hues that still couldn't distract from the ironwoods.

"So," Nicole said, leaning against him. "Can I see them again?"

"Right now?"

"It's just you and me," she said.

He looked around, confirming, and huffed. "All right."

He removed his jacket and sweater, tossed them into the grass and stood there in a grey tee shirt. Tongues of starlight unfurled behind him and feathery shadows formed within the light, stretching wide, forming wings as the light faded.

Nicole opened her mouth but found she was speechless. She stepped closer to him so that she could reach out and touch the dark silvery plumage.

"You can't be real," she muttered through a quiet laugh.

He smiled. "Well, I suppose neither is this then," he said, wrapping his wings around her and she watched in awe as they closed around them like feathered curtains. He slipped his hands into her hair and his fingers on her scalp sent a shiver through her as he bent down and pressed his lips to hers. Her body went hot and her heart ricocheted in her chest. He pulled away and straightened up, his curled mouth out of reach. "What a shame that wasn't real."

The next thing she knew her feet were off the ground, and she was in the air, tilting his face up to hers, her heart so giddy with him that she might have drifted away if she weren't holding his face in her hands. His hands were secured to her waist—her anchor. He pulled her into him, sternum to sternum, ribs to ribs.

Someone cleared his throat and a pair of giggles followed.

They both turned their faces, then looked to each other, laughing at each other's chagrin in the shadowy hideout of Raiden's wings.

"Sorry to interrupt," Leone said. "But if this continues, the camp might be encased in a grassy tomb."

Raiden pulled back his wings, and Nicole dropped to the ground. They looked past Leone, Fen and Asi to see the grass overgrown all around them and reaching halfway up the guards' tents at the perimeter. Finnegan leapt merrily through the grass, appearing and disappearing.

Raiden chuckled, but Nicole simmered with annoyance.

"Another time, I guess," he spoke quietly between them before she stepped away.

"I—uh—think dinner is ready," Leone said, turning hastily and wading through the grass back toward camp.

"Raiden, can we touch your wings?" Asi said.

He shrugged. "Sure."

Fen and Asi hopped and pushed through the grass around their thighs. Raiden turned and they each ran a hand down the back of his wing.

"So pretty," Fen said wistfully.

"Yes, he is," Nicole added under her breath, knowing he would hear and grinning as he pressed his lips together in embarrassment.

"I—um—thank you," he stammered.

Finnegan leapt out of the grass and froze, cocking his head at Raiden's wings and bounding forward with puffed up feathers.

"What's he doing?" Asi asked.

"Hell, if I know," Nicole said.

Finnegan forced his way between Nicole and Raiden. The griffin spread his wings, flashing the blue feathers underneath as he made himself as big as possible.

"Maybe he thinks you're another griffin," Asi giggled.

"Okay," Raiden said and his wings dissolved into light, disappearing into his back once again.

Finnegan cocked his head, folded his wings and turned away, disinterested.

"I guess he's territorial," Nicole said, watching him return to pouncing in the grass.

"Well, I found you first," Raiden said as they headed back toward camp.

"How *did* you meet?" Asi asked.

Nicole smiled at the thought.

"I accidentally ran through a portal," Raiden explained.

❧

Three of the five wagons were already on the other side of the river. Tovar made easy work of floating them across above the water with a hover charm.

"Hey girls," Nicole said quietly, nodding Asi and Fen over as she pulled the cinch strap of her saddle tight and fastened it.

"Yes?"

"What is it?"

"Ask Caeruleus if he'll take you across the river," she said, keeping her eye on Caeruleus well out of earshot as he carried a rolled-up tent into the last wagon.

"I thought we were riding across with you and Raiden," Fen said.

"You're still welcome to, I just think it would be nice to give him the chance to help someone else through the ether for a change," she said, putting on her best pleading sad face.

Asi nodded in agreement and looked to Fen.

"Okay," Fen agreed. "Are you sure we're not going to annoy him?"

"I don't think so," Nicole said.

"All right," Fen said.

The girls sauntered toward Caeruleus.

"Ready?" Nicole asked Imber, taking the horse's reins and walking her toward the river, peeking under the horse's chin to watch Asi and Fen stop Caeruleus and ask him.

Caeruleus shrugged and said something.

Asi continued and then Caeruleus nodded. Guards already had most of the horses across the river, or on their way, the water flowing around the horses' shoulders. Raiden was at the bank waiting for her with Apellon.

"Last wagon is ready to go," Sage called.

"Aren't Fen and Asi coming with us?" Raiden asked.

"Caeruleus is taking them across," she said, watching them walk to the riverbank.

Asi and Fen each took one of Caeruleus' hands and Nicole smiled privately as he looked across the river. The three of them disappeared into the air like flames blown out, and on the other side of the river they emerged from ether. The girls turned and waved at Nicole. She waved back.

"He seems to shift as well as anyone," she said.

"So long as he can see where he's going, he's only ever been able to go as far as he can see," Raiden said, putting his foot into the stirrup and hoisting himself up onto the saddle on Apellon's back.

"Huh," Nicole grabbed her saddle and, with the help of a little weightlessness, pulled herself up easily. She thought about shifting. No matter how far she wanted to go, all she ever had to do was know where she wanted to be and picture it in her mind, or picture the person she wanted to be with, wherever they may be. If Caeruleus could only shift somewhere in his sight, did that mean he couldn't picture places or people in his head clearly?

"Shall we?" Raiden asked, nudging Apellon with his heels.

"Yeah," she agreed, encouraging Imber toward the water with a couple clicks of her tongue.

Tovar elevated the last two wagons with a charm and sent them across the river with the final group of guards on horseback. Loak wadded across, the water only partway up his chest, and pulled any of the horses that were less confident into the water.

Nicole, Imber, Raiden and Apellon brought up the rear of the party as they set out across the Jormungandr. *At least a football field across*, Nicole thought as she eyed the distance. A third of the way across the water made it up to her knees beside Imber's shoulders. The sky was clear, the sun rising into the blue, and Nicole wondered when Gordan and Mitchell would meet up with them.

"Are the fey hostile toward dragons?" Nicole asked.

"I really don't know. The fey are very private. There's not much in the history books about what went on in Meridian—other than how much of the forest was burned."

Nicole's heart sank, of course, there had been an onslaught of fire. How could the fey do anything but hate the dragons? She tried to dredge up her heart and enjoy the beauty of the world around her. The sun glistened on the water. The sky of Veil seemed to be a richer shade of blue. She sighed.

A shadow moving in the water beside her caught Nicole's eye, and she looked just as something broke the surface and flashed across her vision in a blur. It caught the glinting key hanging from her neck and pulled her off her saddle before she knew what was happening.

Realization hit with the crash and gurgle of water in her ears as she tumbled in the current, trying to find the creature still pulling on her key—its chord twisted and dug into her neck. Almost as suddenly as Nicole was in the water, whatever had the key released it. Before she could find which direction was up, flashes of dark eyes peering into hers flickered across her vision, creeping out of the past. Phantom hands from dark waters reached out of her memory taking hold of her limbs, and her heart relived the panic.

No—she refused to return to dark-water nightmares. She wanted the daylight, blue skies and seas of grass. One moment she was slipping through the current, and the next she hit the ground, face in the sweet grass, gasping at the air in the sunshine. *I'm all right,* she thought as she pushed herself up onto her hands and knees, heavy in her soaked clothes, her heart drumming in her head and the rasp of her breaths in her ears. She heard the sound of her name, faint and distant—how far had the river taken her?

When a hand grasped her shoulder and her heart reeled, every muscle in her body tensed. The power inside her snapped, a chord pulled too tight, and fire rolled through her. She heard a shriek behind her, and she threw herself onto her back to see Fen backing away, clutching her hand to her chest, looking at Nicole with a pain-twisted face and watering eyes.

"Fen," Nicole breathed.

"What happened?" Asi asked, running toward them with Caeruleus close behind her.

Raiden, atop Apellon and with Imber's reigns in hand, appeared out of the ether on the riverbank a hundred feet away, the horses rearing and agitated by the shift, but Raiden slid off his saddle before Apellon could throw him. He ran toward them.

Nicole's breaths turned to gasps and her heart clenched; she hurt Fen. Her ears rang and the Council's chamber flickered before her eyes. Her skin crawled like they were inside her again and she shuddered, revolted. She blinked hard and saw Fen's pained face. She hurt Fen.

"Fen—I—" she choked—suddenly Raiden stood bleeding in the dark hall before her. She didn't want to cause the people she loved any more trouble or pain. "I'm sorry." She couldn't even hear herself through the ringing in her ears. *No. I don't want to be here anymore.* When she looked down at her hands, Raiden's sword was there. Frantically, she shook the courts out of her head and scrambled to her feet. *I don't want to be here.*

"Nicole?" Fen said, eyes wide, her gaze suddenly searching.

Nicole shook her head. *I don't want you to see me.*

"Where is she?" Asi asked.

"What happened?" Raiden arrived, panting. Their voices were distant and muffled.

The courts flickered in and out around Raiden. Nicole whirled around, stumbling to get away—running from the present—running from the past.

"Nicole, where are you?!" Asi cried.

"Nicole!" Raiden called, panic creeping into his heart despite Gordan's insistence that the Meridian forest was a safe place. He knew she wouldn't come back, not on her own.

"Nicole, I'm fine," Fen shouted.

"Let me see," Caeruleus implored.

Raiden turned to Fen, who cringed as she pulled her arm away from her chest and opened her hand. Her palm was raw, the burned skin marbled red and white.

"Tovar will have something for that," Raiden said.

"But what happened?" Asi demanded. "I only saw her fall into the water."

"Nixies," Raiden said. "After Nicole fell, one tried to snatch my key too—they love any shiny trinket. We should have had the keys tucked away."

"Nicole showed up on the bank. All I did was touch her—she looked so scared. I know she didn't mean to—" Fen hissed in pain.

Raiden sighed. "Let's go see Tovar."

"What about Nicole?" Asi asked. "Do we really think that man couldn't be here? Is it safe?"

"Gordan thinks so, but I don't know what to think anymore,"

Raiden said, looking toward the trees anxiously. He suspected Venarius was a less of a threat to Nicole than guilt right now.

"We'll go see Tovar," Caeruleus said. "You find Nicole."

Raiden nodded. "Tell them to keep going. We'll meet up… when I find her."

"Should you maybe take Sage and Netti with you?"

"Thank you, but no."

Raiden set off toward the trees, his heart heavy knowing that Nicole didn't want to be found but desperately needed to be. He hoped she would forgive him for not allowing her the solitude she wanted.

He muttered a spell he used once before to find Nicole. "Onthullen troed," the words warmed his chest with magic, and the blue glow of Nicole's footsteps bloomed like flowers in the grass, her stride long and desperate as it disappeared into the trees.

He followed the trail at a comfortable pace, hoping he could give her the time alone she needed and that she wouldn't go too far. Under the gargantuan shelter of the ironwoods, their canopies breathtakingly high overhead. Raiden smiled at the bitter nostalgia of following this spell again, it felt like years ago now since the first time. The trail of glowing blue footfalls gradually bloomed ahead of him into the Meridian forest.

Nicole ran, filling her head with the therapeutic rhythm of her stride and her heart and her breath. Each impact of shoe against the earth fought back the nauseating sensation of the Council slithered under her skin. The piercing ringing in her ears faded, but when she thought of Fen's face the courts would seize her vision again. She blinked—the trees returned and she almost ran straight into one. She avoided it, stumbled and slowed to a stagger. Gasping and angry, she wanted to scream but didn't have the breath for it. Maybe it was wrong to let anyone get close—this was her life now; she was all sharp broken edges. If she wasn't facing enemies, she was fighting nightmares and either way someone she loved ended up hurt—whether trying to protect her, or worse, *by* her—the torture Raiden endured in the courts—near-death by a thousand cuts—Gordan suffering her wounds. Today it was Fen, burned for trying to help because Nicole couldn't handle a few bad memories. Who would it be tomorrow?

Her gasping breaths slowed, but her heart still thundered in the cool shade of the forest. She looked around, realizing she had no idea which way she had come or which way she should go now. Did she want to go back—should she—could she disappear into the forest and live in peaceful hiding for the rest of her days?

A beautiful ethereal glow just beyond the nearest trees caught her eye and she spotted a procession of stunning figures.

The glowing procession emerged from behind the vast trunk of an ironwood, and Nicole was awestruck by them as they drew closer. They moved with an unworldly grace, and in the shadow-veiled shelter of the ironwood trees, the party gleamed. Their clothing might have been made of moonlight. Silver adornments practically dripped like liquid around the form of the smallest female figure. She looked to be ten and she glinted in the shadows. Nicole shrank where she stood; the prospect of being seen had never seemed more terrible to her than now in the presence of their uncanny beauty.

A tall figure with platinum hair falling loose down her back approached the party. She stopped and bowed so deeply that her hair pooled on the forest floor.

"They have arrived, my lady," the woman said as she stood tall once again. "Do you wish to greet the bearers of the keys?"

Nicole pressed herself in the tree behind her, fearing they would see through her invisibility.

"My only wish," said the child replied in a delicate voice, "is to see them pass through Meridian and watch them leave."

"Are you troubled by what the trees have said about her, Lady Day?" A man as pale and bright as the moon bowed a little as he spoke to the girl.

"No," she answered gently.

They continued on. Realizing she'd been holding her breath, Nicole let out the stale air in her lungs. She slumped to the ground, leaned against the base of the tree, and dropped her head back to look up the dizzying height of the trunk. Did she feel so small and lowly because of the gargantuan trees around her? She wasn't sure if she felt wretched and ugly in comparison to the glowing procession of Lady Day and her fellow fey or if she was finally realizing how ugly her world seemed to be now because she was the fera.

She closed her eyes and sighed. If she hurt anyone else that she loved she would finally break apart. There would be no more putting herself back together because there were too many pieces to hold in place now. Her heart finally eased to a sad tempo to mark the time as she sat there in the forest's gentle silence.

With her mind slipping back into the water and tumbling helplessly through memories, she wasn't sure how long she ruminated in the cool quiet air.

A tiny utterance of Raiden's voice—"Hi"—made her eyes burn with both comfort and shame. She pulled her gaze back down from the canopies above to see Raiden standing there—behind him a trail of glowing shoe prints led to her. His gaze searched for her too high.

"Will you let me see you?"

She felt like shrinking into the dirt at the thought of Raiden's eyes on her.

"Talk to me at least," he said.

"How badly did I hurt her?"

"A minor burn that Tovar has already healed by now—she's all right."

Nicole watched his troubled eyes search the air around her. As bad as she felt, she couldn't watch him standing there like that— the sadness in his eyes and his pinched brow. She got up and moved into his arms without thinking how startling a ghostly embrace might be, but he chuckled softly.

"There you are," he said, a smile in his voice. "Are you okay?"

"I'm not the one who was hurt," she said into his sternum.

"That's not true."

She fought hard to swallow back the lump in her throat.

"What happened?" He asked.

Her time in the water made her shudder. "I don't know. I panicked in the water. It feels so stupid to say I was scared by memories, kelpies and mermaid and the Courts."

"It's not stupid," he said, resting his cheek against her head. "You know I don't like crowds."

"I know," she said.

"Haven't I told you why?"

"No."

"I can't stop reliving the day of the massacre in Cantis—around too many people, too much noise, I go right back to that day. I didn't even see it happen locked away in that closet, but I heard an entire city screaming—dying...do you know what helps me stay here instead of going back there?"

Her heart pounded, anticipating the answer.

"You—you holding my hand keeps me from going back to that place. You keep me here."

Her heart raced and she held onto him.

"You keep my nightmares away," she murmured into him.

"We're perfect for each other, don't you think?"

A single tiny laugh slipped out. "I guess I can't argue with that."

"Good, because I don't see that changing...although, I did anticipate getting to *see you* every day, so long as you're here—"

She looked up. "I'm still invisible?"

He smiled at her. "Not anymore." He moved her hair back, and she could see his eyes fall on the branching scar that crossed her collarbone and ended along her jaw. "We have scars, Nicole. You're no less beautiful for this one—" he brushed the scar with his fingertips. "—or any of the ones I can't see. You know that, right?"

Her body bloomed with heat that rushed straight to her face, her eyes stinging with tears.

"Shall we join the others?" he asked.

She looked around. "Can we just disappear into the forest together?"

"I would love to," he said, grinning before he kissed her. "But there are several people who would be heartbroken if they never saw you again, Fen especially—she's very worried about you."

Nicole sighed. "I suppose I have to go back eventually."

"You can't fool me," he said, tightening his embrace. "You don't really want to be alone."

"Fine. I'd miss them too...and the fey probably won't want us to stay anyway."

They didn't have to wander far before the sound of wagon wheels, horses' hooves, and murmured conversation crept through the forest, leading Nicole and Raiden to their party. Nicole could hear Asi and Fen's voices as they walked Apellon and Imber by their reigns at the front of the group.

"Keren would love to be here," Asi said, marveling up at the dizzying height of the trees all around them.

"I wonder what these trees say," Fen mused.

Nicole's stride shortened. She fell a step behind Raiden—her urge to hide was heavy on her shoulders while Raiden held her hand tightly and pulled her forward.

Asi spotted them. "You found her!"

When Fen dropped Imber's reins and ran toward them, Nicole lowered her gaze, her eyes burning again.

Fen hugged her. "Are you okay? I didn't mean to scare you."

"I'm so sorry, Fen."

"I'm all right, look!" She released Nicole and held out her hand. "You'd never know it happened."

Nicole frowned, studying Fen's hand, her soft brown skin unmarred.

"It was an accident, don't feel bad," Fen said, her eyes shiny with the approach of tears.

"It's hard not to," she confessed.

"You don't regret letting us come, do you?"

"Of course not, I love having you here," she said, but the truth of it was the joy of having Fen and Asi around came with just as much worry—and now she was sick with the idea that she might be more of a threat to them than Venarius.

Fen smiled.

Asi, now with Apellon's reins in one hand and Imber's in the other, reached them.

"They're still not too happy," she warned them. "They wouldn't let anyone ride."

"Well, then, we walk for now," Raiden said, taking Apellon's reins.

"Do you know which way we're even going?" Nicole wondered.

"Not at all."

❦

Tovar looked at his compass and scratched his head. "I know we entered the forest heading southeast toward Tine, but now I'm not sure if we're still on track."

"How's that?" Caeruleus asked.

"The compass can't quite settle on North…it looks like it wants to point that way," he said, pointing. "But that's definitely not North."

"How do you know if your compass is broken?" Caeruleus asked.

"North was mostly behind us when we started."

"Just ask for directions," Nicole said. She had her forehead pressed to Imber's as she stroked the horse's neck, hoping to calm her distress from being pulled through the ether by Raiden.

"Ask who?" Fen said.

Maybe Lady Day is still close by, whoever she is, Nicole thought. Surely, they knew how to remain unseen in their own forest.

"If you want to see us leave, we could use some help heading the right direction," Nicole called to those she knew were out there listening among the trees.

Everyone looked around for any sign of whom Nicole might be addressing.

"If there are any fey listening, they must not want to—oh," Raiden said, his surprise drawing everyone's attention to the green-skinned faerie lounging on the back of Imber's neck, its face perched atop the horse's head, blinking entirely-black eyes at Nicole.

"Lady Day said to take you the way you want to go," the faerie said.

Nicole resisted the urge to flinch away from the shining black gaze, much too much like a kelpie's eyes.

"We're headed for Nol," Nicole said.

"Is that the way you want to go?" the faerie asked skeptically, leaning closer.

Nicole's heart gave an anxious pound. Did it *know* she didn't want to go to Nol or had it heard her comment to Raiden about disappearing into the ironwood forest?

"Yes," she answered because luring out her enemy was her only option now.

"Fine," the faerie said, crawling up to stand between Imber's ears and springing off gracefully. Imber didn't seem to notice or care.

"You okay now?" Nicole murmured to Imber. The horse didn't side step away when Nicole stood beside her and placed her hands on the saddle, nor when she stuck her foot into the stirrup, so she hoisted herself up. "That's my girl," she whispered, leaning forward to stroke the length of her neck.

Apellon, however, still wanted little to do with Raiden and kept yanking his reins from Raiden's grip.

"Still mad at me then," Raiden chuckled.

"We'll make better time if no one's on foot," Tovar said. "Let's tie a lead to the wagon and let him follow."

"You can ride with me," Nicole suggested, half joking and patting the back of her saddle.

"All right," he said.

Once Apellon's lead was tied to the wagon, Raiden heaved himself up onto Imber's back and slid into the saddle snug behind Nicole, pushing her pelvis to the front of it. Her face flushed with heat and she bit back a smile.

"Is this okay?" He asked and his voice in her ear sent a shiver down her spine.

"Yeah," she said.

"I can sit behind the saddle," he said.

"No, that's fine." She liked him being close, very much, but she was glad that everyone was behind them and couldn't see her face. The faerie waved from up ahead. Nicole clicked her tongue and Imber set off walking. The movement only heightened her awareness of Raiden pressed against her. She stifled a nervous giggle, the flutter of her heart shooed the gloom from her chest.

His arms slid under hers and wrapped loosely around her, resting his hands in her lap behind her own. She could feel his face in her hair and hear him inhale before he let out a little sigh. Her heart tripped over itself. She felt loved and immediately afraid of losing that…him. She had come too close to that possibility more than once.

Raiden couldn't have been more content to pass the rest of the day pressed in close to Nicole. Nothing put his heart at ease like she did. He so seldom got the chance to soak up her presence this way. Although, he spent each night beside her now, most of that time he was asleep, enjoying her proximity only for a short time before he sank into slumber and after waking up to find her there again.

Since their separation by the Council, they had only brief moments alone, and never the chance to just be. There was always so much to do now—and maddeningly—always people around. He couldn't think of a time he had a chance like this—to relish the warm hum of her magic that he could feel through the contact of her against his chest, just barely perceptible but not unlike the soothing vibration of a cat purring.

By the end of the day, he felt like he could fall asleep there leaning against her, and he almost did until she pulled him back from the brink of dozing.

"Raiden?"

"Hmm?"

"They're setting up camp," she said.

"Are you sure?" He secured his arms firmly around her.

"Yes," she laughed.

"All right," he said with a sigh, straightening up and sliding off the saddle.

Nicole swung her leg over to dismount when a sudden shriek ripped through the air and—startled—she fell off Imber and into Raiden; they both hit the ground.

"No fire!" the faerie wailed at the guards who were setting up a stack of firewood.

"Jeez," Nicole hissed as they picked themselves up. "Scared the crap out of me."

"You heard the faerie," Loak said.

The forest grew dimmer and the full darkness of night settled in quickly, but they weren't left in the dark long enough to summon their own light charms. The moss around the trees and mushrooms peeking out from the forest floor bloomed with blue and green bioluminescence. The forest became its own starry sky and their party stood marveling for a long time before they prodded themselves back to work settling down for the night.

No one felt the need to pitch a tent and close out the world around them. They slept outside in the company of the forest. The air was still and comfortable.

"It's like being home," Asi whispered to Fen where they lay on the other side of Nicole.

Caeruleus was stretched out on his back, quiet, beside Raiden, but he could see his eye looking up into the lights of the forest.

"I wish magic was still a part of the old world," Nicole murmured. "We need it. I think we've been slowly dying without it."

Raiden pulled her closer.

"When we've finished choking the life out of our world will it affect Veil?" she wondered.

"I don't know," he admitted. How connected the two realms were these days—two parts of a broken whole—was a mystery so many books tried their best to solve.

"Is that why the old world was so…dry and barren?" Caeruleus asked beside Raiden.

Nicole tried to smother her laughter in Raiden's ribs and he smiled.

"You were in a city in the Sonoran Desert, Caeruleus, that's just the climate where I live."

"Oh. That makes sense."

Quiet laughter from all of them, even giggles from Asi and Fen, floated up into the lights of the forest.

℃℥

Nicole could feel the earth beneath their blanket, Raiden's breathing beside her, his arm under her pillow. She heard no other sounds around her, no one seemed to be stirring, so she wondered why she was awake—until she heard murmurs and realized that was what had pulled her up from dreams.

"They're this way…not far," the hushed voice crept through the forest.

Nicole opened her eyes. It was morning. The bioluminescence had gone to sleep, and the forest was dimly lit. She sat up and Raiden stirred—rubbing his face as soon as she pulled away from him. The soft crunch of footsteps made her tense.

"It's too early for this," a second voice muttered. Nicole jumped up, recognizing Mitchell's tone and tired inflection.

She spotted them just beyond camp as they stepped into view from behind a gargantuan ironwood. Gordan was leading a half-asleep Mitchell by the hand.

Nicole had to stifle a yelp of joy as she ran carefully through the sleeping forms of the camp to meet them. She threw an arm around each of their necks and pulled them into her. Gordan chuckled. When she released them, she couldn't help glancing down at their hands—still laced together. She beamed at them.

"Please tell me this is really happening," she had to whisper, but Gordan and her brother were absolutely holding hands, and she could barely contain her delight.

Gordan looked down as though to hide the smile on his face, and Mitchell's cheeks went pink as he rubbed the back of his neck. She wondered if they had even discussed the feelings behind their clasped hands.

"I guess it is," Mitchell said. He shrugged, his face getting redder.

"You two finally made it," Raiden said, his voice quiet with morning hoarseness. He pushed his hair away from his eyes, still heavy, and Nicole watched his gaze catch Gordan and Mitchell's joined hands. He smiled. "Glad to have you both back."

A succession of short percussive sniffs just above their heads seized their attention, and when they looked up, Nicole recognized their faerie guide clinging to the bark of the tree beside them. Her little green face was pinched into a scowl.

"You," she said, glaring at Gordan and Mitchell. "You smell like fire."

Gordan shot a quick glance at Nicole. "My apologies," he said.

"We've been in the forge for two days," Mitchell said quickly.

The faerie twisted her face at him and leapt down from the tree to run with an uncanny grace out of sight.

"Is that really why we smell like fire?" Mitchell whispered.

"No," Gordan said. "It's me."

Behind Nicole and Raiden sounds of the stirring camp rose into the air.

"Well, you're here in time for breakfast," Raiden said. "We should make it out of Meridian by tomorrow."

☙

Gordan couldn't help but notice that the faerie leading their party through Meridian kept a close eye on him. He wondered when she would realize he was a dragon and not just someone carrying the smell of an ironworker with him. He sat beside Mitchell at the front of one of the wagons, and by midmorning Mitchell had dozed off on his shoulder after their two-and-a-half days awake in the forge and just an hour of sleep on the Tempest.

Mostly he was glad he could have an eye on all the people he loved all at once again, and didn't mind creeping along at the feet of the ironwood giants, the day passed slowly. He even slept a little, lulled by the peace of the forest and the contentment of everyone around him.

When the forest grew dark and the ethereal lights swelled out of their hiding places, Gordan was reminded of the ruins in the wastelands. They made camp—no tents, just pillows and bed-rolls beneath the cloak of night and dancing forest lights. Gordan lay beside Mitchell—lost somewhere between the sweetness of where he was and the bitter past that he strived to keep behind him. But the lights above his head carried him back to the wastelands, back through the centuries as he fell asleep.

He knew he was dreaming when he smelled the metallic heat

of fire and smoke. The past never gave up trying to find him. Then a firm hand pressed into his chest and jostled him.

"Gordan," Mitchell said his name. He snapped upright, his heart lurching at the edge of panic in Mitchell's voice when he said his name, laden by dread.

A telltale orange glow in the distance met Gordan's eyes, and his chest tightened around his heart.

"No," he breathed.

Nicole sat up, startled from sleep by the crackle of fire in the distance and the heat rolling over their camp. Raiden, Caeruleus, Loak—everyone dragged themselves out of their slumber, waking with alarm as their groggy eyes saw the foreboding glow through the trees.

Gordan stumbled, legs caught in the blanket as he jumped to his feet. The flames in the distance roared alive and hungry. He knew this sound. It wasn't just fire. It was dragon fire. *That can't be.* He ran.

"What are you doing?" Mitchell demanded.

"Gordan," Nicole scrambled to her feet as well, following him.

They didn't have to go far. The flames moved swiftly, closing in on their camp. The intense heat hit them first and Nicole stopped, throwing her arm up to shield her face from it. It was sweltering against her skin but not his. A pulse of magic rolled through the air, pushing back the heat, but as it hit the flames ahead, the fire surged forward.

"It's dragon fire," he shouted over the noise of it. "Magic will only feed it."

The flames twisted and moved around the trees in a long serpentine form. A pointed and horned head and wings that reached up into the canopy and scorched the leaves. The dancing serpentine form of the dragon fire wound around one of the giant ironwoods and its burning white eyes spotted them.

The heat pushed Nicole back as Gordan's shape grew and his wings unfurled. He charged into the fire, and she watched, dismayed, as she backed into a tree, unable to take her eyes away from her friend and the fire lunging toward him, glinting metallic like Gim, only it was nearly twice Gordan's size. She knew she should turn and run, but she froze.

Were angry dragons hiding somewhere in the mainland, or had someone brought dragon's breath into the meridian forest? *It's an immortal flame*, he had told her. How did you beat an immortal flame? Gordan collided with the dragon fire, opening his jaws wide and sinking his teeth into its fiery form. Shock seized her face as she understood what he was doing.

Dragon's breath was immortal; it would consume without end…unless it was consumed. Gordan ripped and tore at the writhing form. Its flames did not deter him. As he consumed it piece by piece, its form shrank and the unbearable heat in the air eased. At last Gordan gulped down the tattered remains of the dwindling dragon's breath, and the flames in the trees turned to docile flickering fires.

Nicole shook herself from her disbelief and let out enough magic to push gravity away and jump through the ether, emerging above the smoldering canopy where she poured her magic into the sky and pleaded desperately for rain until clouds bloomed in the air, smothering the stars and rumbling with purpose just before the water fell.

She took a deep breath and slipped back through the ether to the forest floor where Gordan condensed himself into the shape of a man, stooped and panting.

"Gordan," she reached for him but wasn't sure if she should touch him or not. "Are you all right?"

He shook his head, held up a finger, and turned his face away from her, exhaling a short flourish of fire with a sigh.

"That is never pleasant," he said.

She sagged with relief and hugged him. The rain fell through the bare canopy, and the rest of the remaining fires languished, hissing and shrinking beneath the raindrops. They weren't far from the camp; All were on their feet and staring in awe.

"I knew it," a small voice shrieked. "Dragon," their faerie guide hissed, spitting. Beside her stood a slender white-haired man, his locks nearly as long as he was tall.

"Bringing dragon fire into our forest is punishable by death," the elven man said coldly.

"I did not bring that fire here," Gordan said sternly.

"He stopped it," Nicole added, her voice shaking with anger.

"Dragon fire has *one* source. This is not your kingdom. That key cannot hide such heinous lies, nor does it put you above our laws."

Nicole realized they were surrounded by an army of pale white-haired fey, silver armor gleaming in the night.

"Gordan didn't start that fire," Nicole growled, stepping in front of him. Gordan took her hand, but she would not back down.

"Everyone here can attest to that," Raiden said, stepping up to stand beside her.

"You can try to dress up hate as law all you want, but try to kill him, and you'll deeply regret it." Nicole's power crackled beneath her skin, standing her hair on end, creeping into the air around her and lifting her curls into weightlessness. The earth trembled beneath her feet.

The elven man glared at her and at everyone who stepped up to stand around Gordan—Caeruleus, Fen, Leone, Asi, Tovar, Loak and all their guards. The rain was the only sound as they stared each other down.

"Pack your camp and get out of our forest. You are no longer welcome here," he finally said, glowering.

❧

They were escorted through the night, surrounded by the elven troops until they reached the edge of the Meridian forest. It was a tense final leg of their trek. Everyone stayed close to Gordan and on their guard as they marched. The air was so taught with mistrust and loathing that Gordan's head was pounding by the time they left the forest behind them an hour past sunrise.

Focusing on Mitchell's hand in his and taking solace in the relief seeping into the air as they put Meridian far behind them, he closed his eyes and leaned his head back against the wagon.

"Someone brought dragon's breath into that forest," Gordan said quietly to Mitchell.

"The same someone who would try to bring down the Tempest, I'm guessing."

"My thoughts exactly. Encite conflict with the fey—maybe they get lucky and Nicole loses some of the people closest to her."

Twenty-six

The journey through Nol took three more days. They passed through towns that welcomed them into their inns and celebrated their arrival. Gordan remained in the caravan, and Mitchell, Nicole and Raiden stayed with him, opting to let everyone else enjoy the nicer accommodations and hospitality. They were all anxious for his safety among crowds and the caravans were safer for both Nicole and him. The incident in Meridian left everyone feeling like Venarius was looming overhead and they trusted their spell-protected caravans more than any of the inns offered to them.

As the caravan drifted through Nol's countryside between towns there stood forlorn ruins—as common as the great rocks that rose from the moors like the backs of whales breaking the surface of the sea and the scattered islands of forest—the shreds of razed villages lingering like forgotten cemeteries left to be reclaimed by nature. Some were almost unnoticed, piles of stone too uniform to be natural. A pointed archway refusing to topple, a half-crumbled wall resisting the loss of its purpose to encroaching growth—Nicole knew the history of these remains from the way Gordan hung his head and would not look at them.

They arrived in the city of Tine in the early afternoon on the third day after leaving Meridian. At first people ran to the street to wave, but word traveled faster than they did, and eventually the streets were a roar of people cheering, throwing flower petals, singing the old songs about the keys, waving flags of all colors in welcome to the prophesied kings.

They didn't even need to know the way through the city streets. Their path was laid out before them as the only available option through the streets—any other road choked by crowds—and eventually they arrived at the ornate gates to the palace grounds of Tine, home of Prince Cinder of Nol.

The long avenue across the lush green lawn brought them to the entrance of the sprawling palace. It stretched out luxuriously across the grounds, no towers or spires reaching for the clouds. They were met by two people—a man and a woman standing side by side. There were several more figures lined up on either side of them, but they were not people, they were human-sized cloth dolls dressed in household uniforms—servants without needs.

"That's not creepy at all," Mitchell said under his breath.

Nicole glanced at him and cringed in agreement.

"Welcome, Your Majesties," the man said with a bow.

"We are so pleased to receive you in honor of Prince Cinder," the woman said with an identical bow.

"My name is Thomas, Prince Cinder's right hand," he introduced himself.

"I'm Mirabel. I oversee the household," she said. "No doubt, you will all like some rest after your journey. Our palace hands here will help you with any labor. You will find the stables and barracks on the east side of the palace grounds."

"We have rooms in the palace for everyone," Thomas said. "If you'll follow us."

Thomas and Mirabel turned toward the palace and led them inside. Straight ahead was a set of doors and to the left and right of those grand doors extended long hallways.

Thomas halted and raised his arm in invitation to the left. "This way gentlemen."

In precisely the same manner, Mirabel gestured to the right. "Your Highness, I will show you and your ladies to your chambers, this way," she said with a smile.

The guys drifted to the left as directed, Raiden casting a disappointed glance back at her.

"Actually," Nicole said quickly. "Raiden and I share a room."

Mirabel balked and lowered her voice to a low whisper. "Majesty, here it is quite improper to share a room with a man if you are not married—not that I frown upon lovers—but here— people will say—"

"We are," Nicole said without flinching. The lie hardly mattered to her; they were together, and she wasn't about to let silly social technicalities keep her from her peaceful night's sleep.

"I—I beg your pardon, your highness," she sputtered, turning red. "Please forgive me, I did not mean to insinuate—neither of you wear bands of marriage—I was not told you and the king are married."

"You're what now?" Mitchell asked, spinning around with interest. Raiden and Gordan both stopped beside him, turning curiously. Raiden straightened up, eyes wide and mouth amused. In her agitation, Mirabel didn't catch the confusion among them.

"I'll see to it that your things arrive to the proper room. Excuse me. This way, ladies," Mirabel said, bowing more drastically than before as she whirled around and hurried off. Fen and Asi snickered as they followed, waving to Nicole in farewell.

"Did I hear that we're married?" Raiden asked quietly.

"She was making a big deal about separate rooms," she murmured back.

"Guess that makes this your honeymoon," Mitchell muttered with a chuckle.

Her face flushed with fire and she tried to fight it back. Mitchell's suggestive quips were nothing new, but she glanced at Raiden and saw him glance at her wearing the same embarrassed expression.

Thomas lead them through the long corridors of the sprawling palace, it seemed to be only a single story, but the ceilings were two stories high. At last Thomas stopped outside a door.

"For her majesty's brother," he said and continued down the hall to the next door. "And for you…sir," he said to Gordan before crossing the hall. "For the prophesied kings."

"Thank you, Thomas," Raiden said stiffly.

"Prince Cinder hopes you will feel at home here. You are welcome to explore the palace and the grounds as you please. The Prince will welcome you personally at his birthday celebration tonight." Thomas bowed and left them.

Nicole let out a little groan.

"I'm sure it won't be so bad," Raiden said, unconvincingly as he opened the door to their room.

"Yeah, you aren't expected to wear a dress," she answered, with a bitter laugh as she stepped inside and lost her gaze to the dark wood-paneled rooms, to intricate carved moldings that were leafed in gold, to the diamond-paned windows, and to the painted ceilings high overhead.

"Wear whatever you want. Who is going to stop you?" Raiden said as he followed her inside and stopped beside her to take in the rooms. "Wow."

"Yeah," she agreed.

She wandered deeper inside, past the little entrance chamber, through a sitting room with two couches and a fireplace, and finally found a bed in the third room. There was an ornate tasseled canopy over the bed and from it hung heavy brocade curtains tied open. She turned around as Raiden walked in.

"I can't sleep here," she said, shaking her head.

He laughed. "Why not?"

"I feel like I shouldn't be touching anything, let alone disturbing the bed," she said. She'd only ever seen places like this, carefully pre-served or replicated from centuries long gone in pictures. Just looking down at her hiking boots against the luxurious carpet appalled her. *I don't belong here.* "I think I'd be more comfortable in the stables with Imber, and I bet they're unnecessarily fancy too."

Raiden caught her as she tried to leave the room. "Don't be ridiculous." He pulled her by the arm toward the bed, and she trudged behind him like an anchor. He fell back onto the bed and tugged her down beside him. "See, no harm done. And when you close your eyes, it's exactly like any other boring bed."

She smiled, closing her eyes. "I don't know. I can still hear the luxury," she said, relaxing into the comforter with her hand still in his. Then she felt him move beside her, and his lips pressed against hers. She opened her eyes just as he leaned away.

"Forgive me, I thought I should kiss my *wife* for the first time," he said, leaning on his arm, smiling. "I just found out we're married after all."

She laughed, pressing her hands to her face to hide the embarrassment. "Only while we're in Nol. After this I go back to being your—" She stopped short.

"My what?" he asked, giving her a devilish look that made her heart pound.

She realized that she'd never thought of herself as a girlfriend or called him her boyfriend, not once. Those words felt so flimsy for what she and Raiden were—what they'd been through, and what they were willing to do for each other. "I don't know. Forget I said it. What do labels matter anyway? We're us, we're the same *us* here as we are anywhere else."

"So then, if we're going to say we're married *here*, why not everywhere else?"

Her heart sped away nervously. She pulled her shoulders toward her ears. This is what she had been afraid of—the absurdity of becoming a tangled mess of two psyches that would probably never extricate themselves from each other, a knotted monstrosity of attachment and sentiment that would make life more difficult, a three legged race—"Why not just call ourselves a monster with two heads?"

"As long as it means the same thing," he said through a laugh.

"A marriage can be broken. I don't think you can separate a monster with two heads." It felt as dreadful as it did wonderful. *If one dies, what happens to the other head?*

His hand closed around hers. "Good, I like the sound of that."

☙

Gordan opened his eyes to the brocade canopy overhead, surprised by how tired he had been and how easily he had slipped into a shallow sleep when he had lain down on his bed. His still-dozing mind wavered between feeling like he'd woken up in his past and knowing when and where he was. He never expected to be back, in this lavish world of Nol.

He got up, still bearing the weight of the events on the Tempest. He couldn't wait around for the perfect opportunity to tell her what had happened—there was none. No matter how much he enjoyed that she was smiling more these days, he couldn't let that stop him. She needed to know every move Venarius made. Keeping her in the dark—even for the sake of her happiness—was wrong.

Even as he crossed the hall from his rooms to Nicole and Raiden's rooms, he could tell she wasn't there. The door was open and he stopped to knock anyway. Raiden was seated on one of the couches, peering into his cupped hands when he looked up.

"Gordan," he said, closing his right hand and slipping it into his pocket.

"Where's Nicole?"

"She took Finnegan out to run around the grounds, tire him out before we have to go to the celebration this evening."

"I see," Gordan said, suspicious of Raiden's secretive moment. Raiden could compose his face perfectly but couldn't hide the twinge of shame from a lie twisting the air. Knowing Raiden, Gordan could think of only one thing that would make him feel guilty. "Might I ask what you're hiding?"

Raiden sighed and pulled the object from his pocket and held it up. Glinting in the light falling through the windows behind it was a small crystal ball.

"Raiden, you haven't."

"I check only hours ahead, just for a little peace of mind, nothing bigger than that. I'm not letting myself get lost in the future."

Gordan shook his head sympathetically. "You know I understand your motives, but your sanity isn't the only thing at risk when you get caught up in the Sight."

"I know, but these little glimpses are harmless. The crystal helps me control it. The Sight even forces its way in less than before."

"There's no telling how long we'll be playing this game with Venarius. Are you considering how to adapt to this fight when you're blind?"

"I'm not going blind," he snapped back, exasperated.

"For now, but you know that's where this path leads, Raiden, no matter how slowly you take each step."

Raiden set the crystal down on the low table in front of him and pushed his hands back through his hair. "You sound like my mother," he said, a nostalgic smile pulling at his mouth. Then he looked at Gordan with that sad curl on his lips. "Thank you, Gordan. I do appreciate your concern."

"I take it Nicole doesn't know about that," Gordan said, nodding toward the crystal.

Raiden shook his head.

"Believe me. Secrets are poison."

Raiden sighed.

"I should go find Nicole, I would like fewer secrets in my chest."

"What do you mean?"

"The Tempest was attacked when we were returning from Orodon, and I think she needs to know. Venarius is making strategic moves, and we were unprepared."

❧

Nicole ran, relishing the painful strain of her heaving lungs as she tried to think of the last time she went on a proper run—not running for her life from some enemy or from her mistakes, just reminding herself that her body beloned to her through the burn in her legs and the pounding of her heart.

Finnegan loped beside her and leapt into the air, gliding above the ground beside her for several strides before landing. She put distance between them and he bounded after her, leaping and gliding again, sailing ahead of her. She surged faster and caught up where he landed. When she snatched at his tail, he tore off into a startled sprint.

A burst of laughter impeded her breathing and her posture, but she straightened up and pushed on, spotting a figure ahead crossing the immaculate lawn at a leisurely stroll. As she neared, she could see that it was Gordan.

"Come on, Finn," she said, breathlessly as she sprinted past him to get to Gordan first. The griffin picked up speed and caught her, springing into the air and soaring past Gordan who ducked beneath a wing. She sank to the ground in defeat. "Okay, you win," she said, gasping.

"Hello," Gordan said, peering down at her.

"Hey," she panted, her vision spinning a little as she looked up at him from her back. The perplexed look on his face caught her off guard. "What is it?"

"Nothing, I'm just enjoying you feeling more like yourself. You seem happier."

"Then why do *you* sound so troubled?" she asked, her breaths still heaving.

He frowned and offered her his hand.

"There's something I've been meaning to tell you." He pulled her onto her feet.

"Okay."

"We encountered some trouble on our trip—the Tempest was attacked on our way back from Orodon."

"What?"

"There was another ship. The Council had a whole fleet of ships designed for killing dragons. It would seem with the fall of the Council their remaining fleet is out there for hire."

Nicole's straining heart clenched with dread as it pounded.

"We're fine—obviously," he said. "I handled it. I just didn't want you to be left in the dark. I know it's distressing, but keeping it a secret felt wrong. The bliss of ignorance doesn't outweigh knowing all the moves your enemy makes."

Nicole closed her eyes, breathing deeply. *He attacked the Tempest—did he think that would work, that I was there? What kind of plan is that? It doesn't match his usual patterns. How many more of the Council's ships could he have under his employment?*

"Nicole?"

"Sorry, just thinking."

"Spiraling is more like it."

"You knew I would."

"Yes, and that's why Mitchell didn't want to tell you."

"Of course, he didn't. Mitch thinks that pretending bad things didn't happen makes them go away," she said, well-aged anger sneaking up through her annoyance. *That's how we dealt with Mom leaving.*

"He only wants to protect you from some grief," Gordan said softly. "I certainly understand the feeling. You've endured more than enough."

"Well, it doesn't make it any better, does it? At least, you get that," she sighed. "Thank you for telling me."

"Of course."

"Was anyone hurt? Are you and Mitchell okay? Rhee, Priseil?" Her heart felt like she was running again.

Gordan held up his hands to quell her. "The only one hurt was the Tempest and the remainder of our trip to the palace was slower than usual. But Captain Rhee said she should have the ship like new again in no time."

They were silent and Gordan looked down. Nicole watched Finnegan prancing and gliding around them.

"I am sorry, though, to steal your happiness away like that."

Nicole took a deep breath and let it out. "You don't have to apologize. The fact that I'm feeling more like myself is not because I willfully forgot about the bad things. It's not like I can forget he's out there," she muttered. "I just don't want to let that cloud darken the days I have. Whether any of us like to admit it or not, there's a chance I don't have a lot of time with the people I love. Maybe we don't win, but I'll be damned if I don't live a little until then."

Gordan sighed, a smile on his lips as he trapped her in his arms.

"Gordan, I'm sweaty and gross," she said, turning her face away from his chest.

"I couldn't care less."

"What happened to you not liking hugs?"

"You did."

"All right, release me, dragon," she said, chuckling. "I've got a griffin to tire out before we go to a party tonight."

He let her go, smiling back at her attempted scowl.

Gordan watched her leave, running alongside Finnegan and wondered for himself how she had undone all his work to keep himself alone and safe from loss for the last several centuries. Since meeting her, every time she hugged him, he couldn't help feeling *her* comfort and relief in each embrace. Perhaps her feelings became his own somewhere along the way. He liked knowing she felt better in his arms, and soon he couldn't help craving that comfort himself.

Without a doubt he was guaranteed to outlive the people he loved in this world and anticipating that loss hurt enough, but he thought about what she said and knew whatever time he had with Nicole and Mitchell and Raiden would outweigh that pain. That was the risk of loving in a world where everything was fragile and fleeting. Despite the closeness forged with Nicole, he couldn't deny he was still holding back because of that fear.

❧

Nicole wondered if she had time to take a nap before the ball as she walked the halls back to her room. Her face went hot thinking of Raiden being there. Along the way she studied the suits of armor they had passed and noticed something she hadn't before. Stuffed-cloth bodies like the servants they had seen upon arriving were inside the suits of armor.

It occurred to her that these must move, but what inspired them to move she didn't know. She couldn't help veering away from them as she made her way back to her rooms. When she walked into the sitting room, it looked empty at first glance, the ornate decor overwhelmed the eye.

A body sat up from the couch. "Hey."

She jumped. Then realized it was just Mitchell.

"Jeez, sorry. Raiden said to tell you he went to see Loak and his dad—worried about security detail for the party, I guess," he chuckled to himself.

"Oh…okay," she said—relieved, but still a little annoyed with Mitchell. "I'm going to clean-up." She turned and left Mitchell on his couch. By the time she was sitting in the warm, scented water of the obnoxiously sized tub—more like a small indoor pool—her annoyance had seeped away. She was left fatigued and aching, both her body and her heart.

Mitchell and Gordan had been in danger even when she wasn't there. Infuriating as her brother could be, she really couldn't blame him. *I've done the same thing*—keeping secrets to spare him the burden of worry. Just because he was pissing her off, she couldn't let herself forget the fact that she could have lost him.

The luxury dripping down the walls in this place made her want to get out of the bath as quickly as possible, so she scrubbed with determined efficiency, lathered hastily, and sank below the water to shake the suds from her hair. As the water moved around her, for a split second she thought a hand slid against her skin and she jerked upright, gasping. The splash echoed around the spacious bathroom as she jumped up and searched the tumultuous water, immediately feeling foolish. She hurried out of the bath, leaving a trail of little puddles across the floor to the low table where plush towels were folded neatly.

There were more mirrors in this bathroom than anyone really needed. It felt like a fun-house in an unsettling kind of way. She grabbed a towel and shook out its folds before she dropped her face into it. It was big enough to get lost in and soft enough to fall asleep in.

She squeezed the towel around her hair and combed her fingers through it, realizing that her wet hair was almost to her belly button. How hadn't she noticed it growing so quickly over the last few weeks? She took a folded robe from the table and lost her train of thought when she slipped her arms into the sleeves. The fabric was velvety and slid over her skin with a soothing weight.

When she opened the bathroom door and peeked out, she saw the bedchamber was empty. She wandered through to the sitting room where Mitchell lay lounging on the couch with a leg slung over an armrest.

"Have a nice bath?" he asked.

She wondered if he heard her little splash-fest in the bathroom.

"It was fine," she said, folding her arms against her chest; against the ache inside her. "Did you have anything you wanted to tell me?"

He blinked at her. "What do you mean?"

She looked at him expectantly until he caved, cringing.

He sat up, "Gordan told you about what happened on our trip."

"Yeah."

"Look, it's not like I was gonna lie about it. I figured he was going to tell you since he made such a big deal about it," he said, standing up.

She crossed the room and caught him in her arms. "I don't care. You made it back."

"Well, yeah, thanks to Gordan."

"At least no one was hurt."

He scoffed.

"What?" she demanded.

"Is that what Gordan told you?" Mitchell asked, pulling away with a perturbed slant on his brow.

"Well, he said the Tempest suffered most of the damage."

Mitchell grumbled something under his breath.

"Am I missing something?" She demanded. "Aside from the whole incident."

"No—he didn't tell you the whole story, did he?"

"Not in detail."

"Gordan knew how to deal with the attacking ship. Rhee called it an enforcer or something like that. I guess the Council sent a whole fleet of them to wipe out the dragons once upon a time, and that's how Gordan knew they had a weak point. It only really managed to damage the cargo door. Everyone was okay. But what we can't know for sure is what the plan really was—if they were trying to bring us down or capture us or if they thought you were with us or not…"

"He knew I wasn't on that ship," she said, her heart growing heavy. "He's targeting the people close to me. That's what I've been afraid of this whole time."

"Look, we're sticking together from here on out. We're being careful and smart, okay? There's safety in numbers, right?"

"Yeah," she agreed halfheartedly.

There came a knock at the door, and they looked at each other with curious uncertainty.

"Come in," Nicole called.

The door opened. Thomas appeared, followed by two shapes floating along without assistance. One was a suit tailored into sharp angles at the shoulders, the other was a gown with a severe bodice, the neckline forming a peak pointing up and, in the back, an even taller rigid point that looked like it would jab her in the back of the head if she let it dip back in boredom. The only good thing about it was the color, crimson.

"Your highness, the prince has sent you and the king, as well as your party, the latest in Nol fashion to wear to the celebration. He looks forward to meeting you all tonight."

"Of course. Thank you, Thomas," Nicole said as pleasantly as she could to mask the disgust building in her chest the longer, she looked at the dress.

He bowed. "Master Mitchell, your attire has been delivered to your room as well."

"Great, thanks, Tom."

Thomas nodded, pivoted on his heel, and departed. When the door closed behind him, Mitchell's composure dissolved into snickering.

"Can you believe this thing?" Nicole said, appalled. It looked like it was designed to hold someone hostage.

Mitchell continued to laugh.

"At least the suit looks comfortable, I'd rather wear that," she muttered.

"Why don't you? That would cause quite the stir wouldn't it?" Mitchell said with a laugh, then he gasped. "Idea," he said with a grave voice. "Let's change the dress!"

"I'm listening," she said.

"We can turn it into a suit. I need paper and a pencil."

Nicole sighed and held out her hand. A pencil appeared in it and before Mitchell could re-request the paper, a single sheet fell out of the air like a leaf in front of his face, as he tried to catch it. He set to work scratching the pencil across the paper as he hunched over the low table, looking up now and then at the gown and suit.

"Okay," he said, sitting up and looking at his drawing with scrutiny. "What if you made a few alterations to that monstrosity." He handed her his drawing.

Nicole looked down at the sketch.

"Not a suit, not a gown. It goes both ways you could say," he said with a proud grin.

She laughed. "Yes, you're hilarious, well done."

"Thank you. I know."

"I wonder if this is going to offend people," she said, looking at her brother wearing the same devious look on his face as she wore.

"I hope so," he said, laughing.

❧

After almost getting lost looking for where Loak and the guards had been housed on the palace grounds, Raiden tried stepping through the ether and found that he arrived outside the door of the barracks. *So, they don't bar the ether here*, he thought. He had been trying to shift to Loak, so it seemed the buildings diverted visitors to the door rather than letting them in. *At least not entirely.*

He wondered if he could shift into the palace and made a note to try. A convenience for them could also be an open door to Venarius to get close. Maybe Prince Cinder would enlighten him on what kind of spells were protecting his residence.

Raiden knocked on the door, and shortly, it opened to Loak, hunching a little to see through the doorway.

"Ah, Raiden, come in. We're still getting settled."

"Is my father here with you?"

"No, no. After we finished sorting everything out in the stables and barracks, they put him up somewhere inside near you, the king's father and all," he said, chuckling. "Caeruleus, too. His father has connections with some of the nobility around here, I think."

"That's right," Raiden frowned. "They moved to Nol when they left Cantis." He hoped there wasn't any chance that Caeruleus' father might turn up.

"You should know they told us the guard won't be permitted to attend the party. I was told the celebration will be the safest place in the realm, and the prince does not allow the presence of guard in uniform. It dampens the mood, apparently, makes people feel *less* safe," Loak scoffed.

"Can they attend as guests, out of uniform?"

"That I don't know. Not sure how exclusive this party is. If it's open invitation, maybe."

"Let's see about that. I don't doubt that you're right about our guard not being much use against Venarius, but in civilian clothes they can be our ears among the attendees at this ball. Never know what we might overhear since Dawn has some prevalence in Nol."

"Right," Loak agreed.

"Have you spotted *Nol's* royal guard around here," Raiden added.

"You mean the dummies in armor?" Loak chuckled. "I've seen them. All I can guess is the Prince must trust spells more than people."

"I haven't seen any real people around here other than Thomas and Mirabel."

"You're right, the place is pretty deserted. Strange for Nol, I've always heard this place is a social playground that rarely sleeps."

"I'm going to see about finding my father and Caeruleus before this big celebration starts. This whole place feels like a trap."

Loak frowned. "I'm thinking the same thing."

"I'll see you at the celebration," Raiden said, turning away. He thought of his father and stepped into the ether, unsure where he would emerge. Again, he reformed with a door in front of him and he felt certain now that individual rooms were barred against magical entry. He took the handle but it wouldn't turn. He knocked.

"Come in," his father's muffled voice called from the other side of the door.

Raiden was about to call back, but he heard a click and out of curiosity tried the handle again. It opened and he stepped inside to a smaller but equally lavish suite of rooms as the ones Nicole and Raiden had been given.

"Raiden," his father greeted him with a yawn.

"Did I wake you?"

"I just figured I'd catch a little sleep so that I'll be more alert tonight. Royal parties can go on into the morning and I don't want heavy lids getting the better of me before the night is over."

"That's—thank you. I wanted to talk to you about this place. I don't like how empty it is, and I just wanted to ask you to keep Nicole in your sight if I can't."

"Of course."

"It seems we can't enter anyone's chambers through the ether. There are spells around here that do that much, at least."

"I would bet there are a number of spells at work," his father offered.

"Your door was locked until you said 'come in' a minute ago."

"Could be that the ether is barred to anyone but those the room permits, like the castle. I haven't tried—never learned to shift, myself."

Raiden hadn't stopped to think what being raised a celengel implied. Why *would* they learn to shift when they relied on their wings and valued them so much?

"This place does *seem* perfectly safe, doesn't it?" his father said.

"I'm reluctant to believe anywhere is safe, except for the palace of the keys."

"No doubt the best mentality to have if we're going to confound any traps that might be set for us, but not the best mentality for getting any sleep at night."

"Her safety is more important than sleep."

"How well can you keep her safe if you're exhausted?"

Raiden sighed.

Leone chuckled. "I'm not saying you should let your guard down, but you and Nicole are more valuable as allies than enemies here. This is a strange time in Veil with the Council gone and the keys claimed. Dawn holds sway over many in this realm, but the belief in Veil as a safe haven is just as strong. You and Nicole have support throughout the realm in everyone who has believed in the prophecy of the keys. The rulers are better off having an amiable relationship with you."

"Maybe."

"Here in this realm they have power, Raiden. Dawn wants Veil to return to the old world which means the disappearance of the land they rule over. I think you can trust that the rulers of Veil have a vested interest in the preservation of this realm. Without it they are no longer rulers."

Raiden nodded. He could think of no reason why any of the leaders in Veil would be supporters of Dawn, but that didn't mean Nicole was safe here, or that Venarius didn't have ways of getting into heavily protected places like this palace.

"You have a point, but I don't like how empty this place is."

"It's certainly strange for a royal court, but not having to worry about a court full of strangers surrounding us is certainly something to be grateful for. It doesn't necessarily mean something odd is going on around here."

Raiden wasn't sure if his worries were being assuaged or reinforced. He sighed. "Venarius attacked the Tempest while it was on its way back from Orodon. With our plans to be here in Nol so well-known, I'm inclined to believe he knew full well Nicole wasn't on that ship."

"You think he was making an attempt on Gordan and Mitchell."

"I do."

"I know she's your first concern, but remember that he's not trying to kill her. She's safer than any of us. The people protecting her are his enemies. I, for one, am concerned for you."

Raiden's jaw clenched. "I understand what you're saying, but I need you to promise me that if the situation should ever arise, you'll make sure she's safe even at the cost of *my* safety. Just because he's not trying to kill her like the Council did does not mean she's safe."

"Raiden—"

"The only thing I want to hear is your promise."

His father pressed his mouth into a stern line. "I promise."

"Thank you."

"You're so much like her," his father said softly.

Raiden smiled, realizing he'd said something his mother used to say to him so often. He would say it with her just to annoy her. *I won't lose Nicole like we lost her.* "See you at the ball," he said, turning to go.

"All right, son."

Raiden stepped out into the hall and supposed he should try returning to Nicole's and his rooms through the ether, and he was pleased to find himself standing at the foot of their bed rather than outside the door.

"No, my hair stays down if I have to wear this thing," Nicole said from the other room.

"What thing?" Raiden wondered, wandering out from the bedchamber to find Mitchell and her in the sitting room.

Nicole looked at him with embarrassed discomfort written all over her face, but he couldn't help being stunned by the sight of her in a gown, well, it was partly a gown—it looked more like the suit upon the form beside her. The back of the coat flared to the floor like the back half of a skirt under which she wore tailored pant legs. The jacket was form-fitting and beneath it was a bodice with a V-shaped neckline that nearly matched the collar of the coat as it plunged down to a point right between her breasts.

"Wow," he said, nearly choking on the word before clearing his throat.

"See," Mitchell said. "You look good."

"People also say 'wow' when someone looks ridiculous," she said, and then Mitchell and she both looked to him for validation.

"It's different, but you certainly don't look ridiculous," Raiden insisted, pulling his eyes away from her neckline as his face went hot with thoughts of the parts of her he hadn't seen in so long he was starting to think those early days were just dreams.

"Ha!" Mitchell said triumphantly. "You're welcome."

Nicole sighed. "This is going to be a long night. I already can't wait to take it off."

The Sight seized on his imagination unexpectedly, and he fell into brief vision of buttons being undone revealing bare skin. He pushed the vision away as quickly as he could, turning away from Nicole because Mitchell was right there, and he couldn't stop seeing her slipping that gown off. "Excuse me. I suppose I should get cleaned up," he said.

Nicole watched Raiden disappear into the bedchamber at a flustered pace, her cheeks burning a little as she realized they would be coming back to this room tonight and shedding these ridiculous clothes. The thought hadn't flustered her like this since the week they had met. Everything that happened since the Council stole him away had just been so suffocating. She'd felt so uncertain of everything that those thoughts had been curiously absent. Her stomach clenched anxiously, and her heart raced until she was uncomfortably warm in the suit.

"While we wait for Raiden to get ready, we can practice," Mitchell said.

"Practice what?"

"Dancing, of course—you'll want to get used to moving in that."

"Neither of us knows how to ballroom dance, Mitch."

"Well, then, we can't get any worse, can we? Come on, put on the shoes," he said, snickering.

Nicole looked down at the base of the naked dress form. The shoes provided for her were no less than five inches off the ground, the heel of the shoes floating over nothing as the platform extended down from the arch, like someone decided women should always walk on the balls of their feet and toes.

"I draw the line at the shoes."

"Are you going to go barefoot?"

"Maybe."

Mitchell laughed. "Okay, those *are* a nightmare, conjure up a pair of plain heels."

"Why not flats?"

"You can't wear *flats* with my masterpiece," he said, throwing his hand against his chest in disgust.

"Fine," she said, holding out her hands and pulling a pair of shoes out of the air. She wondered if these were the shoes from the back of her closet at home in Yuma, or just replicas of the cranberry suede pumps that matched the dress she wore at Anthony's wedding. With a snap of her fingers, the pumps turned black.

"I guess those will do," Mitchell said. "At least we know you can dance in them."

"Oh, because I'm sure the prince will have a DJ playing *Cotton Eye Joe*," she said, rolling her eyes.

∞

When Raiden emerged from the bedroom he straightened his black satin coat over the black satin vest and fastened it with the hook and eye. All the gold embroidery made the vest stiff and his sleeves heavy.

"Oh dear, aren't you two quite the pair. Just say 'off with their heads' once for me, *please*," Mitchell insisted, holding up his hands to frame them with his fingers.

"No," Nicole laughed.

"Fine," he huffed. "Now I feel severely underdressed. I better get my fancy clothes on too," Mitchell said, jumping up from the couch and hurrying out of their rooms.

Raiden looked to Nicole beside him and noticed she was taller—her mouth much closer to his now.

She laughed at his perplexed expression. "It's the shoes," she said.

He looked down and spotted the heels on her feet. "Oh."

"You look pretty intimidating in black," she said. "If I didn't know you so well, I'd say you look like a ruthless king."

He fidgeted. The suit fit perfectly but didn't quite feel right. The weight of it seemed to be a reminder of all the eyes that would be on them tonight.

"You're looking forward to this as much as I am, I see," she said.

He grimaced. "He could have a plan for tonight."

"We didn't come for the dancing," she said with a wry grimace.

"I don't know how, anyway. That's not something you learn alone in an empty city," He said with a cold laugh.

"I can teach you," she said, stepping toward him. "It's easy in the other realm." She took his wrists in her hands, lifted his arms and placed them around her waist, then slipped hers behind his back and rocked their embrace gently. They barely had to pick up their feet to sway and turn.

"I was wrong. I think I could dance all night," he murmured, forgetting everything outside their swaying embrace.

"They won't be dancing like this," she said through a laugh.

"Then let's stay here."

"You won't hear me complain."

"Excuse me," Mitchell interjected, standing there in his suit, identical to Raiden's in cut but a deep blue fabric embroidered with green foliage and white flowers. "You can't get dressed up and not go out."

"Sure, you can," Nicole said, turning to her brother.

"I really don't want to go," Raiden said.

Mitchell scoffed. "Jeez, you two were meant for each other."

Nicole glanced at Raiden and smiled.

A knock came from the entrance chamber.

"I see everyone is dressed," Gordan said.

Gordan joined them in the sitting room. His suit was deep plum embroidered with a similar floral motif as Mitchell's. Raiden spotted a swift glance between them before Mitchell stuffed his hands into his pockets and Gordan did the same.

"We can't let this celebration rob us of our wits. The grandeur will be…distracting, to say the least," Gordan said.

"Can we agree that Nicole will have at least one of us beside her at all times tonight?" Raiden asked.

"We should be able to manage that," Mitchell said.

Raiden glanced at Nicole and saw a frown settle on her face. He could see her worrying about them. His hand instinctively moved for the pocket where he tucked the crystal ball but he refrained. "I doubt this will turn into a war zone. You shouldn't have to worry about anything like that."

"I think we all know he took deliberate aim at Mitchell and Gordan. If his strategy is to isolate me—"

"It's not gonna happen," Mitchell said. "We'll stick close together and keep an eye on each other, not just you. Right?" He looked to Gordan and Raiden.

"Right," Gordan said.

Raiden nodded.

"Then I guess…we're ready," Mitchell declared, less than confidently.

Raiden looked around and saw a resounding *no* in everyone's eyes, but *no* wasn't an option.

They arrived to an empty ballroom—silent and dazzling—the floor polished to a mirror-like shine. Its intricate pattern pulled in Nicole's gaze and almost trapped her mind within its fractal patterns. When she looked up, she could hardly count the chandeliers without nearly tripping as they crossed the vast cavern of grandeur.

They crossed the glittering room and approached a slender, high-backed throne where a man sat in deep purple garments with fiery orange hair pouring over his shoulder and a gold circlet crown around his head. Prince Cinder didn't stand, but he spread his arms out wide as they approached, and Nicole could see him clearly, dressed lavishly—dark gold embroidery dripping down his light gold suit and shining in the light like jewelry. His long hair glinted like polished copper in the room. His brows were sharp and angled over gold-shadowed eyes. His skin was flawlessly porcelain, his cheekbones striking. His whole presence was intimidating even seated; she could imagine how much more intimidating he would be standing because the shoulders of his suit were wide and pointed. Even more striking than the features that glinted and gleamed about his person were his dark eyes, standing out in contrast from his pale face and shining makeup. His was a gaze she could feel down her spine when it met hers.

"Welcome to Nol," he said. "It is truly a gift to have the Kings of the Keys here to celebrate with us." He gestured to the ballroom around them and applause broke out despite the space being empty. Then an invisible curtain lifted and all around them the ballroom was suddenly filled with hundreds of glittering attendees, clapping gloved hands, a soft thunder of approval. Nicole tried to smile, but she was pretty sure she looked like she was horrified by the sudden appearance of an audience that had been there the whole time.

"Wow," she heard Mitchell utter to her right.

On her left Raiden's hand found hers and from the corner of her eye, she could see him tense up, but his face didn't betray his discomfort at the abruptly crowded ballroom.

"Tonight, there will be music," Cinder said, his voice carrying jovially through the room and everyone around them laughed as though he'd told a joke. "Please," he said, motioning to Nicole, Raiden and their entourage of Mitchell, Gordan, Fen, Asi, Leone, Loak, Tovar and Caeruleus, to join him beside his throne.

I see what he's doing, Nicole thought. Of course, he wanted them to come for his birthday—it ever so subtly elevated his importance over theirs. If they had visited at any other time, all the focus would have been on them.

Behind Cinder's throne the wall dissolved into a translucent barrier, revealing that the ballroom was deeper still and a sprawling symphony sat awaiting their instruction to play. Cinder raised his hand to the side of his throne and the conductor raised his baton. Music swelled out of the silence, gentle and undulating. The guests drifted toward the throne and waited their turn to step forward and greet the prince. They bowed or curtseyed and wished him a happy birthday.

Nicole noticed people's eyes slipping away from Cinder and toward Gordan as they bowed. Cinder had not acknowledged Gordan's presence in any way, and to Nicole's pleasant surprise, she didn't see any looks of abhorrence or even surprise on their faces. She looked past Mitchell—who seemed to be looking anywhere but toward Gordan—and saw that Gordan was glancing at her.

She reached behind Mitchell and Gordan did the same. She squeezed his hand, hoping he knew how much she needed him here. He tightened his grip as though to answer—*I know*. They released each other's hands and Gordan's returned to his side, stiff beside Mitchell. Nicole shifted her gaze back to the subjects bowing, pretending to be impressed while she leaned a little toward her brother and whispered, "What do you think?"

"It's unreal," he murmured.

"Yeah, nightmarishly," she said.

He smiled, fighting back laughter.

"Ah, Cole," Cinder said of the man who approached next.

Nicole studied the person standing before them—the only person to receive a greeting like that from the prince. Cole was dressed as elegantly as anyone in the room, with golden-brown hair and heavy-lidded eyes that made him look tired. When he bowed, he looked up at Nicole.

"Happy Birthday, Cinder," Cole said, standing tall. "And welcome to the kings," he added with a slow emphatic bow.

He bowed once more and walked away with a trace of a smile in the corner of his mouth. As he passed by just a step away from them, he turned his head and glanced at her once more with his dark eyes. Nicole was almost certain she just witnessed a jab at Cinder. Despite the apparent warmth of their exchange, she detected disguised animosity there.

"Your Highness," doted a man bowing deeply. "King Heimskur sends you his regards and wishes you a most joyous celebration."

Nicole caught herself before she rolled her eyes at the man's swollen syllables. Cinder nodded and the emissary from Taroth walked away, sliding his gaze across Raiden, Nicole, and their company as he went.

"I still want to hit that guy," Raiden muttered to her, and she stifled a laugh.

When everyone in attendance had bowed or curtseyed to Cinder, he lifted his voice effortlessly to address the entire room,

"Let us dance!"

He waved his hand and the repetitious melody that had been playing went quiet. Then a single slinky obo emerged from the silence in the company of a soft low tempo of plucking strings. Prince Cinder rose from his throne and stepped down from the dais. He moved like a dancer, graceful fluidity in every stride.

As the strings joined in, Nicole found it difficult not to sway where she stood. The crowd dispersed into couples and took to the ballroom floor, falling into the sweeping movements of a waltz. Music always had a way of seizing Nicole, imploring her to move or hum. She supposed it was the way the music filled the sparkling cavern of the ballroom and the kaleidoscope of people moving in graceful unison that made the melody so intoxicating now.

"It makes me wish I knew how to waltz," Nicole said.

"Me too," Mitchell agreed.

Prince Cinder glided toward them and smiled, holding out his hand in invitation to Nicole. "You look like you would like to dance, your highness."

Nicole reddened. "I don't know how to—at all," she said, shaking her head and glancing nervously at the formation of dancers floating around the ballroom flawlessly, imagining herself throwing it into a chaotic mess with bumbling steps that even the most proficient lead could not overcome.

"I insist," he said. "You may surprise yourself."

Nicole looked to Mitchell for help but he shrugged. She looked to Raiden who just smiled anxiously. She didn't want to leave him, but she wanted so badly to move with the music—she wondered why the desire seemed to buzz incessantly inside her. She squeezed Raiden's hand before she released it and took Cinder's gloved fingers in her own.

This is going to be a disaster, she thought with dread although she noticed her steps fell into the tempo naturally, matching Cinder's as they reached the edge of the dance space and faced each other.

Her heart raced. *Here we go.*

"You don't have to worry," Cinder said as he took her other hand and raised her arm to rest on his shoulder, placing his hand on her back so that her arm was atop his. With their frame established he pulled her into step with all the other dancers.

She felt the music in her skin and her body sank into the notes, her muscles mirroring the melody. She looked around her at everyone engrossed in the dance, stunned that she was moving as they were. She and Cinder became another turning cog in the clockwork—*but how?* She stumbled.

"If you think too much about it, you'll disrupt the enchantment," Cinder said. "It can be resisted although you seem strongly influenced by it like I am."

"Enchantment," she said, letting out a mystified laugh. "Of course." She noticed that her confidence slackened when she was distracted from the music, but when she listened and let it fill her, her body was almost not her own.

"Most people don't consider it to be a very useful kind of magic," he said with a smile that seemed to be for himself and not her.

"Why? This is the best feeling," she said, closing her eyes and noticing that the music moved her more powerfully.

"I'm glad you think so."

She opened her eyes and gazed around them at the others. There were others with their eyes closed, embracing the music, some with their eyes open and even chatting to their partners. All Nicole wanted was to close her eyes and feel the music until it stopped. When a high soaring brass note rang out in crescendo and fell silent, she felt her heart clench. The strings emerged again from the quiet to climb once more, and she could feel the end of the movement approaching in an ascent to a final note upon the strings. Cinder looked her in the eye. She was struck—there were red striations in his dark drown eyes. She'd never seen eyes like his.

"That was foolish of me," Cinder muttered as the music died. "Forgive me, will you? Act as natural as you can."

"What?"

Cinder tipped toward her and she braced him instinctively, holding their frame in surprise. He was taller than her, but thankfully he was slender and easy to prop up. Everyone around them applauded and the next song began. Cinder reclaimed his weight, stepped away from her and kept her hand to lead her back to the dais across the room. As before, he moved with a dancer's grace.

Is he sick, lightheaded from dancing?

"Thank you," he said, looking ahead and smiling to his subjects who bowed and curtseyed as he and Nicole passed. "For the dance…and your support."

"Um—are you okay?" she couldn't help asking even if it was rather informal and familiar to address him like that.

"Yes, I'm quite all right now. No need to fret, I am merely human," he said quietly between them.

But you don't want your subjects to know it, she thought with a smile. Cinder bowed to her and released her hand then returned to his throne upon the dais. She hurried back to Mitchell and Raiden.

"Hey," she said breathlessly.

"How the hell—you said you don't know how to waltz," Mitchell said.

"I don't. You don't need to," she said hastily, turning to Raiden and taking his hands. "Dance with me."

He gave her an uncomfortable look of doubt.

"Come on," she said, pulling him to the edge of the dancers. She put her hands on his shoulders and pulled him close so she could murmur in his ear. "Close your eyes and listen, okay?"

They took their position, her hand on his shoulder and his on her back, their opposite hands joined. Raiden closed his eyes and the music pulled them both into the dance. He laughed, falling into the steps perfectly with his eyes closed. She smiled, letting the music fill her head, while the sight of Raiden smiling like that filled her chest with warmth. It was like the people all around them weren't even there, like they were alone and the horrors of his past and the future couldn't reach him. She wanted so many more moments like this.

She saw Mitchell lead Fen to the dance floor, and Gordan took Asi by the hand—they were a comical pair of opposite statures. If the evening had been only the music and enchantment, Nicole might have admitted that she enjoyed wearing the key for once, but after three songs of enchanted dancing, they were out of breath. Nicole and Raiden drifted to the perimeter of the ballroom where the fewest people were, giddy smiles still on their lips.

When they spotted the emissary of Taroth and saw that he was wandering their way, they couldn't salvage their joy from the dread of his approach. To her surprise Raiden pulled her in close to him before he acknowledged the emissary's presence with a chilly smile.

"King Raiden," he said, barely bowing. "Wonderful to see your highness again."

"I would say the same of you, but you've shamefully forgotten to greet another king when she is standing right here beside me looking so breathtaking."

Nicole's face burned—where had *this* Raiden come from?

The emissary's pleasant expression faltered, he blinked furiously and inclined his head to her. "Your majesty."

All she could do was nod, biting back her chagrin.

"I see you travel with…unique company," the emissary said. "Unfortunately, I cannot extend King Heimskur's invitation to *all*, but I hope we will have the pleasure of welcoming you and the queen to Taroth." He spoke as though she wasn't even there, looking only at Raiden as he bowed and turned away quickly, no doubt to have the final word after his humiliation.

"I really hate that guy," she said.

"Me too," Raiden agreed. "But it was fun to make him squirm."

Nicole buried a laugh in his chest.

"What's so funny?" Mitchell asked as he and Fen walked up, flushed from dancing.

"Raiden's just picking on the emissary from Taroth," she said.

"He makes me nervous," Fen said with a shudder.

Nicole reached out for Fen's hand. "He has no way of knowing who you are."

"Yeah," Mitchell said, hooking an arm around Fen reassuringly.

Fen smiled.

Gordan and Asi joined them, Asi almost running ahead of him to reach Fen's side.

"There's food on the other side of the room," she said, and Fen turned, bumping into Asi before they hurried off snickering.

"I might have to join them," Mitchell said in a rush as he skipped off after them.

Nicole noted the small affectionate smile on Gordan's face but saw a little sadness in his eyes. "What's going on with you two?"

"We had a bit of a disagreement," Gordan said.

"About what?" Raiden wondered.

"Telling you what happened on our trip back from Orodon," he said.

"That's Mitch for you. He'll get over it," she said.

"All I seem to be feeling from him is annoyance. He hasn't said a word to me."

"Have you said anything to him?" Raiden asked.

"No," he said.

Nicole let out a soft laugh. "Break the silence, then."

Gordan sighed.

A lord and lady approached them, bowing and curtseying with warm smiles.

"An honor to meet you," the lord murmured before he and his wife carried on elsewhere.

"I'm starting to think you were making a bigger deal about dragons here on the mainland than was necessary. No one here has so much as flinched at you," Nicole said to Gordan.

"Don't be so quick to give them credit," Gordan said. "Just as an enchantment in the music can lead you in a dance, it can be used to influence the mood of the room. What we see might not be these people's authentic sentiments."

Nicole wondered if that could have influenced Taroth's emissary into acknowledging her after Raiden accused him of being disrespectful. He clearly hadn't thought his behavior unacceptable, but he couldn't resist a demand for recompense. And if there was, in fact, some peace-keeping influence in the music, what kind of reaction would Raiden have had to the emissary's contempt without it?

"Here you are," Caeruleus greeted, hurrying over as discretely as possible. "I've been listening to the chatter among the guests."

"What have you heard?" Raiden wondered.

"I guess it's tradition in Nol that they don't have a set line of succession. The reigning king goes into seclusion and gives the prospective kings a trial period you could say, to prove who is best for the people and deserves the crown."

"So, Prince Cinder is in the middle of his audition for the king's seat," Nicole reasoned.

"Apparently, Cinder does things very differently. There's talk that the king will chose Cinder's cousin instead."

"Who's his cousin?" Nicole wondered.

"Cole," he said, hushed. "I hear he had a very successful trial regency last year. But Cinder has to contend with the fall of the Council during his trial—unfortunate timing for him."

The gentle intrusion of someone clearing his throat behind them pulled Nicole and Raiden's attention away from Caeruleus. It was Cole.

"Pardon me," he said, bowing. "It would be an honor to dance with her majesty."

"That's certainly true," Raiden said softy, meant for her—not Cole.

Caeruleus glanced at her and nodded toward Cole. They could learn something from him, perhaps. As much as she loathed another dance with a stranger, she couldn't deny that it was a choice opportunity, probably the only opportunity they would have.

"I suppose I'm ready for another dance," she answered, crafting a smile and taking Cole's gloved hand.

The current song drifted into a gradual silence before swelling one last time into a brief crescendo. The dancers stopped and applauded, some remained, others wandered away from the dance floor trading places with those who arrived for the next movement. Nicole did her best to focus on the music as it bounced out of the silence and to ignore her discomfort as she took position with Cole. She could feel his eyes on her face, seeing his gaze clearly enough even on the fringes of her vision as she kept her eyes away from his.

In avoiding Cole's persistent stare, she noticed Prince Cinder watching them. He rose from his throne and moved gracefully around the grand ballroom. Cinder smiled and nodded to the bows and curtsies from his subjects, but his eyes kept glancing at her— no, at his cousin.

She stumbled and remembered to focus on the music, let it seep into her, but she needed to get something from Cole.

"Do you spent much time at court?" she asked. The question sounded as stupid coming from her mouth as she felt in the gaudy layers of fabric on her body.

"I did in my youth," he said. "Cinder and I were raised like brothers. We were once very close."

"But you're not so close now?" she wondered aloud, taking a moment to look him in the eye. His were the same dark brown eyes with red striations as Cinder's.

"No," he said, glancing toward Cinder, perfectly aware from where in the room the prince was watching them. "He has changed and I am no longer welcome at court. I do not believe anyone is anymore, not during his regency, but he still holds parties and extravagant performances to delight the nobles and his subjects."

"How strange," she said, hoping he would continue while she focused on the music. She glanced at Cinder as they danced closer to the prince, and she could see the furrows in his brow before he softened them for a pretty curtseying noble.

Cole remained silent until they glided away from Cinder. "He has secrets—I would be wary of him if I were you. He only wanted you here for your good influence on his royal image, but make no mistake the keys you and the king hold are a threat to the power of every leader in this realm. Power is what they care about most."

Nicole tripped again. "Sorry," she said when he caught her.

"No, forgive me for distracting you," he said, looking up at Raiden watching with Caeruleus. "If you were not married to your fellow king, I would invite you to fall on me as much as you please."

"And yet you just did," she said with an uncomfortable laugh.

His face flushed with chagrin. "Right. My apologies. I would appreciate it if you didn't tell the king I let such an improper thought slip past my lips."

"I wouldn't dream of keeping a secret from him," she said with a devious smile. "Unless you repay the favor."

"Your price?"

She shrugged. "Tell me something interesting."

"Interesting," he said, considering the idea for a measure of music. "What might a fera king who brings down a corrupt government and faces manticores find interesting?" He mused.

She waited patiently, smiling—doing her best not to let it turn into a cringe—at his attempt at, she supposed, flattery. Instead, she kept her mind on the music and danced with him. She was glad the music did the dancing for her and glad they wore gloves, suffocating any trace of intimacy in their clasped hands.

"Let's see…certainly not the Taroth ambassador trying to negotiate the marriage of Heimskur's daughter to Cinder."

Nicole rolled her eyes—*royal courtship, really?*

"And certainly not what the ladies are saying about your attire and your hair."

Nicole let her disgust twist her mouth.

"I thought so—well, perhaps you might find it interesting that Prince Cinder is obsessed with the old world."

"Really?" Nicole couldn't bluff disinterest.

"Oh yes. He collects anything and everything from the other realm. When we were kids, he liked to convince people he was *from* the old world. He studied it incessantly."

"Do many people find the old world worth studying?"

"Only people who think the realms will merge again someday. I personally don't think so. Sure, portals open now and then, but we might as well be talking about an imaginary world. It's irrelevant now, and it has been for centuries. This is our home."

People who think the realms will merge again? That sounded an awful lot like Dawn's philosophy to her.

"Can I assume that was adequately interesting?"

"Yes, that's interesting enough to me, I'm from that imaginary world after all," she said with a chuckle.

"Are you *really*? Don't tell Cinder. You being married might not even be enough to keep him from trying."

"Trying what?"

"To marry you—trust me, he had a mind to do it before your marriage to the king came out. I dare say he'd like to have a wife from the old world even more than he wants the authority that comes with that key around your neck."

Nicole's face went hot. "No one with that attitude deserves any woman's time," she muttered.

Cole laughed. "That's the way royals play, your highness."

"Well, I'm glad I'm not a royal."

"You are now."

"Unfortunately."

"The ruler who has power but does not want it is a rare thing indeed. Power poisons most people, believe me. Perhaps a throne is not to your taste, but isn't the power you possess as the fera intoxicating sometimes? Wasn't it thrilling to bring down the Council and their courts?"

Nicole went cold, swallowing a lump of anxiety in her throat. The influence of the music in her body suddenly felt too foreign, the melody writhed like worms under her skin and the grand room around went dim. She fell out of step as she moved forward instead of back. Her chest bumped into his and in her flustered attempt to return to the flow of the music she stumbled. She tried to compose herself, looking around the ballroom to see the dark hall of the Courts flicker in and out. She looked down at her feet and saw the mirror-like floor fracturing for a split second.

"Pardon me," a familiar voice said softly from behind her, and she sagged with relief before she even turned to see Gordan there.

"I must insist on stealing the remainder of this dance."

"Of course, how can I blame you?" Cole said, stepping back and bowing deeply while still holding her hand. "Thank you, your highness." He stood up and brought her hand to his face to place his lips against her glove before he slipped away through the dancers.

She frowned, turning to Gordan. "Thanks for the rescue."

"What on earth did he say to you?" Gordan asked quietly as he took her trembling hand and pulled her gently into position. Reluctantly she listened to the music and let it guide her once more. With Gordan there the memory of the Courts couldn't cut in, the enchantment in the music felt less sinister. They eased into the flow of the music and Nicole caught a glimpse of Raiden keeping his distance from the crowds and watching her with anxious eyes. She gave him a weak smile, knowing he wanted to be the one who pushed his way through the people to steal her away from Cole.

"You could sense that from across a crowded room like this?"

"Not clearly, but enough to get my attention and catch the look on your face."

"Oh," she knew better than to tell Gordan *it was nothing* when he knew full well something had disturbed her. "He asked me if my power—if killing the Council was intoxicating."

His hand tightened around hers. "I see."

The music faded and Nicole hugged him, a brief grateful embrace before they moved with purpose through the citizens of Nol and off the dance floor. Nicole realized that at some point during the dance she'd lost track of Cinder and found him once again on his throne, his face composed into a mask of pleasant observance.

"I'm so ready for this party to be over," Nicole muttered to Gordan as they headed for Raiden waiting on the edge of the crowd with Caeruleus.

She couldn't help noticing the urgency in Raiden's hand as he reached for hers and pulled her close with the crowd pressing close to them.

"Has anyone seen Mitchell and the girls?" Nicole asked, looking around the sea of faces with a pang of concern in her chest.

"I'm sure he's still with Asi and Fen. I'll find them," Gordan said, slipping away to weave through the onlookers at the edge of the dance floor.

Nicole relaxed a little and glanced at Raiden, his jaw tight and his brow pinched. The band took a break, leaving the grand room to swell with the cacophony of conversation and laughter.

"Cole told me Prince Cinder has quite the fascination with the old world," Nicole said. "And apparently no one is welcome at court while he's regent. I wonder why."

"That is strange. Nol is known for their elaborate social lives," Caeruleus said. "Aside from the kings going into seclusion to test their successors, the royal family has never been reclusive."

"And to have no *real* people around either," Raiden added. "What does *that* mean?"

"I think the question is how do we find out?" Caeruleus offered. "The king is in seclusion, he might not even be on these royal grounds. And the Prince...well, we didn't even see him until tonight."

"Maybe we're making this into something bigger than it is," Nicole suggested. "What if I just ask him?"

The three of them looked over at Cinder seated on his throne, nodding subtly as he listened to the ambassador from Taroth.

"It seems there are lots of people who want his ear tonight," Raiden said.

"I wonder what Prince Cinder could possibly get out of an alliance with Taroth," Nicole said.

"With the Council gone and Candhrid between them, an alliance would make it easy for them to take the state like Taroth is trying to do with Navn," Caeruleus remarked.

"But are Taroth and Nol...compatible?" Nicole wondered, looking around the room. From what Asi and Fen told her, not to mention what she and Raiden had seen from the ambassador, Taroth was a state deeply rooted in a controlling patriarchy. But was Nol any better? She searched the faces of the crowd, seeing women engaged in conversation, wondering if they were free to speak their minds, or was Nol more like Taroth than it appeared. She tried to tell herself those were concerns for a ruler, not for her, but she couldn't stop thinking of Asi and Fen and all the girls left in Taroth.

Gordan spotted Mitchell with Asi and Fen, the girls laughing over the plates of food in their hands. He approached, his chest tightening anxiously around his lungs and heart

"Hi, Gordan," Asi said, smiling.

"Checking in?" Mitchell asked, looking at him with distinct exasperation in his gaze.

"Nicole was a little anxious," he explained. *And so was I.*

"Okay. I better go tell her I'm fine, you know, make sure she knows that no one got hurt while we were here at the buffet," Mitchell said with a quick glare before stepping away.

Gordan understood now why he was mad and sighed.

"What was that about?" Fen asked, laughing.

"I did something foolish," Gordan said and went after him.

Mitchell hadn't gotten too far through the crowd and Gordan wove around the strangers deftly to close the distance between them. He caught Mitchell's sleeve gently in his fingers.

"Wait," he said.

"I won't tell her you lied to her," Mitchell said, turning to him. "But after the crap you gave me for not wanting to tell her about the whole thing…" He shook his head and laughed, but there was no amusement in it.

All Gordan could feel was annoyance, sadness and—

"You don't think it matters that you were hurt?"

—pain…and worry. Mitchell was upset. Gordan couldn't figure out what to say, trying to sift through his own regret, Mitchell's disappointment and concern, and the haze of amusement all around them.

"It matters."

The annoyance dispersed and Gordan was stunned by the sudden warm ache of love as Mitchell pulled his sleeve from his grasp and turned away again. It rang out so clear it drowned out every-thing else in the room for a startling moment. Confusion twisted his stomach. He had thought Mitchell was upset about his hypoc-risy, but he realized now he was wrong. *He's still upset that I was hurt.*

He let out a quite growl of frustration.

"Uh, Gordan?" Asi's voice crept into his ear.

"You're just standing in the middle of the crowd," Fen said.

"Are you okay?"

He sighed. "Yes," he said lifting his eyes from their dazed stare to look at the girls. Then he noticed someone else's gaze on them, the ambassador of Taroth looking their way as he passed. "Let's go. I think it's time we joined Nicole, don't you?"

Gordan kept a carefully crafted smile on his face as he frowned internally. Trying to think of how to ask for Mitchell's forgiveness.

♋

Venarius stood just outside the threshold of the grand doorway as the music and light of the celebration inside the immense ballroom poured into the shadowy hall. He could find her easily, the only one in red as he had specified. Her entire party was in color, easy to pick out from the rest of the guests. They lingered around her as he ex-pected, the brother, the dragon and the king—especially the king.

He pulled a pocket watch from his coat and checked the time.

♋

Nicole felt her eyelids growing heavy as she stood by the throne and listened to the music. Her mind drifted through swaying notes as she leaned a little against Raiden, their hands linked. Then Prince Cinder leaned over the arm of his throne. "Your highness," he said.

Nicole forgot for a moment that *'your highness'* was her—Cinder was speaking to her. "Oh—yes?"

"May I have one last dance?"

Nicole swallowed back the reluctance in her throat. The music and the desire to move to it was still there, but she trusted Cinder far less than she had at the start of this evening. Still, he might be more inclined to talk to her on the dance floor than here while ev-

413

eryone else listened.

"It is your birthday celebration," she said.

He stood and stepped down from the dais to take her hand. Raiden squeezed her other hand briefly before she stepped away, a silent *be careful.*

As she walked with Cinder, a little envious of his elegant stride, she noticed that he kept to the edge of the dancers and did not stop to turn to her. They walked around the dance floor.

"Did you enjoy yourself tonight?" he asked.

"It has been interesting, but I won't lie to you, I find all this more taxing than enjoyable," she said, wondering how much of an influence the music had on her now. Was it just the urge to dance, the lighthearted edge to her exhaustion—could it even be lowering inhibitions and deception?

He chuckled, leading her toward the entrance to the ballroom, the doors standing open. "I'm afraid this is goodbye." He turned to her and kissed her hand. "Thank you, for granting me one final dance," he said and twirled her.

She was caught off guard as the room spun around her. When she stopped and regained her bearings, she couldn't see Cinder any- where, just the doorway and someone standing there—a man. But her head was still spinning, and she closed her eyes to steady herself. She opened them and the doorway was empty, the music played on and she turned back to see the kaleidoscope-crowd of dancing pairs.

Across the room Raiden craned his neck to see her, and she shrugged, confused and heavy with exhaustion. Curious, she turned toward the doorway and stepped out into the hall, looking both di- rections down the identical stretches of dim corridor. No silhouettes in the shadows, no footsteps sounding in the dark silence. A yawn seized her breath and stopped her mind for a moment. She turned back to the ballroom to find Raiden right in front of her. She jumped.

"You scared me," she said.

"Sorry. Did Cinder leave?"

"Yeah," she yawned.

"Strange."

"That means we can too, right? I'm so tired."

"Of course, but we should make sure the others know we haven't just disappeared."

She nodded with a little flare of renewed energy, encouraged by the promise of returning to their room and the bed waiting for them.

✃

Raiden held Nicole close against him, and he looked down the hall, not trusting the shadows. He decided against the long stroll back to their room and pulled them both through the ether into their bedroom. Relief was immediate. In the silence of their room, alone, the suffocating weight of the noise and dense presence of people fell away. He was exhausted but lighter.

"You know, sometimes I forget we can do that," she said.

"Did Cinder say anything to you before he left the party?"

Nicole wobbled, cursed, and kicked off her shoes—her height dropping suddenly. "Not really," she said, fumbling with the front of her dress coat to unfasten the buttons. She wrestled the garment off, shedding the partial skirt, leaving her in the embroidered bodice and closely tailored trousers. "Jeez, that thing was heavy."

Raiden's face went hot as he realized he had seen this moment earlier today. Her snug bodice parted as she plucked each small button, opening the vest. Raiden forgot all about removing his own jacket as he watched the vest open little by little with each button she unfastened. His heart quickened and she looked up at him.

She smiled. "Are you going to sleep in that?"

"Huh? Oh," he said, his face burning.

She shuffled toward the bathroom, fiddling with the last few buttons of her vest.

Raiden set to work removing his jacket, the stiff embroidered vest, the simple soft tunic beneath. Nicole shuffled back out of the bathroom in her underwear, arms crossed over her bare chest against the chill in the room as he pulled the tunic off his back. She held out her hand, and he passed the garment to her. She pulled it on; it fell to her thighs. She turned to the bed, threw back the ornate embroidered comforter and climbed onto the bed, collapsing face down in defeat. He shed his trousers and was left in his boxers when he realized she was falling asleep, and he didn't have the Juno's Tears herb.

"Damn it," he cursed quietly, trying to remember where in the room he left his everyday coat with the herb tucked safely within the inner pocket. He rummaged through the pile of garments he'd tossed onto the nearby chair, but his coat wasn't there. He checked the sitting room and found it draped over one of the couches. As he pulled the wilted sprig of Juno's Tears carefully from the inner pocket, he wondered if the harmful nightmares would ever stop plaguing Nicole's sleep. He wanted to believe it was something he could help her banish for good, like Venarius. Until then he could only be there with her.

When he wandered back into the dim bedroom, he wanted to believe it was safe. He bent over the chair and dug through his clothes until he found the crystal. He looked into the little sphere, peering through the night and into the morning to see Nicole asleep, her arms caught around him while sunlight slipped through the window. He sighed and tucked the crystal out of sight once more before turning to the bed. He slipped the herb beneath one of the pillows in the center of the bed.

Nicole stirred sidling closer as he settled in. His exhaustion caught up with him, and he closed his eyes easily knowing she would be right there in the morning.

Twenty-eight

Nicole opened her eyes, resisting the urge to get up wasn't working. She slid to the edge of the bed and placed her feet begrudgingly on the floor, her head thick with sleep and her body heavy. She wandered into the bathroom, remembering to avoid the bath in the center of the room on her way to the toilet, but when she finished, she thought she heard the faintest sounds stirring in the silence of the night.

She flushed the toilet and shuffled back into the bedroom, pausing in the bathroom doorway to listen. Was the sound still there? *Music—is the party still going?* She couldn't believe it. Curiosity pulled her into the sitting room, maybe she was imagining it— memories of the evening mixing with dreams and lingering in her groggy mind.

Out in the sitting room the music was clearer, and she followed it through the door standing open for her; her thoughts were too wrapped up in the music to notice the mannequin standing innocently in the entrance way as she passed it and stepped into the hallway.

The carpets were soft under her bare feet. The low undulating melody only grew more captivating the dark corridor—notes long and deep that she felt like she could sink into as her feet fell into sync with the tempo. Why would anyone be playing music in the middle of the night?

Her heart struck her sternum with a sudden realization that it was not the party going on into the night. The music slithered through her mind and into her limbs. Fighting the impulse to follow it made her dizzy and her steps unsteady, but the music as it grew louder and she could not ignore it. She couldn't convince her arms to raise her hands to her ears. The music only drew closer and harder to resist as she went, still she fought to the point of staggering.

"Shit," escaped her mouth but she gasped. *My voice!* "Hey," she called, unsure how far away she was from her room, from Raiden, or Mitchell or Gordan. Where was she even headed? "Can anyone hear me!?"

She turned toward an open door and into the ballroom, dim but still glistening. In the center of the room there looked to be an open music box. She knew the music was coming from the box, and felt the pull even stronger than before.

"I can hear you," a man's velvety voice said echoing gently through the ballroom. "We wouldn't want to wake anyone else."

She searched the room in a panic, her heart racing as her head swam in the music and her legs carried her forward. The music—she needed to drown out the music. *Raiden, Gordan, Mitchell, Asi, Fen, Keren, Dad, Bandit, Ashley, Ryleigh, Anthony, Frances, Roxie—* she repeated their names in her head, creating a rhythm, disrupting the melody of the music until she could lift her hands to her ears and finally keep the music out of her head. Her legs were heavy but they were hers again. She kept repeating their names, searching the room for her enemy, but she knew she had to get out, and away from the music.

Whirling around to retrace her steps, she found herself face to face with someone, colliding with him—*Cinder!* Her hands came off her ears in the impact, and he stared back at her with wide bewildered eyes.

☙

Raiden's arm slid across the empty space beside him, and he lurched upright out of his shallow slumber. He blinked furiously through the blurred darkness and could see clearly enough what he already knew—she wasn't there. As he jumped out of the bed, he hoped he was overreacting, that he'd find her in the bathroom. Tangled in the blanket, he stumbled, righted himself and reached the bathroom door to find it silent and empty.

He turned, ran into the empty sitting room and stopped. His heart dropped like a cold stone at the sight of the open door. Lurching forward, he almost ran past the mannequin by the door without a thought. He halted, unnerved—it had been in the bedroom, not here. Then he heard the distant music and hurried into the hall, pausing to listen a moment before feeling the gentle pull to the right. He ran.

A jolt of panic pulled Gordan from his sleep and he sat up, confused, were *his* dreams becoming too real now? Then his keen ears heard footsteps running down the hall, and he lurched out of his bed, realizing someone was awake and there was dread in the air. *Nicole.* He bolted through his rooms and slid into the door as he fumbled with the handle before he managed to yank it open and project himself into the hallway.

From the corner of his left eye, he caught sight of Raiden disappearing around a corner. Gordan chased after him.

☙

Nicole shook her head. The music slithered. Her arms were too heavy to cover her ears. *Raiden.* The melody swooped down into low soothing notes. *Mitchell.* There was comfort in the tempo. *Gordan.* She couldn't string their names close enough together to drown out the music.

"What a surprise to see you here, Cinder."

Nicole looked up—she was blocking Cinder's path, and he looked back at her with wide eyes. She turned with the music to see Cole striding across the dance floor.

"We were going to let Cinder take the blame for your disappearance. The king wouldn't let him have the crown with a scandal like that hanging over his head. That way both Venarius and I get what we want," he mused. "But seeing as Cinder wandered into our private dance, I'm going to have to do things differently. I can only imagine the stories they'll come up with—Nicole and the prince both mysteriously disappearing."

Cole folded his arms and waited. Intent on reaching the melody within the music box, Nicole crossed the floor, because she knew she would be safe there; she would be wrapped in beautiful music… all by herself. Her stride faltered. If it meant no Raiden or Gordan or Mitchell, she didn't want it. She glanced at Cinder and saw contentment on his face as the music lured him to the box. Nicole looked to Cole and her disgust stirred the burning core of magic deep in her belly.

There was nothing more disgusting to her than someone who could betray his own family. She felt venom in her veins, tasted it in her mouth—sour and metallic. Her steps veered toward Cole, and she caught the collar of his jacket in her fists.

"I suppose its safety and solitude aren't so alluring, after all," Cole said. "However, Cinder seems to want everything the music promises." He chuckled.

Cinder reached for the box, and it pulled him in. The lid closed tight and the music stopped. Her head reeled a little in the silence.

"He's not fit to be king. He wasn't born for power—not like you and me."

"You're right," she said. *Maybe I was meant for this.* She released a flood of magic that hit Cole so hard that his jacket slipped from her angry grip. She stumbled back and fell beside the music box. Cole hit the ground, unconscious.

"Prick," she muttered, picking up the music box. She was scared to open it, unsure if Cinder would be released or if the music would just pull her in with him.

Choosing to risk it, she opened the box just an inch and the lid snapped open to spit out an expanding blur of a man. Cinder tumbled onto the floor, and Nicole slammed the lid shut when she heard the music creeping out after him.

"Are you okay?" she wondered, picking herself up.

He rolled over and sat up, blinking and shaking his head. "I suppose I am."

"Here," she said, holding out her hand, but he looked at it with a strange look of dismay on his face.

He can't walk, she realized as she looked down at him. Cinder's behavior throughout the party replayed in her mind. He only got up from his throne when the music was playing, he walked almost like he was dancing. He asked for a final dance but left the party long before the music stopped. *He relies on the music.*

"Nicole!"

Raiden ran into the ballroom, barefoot and boxer-clad. Only then did she realize that she was wearing only his tunic and her underwear. It was the middle of the night. Her mind was finally cleared enough to put everything together. Raiden reached her and closed his arms around her with a sigh. Gordan was right behind him.

"I'm okay," she said, synching her arms around him. She could feel the fear lingering in his shaking muscles. "I'm all right."

"What happened here?" Gordan asked, eyeing Cole's unconscious form sprawled on the floor before picking up the music box.

"Don't open that," Nicole warned over Raiden's shoulder.

Cinder held out his hand in request for the box, which Gordan handed to him with a reluctant look.

"Musical enchantment," Cinder said. "It's something my cousin and I have studied since childhood."

Raiden released her and held tightly to her hand.

Cole stirred and his murmur of discomfort became a crescendo of moaning agony.

"What did you do to him?" Cinder wondered.

Nicole shrugged. "Broke a *lot* of bones…maybe all of them—I don't know."

"He's certainly less fit than I am to be king now," Cinder realized with a bitter chuckle.

Cole groaned.

"What do we do about him?" Raiden asked.

"He's not going anywhere like that," Gordan said.

"I will send some servants back for him," Cinder said.

"Good, can we get out of here?" she asked.

"Forgive me for imposing," he said. "But I do need some assistance."

Gordan and Raiden each crouched beside Cinder, he placed his arms around their shoulders and they scooped him up with their joined hands beneath his legs like a seat. They carried Cinder out of the ballroom, and Nicole followed with the music box in hand, clutching it in a mistrustful grip as she looked back at Cole on the floor. Wondering with a chill down her spine how far away Venarius was at that moment, she looked around the ballroom once more before she stepped through the doors.

Venarius stepped from the dark corner and crossed the ballroom at a slow but purposeful pace, his heels striking the cold polished floor with disappointment. He stood over Cole and looked down in disapproval.

"There…you are," Cole strained to speak and hissed in pain. "Help me."

"I'm afraid I cannot."

"What?" Cole almost choked on the word.

"Your incompetence is of no use to me," Venarius said. "Let this be your recompense for failure."

"No. Wait—Venarius."

"That will be all, Cole. Good luck with your pursuit for the crown." Venarius smiled and left Cole where he lay. "This has been enlightening at least. I'll find another way."

Nicole scowled at the music box in her hands, studying its enticing beauty, and contemplating its contents.

"Cinder, what happened when you were inside the music box?" She wondered as they walked through the silent corridors.

"It was quite lovely actually," he confessed. "There was nothing but the music. I just felt safe and content—something I haven't felt so completely for a long time."

"Your cousin—"

"He can lay there until morning for all I care."

"He said you two were close as kids. When did he become so horrible?" she wondered.

"I suppose when he realized he wanted the crown. We grew up as brothers until the day my father sat us down and told us what he expected of us both as potential kings; since he had adopted Cole, we were both eligible to succeed him."

"It became a competition," Raiden said.

"The worst kind," Cinder said. "Cole set the stakes high the day he pushed me into the path of father's carriage. We had been running to greet him upon his return. After the incident people even said they saw me trip," he said with a sardonic laugh. "I was badly hurt. They thought I was dead before the healer came. They didn't realize my spinal cord was severed. They healed my broken arms, legs, my fractured skull, they healed everything they could."

"And no one ever found out you're paralyzed?" Nicole asked.

"No," he said. "I woke up, knew I couldn't move my legs, but I kept it to myself as long as I could because I was relieved in a way, knowing my father wouldn't ever hand the crown to me like this. I was afraid they would fix me and this would continue. We were only ten, and Cole was ready to kill for what he wanted. I didn't want to play that game anymore. My father kept me secluded 'to rest' after the accident and built this palace where I could get around freely in my chair and where people couldn't see my weakness. There were rumors that I had died." He laughed. "Which I'm sure Cole hoped was true."

Nicole was tempted to march right back to the ballroom to kick him one last time.

"I turned to music as I have always done and discovered that melodic enchantment could move my legs even though I could not."

"But you said you were relieved to be free of the expectation to be king. Why not keep that a secret? Why create this illusion for a crown that you don't really want?" Gordan asked.

Cinder smiled. "After years of experimenting with the music and practicing, I had mastered the enchantment for movement. I guess I didn't care until I realized that this illusion might be possible. Then I couldn't stand to let him win after what he did to me. I convinced my father that this illusion would work, and he consented to give me my trial as regent. As far as my subjects know, I am just a deeply-private man, so long as the other rulers see an able-bodied king."

"Why should that even matter?" Nicole asked. "Who cares if you can't walk?"

"With the Council gone we royal figureheads must pick up the full weight of ruling our kingdoms again, and the people need to believe, more than ever, that we're capable. As my father says, a king in a wheelchair does not command respect of other leaders."

"If this illusion matters to you, rest assured, we'll keep your secret," Raiden said.

"That's right," Gordan agreed.

"Thank you. I don't think I'm ready to let the whole realm know this about me. The way things are—it's peaceful for me. It offers me the comfort and distance I need to be a king. I don't want people's sympathy. I don't want to be surrounded by a court of flatterers and schemers. I even enjoy my life and the responsibilities of the crown like this—well, except for when I wake up halfway across my palace to find my body has been enchanted in the middle of the night."

"You mean you were still asleep when you left your room?" Nicole recalled the surprise on his face in the ballroom.

"Yes, as I told you at the party, I am highly susceptible to music. I believe even more so since the accident because I cannot command my legs to resist the influence of the enchantment."

"You didn't even wake up until I ran into you," Nicole realized.

"That's right, quite the surprise," he said, chuckling. "This way," he instructed, pointing to the right over Gordan's shoulder.

"That would be reason enough to preserve this ruse. Anyone who knew that you use melodic enchantment as a crutch could use it against you," Gordan offered.

"Yes, like tonight although I do not think my cousin suspected a thing before tonight. He's so arrogant. He probably thought I've been afraid of him all these years and that I became a paranoid recluse."

"Doesn't that make Cole a problem now?" Nicole wondered.

"He won't have the chance to tell anyone a thing after we scrape him off the ballroom floor," Cinder said.

❧

After they delivered Cinder to his rooms, Nicole, Raiden and Gordan slipped through the silence of the night and emerged outside their bedroom doors. Raiden and Gordan caught her in a hug at the same time and she relished the soothing weight of their relief in the shared embrace. Oddly enough she was happy in that moment. It felt like the wrong reaction to have when her enemy had come so close to ensnaring her. His presence still seemed to creep through the halls. Fear would have been more appropriate, but she was in their arms—she felt like Venarius couldn't touch her here.

"Can we pretend this didn't happen until tomorrow," she said, laughing through pure exhaustion.

"I'll sleep better outside your door than in my own bed," Gordan said.

"Why not inside on a couch?" Raiden suggested.

"All right," he agreed.

Raiden nodded and opened the door to their room, but stopped immediately. "The mannequin is gone."

"Mannequin?" Nicole questioned. Then she recalled the blank figure by the open door. "That's right…I heard the music and found the door open."

"Sounds like it was a golem," Gordan said.

"Then let's be glad it's gone."

"Maybe we should check the rooms for it first," she said anxiously.

The mannequin was nowhere to be found. They closed the door and locked it. Gordan settled in on the couch facing the door. Nicole crawled into their bed feeling like the blankets and sheets just weren't warm enough or deep enough. When Raiden climbed in, she couldn't get close enough even as he wrapped his arms around her. Exhaustion pulled her to the edge of sleep, but worry had her clinging to consciousness where she knew Raiden's arms were securely around her.

Raiden held her, stuck in a stunned trance of relief.

"We've had closer calls," she murmured against his heart. "Remember the bridge?"

He laughed incredulously. "I guess that's true."

"Did you hear the music?"

"I did, long enough to know where to find you. It was…

enticing."

"It promised me safety and freedom from all this uncertainty and fear. As much as I wanted that I realized you weren't there with me—no one was—I didn't want those good things if I was alone. I'd rather be facing Venarius' schemes every day for a lifetime with you and Gordan and Mitchell. I'll take a close call like tonight everyday if it means being with you."

His heart ached curiously, both blissful and terrified. He had lived a decade with the pain of losing the only person he had in the world and now he lived every day with the fear of history repeating. If he was still alone, he wouldn't know that fear—the torture of every close call—but he wouldn't have Nicole. She was worth all of it. He wanted to say it, but she already said exactly that.

"I love you too," he said and her soft laugh against his chest made him smile.

The warmth of her breath against him lulled him to sleep, and when he opened his eyes again, there was sunlight slipping through the window. Nicole was in his arms precisely as the crystal had shown him last night, and he laughed bitterly, despising the Sight.

A deep inhale broke Nicole's slumber. "What's so funny?" she asked, her voice low and gravely with sleep.

He knew he should tell her. He didn't want to admit he'd been keeping a secret, but he didn't want to lie even more. "I used the Sight last night to make sure nothing was going to happen to you, to sleep a little easier, and I saw this moment, so I went to sleep thinking you were perfectly safe."

Nicole pried her eyes open and looked up at him. He didn't expect her snort of laughter and found himself laughing again with her.

Gordan woke up to laughter bubbling through the door of Nicole and Raiden's room. He smiled at the bittersweet pang in his heart, relieved to feel their little surge of joy which reminded him of Mitchell. He had fallen asleep to the warmth of what Nicole and Raiden shared, woken up to it. He sat up with an aching heart. No matter how scared he was of losing it, he wanted that warmth too and didn't want to pass up the chance to have it.

He got up and walked to the door. Nicole and Raiden's soft murmurs seemed to follow him, encouraging him to open the door and walk down the hall to Mitchell's room. He hesitated, sensing the weight of slumber in the rooms behind the door—Mitchell was still asleep. With a quick sigh he knocked on the door and waited as groggy consternation crept through the rooms followed by the sound of shuffling feet.

Pinching the sleep from the inner corners of his eyes, Mitchell opened the door. When he realized who was standing there, he opened his eyes blinking with surprise.

"Gordan—"

"I'm sorry," he said. "I was selfish. I was protecting myself—I didn't tell her I was hurt because I didn't want to feel her pain. It's bad enough to hurt the people you love but to feel their pain the way I do…it makes it all the worse. I just didn't realize how upset you were by my injuries until—"

Mitchell took him by the hand and guided him into the room so he could close the door. "Look, I don't blame you for not telling her. I'm just not so great at dealing with my emotions sometimes… okay, a lot of the time."

Gordan's heart hammered against his ribs, drumming impatience and longing and, for a second, he couldn't tell what Mitchell was feeling.

"The thing is, I've never had to worry about losing the people I love before, and now I worry every day about Nicole and you. I'm not dealing with it as well as I could," Mitchell confessed.

Gordan's heart yanked him forward like it might escape his chest. He took Mitchell's face in his hands and pulled the two of them together until their lips met. When he pulled away, Mitchell's stunned delight made his heart sputter gleefully.

"That was a pleasant surprise," Mitchell said, grinning.

"I didn't want to pass up this chance anymore," Gordan said, clearing his throat. "That being said, I should tell you—"

"No," Mitchell said.

"What?"

"It can wait," he said, catching Gordan's neck in his hand and pulling him back into another kiss.

Gordan had no inclination to argue.

❧

Nicole sat up. "Do you think Cole is still in the ball room? Should we check?"

"I'd rather stay here," Raiden said, throwing the blankets up over their heads.

She laughed. "What about finding breakfast?"

"All right, you got me there. I'm starving."

"We didn't have dinner last night, did we?"

"No, we did not."

In the silence her stomach made a sound of gurgling dissent, and they both snickered. Nicole threw back the covers and shuffled into the bathroom, catching an eerie memory of the night before as her feet hit the cold tile floor. She bent over the sink to rinse the grease from her face and the lingering trace of sleep from her eyes with cold water. When she stood up, throwing her hair back from her wet face, she noticed her reflection in the mirror.

For a minute she studied her face thinking she looked different, better, less tired maybe. Remarkably, she just felt a little lighter today.

When she emerged from the bathroom, she crossed the bedroom to her trunk, dug out a clean pair of underwear and jeans, and a pair of socks. She changed underwear, stepped into her jeans, pulled on her socks, shoved her feet into her boots and heard Mitchell in the other room.

"Where is she?"

She walked away from her trunk, still wearing Raiden's tunic, and arrived in the doorway to the sitting room just as Mitchell did.

"Hey," he said, catching her in a hug. "You okay?"

For a second, she was confused by his question, but she realized he must know about last night.

"Yeah," she said with a little laugh. "I'm great—it was a weird night."

He released her, chuckling. "Good look, sis."

She flushed and rolled her eyes.

Raiden appeared, still in his boxers and noticed she was dressed. "You don't waste time, serious about finding food, huh?"

"I'm always serious when it comes to food," she answered gravely.

"I guess I better get dressed," he said.

"Wait," she said to Mitchell. "Why are *you* up, and where's Gordan?"

She was pretty sure she saw Mitchell's face redden as he hitched his thumb over his shoulder toward the sitting room.

"What?" She asked—something was up, she could tell.

Mitchell smiled and shook his head. "Finish getting dressed."

Nicole squinted at him through her suspicion and returned to her trunk where she shed Raiden's tunic and pulled on a bra and her mauve sweater. As she headed for the sitting room, Raiden stepped out of the bathroom. She couldn't help smiling at him— taking an appreciative look at him, bare skin the shade of a cappuccino. Her heart tripped itself—there they were, she got lost in the scars, the marks she had left, and she couldn't even count them all. They drew her in closer. She traced a scar with her fingertips and watched the goose bumps raise on his skin. She felt her sting as her hands traveled to touch each one in penance. He was patient, letting her examine the marks she had made until tears fell from her eyes.

He stopped her hands beneath his own and pulled her arms around him before he closed his arms around her, smothering her guilt in his persistent forgiveness.

"The only way you could hurt me is by leaving," he murmured in her ear.

She sighed. It was a relief to breathe him in and press her cheek against his skin. She reciprocated his embrace with a fervent squeeze until he chuckled and before releasing him, she thought, *I love that sound.* A rustle of feathers and fabric drew their attention up to the canopy over their bed where Finnegan hung his head over the side and blinked at them.

"There you are," she said. "Get down from there, Finn, we're going for a walk." She wandered out into the sitting room and stopped in her tracks when her eyes fell on Mitchell and Gordan sitting beside each other on the couch, their hands laced together between them. Mitchell rested his head back, eyes closed, he was definitely up earlier than usual; and Gordan's wistful gaze was called back from somewhere far away to notice her standing there.

She blinked. Her heart swelled at the sight.

Mitchell lifted his head and Gordan blushed. Then a knock at the door stole her attention. She crossed the sitting room and the little entrance chamber to open the door to Thomas.

"Your Highness, Prince Cinder hopes you slept well and has sent a selection from the kitchens if you would like to receive it."

She refrained from saying *hell yes, I do!* "That would be wonderful, Thomas. Please thank Cinder for me."

"Of course." Thomas bowed and directed a procession of the servant dolls into the room with their silver dome-covered platters and delivered them to the long low table between the couches. Then the servants marched back out of the room.

Thomas bustled away and Nicole closed the door. She whirled around and practically ran back into the sitting room, eager to yank the covers off the platters. Raiden walked out of the bedroom and stopped, inhaling the aroma of food in the room.

❦

Between the four of them most of the food disappeared—from fresh fruit and airy pastries, to breads and soft sweetened spreadable cheese, quiches and jam tarts.

"Doesn't this mean that Cinder will be crowned?" Nicole asked, sitting on the floor holding a bowl of blueberries to her chest and pinching several between her fingertips before popping them into her mouth.

"After what Cole did, I would like to think he's lost his chance," Raiden said on the floor beside her.

"Cinder's ruse seems to be a success," Gordan said.

"But for how long?" Mitchell asked. "Secrets get out eventually."

"If he's a good king, it won't matter. The day the secret's out, who he is as a leader will speak for itself," Nicole said. "At least I should hope so." Finnegan nudged Nicole's arm, sending the berries in her hand tumbling away from her mouth. She huffed as the berries bounced on the rug and rolled away. Finn pounced on them. "Yes, I did tell you we were going for a walk."

"We should all go," Raiden said, reaching for a runaway blueberry that had fallen between them.

The palace was probably as safe as it could be from Venarius… today. This storm would follow her wherever she went, but lightning never strikes the same place twice, so why shouldn't they run in the rain, howl into the wind, and laugh despite it all?

"Yeah, let's see what kind of fun we can find around here," she said, standing up. "Venarius' plan didn't work out last night, so it's back to the drawing board for him. I think it's safe to say we have at least one day worry-free."

"Taking an on-going kidnapping scheme a little lightly, aren't you?" Mitchell asked with a chuckle.

"Turn into a paranoid wreck or enjoy time with my favorite people," she said raising her hands to present each option and weighing them against each other.

"Why not both?" Mitchell said enthusiastically.

"I think today I'll just take the latter," she said, taking Raiden's hand and pulling him off the couch, relieved to see his troubled brow had softened; a smile creeping across his lips. That's what she wanted the most—to see him smile and hear him laugh. She watched Gordan and Mitchell stand up, their hands catching each other discretely between them. She wanted to see the people she loved happy; they deserved that. And she could keep the deepening pit of fear to herself to give them that.

⁊

They stopped by the ballroom only to find it was empty which had the strangely comforting effect of making last night's incident seem like just an unpleasant dream. They walked the grounds, the wide lane lined with great oak trees, the garden of fountains, and past the stables and barracks, all the while Nicole left a trail of unruly growth behind her which would probably baffle the gardeners if they were real people.

Finnegan swooped and bounded around them throughout the morning but eventually wandered away.

"Where's he off to?" Mitchell asked.

"I don't know. It's not like I take care of him. He was on his own before. Probably went to find something to eat," Nicole said with a shrug.

"But is that okay? People don't hunt griffins, do they?"

Nicole looked to Raiden.

"No they don't," Raiden said.

They arrived at the opposite wing of the palace where they had returned Cinder the night before.

At first glance the halls in Cinder's wing of the palace looked like the others, but paintings hanging on the walls looked familiar to Nicole.

"Mitch is that—that's a Rembrandt," she said, stopping to stare at a painting of a crowded ship being tossed in a storm, its bow high and its crew in distress. "I'm pretty sure this is a lost painting."

"Really?"

Nicole looked at the next painting and continued down the hall, stopping abruptly at another she recognized. An impressionist scene of a silvery blue bay on a misty morning with a red sun rising over the dark silhouettes of two small boats—she shook her head in disbelief. "This is Monet, I *know* I've seen this in an art book. I think *all* these paintings are from the old world."

"Copies?"

She laughed. "Why do I doubt that?"

Mitchell curiously turned the handle of a door and when the door opened, he turned back to them with delicious intrigue on his face. "Fair game, it's not locked." He stepped inside before Gordan could utter a word of discouragement.

He looked to Nicole. She raised her hand toward the open door, "He's yours now."

An amused huff escaped his lips as he followed after Mitchell. Nicole looked at Raiden who was studying the Monet on the wall closely.

"Hey, you're gonna wanna see this," Mitchell called from inside the room.

Raiden pulled his eyes from the painting.

"Might as well," she said, taking Raiden by the hand and leading him into the room with her.

They stepped into a room like an exhibition hall or a museum. With shelves and tables filled with a catalog of anything and everything from the old world—from historical treasures to antiques to an array of modern plastics.

"Wow, look at this stuff," Nicole muttered.

"Isn't it neat?" Mitchell added, looking pointedly at her before they both let out a laugh.

"He's practically got a department store in here," she said standing before a table of eye-glasses all different frames, from name brands she knew from magazine ads to delicate spectacles that looked like they were centuries old.

"Jeez, how much you wanna bet each one of these represents some poor schmuck who inexplicably lost his glasses?" Mitchell chuckled, picking up a pair.

Raiden picked up a pair of glasses, put them on and Nicole turned into a blurry column, her hair and skin blending together. He shook his head, pulled them off and put them back onto the table.

"They all look new," Nicole said, picking up a pair of square frames and placing them on his face. She tilted her head and looked at him with a smile.

Raiden's eyes went wide as he realized Nicole's face was clearer, startlingly clear. He pulled the glasses off to see the very subtle haze of his vision and put them back on. The clarity made his heart pound—his eyesight had deteriorated, he knew he used to see the world this clearly, how had he not noticed the blurring of Nicole's faint freckles?

"What?" Nicole asked with a chuckle.

"I—these—" he couldn't say it.

She looked at him—her eyes asked before she uttered the words, "Raiden, do you need glasses?"

"No way—really?" Mitchell took the Buddy Holly glasses off his face and put them back hastily.

"I know I used to see clearly, I just didn't notice that—" Over the last few weeks he had grown so used to the blur of tired eyes, but this…

Nicole looked at him—brows pinched, eyes full of understanding—he had told her seers lose their eyesight the more time they spend in the future. "Raiden, how much have you been using the Sight?"

Raiden pressed his lips together, worried she might think this was her fault in some way. After all, he told her that he's used it last night. He'd been using the crystal incessantly since finding it, knowing full well what the cost was, but he was too busy thinking of her, wondering if she would be there in the morning.

"Let me see," Mitchell said, taking the glasses from Raiden and putting them on. He looked around the room and looked at them. "Oh, well that's not so bad really, just a little blurry. Nowhere *close* to being blind." He took them off and handed them to Nicole who put them on.

She looked around the room through the lenses and took the glasses off to look at Raiden, handing them back to him with sadness crumpling her expression. He sighed and put the glasses on, his world was clear again. He wasn't going to risk that clarity any further. Last night was as good as his mother's voice in his ear—*'live in the present'* hadn't resonated with him as a kid. He had no idea how precious those days had been until they were gone. Then he spent a decade in the past. Now he had something in his present that mattered and he was still worrying about the future.

"It's fine," he assured her. "Trust me, it's not going to get any worse. I'll be perfectly all right wearing glasses," he smiled at her, glad to see her so clearly.

"Yeah, don't worry about it, Nikki. That's a good look for him," Mitchell said as he wandered away across the room.

Nicole folded her arms. Raiden raised his eyebrows. She scrunched her face into a frown that lacked real severity. He wished he could hear the thoughts. Her gaze scrutinized him with a gently disparaging slant on her brow, but he was too busy appreciating the light in her amber irises.

The concerned line of her mouth finally curled—that slow creep of her lips from frown to half a grin that always pulled on his heart. "You know, he's not wrong. You do look really cute with glasses."

Raiden smiled as he pushed his hair back, trying to hide the heat in his cheeks.

"Even cuter when you blush," she teased, and she pulled him closer by his hips, pushing his temperature higher.

He couldn't believe how much of her he had been missing in his lost eyesight. Had she always been this beautiful. Of course she had, but—he rolled his shoulders forward and hunched to bring his lips to hers. Heat spread through him, they were pelvis to pelvis and he tensed, this was the wrong place.

"Get a room," Mitchell called.

A laugh bubbled up through her lips against his and tasting her laugh made him shudder. Then she dragged him into the ether.

๑

They fell out of the air, stumbling but they caught each other, mouths fusing again. Nicole's heart raced and her temperature rose. She couldn't get her sweater off fast enough. Her skin burned. The laces of her boots unknotted and loosened, caught up in the pulses of magic pouring into the room. She kicked her boots off—one hit the wall with an obnoxious thud.

"Oops," she laughed.

Raiden yanked his shirt over his head and tossed it as he wobbled stepping out of his shoes. She pulled his face back down to hers again, but her whole body seemed to pulse with the mantra *closer*, her heart lurching at the tug of his hands on her waistband until it was undone. When his hands slid from her hips to her waist and up her ribcage, his palms against her skin, she shivered. His fingers caught the fabric of her bra and he pulled it up. She raised her arms and it was gone.

As he tried to step out of his jeans, he toppled back onto the edge of the bed, sitting there disheveled in boxers with jeans still stuck around his ankles. His glasses were slightly askew on his face.

"Do you want to take these off?" She asked, straightening the frames.

"No," he said, catching her hand. "I want to see you clearly." He looked at her intently, and she remembered that she first met him this close, face-to-face, plunged into that blue-green gaze before she even knew his name. Raiden's gaze fell, and he dragged his fingertip against her bare skin from her sternum to her bellybutton raising goose bumps in its wake. He let out a breath of appreciation that made her giggle.

❦

A black bird peered through the window into their room, but it was Venarius who watched through the creature's stolen gaze in his looking glass. He clenched his teeth as clothes were shed and a yaldson's hands touched what was his.

"Sir," Venarius' apprentice said timidly from the doorway. "We intercepted a letter from the King of Nol to Prince Cinder."

Venarius held out his hand. His apprentice crossed the room hastily to deliver the letter into his waiting hand. He opened the envelope carefully and pulled out the letter.

"It would seem the King has made his decision; Cinder has been named successor. Let's add a little to this letter, shall we?"

Venarius opened a drawer of his desk and retrieved a blank piece of thick parchment to match the royal stationary. He transcribed the king's words, adding the suggestion to Cinder that he send Nicole and her party to Eanna on Nol's best ship as an amends for the unfortunate incident involving Cole. Of course, the King of Nol would object to this arrangement; he cherished his naval fleet and loathed being in service to anyone.

"There," he said as he finished. He waved his hand over the letter and his script took on the staccato slant of the King of Nol's handwriting. He handed the letter to his assistant who proceeded to fold it like the original and place it into the envelope. "Get me the name of our maid in the king's household, I have orders to send her."

"Yes, sir."

Venarius began the letter to his planted agent. No one really needed the king around any longer, especially when he had the authority to stop the allocation of Nol's best ship as a transport vessel that would put Nicole where Venarius wanted her.

∾

"Hey, where did they go?" Mitchell asked, looking around.

"I don't know," Gordan said even though he was pretty certain he did. He cleared his throat—a charge of desire lingered in the air. "I certainly don't mind us being alone."

Mitchell turned away from the wall of instruments and looked over his shoulder at Gordan with a slant of amusement on his mouth. "I couldn't agree more."

Gordan turned his burning face back to the display of hats upon a shelf as he passed. He noticed the perplexing scent of confusion in the air but when he glanced at Mitchell, who was smiling to himself.

"What's on your mind?" Gordan caved under his curiosity.

"I was thinking that dating a dragon might make me more pansexual than bisexual, but what does it really matter anyway? I like you," he said chuckling. "You don't have any reservations about being with a human do you—having a relationship in this form?"

"Not at all, it feels right to me."

Mitchell cleared his throat but a note of anxiety rung through a flutter in the air.

"What do you have to be nervous about?" Gordan wondered out loud.

Mitchell chuckled. "The fact that I can't hide how much I like you from your mind-reading."

"I don't read minds," Gordan said, smiling to himself as he walked the length of the table between them, sliding his gaze over the array of devices like Nicole's cell phone. "I feel emotions. My sense is empathic, not telepathic."

"Okay then, so what am I feeling right now?"

Gordan glanced up at Mitchell, walking along the other side of the table. There was a hum of attraction in the air, an energy that made him tense and shudder with anticipation both enjoyable and torturous. When he caught Mitchell's direct gaze for a startling instant, he felt like he was falling and his heart reeled, his body flushed with adrenaline and his temperature rose. Then they reached the end of the table and there was nothing between them.

Mitchell had a look of expectation on his face, a devilish curl on one side of his mouth, but Gordan stumbled through his thoughts for an answer. "You're—" His head was too crowded with Mitchell to find words for what his body was screaming. He wondered for a moment if it was Mitchell's hunger or his own at this point—he had never known this agonizing draw. He gave up, slipping his hands beneath Mitchell's jaw and pulling him in to place the answer on his lips.

Gordan considered for a moment that the warm wet marriage of their lips might be just as good flying. Had there really been a time he despised the human form? Mitchell's hands found the waistband of Gordan's pants and he pulled their hips together.

"Hello," Mitchell murmured against Gordan's mouth at the building pressure between their pelvises. He was equally surprised to feel the change below his waistband in that appendage he had only ever needed to relieve his bladder.

He cleared his throat. "I'm not…entirely familiar with everything about this form," Gordan confessed, struggling with his words again as Mitchell hadn't let go of his pants and, in turn, he grew increasingly rigid as his heart rate sped with exhilaration.

"Can I please help you get to know it a little better?" Mitchell asked with an ardent glint in his eye.

"Right now?"

"Why not? Who's going to see? The servants and the guards don't have eyes," he said with a grin and a peck on Gordan's lips before his fingers deftly unfastened the waistband of his pants.

Nicole walked hand in hand with Raiden past the old-world paintings as she tried to understand how she could feel like something significant had changed. She wasn't so different than she was an hour ago. She didn't feel like she'd lost anything. How can a woman be less for that intimacy when two people coming together was the very definition of being more?

She had known how much he loved her, *needed* her, but now her heart felt swollen with that connection like a belly distended with dessert. It was sickly sweet, satisfying yet uncomfortable. Fear hit her in sudden bursts because she was perfectly content, happy even—for what felt like a few goddamn moments of relief in a hurricane—she wanted to keep it, and yet she felt the very real potential of losing it with icy keenness.

As they walked, he raised their joined hands to bring hers to his lips like he knew she needed to be brought back to now, to him. The door past the Monet was still open and music wafted out into the hall.

"How long have we been gone?" She whispered to Raiden.

"I don't know," he answered with a guilty smile and a shrug.

They walked into the collection room but did not see Mitchell or Gordan among the horde of old-world treasures. On a table in the far-left corner of the room crowded with instruments from every era it seemed, a record player sat, black vinyl spinning while Johnny Cash's voice filled the air.

"Mitch?"

"Over here," he answered and an arm waved from behind one of the tables in the middle of the room.

Confused, she moved across the room and around the table tentatively. "What are you—" She noticed a Monopoly box on the floor in time to drift over it and step in the narrow space between it and another stack of board games—on the other side of which Mitchell and Gordan were seated side by side on the floor with a precarious tower of Jenga blocks standing in front of them. Gordan looked up at her like a kid caught stealing candy—he certainly wasn't the mastermind of this mess.

"Just showing Gordan how to have some fun," Mitchell said with a sly grin. "What did you think we were doing?"

She masked her chagrin with a smile. "I was thinking Uno. But Jenga is always a good choice."

"Now that you're here, we can play Twister."

"There's not a lot of room in here for Twister and should we even be playing with Cinder's collection of board games?"

"You've already taken a pair of glasses," he said, attempting to pull a piece from the Jenga tower only to topple the whole thing.

"Good point. What other games does he have?"

Mitchell nodded toward the shelf. She hopped and drifted over the collapsed pile of Jenga pieces between Mitchell and Gordan. The shelf was stacked full of board games like a near perfect round of Tetris.

"Also, I think I have a responsibility as your brother to point out how obvious it is that you got laid," Mitchell said with a chuckle.

Laughter sprayed from her mouth as she turned around. "Excuse me?" Her face went hot. "It's not *obvious*."

"Aside from that reaction—and the fact that Raiden looks like he's achieved Nirvana—"

Raiden raised his hands in a gesture of *no contest,* his mouth was half-shameless grin, half-stoic agreement. Nicole nearly choked on another laugh.

"It's been a while since I've seen you float like that," Mitchell said, his tone softening with sincerity.

Nicole puzzled—her brother noticed something like that? Thinking back to the days before Atrium and the days after, he was right. Before Atrium stepping off the edge of gravity here and there was something she did without a thought, but since…

"Don't think too hard about it," he said. "It's a good thing, and we shouldn't pass up good things while we have a chance at them, right?"

She glanced at Gordan, then her brother, sitting close to each other, their thighs touching. "Yeah," she agreed.

"Like teaching Ray and Gordan how to play the best board games."

&

They passed hours in the old-world room, having played Twister— after carefully moving Cinder's tables aside and doubling the size of the playing mat—then The Game of Life and Trouble.

"Hey," Mitchell said, nodding toward Raiden.

Nicole looked beside her to see Raiden had dozed off, his head leaned back against the spines of books in the bookcase behind him.

"I don't think he slept well last night," she said.

"Did any of us?" Gordan offered.

"I did, actually," Mitchell said. "Because no one woke me up for the messed up after party."

Nicole smothered a chuckle, not wanting to disturb Raiden. "It's kinda late, I should go find Finnegan," she said quietly. "Can I trust you to put everything back?"

"Sure, sure," Mitchell said.

"And don't wake him up; he could use a power nap," she added as she got up from the floor, wincing at the stiffness in her legs from yesterday's run and sitting so long.

She was grateful for the chance to move again, walking through the halls loosened up the tightness in her legs as she made her way outside. The late afternoon sun was warm and golden, but a winter chill lingered in the air.

"Finn," she called, making her way across the pristinely manicured lawn and throwing it into overgrown upheaval.

She had feared that love would change her, lead her astray and leave her with an identity she didn't want like her mother had come to realize twenty years into a marriage. Her mother discovered her conviction to be the person she wanted to be and Nicole couldn't blame her for that, but it had damaged their family nonetheless. Nicole had decided she would be better off never losing herself in the first place. She laughed sardonically to herself, *I'm as lost as someone can be*—and it had nothing to do with how she felt about Raiden. She didn't feel altered by loving him. She didn't feel like a captive of his need for her, or less an individual for having been a part of someone else. She felt stronger for it, more comfortable with herself and all her scars and cracks, for being wanted and adored exactly as she was—sharp broken edges and all.

This strange peaceful delirium she'd found as she walked, thinking of Raiden as the breeze moved through her hair and slipped through the fabric of her clothes, didn't erase her scars; it didn't fix her or wash away her fears, but it offered a beautiful distraction at the very least—a safe place to retreat to inside herself.

A glint of gold and blue caught her eye. She looked up to catch sight of Finnegan gliding to the ground and prancing joyously through the grass.

"There you are, I thought maybe you finally decided to grow up and start a life of your own," she said, laughing as he nudged her stomach with his head. She ruffled the feathers around his neck and he purred, a low muffled rattle punctuated with a sweet chirp.

"Nicole," a familiar voice called across the gardens.

She looked around until she spotted Fen waving.

"Hey," she called back and once the distance between them closed, she could see Fen was out of breath. "What have you been up to today? Where's Asi?"

"Oh, we spent the day with Sage and Netti. They taught us some basic combat exercises, but we were over at the fountains just now, and I saw Finnegan fly over. I thought you might be around somewhere," she said.

"Did you two have fun last night?"

Fen's eyes lit up. "Yes! I never dreamed of dancing like that, but—it was so formal. I think the celebration we had back in Keystone was more fun, to be honest."

"Ah, so you like a lack of decorum," Nicole said, laughing.

"I guess so," Fen grinned. "Did you have fun last night? You danced a lot."

"I should tell you and Asi about something that happened last night," she admitted. "Come on."

She and Fen walked back to the garden of fountains where sheets of falling water were the hedges, stone statues instead of topiaries stood, and Asi walked the paths trailing her fingers in the water.

"You found her," Asi said with a smile.

"Hi, Asi," Nicole said.

"So, what happened?" Fen asked impatiently.

"What do you mean 'what happened?'" Asi asked, looking between them.

Nicole told them about the music in the middle of the night, excluding Cinder's secret. "I don't want to scare you, but you need to know that Venarius is always nearby."

"Has Prince Cinder managed to get any information from his cousin?" Fen wondered.

"I don't know. We haven't seen or heard from him at all today. Cole wasn't in the ballroom this morning, but that's all I know."

"I can help, you know," Asi said. "A guy like that might not tell Cinder anything, but I can take memories and maybe we can learn something useful about Venarius."

"Maybe Cole knows where Venarius conducts his business," Nicole said.

"If Cole is still alive," Fen said.

"Do you think Cinder would do that?" Asi wondered.

Fen shrugged. "Would you blame him?"

"I don't think Cinder would risk the rumors of his cousin's disappearance. Killing his competition would only make him look like the weaker ruler." Nicole looked down at Finnegan lying at her feet resting his head on massive paws, dozing…like she'd left Raiden.

"Hey, where's Raiden?" Asi asked.

"With Mitchell and Gordan," Nicole answered. "I guess I better see if I can find Cinder. I thought he would be less reclusive after what happened last night." She knew his secret after all. He didn't need to hide anymore, not from her, Raiden or Gordan.

"Find Thomas," Fen suggested. "He's always running around doing Cinder's errands, right?"

Nicole nodded. "True. He shouldn't be too hard to find. I'll let you know how my mission goes. See you later, my dears."

Finnegan sprang onto his feet and into step alongside Nicole.

She walked through the palace, taking the long route in hopes of running into Thomas or Mirabel, but she made it to her room without any sight of them. After living in their palace for a few weeks, she had grown used to the constant presence of staff; Cinder's palace had an eerie atmosphere staffed by dolls that could see nothing and tell no secrets. So much space and so many doors would denote some relative number of people and so the lack thereof hung in the air incongruently.

When she opened the door, Finnegan bounded inside and flopped down on the rug in the sitting room to roll vigorously on its luxuriousness. She wandered through the rooms found them empty and arrived to the bathroom. While she peed, she eyed the pool-like tub in the center of the bathroom and wondered if she could bathe a griffin in it.

She realized her feet felt heavy as she trudged to the sink, washed her hands, and rinsed her face in cold water. It was late afternoon. The weight of the previous night was catching up with her now. In the bathroom mirror she could see through the bathroom door and the bedroom door as Raiden walked through the sitting room. She dried her face and saw him step into the bedroom, his eyes searching.

"Lose something?" she asked, stepping out of the bathroom.

She could see the tension fall from his shoulders before he smiled and caught her firmly in his arms, lifting her feet off the floor. That tiny nagging fear would plague him as long as Venarius was out there. So, she closed her arms behind his neck and let her head sink into his shoulder, hoping she could banish that fear from their lives someday. Her head felt twice as heavy now. She was liable to fall asleep, yet she had no interest in being set down.

"I'm just gonna stay here, okay?" she mumbled into him.

"That's fine with me."

There came a knock at the door. "Of course," she groaned.

"We don't have to answer it."

She sighed. "We do. I need Thomas to take a message to Cinder."

"All right," Raiden said, setting her down.

With a huff she marched out of the bedroom, through the sitting room, to the door and opened it to none other than Thomas.

"Good afternoon, Your Highness," Thomas bowed slightly.

"Hello, Thomas."

"Prince Cinder would like you to know that he has arranged an informal dinner for you and your entire party this evening at seven," Thomas said.

"Oh," she said, glad to have her chance to talk to Cinder handed to her until she realized they couldn't have the conversation she had in mind over dinner with everyone around. "Thank you, Thomas. Could you let the prince know that we'd like a private audience with him at his convenience?"

Thomas looked skeptical. She wondered if he knew Cinder's secret or if Thomas was kept on the other side of closed doors and written requests.

"Of course, your highness, I will relay your request to him."

He bowed and turned away from the door.

She sighed. "*Your Highness*," she muttered, turning back to Raiden, hooking her arms around his ribs and pressing her face into his sternum.

"You still don't think it suits you?"

"The only thing that suits me right now is you and a nap."

He chuckled.

Fatigue pressed down on her to the point that settling onto the couch with Raiden was as fuzzy and fragmented as a dream. She sank into slumber almost as soon as she closed her eyes.

Raiden remembered that he didn't have the Juno's Tears on him. It was still tucked beneath one of the pillows on their bed. He tried not to worry about it. He could wake her up, and she knew he was there when she fell asleep—maybe that was enough now.

Nicole sank into the kind of sleep where she knew where she was. She still felt Raiden beneath her and the couch against her back amidst the weight of sleep and the shadows of her mind behind closed eyes.

The unseen ghoul in her sleep never seemed to touch her when Raiden was with her, so she could care less if it circled her. She knew where she was—in Raiden's arms. She felt buoyant in this slumber, dipping below the surface of consciousness into dreams and floating back up to the rhythm of Raiden's rising and falling chest beneath her. Then the light pressure of something sharp trailed down her spine, a delicate reminder that made her heart go cold. She shuddered, turning around in the darkness of her dream. It was instinct, nothing was ever there.

Except this time there was. The thing behind her was her, the doppelgänger she had met in her bedroom back home, but she was out of the mirror. Her hand was closed around something invisible. Nicole didn't need to see the blade to feel it. If these dreams had taught her anything, it was that unseen things could still wound you. She shook her head and felt herself resurface to the safe darkness behind her eyes, to the pressure of the couch and Raiden against her.

I have Raiden, he's right here, she thought, opening her eyes to break from sleep only to see she was still there in a half dream, the darkness cradling them both. *Oh no.* She tensed, anticipating the pain, but she felt something warm and wet hit her cheek and she sat up, startled, to see a vivid red slash on his face, yet he lay there unresponsive. Then gash after gash tore into him, at his face, his arms and chest turning his clothing to bloody shreds. *No,* she threw herself over him in an attempt to shield him, *stop it!* Those wounds were meant for her. He didn't deserve this. She wrenched her eyes open again and this time she saw the low polished table and ornate rug beneath it—the sitting room.

Raiden jumped when Nicole jerked upright, gasping, her hands searching him, pulling at his clothes and her eyes wet with horrified tears. He sat up.

"What? What is it?" he asked, shaken, unsure what she was looking for when she placed her hands on his face.

The nightmare lingered in her troubled gaze even as she sighed with relief and sagged into his chest, synching her arms around him.

"Nicole," he implored, closing his arms securely around her.

"It's still there. I can't make it go away," she muttered into his heart.

"What's still there?"

"I have nightmares that hurt me sometimes," she said, barely more than a whisper.

He sighed, understanding now what she must have seen this time in her sleep—what she was searching for when she woke up.

"Gordan told me," he admitted.

Her face crumpled further.

He explained about the herb, about how his mother had used it when he was young, offering her presence when his dreams were too dark and strange for a child.

She listened, her frown wavered and she tried to smile. "You've been spending your nights in that place with me," she let out a short ironic huff.

"Like you said, it's not so bad when we're there together."

She took a deep breath and let it out shakily. "Aren't you afraid…that this might be the rest of your life, my nightmares and my enemies? It might never end."

"That's fine."

She shook her head. "Everything that's happened to you because of me."

"No—because of *them*, Nicole. What about everything that's happened to *you*?"

His question couldn't derail her thoughts.

"You've seen what I can become. I could go so much further down that path before this is over…if it's ever over." She dropped her gaze to the carpet.

Raiden dipped his head to look her in the eye, reading what she didn't want to say in the moisture brimming on her lashes. His heart sank. "I'm not afraid of you, Nicole. The only thing I'm afraid of is you facing this alone."

She lifted her eyes to meet his. He took her face in his hands and wiped the trails of tears away with the sweep of his thumbs. She gave him a feeble nod.

"I can get the herb and we can get some sleep," he offered.

"Yeah." She let out a sigh. "Can we go to your dreams instead of mine from now on?"

☙

Cinder did not attend their informal dinner although the only thing 'informal' about the gathering was the guests and their attire. Everyone arrived in the comfortable clothes they'd worn for the day, the guards in their uniforms sans jackets, Asi and Fen looking like they strolled out of Keren's orchard.

The venue was, in fact, uncomfortably extravagant. As a whole they looked like some group partaking in a pub-crawl that wandered into a five-star restaurant. There were a lot of awkward smiles and shrugs floating around as they pulled out high-backed chairs and settled in at the dramatically long wood table.

But without Cinder or any ceremonious influence on the evening, the excessively ornamental atmosphere faded to the background and the dining room relaxed. While they ate, however, Thomas arrived with a small sealed envelope and presented it so discretely that others would assume he had merely come to check that everything was satisfactory.

"From Prince Cinder, your highness," he whispered with a bow. "I do hope everyone is enjoying dinner."

"Yes, thank you," Nicole said, taking the envelope.

She opened it under the table and read,

Thomas will escort your highness and the king to my chambers after dinner so that we can talk. Gordan is welcome should you wish to include him. Until then,

> *Cinder*

Nicole passed it to Raiden beside her.

⃣

"Have fun with your royal business," Mitchell said as he waved. He strolled down the hall toward their rooms. Gordan watched him go, and she could see the disappointment on his face.

"You don't have to come, you know," Nicole said quietly. "We can fill you both in afterwards. Besides, who knows what trouble he'll get into unsupervised."

He laughed and gave her a grateful smile before loping after Mitchell and catching him by the hand after several strides. Nicole beamed and shook her head.

"What?" Raiden asked.

"Them—being together," she said.

"Shall we?" Thomas said. He walked with Nicole and Raiden through the palace to Cinder's wing. They walked past the old world paintings. Thomas led them several doors past the room of old world collections. He knocked and waited.

"You may come in," Cinder answered.

Thomas opened the door and remained in the hall, closing the door behind them. They stepped into a study that at first glance seemed to be a room made entirely of stacked books—bookshelves wall to wall, floor to ceiling. A wing-backed chair sitting empty behind a table, a perfect setting for the right amount of intimidation to discuss business privately, but Cinder was seated in a wheelchair that Nicole recognized immediately to be from the old world, an ultra-light-weight chair with a minimal back rest and no armrests.

What struck Nicole the most was not seeing him in the wheelchair—even after witnessing his inability to walk the night before—but, in fact, he looked very different to her now than he had in the glittering scene of his birthday celebration. Come to think of it, she hadn't seen him all that clearly last night in the dim ballroom or the shadowy hallways.

The perfection of his presence at the ball—his flawless porcelain complexion, the shine of his hair like polished copper, the pointed severity of his brows and eyes—it was all softened, he was unpolished. His face was covered in freckles and his hair was a more natural ginger-brown without the near-metallic shine. She realized the stunning Prince Cinder they had met last night had been part illusion. He was not dazzlingly handsome, and like his movement to the music, it was all artifice for his image. In fact, the Cinder before them had a far warmer and earnest appearance.

Nicole caught Raiden looking around at the books in a daze of wonder, and she couldn't hold back a knowing smile.

"Welcome," Cinder said, matter-of-factly with none of his flamboyance from the night before. "I regret that I have been so busy today, dealing with Cole is proving to be troublesome."

"What have you managed so far?" Raiden wondered.

"I have him sequestered in a room attached to my chambers. I'm keeping him sedated with musical enchantment. That's the best I can do on my own, I have no talent for any other magic really," Cinder explained. "I have been corresponding with my father all day over the matter of his betrayal. While he has named me the official successor, Cole still knows my secret...so, the real problem is what to do about his healing and his punishment."

"I think we might have a way to help that could benefit us both," she said.

"Go on."

"One of my ladies," she said, almost rolling her eyes at the phrase, "can remove his memories for you. I'm hoping that somewhere in those memories there might be some information about Venarius, how Cole was communicating with him, for how long, and where he might be."

Cinder looked like he would jump out of his chair if he could.

"I would be in your debt for years," he said with a relieved laugh.

"Like I said, it could help us both."

"After the trouble my cousin has already caused, you must allow me to show my gratitude," he insisted. "Even my father thinks we should make amends for what Cole did. Since you're traveling to Eanna for the vernal festival, please allow me to send you in one of our best ships. Ours are truly the safest on the seas. You can travel the coast; it is a far more enjoyable journey than going by caravan."

"We can't fit everyone in the Tempest anyway," Raiden said.

"Our ships are well protected," Cinder added, his voice turning to sympathetic candor. "Given who you're up against, there's possibly no safer way to travel."

Nicole looked to Raiden who clearly didn't need any more convincing than that.

"I guess that's settled, then," she said.

"Congratulations on the succession," Raiden added.

"Yes, that's great news," Nicole agreed. "Isn't it?"

"Oh yes," Cinder said with a chuckle. "I've hardly had the clarity to appreciate it."

"Is this set-up part of your illusion?" Raiden asked, motioning to the chair and the room.

"Yes. On occasion I do conduct diplomatic business in private, but only if I must. Obviously, I have no need for the disguise this time," Cinder said with a flippant wave toward the chair behind the table.

"Your wheelchair," she said. "It's from the old world, right?"

"It is," he said, his tone lifted with interest, and then he looked more closely at her.

"I'm from the other realm," she said. It wasn't like it was a secret.

Cinder's eyes widened a little and a slow smile spread across his mouth. "How could I miss it?" he said. He looked to Raiden. "But you're not—were you wearing glasses last night?"

"Of course," he lied easily and Nicole held back a smirk.

Cinder seemed satisfied by that—not that it mattered since he duplicated the glasses and left the second pair on the table so that Cinder's collection wouldn't be conspicuously incomplete.

"Well, I can't help but find it somewhat portentous that the keys of the realm should finally be claimed and that one of you is from the other realm. Balance indeed."

"I beg your pardon?" Nicole asked.

"The songs, the old rhymes, the prophecy—this realm has been waiting for balance. Let's see, it goes: *Two opposed in harmony will forge the key and unlock our chains.*"

"You know that prophecy?"

"Everyone does, well most people have heard it, and anyone with any sense would remember the words of the last living oracle of our time."

"You mean Althea Gweldith Divale," Raiden said.

"Yes, she left us with our greatest hope. This realm is a product of imbalance and injustice. Undoubtedly it was a haven, but I firmly believe the torn world will heal and be whole again."

She'd forgotten what Cole said during their dance. Cinder believes in the dissolution of Veil, precisely the idea that Venarius founded Dawn upon. Nicole and Raiden exchanged a swift glance of discomfort that Cinder didn't see. After everything that had happened last night, she hadn't considered that Cinder could be a Dawn sympathizer.

"How do you suppose that? You think the prophecy is talking about breaking free from this realm, that Veil is '*our chains*' in all this?" Raiden asked, digging for more.

Nicole swallowed the sudden anxiety in her throat.

"I suppose it would happen the same way the world split in two, gradually and not without its difficulties. I think there will come a time when the old world will be receptive to our return, and it won't be easy. It will take the bravest and most foolish of us to risk the alienation and hostility that chased us away, but I believe the old world needs us. As we return the imbalance will shift, the barrier will weaken, and Veil will turn back into the mist at the edge of reality as it began."

Nicole realized her mouth had fallen open.

Cinder continued. "But Veil must find its own balance first. We had something good—a place to lick our wounds—and look what we did to it. We tore our haven to pieces over petty differences. It's not that everyone must be the same, but if we cannot accept each other in our exile from the old world, then can we blame them for chasing us away?"

"Yes," Nicole said. "You can still blame them. You being awful to each other here doesn't mean the people of the old world get a pass. You don't have to achieve utopia to justify condemning what they did then."

Cinder smiled. "I suppose you're right. What do you think about the old world?"

"It's even worse than before, the religions that chased you all out got bigger and uglier and wars got bloodier. It's strangling itself in greed and hate. It's not the place anyone in Veil wants to return to, gradually *or* suddenly."

"It's dying," Cinder said. "Because it's broken. Magic is a part of the world and to remove it, it's like removing the heart."

A swift knock at the door stole their attention.

"Your Majesty," Thomas said through the door.

"What is it, Thomas?" Cinder asked.

"Your father—the king…is dead."

Cinder's contemplative expression fell into slack shock. He looked to Nicole and Raiden. Nicole saw fear in Cinder's eyes.

☙

Given the confident and almost menacingly beautiful image Cinder had crafted for the people of Nol, there was no doubt what kind of rumors would spread about the death of the king. They would never imagine the Cinder Nicole had seen—the immediate shock of the news, the panic in his breathing, and the grief welling in his eyes. Only she and Raiden got to see the boy who lost his father—who had been trying to beat his horrid cousin at a game for a prize he wasn't yet ready to take—buckling under the weight of it all, sagging forward in his chair, dropping his elbows to his knees and his face into his hands.

When Nicole looked to Raiden, she saw him close his eyes against what she supposed to be the stirrings of his own losses, and she took his hand. They stood there in solemn silence, unsure if they should leave him to process this alone without trying to hide his emotions from strangers.

Then Cinder straightened up, took a shaky breath, and composed himself in mere minutes—a facade Nicole suspected wouldn't last long.

"I hope you can forgive the inconvenience to you and your friend, but I need you to help me with Cole *tonight*," he said, his tone was low and shaky.

It was a strange rest of the evening, hurrying to Asi and Fen's room, whisking Asi across the palace to Cinder's rooms. Cinder stayed out of sight. Nicole and Asi stepped into the small room where Cole lay asleep and the thick music in the little chamber hit them with a wave of lethargy that made them yawn. Nicole closed the music box on the bedside table and the music stopped.

Asi barely touched her fingertips to Cole's face and Nicole waited until Asi took her hand away and nodded.

"He'll be confused when he wakes up here instead of his home," Asi said.

"As much as he deserves every broken bone, I suppose I had better fix him. Cinder can see to it that he wakes up in his own bed."

Asi nodded in agreement, and Nicole scowled at the man before she placed her hand on his shoulder. She was surprised to feel a charge of familiar magic jump through her, and she caught a sudden jolt of the anger she'd felt that night—she hadn't realized her magic could linger like that in someone else. Before he could wake up, she sent a calm wave of energy through her hand and felt it creep through him. She shuddered at the odd intimacy of that connection, sensing every crack and break to undo the damage.

When she was certain there was nothing broken left to mend, she pulled away and opened the music box once more before she and Asi left the room. Nicole walked Asi back to her room.

"Cole's partnership with Venarius was very brief," Asi offered in the silence as they walked. "They only communicated through letters in the week or so leading up to Cinder's birthday."

"I guess that's not surprising," Nicole said, disappointed. "It was too much to hope that Venarius shared any vital information with his lackeys."

"There is a memory of Cole's that I should give you even though I really don't want to," she said, barely audible as they reached her bedroom door.

Nicole frowned and her heart ached—everyone wanted to protect her.

Asi sighed and raised her hand to touch Nicole's forehead with her fingertips. Nicole's thoughts warbled, disturbed by an invading memory—she realized she was lying on the floor seeing a man standing over her in the dimness of the ballroom.

"Your incompetence is of no use to me," the man standing over her said. "Let this be your recompense for failing."

"No. Wait—Venarius." It was Cole's voice.

"That will be all, Cole. Good luck with your pursuit for the crown." Venarius smiled and left. "This has been…enlightening at least. I'll find another way."

The memory raised bile in the back of her throat. It wasn't as though she didn't already know that he would come at her again with another plan, but seeing his face shrouded in the shadows, hearing him say it himself shook her.

"It's strange having other people's memories," Asi said. "I'm used to it, but it's still strange. What was it I just gave you?"

Nicole realized that she truly was giving her the memory, and it was forgotten now to Asi. "Just a glimpse of Venarius," she said. "Thank you, anything helps."

"Good," Asi said, less troubled than before. "Cole's memories of their correspondence are useless, a proposal, agreement, arrangement, everything we already know after what happened."

"I think it's safe to say we know something about Venarius," Nicole said.

"What's that?"

"He doesn't like to get his hands dirty," he said. "He likes to have others do it for him. He likes planning. He likes observing. He's a necromancer—we know he's a pretty powerful guy in his own right, and he was right here in the palace. Don't you think he could have come after me himself with abilities like that? But he likes exhibiting his power over others. It's like he doesn't just want me, he wants to prove something along the way."

Asi frowned.

"Hey," she said, pulling Asi in for a hug. "I'm okay. He may be able to control a lot of people, but that doesn't come close to having people fighting with you because they love you."

Asi nodded.

"Get some sleep, okay? If Venarius wins, it will be because we'll all be defeated by our own sleep deprivation."

"Don't say that," Asi said. "He can't win."

Nicole chuckled. "Okay, but still, get some sleep."

"All right."

Once Asi was inside her room and the door was shut, Nicole practically collapsed into the ether and fell out onto the couch in her room, landing beside Mitchell who jumped, throwing himself onto Gordan beside him.

"Jeez—Nicole!"

"How did it go?" Raiden asked. He was on his feet—pacing, no doubt.

"Cole will wake up at home thinking he's recovered from a fever, but his memories didn't offer much at all about Venarius," she said.

"Other than that, he was too close for comfort last night—he was right there in the ballroom. Needless to say, getting the hell out of here will be a relief."

With the sudden death of his father, Cinder had to get Cole back into the public eye, lest his absence add to the already suspicious demise of the king—who, with a son of only twenty-six, was neither old enough nor ill enough to reasonably die of natural causes.

The days that followed had to be chaos for Cinder hidden away in his rooms trying to orient himself as a fully-fledged king while planning a funeral and a coronation; but for Nicole, Raiden, Mitchell and Gordan the days were suspiciously peaceful which only unsettled them more with each passing day as they wondered what next opportunity Venarius would take.

They soothed their paranoia by spending the days with Caeruleus, Loak and Leone, running drills with the guards and with Asi and Fen. Nicole proudly watched Asi and Fen learn how to take down Caeruleus and Leone. Caeruleus hit the grass ground with a grunt and a laugh, "See, you've got it now." Asi beamed and cast Nicole a sly look.

"I hate to break it to you, Caeruleus," Nicole snickered. "But Asi and Fen were able to kick your butt long before your lessons."

"What?"

The girls giggled.

"Maybe you should give him his memory back, Asi," Fen said.

Caeruleus' mouth fell open, "Oh, no. You mean that day I woke up in Witch Haven? That was you?"

Raiden smothered a snort in his hand. Loak and Leone grinned.

Caeruleus sighed. "All right, let's have it."

Asi reached up and touched his forehead. After thirty seconds she removed her hand and Caeruleus blinked in astonishment.

"Well? What happened, Stone?" Loak insisted.

"Humiliating defeat by a potions master and a memory thief," Caeruleus muttered, his face pink with embarrassment. "At least they're on our side," he added with a smile.

Nicole remembered the day Caeruleus arrived to the orchard looking for her. Keren, Asi and Fen subdued him in seconds with their combined gifts. *They're strong and capable,* Nicole reminded herself to fight against her worries.

"Hand-to-hand combat is just as vital as magic in this world," Loak laughed. "Isn't that right, Raiden?"

Raiden winced, placing his hand on his chest. "Yes, I can still feel that valuable lesson, Loak, thank you."

"You sparred with Loak?" Mitchell laughed. "Oh man."

"Indeed, and he still needs training," Loak chuckled.

"Hey, don't you want to practice too?" Mitchell asked, elbowing Nicole playfully.

She shrugged, smiling devilishly.

"We'll be stuck in close quarters for a while on our way to Eanna, best to train while we have the space," Loak encouraged. "Even a fera should know combat, and I'm happy to teach."

Nicole smiled, "I already know a little."

"Oh, show us, please!" Fen insisted.

She looked to Mitchell who snickered behind his hand.

Caeruleus put his hands up and stepped back, shaking his head, "I'm not looking for a rematch."

"Mitch?" she asked.

"No, I'm good. You're too rough."

She scoffed.

"All right, show me what you've got, little king," Loak said. "No magic."

"Okay," she agreed. Loak towered over her, and she knew she couldn't reach his neck or shoulders without the aid of magic. But his incredible height meant she had an advantage close to the ground. They squared off and everyone around them gawked at size difference, Nicole standing five-six in her hiking boots and Loak a gigantic seven feet.

Nicole eyed her target, mentally running through years of drills with her brothers. Loak made his approach. His arms went to close around her as he stepped forward. She grabbed his right arm at the wrist and elbow and pulled it from left to right across her centerline. He was forced to step toward her. In an instant she released his arm and went for his forward leg, dropping to the ground, hooking her leg around his ankle, trapping his foot beneath her as she grabbed the back of his leg and drove her body forward. She broke his balance and down he went, hitting the earth with a thud. Nicole stood up with a flush of satisfaction burning her cheeks—her heart racing.

Her audience clapped and Loak heaved himself off the ground, nodding with appreciation.

"Well, I think you could teach Raiden a thing or two," Loak chuckled.

She returned to Raiden whose mouth was open, turning from shock to a broad smile. He shook his head in amazement and she fought the blush spreading across her face. He took her hand and pulled her close to talk in her ear. "Any chance you're available for private lessons? Please, teach me a thing or two," he murmured.

Nicole coughed and bit her lips together. "Sure," she said, losing the battle to compose her face.

The ship—named The Nereid—was more spectacular than the palace in the midlands. It had five masts with sky blue sails which looked like silk in the sun. She counted four levels of windows at the stern of the ship, ample sleeping quarters it would seem, but not impressive enough even with the gold gilding on the ornate molding of its balcony railings to outshine the four stacked rows of guns. It looked every bit like a king dripping in gold ready for war.

At the bow of the ship was a stunning figurehead in the shape of a sea serpent. She didn't know what to make of this undeniable image of a dragon. It was a war ship, after all. Was the dragon leading the charge to strike fear into the enemy by emulating the most terrible foe known in all of Veil? Or could there be other sentiments behind that figurehead?

Caeruleus was already on board as was Loak, Leone, Tovar and the guards. He exchanged a few words with Sage who nodded and turned then stopped to wave when she spotted them on the dock. She halted the movement abruptly and cringed, realizing she was breaking Loak's strict code of conduct and hurried off.

"This is the greatest moment of my life," Mitchell muttered to her as Caeruleus stepped off the boat and onto the gangplank to greet them.

"Don't you dare," she said, holding back a laugh.

"Whatever, you were thinking it too," he cajoled.

She shook her head and Caeruleus stepped onto the dock.

"Safe as can be," he said. "Several wards bar the ether against entry all around the ship. There's no sneaking onboard. Tovar checked every inch of it, and the crew has all been inspected for any hint of deception. They are all cleared. Loak has assigned our guards to crewmembers for the duration of the journey anyway, in case of any…external influences."

Nicole thought of Lyana back in Orodon and her brow crumpled for a moment.

"I suppose that means it's time to go, then," Raiden said.

"Ladies," Mitchell said to Asi and Fen, inviting them to go first.

They grinned at each other and practically ran across to the ship.

"Shall we?" Gordan asked Mitchell.

"Why yes," Mitchell said, taking his hand and marching across the gangplank.

Caeruleus raised an eyebrow after them. "When did that happen?"

"I think it happened while they were away in Orodon," Nicole said.

Caeruleus nodded before stepping onto the gangplank and walking back aboard.

"This should be an interesting trip," Nicole said as she and Raiden followed the others onto the ship.

"Have you ever been on a boat before?" Raiden asked.

"Sure," she said. "I've been on ferries a few times. Have you?"

"No, but I used to love watching the fishing ships from shore," he said, a sad nostalgic smile moving his lips.

Nicole imagined a young Raiden sitting on the end of one of those docks in Cantis.

❧

The Nereid sailed along the coast, the constant roar and hiss of the water below them. Nicole found herself constantly looking up into the sky-blue sails. She marveled at how transformative the salty air in her lungs seemed to be, the peculiar effect it had, stirring the magic in her core until it percolated through her skin and when she looked up into the sails, she saw a shimmer across them like she was witnessing the same phenomenon above her.

"There's a lot of magic at sea," Gordan said, and she realized he had been watching her marvel to herself. "The sails catch the magic in the air and retain it."

"I guess that's why I feel like I'm buzzing," she said with a chuckle.

"Look at that water," Mitchell said. "Do you think it's cold?"

"The Avalon Sea is notoriously warm," Raiden said. "At least the books say so."

"We're definitely stopping for a day of swimming—we have time, right?"

"We're not in any hurry, and Cinder said we should enjoy the coast," Raiden said.

Nicole detected a hint of enthusiasm in his voice and realized after half a lifetime spent in books, he was finally somewhere he'd read about and she couldn't keep from smiling.

"Then we should enjoy the coast," she agreed.

☙

Raiden spotted his father gliding over the water, closing the distance. The sun touched the mainland to the west of them as the boat traveled North along the coast. Raiden left everyone leaning against the bow and wandered down to the lower deck as his father swooped in between the sails to land lightly on deck.

"You know, you don't have to spend all day out there keeping an eye out for trouble," Raiden said.

"I just like being out there… making sure you're all safe is a bonus," he said, folding his wings but not concealing them. "It's natural to be in the air. Celengels like to say the sky is inside us—it's in you too, you know."

"I don't fly much," Raiden admitted. "I'm used to having my feet on the ground."

"I understand—it's where everything that matters to you happens to be."

"Exactly."

"I used to hate the ground. If I wasn't in the sky, I was unhappy," he said with a chuckle. "We used to play a stupid game—we called it the dive. We would head for the earth the first person to bail was the loser."

Raiden cringed. "That does sound stupid."

"Yes, well, I have you thanks to being that stupid. I won the dive, but I grazed the ground and let's just say my landing was less than graceful. I beat that lark, though—stars, what was his name? I don't even remember now."

"That's how you and mother met?"

"She found me in a bruised heap on the ground. My hand was badly cut, and she handed me bandages saying she had a feeling she might need them that day, but I probably needed them more," he said, laughing. "And then she just walked away. We were miles from town—I was baffled."

"So, she had a vision and walked all that way to give a stranger a bandage," Raiden said—*that sounds like her.*

"I was curious about how far she had walked, and about her having the bandage. I couldn't let it go and that's that. The more time I spent with her, the less certain I was about going back home. And when I realized I loved her, I couldn't figure out if I belonged in the sky or on the ground."

"She's why you lost your wings?"

"And met Loak…strange the paths life takes, huh?"

"Yeah," Raiden said, watching the sunset.

"You know, to be honest, I've been out there looking for home—Terra Celestia I mean. I want to believe this time they'll help, but I can't say I have high hopes."

"What do you mean 'this time'?"

"I went home to ask them to hide Vervain…"

Because the Council was tracking down seers, Raiden thought. "But they refused," he knew, because his family had not lived in safety among the celengels, they lived in Cantis, as far from the Council as they could be without living in the wastelands.

"Celengels have insufferable egos to match their lofty ideals about freedom. They sneer at the earthbound, their borders and their oppression, but they refuse to allow outsiders to set foot on Terra Celestia."

"I see."

"I like to think that they might make an exception for you and Nicole."

Raiden's heart ached with this tiny sliver of hope.

"We could search together—if you like," his father said.

Could a half-blood celengel convince them to accept Nicole and him? Even if he could, that would leave everyone else she loved earthbound.

"She doesn't want a life in hiding any more than she wants a life on the run," he said. "That's not the solution we're looking for… but, I would still like to see Terra Celestia if we were to find it."

His father smiled wanly.

❧

Nicole thought the ship's crew might roll their eyes at the idea of dropping anchor for an afternoon beside a rocky island, but it seemed that the leisurely voyage to escort the kings of the keys to Eanna was a welcome relief from whatever regimented naval duties they usually performed. They shed their uniform coats and rolled up their sleeves, including the Captain—a short thick man whose graying hair looked like it had never been tamed a day in his life.

"Relieved to be on land again so soon, Loak?" Leone asked with a hearty laugh.

Loak let out a less-than-amused chuckle.

"We'll be back before sundown," Raiden said, turned, and placed a kiss on Nicole's forehead.

"Have fun," she said, her grip on his hands betraying the anxiety she had masked carefully in her voice. "Don't fly too close to the water…or the sun."

Raiden smiled and dropped his forehead to hers. "My wings

aren't made of wax," he said. "But I'll be careful."

She grinned sheepishly and her face went hot as she realized everyone was watching them. She wasn't keen on having an audience when she wanted to jump on him and kiss him on the lips for good measure before he disappeared into the sky. She cleared her throat. That could wait until he returned.

"Good luck finding Terra Celestia."

He smiled, removing his glasses and slipping them into the pocket inside the lining of his jacket.

They all watched from the shore—Nicole, Mitchell, Gordan, Caeruleus, Asi, Fen, Loak, half the guards and half the crew—as Raiden and Leone shrank into the sky. Nicole noticed that the only one who watched them as long as she did was Caeruleus.

"It really is the most incredible experience," he mused with a reminiscent sadness in his voice.

She didn't need Gordan to translate in order to know he was envious as he watched Raiden and his father disappear. He finally turned away. She waited until she couldn't see them any longer.

"Kinda funny, right?" Mitchell said behind her. She turned to see him pull his shirt off and drop it in the sand. "Both our boyfriends have wings."

Nicole snorted. "I guess."

"Speaking of wings," Mitchell said. "Do you ever get tired of the human form?"

Gordan glanced at Mitchell with a tiny smile and an appreciative slant on his brow. "No."

Nicole turned her face away to hide her silent laughter.

Mitchell cleared his throat. "I meant yours," he said. "Cause, you know, if you wanted to relax and stretch your wings, I don't think anyone here would mind."

"I'm not so sure about that," Gordan said, glancing at the present company.

"Then we go to the private side of the island," Mitchell said, snatching his shirt from the ground and clamoring over the smoother weather-beaten boulders that crowded most of the shore around the island. Gordan looked like he was trying to hide how pleased he was as he and Nicole followed.

They made their way around to the other side of the tiny land-mass barely big enough to fit a football field. It didn't have much to offer other than its white rock, shrubs and a few scraggly trees. The turquoise waters lapped in welcome at the shore.

"Here we go," Mitchell said, satisfied with a short stretch of sand in a rocky crook cradling a little bay of water. He tossed his shirt, hopped out of his jeans and sauntered to the water in his boxers.

Nicole was barefoot. She rolled up her jeans to stand at the edge of the water. It was warm like the waters of a Florida beach.

"Aw, come on," Mitchell said. "That's it?"

"What?"

"Swim with me. Please," he whined.

She studied the water, wishing mermaids and kelpies weren't the first images to come to her mind. But she reminded herself that these were not the dark cold waters surrounding Cantis. The sunlit blue-green water rolling in and out around her ankles was that same captivating shade of a certain seer's gaze—warm and enticing. How bad could water the shade of Raiden's eyes be? Her face went hot at such a ridiculously sentimental thought.

"Hello," Mitchell called into her ear.

"Ah—all right," she said. Since she'd rather swim in a suit than her sports bra and thong, she let a crackling burst of energy out and felt her underwear turn into her favorite bathing suit. She pulled off her shirt and stepped out of her jeans, revealing her swim suit.

"No fair," Mitchell said. "You could have conjured mine."

Nicole shrugged. "You didn't ask," she said, turning to the water letting the magic in her flow down her legs. She raised her foot over the water and it firmed beneath her weight, then she took another step, and a third and turned back to her brother, raising her arms triumphantly.

He gasped and cried, "Blasphemer!"

Gordan hid his smile behind his hand as Mitchell crashed into the water at a run while Nicole laughed and screamed when he caught her. They crashed into the water with a great splash and stood up laughing—their amusement was intoxicating, but the thought of transforming was sobering.

Nicole knew his natural form, had met him and loved him first in that shape and then warmed up to him once more in his human form. Still, he couldn't help but swallow back the anxiety in his throat. Wasn't it his human form that Mitchell was drawn to? He'd only seen Gordan's natural form once or twice, briefly, in panicked moments when the stakes were high and the need for transformation was dire.

Gordan didn't want to risk changing the way Mitchell felt about him, but he didn't want to hide part of himself either. Mitchell hadn't shied away from him after seeing the dragon he truly was, and he had been the one to suggest he enjoy the day however he might feel most comfortable.

While his wings had healed since the incident with the Tempest and the enforcer, they were stiff and aching for movement. Nicole and Mitchell were occupied, swimming the deeper water of their little bay while he stood there agonizing over something that was utterly simple.

He transformed—vertebrae and joints popping blissfully until he could spread his wings out gingerly to their full breadth. He tested them with a few tentative beats but felt no pangs in the delicate bones; they had set and healed well despite having to transform in Meridian to take care of the rogue dragon's breath. He let out a low sigh of relief and stretched out to lay across the sun-warmed boulders.

He watched Nicole and Mitchell out in the water, diving down and resurfacing, presenting something found below, their breathless conversation muddled by splashes and the water lapping at the shore. Eventually he closed his eyes and just listened, unsure if time was swift or sluggish.

The disturbance of water growing closer stirred his suspicion, and he opened his eyes to see Mitchell marching onto the little beach.

"Hey," he said breathily, his face flushed pink, but by exertion and sun or the flutter in his chest, Gordan couldn't decide.

Mitchell crawled onto the rocks and settled himself between Gordan's legs to lean against his sternum, and then he sighed. Nicole waded out of the water and smiled when she spotted them.

"Tired already, Mitch?"

"Exhausted," he said—Gordan could hear the shameless lie and satisfaction in his voice.

She laughed and climbed onto the boulders. "Hey, Gordan, have you ever seen Terra Celestia?" She asked.

"I have, only from a distance though."

"Oh. My. Lord—your voice," Mitchell said.

Gordan was suddenly embarrassed about the gravely baritone that came out of his mouth.

"I guess you didn't warn him," Nicole said, giggling.

"I forget how different it is," he said.

"Just keep talking," Mitchell said, his voice profusely appreciative.

Gordan's heart swelled with giddy relief.

⌘

After another swim Nicole sat in the modest little patch of sand between rocks at the shore, and stared out at the sea, her gaze narrowing and expanding like the water on the sand—back and forth between the stretch of blue-green ocean toward the horizon and the shy waves rolling up the tiny beach.

She wondered how Raiden and Leone were doing. She searched for clouds in the blue…fruitlessly, so she studied the shapes of the rocks around the island instead and the way the water moved around them—and the face peering at her from around the rocks just above the water.

Nicole's heart lurched and she threw herself back, away from the water, in a spasm of panic.

"What is it?" Gordan asked, startled by her.

Nicole looked hard, thinking for a moment she had hallucinated the face, but it was still there, mostly human, large eyes blinking back at her—pointing, she replied, "That."

Gordan followed her gaze. "Oh," he said, his voice softening. "It's a merrow."

"A merrow?" Mitchell asked, searching the water for it.

"They can be mistaken for mermaids, but only at a glance—they're benevolent creatures, curious and shy," Gordan said.

"So, they're good?" Mitchell contemplated.

"Well—it's not usually their habit to risk being seen, except to warn people about coming storms, which does lead some to believe merrows *cause* the storms."

"Oh," Mitchell said.

The merrow slid through the water away from the rocks and closer to shore, keeping low in the water. Her skin glistened pale and iridescent, her hair all colors of a desert sunset spread around her shoulders like spilled paint on the surface of the water.

"Um…hello," Nicole said as the merrow blinked at her with its large eyes. She blinked at them and then turned her gaze toward the horizon where endless sea met clear sky. Then she looked back at them, past them, at the ship anchored between the little island and the coast.

"Maybe people get the wrong idea because merrows don't talk," Mitchell remarked given the creature's silence.

"She probably doesn't understand us. She must speak some older language," Gordan said. He called out to the merrow, "A bheil stoirm a 'tighinn?"

Nicole and Mitchell shared a look of surprise. The merrow perked up and dove, resurfacing in the shallows.

The merrow replied, "Cha bu chòir dhaibh fuireach an seo."

"She said we shouldn't stay here," Gordan translated.

"What are you speaking?" Mitchell whispered.

"Gaelic," he said.

The merrow continued. "Bidh mo mhàthair a tilgeil shoithichean an aghaidh nan creagan."

"There must be a storm coming," Gordan said. "She says the

ship will be thrown against the rocks; we need to find a harbor or get away from the coast."

"Innis dhomh, dragan, dè tha i?" Her gaze fell on Nicole who felt the curiosity in the merrow's eyes.

"A charaid ghràdhaich," Gordan answered.

"Tha i a 'falach stoirm a-staigh. Bi mothachail, tha e marbhtach nuair a choinnicheas dà stoirm." The merrow looked over her shoulder once more at the clear blue horizon and sank into the water.

"What did she say?" Nicole wondered.

"She told us to be careful."

"It's still clear as can be out there," Mitchell said. "We must have plenty of time."

"Not as much time as we may think. We should tell the captain and return to the ship," Gordan said.

ʃ

Raiden's mind had never felt so blissfully unburdened. At first it had been strange to fly again, but as he settled into the exhilaration, the wind rustling his clothes, the satisfaction of stretching his wings, it didn't take him long to feel like he belonged in the sky. Just the *thought* of the ground made his heart heavy, but the wind holding him up made him giddy. So, *this* is what freedom really felt like. He forgot they were even looking for anything. What could they possibly need to find? He felt like he lacked absolutely nothing. Could he fly forever? Exhaustion seemed like a foreign concept, and he liked the idea of never setting foot on the ground more and more. He couldn't think of a single reason why he should.

ʃ

The blue-green waters glistened and winked at them as they departed from the little island and moved along the coast in search of the harbor marked on the Captain's map.

"Are we sure we can find this harbor?" Mitchell said.

"Raiden and Leone won't know where to find us," Nicole said, her anxiety crawling up Gordan's spine and doubling his own.

472

"I wouldn't worry about them," Loak said as he point toward the horizon. "That—however—is a more pressing concern to us."

They followed his finger out to where a dark stain bloomed in the blue sky. As it spread, the wind in their ship's sails ballooned backward toward the stern and a chilling gust rolled over them, a sinister hand eager to push them back the way they had come.

"I don't like this wind," Gordan said. The winds usually spoke of odd things and he was used to their whispers, but this wind was incoherent, chanting gibberish as it bent to the will of a spell. "This is a conjured storm."

Above them the sails fluttered and rippled with light and again they strained forward as though they were filled with a strong wind behind them. The ship forged on along the coast, keeping its distance from the rocks only because of the reservoir of magic in their sails.

Nicole looked into the sky frantically searching for Raiden and Leone; everyone's gaze searched for them. Gordan glanced at Mitchell whose face fell with gloom when he pulled his eyes away from the empty sky and saw Gordan's expression.

"What if we don't find the harbor?" Mitchell asked.

"This ship can weather any storm in open water," the Captain said without the slightest pang of concern in his voice. "It's been tested in natural *and* conjured storms alike. We still have time to get away from the cliffs, if we must."

But Gordan couldn't forget what the merrow had said to him, *tha i a 'falach stoirm a-staigh*— she hides a storm inside. He looked at Nicole and the furrowed brow over her searching eyes. *Bi mothachail, tha e marbhtach nuair a choinnicheas dà stoirm*—Beware, it is deadly when two storms meet. He hoped the captain was right about being able to find the harbor in the cliffs.

"They'll be fine," he said, trying not to show how bitter the taste of his own uncertainty was.

"Leone knows how to find his way. If they can't make it back, they'll wait it out somewhere away from the storm," Loak said.

The nausea in the air hit him, and he knew Nicole was far from comforted.

"Hey," Mitchell said, hooking his arm around his sister and leaning his head on hers. "He always makes it back. This is Ray we're talking about."

Gordan hoped that Raiden—like the merrow—had seen the storm and, that he and his father were already ahead of it. He looked back at the little island, a mere pin-prick on the horizon now. Had the merrow not warned them, they would still be on that shore. But would Venarius really try to sink the ship with his most precious asset aboard? Perhaps he believed Nicole would survive, or that he could get rid of some of her protectors even if this proved another failed attempt to reach her.

❧

"Raiden…"

For a moment Raiden didn't even recognize the voice through his confusion; he had forgotten he wasn't alone.

"I think it's time to go back," his father said.

Back where? Raiden nearly asked before he realized he had been so entranced by the sky that he actually forgot about everything— even Nicole. Then a pang of nausea hit his stomach. Now that reality flooded his mind once more, he felt an unnerving change in the air. The wind twisted around them with frantic energy, and the blue of the sky turned a sickly grey.

"Which way?" Raiden asked. He had completely lost track of direction in the delirious bliss of flight.

"The coast is that way," his father said, pointing. They changed course. "Even at our fastest I don't know that we can out-pace a conjured storm."

"Conjured?" Raiden questioned. Then, he noticed the unsettling charge in the air. This meant that Venarius couldn't be far away. "In that case we can just—" His idea died—they couldn't just shift through the ether back to the ship. The spells that barred the ether from their enemies would bar them as well.

"We can fly on to Avalon and wait out the storm," his father said.

Wait it out? Raiden shook his head. "No! Venarius sent this storm—we can't just wait while he's making a move." Racing the storm was their only choice.

"Then we'd better fly!"

The early gusts of the building storm provided them with an encouraging tailwind, but that didn't last long. Soon the winds lashed at them and, despite all their efforts, they couldn't get ahead of the storm as they made for the coast.

"Keep an eye out for the ship. Without a safe harbor they should be heading for a safe distance from the shoreline," his father shouted over the wind.

Searching the churning waters for the blue sails of the Nereid, Raiden frowned. Then the first heavy drops of rain hit them—sporadic warnings that their time was up and that the rain was coming for them. The ship was nowhere in sight.

⁋

Everyone exchanged anxious looks as the captain glared at the cliffs and steered the ship parallel to them. They were all thinking the same thing—shouldn't they turn away from the coast now? The storm was bearing down on them and still there was no harbor to be found.

"There, Captain!" a crewman said, pointing at a distinct pillar-shaped rock in the cliff; it looked like a crudely carved marker.

The captain laughed triumphantly, turning the ship toward the cliff face. At first glance it appeared nothing but a cliff, but the illusion broke as they drew nearer and the ship found the inlet.

Nicole cast frantic eyes to the horizon as the ship slipped through the channel and into a cove surrounded by sheer cliffs. "I still don't see them," she said. "They're not going to be able to find us in here."

The Captain barked orders, "Secure the sails and drop anchor!"

Several raindrops struck the deck igniting a cadence of panic in Nicole's chest as she peered into the sky overhead.

"They'll head somewhere safe outside the storm," Loak said.

"The only way we can be sure they're safe is if they're *here*,"

Nicole insisted. "We can't just assume they're waiting it out somewhere. What if they're caught in the storm?"

"What do you propose we do?" Loak asked.

"We can summon them," Caeruleus said. "The Council did it all the time."

"Yes, with someone's blood," Loak said.

"It's not impossible without it," Caeruleus insisted.

"Tovar, can we do it?" Nicole asked.

Tovar looked uncertain for a moment. "I think so."

"Captain," Caeruleus called, "the ships spells…they keep magic out but do they keep it in? Can someone depart the ship through the ether, or summon someone here from elsewhere?"

"You could leave, but you couldn't return. No one has ever tried to summon someone onto the ship."

"Assuming the ship allows entrance by invitation this could work—who has the strongest connection with Leone?" Tovar inquired.

"That would be me," Loak said.

"Then let's get inside. I have to draw a couple summoning circles before we can—"

The rain came down like a falling curtain, stunning them all with its sudden hissing intensity. Dread lined everyone's faces as the water saturated their clothes. They were sheltered from the brunt of the wind, but the storm was upon them, and Leone and Raiden were likely somewhere in the middle of it.

৩

Leone pointed, the shoreline was in sight—as disheartening as it was encouraging—it was still so far and there was no sign of the ship. A vicious gust of wind surged behind them, throwing them into a tumble for a moment.

"We're close!" Leone yelled, but the rain came down on them— hissing viciously. The wind grew more savage, turning around them, disrupting the rhythm of their wings, throwing them in every direction but toward the coast, pushing them closer to the sea below where the waves reached up—dark swells like grasping hands that fell crashing into each other.

When a wave nearly caught Raiden, he slipped into the ether and back out again high above the waves once more, but his father was still close to the water, struggling against the winds. *He doesn't know how to shift*, he remembered as he dove toward to his father. He could get them both higher if he could just grasp ahold of him.

The wind shoved them together. They collided and an eager wave seized them. Raiden's hand locked around a fist-full of his father's shirt, but they were wrenched apart in the waves. The salt burned his eyes as he saw the blurred form of his father slipping away, swallowed by the darkness of the sea.

Raiden broke the surface, gasping and fighting to keep his head above it as he searched the waves for his father. He dropped below the surface and peered through the biting water for a human form but found none and resurfaced. The water pulled at him, trying to drag him down. He fought, keeping his head above the water and hoping his father would surface as well.

☙

Loak stood inside Leone's summoning circle and Nicole stood inside Raiden's, trying to move with the rocking of the ship and to keep from being thrown off their circles. Water gurgled up from the circle beneath her and her heart lurched, but nothing else happened. Beside her a wave and a man fell through Leone's circle, toppling Loak with a wet smack.

"It worked," Loak said, picking Leone up as he coughed and gasped.

Nicole's heart reeled with panic. "No—Raiden's not here," she said.

"Why didn't it work?" Mitchell asked.

"He must be resisting," Tovar said.

"You can't resist a blood summons. The Council was able to use Leone's blood to summon Raiden," Caeruleus offered.

Tovar shook his head. "It won't work. Raiden and I broke the blood bond for summoning so that he could flee Atrium."

Nicole's breaths felt empty—each one a gasp that didn't steady her. She looked at Caeruleus gazed back with just as much panic in his eye.

"We can try again," Tovar said.

"He'll keep resisting," Leone coughed. "He's fighting the ocean."

Caeruleus strode across the room and took Nicole's hand as he removed a knife from his belt. He stepped close, hiding her hand between them as he cut her palm. She winced.

"Make sure you don't let go of him," Caeruleus said in her ear. She understood. They could summon her instead.

It has to work, she insisted because once she left the Nereid, there would be no getting back through the ether on her own. Her heart was in a panicked ricochet inside her chest as she thought of Raiden and fell into the ether.

☙

No, no, no, he's got to be here somewhere—Raiden's breath was cut short by a wave that shoved him below the surface. The water pulled on his wings, so he called them in, feeling instantly lighter as he fought his way back to the surface.

Nicole wasn't prepared for the violent disorientation of emerging from the ether beneath crashing waves, tumbling in the current that sent her head spinning as she floundered to find which way was up. Her heart raced in an icy panic in her chest—this was a nightmare. She found her way to the surface and gasped, blinking against the salt in her eyes. There he was—searching frantically.

"Raiden!" She was horrified by the distance between them and swam. She didn't know how much time she had, or how soon they would summon her with the blood on Caeruleus' knife.

He whirled around. His eyes were utter dismay and disbelief as he swam for her.

She swam, fighting back the phantoms emerging from her memories with immense darkness of the ocean below her.

"What are you—"

A wave crashed on top of them, and the water buried them together. The current dragged them down, and she peered through

the water, reaching desperately for him, wondering if she was doom-
ing them both. Were the pale faces with black eyes really there in
the water around them or just in her head? She caught a handful
of his shirt in her fist. Afraid to drag him down, she had to believe
Raiden wouldn't let her. Surely, they wouldn't drown together in
the storm sent for her.

They were pulled into the ether and tumbled onto a wooden
floor with a surge of sea water. The relative silence of the cabin was
dumbfounding after the roar of the churning ocean.

"Welcome back," said Loak's unmistakable baritone.

Nicole snapped upright and caught Raiden, taking his face in
her hands and scrutinizing him through her shock and exhilaration.
His eyes were wide open—stunned and blinking. It worked. He
was here. He was safe. She closed her eyes and dropped her forehead
to his, relieved laughter slipping past her lips.

When she lifted her head and looked at him again, Raiden
stared back at her, his mouth slack and his gaze utterly mystified.

Standing over them, Leone cleared his throat, and Nicole
couldn't help smiling at the relief on Raiden's face when he realized
his father was safe. Leone had disappeared in the ocean; she could
imagine Raiden's panic all too vividly.

Leone pulled him off the floor. Gordan helped Nicole onto her
feet.

"Must you two scare the crap out of me every chance you get?"
Mitchell asked, shaking his head. "That was pretty awesome,
though."

Mitchell raised his hand and Nicole did the same, slapping her
palm against his. Her immediate cry of pain mingled with a laugh
as she clutched her cut hand.

"You came to get me," Raiden said, gratefully. He took her
hand, studying the bleeding cut and put it all together. He closed
his hand over hers.

"Don't I always?"

He laughed and her heart almost burst to think of all the times
that sound had nearly been erased from existence.

"We tried to summon you, but you made things rather difficult," Gordan remarked.

The ship rocked. Any remaining tension in the cabin broke as the seawater sloshed around their shoes and the floor titled back and forth beneath them. They were still stuck in the middle of a storm, barely able to stand on their feet, but at least for a moment everyone was all right.

Thirty-two

In their cabin they fumbled and struggled to change into dry clothes as the ship rocked like the floor of a funhouse.

"How's your hand?" Raiden asked as he pulled a sweater over his head.

"Healed, no harm done," she said. "I'd give the whole hand to get you back."

"Please don't say that," he implored.

"It's already said." She closed her arms around him. "I'm glad you're okay."

"Me too," he chuckled. "For a minute there I thought I lost my dad…again."

"I thought I lost *you*."

"That's never going to happen."

Her feet were still so cold from being soaked to the bone in the ocean. The ship tipped just a little as she stood there on one leg to pull on her second sock, and she fell over, taking Raiden with her when he tried to steady her. They just missed the bed, sliding off the edge of it and landing on the floor with a thud.

Nicole groaned. "I give up, I'm staying on the floor," she said into his chest.

"To be honest, I couldn't be anymore glad to be here," he said, chuckling.

"How was your first real flight? You know, before getting caught in this storm."

"It was…" Raiden looked up at the ceiling with a frown on his face.

Nicole sat up, trying to understand his expression. "What?"

"I was free from everything up there," he said, sitting up. He shook his head. "It was the most incredible feeling." He dropped his gaze. "But I forgot about *every*thing."

When he looked at her with pain on his face and guilt in his eyes, she understood. In the bliss of the sky, he had forgotten about all the troubles on the ground, he'd forgotten about her…again.

She shrugged. "Hey, don't feel bad. We all need to escape our troubles now and then."

"You aren't one of my troubles," he insisted.

"I know," she said, halfheartedly. Venarius was their trouble. "But you didn't forget. So, you were distracted by the exhilaration and the freedom. You're here now, aren't you?"

"Well, yes—" he looked concerned.

"And you know who I am," she continued.

"Of course."

"See? What's there to worry about? I don't even have to do anything drastic to jog your memory," she said.

"Drastic?"

"Oh, like kissing you until you remember," she said. "If you didn't know who I was that could be quite distressing—a *stranger* forcing herself onto you."

He smiled. "Come to think of it, there's no telling what I might not remember. Maybe you should jog my memory just in case," he said, pulling her closer.

Her laughter was muffled against his lips.

❧

The storm raged for hours but only threatened to drive them all mad from their rocking ship. The wind howled above their safe haven in the cliffs, but in the cabins below deck, it could hardly bother anyone, save for reminding them that Venarius was out there, conjuring storms and waiting for his chance. Still, they felt safe on the ship hidden away in their high-sided harbor and actually fell asleep that night, knowing the storm would die out before dawn.

Raiden opened his eyes to a vivid blue sky filling the window pane and the dull roar of water churning behind the ship below their cabin. He could feel Nicole's breath against his back, her arm draped over his ribs—her body pressed against his. He lay there, ruminating in the rhythm of her breathing and studying the blue of the sky a little suspiciously until a deep breath disturbed the steady cadence of her lungs. It was late in the morning, he supposed.

"Are we at sea again?" she murmured into his back.

"It looks that way," he said, his gaze departing from the window and alighting on her hand to linger on the white line across her palm. He had forgotten about his plan back in Atrium—breaking the blood bond for Caeruleus and her—a plan that quickly fell apart and entirely from his mind.

A knock at the door sounded before it opened.

"Are you two awake yet?" Mitchell's voice preceded him flopping onto the bed, casting himself across Nicole who protested with a muffled, "Get off!"

Mitchell rolled off the bed and strode to the windows. He threw them open, letting in the salty breeze and the full roar of the water beneath the ship.

"Come on. Venarius' big storm was a bust. The sun's out—we should be celebrating."

Nicole groaned, tightening her arm around Raiden.

Mitchell let out a huff of exasperation and rolled his imploring stare at Raiden, who couldn't bring himself to sympathize with Mitchell's frustration while Nicole was clinging to him. Raiden smiled and shrugged.

"Fine," Mitchell said. "Then I'll have fun without you. I'm going to get Caeruleus to say 'argh' and you're gonna miss it."

Nicole smothered her laugh into Raiden's back.

"Where's Gordan? Why are you unsupervised?" she asked, sitting up.

Raiden rolled back and watched her scrub her fingers through her hair, shaking out the mess of curls gone wild in her sleep.

"He's wandering around the ship like a guard dog—didn't even sleep with me last night," Mitchell said dejectedly.

Nicole sighed, "That dragon."

Raiden couldn't blame him. He sat up, leaned over to pluck his glasses off the chair beside the bed, and placed them on his face. The ritual was still odd to him, but every time the room around him settled into clarity, he appreciated this little annoyance.

⁊

When they emerged from the cabins into the glistening clear day on the Avalon Sea, Mitchell and Nicole searched for Gordan, but Raiden scanned the figures on deck for his father. He spotted Loak leaning against the forwardmost mast and supposed his father might be out on a flight until his gaze wandered up and caught him perched in the crow's nest above.

Raiden drifted away from Nicole and Mitchell, making his way to Loak who nodded in greeting when he arrived.

"He's not out there today," Raiden remarked.

"No, I don't suppose he'll go wandering off anymore after yesterday. He's sticking close."

"You've known him a long time—did he ever tell you about the celengels? What they're like?"

Loak chuckled. "Oh sure, not all that much to tell. The stories about them are pretty on-the-mark, lofty, self-important birds."

"Has he ever told you about flying?"

Loak's laugh boomed, "Get him started, and he won't shut up about it."

Raiden managed half a smile with a sad excuse for a laugh.

"What's going on down here?" Leone dropped to the deck beside them, his wings like a parachute that disappeared into his back.

"Just a chat about flying. I reckon you've got more to offer on the subject than I do," Loak said, clapping him on the back and letting out another hearty laugh before walking away, shaking his head in amusement.

Leone smiled and studied Raiden, "Something troubling you?"

Raiden knew his frown had burrowed its way into his face again. "Yesterday, before the storm hit..."

"Yes?"

"Has being up there ever made you forget everything about your life...even yourself?"

"Ah, yes. The sky has that effect on us. It's in our blood. We're born to be up there."

"You didn't think to warn me that I might lose myself up there?" Raiden scolded.

"It's been so long since I experienced that, I didn't even think of it."

"I felt like it wanted to erase everything about me."

Leone frowned. "I'm sorry, I should have warned you. It's the reason celengels are who they are—that bond with the sky...they're enthralled with that freedom—well, we tend to care very little about anything else."

"Even you?"

"Yes, even me," he admitted, "that is, before I met your mother and Loak and made a life on the ground."

"Don't you feel that way when you're up there now?"

"It's still there. It always will be, but I've learned to keep my thoughts...grounded, and keep my heart close to home. You just have to think about what's down here waiting for you when you're up there."

"I'll keep that in mind."

"The sky is part of who you are," Leone said, attempting a smile. "I hate to think you would disown it after just one flight. Raiden could hear in his voice that he was truly worried. Rejecting that heritage, Raiden would be, in effect, rejecting his father.

"Of course I won't," Raiden said. "But I think it's best if I keep my feet on the ground with Nicole while Venarius is out there."

"I won't argue with that. We're all better off if we stick close to-gether. No telling what he'll try next."

Raiden sighed, "We thought we would be able to draw him out, but he strikes from a distance—never close enough for us to strike back."

Venarius stood with a smile on his face—unseen through the veil of his illusion—as he laughed silently to himself beside Raiden. He looked up at the dim sky above the cliff-sided harbor where the ship was still anchored, the captain standing at the helm unaware that he steered his ship nowhere, a fool playing make-believe.

Arms folded smugly across his chest, Venarius turned and crossed the deck at a leisurely pace until he spotted Nicole. He fell into step beside her as she walked the perimeter of the ship alone, occasionally glancing across the deck at the dragon and her brother.

He watched affection possess her face—the corners of her mouth pulled back in a private smile. Disgust pulled at his. He had not made his creations to live, to love; they were made without family, created with power and a single purpose. Venarius looked around at all the people attached to Nicole. They all muddled what she was meant to be.

He was as fascinated at as he was disappointed with what his creation had become—the only one to escape her destiny long enough for her physical form to expire and journey through Death to return. Death and rebirth changes souls, sometimes drastically and sometimes very little. Venarius wanted to know to what extent his creation had changed.

He suspected she was still volatile beneath the surface, but clearly not as unstable as her predecessors—an advantage, perhaps. He might even consider her stronger than the first of her kind if not for all her attachments in this new frivolous life of hers. Every-one she loved was a point of weakness—all too easily exploited.

The young woman with dark skin and a head of short black coils ran up to Nicole and Venarius stepped aside for her. His pres-ence was unseen, but he was not immaterial.

"Nicole," she said, her voice airy as she panted.

"Fen," she said, with a chuckle. "Take a breath."

"You have to come look," Fen said excitedly.

Venarius watched them go.

Nicole nearly stumbled as Fen pulled on her at a run, and she drifted into the air and let Fen drag her, holding back her laughter.

"What is it I'm coming to look at?" she wondered impatiently as Fen towed her below deck to Asi's and her cabin where Asi was leaning halfway out the open window peering at the waters below.

Their cabin looked out at open ocean from the side of the ship. Fen dragged her all the way to the window, wide enough for two people to lean out side by side.

"Look," Asi said, pointing down at the water.

Nicole expected dolphins and her heart leapt, but when she gazed into the water, she saw forms she couldn't immediately recognize. Though the water was clear, their shapes wobbled beneath the moving surface as the ship went. Nicole was fairly certain she was looking at a pod of creatures that were the forward half of a horse and the tail end of a fish.

"Those are hippocampi," Asi said.

"In Taroth I used to see them playing in the waves near shore sometimes," Fen said. "My father didn't let me make potions, but he always sent me out to find what he needed. My favorite days were when I had to gather herbs near the beach. I like to imagine that the girls who chose those cliffs to escape Taroth are out there swimming with the hippocampi, finally free."

The sadness in Fen's voice weighed on Nicole's heart. She stepped back from the window and let Fen back in to look. They looked down together.

"I think about Taroth a lot," Asi said. "Mostly about the girls there. Sometimes I feel bad that Fen and I escaped."

Fen nodded. "Sometimes I feel like I'm still not free—like knowing there are girls stuck there wanting to get out keeps a part of me there."

Nicole's breath shuddered in her chest, and she trapped the sound behind her lips with her hand, pretending to rub her face. Her eyes burned with sorrow and anger, pained by the desire to do something for all the other girls like Asi and Fen. Perhaps she could, she thought—closing her hand around the key hanging from her neck as always—*but I'm only here to finish this thing with Venarius.* She didn't want to be a ruler. She had no right to be. That wasn't the life she wanted. But how could she do nothing if she had the power to do *something*? Did the keys really mean anything? What power did she really have to change the way an entire kingdom treated its women and raised its girls?

Gordan could not ease the frown from his face as he looked out across the stunning waters. The sunlight glittered on its surface, and the waves tumbled delightfully against the rocky coastline—a playful mockery compared to the deadly storm-tossed sea of yesterday. The sunshine was warm and reassuring, but he thought he heard something in the breeze.

"Hey," Mitchell implored beside him as he laced their fingers together. "You don't have to worry all alone, you know."

"Forgive me," he said, trying to smile. "There's just..."

"What?"

The sails rustled overhead, a spasm in the air, and Gordan looked up. The wind was strangely silent today. He was so used to its constant chatter—*that's strange.* He cocked his head and listened, then for a moment he heard a frantic whisper of gibberish—*just like yesterday.*

"Gordan?" Mitchell implored, his voice heavy with concern.

Dread seeped out of Gordan's bones and his body went cold. He took careful breaths, trying not to react to the panic digging into his heart. *We're still in the storm...perhaps in the eye of it.*

"Where's Nicole?" he asked, looking around. He spotted Raiden with his father, Loak strolling across the deck.

Mitchell looked around too. "She's here somewhere."

Gordan couldn't be sure of anything knowing they were in some sort of illusory spell, but how entangled were they in magic and how close might Venarius be? Driven as much by the need to conceal his revelation as he was by fear for the person he loved, Gordan turned to Mitchell, slipped his hands around his face, and pulled him into a kiss.

A flourish of surprise and giddy delight bloomed in the air and Gordan hated to snuff it out so quickly, but he pulled his mouth from Mitchell's, pulled him close, and murmured into his ear.

"I need you to act like nothing is wrong," Gordan insisted softly. "I think we're still in the storm, in some sort of illusion."

The air went cold with Mitchell's dismay.

"Find Nicole," he continued as calmly as he could with Mitchell's panic seeping through the little space between them. "You cannot look alarmed."

Mitchell answered with an almost imperceptible nod and a deep breath. Gordan let his hands slip from Mitchell's face and stepped back. Other than a slight pallor that hadn't been there before, Mitchell was convincingly composed when he turned away from Gordan. With a pounding heart he watched Mitchell go and then crossed the deck, struggling to keep his stride slow and unburdened as he approached Raiden and his father. He could not take a direct path to them; instead, he resumed the aimless rounds he had been making all morning, to seem like he was none the wiser to their current danger.

Nicole inhaled deeply as she, Asi and Fen watched the hippocampi. The girls rested on the window ledge comfortably and Nicole floated just enough to lean over Asi. The blue of the sky, the warmth of the sunshine glittering on the blue-green water, and the brisk salty air in her lungs and on her tongue—it all amalgamated and swelled in her heart, a moment that was, perhaps, too perfect.

"There you are," Mitchell sighed in the doorway.

Nicole turned toward the sound of Mitchell's tense voice and saw a peculiar look on his face as he stepped into the cabin. She dropped to the floor, troubled by his stiff demeanor.

"Mitchell, come see!" Fen said.

But Mitchell marched across the room and stopped inches away from Nicole to speak in her ear.

"Gordan says we're still in the storm—in an illusion," he said.

Nicole froze, forgetting how to take a breath.

"We can't act like we know."

She nodded and swallowed back her terror.

"What's going on?" Asi asked, turning from the window.

"Raiden's looking for me," Nicole answered. "Why don't you come with us." Maybe they were safer here, locked in their room, but she didn't want to leave them alone or let them out of her sight. She didn't want them stuck in here if anything happened to the ship. Her heart clenched with dread.

The girls agreed and followed, blissfully unaware. As they left the cabin, Nicole spotted Caeruleus retreating into his.

"Caeruleus," she called before he could close the door and immediately realized she sounded too urgent.

"Yes?"

"Oh, we need you up top," she said, trying to recover her nonchalance without cringing.

He gave her an uncertain look, but stepped out of his room and closed the door. "All right."

Raiden spotted Gordan and was glad to see him approaching, but surprised to see him alone.

"How is it you came to keep the company of a dragon, son?" his father asked beside him.

He could laugh about that night now. "That would be thanks to Nicole. We found him in the tower on Cantis. He was being kept by Dawn. She freed him, so he had a debt to pay."

"Did he ever tell you why Dawn was keeping him?"

"He said he didn't know."

"You trust him?"

"Completely," Raiden said, looking his father in the eye.

Leone nodded.

490

Raiden turned his gaze to Gordan and was surprised that he didn't stop until they were nearly chest to chest.

"Raiden," he said, leaning to speak into his ear swiftly and quietly. "We're still in the storm."

Gordan leaned in and away so fluidly it was more like a greeting, almost an embrace. No one would have suspected an exchange, let alone heard the words that plunged Raiden's heart into cold water. Raiden struggled to keep his breathing slow and even as he studied the ship around them, the clear day, the sunshine—if they were in the storm, it was an illusion. He needed to know how much of it was false. He glanced at his father—who was real? And Venarius had to be somewhere nearby.

"Where's Nicole?" Raiden asked calmly while panic closed around his lungs like an iron grip.

"With Mitchell," Gordan said. "What are our plans for the rest of this trip? Will we have the time to visit Avalon on our way, or will we go straight to Eanna?"

"I—" Raiden felt like he was drowning where he stood—in fear and uncertainty. What was the plan? There was an illusion wrapped around them, and their enemy could be anywhere. The only advantage they had was their feigned ignorance. Then he spotted Nicole with Mitchell, Asi, Fen and Caeruleus walking across the deck. He could see it in her eyes. She knew, and so did Mitchell. "I think we should ask Nicole, and see what everyone else thinks," he said, nearly stumbling over the words.

Nicole's heart pounded. Fear summoned up something between a daydream and a memory. For a moment she was a cowering child without an identity—all alone with too much power to control. She stepped a little closer to her brother and took his hand. She was still afraid, but the phantom of the fera's life faded, and she was just herself, clinging to her big brother's hand and trying to feel brave.

They crossed the deck, and she could see the tension in Raiden's and Gordan's shoulders.

"Perfect timing," Gordan said.

"We were just discussing our plan," Raiden said, his voice was tight and unlike his usual warm tone.

"We have the opportunity to visit Avalon," Gordan suggested.

"It's out of our way, but we have the ship and the time," Raiden added.

Nicole felt her breathing grow deeper and shakier. She knew they were draped in an illusion, but she didn't know what would happen if they broke it. Outside the illusion they were presumably still trapped in the storm, but what else lay outside the illusion? There was no way they could keep up the charade of ignorance once it was gone, and Venarius would surely know when the illusion was broken. But perhaps she could peak through it.

"Well, what does everyone think?" Gordan asked. Nicole realized she had forgotten to answer Raiden's question. She just couldn't keep up the decoy conversation.

She couldn't even follow everyone's voices around her, they were real. She looked at Raiden, into his anxious teal eyes, then Gordan, they were real. Where was the illusion? She thought, glancing around. Not the ship—but they were still in the storm—then the sunshine, the clear waters, the coast drifting along beside the ship, that was all illusion. She took a breath and clenched her teeth, unsure if she was prepared to see what was really all around them as she coaxed her magic out of her core, and it struggled through the icy presence of dread.

Her magic warmed her, steadied her and as she blinked the day grew dark. Her heart lurched at the sudden appearance of a figure standing there among them, watching her. She knew who this was. She had to wrench her eyes away and lock them onto Raiden, she forced a smile onto her face. If she made eye contact with him, he would know. So, she fought to contain her raging heart and panicked lungs beneath a pleasantly composed face. *He's here—he's right there.* She looked around at everyone she loved within his reach and felt her body shudder with something savage. She squeezed Mitchell's hand, looked to Raiden and then to Gordan before she looked directly into the face of Venarius. A pulse of trembling power

rolled off her and knocked everyone around her to the deck—
pushing everyone she loved away from Venarius' reach.

Venarius was not one easily taken off guard, but when Nicole turned
her gaze to him and looked him dead in the eye, he was surprised—
seized by a hand of magic, his body crushed in the pressure of her
clenched fists. Every person around him save for Nicole was
knocked down by a pulse of power, and they slid across the deck
far from his reach as the ship moaned and planks beneath his feet
splintered.

Her chest heaved with labored breaths, and she glared at him
with murder in her gaze. His body protested in pain, his bones
bruised and cracked, his blood raced with a sensation long unknown
to him—fear—he realized with a delightful tremble. He might have
laughed if he had had the air in his lungs to do it.

The deck of the ship split open like a terrible mouth full of
splintered teeth, and her invisible grasp tightened. He smiled, de-
lighting at the idea of watching her rip the very ship in half and cast
her loved one's into the sea herself. Self-preservation was not so
strong as the exhilaration of seeing his creation emerge before him,
to feel her breath-taking power in waves of delicious crushing agony,
to look into her eyes burning with a rage he wanted to possess.

She was far more glorious than the one before her, and she
hadn't even lost control yet. But as much as he relished the shudder
of ecstasy and adrenaline swelling in his suffocating body, he knew
he must concede the day to her and consider a better approach to
claim what was rightfully his.

Gordan realized too late what Nicole had done, what she could see.
In an instant he and Raiden were pushed aside and the air trembled
with rage and magic. The bright blue sky melted away and the
churning grey clouds of the storm loomed overhead, the sheer cliffs
of the natural harbor were all around them. Deafening over their
heads, thunder cracked.

He picked Raiden up. They were stunned to see Nicole standing before a figure locked in her grip as the ship moaned and the deck warped beneath them. She had him—Venarius. Planks snapped, bending upward, twisting around them. The nearest mast sank and the deck buckled beneath it. The mast fell and then Venarius slipped away into the ether.

Nicole's venomous glare turned to shock and she shook, letting out a cry of outrage. The deck buckled further and her anger only grew. She might destroy the ship.

He lunged forward, sprinting across the deck and grabbing her by her shoulders.

"Nicole," he snapped at her, "the ship."

She looked at him, then looked around her, and shame dampened her fire. She took several deep breaths.

"Are you all right? I'm sorry," she said, shaking her head and fighting back her angry tears.

He sighed. She was apologizing for failing. "Don't be," he insisted. "Everyone's fine. What other way was there to escape that?"

She opened her mouth but didn't have a word to offer. Then Raiden was there with his arms around her in a blink. He gasped like he hadn't been able to breathe until he had her in his arms. Words were scarce on the mangled deck of the ship. Raiden held Nicole tightly and she buried her face in his shoulder, her feet dangling.

"I had him," she murmured, a pitiable sound.

Raiden looked at Gordan over the top of her head, his breathing still quick with lingering fear. A warm hand closed around Gordan's, and he turned his gaze to Mitchell whose mouth was slack and his eyes glazed with shock. Gordan peered across the deck of the ship to the stunned faces of Fen and Asi, the vivid blue surprise in Caeruleus' single eye, and the baffled expressions of Leone, Loak, and the mortified crew.

Thirty-three

The captain assured his passengers, "The ship's enchantments take care of the damage; we'll just be here for a few days while she sort's herself out."

What he meant was that the wood of the ship was still very much alive, so broken wood sprouted and joined itself back together. Planks untwisted themselves slowly like the creep of vines, and the gaping splintered maw she had created in the deck gradually closed itself—a scab forming over a wound. The ship remained anchored in the little harbor while they waited. The captain refused Nicole's offer to speed up the process, insisting that the ship's spells worked best on their own and tampering with them could affect all the spells knitted together to make the ship the magically intricate vessel that it was—but she couldn't squelch her suspicion…and guilt that he didn't want her meddling with his ship any further after she had done the damage in the first place.

Everyone was on-edge even after the storm cleared, plagued with a persistent uncertainty as to whether or not they could believe the sunshine and clear sky this time. Gordan assured them that there were no spells in the wind. Their quiet harbor was, indeed, all that it appeared to be.

Nicole trusted Gordan when he said the coast was clear, but she stayed in their cabin, only venturing out to the balcony, partly because of the sideways glances the ship's crew gave her and mostly because she needed to sulk.

I had him. She let out a guttural sigh, hating how close she had been to freedom from this absurdity only to watch it slip away. Movement in the sky caught her attention, and she looked up to see Leone departing. She watched him a moment as he shrank into the sky alone, admittedly relieved that Raiden wasn't with him. Dropping her head to her folded arms against the carved wooden railing, she thought, *no matter how hard we try, this will drive us all mad eventually.* How long before the worry crawled into their bones and turned to paranoia?

She couldn't stop thinking about that moment—finally seeing looking into Venarius' his pale blue eyes. He hadn't been what she expected—not that she had been expecting some terrifying monstrous visage. He looked like any middle-aged Caucasian man—like a father she might see at a grocery store—a long nose that may have been broken once, his hair mostly white and shorn close to his scalp which minimized his receding hairline. The grey and white scruff on his face had been longer than his hair. This was their foe—necromancer and infamous leader of Dawn?

A pair of arms slipped around her—Raiden latched onto her.

"Hey," she said, chuckling when he let the weight of his torso sag completely onto her back. "I just saw your dad leaving."

Raiden removed himself and she straightened up to turn into his chest, deeply disturbed by how close Venarius had been to him and to everyone she loved.

"He's going to Eanna to let them know what happened. We thought it was only fair to warn them about Venarius so that they might be prepared, or even have the opportunity to rescind their invitation to the vernal festival should the queen wish it."

That seemed fair; she nodded against his chest—hopeful that Eanna's Queen would withdraw the invitation so that they could return to the palace in the midlands. Nicole wanted to send Asi and

Fen safely home to the orchard with Keren. They were still shaken up by the scene on deck with Venarius, and Nicole couldn't help think they feared her now. They had never seen her like that; neither had her brother. *I probably looked scarier than Venarius to them.*

"Gordan and Mitchell wanted me to ask you if they could come in," Raiden murmured.

"What? Of course, they can," she said, pulling away from him. "Guys," she called, suspecting they were outside.

The door opened and Mitchell stepped into the cabin, followed by Gordan. Her brother crossed the room, raising his arms to throw them around her and swing her off the floor.

"I'm so proud of you," he said in her ear. She was startled by the sob his words conjured up in her lungs as he bear-hugged her.

"I think you may have scared him off for a while," Gordan said with a smile. "I sensed a note of fear in that man."

"I bet he pissed himself," Mitchell muttered with a chuckle and set Nicole back down. She allowed herself a tiny satisfied smile.

Nicole let out a weak laugh. "He wouldn't be the only one. The crew is definitely scared of me now, and the captain is pretty sour about the ship."

"Forget them," Mitchell scoffed.

"We literally have to share the ship with them," she laughed.

"Then let's get off this ship," Raiden suggested.

∽

Nicole looked up to the top of the cliffs where Gordan was perched after his swift climb up the cliff face in his dragon form. She lay on her back in the dinghy, her legs bent over the side. Raiden tied their little boat to one of the rocks at the base of the harbor's cliff walls just beside a low cave, its wide mouth mostly filled with water.

"All right who wants to explore the cave with me?" Mitchell asked.

Nicole turned her head and watched him pull his shirt off as he sat on the edge of the dinghy in his neon green dino-print swim trunks.

"Given how our day started, maybe we should pass on mysterious caves that scream monster lair," she teased her brother.

"Oh, come *on*. You're scarier than anything out there. I know it and you know it," he said. "Just embrace it."

Nicole sat up. "Ouch, thanks Mitch, that's so encouraging and not at all insulting."

"What's insulting about being a badass?" he asked, looking her in the eye. "Please, tell me."

Nicole laughed and shook her head, undeniably perplexed by his request. After all he was kind of right—should she be afraid of mermaids or sea monsters that might be lurking in that cave, when she knew they should be afraid of her, knowing what she could do, what she *had* done to those who tried to hurt her or someone she loved? She scowled at him. Mitchell being right annoyed her.

"That's what I thought. Now are you going to chaperone your helpless brother in that monster lair or not?"

"Why are you like this?" Nicole asked.

Mitchell ignored her and turned to Raiden. "You'll come, won't you, Ray?"

"Sure," he said, pulling his shirt off and leaving only the turquoise swim trunks she had conjured for him.

Nicole glanced at him and couldn't stop the little grin from possessing her face—there was something about that caribbean green against his brown complexion.

"I bet now you want to come," Mitchell teased.

Nicole rolled her eyes to her brother across the dinghy and let a little pulse of magic roll through the air. He fell back into the water, a shout of surprise barely escaping his mouth before the splash.

☙

Mitchell barged into their cabin, and Raiden jumped as he pulled his trousers up, startled by the sudden entrance. Mitchell was carrying with him a large plank.

Nicole dropped the book she was reading onto her lap. "Mitch, what the hell?" she demanded.

"Look what I nabbed," he said, snickering as he heaved it

through the cabin onto their balcony. "They were preoccupied with propping up the mast."

"Why would you take that?" Raiden asked.

"*Where* is Gordan?" she asked.

Mitchell sagged in frustration and sighed, ignoring Nicole and answering Raiden, "We're gonna set it up and walk the plank, obviously."

Forehead creased with confusion, Raiden asked Nicole, "Is he joking?"

She laughed. "Oh no, he's serious."

Gordan arrived with what looked to be a rolled-up rope ladder under his arm. "I found the ladder but I don't understand—" he stopped when he spotted Mitchell at work across the cabin.

"So, you're an accomplice this time," Nicole said.

Mitchell shoved the plank through the bottom gap in the railing and dragged Nicole's trunk through the cabin to position it atop the back end of the plank as a counterweight and a means over the railing.

"Done," he said, his breathing heavy from the effort. He spotted Gordan and crossed the room briskly to take the ladder from him. "Thanks," he said, pecking him on the mouth.

"What's he doing?" Gordan asked.

"I think you're about to see," Nicole replied.

Mitchell threw the metal hooks at the end of the ladder onto the rail and tossed the bundle of rope off the balcony. He yanked off his shirt. He wore the swim shorts she'd conjured for him the day before. He climbed over the trunk and balcony rail. He walked to the end of the plank, looked down and stepped off.

They heard him crash into the water below and a few seconds later came an exhilarated cheer. A minute passed, then Mitchell appeared dripping wet at the top of the ladder and climbed onto the balcony.

"You're just going to sit there?" he panted. "I know you want to join me."

Nicole grinned and jumped off the bed, leaving her book

behind and conjuring her bathing suit onto her body beneath her clothes before she jumped out of her pants and threw off her shirt. She climbed over her trunk and onto the plank on the other side of the balcony.

She held on to the rail and looked down. It looked higher than she had expected. She always hated the high dive, but if Mitchell could do it, then she could too. She'd spent her whole life following him—determined to prove she could keep up, be just as strong, and just as brave. She smiled to herself and wondered if anyone ever really grows up. She walked to the end of the plank and stepped off, crossing her arms tight to her chest as she fell. Her heart pounded. The water broke and roared in her ears. Bubbles gurgled and hissed around her, dissipating into the silence below the surface. The depth of the harbor chased her back to the surface, and her reeling heart propelled her clear out of the water. She let out an embarrassed laugh as she hovered over the water. She rose up to the balcony easily, leaving her anxiety below her.

When she landed back on the plank, Mitchell was standing there on the balcony. "Peter Pan, you've sure changed."

She bent over with laughter and almost toppled off the plank again.

"What's going on in here?" A voice asked from the doorway.

All eyes turned to see Caeruleus peering into the cabin curiously.

"I guess we're going swimming," Raiden told him.

"Come on, Stone, we'll teach you how to cannonball," Mitchell said.

"To what now?"

Raiden shrugged.

Nicole nodded encouragingly at Caeruleus and thought of Fen and Asi. She stepped off the plank and drifted down to the windows of the cabins below. Through the window she saw Netti and Sage chatting on their beds, so she floated over to the next window and found it open. She peaked in and saw Fen lying across her bed while Asi, seated on the floor against the foot of Fen's bed, wrote in a small notebook.

Nicole knocked on the window frame and waved. "Hi, girls."

They looked up, startled to see her at the window, no doubt.

"You fly?" Fen asked.

"Sometimes I can," she said. "We're going swimming if you want to join us."

They exchanged an excited glance.

☙

The Nereid was on its way the third day. The captain set a direct course for Eanna across the Avalon Sea. It was apparent he was done being the escort of the fera king and all the trouble that followed her.

Leone arrived around noon with news from Eanna. Nicole had hoped to hear the queen wasn't up for the increased risk of having the fera in her stead after hearing of Dawn's involvement and Venarius' cunning attempts.

"Queen Belen has sent her own ships to escort us the rest of the way to Eanna," Leone said.

Raiden remarked quietly to Nicole, "Then I guess we're still going."

"The queen isn't concerned at all about Dawn?" She asked Leone. Admittedly, she still wanted an excuse to return to the safety of the palace. She also worried for the people of Eanna and for the queen. She was rethinking her brazen plan of baiting Venarius out into the open. There was no telling when he might choose a kick-down-the-door-leave-no-survivors tactic to get what he wanted.

"Not in the least," Leon answered. "Her ships will likely meet up with us tomorrow morning. The queen told me she's eager to meet you—now more than ever."

☙

By sunrise the next day four ships with vibrant fan-shaped sails were spotted on the horizon. By the time the Nereid reached the four vessels from Eanna, they had turned around to fall in beside the Nereid and flank her, a pair on either side. Aboard Queen Belen's ships the crews waved in greeting; and Nicole counted mostly women. The remainder of their journey to Eanna was quiet. It took another full day and night; the following morning the coast of Eanna bobbed on the horizon.

Nicole was as happy to march off of The Nereid as the captain undoubtedly was to see her go. She had no idea that they would be getting right back onto another boat because to get to the capital of Eanna, they would have to travel the canals.

"This way, Finnegan," Nicole said. "Maybe I should have a leash for him," she added, laughing as Raiden nudged the griffin on his left while she prodded him from the right to keep him on track toward the boat.

She marched onto the smaller boat with its wide rectangular sail. Finnegan jumped excitedly onto the deck and bounded around several women standing there waiting to greet them. The most prominent figure waiting for them as they reached the end of the plank onto the boat was a woman with her hands clasped at the small of her back—her posture comfortably authoritative. She was young, her complexion brown and warm as she smiled, her rich brown eyes followed the griffin. Thick brows twitched with amusement as she watched Finn investigate the deck of the boat.

"Welcome, Kings Nicole and Raiden, it is my honor to escort you to Hypatia at Queen Belen's request. My name is Akarsha, head of the Queen's Guard."

"Thank you, Akarsha. I'm sorry about him," Nicole said.

"Not to worry. I don't think any of my ladies will mind," she said, glancing over her shoulder at another woman, similarly dressed, bent over Finnegan and scrubbing his neck.

"Is this where the party is?" Mitchell asked. Nicole turned to see Gordan and him step onto the deck hand in hand.

Nicole saw it on Gordan's face—discomfort. When she looked back to Akarsha, her warm smile had fallen to a stiff expression.

Nicole straightened up. "Akarsha, this is my brother Mitchell and my dearest friend Gordan."

Akarsha nodded slowly. "Pleasure to meet the prince and the dragon who saved King Eisen and his daughter."

They had heard about what Gordan did in Orodon then, but clearly mistrust persisted among them.

"Permission to come aboard," Loak's low voice shook them all out of tense silence.

As everyone filed onto the boat and Raiden stepped in to introduce Akarsha to Loak as their Captain-of-the-Guard, Nicole pulled Mitchell and Gordan aside.

"What the hell was that?" Mitchell asked.

"They don't trust me," Gordan said with a shrug, used to such sentiments.

"They don't know you like we do," Nicole assured him.

"Don't push matters, Nicole," Gordan implored. "They're tolerating my presence. That's good enough."

She frowned. Gordan didn't begrudge anyone their hatred of dragons. He didn't oppose the exile of his kind. He didn't seem to think they were worthy of forgiveness. She wondered if he was being far too harsh on the whole of his kind or if she wanted so desperately to believe there were dragons who were unjustly vilified, that she was letting her love for him make a fool of her. They weren't talking about the crimes of a long-gone generation, after all. Every dragon in exile—Gordan included—was around during the war, and he had said once before that they all played their part in the fire and bloodshed.

"Listen," Gordan said. "I have you and Mitchell and Raiden— your trust is what matters to me. I couldn't care less about having theirs."

She managed to smile but couldn't quite recover the hopes she had had for Eanna when they arrived. Since Queen Belen's ships joined them at sea, Nicole had believed she could like this royal state, ruled only by a queen. Akarsha had said it herself, word of Gordan's deed in Orodon had reached them, yet he couldn't be trusted for what he was—a dragon. Nicole simmered with her annoyance until Gordan nudged her.

"Don't hate them for the way they feel about me," he insisted. "Raiden felt the same way, remember." He offered her a smile.

His smile was impossible to resist. Sometimes she couldn't believe he was the same chilly-voiced dragon she had met not so long ago. He smiled so often now and it lifted her spirits every time. She sighed, "True, and he was way more of a jerk about it."

They laughed and her mood lightened.

❧

The palace of Hypatia was more like a sprawling temple complex. The boat docked in a little port when it could go no further. Narrower channels branched off into the royal grounds. They transferred onto long slender boats that took them through the pristine stone-lined waterways into the grounds.

The channels weren't just a practical waterway around the royal estate, they also connected countless pools among the pillar-lined structures which created the illusion of alabaster temples floating impossibly upon the water—stone lily pads in serene ponds.

Akarsha stood formally at the back of the lead boat upon which Nicole, Raiden, Mitchell, Gordan, Fen and Asi sat marveling at the maze of channels and pools. The boats seemed to guide themselves, though how they knew the destination wasn't clear.

Caeruleus, Leone and Loak occupied the boat behind them, Loak's stature and weight allowed for only the three of them. Tovar, Netti, Sage, and three more guards followed in the third boat while the remaining guards were in the last boat.

They arrived at a square pool where all four boats could fit lined up side by side, but without much room left. Facing the pool were four houses in a half circle. Behind these was the largest structure—a stone temple at first glance, curtains of airy fabric gently waved at them in welcome from between the pillars—and beside it to the left and right were two smaller but identical structures.

"Wow," Nicole said, staring at the cluster of buildings rather than stepping off the boat. Raiden tugged on her hand and led her off the boat in her stupor.

They followed a stone path from the pool up to the central structure, apparent by its size and position that it was intended for Raiden and her. Unlike their rooms in Nol dripping in gold moldings and luxurious trappings, they walked into an extravagance of space and light as they passed through the pillars and linen curtains of the entrance way. There were hardly walls to speak of; instead, slender vertical shudders opened to let the breeze dance freely through the interior and could be closed to form a wall of privacy.

The inner space was divided by stone walls, but the doorways were tall and wide and filled only with curtains instead of doors. Sun spilled in from skylights in the flat stone roof. As they stood stunned in the entrance of their lodgings, Akarsha cleared her throat behind them.

"I'm sure you would like some time to settle after your journey," she said. "You will have your privacy here, of course, but I patrol the grounds with my ladies should you need us. The grounds are completely open to you and your people. Queen Belen would like you to enjoy the gardens as you please, and she takes great pride in her aviary should you find yourselves wandering."

"Thank you," Raiden said.

Akarsha nodded with a cordial smile and turned on her heel to depart, whipping a long, thick black braid as she went.

Nicole wandered deeper into their rooms, through the curtains and past painted pillars until she found a large low bed, a simple wooden frame raised barely a foot off the stone floor in the center of the back room. She sank onto the mattress and sighed in relief to finally lie down and not feel the world rocking beneath her. The bed was gloriously still.

As heavy as her mind suddenly felt and as ready as it was to sink into the bliss of the rock-steady darkness behind her eyes, it wouldn't relinquish its hold on Akarsha's reaction and what Gordan had said.

"I take it you found what you were looking for," Raiden's voice tugged at her thoughts.

She opened her eyes. "I didn't realize how sick of the rocking I was until now."

Raiden sank down beside her and sighed. She rolled toward him and pulled herself close, craving the reassuring pressure of contact, to anchor her battered and tattered psyche back to her body.

"Do you think Akarsha and her guards escorted us because of Venarius—or because Gordan is with us?" She wondered aloud.

"What makes you ask that?"

"Gordan could tell they don't trust him."

"Unfortunately, I'm more inclined to think they're watching him," he said.

"Me too. It bothers me," she said. Raiden pulled her closer. Nicole continued, "And it bothers me that it doesn't seem to bother Gordan. He knows he wasn't a part of the war, but he just accepts it."

"If he was a part of it, do you think he would tell us?" Raiden wondered. "Maybe he accepts their hatred because he feels he deserves it."

"You think he might have lied?"

"Sure, it's possible. I certainly didn't think him capable of anything else when we first met. *If* he lied, it was because he didn't want to jeopardize something important to him."

Nicole's face pinched with distress. She loved Gordan and supposed she would forgive anything in his past; but was that selfish of her if he had carried out orders, burned forests, whole towns and killed innocent people—even if he had been *forced* to do so? She was ashamed to entertain the notion at all. Gordan, who felt the emotions of others like they were his own, couldn't have done anything so terrible. She knew him. Her heart nearly burst with furious certainty. Whether he had been completely honest with her or not, he wasn't a killer.

"You trusted him when no one else would. I'm not sure I would blame him if he kept a secret that he thought might risk that," he said softly. "Not when I did the same thing."

She sighed. "I like to think he trusts me enough not to keep secrets."

"We've all kept secrets from each other, haven't we?"

"Yeah," she agreed.

"It's not always for lack of trust that we hide things. Don't ever doubt that he trusts you; he trusts you more than anyone in this world."

"Sometimes I imagine where I'd be without either of you—dead or already with Venarius maybe," she muttered cynically.

"I think you're completely forgetting to factor yourself into this alternate reality. If I weren't around and you wandered into Cantis alone, I bet you'd have handled things a lot better without the mess I was making. Caeruleus would probably be dead though."

Nicole let out an appalled laugh. "That's awful! He's your best friend."

"Look, you started this game."

☙

Gordan and Mitchell agreed to share one of the two rooms in the smaller structure flanking Nicole and Raiden's. Asi and Fen settled into the other room in the house. Loak and Leone took one room of the other side house while Caeruleus took the other. Their guards spread themselves comfortably between three of the four small houses, while Tovar took the fourth—unpacking the good amount of his workshop which he had brought with him. From their cluster of buildings, Gordan could feel a collective sigh of relief and the weight of fatigue in the air as everyone settled.

"Do you think this place is safe?" Mitchell asked from a pile of sitting pillows.

"I feel like I don't know what safe is anymore," Gordan admitted.

Mitchell held up his hand to him. Gordan thought he wanted to stand up and offered his hand only to be pulled down into the pillows beside him.

"Together is safe," Mitchell said.

Gordan supposed he was right; all they had was each other. Every attempt Venarius had made thus far was confounded because Nicole had people with her.

Venarius liked this game. The way Gordan saw it, Venarius clearly relished strategy, planning, and flaunting his influence and reach when he easily had the ability to get close to Nicole. Gordan supposed Venarius fully expected to be the winner, and he might not tolerate a worthy adversary for very long. *If he can't win by playing strategy who's to say he won't knock all the other pieces off the board in a rage to take the queen—rules be damned.*

"Should we go see what they're up to?" Gordan asked, tucking his chin into his shoulder to glance down at Mitchell beside him only to find his eyes were closed. Mitchell's contentment filled the room and soon Gordan felt himself dozing off as he considered Mitchell's words—*together is safe.*

Thirty-four

Nicole was close to drifting off behind her closed eyes when she heard two familiar voices.

"So far, I think I like it here," Asi's voice from outside wafted through the open shutters on the breeze.

"I spotted some henbane growing around one of the pools on the way in," Fen said excitedly. "I wonder if we can gather some."

"Keren always said she liked Eanna, lots of her favorite herbs grow here."

"We should bring some home to her. I bet she's running low."

Nicole sat up, careful not to disturb Raiden but he wasn't asleep.

"Where are you going?" he murmured, his eyes still closed.

"Just for a walk with Finn and the girls," she said, leaning down to brush her lips against his.

His arm snuck around her waist to prolong the kiss a little longer. She laughed quietly and pulled away. "Get some sleep," she encouraged.

He sighed and opened his eyes. "I should go have a chat with Tovar about how safe the grounds are, and check in with Caeruleus, and dad," he said.

"All right, see you later," she said, hopping off the bed and hurrying through their temple-like rooms. Finnegan jumped at the sight of her and abandoned his inspection of the rooms to follow her down the four steps to the path. Asi and Fen hadn't gone far and Nicole caught up with them at an easy jog.

"Hey, you two," she called.

"Nicole—"

"Isn't this place beautiful?" Fen sighed.

"It is pretty incredible. Should we wander around?" As much as she wanted to trust the beauty around them, she was anxious to watch out for her friends.

"Yes!" Asi jumped.

The royal grounds of Hypatia were otherworldly. It was a land of water—pools filled with plants and pools where statues were stone dancers weightless on the glassy water. At times the path would cross sprawling ponds by way of stepping stones. The tops of submerged columns disappeared into the green water where large koi swam lazily. Finn pranced and pounced around them as they wandered through the gardens.

"I don't think I've ever been anywhere more beautiful," Fen mused happily—then she gasped. "That's Caenis Wish!" She sprang across the last of the stepping columns toward some low plants growing beside the path ahead.

"What's that for?" Nicole wondered as she hopped and glided over the last two stepping stones.

"It's an herb for transformations. It will change your sex."

"Wow, to think it's as easy as an herb," Nicole said. "Is it a temporary?"

Finn barged in to inspect the herb at the center of their attention, pushing his way under Nicole's hand. She patted his head fondly.

"Permanent," Fen said. "And you have to brew it a special way. It's not exceptionally difficult. Actually, it's harder to find the herb than it is to use it properly."

"Well, you can't find it in Taroth anymore. People used it all up decades ago to turn their unwanted daughters into sons," Asi said, a hint of disdain in her voice.

"That's awful," Nicole murmured sadly.

"That herb should only be used by people who want to change for themselves," a deep feminine voice said gently.

The three of them looked up and saw a stunning woman on the path. Nearly transparent robes hung around her full figure as light fell through the fabric and revealed every robust curve of her silhouette. Her hair—a crown in itself—would put a pharaoh's golden headdress to shame. Locks of black hair twisted into thick ropes hung around her shoulders, and dangled almost to her waist. Without a single ornament of gold upon her person, it was clear she was Eanna's queen.

Nicole was captivated, most of all by her face. Just below her hairline Nicole saw what at first glance looked like a lace band in place of a coronet, but then she recognized the other patches of ivory in Queen Belen's deep brown complexion. When she smiled, her warm brown eyes squinted, and laugh lines creased her face.

"Queen Belen," Nicole dared to greet the woman, whose presence was an intimidating combination of inviting warmth and regal command.

"You may call me Belen if I may call you Nicole," she answered. "And who are these beautiful ladies?"

"This is Fen and Asi," Nicole said.

The girls bowed hesitantly.

"A beautiful family, I must say," Belen said. "Though I've heard yours is much larger and rather more colorful still—is it not? A celengel, a giant, even a dragon."

A giant? Nicole was perplexed for a moment before realizing she must be referring to Loak.

"You've brought quite the mix of people together—a former agent of the Council and a rebel from Atrium as your emissaries. You've been a king for such a short time, but I've heard so much about you already."

Nicole flushed with heat. She didn't know a thing about Eanna or Queen Belen.

"Your highness," Fen said. "May I gather herbs from your gardens?"

"As much as you wish, child," she said with a chuckle.

Fen looked to Asi excitedly, "Let's go get my herb basket."

They caught themselves before they turned to run back across the stepping stones and hastily curtsied to Queen Belen. It looked like a familiar movement to Asi, an awkward unpracticed movement to Fen.

"Thank you, your highness," Fen said.

"My dears, you may call me Lady Belen. Now, please, no more curtseying. Enjoy yourselves."

They beamed and set off across the stepping stones. Nicole laughed to herself. *Looks like they forgot all about me,* but she was glad to see them so happy. Finn chased after them, feeding off their excitement.

"I've heard about your troubles on the journey here," Belen said.

Nicole swallowed back the bitter taste in her mouth. *Troubles* made the narcissistic necromancer on a power trip sound so trivial—but, then again, it was starting to feel so commonplace in her life that maybe it was.

"To be honest," Nicole said. "I wanted to take Asi and Fen home. I put them at risk…well, my *troubles* put them at risk."

"As I hear it, you are the one who keeps your family safe," Belen said. "That seems to be what you do best."

"Not always," she answered heavily.

"No one is perfect. I have failed my people more times than I can count in my thirty-three years as queen."

"How old were you when you became queen?"

"Oh, about your age I would say. You're…twenty?"

"Eighteen," Nicole said. Though her eighteenth birthday seemed like years ago, she suddenly felt so juvenile. Why the hell was there a key to an entire realm around her neck?

"It intimidates you," Belen said, nodding toward the key hanging against Nicole's chest. "That's understandable. To inherit something as complex as this broken realm…" she shook her head. "It has been hard enough to lead Eanna, navigating the wavering presence of the Council and their faltering authority in the realm. They unified Veil but the old kingdoms—their values, their traditions—crawled out of the ashes after the dragon wars. People wanted the comfort of unity, certainly, but they wanted the sense of normalcy most. They wanted things back the way they were."

"But they can't have it both ways," Nicole said.

"And here we are," Belen said. "Arguably a more broken realm than we were before; peace and trade deals enforced by the Council hanging precariously in the void they have left behind."

ↂ

Raiden stepped into Caeruleus' room. "Ruleus, you in here?" There was no one in the front half of the room, only sitting pillows around the low table.

"I'm here," an answer came through the curtain that divided the large space into a sitting room and a bedroom. Caeruleus stepped through the parted fabric rubbing his eye, wavy black locks hanging over his eyepatch.

"Did I wake you?"

"No not really," he said. "I just made the mistake of lying down."

"I checked on Tovar; he's unpacking happily. He seems to be enjoying all this firsthand perspective on the royal states."

"Yes, I know. He'll talk about 'recording the history being made' any chance he gets," Caeruleus said with a chuckle. "Knowing you is the best thing that could have happened to the guy."

Raiden laughed. "He's been far more help to me than I have been to him."

"I wish I was half as much help," he said with a dismissive shrug. He put on a smile, doing a poor job of hiding his disappointment—Raiden knew that look even after all the years apart.

"What makes you think you aren't?"

"Come on, Ray, I don't have much to offer—not book smarts or spell craft—"

"You're worth more than those things, Ruleus. Do you need me to remind you of all the times you kept me company when I couldn't sleep at night, or all the times you helped me forget there was someone missing from our home, or the all the times you took the blame for the trouble we made because you knew Mother would be easier on you?"

Caeruleus laughed. "What you're saying is that you're stuck with me because of sentiment," he said, shaking his head as he crossed the room. Raiden hooked an arm around his neck.

"You're important is what I'm saying. Don't forget you're the reason I wasn't lost at sea. Sending Nicole was your idea."

"That's true."

They stepped outside and couldn't help overhearing half the conversation from the neighboring room.

"Raiden still doesn't know? Leone, I thought you'd have told him by now," Loak's voice carried past the pillars and through curtains.

Raiden looked to Caeruleus beside him.

"Tell me what?" he asked as he walked up the steps and strolled inside where Loak and his father were standing.

They shared a look of brief surprise as Raiden and Caeruleus walked in, but Loak immediately turned a smug face back to Leone.

Raiden pressed, "What don't I know?"

Leone took a deep breath. "We worked for Dawn as double agents," he said.

Raiden's mind went silent for a stunned moment. "Why?" he demanded.

"Because of your mother. The Council was rounding up every seer across Veil. They paid informants well, and I needed help hiding her. We knew the seers were prisoners, but I couldn't take on the Council myself. Even with Loak's help we were out of our depth. After the celengels denied us refuge on Terra Celestia, I offered my assistance to Dawn in exchange for hiding her from the Council."

He felt like he was sinking for several seconds. His father had worked for Dawn. He finally managed to dig words out of his shock. "How did you help them?"

"I released the fera into the other realm as I was instructed," Leone said with a sigh. "And a few years later I stole the journal from the archives."

Raiden took a deep breath and pinched the bridge of his nose. A bitter smile curled on his mouth.

"Does Dawn still keep tabs on you?" Caeruleus asked.

"I honestly don't know. I've been useless to them since I went down for treason. My contract was for my role as double agent. Dawn relocated and cloaked our home in Cantis, and I received my orders to frustrate the interception of the fera and ensure her escape. Venarius used me here and there but with the fera safe from the Council for the time, he only had need of me for one last thing—stealing the Hessian journal brought everything down around me. The Council launched an investigation; they learned of my first betrayal with the fera from my memory evaluation. That was it; Dawn would not assist me after that. Payment for my service had been protection of your mother and you. The transaction was done. I had nothing more to offer them from inside a cell, and there I stayed."

"They contracted me after your father was arrested," Loak said. "I was their eyes and ears in the courts. The Council kept a close eye on me after your father's arrest. They evaluated my memory—and thankfully because he kept me in the dark I was cleared—but they still monitored my apartment and had fellow agents watch me."

"How would Dawn contact you?" Raiden asked.

"Letters. They had the Council's messenger in their pocket."

"So, messages from Dawn looked like messages from the Council," Raiden supposed.

"Exactly."

"But you've not had word from them since?" Caeruleus wondered.

"Not since before the fall of the Council. They have nothing to hold over our heads anymore. Our contracts are completed," Loak said.

"How sure can you be that Venarius doesn't have some kind of link to you through those contracts?" Raiden worried.

"Not as sure as we'd like to be," Loak said, giving Leone a stern look.

Raiden took a deep breath. "I think we had better inform the queen and her guards. For the sake of everyone's safety, they should know the extent of what they could be dealing with."

❧

Nicole walked stiffly in the silence beside Belen. The beauty of the gardens couldn't relax her. Key or no key, she didn't feel like she belonged in the presence of a queen. Finn came swooping back to her side, nudging her hip hard enough to break her stride.

She laughed. "Yes, hello," she said to him, scrubbing his neck and ruffling his feathers.

"A peculiar companion," Belen mused. "Almost as peculiar as a dragon."

"Is he?" she asked, feeling her chest tighten with the mention of Gordan. What was Belen's sentiments about his presence in her home? Fearing the discomfort, Nicole didn't want to lead the conversation toward her friend. "I don't know anything about griffins," she admitted. "Other than he likes to hog the bed, and he's apparently going to double in size."

Belen chuckled. "That is true. Griffins are usually solitary creatures. It's in their nature to claim a territory and protect it for their lifetime. This behavior is very strange indeed. He is an adolescent and should have found himself a territory by now."

Nicole found it much easier to talk about Finn. "He accidentally found himself a portal to the old world a couple months ago and ended up in our house. I imagine it was a little traumatic ending up in a strange place, and being chased by our dog. He was small enough then that I could pick him up and return him to Cantis. I assume Cantis was home because that's where he found me the second time, and he managed to follow me back to the palace. I keep expecting him to decide he's ready to head out. He does wander off to find food, but he keeps coming back so…" she shrugged.

Belen nodded. "Perhaps he's not acting strangely at all, if he has confused you with a place to call home instead of finding a mountain somewhere."

"You mean he's decided *I'm* his territory," she said, letting out a nervous laugh.

"I suppose you are. If you provided him safety, he could easily attach himself to you. It's rather unconventional, but it must make sense to him."

Nicole smiled at Finn, her heart swelling with relief at the idea that she was a safe haven rather than the pit of danger pulling everyone into its void.

She and Belen fell into silence again. Nicole couldn't think of anything to say. *What do you say to a queen? I shouldn't even be here.* She closed her hand around her key, wishing she could crush it into dust and walk away from the whole charade.

A cottontail bolted from a bush. Finn scrambled after it, leaping into the air as he gave chase and swooping toward the ground only to miss. Finn wandered off in pursuit. Nicole felt the weight of the titles between Belen and her settle on her again.

Nicole was content to study the beauty around her and leave the silence between her and Belen unbroken as they walked along a path through the grounds. She didn't want to pretend to be a king anymore.

"We don't have to be rulers, you know," Belen said, startling Nicole from her thoughts. Was Belem reading her mind?

"Pardon?"

"Just because you are one of the prophesied kings of the keys and I am the queen of Eanna doesn't mean we must speak of royal duties. We are free to be two women sharing each other's company. There is so much more we could talk about."

"Right," she said, even less sure how to fill the silence now. Belen's warm presence was vast and beautiful, both maternal and girlishly playful, but Nicole felt herself shrinking in Belen's company.

"Let me ask you this. Who are you, Nicole?"

She laughed nervously. "I'm not entirely sure anymore," she said.

Belen turned her eyes to Nicole for a moment and smiled. "I think you are, but you're reluctant to embrace it, or perhaps just hesitant to let others know what you know."

She had too many thoughts to know what to say.

"I understand. You don't know me well enough to expose your heart. What matters is that you know, and the people who matter to you know as well."

"I do have a few of those," Nicole offered. "I'd be lost without them."

"Will I get to meet them?"

"They're here with me. My brother Mitchell, Gordan and Raiden."

"Ah, yes, your fellow king," Belen said. "A rumor from Nol beat you here."

Nicole flushed with heat, though it wasn't a rumor, it was true enough. *He's my—we're—together…dating…married?* None of that sounded right.

"I see," Belen said. "Having a lover is still very new to you."

Nicole was sure her face couldn't burn any hotter. She cleared her throat. "You could say that." Having someone point it out was something new.

"My dear, there's no need to be embarrassed. You only get to discover these things for the first time once. What I would give to relive some of my first experiences with a lover," Belen said wistfully. "I hope you'll both partake in the ceremony at the festival."

"Ceremony?"

"Forgive me, I forgot you are not from Veil. The vernal festival is a celebration of Spring and the abundance of the womb of the earth. During the ceremony of flowers, women who wish to embody the sacred Mother chose a partner to lie with in an exaltation of the earth."

"Oh," Nicole said.

"It is a private worship of life, only the ceremony of the women choosing their partner is public."

"That sounds…beautiful," Nicole said.

"It is. It is one of the most sacred rituals in Eanna. Naturally, many women participating already have lovers with whom they celebrate, but there certainly are those who do not, like myself."

Nicole caught sight of several people traversing a path a couple of pools away. It was Raiden, Caeruleus, Leone and Loak. Raiden waved.

"That must be the king," Belen said.

"Yes, that's Raiden," Nicole said, feeling like she couldn't say his name enough—the sound of it pulling at the corners of her mouth.

Their path intersected with the men's path, and Nicole could see Raiden's stride lengthen to meet her. They halted their instinct to lock together, their momentum stopping awkwardly—they had an audience. Raiden took her hand, lacing their fingers together and bringing it to his lips in a discrete greeting.

Nicole fought her lips urge to smile with an introduction, "Raiden, this is Queen Belen."

"A pleasure to meet you," Raiden responded, bowing his head. "And an honor to be in Eanna during such a sacred celebration."

"All of Eanna has joyfully prepared for your arrival. The festival this year will be truly special," Belen said. "Now, I have met your father and your emissary before, but your tallest companion I have not."

"This is Loak Clyson our Captain of the Guard," Raiden said.

Loak bent down in a bow, "Your Highness."

"Sir, I'm afraid you are the highest of us all," Belen said with a tiny smile.

"Your Radiance, then," he said, straightening up.

Belen's smile broadened while Nicole, Raiden, Caeruleus and Leone all changed amused glances.

"What a delight to have new faces at the festival this year, and quite the treat to have you all here in my gardens. I trust you have everything you need."

"Actually, we were hoping to speak with you and the captain of your guard about the potential risks of our stay here," Raiden said. "Our presence in Nol, unfortunately, put Prince—uh, King Cinder—in danger alongside Nicole."

Belen nodded, "I see. The safety of everyone here is certainly very important to us, as well as the security of the festival and everyone in attendance. We should find my ladies training about now."

⸲

Gordan heard the excited chatter of Asi and Fen just outside before he opened his eyes.

"No, I've got to make room. We haven't even been back to the pool near the henbane yet," Fen insisted.

"You know Tovar keeps fresh herbs; he might help us charm a box or something to keep some fresh."

"Oh, that's true, I didn't bring mine from home. These ones we can lay out and dry right away."

Gordan opened his eyes. Mitchell was asleep, his face pressed into Gordan's chest.

"Mitchell," Gordan whispered. "we dozed off."

"I'm trying to stay that way," he muttered.

Gordan chuckled, jostling Mitchell.

"It sounds like everyone's out there exploring the grounds. I don't feel Nicole or Raiden nearby," Gordan said.

Mitchell sighed and sat up. Gordan saw so much resemblance to Nicole in his groggy scowl.

"Without us?" Mitchell heaved himself off the large sitting pillows and onto his feet.

"I thought you wanted to sleep," Gordan teased.

"Are you kidding me? Nicole and Raiden need us around. After last week there's no telling where that psychopath could show up."

Gordan was perplexed by the simultaneous severity and facetious lightness in Mitchell's tone and could only let out an anxious laugh. He wasn't wrong, after all, about Venarius' ability to get close to Nicole when they least expected it. Why should Eanna be any safer?

"Shall we go for a walk then?" Gordan stood up, rolling his head and shoulders, popping the joints of his compressed form.

"Yeah, beautiful day for a rescue mission," Mitchell muttered.

ଏ୬

A line of women stood facing a line of targets across a flat open field poised arrows upon the strings of their bows, holding them first above their head and lowering them as they drew their arrows back and took aim. Their bows were taller than the archers. They set, drew, and released their arrows with such fluid grace that they seemed to be performing a dance.

Nicole was stuck in a stupor of admiration beside Raiden, Caeruleus, Leone and Loak. Belen spread her arms in greeting.

"The most beautiful creature is a dangerous woman," the queen said—reciting some kind of proverb, or riddle, Nicole thought—and the woman overseeing the lines of archers turned to her queen with a smile.

At first glance Nicole thought it was Akarsha, but this woman's black hair was loose and straight, just grazing the tops of her shoulders. Her brown eyes were dark and magnetic. She wore the same garb as all the other archers—dark blue pleated trousers that created the illusion of a full skirt hanging to their ankles and showing their bare feet—a white short-sleeved wrap tunic over which was secured a brown leather guard for the bow string—a four-fingered glove on one hand.

"She is dangerous only to those who do not see her beauty," she answered and inclined her head respectfully. "My queen."

"Amulya," Belen spoke, her voice rich with fondness. "The Kings of the Keys are finally here, and you know how I delight at showing off my lovely birds."

"The Queen's Kestrels are sharp and fit as ever today."

Belen turned to Nicole and Raiden. "Akarsha and my personal guard escorted you to Hypatia, but Amulya here is the captain of my elite archers. They are the ever-present eyes watching over these grounds. They are swift and silent—the most dangerous force in all of Veil."

"Except, perhaps, the fera," Amulya said, stepping forward. "I envied my sister a little for getting to escort you here. It's a thrill to finally meet the woman who put an end to the Council."

Nicole's face went hot. "I'm afraid you may have been told some profoundly exaggerated story. It wasn't some noble revolution," she said, swallowing back her embarrassment. "I only did what I had to—to take back my body and my life."

"Oh, but my dear, that is precisely why you should be celebrated," Belen said, taking Nicole's hands. "That *is* noble. You say you *only* took your life back? There is not a more heinous crime in this world than to rob someone's sacred right to their bodies or lives. We all belong only to ourselves. *That* crime is the only one that earns someone the penalty of death in Eanna."

"You took back what is yours *and* the justice you deserved," Amulya said.

"And in doing so, you gave Eanna back to her people. Like it or not, you are a saint here," Belen said, lifting Nicole's hands and then releasing them.

Nicole's face couldn't burn any hotter. That title was even more mortifying than king.

"Rest assured, you are safe in Hypatia. Venarius could never get close to you here," Amulya said. "Never less than forty of us are on patrol around the grounds at any time."

"I'm curious, what kind of arrows do you use?" Loak asked.

"Well, I can't disclose everything, but we carry a variety of spell-laced arrows from light charms to immobilizing hexes," Amulya explained.

Nicole could feel the lag in attention at last—her escape—and turned to Raiden. He chuckled at the private horrified expression she gave him, so together they drifted away from the Loak, Amulya and Belen's conversation.

"You can enjoy the peace and quiet before the festival knowing these grounds are secure," Belen assured Loak.

"The recognition you deserve makes you uncomfortable,"

Raiden informed her.

"I don't want any recognition. I don't want to be anyone's saint, or anyone's king," she said, letting out a sigh of exasperation. "I just want to be Nicole."

"How does one *be* Nicole?" he inquired.

She chuckled. "Like this." She spread her arms wide and held them out, closing her eyes for a moment with a smile. If only it were that simple, to just be, no keys, no enemies.

"I see," he said. "Does it include this?" He hunched down to close his arms around her torso and straightened up, lifting her off the ground.

She draped her arms around his neck and sank into his embrace. "Yes," she said. "Yes, it does."

☙

"Do you have any idea what this festival is going to be like?" Nicole asked Raiden, wondering if he knew about the sacred celebration.

"I've been told about the customary activities," he said, a smile on his mouth as he pulled his festival tunic over his head. The cream linen was light, embroidered in intricate patterns around the cuffs of his sleeves and his collar.

Nicole was pleasantly surprised by the dress Belen had given her. The simple silk column dress was loose and draped at the neckline. The band that held the dress up, tied behind her neck, wrapped down the front of her shoulders, under her arms to her lower back where the band crossed and tied at her waist. Her arms were bare and the branching scar up her arm had faded from its original wine red to a faint pink.

As she finished tying the slender sash, she looked up and caught Raiden's gaze. She smiled. "Belen asked me to meet her before the festival," she said.

"I'll be here, thinking of you in that dress," he said, falling back onto their bed with arms outstretched, landing with a sigh to make her laugh.

It worked. "Okay," she snickered. She left their room and followed the paths through the pools to the gardens where Belen had asked her to meet.

Belen strolled among her flowers, giving them focused attention as she went; then she spotted Nicole.

"There you are—come, come," she said, waving her over. "I thought that dress would suit you, and I was right."

"Thank you. I'm surprisingly comfortable in it," she said.

Belen smiled at her, studying Nicole for another moment, her long wild curls hanging to the middle of her back now, the silk falling down like milk around her body, her bare shoulders and arms. She nodded in appreciation.

"Now…" Belen began, motioning a sweeping hand at her garden. "I asked you here to choose your flower. This is a very special part of the festival; the flower you choose, you will give to your partner for the ceremony. Take your time and pick the one that feels most like *you*."

"All right," Nicole said hesitantly, looking around at the vibrant array of flowers; some she could name, others she could not. They both considered the flowers for quite some time and every time Nicole passed them her eye gravitated toward the pale orange lily-like flowers with six wide petals. She took hold of the stem and broke one free.

"A rain flower," Belen said thoughtfully.

Nicole supposed it meant more to Belen than it did to her. Nicole tucked her rain flower over her ear.

"For me, I think…" Belen reached for the vines clinging to one of the pillars around the garden and plucked a passion flower for herself and tucked it into the neckline of her white dress. "There, now we're ready for the festival."

❧

"Wow," Gordan said as Mitchell stepped through the curtain between their bedroom and the sitting room, he was wearing an airy white tunic and white linen pants. "You look beautiful."

Mitchell flushed. "No fancy clothes for you?"

"It would be best if I stay in during the festival. I can't bring myself to ruin such a precious celebration for these people. They certainly won't like seeing a dragon there; plus, I won't enjoy that kind of attention," Gordan said.

Mitchell frowned. "Then I'll stay in with you."

"I think you should stay close to Nicole tonight. I'll be fine on my own for half a night," Gordan insisted with a smile.

He sighed. "All right."

"After the festival we go back to the midlands," Gordan said. "And we'll have ample time to ourselves."

Mitchell tried to scowl, but the room filled with a haze of satisfaction. "Good."

"You should go or you'll be late," Gordan said.

"Fine, fine." Mitchell waved as he trudged through the curtains and down the three steps outside.

Gordan sighed and sank into the cushions. Then he heard feet upon the steps again and Mitchell's distinct presence swelled around him once more.

"I forgot something," he said, stopping behind him.

Gordan dropped his head back to look up at him, and Mitchell bent over him to kiss his forehead. "Don't miss me too much," he said as he stood and whirled around to leave once again.

Gordan smiled, knowing Nicole's heart was most at ease with her brother around—she smiled more, she laughed more, and she needed both now.

Thirty-five

Everyone walked across the grounds toward the festivities together—Raiden, Caeruleus, Nicole, Mitchell, Asi, Fen, Leone, Loak and all the guards. Tovar was eager to observe the festival himself and write first-hand about it. The guards were dressed to revel, but they were always watching. Raiden held onto Nicole's hand, already anxious about heading into a crowd, but to their relief their arrival wasn't announced. Those who spotted the keys hanging from their necks would nod respectfully toward them, but they were guests at the festival like everyone else. Everyone was here to celebrate the fertility of the earth, not royalty. Not even Belen's arrival stole any attention from the reverie.

The festivities started with the lighting of a great bonfire as the sun set. There was mead to drink, fruit and meats to eat, and lively music luring people to dance around the fire. Raiden found he enjoyed the lot of it without people approaching them to bow or praise them for the keys hanging from their necks. They were just Raiden and Nicole.

He watched Mitchell drag Nicole into the dancers to try his best to imitate the steps of those around them until she was laughing too hard to continue and escaped back into his arms.

526

Mitchell trotted after her. "Let's teach Ray. The steps are actually pretty easy."

"Want to?" She asked, her cloud of curls hanging tousled around her face—cheeks pink from dancing and eyes bright with adrenaline.

"How can I say no," he said with a smile.

"You too, Stone, come on," Mitchell said, pulling Caeruleus by the sleeve.

Nicole and Mitchell taught Raiden and Caeruleus the boisterous dance, tripping each other more often than not, but laughing and enjoying the music all the same. Mitchell jumped in between Raiden and Nicole, so she danced with Caeruleus. Raiden was so delightedly distracted by his two best friends laughing together that he failed horribly at the dance steps and collided with Mitchell.

"You're hopeless," Mitchell said through a laugh, pulling on his arm and swinging him toward Nicole. Fen snuck in and stole Caeruleus before Mitchell could join him again, and Asi hopped in front of Mitchell. They danced until they were breathless, hungry and lightheaded.

"Which way is the food?" Nicole asked, looking around as they made their way through the people of Eanna—a beautiful spectrum of brown faces, warm and welcoming, all wearing shades of white to cream to yellow.

Raiden looked around and bumped into a woman with feathers adorning her raven hair. "Pardon me," he said, but she just smiled and nodded as she went on her way.

"Oh, it's over there," Nicole said, pointing in the opposite direction.

They turned around and Raiden noticed the same woman, recognizing the feathers in her hair as she leaned in close to Mitchell for a brief moment, saying something to him in passing.

"I think we've determined the food is this way," Raiden said as they ran into Caeruleus, Fen and Asi who had been close behind them.

"This way, Mitch," Nicole said, so he joined them.

Leone was loitering by the food, eating a pear.

"Enjoying yourselves?" he asked between bites.

"We are, surprisingly," Raiden answered.

"You and Loak both," his father said with a grin as he nodded with a pointed look toward the many blankets laid out around the roaring bonfire. Loak and Belen were seated together, gesturing and nodding in deep conversation.

Nicole noticed Mitchell was staring in the complete opposite direction of the food.

"Hey, you said you were hungry," she said.

His eyes searched the people dancing and milling around the fire. "Yeah," he said as he turned back to the food and grabbed a turkey leg.

Nicole leaned in and scavenged as big a bite as she could, expecting his outrage only to see he was searching the faces around them again. She followed his gaze and noticed several people looking up and pointing at the moon, now risen in the sky. This seemed to be the catalyst to the ceremony because Nicole spotted one woman plucking the flower she wore on her dress and offering it to the man beside her.

Her chest went hot and she watched several more women do the same. Near the bonfire Loak nodded to Belen as she handed him the passionflower she picked earlier. Two women smiled at each other and traded sunflowers. Nicole reached for her hair, afraid she might have lost hers when they were dancing, but her fingertips found the soft petals still there. She removed her flower from her hair, her curls grasping at it, but she noticed Mitchell had slipped away. She spotted him standing with a woman who handed him a marigold.

Without a thought she marched through the people, stomping through the grass with her bare feet to get to Mitchell. The woman turned and walked away, throwing a smile back at him over her shoulder as she went, but Nicole stepped in front of him pushing him to a halt with her hand flat against his chest.

"Mitch, what are you doing?" Nicole asked, eyeing the flower he twirled in his hand.

"Enjoying the party like everyone else."

"No—what are you doing with someone's flower? You know what that's all about, right?" She was sure he must not know; if he did, he would have refused that stranger's offer.

"Yeah," he said with a shrug.

"Excuse me?" She smothered her outrage into a hiss. "You and Gordan."

"Well, yeah," he said. "But, come on, I'm just joining in on the sacred celebration. It's an honor, right?"

"Wait, that's not the point. You don't *have* to just because someone extended the invitation, you—"

"Relax, I want to. It's just a little fun—catch up with you in a bit," he said hastily with a grin and an anxious searching glance through the crowd as he hurried away.

"Mitch," she called after him in outrage. "I can't believe him," she muttered under her breath, losing sight of him as he weaved through the people after the woman. Her heart broke a little, thinking of Gordan waiting patiently back in their room. Then she gave in to disgust. She had a mind to march after Mitchell, drag him away from the party and throw him into one of the ponds with the rest of the scum. She searched for him with fervent annoyance, but with everyone wearing shades of white and cream and yellow her gaze was overwhelmed by the sea of linen-draped bodies.

She could easily spot Loak among the revelers, head and shoulders above everyone else. She decided to push on the direction Mitchell had gone, hoping to spot him, hoping he wasn't already in some private place with Marigold. Part of her brain wondered if this was her business—how would she know if Gordan and Mitchell had an open or closed relationship, or an agreement that he could partake in the sacred worship tonight? But another instinct in her gut insisted this wasn't right—it wasn't like Mitchell at all.

"Caeruleus," she practically cried out when she spotted his one piercing blue eye peering out through his shaggy black waves.

"What is it?" he asked. She knew he could see the distress on her face.

"I lost Mitchell a minute ago. Did you see him go by?"

"I didn't," he said, scanning the people around them.

"Damn it," she whispered, mostly disappointed but she couldn't shake the little nagging worry.

"There's Raiden," Caeruleus said, nodding as he made his way through the people.

Nicole turned to follow when a letter flitted out of the air in front of her nose and fell to the ground. Startled, she stood there looking down at it for a confused moment. Then she snatched it up in a hurry as a pair of bare feet nearly trampled it. When she read her name on the folded parchment, she could only stare at it for a moment before turning it over and peeling the wax seal back to unfold the letter.

Your brother has joined me for the evening. His wellbeing depends on your adherence to these simple instructions. Speak to no one. Leave the festival and let no one follow. Go to the queen's aviary. We're watching.

Venarius

Nicole took a shaky breath, horrified, her stomach twisted into a sickened knot; she thought she might puke. She had *just* seen Mitchell minutes ago, it had to be a lie. But her eyes fixated on the last words. If they did have Mitchell, she couldn't risk his life. She glanced up, seeing that Caeruleus was more than twenty feet away, unaware that she wasn't behind him as he greeted Raiden.

She had to force her lungs to keep their rhythm as she coaxed her feet away from the lights and the celebration. *Let it be a lie*, she thought as her dazed march quickened into a frantic run along the paths. *Please let me hand myself over for a complete lie.* Either way she knew where she would end up tonight, she didn't want Mitchell to end up in the fire with her.

She ran on the balls of her bare feet. The full moon overhead was enough to reveal the paths before her. She had to pull up the fabric hanging around her legs and in crossing a stepping stone path through one of the garden pools, she missed a stone. Her shin struck the stone hard as she fell with a crash, letting out a cry of pain beneath the water before she staggered to her feet in the thigh-deep pool and back onto the stepping-stone path, limping the rest of the way, gasping in panic and pain.

The aviary was distinct—the tallest structure in the center of the grounds—its glass dome catching the moonlight. Water dripped from her hair and dress as she reached the doors—she was sure they would be locked. Her hand found the handle—a long, curled lever—and as she turned it downward, the whole night turned upside down.

❧

Raiden threw an arm around Caeruleus, relieved to find someone he knew at last. "Have you seen Nicole? She disappeared on me."

Caeruleus turned to look behind him, looking immediately confused. "I just—she was right behind me a second ago. She was looking for Mitchell; I guess she lost him."

Raiden frowned; they had promised to be sure one of them was always with her. "Which way?"

Caeruleus nodded in the direction he had come from, immediately Raiden pushed his way through the people. Raiden veered toward the edge of the crowd as he searched for the head of wild curls.

When his bare foot stepped on something dry and crinkly instead of the cool springy grass, he looked down to see an unfolded piece of parchment. He almost ignored it, except Nicole's name written on one side struck his heart. He snatched up the letter, flipped it over, and read it.

"Ruleus," he said in a panic and Caeruleus whirled around, alarmed by his voice.

Raiden couldn't utter a single word, he couldn't pass him the paper, or even let go of it. He turned and stumbled forward into a run, knowing his friend would be behind him as he sprinted down the paths across the grounds to the aviary. He could hear Caeruleus' panting over his shoulder as they ran. When they reached the doors to the aviary, one of the handles was entirely gone.

He took hold of the other handle, opened the door, and stepped inside. The shadows of plants surrounded them; the silence of moonlight fell in through the glass dome. There was no one here, not even a single bird seemed to be disturbed from its slumber. No one had been here at all.

"Ray?" Caeruleus spoke between heaving breaths.

"No," he exhaled.

"Raiden, what does it say?"

"He has them both." Saying it out loud broke his composure. He brought his shaking hands to his face, pushed his hair back, and realized his lungs had frozen. Finally, he took a breath and let it out, shuddering.

☙

Nicole fell to the floor with a wet smack, shivering as she pushed herself up. *The door handle*—she realized, releasing it from her hand. *They planted a shift token.*

"Welcome, that's quite an entrance," said a soft raspy voice.

She knew who to expect when she lifted her head. She scowled into the face of the man she had nearly crushed on the deck of the ship. "Where's my brother?"

Venarius tossed something toward her and a marigold fell to the floor at her feet.

"He's somewhere safe—for now—in the company of the siren who gave him that."

She stared at the flower, blurring as her eyes burned with tears and anger. *A siren.*

"Nicole," Venarius said, his voice was accompanied by footsteps. She looked up to see him walking toward her. "You're home now, this is where you belong."

"I want my brother to be returned safely," she demanded.

"I'm afraid it's a little late for negotiating, my dear. He belongs to her now. Rest assured, he will be alive and well as her pet, so long as she decides to keep him."

"Keep him?"

"Men enthralled by a siren will waste away if she does not sustain them. The only way to free a man from a siren is to kill him… or her."

The air fell from her lungs as Venarius stood over her. He reached down and lifted her chin until she looked up at him.

"But I'll let you see him one last time after we're finished here," he said.

Finished?

"This won't be forever," he said, raising his other hand in which a light glowed against his palm, some sort of insignia. He took her wrist, pressing his palm to her skin and his grip was an ice-cold vice. She gasped at the burning cold. It was a sudden, thought-shattering pain that swallowed her whole. All she could feel was the acidic burn when he released her wrist, leaving the insignia of light on her skin. The light faded and the icy pain sank deeper, spreading through her, sending her body into a violet shudder against the cold wave that chased her power into her core and settled there.

She shivered. Her clothes were soaked and her body was like ice from the inside out. Like she was turning to stone, her limbs grew heavy and her muscles stiffened. She sank to the floor, trembling, weak, nearly numb.

"Tell her to bring him in now."

Venarius' voice was muffled like her head was under water. *Mitch!* Her body was too heavy to lift off the floor. Her arms shook as she pushed against the polished wood, but she heard the creak of a door open and lifted her head enough to see two blurry figures enter the room, one clinging to the other.

Nicole blinked furiously and her vision cleared. Mitchell looked markedly changed in less than ten minutes from the last time she had seen him. His eyelids looked heavy and his postured sagged, not unlike the Mitchell she knew when he had had a few drinks. He didn't take his eyes off the woman with him, his arms caught around her frame while she humored him with indifferent strokes through his hair with a half-amused smile on her face.

"There now, you can say goodbye," Venarius said.

She couldn't make her mouth form Mitchell's name, and her eyes burned with the effort. It was the only warmth she could feel.

"Take him to a cell," he said. "Azra, love, you may go."

Nicole shook her head lethargically and sent the room rocking around her. "No," she could barely get the word out. Two men pried Mitchell away from the siren and held him by the arms as she sauntered away, walking past Nicole—struggled to sit upright. Mitchell writhed frantically, resisting more the further the siren moved from him until he was in a crazed fit of desperate panic, lunging, jerking and crying out in the men's arms. He didn't even see Nicole there on the floor, his eyes were frantic and fixed on the siren walking away.

"You'll realize soon enough that this is all for the best," Venarius said.

As they wrestled Mitchell from the room, he shouted and sobbed, and the sound crushed her because it wasn't for either his own fate or hers. He didn't even know she was there and didn't know he wasn't going to see Gordan or his family again. No one but the siren existed to him anymore. Nicole choked on her own sobs, nauseated by where she had led her brother, how his life would end thanks to her. She felt her stomach heave and her vision went black as she retched.

☙

Gordan looked up from the book in his hands. Suddenly, there was a pervasive gloom in the air that sent a chill down his spine. He jumped up from the cushions and dropped the book as his heart quickened with foreboding.

Raiden's voice called, heavy with dismay, "Gordan!"

He nearly tripped over a cushion in his haste, striding across the room, almost running by the time he made it outside and stopped, hit by the cloud of sorrow and shame in the night as Raiden stopped on the path to look up at him. Gordan's heart dropped—his dread confirmed by the pain in Raiden's wet eyes.

He shook his head before Raiden could even speak.

"Venarius has Nicole…and Mitchell."

Gordan's heart crumpled. He wasn't sure what was keeping him upright anymore—he swayed in the flood of Raiden's shock, pain and anger…as well as his own. His head pounded with it, and he cringed, dropping his forehead into his hand.

"We can get them back, Raiden," he said, wincing. He had to believe that or be crushed by the alternative.

Raiden nodded, pushing his hands back through his hair.

❧

Now and then Nicole opened her eyes to a fuzzy world around her, to sounds she couldn't interpret, and to the horrible thought of Mitchell being dragged away—to wither in a cell. When she was awake, she could feel the weight of her body. It ached with her power balled up tight and locked away, frozen over inside her. *He sealed my magic*, she realized. She found relief only when she sank back into unconsciousness.

Every time her mind surfaced, her heart was crushed again by Mitchell. *This is my fault. He's gone and it's my fault. That should be my fate, not his.* She just wanted to go into the dark and never come back out.

She recognized Venarius' soft rasp. "How is she today?" His voice sickened her more than the seal.

"Deteriorating," a woman answered.

"She's no good to me if she doesn't even have the will to withstand a seal until I need her," he said.

The woman spoke, "Perhaps you made the wrong choice in how you handled her brother—taking him away from the siren like that."

"I needed to break her," Venarius explained.

"Congratulations. You did…and now she's letting herself die. I wouldn't be surprised if she was doing this to spite you." The woman's voice was indifferent.

"Summon Azra then. We'll return the brother to her. If that doesn't stabilize her condition, I'll have to erase her memories entirely. They're just so…feral when you wipe away their identities."

Nicole shied away from their voices and returned gratefully to unconsciousness.

✧

Nicole opened her eyes for a brief moment and squinted skeptically at the face she saw, blinking for good measure.

"Hey," Mitchell said. Dark bags sagged under his eyes, and he looked paler than he ever had in his life.

"Are you really here?" She didn't recognize the rasp that was her voice.

"Yeah. I'm here."

"Did they hurt you?"

"No. I'm all right. What about you?"

"Tired," she said. "Glad you're here."

"Me too. I'm sorry I was gone."

"It's not your fault," she said, closing her eyes. The warm tears that slipped out and slid down her face were hot against the chill of the seal's magic in her skin.

"Hey," he grabbed her hand and squeezed. She opened her eyes. "We're gonna get out of here, Nikki," he whispered. "They'll find us."

She nodded, closing her eyes again.

"I need you to say it," he insisted.

"They'll find us," she said. Those feeble words on her lips lifted the weight on her heart for just a moment before she fell back to sleep, already sure he was just a bittersweet dream.

Sleep was restful for the first time. When she opened her eyes again, Mitchell was there, looking more like the Mitchell she knew.

"Hi," she said.

"Welcome back."

She pushed herself upright, and Mitchell leaned over the bed to hug her. "I thought you were a dream."

"I've been known to have that effect on people," he joked, squeezing her hard.

She smiled feebly. He released her, and she leaned back against the headboard.

"Looks like they've decided I'm more use to them here with you," he said with a wry curl in the corner of his mouth.

☙

Curled up on the bed where Nicole had last slept, Finnegan let out a quiet whimper and a sigh as he watched Raiden pace their room furiously. Raiden held the small crystal ball in his shaking fist. Every vision that showed him something he didn't want to see filling him with the burning urge to break it—hallways filled with smoke and fire, the woman with silver hair in his arms, himself pacing his room. He looked for Nicole but the crystal showed him darkness, her lying in a bed, Venarius speaking in her ear. Raiden's skin crawled. He nearly hurled the crystal against the stone wall. But his need for any glimpse of her kept it locked safely in his trembling hand until he had the courage to look into it again.

He was as desperate as he was horrified to know what was happening to her there in Venarius' hiding place. He looked into the crystal again, and saw Venarius' hands on Nicole's shoulders as he spoke to her. Raiden shuddered with disgust and rage that he wasn't able to step into that vision and break those vile hands for touching her. His stomach turned as he wrenched his cowardly eyes away from the crystal. *I can't*, he shook his head, but there had to be something—anything—that might tell him where they were.

"Raiden," it was Caeruleus' voice. "You have to stop, you—really, you should at least eat something."

"I can't. I have to keep looking."

"You'll go mad inside that thing," he nodded at the crystal.

"Whatever it takes to find them." He swallowed back the shame in his throat and looked into the crystal again.

Just yesterday there had been only darkness in the crystal when he searched for Nicole and Mitchell. He didn't know what changed, but today the crystal finally found them. The visions were clear, but they flickered back and forth, different possibilities. He saw blood streaming from Nicole's nose and off her chin, and his heart seized. He saw her fall to the floor screaming; he wanted to do the same.

He pulled his eyes away—Caeruleus was still there, watching with his face twisted in pain.

"Ray," Caeruleus pleaded.

Raiden straightened up, steeled himself and looked again.

He saw her writing something; no, she was signing a contract. *No!* The visions shuddered between her looking well in the rooms of some lavish house and her wasting away in a bed. His lungs tightened as the visions lurched back and forth between possibilities so quickly that he saw only seconds at a time, a shadow of herself curled up alone, Mitchell sitting beside her bed while they talked, a man's shadow moving in a dark bedroom—the rustle of sheets in a feeble struggle. His thundering heart stopped cold—a tear sliding across Nicole's temple and into her hair as she lay staring at the dark ceiling. He couldn't keep up with the shifting futures. He saw her step outside, sunlight hit her face, her eyes glazed over as she looked out upon the sea, a cliffside view. Then she was back in the bed, a withered shell of herself.

"Okay—Ray, enough!" Caeruleus smacked the crystal from his hand. The crystal sailed across the room into the wall, and Finnegan sat up, alert at the sound of crystal striking stone.

Raiden stood there his lungs frozen around a breath going stale as he realized there were tears on his face, his eyes burned, his heart ached, his stomach churned, and his body shook.

Caeruleus let out of sigh of exasperation and relief.

Raiden let the air from his lungs carefully, and took a deep breath, flinching at the fragments of futures too small and sharp to brush away, they sank like slivers into his heart. An unsettling nausea spread through him as he clung to the glimpse of Nicole staring at the ocean beyond the cliffs—her eyes darker, dark circles beneath them, their exuberance and defiance snuffed out. He didn't know which Nicole he would find when he got there, but he knew now Venarius had them somewhere on the coast.

"They're on the coast," he said, the words thick and strange in his throat.

"What?"

"I saw her outside. Venarius is hiding them in a mansion on the cliffs along the coast…that could be most of Taroth or even Nol," he said, still trying to wade through the disconcerting glimpses he remembered.

"That's something, Ray. That rules out a hell of a lot of Veil," Caeruleus said encouragingly.

"Sure," he agreed, trying to forget the silhouettes in the darkness.

☙

Every time Nicole opened her eyes, Mitchell was there. Sometimes just lying there beside her, other times slumped over in the chair beside the bed, lost in worry and rubbing his temples. Still, other times he wandered around the room like he was doing now. Seeing him always pushed back the fog in her brain. She sat up.

"Hey."

Mitchell spun around, turning his worry-furrowed face into a soft smile for her, "Hey."

"Do you stay in here all the time?"

"Yeah, I mean…they put me in the next room. There's a bunch of rooms connected, but eventually you hit locked doors. It's still a cell really."

There was food on the bedside table, and she looked at it without interest. Her stomach had been silent since Venarius placed the seal on her.

"You need to eat that," Mitchell said with a stern frown on his face.

She knew he was right. She tried not to cringe at the baby potato as she picked it up to consider it. It was room temperature, but its crispy exterior and herby aroma would normally have interested her.

Mitchell watched expectantly until she put it into her mouth and chewed. She felt like it would be easier to choke down if it had been tasteless instead; the flavor was overwhelming to the point of being sickening. With one little potato down she felt queasy, but Mitchell just nodded toward the plate.

"Go on then," he said.

She sighed and picked up another baby potato, but remarkably as she forced it down and then another, her appetite crept out of its dormancy. She was tired. She was always tired now. Her arms felt full of lead and picking food off the plate took more energy than it should have. Even keeping her eyes open was work, so she closed them as she chewed.

"They really did a number on you," Mitchell said.

"He sealed my magic. It makes me feel sluggish and heavy and just…tired."

"So, you can't use it—like before when your magic was locked away, and we didn't know it was there?"

"This is so much worse—like how I felt right before my powers emerged. It's like all the energy in my body is gone —it's crippling."

The sound of a door opening a couple rooms away made Nicole and Mitchell lock eyes. Her heart clenched, worried they were here to take Mitchell from her. Two large men and an almost equally large woman strode into the room. The woman approached the bed, and the men moved toward Mitchell. The woman scooped Nicole off the mattress easily.

"Hey!" Mitchell lunged to get past them, but the men blocked him into the corner of the room as the woman carried Nicole toward the door. She couldn't fight out of the woman's sturdy arms. Mitchell tried to get past the two men who were more like walls in his way.

"No—where the hell are you taking my sister!?" He shouted. "Get off me!"

"Mitch, stop," she pleaded as her stomach twisted around the food. She didn't want him to get hurt for picking a fight he couldn't win. Even worse, she didn't want to go wherever the woman was taking her.

She wasn't sure if she blacked out during the trip. She just remembered resisting the nausea churning in her belly; then it seemed jarringly sudden that the woman set her down in a dark blue tufted velvet chair and walked away.

"I'm told you're feeling better," a familiar voice greeted her from somewhere in the room.

She looked around anxiously and found him sitting at a large desk, looking over an array of papers.

"I'm glad," he added.

I don't care, she thought, scowling.

"I thought we should spend a little time together, seeing as you're integral to our endeavor to free this realm. I want you to know that you're not some kept dog here. You're making a noble cause possible, and for that you are truly held in the highest esteem by Dawn."

Does he think I can be flattered into being a willing participant?

Venarius put down his pen and stood up. He wore a pressed white shirt—sleeves neatly folded up—and a black vest, a black jacket on his chair. He turned toward her and crossed the room, the heels of his polished shoes knocking against the hardwood until they hit carpet and went silent. Her heart lurched a little, and she pulled her legs in close to her body, pushing herself back into the chair as far as she could go.

"It's such a shame I have to keep you like this," he said, the disappointment on his face was convincing. He reached out, but she couldn't lean any further away. He touched her cheek; she turned her face away to escape. Then he dropped his hand to her shoulder and her body tensed as she was disturbingly aware that there was only a gauzy shift on her body—a garment she didn't remember putting on herself. When—*who* had taken off her clothes and dressed her in a flimsy nightgown?

"Such an unassuming appearance. You'd be like any other unremarkable human if it weren't for what you are beneath all this. *I made you*," he said quietly. Her stomach clenched in repulsion.

He walked around the chair and stood behind her, placing his other hand on her other shoulder before he leaned down to speak beside her ear.

"It's a travesty that you've lived your whole life until now not knowing what you really are. Hessian merely hoped to create a soul, a replica of those frail imperfect beings, but thanks to *me* we made a force to be feared, even revered. You are chaos, my dear—pure beautiful chaos, the driving force of all things, in a physical form."

His hands slipped down her arms and her skin crawled. She tried to sink deeper into the seat cushions, to sink away and disappear. Her body was too heavy to do anything else. Cold terror spread from his touch, and she held as still as death hoping he'd walk away, hoping that the large woman would return to carry her back to her room.

"The world sprang from chaos. It is creation and destruction, and I bottled it. I wish I could have seen you in your glory when you destroyed the Council and their courts," he continued. "If ever gods have existed, you are the last of them, my dear, and you're mine."

Venarius' hands crept from her arms to her chest, sliding down her abdomen. "You were made to be so much more than this body, my love," he murmured. "You're not for that fool's bed."

Raiden—tears fell from her eyes. She held her breath, shaking, hoping consciousness would stop, and she wouldn't have to be here or feel this monster's hands move past her bellybutton.

His hand crawled further, between her legs, impeded by the fabric of her shift. The delicate cloth deterred his advance but did not shield her from the violation of his touch as he dragged his hands back up her chest. She felt her stomach spasm and a shudder rolled through her from deep in her core. Her head spun. He stood up and walked back to his desk.

"Back to bed for you. We have all the time in the world to talk," he said. At that the woman reappeared—had she been standing at the door watching him violate her?

Nicole had never been more relieved to be in a stranger's arms, but with her revulsion still fresh on her skin and the motion of the woman's stride rocking her, she felt the food in her belly creeping upward. She swallowed down the rising bile.

This trip seemed to go on forever and she wished she could slip into unconsciousness, but she was afraid Venarius would be there when she closed her eyes and surrendered to the dark. At last the woman walked through the doorway into familiar rooms and carried her back into the bedroom where Mitchell was still in the company of his two large attendants.

They pushed Mitchell back into the wall when he tried to get past them.

"Nicole," he said, throwing his elbows and shoulders uselessly against the two massive men. "Are you okay?"

They held him back as the woman placed Nicole on the bed—she fought to keep her food in her stomach as the woman left. The men released Mitchell. He staggered forward and bolted across the room—dropping to his knees beside the bed to look into her eyes.

"Where did she take you?"

She stared into the blanket upon the bed, her eyes attempting to get lost in the weave of the threads. "To Venarius."

"What happened?" he demanded with horror shaking his words.

She realized he could see it on her sickly face, the sweaty sheen of nausea, the horror and disgust in her watery eyes.

Mitchell trembled, leaning closer and taking her hands in his. "What did he do?"

She closed her eyes, fighting back tears and the truth.

"Nicole," Mitchell pleaded and she could see he was distraught from being trapped in here while *something* happened. Tears ran down his face. "Did he touch you? Did he—"

"No." She shook her head and squeezed his hand. "No," she insisted. "He said awful things, and with the seal…he just made me sick, literally." She managed a convincing chuckle and again swallowed back the urge to puke.

What happened would destroy Mitchell. She couldn't do that to him. He sagged, dropping his head into her lap and sobbing quietly before he picked himself back up and pulled her into his arms. As sick as she felt, she refused to let her food resurface. She needed that food. She needed what strength she could muster because there was no telling how long it would take Raiden and

Gordan to find them or how many times she would have to visit with Venarius. She knew what he would try to do sooner or later.

"I'm sorry, Nikki." He crushed her in his arms. "I'm sorry."

Her body was so heavy now that she felt herself turning into dead weight in Mitchell's embrace. He must have noticed too. He eased her back onto the bed and sat beside her, holding her hand fiercely as she fell asleep studying the deeply troubled lines on his face.

Tovar pressed his lips to his fist in thought. "We already know Venarius has the ether barred. We cannot get in and we cannot summon them. Even if you were to make it inside, we should assume you won't be able to shift out, or that there's the risk of being redirected."

"I've encountered that trap once already," Raiden admitted.

"We need a plan to get everyone out and somewhere safe," Tovar said.

"The palace is the safest place we have," Raiden said.

"How do we even know how far a redirection trap might extend around their hideout?" Gordan wondered.

"For that matter how do we know a similar trap hasn't been set around the palace, a net waiting for you to jump into it…Or anywhere we might think to retreat to for that matter," Tovar's brow creased and he slipped into troubled thought. "He has had time to prepare."

"Then we need a safe way to travel and perhaps a decoy," Gordan said. "He won't easily give up on what he thinks is his. He'll pursue us."

"Can we cloak the Tempest, Tovar?" Raiden asked.

"That would be difficult to do quickly, total cloaking of the Tempest and all its spells, power source, engines…a sea-faring ship would be simpler—you did say she's somewhere near the coast. And the ocean would also be a cloaking advantage. There's a lot of magic out there, the sea tends to confuse tracking spells that he might use to follow you."

"We'll need a couple ships," Gordan said.

"Then let's visit Cinder."

Ↄ

The smell of food, something warm and sweet, woke Nicole. She opened her eyes, surprised to feel a pang of interest in her stomach. Mitchell was asleep, bent over the mattress from his seat in the chair beside the bed. She looked around the room but caught no sight of whoever delivered the food to the bedside table.

She sat up carefully trying not to disturb Mitchell, but he lifted his head nonetheless.

"Hey," he said, fighting the weight of his eyelids. "What smells good?"

"They brought something," she said.

He turned and pulled the cover off the platter, crowded with half a dozen glistening buns filling the room with a sweet aroma of butter and yeast. "At least the food is good," he said unenthusiastically.

"How long have we been here?" She asked.

"I'm not sure how many days I spent in that cell," he said bitterly. "But I've been with you for three days—four today, I guess."

"So, a week, maybe?" She let out a sound of disgust and folded over, burying her face in the bed and hating the thought of what that time was doing to Raiden and Gordan. "They probably haven't slept in a week," she mumbled into the comforter.

"They'll find us."

"We have to do something," she grumbled.

"You can start by eating," Mitchell said. "What can you do when you're so weak that you're stuck in bed?"

She sat up with a huff and took one of the buns off the platter, pulling it apart to expose a thick purplish-red bean paste inside… *we're on the inside now.* "I can get close to him."

"Who?"

"Venarius. Yesterday, I was taken right to his study." Her stomach clenched at the thought.

"I don't like where this idea is headed," Mitchell said, taking one of the buns.

"His guard is down. He thinks he's won. I've got an opportunity here," she said.

"To do what? Do you think you can kill him while you're in this state?"

"No—I don't know what, but as long as we're here, we can learn something, like why he had Gordan locked up in Cantis, or where his other hideouts are, or who his supporters are…*anything.*"

She took a bite of the bun—a buttery bread concealing a soft gritty sweetness of bean paste in the center. *And if I get the chance to kill him, I'll take it.*

She managed to get two of the bean buns eaten before the sweetness was just too much. When she scooted to the edge of the bed and placed her feet on the floor, Mitchell tried to pick her up as he usually did to carry her to the bathroom.

"Let me try," she insisted.

"Okay," he said, pulling his hands away but standing close.

Her legs felt heavy and half asleep. She felt nothing but pins and needles in her muscles with each step. Her head pounded after several small steps. The bathroom was only five feet away but felt like twenty. At last she stepped into the bathroom and clutched the sink in triumphant exhaustion.

"Not bad," Mitchell said behind her. "At least you're as strong as a gran—*Nicole.*"

She felt it, the hot stream from her nose, running over her lips and down her chin. She peered into the mirror to see the brilliant red trail of blood dripping down her face and into the sink.

"That was harder than I thought it would be," she said with a sardonic laugh, looking up at Mitchell through the mirror.

By the time she was done in the bathroom and her nose had stopped bleeding, her nightgown had several red drips down the front and Mitchell carried her back to the bed.

Realizing he was no longer wearing his white clothes from the night of the festival, she asked, "Did they give you clothes to wear?"

"Yeah, just a few pairs of pants and a few shirts—want to change?"

"Please," she said. "I feel naked in this stupid thing."

Mitchell disappeared into the next room and returned with pants and a shirt almost identical to what he was wearing. The grey-blue shirt was more substantial than the flimsy nightgown, and though it was loose on her, she felt much less exposed. The brown pants were a little big, naturally, and too long, but she rolled them up and tucked in the excess shirt to fill in the space in the waistband. Being in real clothes made her feel safer somehow.

Getting the shirt and pants on was almost as difficult as walking to the bathroom had been; she fell back onto the bed with a sigh, ready to sleep again.

"Better?"

She smiled, "Yeah. I don't feel like a ghost anymore." The fatigue of the seal and her frail exertions were already pulling her back into unconsciousness.

⁂

Gordan was relieved to be alone with his own sickening worry and without the added torture of Raiden's. He did the only thing he could do—search from the sky. With the salty gusts rolling off the ocean and filling his wings, he flew along the coast, unsure if he would be able to sense Nicole or Mitchell even if he were soaring over them now.

It occurred to him, that perhaps despite how desperate his heart was to sift through the atmosphere for a trace of Nicole or Mitchell, it might not be the way to go about finding them. Perhaps he should be looking for something else. He had only ever been in Venarius' presence very briefly, but he had known another nec-romancer well and even centuries later he could remember the peculiar aura of a soul with an ambiguous tether to the world of the Living.

∞

Nicole awoke surprisingly clear-headed and sat up. Searching the room for Mitchell was always the first thing she did. She could hear his breathing, but when she didn't see him, she crawled across the bed and found him shirtless on the floor doing push-ups. For an envious moment she watched, hating the lethargy and lead limbs from the seal all the more.

He sprang up onto his feet and caught sight of her. "Hey, welcome back."

They heard the sound of hinges as a door in the far room opened. They looked at each other tensely, and Nicole knew Mitchell was wondering the same thing she was—it was like they knew she was awake. Were they watching or listening and if so, how often?

"Don't provoke them," she pleaded.

Mitchell frowned at her as their three unwelcome visitors strolled into the room. He took a slow breath, struggling to accept these terms of their captivity. The two man-shaped walls loomed nearby as the woman retrieved Nicole and made sure to avoid any eye contact. Nicole looked to Mitchell as the woman scooped her up and carried her from the room. His jaw clenched and his nostrils flared as he glared daggers at the woman's back.

Nicole tried to concentrate on her surroundings this time, to pay attention to the halls and memorize the way between her rooms and Venarius' study, but her mind kept slipping back to the woman hauling her off to Venarius. Nicole couldn't fathom what someone like her thought about while she carried a kidnapped woman to her captor—did she think at all? Maybe to these people she wasn't even a person, just a tool that belonged to their leader, but if this woman really believed that, would she try so hard not to look Nicole in the eye when she was carrying her like a child?

Nicole didn't make any effort to hold onto the woman or make her task any easier. She kept her arms folded against her chest, glad she was wearing Mitchell's clothes now and not that willowy shift.

When they arrived to Venarius' study, the woman entered without a knock or word, deposited Nicole on the same chair as before, and left.

Venarius sat at his desk writing something with slow careful penmanship as a young man stood beside him, eyes held carefully down. When Venarius folded the paper and handed it to the young man, he took it, poured a tiny bowl of wax over the edge of the page and then pressed a gold seal into the red glob. When he removed the the seal from the wax, the impression of the insignia glowed, and he held up the letter to the air before it disappeared in a wisp of white smoke.

This went on for three more letters, Venarius wrote—mostly a few brief lines it seemed—he folded each page and handed it to his assistant who sealed it. She was certain he had to be corresponding with followers and that seal pressed a spell into the wax that carried the letters to whomever they were addressed. Were they merely addressed to a name—could the magic be so simple?

Nicole watched the young man each time, straining to see every little thing, but all he did was press the seal into the wax. The spell seemed to activate as the wax cooled. Nicole was certain this meant the letters were exempt from whatever protections and barriers there might be around this place.

"That will be all, Josser."

The young man nodded gravely and left, keeping his eyes down and his steps quick.

"There's always work to be done," Venarius said with a sigh that sounded like satisfaction to her. "My, don't you look better today? I was afraid we pushed you too far yesterday. I know the seal is a heavy burden, but you won't have to endure it forever."

Empty promises to gain cooperation, she thought, trying not to scowl. She didn't want to look at him, so her eyes lingered on his desk instead, finding interest in the old worn journal lying there. She knew what it was instantly—the Hessian journal.

"It must be a lonely feeling, having no others like you," he said. "I'm sure you know by now that wasn't always the case."

You don't need people to come from the same place or live the same suffering to be like you, she quipped to herself. *I'm not alone. I have Gordan, Raiden, my brother, Fen, Asi—*

"You'll have companions soon enough," he added, and his words turned her heart into a knot. "It has taken me quite some time, but my dear friend Hessian—your *other* creator—can no longer conceal his secrets from me. He caused us all an undue amount of trouble, freeing our creations and disappearing like that. Fool, he even thought the Council would help him protect them, but they took his journal and set out to destroy our hard work."

Why does he talk like he was the one who created the fera? Nicole puzzled with sluggish confusion. He couldn't be that old—he looked to be in his fifties maybe—but the creators of the fera would have to be pushing one hundred and fifty. Wasn't this man supposed to be the great grandson of the man who helped Hessian create the fera?

"I'm sure he regretted his betrayal more and more with the destruction of each of our creations. He was very…fond of them. He considered them his children of sorts."

Venarius picked up the journal and held it up. "We often debated which art was superior, alchemy or necromancy. While I must concede to him in his methods of protecting his work for so long, his craft was outmatched by mine in the end. Hessian withered away in hiding, teaching apprentices in secret while I have lived three full lives now in pursuit of my goals. I have built the greater legacy."

"Three lives?" the words slipped out through her haze of disbelief.

An arrogant smile crept across his face. "When you know the secrets of death, there are ways around the inevitable. My body was doomed to expire, but a body is merely a vessel. It is simple enough to find another. Family makes it all too easy with their sentiment and attachments. It's a trade. Most souls imprint upon their bodies and reject other vessels without being sealed inside. What makes necromancer's unique is that we do not so immutably bond to our vessels and can move freely from them as we please. That is the reason we can travel into Death. My first trade was with my son. I had him very late in life and we might as well have been strangers. Still, he sat beside my deathbed dutifully."

Nicole's stomach clenched. *He trapped his son's soul in his dying body.*

"I was able to use that body for 60 years before I had to make my second trade. My son's grandson was my only visitor by those days—he was a child with an obvious fascination for this dying man called grandfather. He might have been suited for the craft himself, but I needed his lifetime more than he did."

Horror crawled through her. So Venarius *was* his great grandson—in body—and the infamous founder of Dawn in mind and soul. *It's like he expedited reincarnation, instead of dying and coming back he jumps to a young living body he can get his hands on and he remembers who he was. He'll just keep on living other people's lives.*

"And thanks to the time my son and great grandson granted me, I was able to mend Dawn's dream. I have deciphered the journal with the knowledge from our resident apprentice to Hessian's last student," he said with a chuckle.

Nicole frowned, the apprentice Raiden met in the rebel's cell. "But the apprentice told Raiden they didn't know enough to decode it."

Venarius laughed. "That little fool thought Raiden was a trick, an elaborate act to get some confession from her. To her credit she maintained her naivete to the very end. But no matter, I am only a patient man to a point. She ran out of time to help me willingly, so I had to take what I needed by force. Unfortunately for her, to uncover *all* a mind's secrets you have to break it. She threw away the better part of a lifetime for nothing."

Not for nothing—to keep you from creating more victims, Nicole thought, but now he could. Venarius had everything he needed to bring more fera into existence.

"I think, perhaps, it would be a comfort to Hessian to know this time around our creations will have someone to guide them. A mother—in a way."

Nicole realized he meant her. Her heart was a stone in her chest. This was where he had her. Could Venarius possibly know her well enough to see that she wouldn't abandon children, new fera, brought into a world terrified and intended only for their own exploitation. They didn't have to exist yet for her to know she could not leave them even if it meant never seeing Raiden or Gordan or her father again. And if they managed to get Mitchell and her out, what could they possibly do to stop Venarius from making more fera? How could they stop him once he had innocent children as his weapons? They would never get to him again if they had to go through children to do it.

I have to get that journal—it was her only option.

"Pardon me, sir," a voice said from the doorway.

"What is it?" Venarius answered impatiently.

"Something very large has been getting close to the cloaking spells…repeatedly," said a woman's voice and Nicole turned to see it was her chauffer.

"Please excuse me, I'll be gone only a moment," Venarius said.

Nicole's heart reeled. *This is a trap*, it couldn't be real. She pressed herself back into the chair as he walked past and left the room. She strained to hear their footsteps disappear, drowned out by the pounding of her heart. The desk wasn't far, the candle heating the bowl of wax still lit. All she had to do was burn it, but she had to get there first.

Taking furious breaths, she gripped the arms of the chair and heaved her lead body onto her feet, leaning into her strides. For as much as she felt like she was sprinting for the effort, she staggered across the room and barely made it to the desk still on her feet. Her head throbbed, her ears rung, and her vision wobbled. *Just burn it, even some of the pages might be enough.*

She dropped her hand onto the journal and pulled it toward her, realizing with sickening dread that Venarius needed her, but if she destroyed the journal, he would punish her the only way he could—Mitchell. She held the journal, gasping. If she burned it, he would do the same to Mitchell. She couldn't.

Warmth slid from her nose and over her lips, a vivid drop of blood fell, hitting a blank sheet of paper. Her eyes locked on it, then she searched the desk for Venarius' pen and snatched it clumsily.

Leaning heavily on the desk as she fumbled with the pen, she wiped the dripping blood across the back of her left arm. She wrote in a scrawl she could barely recognize as her own as she put Raiden's name down.

She could barely see straight by the time she got to signing her name on the page and only managed the first letter when her anxious heart insisted, she had no more time. She folded the page in haphazard thirds, picked up the bowl of wax in her shaking hand, dribbling wax across the folded paper before getting a proper pool where she needed it. She put the bowl back and picked up the seal, pressing it anxiously into the wax as she looked up at the door, knowing she wouldn't hear their footsteps in the hall over her pounding heart.

When she removed the seal from the wax, she blinked at the impression but couldn't make it out. It glowed and she picked the letter up, tossing it into the air before it slipped into the ether. She set the seal back where she found it, gathered the three pieces of blank paper marked with incriminating drops of blood and wax. She folded them hastily and shoved them into her pocket.

She knew she wasn't going to make it back to the chair, and she didn't want him to know she'd been at the desk, so she staggered toward the door as far as she could get before her legs were too heavy to lift and they were too tired to hold her up. She sank to the floor halfway to the doorway, crawling as far as she could, heaving air in and out of her lungs, her nose bleeding onto the floor.

"Do we take any precautions?" a voice came from the hallway.

"No, this is nothing to worry about. We are still perfectly protected; nothing can get in," Venarius' voice answered, drawing nearer.

"Of course, sir."

"I'm impressed," he said, his voice directly overhead. "That's farther than I would have thought you could get. You certainly didn't think it through, but I admire the effort." He chuckled. She wished she could punch him in his arrogant mouth. "At least that lesson is learned, now, isn't it?"

"Shall I take her back?"

"Yes, the brother can clean her up."

Her head spun as the woman gathered her up from the floor and lifted her. Her mind was a storm of triumph and failure, relief and horror—she'd had the journal in her hand, but it might as well have been indestructible because as long as she and Mitchell were here, she could do nothing without inviting retaliation upon him.

Nicole expected the look on Mitchell's face when the woman carried her in, blood smeared on her mouth and chin, drops on her shirt and a streak across her arm. She kept her best poker face while the woman set her down and left with the two blocky men.

"Jeez, Nikki, what the hell?" He said in a quiet voice that shook.

She opened her arms, and he took the invitation readily, closing his arms around her.

"I think I got a letter to Raiden," she whispered in his ear.

A sharp breath caught in his throat and he squeezed her tighter.

೧

Raiden paced the colonnades between his rooms and the gardens, waiting for Gordan to return and for word from Tovar that the ship was finally cloaked. He pushed his hand back through his hair every several strides until a letter slipped out of the ether and dropped at his feet.

He stared at the folded and sealed paper, feeling a sense of urgency from its manic appearance—uneven fold and spilled wax. Then his heart struck his ribs. He snatched it off the ground and stared at the seal, feeling himself grow cold at the sight of the unique design. He had seen this seal before—he remembered holding an envelope with this seal in his hands as a boy; it had come for his mother.

He swallowed the nausea in his throat, peeled the wax seal off, and unfolded the paper. His stomach tensed at the blood on the page—still damp—smeared by the writer.

RAIDEN ALDOR CAEL,

WE'RE OKAY. MAGIC SEALED. RETURN TO SENDER.

N

The air escaped his lungs. He almost forgot how to inhale through his dizzying relief. He read the first two words again and again—*We're okay*. His eyes burned. He had to pull his glasses off his face to wipe the tears away so that he could see the letter again clearly. *Return to sender*—some kind of magic had carried this letter out of the protected location. That magic was their way in—he just needed to reverse it.

He choked on a sob, distress and relief contending for his heart as he poured his gaze over Nicole's writing and blood on the page. It was easy to spiral into what he didn't know—what was happening to them there, how had she managed to send this letter? At least for now he knew all he needed to know, they were all right, and more importantly, he had a way to get to them. What still remained was arranging their means of escape.

Nicole's letter did not ease his sense of urgency; in fact, it crushed him with a heavier anxiety. The magic inside her had been sealed once before and that had nearly killed her. Venarius clearly didn't care what lasting damage might be done to Nicole's body or mind because her power would still be there for his purposes.

Raiden folded the letter up carefully and took one last look at the seal before tucking it into the inner pocket of his jacket. He hoped the ship would be ready by the time Gordan returned because Raiden couldn't allow Nicole to endure that seal any longer. And while he had time, he needed to speak with his father. He slipped through the ether before his decision was made.

"Dad," he said, materializing behind Leone as he walked down one of the vine-covered walkways.

Leone turned, startled.

"Raiden—"

"Do you recognize this seal?" Raiden asked, holding out the

letter.

His father took the letter and frowned.

"It's Venarius' seal. He contacted you?"

"No. Nicole sent it. She doesn't have a lot of time, but I need to know why Mother would have received a letter from Venarius."

"What do you mean?"

"Before she died—I remember her getting a letter with *this* seal on it. I didn't understand it then, but she was in contact with him."

"I don't know what to tell you. As far as I knew, she never had contact with Dawn. Their contract was with me."

"Wouldn't Dawn have been just as interested in seers as the Council? You don't think they would have contracted her for the Sight?"

"Dawn wouldn't have had any use for a contract with one seer in hiding when they had their own people inside the courts. They let the Council's seers do their jobs and, thus, learned what the Council learned."

Raiden frowned. That didn't satisfy him. There was a reason she was communicating with Venarius. He fell into the ether and his feet hit the dusty floor of his childhood home with a loud thud. Impatiently, he waved his hand, throwing a light charm into the air as he lunged for the little table beside the chair in the living room. He pulled open the drawer and sifted through the contents—dusty bits and bobs but no envelope.

He shifted upstairs and bent over the table in the hallway, rummaging through the slender drawer. His heart lurched at the presence of a few letters, but they were from his father—none of them had the seal.

Without even closing the drawer, he turned toward his parents' bedroom and stormed inside to the desk. He yanked open every drawer and pulled out everything—searching with meticulous anxiety. Then there it was—in his hand as suddenly as the letter from Nicole appeared before him. It was old, the parchment discolored, the wax seal dry and cracked, but there it was, identical to the one he had just received. *I didn't imagine it.*

He opened the letter.

Vervain Aldora Divale,

We intercepted your warning to the Council about the fate of Cantis. As noble as it was to expose yourself as a seer—I am afraid I just cannot allow you to jeopardize my plans. If you want to ensure the safety of your son, you will do so with your silence. We will be watching and listening. Take care.

Raiden jerked the letter away from his face and lunged back through the door. He stopped cold in the hall, spotting the new door that didn't belong in memories of his childhood home—the door Nicole had put there, leading to her chamber in the palace of the keys. It reminded him—he looked across the hall at the door to his bedroom—that door would now take him back to Yuma—home—to where Nicole and Mitchell's father waited, not realizing his children were lost. *No—we'll get them back.* Raiden insisted, swallowing the lump of doubt and dread in his throat. He didn't want to walk through that door to tell Michael they were gone—that he had failed to get them back. The sight of the door pained him and responsibility pressed on him. He had to close his eyes to break away from it and to step back into the ether with even more determination to get them back.

He emerged from the ether to land by his father's side. He thrust the old parchment at him.

"I always thought she knew what was coming," Raiden said heavily.

Leone read the page with a furrowed brow. He lowered the letter. "We try our best to do what's right, Raiden. We don't always succeed."

"That's not an option this time," he said, looking his father in the eyes.

His father nodded.

Thirty-seven

Gordan swooped down toward the royal grounds of Eanna, his heart pounding with anxiety and exertion. He landed upon a garden path, transforming hastily, his hastily-conjured clothes askew. He straightened the white turtleneck and tugged on the sleeves.

"Gordan!"

He wheeled around, startled by the exuberance in Raiden's voice, and concerned to see him running toward him in the same maroon sweater and jeans that he'd been wearing the last three days.

"What is it?" Gordan asked.

Raiden hardly slowed, running headlong into Gordan and seizing him by the shoulders, his blue green eyes wide and watering. Words tumbled from his mouth so quickly all Gordan heard was a jumble of breathless excitement. Even his emotions in the air were an inexplicable jumble.

"Slow down," he begged.

"We have a way in," Raiden said. He dropped his hands and pulled a letter out from where he had tucked it into his waistband. "She sent us a way in."

Gordan took the letter, turned it over in his hands, read it, and understood with a surge of painfully delicious hope that burned his eyes. He nearly forgot what had been on his mind when he arrived; then, it hit him.

"Raiden, I think I was close to where he's hiding," he said.

"You think?"

"It's a hunch, I detected something peculiar and grew disoriented after getting closer to the source; it could have been him. Wherever they are is heavily cloaked. I didn't see any houses, but I'm pretty certain I was repelled by a spell."

"You remember where this was?"

"Yes, I'm sure I can find it again."

"Good, we have to know where we're going. We have one shot at this," Raiden said.

Gordan nodded. "Are we planning an escape or a fight?"

Raiden sighed, avoiding a direct answer. "It's likely the best chance we have to take care of Venarius. I doubt we'll get this close again with the element of surprise, but we wouldn't stand a chance without Nicole, and she's in no condition to fight."

"As much as I want to see Venarius dead, I think rescuing Nicole and Mitchell is more important."

"Then we plan to sneak them out, but we go in prepared for a fight."

"When you reverse the spell that sent this letter," Gordan said, handing it back to Raiden. "It's going to take you directly to her. Remember, there's a chance that could mean directly to Venarius. How do you think she sent this?"

Raiden sighed. "She used his seal. She had to be in his study."

They both knew she hadn't been there by accident. As strong as she was, under a seal she would be lucky if she was able to walk on her own. Gordan could feel how unnerved Raiden was by the idea and tried to derail those horrified thoughts.

"What time did you get this?"

"It was," he shook his head, thinking. "Around three o'clock."

Gordan was struck by the coincidence. "That's about the time I was repelled from the cliffs. I'm starting to feel pretty certain that's where they are."

"I am too."

☙

"Is it just me, or is the waiting worse now that we know they have the means to reach us?" Mitchell murmured between them.

"It's definitely worse," Nicole agreed. It had been difficult to sleep—even for her.

She couldn't stop thinking about the journal. If Venarius knew it was gone, he would lash out and she would have no way to hide it from him. She couldn't safely destroy it even if she got close to it again. She couldn't risk Mitchell's safety. It was impossible to know when Raiden and Gordan would come for them, and timing her removal of the journal with their escape was a fantasy, but they would surely come soon.

Her gaze always devoid of interest, Nicole looked around their room. A cluster of books sat atop a dresser. She noticed that one of the spines was slender and tall among the shorter thick volumes, not unlike the Hessian journal.

"Hey," she said, sitting up. "See that book, the tall one?"

"Yeah," Mitchell answered with disinterest.

"Can you get that for me, I want to see something."

He sighed, retrieved the book, and flopped back down on the bed, "What are you thinking?"

She turned the book over in her hands. It didn't look anything like the old worn-out journal, but it was the right size. She took a firm hold of the pages and pulled until the glue holding the sewn edges of the pages to the spine split.

"Where'd that nightgown go?" She asked, leaning over the bed and spotting the ruffled hem peeking out from under the bed. She snatched it and sat up, that alone had her breathing labored. She found a weak point in the hem and ripped the garment apart—the rending fabric cut through the silence and was satisfying to her ear. In no time she had two good long strips of cloth.

"Okay," Mitchell said, confused.

"What if I can take the journal without it looking like I took the journal?" She explained.

"Oh," he said, his confusion melting into enthusiasm.

"Will you help me tie this to my leg?"

"Yeah." He scooped her up and carried her to the bathroom.

She had to keep in mind that the pages couldn't be noticeable when she was carried, so she tied the fabric to her leg and tucked the book pages in toward her inner thigh where it wouldn't be felt when she was carried by the woman who chaperoned her through the halls. Mitchell carried her back to the bed and set her down.

"I couldn't tell it was there," he said as he gathered up the unused scraps of the nightgown and stuffed them under the bed.

"Good," she said, her heart pounding anxiously. She still wasn't even sure she wanted to do this.

A silver covered platter materialized on the bedside table.

❧

"Are we going in with swords drawn to take out Venarius or are we rescuing them quietly?" Caeruleus asked.

"I can't risk a fight with Nicole and Mitch in there. We have to do what's best to get them out safely."

"Is the ship ready to go?" Caeruleus asked.

"It is, and thanks to those sails it can be there in a few hours," Raiden answered.

"When are we doing this then?"

Raiden turned the small crystal ball over in his hands. He needed the Sight now more than ever, but he wasn't sure if he should trust it. Could they rely on what he might see or would it lead them down the wrong path?

❧

Nicole shook her head. "Mitch, I don't know how long the decoy will go unnoticed. Assuming I even get the chance to swap them. We don't know how long we might be waiting for Raiden and Gordan to show up."

"You sent that letter yesterday. You know they've been putting together a plan this whole time. Do you really think it will take

them long now that they have a way in?"

She sighed. "No." But she was terrified of risking Mitchell's safety again.

"If anything, we don't have a lot of time for you to do this. If you get the chance, you have to take it."

She knew that woman would come to take her to Venarius and her heart thudded in sick anticipation. They waited what seemed like hours until Nicole thought she might be wrong about being taken to Venarius today. Then her escort arrived and her heart dropped into the pit of her nausea.

Nicole was better at staying awake and paying attention to the route to Venarius' study, but yesterday she had turned left out of their rooms and today her escort went right. Nicole noted a porcelain swan on a narrow table, but eventually she realized she saw the same painting of a deer twice—was this woman walking her in circles on her way there?

When at last they arrived, Nicole was set down in her usual chair inside Venarius' study, she resisted the urge to adjust the pages tied to her leg.

"Welcome back. I see your brother cleaned you up nicely. At least he's doing his part," Venarius said from the chair behind his desk.

She clenched her jaw until her teeth hurt and her ears rang.

Venarius stood and he sighed, trying to sound concerned, but it only sounded calculated to her. "It's time you understand what your purpose really is, Nicole. What Dawn is working toward isn't some terrible scheme. It's freedom." Today he wore a three-piece suit in its entirety—dressed to impress—was it for her?

Nicole watched him sink into his self-aggrandizing speech and tried to think of some way she could get him to walk out of the room long enough for her to steal the journal pages.

"I know you share Dawn's feelings about the world," he said.

You don't know shit, she thought, struggling to keep an indifferent expression on her face.

"You're afraid the old world is dying without magic."

A chill slithered down her spine to hear him recite what she had confessed to Raiden in the Meridian forest. Had he been there too—listening—watching?

"The world wasn't meant to be torn in two, and your world has suffered more from the amputation of magic than we have from our exile here. Dawn believes in restoring the world—the balance. Your purpose, and the purpose of those like you yet to be, is to weaken the barrier between Veil and the old world so that it will crumble and magic can return."

"Not everyone wants this sanctuary here to be erased," she said.

"Not everyone wanted to be here in the first place," he countered. "Some may not like it, but it can't be denied that this realm was never meant to be, and the world we used to call home is dying without us."

She didn't want to believe him, but she did.

"You said you wished the old world still had magic. We want the same thing, you and I. You can be a part of fixing what has been broken for too long. This doesn't have to be a prison. I don't have to be your enemy."

"What would I be agreeing to?" she wondered, buying time in this room, time to think of some way to get him out of it.

He paced, his footsteps silent on the carpet. "You would agree that you belong to me, that I grant you freedom so long as you come when I call. Your life wouldn't change all that much. You'll help me guide the new generation of your kind, and when we're ready, we'll spread enough magic through the old world to wipe the barrier away."

She thought about it. Was there some way she could agree and get close enough to kill him?

"You can't live like this for long, Nicole. A seal on someone like you will kill you slowly, eat you from the inside out. I hate to see you this way."

"You're going to let my brother go, too? You're not going to keep him as collateral?"

He chuckled. "I don't need collateral. We deal in contracts here.

The kind you can't break. Every stipulation is clearly stated—you agree to come when summoned, to obey direct orders, to preserve my life as you would yours; and I agree to grant freedom to your brother and you."

Her heart sank, but her mind raced. *Get him out of the room.* "Could I have some time alone...to think about it?"

He smiled. "I suppose that's fair. You deserve to consider this offer uninfluenced by me or your brother. The decision is yours." He stood up and left the room with a confident smirk on his face.

He left. He really left. Her heart reeled. She took a few long steadying breaths because she had to make her way across the room to the desk first. She slipped her feet off the chair and onto the floor, pushing her weight upright for a wobbly second. *I've done this before*, she thought fiercely, taking a deep breath and marching toward the desk. Arriving at last, she steadied herself for a moment and checked her nose for blood—it was still dry.

She had to fight her urge to hyperventilate as she opened the drawer and found the journal exactly where she had seen him drop it. First, she slipped the decoy from the fabric ties around her thigh and laid it on the desk. Then she grabbed the journal from the drawer, opened the cover, grabbed the pages and pulled. The journal was old—glue brittle and weak—and the pages peeled free with ease.

Her heart pounded furiously as she placed the decoy pages into the journal cover—practically perfect—and put it back into the drawer. She snatched the journal pages and pushed them down into her pants, fumbling with the cloth ties around her leg and curling the pages against her thigh to pull the ties up, snug and secure around the pages. She swayed on her feet without a hand on a steady object. She nearly fell before she had the pages secured to her thigh. By the time she was done, she was out of breath. Panting, she eyed the chair across the room—she still had to make it back—it looked so far. Her nose wasn't bleeding yet, though, and she felt powerful despite the weakness of her body.

Setting her sights on the tufted armchair, she marched back as quickly and steadily as she could, catching herself on the chair as she collapsed into it. *I have the journal,* the thought bounced around her spinning head. She pushed herself upright in the chair and pulled her legs up to her chest, her arms wrapped around them as she tried to slow her breathing. *I really did it.* Blood slid over her lip before she could pinch her nose shut. Her head was still pounding, and the blood snuck past her fingers. She wiped it away as best she could, looking at the red stain on her hand. The sight unnerved her. Could this really be a victory—would it work? Then it occurred to her that she still had to give Venarius an answer; he would expect it when he returned. Her heart pounded with worry. Would he see the blood and suspect something? She wiped her face on the dark fabric over her knees.

How would he take her rejecting his offer? He could threaten Mitchell's life if she didn't sign a contract—then what? Would he humor her if she asked for even more time, another night, or to tell her brother first? If she said yes, he might insist she sign it here and now. She was stuck. *No, no, no,* this is not how she planned it. This was—

Two figures lurched out of the ether and she jumped, smothering her gasp behind her hand. She knew the heads of auburn and black hair before they turned around. Raiden lurched toward her, and swooped in as she threw her arms open. Tears came too swiftly to stop them, and she could feel his gasp in his chest as he pulled her out of the chair.

His arms locked around her and she shook. Her fear of the future still clinging to her even though Raiden's arms promised it couldn't reach her now. No, she was more terrified than before.

"I've got you," he murmured.

"He's coming back," she said frantically. "Mitch—he's back in our room."

Raiden held her tight, as they moved to the door. Caeruleus checked the hall and nodded.

"Where?" Caeruleus whispered.

"I don't know the way back," she admitted.

"We'll find him," Raiden whispered.

They stopped at every corner. Caeruleus pulled a handful of fine sand from a satchel hanging at his side. He threw it into the air as someone rounded the corner making him fall to the carpeted floor with a thud.

Venarius walked back into his study and stopped cold when he saw Nicole was nowhere in sight. He wheeled around and stormed down the hallway, shaking with anger. *How?* Well, he knew where she was headed—she wouldn't leave without her brother.

Caeruleus snuck up behind the guard walking down the hall ahead of them, tapped her shoulder and blew the sand into her face as she turned around. With a fleeting swell of satisfaction, Nicole watched the woman who had carried her to Venarius topple to the floor face down.

"There," Nicole hissed when she spotted the porcelain swan on a small table. "It's that way." She scowled gratefully at that stupid swan as they passed.

They weren't halfway down the hall before the door to her room opened. Caeruleus and Raiden stopped. Nicole's heart clenched when Mitchell stumbled out into the hall followed by Venarius. Mitchell straightened up, wearing defiance on his face until he saw them down the hall. His eyes met hers and she saw his heart break. Venarius drew a black-bladed knife, and she threw herself out of Raiden's arms.

Venarius threw his arm around Mitchell so fast that she didn't see the blade, but she saw the sudden flash of red. She screamed, staggering to the floor as Mitchell dropped. She felt Raiden's arms wrap around her as she shook, agony more terrible than a human voice could contain clawing at her throat. The world went blurry, it went red, and she screamed until she turned to fire and felt something break inside her.

A distant scream wavering in the air pierced Gordan's heart and his legs buckled beneath him where he waited outside the mansion, the ships waiting for them below the cliffs. The sound didn't stop. He shuddered, knowing it was Nicole, knowing they'd lost someone, watching in utter dismay as the mansion erupted, creaking, snapping and moaning into a spinning storm of wreckage.

Waving debris away with his hand and clearing his path toward his study, Venarius walked through the destruction. Half the mansion had been swallowed up by the earth, luckily many rooms, including his study, escaped the pit. Smoldering beams, charred stones, disfigured furniture—all drifted through the air as he picked his way to his heavy oak desk, broken in the middle, the legs snapped. He wrenched open the top drawer with a moan, relieved to see the journal had survived the destruction.

As much as he hated to lose, for all intents and purposes, he had what he needed. He could accomplish his goals without her, without all the trouble that came with her. He pulled the journal out of the drawer and knew it would be more prudent to focus on his new creations than punishing the old one and those she loved. As he walked away from his desk, the sound of paper slipping to the ground in a flutter stopped him cold.

He looked down at the empty journal cover in his hands and then down at the pages on the ground and saw the title page of a modest novel at his feet. His breathing quickened as he stooped down to pick up the pages, his hand shaking in outrage at this trick. *Fine*, he wouldn't let her walk away from her fate.

"Sir?" his apprentice asked timidly.

"We're done here," he said, gripping the journal cover and the decoy pages fiercely.

❧

Caeruleus watched, leaning against the door of his cabin as Raiden paced inside, passing the bed again and again. Nicole was safe next door under Gordan's watch and still asleep since the destruction of the mansion the day before. Venarius would follow, they all knew he would, and they had to be ready. But Raiden struggled to pull his thoughts from the rubble—that horrible moment ringing sharp and constant in his mind. He wished he could stop seeing it—Mitchell's face and the swift blur of the knife.

He sank to Caeruleus' bed, dropping his face into his hands. His eyes burned but his tears were spent. "I made the wrong choice," he said.

"Ray," Caeruleus implored gently.

"Why didn't I look further ahead in the crystal? I shouldn't have jumped at the first opportunity."

"You saw what was happening there with Venarius—we had to take that window. If we hadn't there's no telling—"

Raiden flinched. "But we did and Mitchell is gone!" he snapped, lifting his wet face from his hands.

"We can't change it, Ray," Caeruleus said mournfully.

Raiden nodded. He swallowed back the lump in his throat. It was just too painful to accept—almost as agonizing as replaying Mitchell's final moments. He shook his head. Their failure sank into his heart, weighing it down as he struggled to imagine a world without Mitchell in it. Raiden couldn't think of Mitchell without hearing Nicole's laughter—would he ever hear that again? It hit him with a shudder and another wave of tears. Mitchell was gone.

Nicole knew she was on the ship before she opened her eyes from the gentle rocking of the bed, the distant rush of the sea outside, and smell of salt everywhere. The darkness of sleep had been only that— darkness, emptiness, no doppelgänger, no unseen blade. She wished she could believe it had been a bad dream, but her body felt brittle and bruised. Even closed, her eyes felt sore and swollen. She couldn't convince herself the terrible images haunting her mind hadn't really happened.

She heard a faint knock and, strangely enough, Mitchell's voice. *Are you awake yet?*

She opened her eyes to the familiar cabin. It was empty and silent. She was alone. She was not waking from a nightmare. Her eyes burned painfully, so she closed them. Another faint knocking—the countless sounds of a ship at sea sounded almost like footsteps. The window whined and a robust breeze whirled around the room.

Come on—we should be celebrating. Mitchell's voice sounded like Déjà vu.

She opened her eyes again to see the window swinging by itself in the breeze. *He would think that,* she thought. Escaping Venarius, stealing the journal, he would have cheered—but those were empty victories now.

A full bladder pushed her out of bed, igniting muscle memory through her barely conscious daze. The warmth in her core, though small and quiet, was there—her power no longer sealed inside her. Though she was tender—everything ached—she could move her legs easily. Each step was stiff but not heavy, in fact she felt so unnaturally light now that she wondered if she was dissolving away.

As she stepped into the little toilet closet, she passed the narrow basin sink and didn't even glance at the reflection that passed in the mirror. She looked down to unfasten her pants, and she realized she was still wearing the clothes Mitchell had given her. When she pushed them down to sit, her mind froze at the sight of the journal pages still tied against her thigh.

The pages were warm with her body heat. She tugged them free of the torn cloth strips. Her prize—she stared down at the manuscript in her lap and only felt disgust. She threw it out the bathroom door in a flutter and it landed with a slap against the cabin floor. When she stood in front of the sink and looked up at the mirror, she wasn't sure what she expected, but she was confused and slightly horrified by the creature she saw.

It was her in some semblance, but the eyes were blood red instead of white around the irises. *Hemorrhage,* the word crept out from the back of her mind when she remembered how the effort of just walking across the room had made her nose bleed while her body bore the stress of her sealed magic.

She blinked and the doppelgänger in the mirror didn't change. It didn't look quite human, nor did it feel human anymore. Unnerved and a little nauseated by the gentle rocking of the cabin, she turned away from her reflection and walked mindlessly back to her pillow, not remembering the steps between sink and bed by the time she sank back into the mattress.

The sound of paper sliding against wood touched her ears, and she knew someone was there before he spoke.

"Nicole?" It was Gordan's voice, fragile and shaky.

"It's the journal," she said, not wanting to speak what was devastating them both.

He crawled onto the bed and settled in behind her, but she couldn't bring herself to roll over and face him. She couldn't look him in the eyes and see Mitchell's absence there. She had a vague idea of days passing as the sky was sometimes bright and blue outside the window, other times it was an inky black shadow pressing in against the glass.

Sometimes Gordan was there lying beside her. Other times Raiden would be there. She couldn't hold them tight enough. When one was with her, she knew the other was probably on deck—worrying… watching. When would Venarius come? The question haunted her thoughts like Mitchell's final moments.

They brought her food that she would have turned down, but she kept hearing Mitchell's voice fresh in her mind, *you need to eat that*. She did because it was the only way to silence his nagging concern in her head. She couldn't take it, his voice tore her heart to shreds, so she ate and went back to sleep to search the darkness. *Where are you?* She was ready for her penance, to bear it all, every wound she had caused— Raiden's, Gordan's, Fen's and Mitchell's— she yearned for every last cut.

∾

Raiden felt the mattress move, the bedframe creak, and opened his eyes to see Nicole was no longer curled up against him. He leaned away from the headboard and scanned the cabin to find her at the window, looking outside.

"Can we go outside?" she asked, almost like she was talking to the window instead of him. "I hate it in here."

He threw his legs off the bed and stood up in one lithe movement to cross their cabin. "Of course we can," he said.

She turned away from the window, her arms folded tight against her like a shield. The corners of her mouth pulled back, but the attempt at a smile was really just heartache stretched thin on her lips. She didn't unfold her arms, but she leaned on him a little. He put his arm around her shoulders to steady her.

"The Tempest is waiting for us in Eanna," he said as they made their way upstairs to the deck. She nodded.

Once they were on deck, she eased away from him and he released her, his hand lingering reluctantly on her shoulder as long as it could. He kept his eye on her as she made her way toward the bow and turned her face into the wind. A hand came to rest on his shoulder and he turned to see Gordan was there beside him. His eyes were bloodshot and his eyelids heavy.

Nicole wandered toward the bow, drifting to peer over the side and down at the water below the anchor waiting for its time to drop. Her gaze fell to her feet, bare against the wooden deck. She hadn't noticed, they didn't seem to feel the cold. She realized curiously that she hadn't felt anything after escaping the stale cabin below.

She turned her face into the wind but wasn't invigorated by it. Her hair whipped and her clothes flapped, salt hit her nose and tongue, but it was all lackluster sensory information to her now. A leathery orange-brown length of seaweed near her feet pulled her absent-minded hand toward it and she picked it up, popping the floats in a trance, feeling the pressure build between her fingers before the little orb burst with a sharp crack. Once she popped every float, she tossed the seaweed into the air over the side of the ship and watched it flail and fall into the sea. The waves churning around the ship sucked it down—*gone, just like that*. Her mind crawled painfully back to Mitchell. Escaping the grief-saturated air of her room offered no escape from his absence. *I need help*, she thought. He had always been there. There could be no such thing as a world where Mitchell wasn't there when she needed him. *How do I stay here? How do I do this?* She didn't think she could take any more, not without him.

"You should get some sleep, Gordan," Raiden said.

"I don't know that I could even if I wanted to," he said and glanced across the deck at Nicole's back.

"I don't want to alarm you, but we shouldn't let her be alone… not even for a minute." Gordan felt Nicole's anguish. It had settled into something quiet, growing deeper every day, and she was standing on the edge of it. Its enormity pressed on him and sometimes he found himself gasping for air. If he was being honest, he was a little afraid of sleeping under that weight. Still, he hadn't slept since Nicole and Mitchell were taken from the festival. His body would sleep eventually, whether or not he went willingly.

"Stay with her, then," Raiden said. "I'll wake Caeruleus. It's your turn to get some sleep, or at least try," he insisted, turning to descend the steps.

Gordan sighed, watching Raiden go for just a moment before he turned his eyes back to Nicole anxiously as she stood at the side of the ship watching the sea, squinting into the wind. His throat tightened around words he couldn't say. He knew his time with Mitchell would be all to brief, but…*I didn't get to say goodbye.*

Raiden was only a few steps below deck when several ominous thuds overhead startled him and he wheeled around to see Gordan tipping toward him into the stairway. Raiden lunged forward. Gordan toppled into his arms. Raiden fell back into the wooden rail— hissing through his teeth—trying to hold on to Gordan and catch himself before they both tumbled down the stairs. Gordan was asleep.

"Gordan!" Raiden said, giving him a shake—no response. "Caeruleus!" he yelled as he sidled out from beneath Gordan and left him slumped against the railing on the stairs. He ran back up to the deck to find it riddled with sleeping forms.

"Evulgo," he said in haste and the spell rolled through air, over the deck, revealing the standing form of some stranger near the bow as he stooped to drag Nicole off the deck and throw her over his shoulder.

Raiden reached behind his neck only to realize he wasn't wearing his sword as he lurched forward, racing to reach the stranger before he made it to the plank across to the enemy ship, wobbling beneath its failing cloaking spell. He reached out and caught the man's braid, pulling back on it hard.

"Put her down," he demanded, his voice breathless.

But the man smiled smugly and complied—heaving Nicole forward, off his shoulder over the side of the ship.

"No!" he cried. The man wheeled around, seizing on Raiden's shock. The man lunged, a knife in hand, and Raiden bobbed aside, narrowly avoiding the knife's plunge toward his neck.

"*Decerpo*," Raiden cast, and the knife disappeared from his foe's hand to appear in his instead.

"Ray!" Caeruleus called across the deck.

The man lunged again without realizing his knife was gone. Raiden stepped directly into his path and pushed the knife up through the man's jaw.

"Water! Wake them up!" Raiden shouted back to Caeruleus as the man gurgled and stumbled forward, falling into a heap on the deck. Raiden lurched forward, leaning over the side of ship to peer into the water. A simple sleeping spell would have been washed away immediately—but there was no sign of Nicole in the water.

Thirty-eight

The slumber broke as the water swallowed her. She blinked through the sting of salt in her eyes. Entranced by the light wobbling through the surface above her. She couldn't muster up the desire to stop herself from sinking. She sank and there was no one there to pull her back up. She was alone at least, not dragging anyone else down with her this time and that thought was peaceful. The darkness at her back welcomed her, and all the monsters in her memory were there waiting kindly.

Why shouldn't she? Up there, something even worse was waiting for her in the sunlight. If she went back, he would keep coming for her and people she loved. If she let it end now, they wouldn't be in anymore danger. If Mitchell could do it, then couldn't she?

Her lungs pulled helplessly for air and a dark shape moved through the water beneath her. *You're scarier than anything out there,* Mitchell's voice insisted. A tentacle crept past her from the depths reaching toward the surface. She looked up at the two ship hulls above her—people she loved on one. Was Venarius aboard the other? Anger stirred in her chest. Of course he was; he was always close. The shorter narrower hull above, that's where he waited. She would drag it down with her if she could. *Embrace it*—Mitchell's memory hurt more than her straining lungs did, more than the acidic burn in her heart and the salt against her eyes. The man who took him was up there. Something pushed her, prodding her in the back, gently reversing her descent as another tentacle reached past her. *Embrace it.* She pulled herself toward the surface. The light above erupted into bubbles as a body crashed into the water—Raiden.

He caught her arm and pulled her swiftly to the surface. They gasped. Oxygen hit her brain and sent it spinning. They bobbed between the two ships and Venarius stood glaring down at them from the deck. Nicole smiled up at him, her face tight with pure derision, her mouth devoid of humor. The first dark tentacle reached up and grasped the side of Venarius' boat. He threw his startled gaze down to see the second tentacle. His composure cracked as his crew shouted.

"Leviathan!" they cried and several more tentacles emerged from the water and the ship's hull moaned. Raiden started, pulling her closer.

"Ray!" Caeruleus shouted above them. He dropped a rope ladder. When they both had hold of it, it undulated with the life of a spell and pulled them up onto the deck.

The captain moved the ship away from the enemy as the leviathan embraced Dawn's vessel and pulled them into the deep. She was sure Venarius was no longer on board that ship as it buckled and sank in the churning waters.

"Too bad he didn't go down with it," she muttered as the bubbling and churning water disappeared in the growing distance.

❧

Nicole returned to the cabin and slipped into the darkness of sleep again like the warm welcoming waters of a bath. In her dream she walked until she heard her footsteps double and she turned around. There she was, her doppelgänger, unseen sword in hand. Nicole turned her palms out in invitation and watched her double walk toward her, into her. She heard the clatter of a falling blade and looked around her feet, but there was nothing. When she raised her gaze, someone else stood before her in the darkness. His face made her stomach churn. He raised his knife, suddenly Mitchell was there. She woke up retching.

Gordan was startled when she woke up heaving although her stomach had nothing to purge. He watched over Nicole anxiously. Something had changed—her near constant sleep and her silence were the same—but below the surface there was an unsettling shift. Her pain grew darker and quieter, it blackened and simmered into something strange, muddled, like grief and hate and love and rage were all the same force now.

When he settled onto the bed beside her, she opened her eyes. They were steady, almost blank as she looked back at him. She slid her hand across the space between them and took his hand.

"I'm sorry," she murmured.

His heart clenched. His throat constricted. His eyes burned, and closing them did not stop the tears. He had been waiting to be there for her when she was ready to let out her grief. He had braced himself for the cascade of *her* pain, not expecting her to open *his* wound and expunge his festering sorrow with two delicate words.

❦

They sailed the entire way back to Eanna and took the canals to Hypatia as they had before. Raiden was so worried about traps laid by Venarius that the ether itself could no longer be trusted. They had no way of knowing how many precautions Venarius had taken or how many traps he might have set—like the one that sent Raiden into a cell when he tried to leave Tovar's shop back in Atrium. They didn't want to risk falling into a similar trap waiting for them to take the easy way back to Eanna or the palace of the keys.

Nicole couldn't manage to care either way; in fact, the familiar journey to Hypatia had an uncanny way of blurring the lines between now and their first arrival so that she could believe for a moment Mitchell was standing beside Gordan to her right. She knew if she leaned to look past Gordan, he wouldn't be there. Looking for him broke the spell, and the brief moments where the past seemed to coexist with the present, like they could both be true, both troubled and soothed her.

They made it to their cluster of houses on the grounds of Hypatia, and it was so unchanged that she didn't know *when* she was anymore. Raiden led her by the hand to their rooms, and she walked through them slowly, unsettled by it all. They felt like a dream, each step she took was suspended between the present world with its strange void left by Mitchell and the past that seemed so tangible where he was alive somewhere out of sight. It seemed unfathomable that the world could be utterly unchanged by his death.

She stepped through the curtain into the bedroom and saw Finnegan curled up tightly upon their bed. He raised his head from sleep when she sank down onto the low bed and lay down beside him. Rather than his usual exuberance, Finnegan tilted his head at her and regarded her somber countenance with a gentle purr. He lowered his head back down, and she stroked his neck until the low rattle of his purring filled the silence.

"Raiden!" She recognized the distant shout as Fen's. "Are they back?!" she asked breathlessly, her voice clear and close this time.

Nicole winced.

"Nicole's here," Raiden answered heavily.

There was silence and Nicole knew the look on Raiden's face, knew Fen could see it written there, hear it in the omission of Mitchell's name from his answer.

"No," Fen said, her voice shaky. "No, we can't lose Asi *and* Mitch."

"What do you mean 'lose Asi,'" Raiden hushed his urgent voice, but the breeze shudders were open and his voice carried.

Nicole's temperature spiked, and she climbed off the bed hastily, ignoring the subtle tilt of the floor beneath her feet as she stormed through the room.

"The emissary from Taroth recognized her in Nol. He and Asi's father came to see Queen Belen. They took Asi back to Taroth," Fen said through tears.

Nicole walked outside—her mind set on finding Belen. She marched down the steps, and onto the path through the gardens and pools.

"Nicole, wait!" Raiden called.

She didn't slow her pace. Struggling to remain a semblance of calm, she forced her breathing into a slow steady rhythm. Her eyes finally fell on the aviary and her heart raced. Approaching the doors to the aviary again made her heart pound. The darkness of night flickered in her vision but she shook her head and marched toward the doors. They were open this time and she could see Belen ahead of her.

When Belen caught sight of Nicole, she jumped, throwing her hand against her heart. "Nicole, my dear, you're—"

"You let them take Asi?" Her voice shook with anger and panic.

Belen wore her shame in the open. "You have to understand my position. I could not deny them—"

"You *know* what Taroth is like."

"She is a citizen of Taroth, not Eanna. They threatened war, Nicole. Eanna cannot endure a war right now. I have to look out for my people."

"It comes down to borders, then? Only the people of Eanna are *yours*—all the others out there be damned. For all your talk of the freedom everyone deserves, *the sacred right to ownership of ourselves*," she spoke Belen's own words with venom. "That's all worthless because Asi wasn't born in Eanna?"

"Nicole, I—"

"It would be different, though, if they came and dragged away one of *your* people. Isn't that right?"

The birds were screaming and flapping in agitation. From the corner of her eye, she could see the lush vegetation of the aviary sag and wilt, leaves browned and curled.

She didn't want an answer; she wanted to get Fen home. She needed the people she had left to be safe again. When she turned around, Finnegan was standing behind her. Just outside the doors to the aviary stood Raiden and Fen holding onto Gordan's hand with both of hers.

"We need to go home," she said as she passed through the open doors. "Then we're going to Taroth."

❧

The Tempest was mind-numbingly silent the whole way back to the midlands. No one knew what to say to anyone. Nicole knew Caeruleus had shared the latest news with everyone by the looks she received from Captain Rhee, Priseil and Andrus. She knew they wanted to express their condolences, but they seemed to know silence was gentler. There was an anxious tension in every corridor and room aboard the Tempest; everyone wondered if Venarius would attack; they all just wanted to be back at the palace where they could finally sleep and where the word 'safe' meant something.

Raiden's relief was palpable to Nicole when they walked through the doors of the palace. Nicole's pit of dread deepened with every step because she had to escort Fen back home to Keren's cottage in the orchard, and they would have to tell her that Asi had been taken back to Taroth. Nicole held onto Raiden's hand as they made their way through the palace.

"I'm going to have a word with Tovar about going to Taroth," Raiden murmured to her. She nodded, releasing his hand as they reached the door to Tovar's workroom.

Raiden watched Nicole, Gordan and Fen walk on as he stopped at Tovar's door and knocked, even though it was open. Tovar looked up from the book in his hands. His eyes lit up with surprise.

He set down his book. "Raiden," he greeted somberly.

"Tovar, will you send a letter to Taroth, please?" he asked. "We want to take the king up on his invitation."

"Certainly—"

"Thank you," he said with tired sincerity.

"When were you thinking of visiting?" he wondered.

"Immediately," Raiden said.

"So soon after—" he let his remark fall silent. "I do hope you try to get some rest. I did a thorough check around the palace; there don't seem to be any traps, no redirection spells. It's safe to come and go as usual."

"That's good to hear. I don't know what we'd do without you, Tovar."

"You wouldn't have the chance to get any rest," he said with a smile. "You need it."

Raiden returned a grateful nod and left the workroom to catch up with the others.

☙

Nicole held Fen's hand as they made their way into Nicole's grand room where the door to Keren's cottage waited. They had to tell her that Asi was gone. Her eyes burned with pain as she glanced at the door to Cantis. After, she would have to tell her father that Mitchell wasn't coming home, but she shoved that thought away quickly.

"What do we say?" Fen asked, her voice trembling.

"That we're going to get Asi back," Nicole said. A bitter tear slipped from her eye. She flicked it away before she reached for the door. She couldn't make that promise to her father, and the thought of telling him what she and Fen were about to tell Keren pressed on her. She felt like she was suffocating. Finn walked beside her, keeping in contact with her hip as they went. She suspected the griffin sensed the morbid aura in the air—he had not been his usual energetic self since she returned to his side.

Nicole spent a long time in Keren and Fen's arms after they delivered the news. She didn't want to go back to the palace, but she had to get Asi back. *I exposed her*, she thought. *This is my fault. I have to fix it.*

"Keren? Can Finn stay with you," she asked, looking sadly at the sweet creature—the only one whose life she hadn't destroyed yet. She knew she couldn't have him tagging along in Taroth as delicate a mission as that would be. If she could save one life from being pulled in to the misery, that would be something. Finn lay on the ground as Shio pounced at him despite being dwarfed by the griffin. Finn could easily pin the fox down with one massive paw but instead kept both paws on the floor while he and Shio

581

wrestled.

"Of course he can stay."

Finn looked to Keren then sprang up onto all fours.

"Come on, Finn," she said, moving to the front door. He followed her outside.

She walked across the open grass in the center of Keren's orchard, the trees all shushing and swaying cheerfully in the breeze, waving at her like a friend. She had awakened them from their winter sleep early when she first came to the orchard, and Gordan had said he felt her presence here when he was searching for her. She took a deep breath and exhaled shakily. Her magic stirred, but it wasn't so eager to bloom from her core. The trees whispered to her, unintelligible nothings. She had to delve deep and drag her magic up like an old iron anchor from a black sea. Finally, the crackling warmth swelled out of her core, and she let it pour through her into the earth. Fen flopped into the grass and rolled vigorously. The trees shuddered delightfully, but she only felt exhausted and drained as her power recoiled into its hiding place, leaving her baffled and frustrated. It had been so easy before. *I can barely do this*. How could she get Asi back if she couldn't do something this simple?

"Finn," she said, kneeling down. He pushed his head into her chest, and she buried her hands into the soft plumage of his neck. "I need you to protect this place—I know you understand me."

He raised his head and blinked at her. Large yellow eyes met hers.

"You keep them safe. Don't let Fen be alone."

Finn closed his eyes and pressed his head to her sternum again.

☙

Gordan waited behind in Nicole's room. Trying not to see traces of Mitchell everywhere he looked. He sank into the giant pillow bed and closed his eyes. A rhythm of footsteps from the hallway announced Raiden's arrival before the tense gloom rolled into the chamber. Gordan wondered when he learned the precise rhythm of Raiden's stride.

Raiden crossed the chamber without a word and collapsed onto the pillow with a sigh. Just having him there beside him in the silence made Gordan feel a little better. He must have drifted in and out because it seemed like only minutes later, he heard the door inside the room open and close again. Only one set of footsteps returned.

He didn't open his eyes. Nicole fell down onto the pillow between Raiden and him.

"Fen?" Raiden asked.

"She's staying home with Keren," her voice was muffled a little, her face in the pillow. She sighed.

Then he felt her hand pull on his shirt. Gordan opened his eyes and turned his head to see her tug on Raiden's shirt. He sat up and scooted closer to her as she settled prone into the cushion, her arms tucked entirely under her torso. There were a few inches between them. He shifted himself over until his side pressed against hers. He could feel her relax into the pressure of being pressed between them. Her quiet relief helped him close his eyes again.

❧

Raiden woke up to a full bladder and a pang of hunger. Wondering what time it was, he found his way through the dark to the bathroom in Nicole's chambers. When he returned to Nicole and Gordan—Nicole on her belly and Gordan on his side, an arm thrown across her back—he sighed and left them to venture downstairs to the kitchens.

As he made his way through the palace, he was sure it was the middle of the night. The corridors were silent and gentle night lights lit the way. He was glad to have empty halls to himself—realizing how much he missed the quiet, so he reveled in it only to find himself wishing for those quiet days with Nicole and her family. The fond thought turned cold and sharp—they would have no more of those days.

He wandered into the kitchens, warm and aglow with the firelight from the ovens. Someone was seated at one of the tables with a mug in her hands.

"Gwyn," he said.

She looked up, the curtain of her hair colored orange in the light. "Raiden," her voice was sorrowful and he knew why.

"I take it you couldn't sleep?"

"No. How is Nicole?"

"I think she nearly gave up on what's left here for her. I'm fairly certain the only thing keeping her here is anger."

"She has you and Gordan. Revenge can't mean more."

"You've never lost family at the hands of someone else, have you?"

She sighed and blew into her steaming mug before she answered, "No."

"When the person responsible is still out there, that's all that matters to someone with a wound this fresh. And if she needs anger to keep her going, I can live with that—so long as she's still here. I stay with her, even if revenge matters more than me."

"I finished the sword Mitchell and Gordan and I made together, but I don't know how to give it to her now that he's gone. I'll be handing her a reminder of him."

"That's exactly why you *should* give it to her."

"I don't feel like I know her well enough to give her something like that. It wouldn't be so painfully intimate if he was still here. Please, can you give it to her for me?" Gwyn's eyes glistened with tears that she tried to blink back.

"Of course, Gwyn."

She cleared her throat. "I'm sorry, you probably came down here for food—I don't mean to keep you."

"Don't worry about it. My appetite seems to have vanished."

"You should eat something anyway," she said before taking a drink of her tea.

Raiden looked around and spotted a basket of pears. He took one and raised it for Gwyn's satisfaction.

"It's a start," she said.

"I'll come back for breakfast in the morning to get something for them too. They might not be ready to endure everyone's sympathy."

"If you're heading back, can I give you the sword?"

"Sure," he said, passing the pear back and forth between his hands as she got up from the table.

They walked in silence upstairs from the kitchens to the first floor and then to the second, past Tovar's workroom door and finally to Gwyn's. She opened it and invited him inside with a nod. He stepped through the doorway and waited, still switching the pear from hand to hand as she went to her cluttered work table.

"I sent a cast of the sword to a leather worker in town who is making a scabbard for it, but I think she should have this now," she said. She fussed with wrapping the sword in a long piece of cloth before carrying it across the workroom. He set the pear down on the corner of the table so that he could take it in both hands.

"He was so excited about this," Gwyn said, shaking her head. "I'm sorry he doesn't get to see it in her hands."

"Me too," he said. "Thank you…for having a piece of him we can give to her." She walked with him out of her workroom and into the hallway. He watched her close the door before she turned the opposite direction toward the first floor.

"Are you going back to the kitchens?" he asked.

She chuckled. "It's the strangest thing…even though I have my own room and workshop, I just like being down there with the ovens."

"You're not even going to try to sleep tonight?"

"It would be a waste of time at this point—too much on my mind. Good night, Raiden."

❧

Gordan opened his eyes, confused for a moment to find his vision blurred with tears that fell as he sat up blinking. Nicole was sitting on the edge of the massive pillow, a long object wrapped in cloth upon her lap. He spotted the sword hilt peeking out of the fabric. She stared at it for a long time until her eyes welled. Sitting beside her, Raiden looked to Gordan with an uncertain frown. Gordan could feel his regret.

When Nicole finally unwrapped the cloth, Gordan held his

breath, anxious to see what he and Mitchell had created together. The cloth slipped away from the single-edged blade. The top of the blade curved slightly downward from the hilt and back up subtly before its point. The cutting edge of the blade formed a graceful S curve up from the hilt where the blade was narrowest and back down toward the end where it was widest before its sharpened point. Between the rippling striations of the doragonian steel and the shape of the blade, it looked like it was moving even in its stillness.

The grip was dark polished stone that came alive with vivid colors as light hit it—this was the black moonstone Gwyn had planned to use as the main component of the wand in the core of the sword, extending into the blade. The whole hilt curved like a C around the wielder's fingers. Nicole ran her fingertips against the dark steel. Gordan could feel her swell of adoration for the work of art in her lap, but it was salt in her wounded heart. She pushed the pain back down and blinked the wetness in her eyes away.

"Nicole?" Raiden broke the silence reluctantly.

"It's beautiful," she nodded. "I can't believe he doesn't get to see it."

A knock at the door pulled Raiden from the bed. Nicole couldn't take her eyes off the sword—no doubt seeing Mitchell in the long, curved lines of the blade like Gordan did. She reached for his hand, and he gave it to her gladly, feeling all the pain she would not let him see. Raiden returned with a basket of pears and half-moon hand pies. A brass and leather scabbard for the sword was nestled inside among the provisions.

When Nicole reached for the scabbard a familiar gold-scaled dragon in miniature scurried out from the basket and onto her hand. She took the scabbard and slid the sword into it. Gim wrapped himself around her wrist; her sorrow burrowed deeper, sinking teeth into her soul. Gordan watched her hands grip the sword until they trembled. He didn't know how to step in, or if he could even pull her up out of this desolate anger.

She took a breath and set the sword down on the bed between them. Gordan's eyes couldn't give up the sword. He touched the hilt and slid his other hand beneath it. The weight of it in his hands pressed on his heart. He wanted to cherish it and, at the same time, destroy it. It was a piece of Mitchell but it wasn't enough of him.

"I should go shower…I smell pretty awful," Nicole muttered as she stood up and walked toward the bathroom.

Raiden sighed and Gordan finally tore his gaze from the sword.

"I thought losing my mother was the worst pain I'd ever know, but watching Nicole endure this," Raiden said, shaking his head, "I'm useless."

"You're not. It might not seem like we're any comfort, but she would be so much worse alone," Gordan said. "I would be lost again without you two here."

"Every day that Venarius is out there will keep Mitchell's death fresh," Raiden said. "And I know too well that anger seems like the only balm for it, but it's a poison in large doses. I wonder how long she can withstand it."

Gordan nodded, "We'll find him."

"I worry that he'll find us first."

❦

Nicole squeezed the towel around her hair in the warm misty bathroom. She dropped the towel and held out her hands to summon her clothes but found she had to reach far deeper than usual to find the warm core of magic. Once a well of vibrant energy, she struggled to draw it out. Her body tensed and shook with the effort to force that power into her hands. The wad of garments finally fell into her hands, and she let out an exasperated breath of relief.

She didn't have to wonder what was wrong with her. As much as she wished she could blame it on some residual trace of Venarius' seal, she knew she had broken it, destroyed it. When she looked into the mirror and wiped the fog from the glass, the eyes that looked back at her were almost entirely clear of blood, the unsettling red gaze was gone, but she still felt like two different people were standing there looking at each other.

You endured a whole life of this, she thought of the fera before her, *but you never had anyone to lose. I can't do what you did.* No matter what it would take, she had to stop all of it—Venarius, Dawn, the fera and their purpose—but she had to keep herself together to do it, and she had to get Asi back first. *I can't keep sinking.*

She wandered out of the bathroom, willing a little more magic into her fingers as she scrubbed them through her hair, drying her curls. When Raiden and Gordan looked at her, she knew their conversation had ceased because they had been talking about her, or Venarius, or something they thought might weigh too hard on her heart. They were so worried about her. A sad smile pulled at her mouth. *I could lose them too.*

When she reached the bed, she stepped between them and bent down to pick up the sword. She had to memorize the weight of it, know the feel of it against her back, learn how to move with it because her life really was war now. *You're goddamn right it's war,* Mitchell had said, and she could almost smile at the memory.

She turned to Gordan and hugged him. "Thank you," she said into his heart, the sword in her hand behind his back. He closed his arms around her, gently at first, then his arms tightened and trembled. She knew the feeling. He let her go at last, and she pulled the strap of the scabbard onto her body, situating the sword on her back.

She turned to Raiden, and he reached for the buckle on the strap across her chest, adjusting it a couple holes tighter. "There," he said, and she caught his hand just to hold onto him. She laced her fingers through his and pressed her cheek against the back of his hand.

"It's not likely our trip to Taroth will stay a secret," she said. When she looked up at Raiden, she caught his eyes meeting Gordan's.

Raiden agreed, "If Venarius doesn't find out we're going, he will certainly know once we're there. Dawn has a pervasive presence in Taroth."

She took a deep breath and let it out. She kissed his hand and released it, then bent down to take a moon pie from the basket. "I should go thank Gwyn," she said, making her way toward the door.

❧

Venarius sat at a new desk in a new base of operation for Dawn. He stared at the shell of the journal. It was fitting that something he created would be so clever, but the game grew tiresome now. He had been robbed of his victory and the journal. His unfortunate attempt to catch them at sea had been far too hasty. He had let his emotions push him into action prematurely. He wouldn't make that mistake again.

This time, at least, he had a new advantage. Nicole was damaged by her brother's death, and now, it turned out, he had a way into the palace and past the protections. He was tired of the people closest to Nicole; they were problems that needed to be removed. Still, he supposed he had one chance to use the loophole that had been given to him. Once they realized how he managed to get past the spells, they would see to it that he couldn't exploit that weakness again.

❧

Nicole knocked on the door of Gwyn's workshop. A minute later the door opened and there stood Gwyn, her silver hair hanging loose around her collarbones. All Nicole could see was Raiden's future standing in front of her and think—*he deserves love*. She didn't want him to be alone if she wasn't here when this was all over.

Eyes widening with surprise, Gwyn greeted her, "Nicole."

"I wanted to thank you for my sword."

"Please, it was a pleasure to work with your brother. He had so many ideas…a lot of rather strange ones too."

Nicole smiled. "That's Mitch," she nodded in the silence for a moment. "Actually, I was hoping you could help me familiarize my-self with how it works; plus, I thought you would want to see it in action, you know, for research."

"Yes, I do," her voice swelled with appreciation.

"Great," Nicole struggled to keep her smile from falling. For Gwyn this was her budding dream, her passion—Nicole didn't need to smother that joy, but for her this was for Raiden and Gordan, for Asi and Fen, this was for Mitchell and ending Venarius.

೧

After Gordan left to take up patrol of the world outside the tower and had taken a couple moon pies with him upon Raiden's insistence, Raiden tried to clear his own head with a shower. He emerged clean, but his mind was even more troubled than before. They had a rescue mission to worry about, but there was a very real chance that Venarius could see an opportunity to strike again. He grew less and less confident that they could handle both should Venarius make a move. If Nicole didn't venture out into the open again, would Venarius sit back and wait?

He needed to talk to Nicole. They needed a plan—even if plans had yet to go as intended. Raiden made his way through the palace to the second-floor corridor and knocked on Gwyn's door. After a long wait he realized no one was there. Perplexed, he wandered down the hall to Tovar's workroom.

He knocked.

"Come in, Raiden."

Raiden opened the door and stepped inside. "Tovar," he greeted.

"I hope you're rested," Tovar said. "Because Heimskur is preparing for your visit."

"He replied already?"

Tovar held up the envelope. "I'm a little surprised as well, to be honest. My guess is that he wants to have your ear while you're still green. The sooner the better for him before you and Nicole have established solid alliances, or amassed substantial troops—"

"Or visited the state Heimskur is trying to quietly assimilate. My guess is he wouldn't want us to visit Navn before he had the chance to tell us all about what's 'really' going on there."

"Very likely," Tovar agreed.

Raiden sighed. "How do we even go about this, Tovar?"

"My suggestion would be to go there and make as little a stir as possible. As wrong as it may feel to abide by their customs and talk allegiance with Heimskur, the less you disturb them the better opportunity you will have to find Asi and get out discretely."

"It's a good thing we already know that we don't want anything to do with Taroth because we'll certainly be leaving as enemies."

"I would recommend taking only male guards with you; try to do things the way they do things," Tovar said cringing.

"All right, I'll add Loak to my list. I was actually looking for Nicole."

"Well, she was next door with Gwyn for a bit and then I heard them head downstairs."

"Thank you, Tovar."

❧

Nicole held the sword and found it already felt at home in her hand. She also found she already disliked handing her sword over to anyone else's hands, even someone she trusted like Loak. She couldn't take her eyes off the blade—the downward curve of its back, the S curve of its edge; there wasn't a single straight line in the sword—from hooked hilt to sharpened tip.

"It's impressive," Loak remarked, nodding as she set the sword in his open palms.

Gwyn beamed beside Nicole.

Loak looked at Gwyn and asked, "You didn't design this, did you?"

"No," Gwyn said, giving Nicole a quick glance.

"Mitchell did," Nicole explained.

"Well, a blade like this is shaped to distribute its weight in a way that gives it the momentum of an axe. You can thrust with it, of course, but this beauty is built for downward swings."

"And," Gwyn said pointedly. "Don't forget it's not just a sword. It is effectively a wand, it should be able to retain power like a reservoir as well as direct it. You have to treat it like an extension of you."

"I think we can agree on that," Loak said, handing the sword back to Nicole. "Would you like to jump into some fundamentals?"

"That's why I'm here," she said, trying to summon enthusiasm into her flat voice.

✂

Raiden stopped at the throne room and leaned against the closed door to peak in through the open door. Inside were Nicole, Loak, Netti, Sage, Andrus—swords in hand—and Loak standing there with folded arms as his instructions boomed through the room. Gwyn sat watching intently from the steps below the thrones. He didn't feel like interrupting, pulling Nicole from her distraction. He turned away from the doors and set out to visit the Tempest on the hill behind the palace and consult Captain Rhee about their trip to Taroth.

✂

Nicole was tired, everyone was, but even after deciding that was enough for today, she didn't want to put the sword down or even into the scabbard on her back. Was it a link to Mitchell or the fact that her own blood was sitting in its core? It felt like Gwyn managed exactly what she set out to do, this creation didn't just function like an extension of her, it felt as much as a part of her as her bones… or her heart.

It scared her a little—the idea of releasing it—still, she convinced her hand to guide the blade back into the scabbard. The movement was awkward, and she determined she needed to practice removing it from and returning it to the scabbard.

"Raiden, you missed training—stars know you should have joined us," Loak said with a boisterous chuckle; Nicole looked up to see Raiden trying to smile at Loak's remark as he crossed the throne room, mostly he cringed.

"Next time," Raiden said. "I've got some news."

"Good or bad?" Andrus wondered with a good-humored tone.

"That's hard to say; we've had a reply from Heimskur, and they're preparing for our visit in Taroth. I've spoken to Captain Rhee. She says the ship is good to go whenever we're ready."

"Oh," she said. "Then I guess we should grab what we need. The sooner we get there, the sooner we find Asi." She nodded and marched toward the doors of the throne room.

She heard a couple murmurs behind her but let her footsteps drown them out. A pair of feet jogging to catch up with her joined the cadence.

"Can we talk about Taroth?" Raiden asked.

"What about it?"

He was quiet a moment. She wondered if he was second-guessing the suggestion that she stay behind or just trying to work up the nerve to say it.

"It's not going to be pleasant there," he said. "You already know how they treat women, but for the sake of concealing our intent, we're going to have to try our best to go along with their rules. The less attention we draw, the better our chance at figuring out where Asi is and getting her out."

She let out a near imperceptible laugh through her nose. "Yeah, that's not going to be fun, but you're right. We can't make a bunch of waves and expect to sneak around and kidnap someone."

Raiden's hand closed around hers.

"I thought you were about to say I shouldn't go," she admitted.

"You would be safer here," he said. "But I think you need this."

"I'm already packed, so guess we're leaving right away," she said. "First, I have to say goodbye to Gordan." There was no way he could come to Taroth—they all knew that—but she hated the idea of leaving him here to ruminate in Mitchell's absence without her.

During the flight to Taroth, Raiden watched Nicole pace. She paced their room, the deck, the corridor. Now and then he could catch her in an embrace, but he knew that forced stillness let her sink back into thoughts of Mitchell. He knew what she was doing. He had done it after his mother's death—buried that loss in purpose. He had no choice, he had no one's arms to seek comfort in, he had to survive, he had to make things right. Anger was easier to live with, until he just buried all of it and found solace in feeling nothing. Now he was torn between watching Nicole bury her sorrow in distraction and giving her what he didn't have then, what he had needed most facing that storm of grief.

As much as he wanted to wrap his arms around her, he felt guilty whenever he did. Trying to comfort her only pulled her from her distraction and back to her sinking misery, so he let her distract herself. For Asi's sake, maybe it was best that Nicole didn't face that sorrow as dangerous as that could be. *She doesn't get the luxury of falling apart, not while Asi needs us, or while Venarius is coming for us.* When would she, though?

They flew through the night and sharing their narrow bed, Nicole clung to him like never before. He wondered if she slept at all because her arms didn't seem to loosen once through the night.

⁂

In the early evening the second day, they reached Taroth. The royal city of Pharos lay on the end of a long hook-shaped peninsula. The majority of the western coast of Taroth was lined by white cliffs. The Heimskur's castle sat perched at the very point of the hook, luxurious green grounds lay around it, but the north wall of the castle looked almost as though it had been part of the very cliff-face, turning from rough weather-worn rock to smooth polished stone. The Tempest swooped around the cliffside castle as it approached the grounds for landing—Nicole couldn't help think of the castle back in Cantis, sitting upon its cliff like a crumbling gargoyle.

Nicole went to her trunk in their room, placed her sword inside and morphed her mauve sweater into a simple dress fitted at the waist so that the flared skirt hung over her leggings and boots. *Good enough for now*, she thought, running her fingertips along Gim's scales as he dozed around her collar bones.

Standing beside Raiden and Caeruleus with five male guards around them, she tried not to wear an outright scowl on her face as she as the door of the Tempest's elevator opened. Welcoming them to the royal state of Taroth was a single well-dressed servant.

"Welcome your highness," he said.

He's only talking to Raiden, Nicole noted, a bitter smile curling her mouth. Raiden's hand squeezed hers.

"I'm here to show you to your rooms; please follow me."

There was no welcome to speak of as they were led into Heimskur's towering castle. They didn't walk through any central doorways or corridors. They saw very few faces on their way through the maze-like passages, and the faces they did see were all servants, dressed in the same uniform as their guide.

As their guide led them through the corridors, they all got their first—several—introductions to the visage of King Heimskur. There was an abundance of paintings along their route and studying them all briefly in passing was enough to know Heimskur's face more than they cared to. Every painting showed him in enough embroidered garments to nearly double his size, large sleeves, perhaps meant to create the illusion of muscular arms beneath. The crown he wore atop his almost white, blond head was about as big as a crown could practically be. He had a pale face, a smug mouth and an arrogant brow. He seemed to be partial to the color orange as his lavishly adorned garments in most of his portraits were orange, dripping in purple gems and gold buttons.

To Nicole's surprise there were a few portraits along the way in which Heimskur was not alone. There was one picture where a woman sat beside him, but a delicate veil of black fabric had been attached to the frame to hang over her face. Nicole could just make out the features of a face through the slightly sheer veil of mourning, but not well enough. She puzzled over the black veil as they continued, but eventually spotted another. The queen's face was veiled again in this family portrait. There was a rosy-faced infant in her arms. Heimskur's expression never seemed to change. He looked odd beside his wife and child with such a look of self-importance on his face, nothing like a father.

A third painting of the royal family stopped Nicole for a moment and she stood there looking up at the massive frame. The queen was veiled in black as the other portraits were, but the princess looked to be six or seven. She didn't smile. What little girl could with the heavily-ringed hand of a father like Heimskur bearing down on her slight shoulder? Her hazel eyes were sad, framed by long shining brown curls, a glistening gemmed bow in her hair. Raiden stood beside her, dragged to a stop by her curiosity and their joined hands. Caeruleus slowed to a halt as well, then their guide cleared his throat, pulling them away from the royal family of Taroth and back to their trek through the castle's maze of corridors.

The three of them cast several uncomfortable looks at one another and couldn't have concealed their relief if they tried. Finally, the servant stopped at a door.

"Here we are," he said. "These are your rooms. This floor is yours, chambers for servants and guards just down there. Dinner will be brought up at seven," the servant said with a bow and away he went.

"That is the coldest reception I could have imagined," Caeruleus said with a baffled chuckle.

"Oddly enough, this is my favorite royal reception we've had," Nicole muttered.

Raiden laughed. "I don't miss the pomp and excitement at all."

"Payback for how you treated his emissary in Nol, I bet." Caeruleus said, his shoulders shaking with silent laughter. "Imagine how satisfied he must be with himself, thinking he's irritated you."

"Only to give us the most comfortable kings' welcome we've had yet," Raiden added.

They had already discussed the likelihood that Heimskur would have listening charms throughout his castle and all direct mention of Asi had to remain on the Tempest.

"I guess we get settled in then, and enjoy an evening free of diplomacy," Nicole said, opening the door to their rooms.

ᛒ

Raiden thought he was used to waking up in new places, but the unfamiliar room around their bed when he opened his eyes was slow to creep out of his memory. He sighed, dreading the day to come already, and glanced at Nicole beside him to see her eyes blinking.

"You're awake," he said, wondering again if she had slept.

"It's hard to sleep here," she said. He knew she didn't mean the bed, she meant being here in Taroth, sleeping felt like a betrayal of their mission to find Asi.

"Maybe we'll sleep better tonight," he suggested, but it felt too foolish to hope they would be leaving Taroth so soon.

"Have to get through today first, your highness," she said.

He let out a soft laugh but noticed she wasn't smiling.

"Time to get dressed, I guess," she said, sitting up and swinging her bare legs off the bed.

He climbed out of bed and glanced across the room at Nicole, his gaze catching the skin of her back before the fabric of her dress fell around her. He got dressed in the best clothes he had, gifts from Cinder.

As he straightened the folded cuffs of his jacket, a knock at the door disturbed the silence. He expected Caeruleus as he made his way through the rooms and opened the door, but it was one of the castle servants. Beside him a female servant stood, her head bowed and a bulk of fabric folded over her arms.

"Your highness," he said. "Good morning. The king insisted that your queen have the best garments among the ladies for her reception here at court."

"Oh," he said, a little perplexed by the woman's firmly downcast gaze. "You'll find Nicole getting ready in our room."

The woman gave a little nod, never lifting her eyes, and hurried past him in to their rooms. *Here we go,* he thought. They had to act like they cared about being here, like they wanted to hear what Heimskur had to say.

"If you're ready, I will escort you down to the hall for breakfast."

"I'll wait for Nicole," he said.

"It is customary for the ladies to meet and socialize before breakfast. The men are not allowed to attend."

"I see. Then excuse me a moment," Raiden said, turning to march through their rooms once again.

The woman attending Nicole jumped when he stepped into the room as she worked to fasten the line of buttons up the back of the bodice of a gown. Light cast a sheen on the fabric, grayish purple, like dried heather. Nicole looked up and he could see the disgust hiding behind her composure.

He was stunned for a moment to see the neckline swooping across her breasts—pushed up to appear larger—the bodice synched tight around her waist. It wasn't strange to see the shape of her body, sleeves clinging to the curve of her shoulders and arms, or the skin of her collar bones, but the dress turned her into another person. He supposed the dress was beautiful, but she looked so unlike herself in it—rigid and weighed down—that he didn't like it.

"Apparently the ladies meet in private before breakfast here at court. I'm not invited. See you in a bit." He slipped his hands around her jaw to place a quick kiss on her lips and whisper in her ear. "Good luck." The woman's gaze widened, boring into the floor like she hadn't seen what transpired between them.

"See you later," she said back.

He returned to the servant waiting at the door and found Caeruleus there as well. He hoped between the three of them, they could figure out where Asi might be, which meant learning about Heimskur's revered court healer who erased memories.

"All right," he said to the servant who nodded and turned to march down the hallway.

"You ready?" Caeruleus asked.

"Not at all."

Nicole took a deep breath, trying to think of something to say to the poor woman who seemed terrified to lift her eyes higher than the dress as she helped Nicole sort out all the buttons and hems. When she turned to the mirror and finally caught a look at what Raiden had seen, she understood the look on his face.

Really? She stared at the dress, dramatic sweetheart neckline skirting the edge of appropriateness across her breasts. She was expecting something prudish, a collar up to her jawline. *Maybe this is some sort of mean joke,* she thought. *I'll show up looking like a harlot among the ladies of Heimskur's court.*

When she was done pinning Nicole's hair into some kind of twisted form behind her head, the woman bowed a little and hurried from the room, leaving Nicole there in a gown and no idea what to do. She lifted her hands and looked around. *Is she not allowed to talk to me?*

"Ready, Gim?" she asked. She wandered through their rooms to the door, and when she opened it there was a male servant waiting there.

"Good morning, your highness. Please follow me, the ladies are waiting to meet you."

Nicole felt the key bouncing against the bodice of her dress as she walked; it was still worth a 'your highness' here in Taroth. She followed the servant, trying to remember the turns and corridors they took through the castle but knew she was already lost. If Asi was somewhere in this place, finding her was going to be a nightmare.

"Here we are," the servant said, opening a door for her and bowing his head as she stepped inside. He closed the door behind her, and she stood before a room of several ladies in gowns of subdued colors.

All eyes were on her.

"Good morning," she said, at a loss for any kind of etiquette at this point. She already felt like a fool in the dress, so what did it matter what she said at this point?

Two of the ladies who were already on their feet, crossed the room to greet her.

"How wonderful to meet you, your highness," a red-haired woman said as she curtsied.

"Please, you can call me Nicole."

They giggled to themselves.

"My name is Scilla," the woman said and introduced everyone in the room quicker than Nicole could assign names to faces. "This is Aster, Nerine, Poppy, Tithonia, and Honesty."

Nicole was too distracted by the ornate gowns in the room. Necklines cut to display, embellished bodices for emphasis, severely synched waistlines. She was indeed dressed like the lot of them, ready for a parade of the bosoms.

"Forgive me, ladies, I've never been surrounded by such well-dressed company for breakfast," she said, shaking herself from her gawking stupor. They smiled—among them someone giggled and, to Nicole, it sounded derisive.

"Is it time for breakfast yet? I'm rather hungry this morning," one woman said, and Nicole regretted not paying attention to their names.

"They should bring it shortly," another answered, sounding a little terse.

Bring? Nicole thought. "Aren't we meeting the men downstairs for breakfast?"

"Dear me, no, we would be far too much distraction," Scilla said with a good-humored shake of her head as she sat down on the long couch beside two of the other women.

"A distraction?" Nicole questioned.

"They like to discuss important things at breakfast, your highness."

"Oh, right," she said, trying to swallow back her sarcastic bite.

"We are invited to the hall in the afternoon, by then the men enjoy a little respite from more serious matters of the court."

"My favorite part of the day," another of the ladies chimed in.

"Oh, what is it like? Just mingling, some music, dancing?" Nicole tried to imagine, would Asi be there? Was she locked away or being forced to assume her role as a lady in this place?

"We enjoy a stroll about the hall and they enjoy our presence."

"But you don't interact at all?" Nicole asked.

"Of course we do. We provide the company of beauty and they gaze upon us," the woman in the center of the couch said, giggling. "Yesterday the Duke of Blackwater's eyes lingered on me several times."

"His gaze is not so hard to catch as Lord Rariton's," the blond woman beside her said with a scoff.

"Well, anyone's gaze is easy to obtain when you make indecent eye contact."

Indecent eye contact? Nicole almost made a face. "I'm sorry, I wish I knew your etiquette better. What is the difference between indecent eye contact and decent eye contact?"

"Any eye contact with a man who is not your husband is indecent," said Scilla on the end of the couch, looking pointedly at the blonde on the other end. "A work of art does look back at its admirers," she explained. "A painting or a statue cannot reciprocate the gaze of onlookers. *That* is the different between a lady and a whore."

Nicole's eyes went wide with disbelief and outrage. She had to swallow back her disgust and push this conversation closer to Asi.

"What else do you ladies enjoy here?" she asked, hiding her clenched fists in the amble folds of her skirt.

"There's the Queen's Garden. The king commissioned it in memory of the late queen—rest her soul—and it is only for the ladies at court to enjoy."

"I did not know about the queen," Nicole said—that confirmed her suspicion about the black veils over the queen's images, but why veil her? Why hide her memory so blatantly?

"We shouldn't speak of her," Scilla scolded quietly.

"How can we not? She wasn't just another cliff maiden; she was the queen," said a soft-spoken brunette.

"Cliff maiden?" Nicole's heart sank into the cold stories Fen and Asi had told her about Taroth.

"She jumped," the blonde woman whispered to Nicole, barely audible.

"Poppy," Scilla scolded under her breath.

A woman who looked to be the oldest in the room—as beautifully adorned as any of them, but strands of grey hair in her golden locks gave her away. "Shame on you for talking like that. Queen Diona's memory deserves more respect. What if the princess were to hear you saying such ugly things?"

That poor little girl, Nicole thought, thinking of the sad sweet face she'd seen in a portrait last night.

"But it's true," Poppy insisted.

"We shouldn't say ugly things even if they are true," Scilla retorted.

Nicole took a careful breath. "Loss can be...unbearable," she said. "I lost—" the words formed a lump in her throat. She didn't want to say it out loud, but she needed to ply sympathy from these women. "—my brother." The words still hit her chest like a battering ram. *Come on, tell me what I want to know,* she thought.

Several soft gasps answered her.

"I've heard there's a healer at court," she added, hoping for something, anything. Would they spill or play dumb?

"He's a miracle worker," Scilla said.

"I was never happier than after I saw him last year, and I finally had my first child after that."

"We're lucky to have him," Poppy said.

The fervent nods of every woman in the room horrified Nicole. Had they all seen him? What were these women erasing from their memories in order to be happy? She couldn't keep looking at them without wanting to break down and scream. A knock at the door came and it opened. A line of servants entered with platters under silver domes. In the sudden flurry of activity, she moved toward the door, slipping out into the hallway after the last servant marched through.

She huffed, shaking her head as she turned down the hall and let her frustration out in her stride. Her skirt swished and hissed around her maddeningly as she wandered, trying to remember the way through the corridors. But when she turned a corner and saw only a short hall and a dead end with a little window looking back at her, she was so annoyed and frustrated that she wanted to rip the noisy skirt apart.

Instead she let her magic out in a swift hot wave. The outer skirt flared up as though caught in a gust and the petticoats beneath disintegrated leaving the skirt to fall back down around her legs. The material split down the front and back and wrapped around each leg, forming pants. She looked down her nose at her exposed breasts and watched the neckline crawl up over her collarbones. Then she glared down at the slippers on her feet and dragged a little more magic from her core to turn them into boots. Nothing felt better than letting her anger echo in the hallway with every fierce heel-strike of her stride now that she wasn't in those stupid, flimsy slippers. She pulled the pins from her hair and dropped them onto the floor as she went, shaking her hair out irritably. Her eyes burned and she tried to ignore the wet trail of rogue tears.

Nicole stormed down the hall and around another corner directly into a young man's path. He stopped abruptly at the sight of her, and his wide eyes clued her in to what a sight she was—gown turned pantsuit and boots, her curls down and unruly, her eyes pink. The anger on her face could only look like pure madness to any man in this place. This one had a boyish softness to his face—she supposed he could only be fifteen. His brown hair was cut straight across his forehead—disheveled above his stunned eyes.

"Do you know your way around this place?" Nicole asked in terse exasperation.

"Yes," he answered apprehensively.

"Great. What's your name?"

"Evren."

"I'm Nicole."

"*Queen* Nicole?"

She sighed. "*Just* Nicole." The key hanging against her belly was confirmation enough. "How the hell do I get to the central halls?"

Evren looked around. No doubt he'd be in some kind of trouble for helping an uncouth woman, key of the realm or not, wander where she wasn't supposed to, but surely not too *much* trouble. She would likely bear the blame; they would be lenient for a young man.

"You just have to follow the—"

"Great. Lead the way," she said, hooking her arm around his and turning him back the way he had come. "This palace is ridiculous. I still don't know where I'm going once I'm downstairs."

"Are you trying to find King Heimskur and King Raiden?"

"Actually, I'm looking for someone else. The royal 'healer' I guess. Do you know where he is?"

"Why would you want to see him?"

"He can help me with a problem I have," she said, turning a lie into the truth.

"If you say so," Evren said. "The healer's home is on the other side of the palace grounds."

"Great. Let's go."

They walked in silence, Nicole stealing peeks at Evren and noticing his quick glances at her. He looked like he didn't get out much—such a pale complexion.

"You know your visit is a secret, right?" Evren said. "No one in Taroth outside the palace knows you're here."

"Is that so?" Nicole said, amused enough that she almost felt inclined to smile.

"He doesn't want his kingdom thinking he's aligning himself with you."

"Oh, I wonder why," she said facetiously.

"He told Taroth you led the rebels against the Council and murdered them…that you're taking over the mainland with coercion because everyone's afraid of the fera—even though you and the king have the keys to the realm."

Nicole couldn't hold it back, a snort escaped her nose and a burst of laughter followed; it was joyless, bitter and cynical, nearly unhinged.

Evren looked at her with his face furrowed. "What about that is so funny?"

"It's—" Nicole gasped. "So stupid—it's like high school." She laughed.

"High school?" he repeated, confused.

"Forgive me," she said, struggling to turn her laughter into steady breaths. "I'm losing my mind—I thought I was so far from childish absurdity like that. I thought the girl who lived my old life was gone, but I keep finding slivers of her."

"You mean you? You thought you were gone? I don't understand."

"It's not important," Nicole said with a shrug. "But you certainly know a lot about the king—if he doesn't want his people knowing all that, you must be listening to things you shouldn't."

His eyes widened.

"Am I right? I doubt many here are privy to the king's lies."

Evren's face turned red—his embarrassment betrayed by his fair complexion.

"How much trouble would you be in for telling me all that?"

"A lot."

"Well, since I kind of like you, I'll try to keep you out of trouble," she said with a wry chuckle, knowing she was leading this kid into deep shit. "I won't tell a soul."

They made their way out of the women's wing and to the main halls below.

"We have to cut through the gardens," Evren said. "But, uh, they're for the women, so I shouldn't be seen in there. You probably shouldn't be either, looking like that."

"The gardens should be empty, right? All the ladies were upstairs last I saw them," Nicole muttered. "I can't imagine living here."

"It's not so bad. I can go almost anywhere I want," he said.

Of course you *can.* Nicole withheld her urge to glare at him; he was helping her, after all. She would be no closer to finding Asi without him, and she felt bad for Raiden for having to muster up convincing diplomacy for Heimskur. How awful was it to be alone with that pompous clown? The sooner she found Asi, the sooner they could leave this place and the sooner they would be back with Gordan.

Annoyed as she was, she couldn't deny she was lucky to have someone to lead her through the castle. It was, frankly, impressive that anyone could remember this maze of corridors, staircases, and doors. Nicole couldn't even fathom where they were until Evren opened the castle door and she recognized it as the one they had been escorted through upon their arrival the night before. Finally, they were outside in the sunlight.

The Tempest was still sitting where they had left it, and to Nicole's surprise one of their guards was standing at the elevator door, a silent reminder that they could not trust this place or anyone in it. She glanced at Evren and wondered if she should erase his memory before they left, but she would have to find Asi *and* get her back before that.

"There's the garden," he said, pointing to the crisply groomed hedges ahead. An arch of stone dressed in ivy stood as the doorway through the chest-high wall of dense foliage. "Careful, they're thorny hedges."

They moved through the garden, ducking to stay below hedges and crouching behind rose bushes to peek around corners before proceeding. Nicole glanced into the greenery at the sound of its creaking, creeping toward her tentatively and she remembered a time when it would have twisted and bloomed fervently in her presence. *Maybe even the plants are scared of me now.* She looked to Evren for his go-ahead nod, but saw his gaze locked on a garden statue across the path.

It was a woman in an intricately carved gown, standing tall yet demur, her hands folded respectfully against her skirts. From where they were crouched, Nicole could read *Our most beloved Queen Diona* on the plaque.

"So that's what Heimskur's wife looked like," Nicole said.

"She didn't look like that," Evren said, frowning at the solemn stone beauty. "She smiled—all the time—even when she wasn't supposed to; there was always a smile hidden in the corner of her mouth."

"I guess you really—" Nicole stopped, stunned by the redness in Evren's eyes. She was touched that the late queen was so well loved, but her heart panged with suspicion. She looked closer at the boy, seeing an unmistakable likeness to the small child in the painting of the royal family. The shining curls and sparkling bows were gone, but those hazel eyes were unchanged. She hadn't bothered to ask how long ago the queen had passed. The veiled pictures made it seem so recent. Nor had she asked how old the princess of Taroth was currently, no longer the small girl in the portrait she'd seen. "Evren?"

"Hmm."

"Are you the king's daughter?"

"No," Evren said angrily. "I'm *Diona's* daughter." She nodded toward the stone queen. "Come on."

Evren moved across the path and crouched behind the wide pedestal beneath Queen Diona. At a loss for words, Nicole followed, trying to catch up with this revelation.

"Hold on. You can actually walk around here and *no one* recognizes you?"

"No, they don't. It would never occur to them. They see my hair and my clothes and see a boy. People can look right into my eyes and don't suspect a thing."

"How long?"

"Four years—since my mother's death. Honestly, I feel more like myself this way. It's not just the freedom I have, being called *son* and *young man* feels just as right as being called Diona's Daughter."

Nicole shook her head, heartbroken for Evren. The women had told her about Queen Diona and her leap from her tower. "I'm sorry."

"She didn't jump like they say. She would never."

Nicole frowned. "Then you think—"

"My father. Maybe he pushed her or *made* her jump, but I *know* she would never kill herself. She wouldn't leave me."

They were silent a while. Nicole wished she could affirm the idea that mothers wouldn't leave their daughters.

"She used to tell me 'We may fight our battle silently at times and seem not to fight at all, but we never give up.' She wouldn't have jumped."

"I'm so sorry, Evren. I know what it's like to lose the person you need the most." Nicole swallowed back the lump in her throat.

"Who…did you lose?" Evren inquired gently.

"My brother," she said. She didn't even feel the burn in her eyes or the tears on her cheeks, but she looked down and saw the drops of wetness on the stone beneath her and wiped at her face.

"Is…that why you want to see the healer?"

Nicole looked up at Evren in dismay—*forget Mitchell?* "No," she answered too loud and cringed, lowering her voice. "No, we're here to find a friend. The healer's daughter managed to get out of Taroth some time ago, but because she was with me, someone recognized her and they brought her back to Taroth—and I wasn't there to stop them. We're here to take her back home…to her family."

"Oh," Evren said, then looked around the pedestal and nodded.

They stood and ran, half crouched, down the path to a nook in the hedge.

"Do you think," Evren said as they caught their breath. "I could come too?"

Nicole stared back at her, blinked, and let out a breathy laugh. *She's willing to run away with complete strangers to get away from this place.* Nicole thought of what Keren had said when she recounted discovering the stow-away girls—that she couldn't return Asi and Fen to this place. How could she deny Evren a way out?

"We're already kidnapping, right? What's one more?" But her sardonic cheer made her heart sink. What about all the other Fens and Evrens here, the Dionas, the women having their pain erased over and over to live it again?

"But before I go, there's something I need to do," Evren's voice pulled Nicole back out of her head.

"What?" she asked, certain it couldn't be good.

"I've had this truth potion for two years now waiting for a chance I could slip it to Heimskur and find out what really happened to my mother that night."

"Evren, that's a huge risk, and we won't have much time once we get Asi."

"It shouldn't be hard. I don't have to hide anymore. I've had the plan for years now. My mother's chambers were right below his; you can get to his balcony from hers with a simple rope ladder. He always takes his dinner in his rooms. With a way out I can finally confront him."

"If this is something you have to do, then you have to do it, but if the man is capable of killing his wife then he won't have any qualms about killing you. They don't seem to care much for daughters here."

Evren spit out a dry laugh. "I'm prepared for that," she said, and pulled out a little pouch. "Sleeping powder—its disturbingly easy to acquire, the men seem to pass it around often. I've been planning this for a long time."

Nicole sighed, knowing—*feeling*—exactly why Evren needed this. "Raiden and I could wait in your mother's rooms in case you need some backup."

"He won't see it coming; he's blinded by his own ego," Evren said with an eye roll.

"If we can find Asi then tonight is the night."

"If she's here, we'll find her. Oh—let's go," Evren whispered.

They reached the rose archway out of the garden and relaxed into an easy run until they were down the path.

"There," Evren said, pointing. "That's the royal healer's residence."

Across the lawn was a house—modest only in comparison to Heimskur's castle—a small mansion. Then Nicole spotted a familiar head of wavy raven hair headed their way, and a single blue eye wide and staring at her.

"What are you doing out here—who's this?"

"This is Evren. We're looking for Asi," Nicole said curtly.

"*I'm* looking for Asi," Caeruleus said. He looked her up and down. "What are you—you're going to draw attention to us."

"Then I guess we're all looking for Asi now."

"How do you know this kid can be trusted?"

"I'm nineteen," Evren said flatly.

"You sure don't look nineteen," Caeruleus muttered.

"You look like you don't see very well," Evren muttered back.

Nicole choked back a laugh and Caeruleus glared, his cheeks turning pink.

"Sorry," she said, failing to hide her smile. "Evren is coming with us when we leave. So, yeah, ratting us out wouldn't be a great idea."

Caeruleus answered with a resigned sigh, "Fine."

They approached the healer's house from the side.

"How do we get her out of there? We don't even know which room she's in," Caeruleus said, nodding to the house and all its windows.

"I can be a distraction and get inside," Nicole said. "You two see if you can find another way in or figure out which room is hers."

"What are you going to do?" Evren asked.

"Consult the healer," she said with a shrug.

610

Evren gave her a concerned look and glanced at Caeruleus, who pinched the bridge of his nose.

"Maybe we should have Raiden with us," Caeruleus said.

"We should have a lot of people with us," she said severely as she turned toward the path that led to the front of the house. Her heart ached like it was rending in two again, but she fought it back for Asi.

Caeruleus stared at Nicole's back as she went, and he took a deep breath. This was a bad idea. Raiden should be here, but he wasn't and they didn't have any better option at the moment.

"I thought you might lose the other eye for a second there," Evren muttered.

"Yeah," he agreed—he had seen her rage at work. "Her brother was killed two weeks ago, her anger is understandable."

"Two *weeks*?"

"Come on, let's get to work. Does the healer have many guards?"

"The grounds are so well protected that he doesn't really need them. That's why he lives here now. He used to live on an estate on the southern coast, but he moved here after his daughter was kidnapped—so he claimed."

Caeruleus scoffed. "She ran away with another girl from Taroth—but they wouldn't want anyone to know that, would they?"

"How did she end up with Nicole?"

"As I understand it, Asi and her adopted family took Nicole in when she was being hunted by the Council. I didn't really understand why they would take that risk then, but knowing who they are, it's really no surprise they sheltered Nicole."

They walked around the house, peeking through the windows to be sure no one would see them walking past.

"How did her brother die?"

"Dawn had Nicole and her brother. When we went in to rescue them, we failed to reach Mitchell before Venarius did. He killed him right in front of us." Caeruleus said, the words growing thick in his throat. Not that they had been close, but Caeruleus thought he lost his brother once—he had tasted the pain Nicole couldn't escape now.

"That's awful," Evren said, frowning.

"Her devastation was…terrifying," Caeruleus admitted.

"What was her brother like?"

"He could *always* make her laugh," he said with a heavy smile, thinking of his youth—bright memories with Raiden and his mother, they laughed so much then. He glanced at Evren and saw him wipe at his eye. He wondered how such a caring young man grew up here in Taroth?

"So, you're running away with us, huh?" Caeruleus asked.

"Still don't think I can be trusted?"

"I can believe it," he said with a wry smile. From what he had seen people were drawn to Nicole, and she couldn't seem to ignore anyone who needed help or…a family. Evren must not have that if he's willing to run away with a group of strangers. "I had a pretty awful home life growing up. I understand needing to escape your home to find a new family. Raiden and his mother sort of adopted me; they made me wish I didn't have a father *at all* rather than the one I had."

"So, your dad's horrible too?" Evren said with a dry laugh. "I guess I'm in better company than I realized." He tried the handle of a side door. "Locked."

Caeruleus peeked inside the next window and spotted a servant guiding Nicole into the room; he put his arm out, caught Evren, and pushed him back against the house beside him.

"We've got to go under this one," Caeruleus said, nodding at the window.

They got down on their hands and knees and crawled beneath the window.

"What about the second story?" Evren said as they stood and brushed their hands off against their trousers.

Caeruleus looked around—there wasn't a single tree to help them—then at Evren. His frame was petite, ideal for lifting, *and kind of cute.* He cleared his throat—*not the time for that*, he scolded himself.

"You look fairly light—you're not afraid of heights, are you?"

Evren made a slightly offended sound. "Boost me up."

Caeruleus cupped his hands together and lowered them for Evren to step into. He was right that Evren was easy to hoist up.

"Can you reach?"

"Yes," he said. "Hey—it opened."

"What?"

Before he knew it Evren's weight disappeared from his hands.

"Evren!" Caeruleus hissed, but he was already inside the house. "Great."

☙

Nicole knocked on the door and waited stony faced. A man dressed in simple tan and brown clothes—*servant*, she thought—opened the door and looked at her with wide eyes and high brows.

"I'd like to speak with the royal healer," she said, and her lips spread with smug satisfaction to see the man's scandalized gaze look down to her feet and back up, stopping at the key for a long second.

He cleared his throat, "Right this way…your highness."

For once she could appreciate having the key around her neck as she stepped into the house. He closed the door and led her into a sitting room off the entrance hall.

"Please, make yourself comfortable, your highness; I shall tell the master you've come to call."

She didn't sit down. *He'll probably be 'too busy' to see me,* she thought wryly as she looked around the room. She just needed to get an idea of what was going on in this house—could Asi hear what was going on downstairs from her room? She figured she would be lucky to have five minutes before that servant came back to tell her his master wouldn't be taking visitors—especially unscheduled ones.

Movement at the window caught her eye, and she glanced up to see Caeruleus standing there staring at her, his blue eye wide and ablaze. She gave him a questioning look—where was Evren? He pointed up. *Up, what does that mean?* She shook her head and shrugged, but when he dropped to the ground below the window, she realized footsteps were approaching behind her.

She turned, expecting the servant and was surprised to see a luxuriously dressed man with Asi's black eyes.

"What an unexpected honor to be visited by the queen," he said. "The king isn't here with you?"

Nicole's heart struck a chord of warning in her chest. "He is discussing matters of the realm with Heimskur today."

"There's only one reason anyone comes to see me," he said.

"Yes, I've heard about what you do," she answered, remembering vividly how Asi had erased Caeruleus' and Cole's memories with a simple touch. "And I wanted to know more about it."

"I see." He walked slowly around the room. She matched his meandering pace to keep much more than an arm's length between them. "I heard you recently lost your brother."

She flinched.

"It's perfectly reasonable to want relief from that kind of pain," he said.

He knew she was here for Asi, but he was clearly enjoying this pretense, a sadist pushing his finger into a wound.

Nicole steadied her voice, "Some people would rather keep their memories even if they hurt."

"But for most a wound that deep will only infect the rest of their lives," he said with a solemn nod. "In my experience the best treatment is always removal of those cancerous memories. Every patient I have treated has come to me with wounds and gone home completely healed and happy. As a healer, I must consider what is best for their quality of life."

Nicole's blood turned to venom. "What kind of healer treats a burn and then sends the patient back into the fire?"

His eyebrow twitched. "With all due…respect, your highness," he said, looking her up and down with thinly masked disdain. "The people of Taroth are none of your concern. That key, your name, all your power, none of it matters here. Maybe you should concern yourself with the flames that took your brother, lest that conflagration consume any more people you love."

She took a deep breath, swallowing back the acidic anger in her throat. *He's with Dawn*, the fact that she was here alone with him finally twisted her stomach. Venarius' voice crept out of hazy memories...*otherwise I'll have to erase her memories entirely...they're so feral without identities*. Asi's father was within arm's reach, and she stumbled backward to regain the space between them to keep away. Would this man even hesitate to erase Asi's memory, erase her defiance, the moment she returned? They still didn't know if Asi was even here in this house. She found it difficult to hope that this man might have allowed Asi to keep her identity. With her memories she would have to be a prisoner, without them she would return to her life before her freedom. *I might be a stranger to her.*

Nicole shook her head. Even if he erased all of Asi's life after escaping Taroth, Nicole knew her, she didn't want to be here, that's why she had run away with Fen. The possibility that Asi might not remember didn't change their plan to get her out, but Nicole had to get the hell out of this house.

❧

Caeruleus moved carefully around the outside of the house, hoping to see Evren at one of the windows, listening for the commotion of an intruder being discovered. *He's going to blow this for us*, he thought, cursing under his breath as he snuck back to the window where he had seen Nicole.

He peeked in and saw the slow unsettling dance between Nicole and Asi's father as he moved toward her and she kept the distance. *He can erase memories too*, Caeruleus reminded himself and hurried around the house, ducking below the windows as he made his way to the front door. But before he could lift the door knocker, the door opened. Nicole started at the sight of him. He was sure he saw panic in her eyes.

"Caeruleus—is Raiden looking for me?"

"Uh, yes, he is."

Nicole stepped outside and Asi's father watched her go with a stern glare before his servant shut the door.

"Where's Evren?" she hissed.

"Somewhere in the house," Caeruleus whispered back.

"What?! What do you mean in the—how did you even—"

"I boosted him up to look in a window—"

"Relax, I'm right here," Evren said, rounding the corner of the house.

Caeruleus sighed, dropping his head back.

"Tell me you found her," Nicole said, taking Evren's hand.

"Let's continue this conversation somewhere else, shall we?" Caeruleus said, leading them away by the shoulders and looking back at the house uncomfortably.

They made their way across the grounds.

"Asi was there, second room to the left of the second-floor landing. They don't seem to have any guards in the house. Just a few house keepers."

"That should be easy enough to handle when we're ready to go," Caeruleus said.

"Yeah, that's all we really needed, to find her. We shouldn't waste any time. I'm sure her father knew I was there sniffing around to find Asi."

"He might move her if he suspects we'll try something," Caeruleus suggested.

"Then we have to get her out tonight. I'm sorry that's not a lot of time, Evren."

"I've been ready to confront him for a long time."

"Confront who?" Caeruleus wondered.

"My father. If I'm finally getting out of this place, it's going to be after I look him in the eye and tell him to sard himself."

Caeruleus couldn't help letting out an envious chuckle. He wished he'd had the courage to do that before he had left home.

Raiden wasn't sure how long he had already endured Heimskur but he was exhausted and his mind was numb after the barrage of Heimskur's circuitous redundancy about how much the state of Navn was benefitting from Taroth's assistance. He was vague about what kind of influence Taroth made and dismissive of Raiden's questions.

"I think we'll have to visit Navn ourselves and hear from them," Raiden suggested.

"We can both agree it's in everyone's best interest that my men stay in Navn even if they want to adopt the rule of the keys. They were unstable without the Council's structure. I prevented a lot of chaos there. Consider it a favor. You certainly don't have the manpower to enforce order like I have, do you?"

Raiden smiled and lied. "We're recruiting and training more every day."

"Splendid. We have an understanding then."

"Seeing as Nicole was not invited to this meeting, I won't have an answer for you until I talk to her about everything we've discussed," Raiden said.

"Come now," Heimskur said. "You needn't trouble her. Fragile creatures are not suited for judgements like these. I would consult my cook about food but not matters of state. I am asking what you think. I have no need for what a wife thinks."

"She has the same authority as I have."

"She has the other key to be sure, but a knight and a fool are not equally matched merely because they both hold a sword," Heimskur said, chuckling. "I have chosen to respect your…authority in this realm. I think it's only fair for you to meet me half way and respect that I do not feel a woman's opinion is needed here. I need only yours, and with your queen so recently losing her brother, I dare say she will only bring irrelevant emotion to this matter."

Raiden tensed. News of Mitchell's death could only have arrived here through one channel—a direct link with Dawn.

"Without a woman you couldn't exist," Raiden said. "How can you suppose they are less than you?"

Heimskur laughed. "Food is undeniably a precious thing, but that doesn't mean I want the dirt from which it springs on my hands."

Raiden clenched his jaw and his fist tightened furiously as he took a deep breath.

"Now, now, I respect that outside Taroth there are different sentiments, daughters raised the same as sons, women with authority over themselves and even others—like your queen." He wore a lavishly smug smile on his face, no doubt sure that any lie was made true by his voice.

"No, you don't," Raiden said. "If you respected the idea of raising daughters the same as sons outside of Taroth, you wouldn't raise them like cattle here. Your inability to control people beyond your authority does not count as respect."

Heimskur's smile fell flat.

"Please excuse me. I would like to speak with my fellow king," Raiden said, refusing to even incline his head toward Heimskur as he left the room—hands still clenched and shoulders tense. If he stayed another minute longer, he would have hit Heimskur as hard as he could, and they would have been forced to leave. He could make him wait at least—waste his time while they searched for Asi.

❦

Evren led Nicole and Caeruleus back to their rooms. Nicole followed, lost in thought. Evren and Caeruleus' conversation was only indistinct background noise to her thoughts about Asi and memories and Mitchell. How could someone who permeated your entire existence even *be* erased without wiping away her identity completely? They couldn't. Raiden had done it and it worked because she had been a sudden flash in his life, a mere week of startling change, easily cut out. Even now, nearly three months could be erased with only the consequence of lost time. They made it to their rooms, and she wrenched herself away from those bleak possibilities.

"I should get ready," Evren said. "I'll meet you back here."

The door to Raiden's and her room opened before she could touch the handle—it was Raiden.

"There you are," he said. She watched the tense muscles of his face fall with relief and her heart ached. She put him through so much. "I looked everywhere until a servant thought I was lost and *kindly* led me back to our rooms." Then he noticed her ensemble, his gaze sliding down and back up with an amused smile.

Raiden's eyes shifted to Evren standing beside Caeruleus, then to his friend. A quizzical look passed Raiden's face, and Nicole glanced curiously at Caeruleus; for a moment she thought she spotted a flush in his face. He cleared his throat to disturb the silence, and Raiden smiled, gesturing for everyone to step into their rooms.

"Who's this?" he asked as he closed the door.

"Evren," she said, extending her hand to Raiden.

"The heir to the throne of Taroth," Nicole added.

"Oh," Raiden's eyes lit with surprise.

"Heir? But I thought the king only has a daughter," Caeruleus balked and Nicole smothered a smile in her hand. "Why did you let me think—" he sighed.

"You can still call me *he*," Evren said. "Both feel completely natural to me. This isn't a disguise; this is who I am—it just so happens that it allows me a little freedom here."

"But not enough," Nicole said.

"No. I can only be part of who I am here. I've got to get out of this place."

"Couldn't things change one day?" Raiden asked. "After all, you are the only heir."

"Father's advisors want him to make someone else his successor, some cousin of his who has several sons to take up the crown. I think the only thing stopping him is his ego—he hates the idea of his bloodline giving up the crown—not to mention he hates his cousin. So, he ignores his advisors for now and has been trying his best to father a new heir with as many mistresses at court as he can."

"The state of succession aside, it's probably best if you aren't in Taroth," Caeruleus suggested. "There's no telling when those advisors will decide eliminating the heir is the best way to ensure the succession goes the way they want it to. You can always return to claim the throne when the time comes."

"Sounds like you're coming with us then," Raiden said. "But there's the matter of why we came here in the first place."

"About that—I hope you sorted everything out with Heimskur," Caeruleus said.

"You found her," Raiden said.

"Thanks to Evren," Nicole said. "We can leave tonight."

"What's our plan then?"

☙

Nicole and Raiden waited in nerve-wracking silence on the balcony below Heimskur's while Evren scaled the rope ladder to the king's rooms above as they listened to cutlery clinking against china.

"Are we sure she has this under control?" Raiden asked.

"She has a truth potion and sleep powder with her," Nicole explained. "She'll get her answer and put him to sleep."

The ladder moved gently in the wind of the night and they listened anxiously.

"And what are you doing here?" Heimskur's voice came muffled through a full mouth. "Come to kill me and take the throne?" He chortled.

"I don't want your throne. I just want the truth," Evren said.

"Rather proud of yourself, aren't you?"

"I just need to know what really happened to my mother."

Heimskur laughed. "A truth potion? You stupid girl. Going through all this trouble to find out what you already know. There is no secret. She jumped."

"She would never do that," Evren's voice shook. "Drink it."

"Fine," he laughed harder.

There was silence for a few moments. Nicole and Raiden frowned at each other through the dark.

Evren finally asked, "Did you force her to do it?"

"I might have if she hadn't done it herself. She marched to her balcony and she jumped. That isn't what you thought you would hear, is it? She abandoned you all on her own."

Nicole's hand found Raiden's hand and he squeezed it.

"No. You still did it to her," Evren said, "With the life she was forced to lead—that we're all forced to lead."

"It's you who make yourselves miserable trying to deny your lot in life. What place is there in this world for a girl pretending to be a boy?" he scoffed.

"I'm not pretending to be anything. What you see is who I am."

"Your mother should have taken you with her," Heimskur said.

"It's a good thing I'm leaving then, I'm glad I have your support in that, at least."

"We both know what's best for girls who don't want the life given to them," he said flatly.

Nicole's heart raced. She didn't dare to breathe as she let go of Raiden's hand and leaned over the railing to look up, trying to see impossibly around the balcony. Evren should be coming back, she should have put Heimskur out with the powder. The light of Raiden's wings unfurling flashed in the darkness.

"Feel free to join them," Heimskur said.

From below Nicole spotted movement and her heart clenched—the large human mass of Heimskur had Evren's petite form in his arms, her head lolling. Then he hurled her over the railing.

Nicole gasped and lunged for Evren who fell well beyond her reach. Raiden grabbed Nicole's collar and yanked her back before he threw himself over the railing, wings poised behind him. Stunned, she rolled onto her hands and knees, jumped to her feet and ran to the railing, folding herself over it. She peered into the night toward the sounds of the crashing waves roaring far below— nothing. Her breaths turned short and fast as she straightened up and searched the sky hanging over the ocean and saw no movement. *Where are they?*

Her panic caught fire and she shuddered with anger, whirling around and storming through the silent rooms then out the doors into the hall where Caeruleus stood keeping watch.

"Nicole—wait, what happened?"

She couldn't answer. She didn't have the words.

"Where's—" he was startled into silence and stepped back from the look in her eyes. The intricately woven fibers of the carpet beneath her feet glowed red, burned and blackened as she left him behind. She heard his swift footsteps catching up to her.

"What happened?" Caeruleus demanded as fiercely as he could through a hushed voice in the quiet halls.

The words crowded in her throat, and she couldn't get them out. He caught her shoulder.

"Nicole—"

She had to swallow back the bile in the back of her mouth. "He threw Evren off the balcony."

Caeruleus froze, his eye round in dismay. She turned back to her march, knowing she wouldn't find her way through this place by guessing. She placed her hand on the wall, running it against the cold stone, letting her magic seep into the castle, crawling through the walls until she had a picture of the maze and the route to king's chambers clear in her head.

"Wait—" Caeruleus lurched out of his shock behind her, his hasty steps catching up once more. "Where's Ray?"

"He tried to save Evren," she said, her voice a growl.

"Tried?"

"I don't know—that man—he," her words were lost in a seething wave of heat. She strode as quickly as she could without breaking into a run as she found the staircase upstairs.

"What do you think you're going to do? Nicole, we should be looking for Raiden. We have to get Asi, not make things worse—"

Caeruleus stopped, halting halfway around the corner where they could see the corridor to Heimskur's chambers and the two guards standing—one on each side of the door. He jumped back, but Nicole continued without breaking her stride. Trembling with rage, she struggled to move her body at a careful polite pace as she approached the doors to Heimskur's chambers.

The pair of guards stood statuesque. Their stony expressions faltered in surprise when they saw her. Their eyes shifted first to each other then back to her. They knew who she was, but what did they make of her arriving here alone, she wondered.

"I'm here to see the king," she said, her voice breathy with an effort to maintain her composure. *Let them think it's a tryst,* she thought wryly as she let out a wave of influencing magic, fighting the disgust that twisted her stomach and nearly turned her mouth into a sneer.

One of them cleared his throat and stepped aside, opening the door behind him and motioning her to enter. He shut the door behind her, and she took a deep shaking breath.

"Now this is a far more interesting surprise," Heimskur said, spotting her as he crossed his chambers with a smug smile on his face. She had seen his pompous expression in so many paintings throughout the castle that she didn't even feel like she was seeing this man for the first time.

"What could possibly bring you here to see me at this hour, alone?" He chuckled. She swallowed back her bitter disgust as he looked her up and down. "You're not bad to look at but not tempting enough for the trouble."

Nicole could barely breathe through her revulsion and rage; it smoldered in her chest and she wondered if her heart would turn black from it or if there would be anything left after it was all over and Venarius was finally dead.

"I'm here for Evren," she said. "And every girl prisoner here."

Everything in the room shuddered, furniture, vases, paintings. *For Asi. For Fen. For every woman who would rather die than live here. For every girl who will be born here. For everyone woman ever told she belongs to a man.* Was she any better than Belen if she only came here to save Asi, and only smuggle out Evren because she had *asked* for a way out when she knew she could do something to change things even if it was messy? Even if it made her a murderer?

He laughed heartily. "That key around your neck doesn't give you any real authority here. It's a joke. What does it matter to you?"

"You take their freedom. You take their voices. You're the worst kind of vile."

"I'm afraid you can't intimidate me," he said with a snide grin. "I wear an amulet to protect me from magic, its sewn into my clothes. So what does that make you—without the power of a fera—without the authority of your silly key? Just a woman full of nonsense."

Nicole smiled, looking at a pompous man who had never been challenged in his life, never been pushed, never had to pick himself up from the dirt, never had his crown knocked off his head. He wasn't particularly tall, having only a few inches on her at most. Right now, the worst thing about this place was the best thing about it. *I'm just a woman.*

"You may see yourself out," he said, raising his hand to present the door.

It was so easy to grab his hand and bend it back toward him. He cried out, dropping to his knees.

"I'm not done," she said, pushing his hand back further as he yelped. Behind her she heard the door handle jerk, and the muffled thuds of an altercation through the door, but Heimskur's cries drowned it out as he squirmed.

❧

Raiden was stunned to find himself caught by a spell, suspended in the air beside an equally stunned Evren. They had plummeted toward the rocks and the ocean, the ether of Pharos was barred, and he knew he wasn't going to reach Evren, but he couldn't bring himself to stop reaching. Then, suddenly, the whipping wind was gone.

"What happened?" Evren asked, looking around dazed. They were in a cave it seemed, lit with the warm light of little fires. The frantic rhythm of footsteps approached, and someone came running, skidding to a halt.

"Everyone okay?" the girl asked, reaching up to pull Evren by the hand out of the suspension spell.

Once Evren had both feet on the ground, the girl reached out to take Raiden's hand but then noticed his wings. "Whoa. You're not a jumper." She pulled him out of the spell and he was glad to have his feet hit the ground.

"I beg your pardon?"

"Did you try to save him?" she surmised. "Not many young men take this way out you know, at least we're here though."

"Where is 'here'?" Evren asked.

"A cave in the cliff. We've been expanding and connecting them for years."

"Ginette," a frantic voice echoed in the tunnel. "Who is it?" A woman came around the corner at a run and stopped abruptly.

"Mother?" Evren's voice trembled and the woman's eyes watered as she stumbled forward to catch her child in her arms.

"Evren—my beautiful child, look at you, you're so handsome." The woman laughed and sobbed at once.

Raiden's breath caught in his lungs—watching a mother who had been long gone embrace her son. He dropped his gaze from the bittersweet sight as Evren's mother kissed his face. His memories of his mother's embrace were like an old blanket, tattered and threadbare, no longer able to warm him—memories would never be enough, no matter how sweet they were.

"Oh, my sweet Evren," her mother said, stroking her hair. "I'm sorry. I'm so sorry I left you there."

"You jumped," Evren said.

"I did. We all did. Women of Taroth have been taking that way out for so long. And as hard as I tried to change things, the pushback was always too much to overcome. I realized we had to change our methods. We needed to save those girls who saw no other way out and give them a chance, to heal, to fight."

"But why not bring me with you?"

"They think we're all dead. I didn't want to take your right to the throne from you. Whether Heimskur likes it or not, you're his only heir. Try as he might, he won't father any more children," she said with a smile.

"A curse?" Raiden guessed.

"A potion, I made him infertile after Evren was born," she said. "I know things cannot change without us fighting up there, but my place is here, to catch those who cannot endure it any longer. I hoped that I was planting a seed of defiance in the hearts of those I left behind."

Left behind, Raiden's thoughts snapped back to Nicole up in the castle. "Nicole might be thinking the worst right now," Raiden said, looking up toward the ceiling of the cave.

Evren's eyes went wide at the thought, remembering how things had ended above on Heimskur's balcony.

"How do we get out of here?"

"Ginette can show you the way outside. We aren't far from the palace. Evren, you should go back."

Evren laughed. "That should give him a good shock. I wonder how well he'll handle a daughter he can't kill."

"*Kill?*" Diona's outrage startled everyone.

"I fumbled my sleeping powder and he threw me off the balcony after I confronted him about your death."

A man's distant scream suddenly erupted in the cave as a fat and overly adorned figure fell through the ceiling and bobbed, squirming, in the suspension spell. Heimskur's face was bloodied and swollen, his robes and jewels were the only things that made him recognizable. A moan gurgled in his throat. He coughed, gasped, and choked until he fell limp and hung there in the utterly stunned silence.

Everyone stared, eyes wide, mouths falling open in shock. Raiden swallowed the lump in his throat, worried that grief for Evren had pushed Nicole headlong into the bottomless hole left by Mitchell.

"The way out, please," he insisted. "Quickly."

Diona pulled herself from her astonishment. "Ginette—send the message through the tunnels, to *everyone*—we need them all here. Now. As fast as you can."

"Yes, Ma'am," she nodded, bolting down the tunnel.

"I'll take you back," Diona said to Raiden with a solemn look and turned toward the tunnel with a sigh. "We're not ready for *this*." They all stared at the body of the dead king.

"For what?" Evren asked, finally pulling his bewildered stare away from Heimskur as he hurried after them.

"You may be the rightful heir, but they'll try to stop you, Evren, and they can. His advisors, his guard. You're one person—you need an army to take what's yours. I cannot give you legions of uniformed soldiers, but there are a few thousand of us now with fire in our hearts and steel in our hands."

"Heimskur has most of his legions 'keeping order' in Navn right now," Raiden offered as they made their way through the tunnels to the exit. He grew more anxious with every turn, the tunnel seemed to go on and on when he needed out.

"They won't make this easy, it's going to be a race. Can we get our people to Pharos before they get their men from Navn?" Diona wondered.

Raiden heard but his mind was more concerned about the race to get to Nicole before her grief could consume her.

❧

Nicole sat on the steps between two rooms in Heimskur's chambers, listening to the sound of her labored breathing, counting the tempo of her heartbeat throbbing in her fingers as she turned his crown over in her hands. She couldn't bring herself to care at all. Watching him fall should have been satisfying at least, but she couldn't even feel that.

"You may have started a war," Caeruleus said, sagging with exhaustion onto the low table by the doors.

She sighed and stood up, tossing the crown toward the balcony to hear it clang against the stone and slide across the floor.

"I didn't start this one."

"Nicole?" Raiden's voice called in the distance, wafting in from outside. She turned her head to see him on the balcony looking shaken—without Evren.

Her face crumpled.

"Evren is alive," he explained hastily as he strode into the golden light of the king's chamber.

She sagged with relief as he crossed the rooms and took her face in his hands, pressing his forehead to hers.

"You scared me there," she admitted.

"I'm sorry."

She took a deep breath and let it out with her disappointment. Raiden let his hands slip from her face and he looked down, taking her hands gently to study her raw knuckles, reddened more by Heimskur's blood than her own.

"They hurt?"

"A little," she lied, but telling him she couldn't feel anything might worry him more than her pain ever could.

He muttered something and brought her hands to his lips, kissing the back of each one. A charged warmth spread through her hands, chasing away the ache and healing the skin across her knuckles.

Raiden sighed, but she couldn't read him. He looked around the rooms and she did too, wondering what he thought of her as he took in the blood smears on the polished floor and the six palace guards lying scattered around the room—the first two who had been outside the door had to be dragged inside to keep them from alerting any more than the two more pairs who had been alerted to the sounds of Caeruleus trying to stop Nicole inside the king's rooms. But in taking care of the guards, Caeruleus couldn't stop her. By the time he dealt with them, she had Heimskur over the rail of the balcony. He sat hunched over on the low table by the doors.

"Caeruleus helped," she said.

"She was a little preoccupied," he said, raising his head. "Where's Evren?" he wondered.

"With his mother."

"Wait, what?" Nicole shook her head. That answer sounded more ominous than reassuring. She didn't understand.

"I'll explain on the way—we should go get Asi before more guards figure out what's going on, and this mess gets out of hand," Raiden insisted.

Caeruleus scoffed. "She beat the king to a pulp and threw him off a balcony. It's already out of hand."

She rolled her eyes, "Let's just go."

❧

Raiden knocked on the door of the healer's house and the three of them waited.

"I don't suppose any of those guards have woken up yet," Caeruleus said. "It's still quiet."

"Who do we have to worry about in there?" Raiden asked.

"Just Asi's father and the servants," Nicole said. "There aren't any guards inside."

"No, just the ones outside who will hear us talking," Caeruleus muttered.

The door latch clicked, and they all tensed before the door opened.

"Nicole!" Asi cried, lunging through the door and seizing her in a hug.

Nicole synched her arms around Asi in stunned relief. "Oh—you remember."

"Hold on," Caeruleus said, leaning into the door to peer into the house. "How did you—"

"I had a little help," she said. "Evren found my room earlier and got me out of my bindings. Loak was right—being small and unassuming is a wonderful advantage. Father didn't expect me to be untied," she said, grinning. "And the servants were all busy packing."

"Packing?" Nicole asked, leaning to peer into the house. There were white sheets thrown over the furniture she could see in the entranceway.

"Yeah, they were getting ready to take me back to our old house on the southern coast. I went ahead and took their memories of me being home at all. They'll wake up like I've always been gone."

Nicole gave Asi a proud squeeze.

"Good," Caeruleus chuckled.

"Some missing time will hardly be noticed when they wake up to the news that the king is dead," Raiden added.

"What?!" Asi balked. "How did—"

"Long story, we should really get the hell out of here. This place is going to turn into chaos," Caeruleus said.

"What about Evren? We don't know how many people Diona can have here in a short time," Raiden said.

"I'll stay," Caeruleus nodded. "You three can get out of here. Leave the guards, there are fifteen of us at least who can stick to Evren while the queen gathers her people along the coast and moves them here."

Asi stepped away from Nicole and threw her arms around Caeruleus' waist. He looked at Nicole and Raiden with astonishment on his face.

"Thank you Caeruleus, please be safe," Asi said.

"I'll be fine—we'll be fine," he said, nodding. Nicole could hear his doubt.

They made their way across the grounds in grim silence, returning to the Tempest. The guards on the Tempest disembarked to stay behind with Caeruleus. Before they stepped into the elevator, Raiden pulled Caeruleus into his arms for a firm embrace. "Be careful," he said and released him.

Nicole couldn't ignore the pang of guilt in her heart—more danger, there was always more.

Captain Rhee took Nicole, Raiden and Asi beyond Pharos where they could disembark from the Tempest and step into the ether. Raiden took Asi back to the palace of the keys. Nicole, however, asked Rhee to wait for her as she slipped through the ether to Eanna. She arrived in the rooms she had shared with Raiden and tried not to look around as she crossed the grounds. She figured it wouldn't take long for the Queen's Kestrels to join her.

"Nicole, your highness," a woman's voice addressed her from behind. "What brings you back to Hypatia?"

She turned to see Amulya with four of her ladies, holding arrows against their bows carefully, not ready to shoot, but not completely relaxed. She could see the uncertainty on their faces, and she understood—she had left Eanna angry with Belen, and her return in the middle of the night couldn't look benevolent at all.

"We got Asi back," she began, wanting them to know that she hadn't returned carrying her animosity. "The king of Taroth is dead, the queen and the rightful heir need Eanna's help."

Amulya's posture went slack in surprise, and her kestrels relaxed their bows as well.

"Can you take me to Belen?" Nicole requested.

Amulya gave a single stern nod and set off at a brisk pace across the grounds. Nicole followed anxiously, growing tenser with every passing minute. The serenity of the gardens beneath the stars could not ease her. The chirps of crickets and frogs in the cool night air could not soften her severe focus. They reached the queen's quarters where Akarsha stood outside, surprised to see Nicole escorted there by her sister. Amulya spoke quietly to her sister and Akarsha disappeared into the queen's quarters. A few minutes passed before Belen emerged, robed in sky-blue linen, her face creased with concern.

"Nicole," she said her name like a patient mother.

Nicole swallowed back a lump in her throat. She didn't have time for sentiments or apologies. "We need your help," she explained and hurried through the events of the last hour. "You couldn't bring yourself to defy Heimskur to defend the liberty you claim to value here in Eanna. I think you and I both know it is in Eanna's best interest to see Evren take the throne in Taroth instead of Heimskur's cousin. You have another chance here," Nicole said. "Will you cower or will you help?"

Belen nodded earnestly, "Of course we'll help. Amulya will bring the kestrels to aid Caeruleus and your guards in protecting Evren's bid for her rightful place on the throne."

Nicole tried to soften herself toward the queen, but she knew this enthusiasm was about political advantage first and foremost.

She turned to go and paused, "Thank you," she offered.

"Nicole!" Belen said with soft urgency. "I am truly sorry—about your brother and Asi. I'm glad you've gotten her back home safely."

She struggled to acknowledge Belen's sentiments with a smile. Nicole knew she was trying to make amends; but Nicole didn't care, she just wanted to get the Queen's Kestrels back to the Tempest where it waited outside Pharos. The sooner they were on their way to Evren's aid, the sooner she could return to the palace of the keys and be sure Gordan was all right.

Forty-one

Nicole climbed the stairs to the tower, anxious to see Gordan. She shouldered the door in the floor open and straightened up into the circular room. It was almost surreal to find him exactly as she had imagined him, sitting on the floor at the open window, one leg dangling out in the open air.

"Asi is safe and sound with Fen and Keren," she said, climbing into their sanctuary.

Gordan unfolded himself and stood up. He crossed the room and draped his arms around her. "I knew you'd find her." She sighed in his arms and heaved the whole story of Taroth off her chest. He didn't release her for a moment of it.

She had finished what she set out to do, and now that she was back, she knew she couldn't postpone the horrible task of returning home to Yuma any longer. The moment they left this tower she would have to make that trip.

"Gordan, I have to tell my dad," she choked.

He squeezed her harder.

"We'll go together—all right?"

She nodded. They didn't know how to let go of each other for a long time, like they weren't sure they could hold themselves

633

together on their own anymore; if they broke their embrace, they might finally fall apart.

"We used to hide from the world together," she remembered.

"Who?"

"Mitch and I—when we were little. We would build forts and hide inside. Something as silly as stacked chairs covered in blankets could block out anything bad." That's where she wanted to be— more than anything—and her shoulders shook with silent sobs.

"Would…you show me?"

She looked up at Gordan and saw his eyes welling—he wanted to get closer to Mitchell, even in his absence, even if it hurt.

❦

"Here you are," Raiden said gently as he straightened up through the hatch-doorway into the tower. He stopped, puzzled by the sight of Nicole and Gordan hunkered down inside a makeshift shelter made of pillows, blankets and chairs that had been conjured into the tower.

"What are you two doing?"

"Just showing Gordan what a pillow fort is," Nicole explained. "Mitchell and I used to make them all the time." Sadness lurked in her voice, making it waver a little.

"Is there room for one more?"

"I think we can fit you in," Gordan said.

Raiden crawled into the mouth of the soft cave they had built to find a little group of firefly lights hovering in the draped blanket ceiling of their safe haven. He settled in on the opposite side of Nicole, sandwiching her between Gordan and himself.

"I have news from Caeruleus," he said, fishing the letter out of his pocket.

"It's good news," Gordan assured Nicole quietly.

"It is," he agreed as he unfolded the letter and read it out loud.

Nicole & Raiden,

Evren is well. The guards and I are returning to the midlands tomorrow, but I wanted inform you immediately of matters in Taroth.

In the last three days Queen Belen's Kestrels have stayed by Evren's side. The guards and I have assisted, clearing the king's guards from the palace, along with his advisors. Captain Rhee and Priseil set out to transport Queen Diona's people up the coast. As the many women and young men thought lost to the cliffs have made their way north in support of Evren, a remarkable number of women—those infant girls turned to boys by the abuse of Caenis Wish herb in this kingdom—joined the ranks of support. This is certainly not over, but Evren has a formidable militia building around him. I think it best to remove myself and our men. This is their fight now and I don't want our presence to color Evren's move for the throne as being controlled by outside authorities.

We've heard word that the king's advisors have gone to Heimskur's cousin in the north of Taroth, but they are still scrambling to retrieve Heimskur's troops from Navn. Word of the king's demise has resulted in a significant number of deserters—perhaps more women trapped in bodies changed by their parents, or men like me or Evren finally encouraged to dissent. Either way, when they finally organize their opposition to Evren's birthright, they will find he already has the throne and has an army waiting to meet them. I am not worried about leaving Taroth.

Evren has asked me to convey his gratitude and regards. He hopes we will return in the future for a far more peaceful visit. I will see you soon.

Caeruleus

Raiden folded the letter. He sighed, sinking into the peace of silence inhabited by people he trusted, of the pillows and blankets around them and of the lazy firefly lights above them. He didn't want everything outside this soft place to exist anymore—the palace of the keys, the political squabbles of a fractured realm, or Venarius and Dawn. He lay there in bittersweet contentment—they could not hide wrapped in a pretty illusion of safety and nostalgia—not forever at least…but maybe…just for now.

They sank together into that sweet silence. He didn't need

Gordan's gift to see the numbness in Nicole's eyes when she turned to him and looked at him; he knew it well. *What do we do from here,* he wondered. Let this palace become their prison, their tomb, the only place they were beyond Dawn's reach? He was most afraid of Nicole deciding to go after Venarius. He knew it was there festering in her wounds. *She won't heal while he's alive.* He realized with a pang of guilt that she might never heal from this. He looked around at the memories she rebuilt around herself, but Mitchell would always be missing. He glanced out the opening to their fort and through the tower window at the sky. He watched the blue for a long time, knowing it would welcome him, erase everything from his mind and heart if he let it, but he'd never abandon the people he loved for that freedom.

Then a familiar shape swooped past the tower. The Tempest was back. Raiden had no idea how long he had been in the tower.

"They're here," he said. He knew Nicole didn't want to leave, neither did Gordan. "I'll go welcome Caeruleus." He kissed Nicole's cheek swiftly before slipping into the ether down to the throne room.

"Should we join him?" Gordan asked.

Nicole rolled over to face Gordan. She only ever saw Mitchell's absence in his eyes when he looked at her now, and she felt awful knowing she reminded him of what he had lost.

"I can't keep putting off going home," she said. It was the only thing on her mind. She had lost count of how many times in the last four days she mustered up the courage to walk back to her rooms to stand hand-in-hand with Gordan and Raiden before the door to Cantis, only to crumple under the agony. The only thing she could do was rationalize her cowardice as gifting her father with more time believing both his children would return home. She knew the day she delivered the news would be the day the light in his eyes would die, the day he finally looked at her and saw her for what she is now—the cause of pain and destruction no matter where she goes. It felt like a long time passed in the silence.

The palace walls shuddered with a low resonating boom, and they whipped their gazes to each other as they lurched upright. Nicole took his hand frantically before falling into the ether, letting her key drag them down to the throne room. They emerged from the ether into a strange reddish fog—she couldn't even be sure they were in the throne room.

"Raiden?" Nicole shouted. *Answer*, she begged as she ran into the creeping cloud.

"Don't breathe it in," Gordan warned.

She pulled her shirt over her mouth and had to concentrate on expanding her magic around them—parting the fog.

"Raiden," she screamed.

"Maybe he wasn't—"

"Nicole," a heavily muffled voice called from all around them.

"You try that way," Gordan said and plunged into the fog in the opposite direction, shielding his nose and mouth with his shirt.

She hurried forward, pushing at the fog that seemed to push back. When she saw a human shape, she rushed toward it until the red cloud rolled back. Unbelievably, Mitchell stood there. She froze and her heart dropped. He was blank—his amber eyes blinked but did not emote, his movement was too controlled. The sight of him, knowing so clearly that her brother was not there, made her muscles weak. He looked at her without even the slightest recognition in his eyes.

"This can continue, or you may come find me," it was her brother's voice, but its rhythm and tone were wrong—she knew the words were Venarius'.

As her empty brother walked away, she was too disturbed to do anything, too shocked to call out or remember to keep the fog at bay as it crept back around her and swallowed her.

Gordan came upon the hazy shapes of two bodies, one bent over the other and could not make out who was whom until he was practically on top of them. Raiden lay on the floor unconscious and bleeding from a wound in his side, while Caeruleus could only hold his shirt over his mouth and his other hand against Raiden's wound.

"Help me stop the bleeding," Caeruleus said.

Gordan dropped down and pressed his free hand against the bloody opening in between Raiden's ribs and hip while Caeruleus moved his bloodied hand to shield Raiden's nose and mouth from the fog.

"Nicole!" he shouted before taking a deep breath and removing his hand from his mouth to let a surge of fire out.

Nicole heard the sound of her name wrap around her in the fog and realized both her hands were on the cold stone floor. She gasped inside the cloud. An orange glow flourished deep in the haze, and her brain finally placed the voice—Gordan.

She wrestled her senses back from the depths of her horrified stupor, pushing the heat out from her core until the prickling warmth ballooned around her once more, chasing back the unknown miasma. A breath of clear air and her wobbling vision grew still enough that she could get to her feet and veer in the direction she had seen the glow. The fog retreated and she found them—Caeruleus and Gordan kneeling over Raiden, a pool of blood beneath him.

With the air cleared around them, they dropped their hands from their mouths and pressed them to Raiden's wound.

"I think it's a leech curse; the wound won't clot or heal—we need fresh nettle," Caeruleus said.

"We've got to get him out of here first," Gordan said.

Nicole sank down, pressing her hand over Caeruleus and Gordan's hands and in a dizzying instant they found themselves on the large pillow bed in her chamber. She stumbled toward the door to Keren's cabin, her hand—slick with Raiden's blood—slipped on the knob. After wiping it frantically against her clothes, she tried the knob again. Finally, she wrenched the door open and lunged into the living room.

"Keren!"

The living room was empty. She ran into the kitchen. The

kitchen was empty.

"Fen! Asi!"

"Is that Nicole?" Their voices were faint from outside.

"Nicole?"

She ran back into the living room. Keren lurched through the front door, Asi and Fen at her heels.

"What's going on?"

"I need nettle—it's Raiden," she said breathlessly.

Keren's eyes went wide, and she pointed toward the stairs. "What happened?"

They ran upstairs and down the hall to a door, behind which was the ladder to the roof and the garden.

"There was an attack—" Nicole's mind seized on the memory of Mitchell. "Raiden's wound won't stop bleeding. Caeruleus thinks it's leech curse."

"It's quite common to lace blades with a leech curse," Keren replied as she hurried to the back corner of the rooftop garden where a couple green waist-high stalks stood upright. "But I thought the palace was safe; you said people couldn't get inside with the intent to harm you or take the keys."

But this assassin had no will of his own. Perhaps a puppet on a string with no intent couldn't trigger the protection spells.

"Was it just the wound?" Keren asked. Nicole watched her reach for a hand-sized leaf near its base the whole stock curled, whipping at her as she snatched the leaf away.

"There was a red fog," she said, her eyes locked on Keren's hands as she plucked two more, the stinging nettle snapping across her knuckles and Nicole thought she heard it hiss. "When I breathed it just for a minute, my muscles went weak and my vision shook."

"Someone wanted to be sure he bled out," Keren said as she crossed the garden and pushed the leaves into Nicole's bloody hand. "Place them on the wound. It removes curses, like sucking out poison."

They hurried back down the ladder and downstairs.

"Fen and I will be there as soon as we can," Keren said as Nicole ran back through the door into her chamber.

Caeruleus and Gordan still had their hands pressed against Raiden's side.

"Here," she said.

Caeruleus turned, pulling a hand away from Raiden to take a nettle leaf and press it against the wound with shaking hands. Beneath his bloody hand, the leaf turned black. Caeruleus tossed it aside and reached for another one. This leaf darkened slowly and the bleeding slowed as well. When the second leaf was black, Nicole handed him a third leaf. The bleeding had nearly stopped and only the serrated edges of the leaf blackened.

Caeruleus took a deep breath and let it out. "I think that did it. Without the curse we should be able to heal the wound."

"Nicole?" Gordan spoke her name to shake her from her trance, staring down at Raiden, the wound, the unnerving amount of blood soaking the cushion beneath him. Lying there, unconscious, he already looked dead to her terrified mind. She dropped beside him, suddenly afraid that he had bled out before their eyes while they thought the nettle was helping.

She stooped beside him, pressing her fingers under his jaw and sagged with relief when she felt the slow pulse there. A tiny sob slipped past her lips as she moved closer to Caeruleus, placing her hand over his on Raiden's wound. The swell of her magic from her core came with a rush of tears.

☙

Gordan and Caeruleus moved Raiden to his chamber. Nicole could only sink to the floor beside the large cushion and stare at the red stain upon it. She looked down at her bloody hands lying helplessly in her lap. She wiped them halfheartedly on the edge of the pillow, but more blood remained than came off.

This may continue, or you may come find me, Venarius had said through her brother's body. She hated that he not only stole Mitchell from her, but sullied his voice too.

"I won't keep doing this," she said, her voice hoarse and exhausted.

She got up, went to her traveling chest, and opened it to see the pages of the Hessian journal still sitting on the top where she had dropped them.

"Gim," she said. She plucked him off her chest and held him out on her palm, presenting the journal pages. What would Venarius trade to get this back, she wondered?

He spit a little tongue of fire at the pages and the bottom corner caught, pages curling and blackening as the flames licked up the outer edge. She held the thread-bound edge securely, watching the flames grow excitedly, creeping toward her fingers, consuming the precious knowledge penned on those pages more than a century ago.

Not until the fire brushed lightly against the tips of her fingers—just as whisper of pain—did she drop the journal and watch the rest of it burn at her feet. *This ends with me.* She raised her hand to study Raiden's blood drying in her nail beds and her life line. *He'll trade Mitchell for a journal that doesn't exist.* She stared down at the ashes, the secrets to her existence—gone. *I'll sign his stupid contract—contracts can be broken after all.* She thought of Caeruleus defying his blood contract with the Council. There would be repercussions. If Venarius thought her life being tied to his would stop her from killing him, then he might let his guard down enough for Nicole to prove him wrong. She knew Gordan and Raiden wouldn't approve of her plan. She remembered her promise to Raiden that she wouldn't face Venarius alone—*promises are breakable too.*

༄

Gordan stood over Raiden. They cleaned him up. His wound was healed, but he was still unresponsive. Caeruleus, Loak, Leone and every guard were busy searching for the attacker and how he could have possibly gotten inside. Gordan knew he had seen the fuzzy shape of someone in the fog when he ran through the throne room.

They thought they were safe here with all the magic in these walls. Gordan sighed and turned away reluctantly, knowing he needed to check on Nicole, but he did not want to leave Raiden unaccompanied. Pained—he resolved to stay by Raiden's side and keep him safe, despite knowing this was the worst time for Nicole to be alone. He would check on her when someone else could watch over Raiden.

Splashing water echoed in the high ceiling of Nicole's bathroom as she scrubbed away Raiden's blood, she felt like she had nothing left but anger. Her reflection looked unhinged—bloodstained sleeves, wild hair, drained eyes. She pulled off her stained clothes and threw them into the sink before she left the bathroom. She refused to let Venarius hurt any more people she loved. No one else needed to die. They were just lucky Raiden wasn't with Mitchell now, and if she did this right, she could fix the damage already done.

She never wanted to be the kind of person who leaves the people who need her, but she couldn't watch anyone else die. She could face death. Mitchell had done it, so could she if it meant saving them all.

At her trunk she dug out her thick grey running leggings and a black long-sleeved shirt. She yanked her clothes on. Then she shrugged on her denim jacket. Gim emerged from the trunk and scurried up her leg, disappearing beneath her jacket.

Fen and Keren stepped through the door into Nicole's chamber as she tied her boots.

"How is he?" Fen asked, holding a bottle as tall as her hand filled with peach toned liquid, it glowed a little as it sloshed.

"The nettle worked and his wound is healed, but he's still out cold," Nicole explained as she stood up, following Fen's horrified gaze at the bloodstained bed. "He's next door in his room."

"I have a purifying potion that should clear his system. Not knowing what kind of miasma it was, this is the best I can do. It should do the trick."

"Thank you, Fen," she said, leading them into the hall.

"What about you?" Keren asked. "Are you all right?"

"I'm fine," Nicole lied and didn't feel a thing.

"You said you breathed some of it too," Keren said.

"Everyone exposed to the miasma should take some of this even a little can linger in your body and it could affect you when you don't expect it," Fen said as they walked into Raiden's chamber.

Caeruleus looked up from the chair beside the bed and stood. "How can I help?"

"Help me sit him up and give him this," Fen said.

Nicole and Keren watched as Caeruleus and Fen carefully coaxed sips of the potion into Raiden's mouth until she was satisfied with how much he had ingested—almost half the bottle.

"That should be enough," she said. "Now you." She held the bottle out to Caeruleus. "One big mouthful."

He didn't question her as he took the bottle and tipped it back. Fen took the bottle from him and handed it to Nicole. Dutifully, she took her swig—the taste of sweet green honeydew melon hit her tongue—and handed it back. The potion hit her stomach and grew warm.

"Where's Gordan, he needs the last of this," Fen said.

"He went up to the tower to search the hills around the palace," Nicole said.

"I know the way, stay with him," Fen insisted. "He should wake up soon."

Caeruleus looked at Nicole and nodded toward the chair. She dragged it a little closer to the bed and sat down, thinking of Mitchell beside her bed until her eyes burned. She couldn't take any more of this. Caeruleus sat down on the floor, leaning against the end of the bed.

"I think I'll go make everyone some tea," Keren said softly, placing a hand on Nicole's shoulder before she left the room and headed back to Nicole's chamber.

Nicole slid her hand across the bed and closed her fingers around his. She closed her eyes and felt warm drops fall, waiting for him to wake up so she could say goodbye. She should have asked him to leave her alone the day she met him. She should have left him in the forest back in Cantis, closed the portal and never looked back. It would have been so much easier to leave him then.

Venarius pulled a gold pocket watch from his vest and flicked it open. Its face glowed as the second-hand ticked. He waited with a satisfied twist on his lips. His puppet could slip through the protection spells with a cursed blade completely undetected. It would have been easy to kill the king as instantly as the brother, but a little more show for Nicole was worth it. He would bleed out in minutes. Venarius wanted her to see it. He wanted her to walk through his blood—let her defiance drown in it. *She will come willingly.*

The puppet returned and he chuckled. "She couldn't destroy you." *Love makes this too easy.* "Shall we wait somewhere private for her? She join us shortly, she need only step through the ether, after all," he said.

Forty-two

Nicole stepped out of the ether into a forest, it was unfamiliar and nowhere near the palace.

"Venarius," she said, a threat in her voice. "I know you're here… I want to end this."

He emerged from the trees calmly. "And how do you propose we accomplish that? Have you come here to kill me?"

"No. I'm here to give you what you want."

"Is that so?"

"I'll hand myself over to you to stop this. You can have your precious creation."

"And what do you get out of this deal?"

"You'll bring back Mitchell and let him go. You won't harm him or Raiden or anyone I love. I want you to swear that you *and* your people will leave them alone."

"Now, you see, there's a problem with that arrangement. Even under our mutual agreement, *they* won't give up on you. They'll search until they find you again, and if they try to steal what's rightfully mine, I will be forced to kill them."

"Well, then, I have incentive to keep them away, don't I?"

"You'll stay with me? You'll do whatever it takes to keep them from finding you—even keep them from hurting me?"

"That's my deal."

Raiden wrenched himself free of the vision, throwing himself upright in disbelief and horror.

"Raiden," Nicole said, startled.

Caeruleus jumped up from the floor near the foot of the bed.

Raiden took her hand and squeezed it hard, unable to release the words trapped in his chest.

"I should go get Fen and Gordan," she said, standing, pulling her hand from his.

His heart reeled. He couldn't let her walk out of this room.

"Nicole," he finally choked out, throwing his legs over the side of the bed and heaving his body onto his feet.

She turned and started, reaching for him anxiously. "Raiden— you shouldn't—"

He caught her face in his hands, stopping her words with a kiss. The heat of magic and panic welled up in his throat, flooding his lips until they burned. Sleep—an unspoken spell of heavy slumber—was the only thing he could think of in his groggy, troubled mind, his heart still reeling from the vision.

The weight of her body sagged against him as the sleeping curse seized her. His arms caught her, but he was too weak to hold both her and himself up. He sank to the floor with her.

"Ray," Caeruleus said through quiet shock. "Did you just—"

Gordan and Fen walked into the chamber, stopping at the sight of them.

"What happened?" Fen asked incredulously.

"Raiden," Gordan's voice was heavy. "What have you done?"

"She—she was going to find Venarius—I saw her hand herself over to him—I just couldn't—" Raiden shook his head—he had to stop her.

Gordan knelt down and gathered Nicole up into his arms. "Well, it's done. Seeing as you're making these decisions alone, what would you have us do now?"

"The palace isn't safe anymore," Raiden said. "We can't stay here."

"You're not wholly recovered," Caeruleus insisted as he helped Raiden to his feet.

"I think I know a place we can go. No one will even know we could be there," Raiden said.

"No one will look for you at all if they think you're still in the palace," Fen said.

☙

Nicole was unnerved to find herself in the familiar dark haze of sleep. She didn't remember going to bed, she couldn't even imagine sleeping with everything that happened to Raiden and—

"What a surprise to meet you here of all places," a chilly voice familiar to her ears spoke behind her. She turned toward the voice in the darkness.

"Amarth," she said, recognizing the ghostly adolescent she'd met in Cantis. "Why would I be dreaming of you?" she muttered, mostly to herself. She hadn't seen him since her first several days in Cantis.

"You're somewhere far deeper than dreams. This is a place on the fringes of Death, at the water's edge so to speak. A sleeping curse isn't quite death after all but close enough. Who would have sent you here, I wonder?" There was a devious smile on his face.

"A sleeping curse—" she said, a wry smile pulling at her lips, poisoned apples and spinning wheel spindles, how could Venarius have—Nicole gasped at the faint warbling tenor of Gordan's voice in her ears.

"You know I'd do anything for her too—but not this," Gordan said.

Raiden's voice sounded weak. "I didn't have a choice. She was handing herself over to Venarius."

"No—she was planning to. You *had* a choice, Raiden."

"Are you going to stand there and claim you wouldn't have tried to stop her from doing it?"

"Of course, I would have—by talking to her. You *cursed* her, Raiden. You took away *her choice* in the matter."

Nicole shook her head—*Raiden did this?* She remembered burning the journal and making her decision. Then she was sitting at Raiden's bedside. She remembered him waking up, getting out of bed, and he kissed her, after that—this place. A kiss? He had cursed her with a kiss? Her disbelief burned. Nicole seethed, trembling as their voices continued to wobble through the darkness.

"I panicked—I had to kept her safe," Raiden said.

"And what do you think *she* was trying to do?"

"It was the right thing to do."

Nicole shook. *The right thing to do?!* She couldn't believe what she was hearing. She couldn't stand the agony, the anger. Her plan to save Mitchell, to keep everyone she loved safe, had been ripped away from her. She was a prisoner in her own body, this was Atrium all over again.

"I was going to get him back!" She screamed, her head was swimming in rage, and it pounded as her heart buckled under the weight of losing Mitchell all over again. She shuddered. "You stole my chance to save him!" She roared at the top of her lungs.

Gordan trembled, his disappointment twisting into anger so suddenly that he glanced down at Nicole in dismay. Despite the peaceful look on her face, he knew this was not his own anger. Behind her sleeping mask she was furious, she could hear them.

He shook his head, trying to quell the surge of Nicole's emotions seizing him. Before he could think his hands lashed out, both palms striking Raiden's chest. Raiden hit the wall—utter shock in his wide eyes.

Gordan couldn't breathe, stunned by the tears that welled up hot and sudden in his eyes as he looked at Raiden. He fought to pull in a breath, gasping.

Nicole carefully pried her trembling fists open.

"If I wasn't already long-dead, I might be frightened of you," Amarth said.

"There's no way out of this place?"

"Unfortunately, you'll be stuck here until the curse is lifted," Amarth said.

"There's no other way?"

"No—would you prefer to be alone with your betrayal?"

She glared at him.

"I suppose that is a yes." He turned away.

"Wait," she insisted and he turned back around. "You said this place is on the edge of Death?"

"I did."

"Does that mean I could find my brother?"

"I'm afraid not. He won't be here."

"Why not? You're here," she said irritably.

"Death is a difficult realm to navigate—even for keepers. I've been wandering around here for centuries. He is most likely still coping with his departure. It's not easy, especially for those who die violently—"

"Stop—I get it," she said, crouching to the ground and sitting in what looked like black sand but felt like nothing. She buried her face in her folded arms.

☙

As Raiden left the room, Gordan sat beside Nicole's bed, frowned and winced at the despair he could feel rending her heart. He took her hand, hoping she could feel him there since she had undoubtedly heard their conversation.

"I don't know what's right anymore, Nicole," he said. "I would trade places with you if I could." He sighed.

Raiden paced down the hall. *I had to stop her*, he thought, but his certainty was shaky. He knew he should wake her up, but in his haste, he didn't think about how the curse could only be overcome by something stronger than the fear and desperation he used to cast it. If he woke her up there was nothing stopping her from going ahead with her plan, and that fear had cast this curse. His love for her, his shame for this mistake, nothing felt stronger than the fear of losing her—so how could he break his own curse?

He sagged against the wall and sank to the floor. "What if I can't?"

Gordan couldn't risk flying from Witch Haven to Keren's orchard, so he shifted through the ether even though he despised it—it always made him sick. Being a passenger through the ether was one thing, shifting on his own was difficult. His altered form often could not hold under the stress and he reverted to his natural state—it happened to his advantage when shifted from the palace tower to Orodon. When he arrived outside the front door of Keren's cottage, he had to take several deep breaths and reclaim his human form. Today, at least, only his clawed hands and tail that slipped out of form. He knocked on the door—even though Keren had told him more than once that he could let himself inside.

Asi answered the door and hugged him.

"Hi, Gordan," she said. "How are they?"

"Raiden has his strength back, but he wanted to stay with Nicole," he answered. "I didn't have the heart to say no."

Asi asked, "Is she…—"

"—Still asleep," Gordan affirmed.

They went inside. "How long are you going to pretend Nicole is taking care of Raiden in her room?"

"I really don't know," he admitted as he opened the door and stepped into Nicole's chamber back at the palace.

As planned, Caeruleus knocked precisely at noon and Gordan opened the door.

"How are they?" he asked.

"Raiden's recovered, Nicole is still asleep."

Caeruleus sighed, "He still can't break the curse?"

"No."

"Well, the whole palace thinks she's in here keeping Raiden safe."

"Good."

Raiden held Nicole's hand, trying to banish the fear that had cast this curse. *She won't leave us.* He had thought he was protecting her then, but now she was stuck in a curse, unable to fight. *She won't leave.* Venarius would love to find her this way. He had to wake her up—if not for that reason than just to hear her voice again. *She won't leave.* Sure, she was here, but she was still as good as lost if he couldn't break this curse. *She won't leave.* He had to wake her up—if not to hold her than to say he was sorry. He brought the back of her hand to his lips. *What if she won't forgive me?*

He lowered her hand and waited, holding his breath, but he knew his lonesome need for her company and his guilt were still too weak to break the curse. He let out a groan, released her hand, and stood up to trudge out of the room and pace the dust-veiled house.

This felt too much like his time alone in Cantis. When his mother was gone, the rooms were no different, yet he almost didn't recognize the house he called home after that. The life it once sheltered lingered in the rooms like a ghost. Here, every room was a stranger to him, yet the knowledge that his family had lived in this house hung from the furniture with uncanny familiarity. He wondered if he might find traces of his mother. Which room had been hers as a girl before she and her mother went into hiding from the Council's search for seers? He could feel whispers of the past in his mind the same way the Sight crept in from time to time.

As he passed a door left ajar, from the corner of his eye he caught a faint orange light trembling within the shadow. He pushed the door open and puzzled over the lit candle sitting in a little puddle of its own melted wax upon a table in the center of the room. He turned his head to listen in the house, but silence reigned. When he looked back into the room, the candle flame was gone. *It must have blown out by a draft*, he thought even though he didn't smell the telltale note of smoke in the air. A dark blur bolted from the room between his ankles.

A cat. He wondered how many animals had found their way

into this old house over the years although he would have expected to hear more strange sounds from birds and mice if there was, indeed, some way inside the manor. Nor did it smell of decades of sheltered animals. He wondered what the cat subsisted on; maybe it hunted outside.

He glanced into the room again but felt more like an intruder than a Divale, so he didn't wander in—*this isn't my house...even if mother did spend her childhood here.* If anything, it was the cat's house now. Still, he wondered about the candle. Perhaps some old charm that still had a little life in it had been awoken by the presence of people in the manor. There was no telling what withered household magic might still be sleeping beneath the dust in these rooms.

In his need to pace, he made several turns back and forth across the second-floor hallway outside Nicole's room until the knocking of his shoes against the bare wood floor started to sound like a ticking clock which drove him just a little mad. So, he wandered downstairs to pace through the foyer where his anxious footsteps were muffled on the faded carpet.

As he paced, he passed a long bookcase packed with tomes that kept catching his eye. At last he stopped to look closely at their spines. There were some titles he recognized; most he did not. Books were never unsure of themselves—they offered answers and company. Although he wanted to pull each book off the shelf, he couldn't bring himself to retreat into the comfort of untraveled pages while Nicole was locked inside a curse alone. He huffed and turned away from the bookcase to see the cat sitting just a step away in the middle of the foyer rug looking at him.

It didn't run from him this time. Stunning pale greenish blue eyes—eyes like his own and his mother's—peered at him from a deep brown round face. Its body was a light cream color, but its legs and tail were dark like its face.

"Hello again," Raiden said.

Then Gordan stepped awkwardly out of the ether into the entrance way. Raiden looked up to meet his violet gaze.

"Raiden," Gordan greeted. "I see you finally met the laranimus."

A house spirit? It seemed like an ordinary cat to him. "How can you tell it's a laranimus?"

"I can feel it around even when it's not corporeal—that, and its presence is far more…human and complex than an ordinary cat," Gordan explained. "I'm surprised today is the first you've seen it. It's been sitting with you while you slept the last two days."

Raiden dug into his memory for what he knew about house spirits—the lingering presence of ancestors that manifest when a family inhabits a home for generations. A house spirit wasn't any one family member's lingering soul, not a ghost, but an amalgamation of emotional and psychic imprints left behind by people who call the same place home. After many generations a laranimus could manifest corporeal forms such as animals, dolls, small humanlike figures, and fire…or lit candles.

"Huh," he said. He looked at the cat, still looking perfectly ordinary as it blinked slowly back at him. Then the cat's form turned into a wisp of smoke like a candle going out.

"See," Gordan said. "Caeruleus said he'll be back at Nicole's door in three hours with some food from the kitchens. He'd like to see that you're all right."

"Sure, I'll go next time. What's in the basket?" Raiden asked, spotting it in his hand.

"Apples, eggs, pickled vegetables and milk from Keren," he said.

"I'll put it away," Raiden offered, holding out his hand. Gordan passed him the basket. "I was going to make some tea for something to do anyway."

"I'll be upstairs with Nicole."

Raiden dropped his head back in frustration before he shuffled toward the kitchen. It was like walking into the past when the house had been alive since Raiden had cleaned it after he couldn't bear to lie in bed with nothing else to do. He set the basket on the counter, removed the ceramic jug—it was cold, charmed to remain that way—and the hefty jar of pickled vegetables. When he pulled the eggs out and set them onto the counter, the cat was there.

He reached out and hesitated, not sure if he *could* touch a laranimus, but it didn't flinch or disappear.

"May I?"

It blinked. He placed his hand on its head. Its fur was as warm and soft as it appeared. In the light of the kitchen, he could see its Siamese coat and Divale eyes more clearly. A brief smile broke his melancholy. He returned to his task, filled the kettle with water and set it upon the stove. When he opened the cupboard, he plucked two tea cups from the shelf, then thought it would be wrong not to make a third cup of tea just in case and took a third one down from the shelf.

The laranimus sat on the counter watching him, so he grabbed a saucer before he shut the cupboard door and set it on the counter in front of the cat. He tipped the jug of milk over the saucer and filled it half way, then put the jug back and went to the pantry for the tin box of tea.

He made the three cups of tea and the laranimus drank the milk, licked its lips, cleaned its face and jumped down from the counter.

"Thank you, dear," he heard before the cat disappeared in a wisp of smoke halfway across the kitchen floor, leaving him to stare at the empty spot for a moment before he could return to what he was doing.

The tea was ready and he snapped his fingers over one, it disappeared in a blink. He did the same to the second cup, sending it upstairs with the first. Then he picked up the third and sipped it halfheartedly.

Gordan watched the second cup of tea appear on the table beside Nicole's bed and sighed. He picked up one of the cups and watched the other sit there, a sad testament to Raiden's guilt and hope. Maybe expecting Raiden could overcome this curse was wrong, after all there was someone who could likely break the curse. If anything could be stronger than Raiden's desperation to keep Nicole from leaving, it would certainly be Michael's love for his daughter.

But the idea immediately hit Gordan with the horrible truth

that Nicole's father still didn't know about Mitchell. If they brought Nicole back home, they would have to tell him. He hung his head over his tea and hated himself for his heart's cowardice. They would have to tell him eventually, but it felt like that day would make Mitchell's loss too real to bear.

❧

Raiden stepped through the threshold between Keren's cottage and Nicole's chamber in the palace for the first time since the attempt on his life. The bloodstained cushion had been disposed of and the silence between the hanging fabrics made him wish Nicole was there. He shut the door to Keren's living room behind him and glanced to the door just two paces away that led home to Cantis.

He didn't have to wait long. A knock at the door came, and he crossed the room to open it. There was Caeruleus, the relief on his face made Raiden smile.

"Stars, it's good to see you on your feet," Caeruleus said, stepping into the chamber with a cloth sack that smelled of fresh bread.

"I wouldn't be here without you," he said, hugging his friend.

Caeruleus shut the door, "I don't trust this place anymore."

"You didn't see who it was that day, did you?"

"No. I heard the boom and ran. The fog was spreading when I got there. I just went directly for the center of it and found you. Whoever it was could have walked right past me."

Raiden took a deep breath. "What do we do, then? We can't keep up this act forever."

"No, we can't, and if Venarius could figure out how to get someone inside and mask the intent to kill you from the palace spells, he's certainly figured out a way to know what's going on in here."

"At least for now he thinks we've locked ourselves inside, but I can only be recovering for so long."

"Well, for now we'll stretch this out as long as we can," Caeruleus said, handing him the sack. "Loak thinks the attempt to get rid of you could mean Venarius is preparing for a bigger move. He's removing the people closest to her, the ones who have gotten in his way. Eventually, he'll get tired of games and just come for what he wants."

"As long as he thinks she's *here*, she's safe at least."

"Tovar has been driving himself crazy checking the spells of the palace and trying to find loop holes and cast some patches, but I doubt we can call this place 'safe' again."

"Please be careful out there," Raiden said.

"Hey, I'm not the one with the target on my back—remember?"

"How could I forget?"

Caeruleus lowered his voice. "*You* be careful. Don't set foot outside that house. Just because everyone thinks you and Nicole are locked in this room doesn't mean someone in Witch Haven couldn't spot you. There's no telling where Dawn is."

Raiden forced a smile and pecked him on the cheek. "Yes, mother," he said somberly.

"I'm serious, Ray."

"I know, I know." He clapped Caeruleus' back. "Thanks for the bread."

"I'll be back tomorrow morning at nine."

"All right."

Caeruleus let himself out and shut the door. Raiden returned to Keren's house where Asi and Fen were waiting with a potion they hoped might awaken Nicole. He promised to try and thanked Fen for her effort, trying not to let his doubt prematurely dash their hopes.

He shifted back into the manor, brought the bread to the kitchen and carried the potion upstairs, knowing it wasn't likely to work against this heavy curse. Still they tried, coaxing the potion into her mouth in tiny careful sips.

Nicole only stirred, turning in her sleep. The curse clung to her as desperately as ever. Raiden groaned and left the room before he could see the disappointment in Gordan's eyes. He turned down the hall and saw the cat sitting ahead of him. It blinked at him once, then it stood up and walked lightly into the nearby room.

Raiden kept walking, noticing the flicker of candlelight as he neared the open door and looked in. This time he stepped inside, taking the gentle encouragement. The candle burned on the table in the center of the dark room. He flicked on the light overhead and when he looked to the table once more, the cat was there instead of the candle.

In the light he recognized the telltale shape of a spherical object beneath a thick velvet cloth—a crystal ball that looked like it would fit in his cupped hands. He had no intention of removing its velvet covering.

"Is that what you brought me in here for?" he wondered, nodding toward the crystal ball. "I'm sorry, I don't want anything to do with it."

"It's yours whether you like it or not," the cat said, it's voice familiar and comforting. "You are a Divale."

"You *do* speak," Raiden retorted.

"Everything speaks—not everyone knows how to listen."

"Is it lonely, being the spirit of an empty house?"

"I am all the company I need. I am Althea, and Eleanor, and Ismene, and Sybil. Every Divale woman born and departed in this house is me."

He wondered if that included his mother.

"For a long time, I thought you were the only prediction Althea had gotten wrong," she said.

"Me?"

"She saw a son in her future, but it would seem much farther in her future than she anticipated. She was heartbroken, thinking she had erased you somehow, but seeing you here—I no longer feel that sorrow in me."

"I wish I knew more about this family; my mother had to keep us safe."

"You can know them just as Althea knew you," she said.

"With the Sight?"

"The Sight allows us to see beyond time. It is a telescope you can point in any direction, not just forward. Many seers never realize this. Most people are so concerned with what is to come they forget to consider the significance of what lies behind us."

"I've had a vision of someone's past before," he said, bemused. "Not just her past, but her past life as well."

"It is unwise to dwell in either, but the past often tells us far more about what is to come than looking into the future does. It is the defining difference between a seer and an oracle. Althea would be proud to know you are so proficient with the family gift."

Raiden spit out a laugh. "I'm not proficient. I can't control it at all."

She chuckled softly. "Son, no one can control the Sight without a crystal. Your mother had to protect you from our heritage somehow."

"So, she told me she renounced the Sight and insisted I live in the present," he said.

"A lesson every child of the Sight must learn. She might have taught you when you were old enough to appreciate the risks and practice cautiously. Of course, seers are free once again."

"How do you know that?"

"You could say this old house has ears," she said. "The Council's fall was all the people of Witch Haven could talk about after it happened, and people still walk by the manor from time to time."

"Oh…well, I don't know that I want to start practicing now. My vision has already suffered from using the Sight, and I did something very wrong because of it." He adjusted the glasses on his face.

"My boy, that's because you were dwelling in the future, not because of the Sight. What about the future mattered so much more than the present?"

Raiden glanced toward his shoulder and Nicole's room down the hall.

"That young woman," she said. "The one you cursed."

"I needed to know she was safe. I couldn't let what I saw come to fruition."

"Yes, and look where agonizing about the future has gotten you both."

"I'm trying to fix it."

"Not everything broken can be mended," she said gently and

jumped down onto the floor. "And even if you manage to, nothing is ever the same as before it was broken." She crossed the room, rubbing against his leg as she left.

He swallowed the lump of anxiety in his throat, his gaze resting on the velvet-draped sphere upon the table.

Gordan stood up, squeezing Nicole's hand before he let it go and left the room. It had been some time now since Fen's potion failed and Raiden retreated in shame. Gordan tried not to listen to his conversation with the laranimus down the hall, but he couldn't stop himself from hearing. Now he could tell Raiden was ruminating down the hall. He didn't want to leave Raiden alone for long, just like Nicole, so he made his way to the other end of the hall where the door was open.

When he stepped into the room, Raiden was leaning forward, his hands gripping the edge of the table fiercely as he peered into the crystal resting in its silver bowl of black sand. Gordan wasn't thinking as he crossed the room and the indiscernible shapes in the crystal became clear—dragons. They filled the sky, leaving the wastelands behind them and descending upon the mainland.

Forty-three

Raiden looked up from the crystal, his hair hanging over his shocked eyes.

"That can't be," Gordan said adamantly.

"Explain to me what you saw then, Gordan, because I saw a sky full of dragons heading right for us."

"They don't *follow* the dragon king anymore; our losses were too great to lead another war like the first one."

"Perhaps someone has been inspiring them lately. The Council is gone and the realm is in pieces again, just like the first time."

Gordan shook his head. "The last time I was there they were not so discontent as that. Most of them weren't even a part of the first war. I can't imagine they could be convinced to do this."

"Gordan, you just *saw* it," he said. "It looks like they are more bitter about exile than you thought."

"But to believe war is the only other option…" he shook his head. "Maybe I can convince them that there's another choice besides exile or conquest, that they could be welcome here one day…forgiven even."

"And if you can't?"

"If I can't, we both know what happens."

Raiden took a careful breath, "What happens to you if you challenge them and they don't change their minds?"

"I don't know. I thought I knew how they felt before, and now…I just don't know."

"I should go with you, Caeruleus can—"

"You need to stay here and wake up Nicole," Gordan said, his voice cold and stern. "We need her." He walked out of the room and turned down the hall toward Nicole's room.

Gordan stood over Nicole. She looked so much like her brother while she slept with a nest of wild curls around her painfully familiar features. He leaned over her and placed a kiss on her forehead. His eyes burned with the memory of his last moments with Mitchell. It felt like a curse even crueler than endless slumber to give her the same farewell, not knowing what awaited him in the wastelands or if he could stop what might be coming for them all.

"I hope this isn't goodbye," he said softly before he straightened up and left the room.

He walked down the hall to the room where Raiden stood, still leaning on the table before the crystal ball.

"I'm leaving," he said. "Don't do anything stupid if you can help it."

Raiden let out a bitter laugh through his nose. "All right."

"Try to get some sleep, would you?"

"I'll try. Be careful, Gordan," Raiden said, looking up at him with a grave expression. "She can't lose you, too."

Gordan winced at the pain ringing through the room and nodded in farewell. This matter was far too urgent for the long trip back to the wastelands—and if he was spotted in the skies would compromise their hiding place. He sighed and twisted uneasily into the ether.

∽

Nicole stood at the water's edge, staring toward the horizon. If they were the waters of Death, then Mitchell was out there somewhere. If she stepped out into those waters to find him, she supposed she would die. That was certainly a way out of this curse, but it wouldn't get Mitchell back. Her heart languished in anger, bared from her body—just as the Council had done, as Venarius had done—but this time it was Raiden. The curse wasn't sleep—it was being trapped in an endless, impossible effort to reconcile the person she loved with something so appalling—Sisyphus pushing his bolder toward the mountaintop again and again—never succeeding.

Then, after what felt like an eternity of numbness, sensation crept through her body. She could feel her own weight again and she felt heavy. When she looked down, her feet were sinking into the sand. She tried to pull them out and only sank deeper, grasping helplessly at the sand around her as it swallowed her up until she slipped entirely into total darkness and pressure all around her, buried alive. *No*—she realized she wasn't buried, she was beneath a thick blanket and her eyes were closed. For a moment she felt like she couldn't remember how to open them and wondered if she was still trapped in a paralyzed body, but her eyelids slid back and a blurry room greeted her.

She was caught in a tug of war between sleep and consciousness, sitting up before she could be sure she was awake. The room wasn't clear enough to convince her, but she could smell dust and hear the blanket rustle as she stirred. She rubbed her eyes and realized they were wet with tears—that was why the room was so blurry. Her breaths were slow and shaky with simmering anger. She could leave and they wouldn't know until she was gone. She could find Venarius if she wanted to, get Mitchell back. Her plan was still viable, but she had to look Raiden in the eye.

Moving her body felt strange, and she wondered how long she'd been asleep as she threw back the blanket and swung her feet onto the floor. She looked back at the bed, half expecting to see her body lying there still as it had been in the Courts. *I'm really awake.* There were no shoes on her feet, and she looked around, growing increasingly agitated. Across the room her denim jacket lay folded over the back of a chair, her hiking boots sitting beneath the chair. Once she yanked her jacket on and had her boots back on her feet she stepped through the doorway into the hall and looked around, realizing where she was.

Wandering down the hall, she checked each room. Then she stopped in a doorway and there he was, his head hanging as he leaned over a table in the center of the room. At the sight of Raiden her heart lurched in a way it never had before. She was pained and sickened. She stopped in the doorway.

He looked up, startled at that the sight of her. "Nicole." He took two steps toward her and stopped.

Looking at him after what he did tore the pieces of her heart into smaller shreds. "How could you do that?"

"Listen—"

"No. I don't need to hear how much you love me. That doesn't make it okay, Raiden," she said, her voice quiet and shaking.

"I'm sorry. It happened so fast, I wasn't thinking—I couldn't lose you, Nicole—and I'm not the only one who needs you—"

"You don't hold someone you love captive. You don't get to take control of my *life!* Congratulations, you're *just* like the Council and Venarius."

She watched those words crush him, and she swallowed back the pain of seeing him endure something worse than countless strikes of his own sword.

"Do you know what it's like to have your own body taken from you? The Council took it from me. Venarius took it from me. And to be stuck in that…fucking limbo *knowing* that *you* took it from me too."

His composure broke. Tears welled in his eyes. "I'm so sorry. If I could undo—"

"You can't," she said. "You didn't even wake me up, did you? How long were you going to leave me like that?"

"I tried—"

She shook her head. "Where's Gordan?"

Raiden swallowed hard. "He left for the wastelands."

"*What*—when?"

"Maybe ten minutes ago."

"Why?"

"I had a vision of an uprising among the dragons, and he went back to intervene. He's hoping he can convince them that there's a future for them other than exile or war."

Nicole looked to the ceiling and took a deep breath. "Where's my sword?"

"Under the bed where you were sleeping."

She turned and walked back to her room.

"What are you going to do?" Raiden questioned as he trotted after her.

"Gordan shouldn't be challenging the dragon king alone. Do you think they'll believe him? If we want to convince them they have allies here, one of us should be there. And if the dragon king is still feeling bloodthirsty, maybe he will help us hunt down Venarius just for the sport of it—call it a trade for diplomacy," she muttered as she stooped to reach under the bed.

"Or he might see an opportunity to take the realm again when he sees that key around your neck. He might try to kill you instead."

She stood, sword in hand. "He can fucking try," she seethed. "I need to be with my friend in case anything goes wrong." She pulled the sword onto her body.

"Please don't go." He caught her by the hand.

She closed her eyes, not wanting to see the sorrow in his gaze because she might cave. "It's too late for that, Raiden. I need to be anywhere but here."

She pulled her hand away and thought of Gordan as she turned away and into the ether. The rush of slipping through the distance was not the same—her heart weighed on her like an anchor and she couldn't keep her mind from returning to Raiden. Her focus wavered between Gordan and Raiden—she fell out of the ether and hit the ground, opening her eyes to find her face in the dirt. She pushed herself up on shaky arms and sat up to look around.

There was a great plain around her, sparse grasses waving sadly in the breeze. In the distance a wall of mountains. This had to be the wastelands, she had only made it part way to Gordan.

"Damnit, Raiden," she cursed quietly, pushing her hands up her face. After a deep breath she stood up. She wouldn't risk shifting again when she couldn't focus, not wanting to end up torn apart in the ether between getting to Gordan and how wrong it felt to leave Raiden like she did. A little groan of frustration escaped her and she trudged forward toward the mountains. *That's where the dragons are*, she knew—she wasn't that far away.

ↄ৲

When an impatient knock from downstairs banged against Raiden's thoughts, he lifted his head off his folded arms and looked toward the door. Confused, he stood up and hurried downstairs to the front door. He lifted the little brass peep hole cover and through the clouded glass he could just make out Caeruleus, his black hair and intense blue eye looking straight at him.

Raiden turned the knob and opened the door.

"You were supposed to show at the palace hours ago," he grumbled as he stepped over the threshold.

"Right, sorry," Raiden closed the door, realizing he had no idea what time it was or how long it had been since Nicole left.

"Why the hell would you scare me like that?" Caeruleus demanded, then the annoyance fell from his face when he looked Raiden in the eye. "What's wrong?"

"I had a vision of dragons invading, Gordan went to the wastelands to intervene, then Nicole woke up—"

"How did you finally break the curse?"

"I didn't actually, I think Gordan did."

"At least she's awake."

"She was so angry, she could hardly look at me."

"You cursed her, Raiden," Caeruleus said uncomfortably. "She's going to need some time."

"I know, but what if we don't have time? She's in the wastelands with Gordan trying to stop a war before it starts. Venarius has a way into the palace. We know he'll try again, and he'll hit even harder than he did last time."

"Look," Caeruleus said, placing his hands firmly on Raiden's shoulders. "You will have time, but you can't sit here driving yourself crazy. Think. What can we do with what we know and what we have?"

Raiden sighed. "We should contact Eisen, Belen and Cinder. If Nicole and Gordan can't change the dragon king's mind, then we better find out who our real allies are."

✑

Nicole marched with anger and disgust in her strides. With every step she felt worse about causing that look on Raiden's face and grew more infuriated with herself. She missed him. The last time she had seen him she'd nearly lost him, but she was unbelievably mad at him, at everything, at the whole goddamn world.

She took a deep breath and held it in, dropping her head back with the urge to scream but letting it whoosh out silently. *I have to focus on Gordan*, she thought, looking ahead to the mountains looming just a few miles in the distance. Her eyes wandered the plain around her, and she realized she wasn't alone out here.

Across the sparse flat earth were fragments of a world she recognized, broken yet unmistakable structures of the old world scattered and half buried here in the wastelands. It was like standing in a tattered history book while someone flipped the pages. There was an Egyptian temple, swallowed by the sands of the changing world and left here. There were rings of pagan stones that looked like they belonged somewhere in a sea of green, not this parched landscape with pale sad grass growing feebly in the shade of ruins.

Her mind slipped back to Raiden. Were they in ruins now—or did she just feel that way looking at the broken shells of once vibrant thriving places, safe havens and sacred houses, left abandoned? A future without Raiden sounded wrong, but everything was wrong now without Mitchell. *Find Gordan,* she thought, that was all she had to worry about. Once she did, and they dealt with this mess, then she could figure out what was left of their relationship.

✑

Gordan stretched his body, shook out his wings and settled into his

666

natural stature, knowing that so many of his kind were put off by dragons taking the shape of men, and if they were on the cusp of a second war, then arriving home looking like a man wouldn't help his cause. He didn't have to wonder where the hostility toward the mainland had survived among the dragons, they lived on the fringes of the mountain range—the rogues as the more penitent and indifferent dragons called them.

He hadn't seen a single one and that troubled him. They might be among the others, cultivating their hatred in more minds, rekindling the dying embers of the dragon king's crusade.

"Looking for anyone in particular?" A rumbling voice asked before a spiny dragon crawled lazily over a formation of rocks.

"No," Gordan said.

"But you've been searching so carefully," another hissing voice came and two more dragons crept out of their hiding places. Their distaste permeated the air.

"I see you're gathering," Gordan said. "What could the occasion be?"

They exchanged glances around him, the air thickening with odium and amusement. "A welcome party," the spiny dragon said. "Isn't that how it ought to be?"

"How thoughtful," Gordan said, darkly as they closed in slowly.

They lunged, falling in on him all at once. Fire was useless on fellow dragons. He weighed the risks of transforming into a man—a weaker form, yes, but smaller and more agile. Then one of them fell away from the fight hissing savagely and Gordan caught a glimpse of a severed tail bleeding on the ground. A startling wave of anger cut through the air, carrying a familiar frequency of pain with it.

He searched for her, but the three remaining rogues converged on him. The wingless drake suddenly went sailing through the air and over the nearby ledge. A set of jaws clamped down on Gordan's neck only to slacken immediately—the dragon dropped to the ground with a familiar glinting sword hilt protruding from its eye. The remaining spiny dragon backed away, now realizing it was outnumbered.

Gordan looked down and found Nicole standing in front of him. Her stance squared toward the remaining dragon. She glared at it as it scrambled over the rocks and out of sight. Then she whirled around, throwing her fiery gaze up at Gordan.

"What the hell was that about?" she demanded.

He could feel that she was still seething and he suspected it was so much more than the rogues endangering his life that stoked this fury. Her expression softened when he lowered his head to her.

"They don't like me," he said.

"Oh, is that all?" She rolled her eyes, but beneath the surface she was shaking, and he could feel her muscles trembling as she closed her arms around his muzzle and rested her face against his forehead. "Are you okay?"

"I'm fine. Are *you*?"

"No," she said, her voice breaking as she released him. "Gordan, he—" she shook her head. "I don't even know how long I've been asleep!"

"Five days," he said.

"Five?! Why didn't you wake me sooner?"

"We tried. Curses are tricky. To break them you need something stronger than what was used to cast them."

"How did you wake me up then?"

"You mean Raiden didn't?"

"No."

"All I did was kiss you goodbye." Had his heartache done it?

"I just can't believe he would—" A spasm of outrage shook her.

"He's felt terrible this whole time. Once he cast it, he—well, he couldn't break it. He did try, countless times. He wasn't thinking, Nicole. We've lost you once already, I know the panic he felt."

"And that makes it okay?"

"No. But I'm curious, were you going to tell us or just disappear?"

"I would never leave without saying goodbye." There was nothing but honesty in her voice. Her heart was a sun radiating the

668

heat of pain, anger, and sorrow, and he couldn't look her in the eye without being hit by the full force of it.

"He crossed a line, but—"

"He loves me," she said, impatiently. "I know he does. I'd rather just deal with something else right now, like having a chat with the dragon king about this invasion Raiden saw."

Gordan sighed as fear crept into his chest and turned his heart cold. He wasn't ready for this.

❧

Lying on Gordan's neck as he carried her over the mountain range of the wastelands, Nicole felt at ease for the first time since…she couldn't even remember. The ridges and valleys went from great exposed formations of sandstone to gradually greener expanses of peaks and slopes where grass and trees grew among the rocks.

When they soared over a line of peaks, below them in a valley circled by mountain ridges a blue lake glistened. In the stone walls around the crater lake were countless cave mouths and a single structure that was beautiful and perplexing to behold. Nicole couldn't quite decide if it was a palace or an abstract sculpture of volcanic glass. It stood severe and pointed. Sunlight flashed off its surfaces.

He glided down to the ground and landed beside the lake. There wasn't a single dragon anywhere besides him. Nicole slid off his neck with an anxious pang. *Where are they?* She tried not to think of ambushes as they walked in silence toward the palace of black glass.

They walked up the steps and the doors opened for them. Gordan transformed without breaking his stride as he went from dragon to man, donning familiar clothes that made her heart clench—Mitchell's jeans and dark teal plaid shirt. Nicole walked beside him, throwing timid glances around and growing confused by the emptiness of this place.

Across the hall stood a massive throne.

"There's no one here," she muttered.

"There never is," he said as they walked.

She stopped when they reached the bottom of the steps below the throne, but he marched up the dais and turned back to her. He sat down and she tensed, looking around for some sign of outrage before she looked back to him. He looked back, his face slowly crumpling. Then it sank in.

She let out her stale air and took a stunned breath. "*You*—this whole time?!"

"I'm not who you think I am," he said, shaking his head.

"You're *not* the dragon king?"

Gordan took a deep breath. "Unfortunately, I am," he said. "But I'm not the one who started the war. The only way to end it was to kill him. I didn't do it for this throne—I did it for the innocent lives being lost. I just wanted it to end. Yes, I have the right to sit here, but this throne, this palace, it comes with a legacy I didn't want."

Nicole took shallow breaths—the empty hall was spinning. "I need to sit down," she said, sinking to the bottom step of the dais. Gordan rose from the throne and stepped down to sit beside her.

"I just wanted to forget my past," he said quietly. "When we met, I felt like I finally had a chance to erase it. I didn't want you to see me as the dragon king. I liked just being Gordan."

"You *ended* the war, Gordan. A dragon ended the war, don't you think everyone should know that?"

"Oh, people knew, but the Council silenced it until it was forgotten. They wrote a new history. Besides, the dragon king couldn't have accomplished so much without my help," he confessed. "I made the armor and the weapons they used to devastate Veil."

His eyes were brimming, his face crumpled as he met her gaze.

"I can't take the weight of those lives off your shoulders," she said. "But I still love you. You may not think you deserve forgiveness, but the people of Veil might…if they knew."

"Could *you* forgive me?"

"Me? What on earth for?"

"Can you still love me knowing that I established the Council and handed the realm to them. I gave them their authority," he said. "I had no right to keep what my predecessor had taken. I thought Veil was better left to the people than the monarchies that tore it apart to begin with—I was wrong."

Nicole fell silent, trying to absorb the connection between the people who hunted her relentlessly and her best friend who had been her emotional shield through it all. An ironic laugh slipped past her lips.

"You're laughing?" he asked, incredulously.

She wasn't sure, her lungs heaved out bursts of disbelief, laughter perhaps, or sobs, or both and she couldn't stop. It was all too much for her to hold inside her chest without breaking. So, she laughed, her heart so utterly baffled that she could feel the creep of madness in it.

"Nicole?"

She sighed. "Gordan, you did what you thought was right for Veil. You're not responsible for what the Council did after power and prophecies went to their heads," she said. "You—"

"Elisar," a woman's cool voice spoke.

Nicole looked up to see a breathtaking woman. There was an iridescent sheen to her porcelain skin and red silk fell like liquid off her slender form. Her hair was straight black satin. Her single-lidded almond eyes made her gaze sharp. Her stoic beauty seemed carved delicately in stone and her pale jade irises were captivating.

Gordan stood and Nicole followed suit uncertainly.

"Bein," he answered, bowing his head. "I ran into four of our rogues on my visit to the outer ridges. They are rarely so social."

"They still don't show their faces here," she said flatly. "I do hope you weren't hurt." Nicole didn't hear a shred of sincerity in her voice.

"Not at all, but I suspect they have been gathering."

"Why should that matter? There aren't many of them."

"No, but if they have been persuading others..."

"*You're* the king, Elisar. These matters are yours. If you're so concerned about rogues leading them astray, why haven't you been here? You haven't acted like a king for centuries—why the sudden urge to lead them now?"

"I never thought they could be so stupid to be coaxed into a war again, and with fewer numbers than the first time."

"Thank the stars you've returned, then."

Nicole's eyes widened at the disdain in Bein's voice. *Who the hell is this?*

"Thank Nicole," Gordan said, glancing at her. "She's the reason I was able to return home."

Bein turned her eyes to Nicole. She felt a chill from her pale green gaze before it shifted down to the key hanging from her neck. "And a king of keys it would seem."

Gordan nodded, "She is."

"Yet another surprise, Elisar. You disappear for a decade, and now it seems while you've been away, you've managed to form an alliance with Veil. What an exciting time for us. You must have so much to discuss. Excuse me." Bein turned and drifted away.

"Uh…Elisar?" Nicole whispered, turning her questioning eyes to Gordan. "When were you going to tell me your *name*?"

"I had hoped to bury it in the past, but here I am. To be honest it doesn't even feel like mine anymore."

Nicole looked at him, testing the name—*Elisar the Dragon King*—but it just didn't seem to suit him. He would never be anything but Gordan to her. "Who was that, anyway?"

He let out a dry humorless laugh. "The queen."

"Queen?" She seemed more like a venomous sibling. "You have a *wife*?"

"Consort. Is it really that surprising?"

"Well, yes…considering you and—" she didn't want to invoke their heartbreak, but it was already done even in the silence.

"It was a political partnership," Gordan said. "I wanted the influence she had among our kind to instill a sense of peace here, and she wanted the status of queen. There was never any pretense of love between us."

"No kidding," she muttered.

"Seeing as we have secrets out of the way," Gordan said with a smile. "What was it you wanted to talk to me about?"

"Oh," she let out an incredulous laugh. "Right. I was going to ask you to help me find and kill Venarius instead of starting another war…are you interested?"

"I think I can oblige that request," he answered with a smile, "If you'll address the dragons with me. I think between the two of us, we might be able to assuage some degree of the hostility someone has been cultivating here."

"That was unexpectedly anticlimactic," she said, still struggling to assimilate this new information and settle her mind. Gordan wasn't any different, he was still her best friend, if anything this only proved everything she knew about him to be true. But she felt so lost, there were too many emotions clashing in her chest, congealing into something toxic. Her confusion wasn't about Gordan. It was Raiden weighing on her heart. She turned to Gordan and dropped her forehead against his sternum.

"Forgive me…for keeping such a big secret from you?" Gordan asked.

"Of course," she said, a tide of heartache shaking her voice and burning her eyes. When his arms wrapped around her, the tears finally fell.

"What about Raiden," he wondered.

The sound of his name cut into her heart like the thought of Mitchell did. "I was a prisoner in my own body, Gordan. I can understand vile people like the Council or Venarius doing that—but knowing he could do something like that to me…"

"There's no doubt he chose the worst way to intervene, but any of us would have tried to stop you, Nicole, even Mitchell if he could have."

Her words were caught in her throat. *It was the way he did it.*

"He was as scared of losing you as you are of losing us. I know you understand how he felt. You've lost Mitchell and almost lost Raiden. Yes, he made the wrong move in his desperation to keep you with us—not unlike a plan to protect the people you don't want to lose by abandoning them."

"It's the only solution to fix this. I know it would make me horrible to hurt you all, and I know full well what's it's like to watch someone you love walk away from your family, but you would all be safe…and Mitchell would be alive."

"We would all be alive, sure, but what good is that if we lose you and you lose us?"

"Mitchell would be here," she sobbed into his chest. "And I wouldn't have to live knowing he died because of me." She realized how selfish that was, to trade their pain of losing Mitchell for losing her just so she didn't have to endure it anymore. Trading places with Mitchell—to force him to live in a world without his sister because she couldn't take the pain of a world without *him*—would be selfish, simply a transfer of pain from herself to everyone she wanted to protect. Nobody would win.

His embrace tightened around her. "It is *not* your fault. Venarius is the only one responsible. I'd rather die to end him than give you up in exchange for Mitchell—and you know, Mitchell would be furious."

She nodded.

"I know that you don't have enough room in your heart for this pain, that you have so much anger inside you it hurts to breathe, and that you're terrified of losing anyone else. I understand, and it all makes what Raiden did even harder to bare, but I can feel how much you love him."

She closed her eyes to keep tears back, but they fell anyway. The thought of walking away from Raiden forever hurt more than what he had done.

"I don't want to lose him."

Gordan stepped back and placed his hands on her shoulders. "If you don't want to lose him, forgive him. Then we'll see this through to the end—together."

Nicole closed her eyes. Forgive him—she could, but it wasn't simple. Deciding to stay with him, accept his apology, and forgive, that didn't make the pain go away. It would take time for that deep bruise to fade. She took a deep breath and huffed. Was there any part of her heart that wasn't bruised or broken anymore, some small untouched corner she could turn to and find her way back after all this? Would they even make it to the end of this together?

"How are we going to do that?"

"To start, you and I can find out what's really going on here among the dragons. Hopefully, Raiden is going to contact your allies. Caeruleus has been keeping up pretenses that you and Raiden are still in the palace."

"We really are preparing for war," she said.

"It does feel that way, and I don't want my kind to be on the wrong side of it again."

❧

Gordan walked alongside Nicole as a dragon, wearing the gold sheaths on his horns for the first time in centuries. The others didn't know his human likeness, so he needed to appeal to them as their king and hope that banner still meant something to them. Gordan and Nicole walked along the shore of the shining crater lake.

"I do believe I owe you a debt, yet again," Gordan said, pleased to see the smile that crept across Nicole's mouth.

"You can pay me back by living," she said earnestly.

His heart panged and he smiled. "Must you always change the terms of recompence."

"There are too many things I can't change," she said, her voice tight with pain.

"And there are things you can," he reminded her. "I used to think there was no redemption for us and that Veil would never welcome us, but you changed my mind. You proved me wrong by trusting me. You changed my life, you gave me a family, you defended me when others would condemn me." *You're the reason I had Mitchell, no matter how briefly*, he thought, but those words caught in his throat.

"You know I wish I could tell the dragons it's safe for them on the mainland," she said. "But there's still so much prejudice. Even when you're by my side I can't always protect you from it—what about them?"

"Maybe not all of Veil is ready, but you've never given up on the idea that hate should be fought and hearts can be changed. It's not going to happen quickly."

"You think that's going to be enough for them? To hear that

maybe things are starting to get better because one person is stubborn as hell and wants things to change?"

"Why do you think that's so insignificant? That means everything and not just because that key gives you the power to influence that change."

She sighed. "No matter how many times people call me a king of the keys, it doesn't make me good at this. I've never done this sort of thing—addressing a crowd."

"You already have."

She halted and locked her gaze onto him. "I beg your pardon?"

"We're in a stone bowl beside a lake, Nicole. Sound carries pretty clearly, and dragons have very keen hearing. Most of them already heard you."

She looked at him, her face flushing with embarrassment.

"Would you have preferred I summon them all from their homes to gather around for a speech?"

"No, but I thought I would get to meet them."

"It looks like you will," he said, nodding toward the caves in the crater walls. Hundreds of curious faces peered out from them.

Nicole looked around. Her eyes lit with awe. Gordan couldn't help reliving the moment he had first laid eyes on her when she had discovered him in his cold wet cell. He never would have thought then that he had found the most important person in his life. He had looked for acceptance among his own kind for so long, only to find it where he least expected.

Here and there a few dragons crept out of their hiding places to get a better look at Nicole. Several of the young peeked out from beneath their elders and ventured from their caves eagerly. Gordan watched, scared that the glow of timid hope from the stoic faces of his fellow dragons might be a figment of his hope-weary imagination.

Nicole's breath caught in her lungs when her gaze met the faces of countless dragons looking out from crevices and caves in the crater walls and from behind piles of rock—the wide, flat and bearded faces of dragons from Asia; the long, pointed faces of dragons from European fairy tales; the vibrant colored faces of feathered serpents. Even from a distance she felt small and though many emerged from their caves, most of them didn't venture any closer. Several young dragons, dwarfed by the adults, showed little apprehension as they wandered away from their elders and toward the lake.

She looked to Gordan, her eyes round with amazement while her heart fluttered nervously.

"Elisar, you were gone a long time," said a red-scaled dragon trotting over on two legs, hopping onto larger rocks and off again.

"Everyone said you were dead," another dragon said, almost cheerfully as it bounded toward them. Its jet-black scales glinted in the sunlight.

"As it turns out, I'm not," Gordan said. "I was only lost for a while. This is Nicole. She found me."

"Does she change shape too?" Red asked, looking at her closely as he paced around her.

"No, I don't," Nicole said with a chuckle. "I'm stuck like this."

"She's human," Gordan said. "She's one of the kings of Veil, too."

"Is that really one of the keys they tell stories about? I thought it would be bigger," Jet said, shouldering Red aside to look more closely at the key.

"Aren't there supposed to be two?" Red interjected.

"Where's the other one?" Jet pressed.

Nicole glanced at Gordan, her heart clenching around the thought of Raiden.

"Our friend Raiden has the other one. He's back on the mainland waiting for us," Gordan answered.

☙

Raiden looked through the books in the foyer and huffed in frustration. He couldn't find the book he wanted and he knew he had read it before. It was back home in Cantis somewhere. He was sure.

"I'll have to go get it," he muttered to himself.

"Go where?" the cat asked.

"Home, to Cantis I mean," he explained.

"I'll come with you," she said.

"I didn't think a laranimus could leave its home."

"But the house in Cantis is your home and it was Vervain's home after leaving this manor. Therefore, I am as connected to that house as this house." She jumped onto his shoulders.

"All right then," he said, *who am I to argue with a laranimus?* He took a steadying breath before he stepped into the ether. The cat's claws seized his jacket as the distance tried to scatter them before he stepped into the hallway outside his childhood bedroom.

The laranimus jumped down from his shoulders and looked around with interest. She turned curiously to the door to his childhood room and walked into it, turning to a wisp of smoke that passed through the door. He almost followed before he remembered that if he opened that door, he would find himself in Yuma. He sighed, too cowardly to think of Nicole's father, and turned to the bedroom across the hall, his parents' room which had been his own for the last nine years of his life.

He stepped inside, pondering the fact that since meeting Nicole, he hadn't slept in the same bed for more than a couple weeks before having to relocate and sleep in a different bed. This room still felt like his safe haven. The sight of his books welcomed him and reminded him why he was there. He set to work searching for the book he wanted.

Nearly thirty minutes later the cat wandered into the room.

"This house has known far too much heartache," she said.

"I won't disagree with you."

The laranimus walked around the room and leapt onto the bed, surveying the scene around her. "Goodness, look what you've done in here," she said. "Have you found what you came for?"

"Not yet."

"I wonder why," she said, her gaze moving across the stacks of books.

A feeble laugh escaped his lungs because she sounded like his mother. She jumped onto his shoulders again, rather more affectionately this time. He could feel the vibration of purring against his neck and he felt warm—the way he used to feel in his mother's arms.

"Here it is," he said, spotting the book and pulling it carefully from the middle of a massive stack, pushing the books back with an unspoken spell when they tipped toward him. "All right, let's get back."

He stood, reaching up to place his hand on the cat's back as he slipped through the ether back to Divale Manor.

Nicole and Gordan walked back into the palace of black glass together. He transformed and she couldn't help notice again that the clothes he manifested were Mitchell's. She couldn't believe how much the last few months had changed him. When she first laid eyes on him, he had been a prisoner, but not some unknown dragon, he was the king.

"Gordan," she said.

"Yes?"

"You always told me you didn't know why Venarius held you captive."

"That right."

"But you're the king, doesn't that have to be why?"

"I can't say whether or not they knew that," he said. "I had a bad habit of checking on the mainland—I can't tell you how many times I was nearly killed. I was foolish enough to keep hoping someday hate wouldn't be the first thing I inspired in people. Dawn caught me on the coast of the mainland. I didn't expect to live long, but instead of killing me, they kept me in chains."

Nicole frowned, puzzled. "If they ended up with the dragon king purely by accident, that still leaves the question of why they

680

wanted a dragon."

"I wracked my brain for ten years trying to understand how a dragon could be valuable to them," he said. "Someone like Venarius could have any number of reasons or none at all."

"That's an incredible coincidence," she said.

"I'm the only dragon foolish enough to risk visiting the mainland since the wars. I had close calls before that, it wasn't an unlikely opportunity."

Nicole looked at him skeptically.

"You think they knew," Gordan suspected.

"Let's say they did," she suggested.

"If they did, we have to assume someone told them who I was," Gordan realized.

"And at the time the only people who could have know who you were would have been the dragons here and the Council, right?"

He nodded, "But we can rule out the Council seeking out Dawn for help."

"Which means someone here told them."

He inhaled deeply and sighed. "Did you seek out Venarius or did he come to you, Bein?" He turned his head toward the twisted glass pillars lining the hall, and Bein stepped out from behind one.

"You didn't want this crown anyway," she said. "You just want us to sit here in our humiliation. I want to *lead* them."

Confounded, Gordan shook his head, "And I was in your way? You're already the queen."

"Yes, but they accept this shameful exile because of you," she strode down the corridor to stand before him, eye to eye. "I want to lead them to something better."

"Another war?"

"No—out of exile. We are going to free all of Veil," Bein insisted, raising her arms—her long silken sleeves waving emphatically.

"I see, Venarius came to you then. He knew what he wanted. He loves a premade army he can manipulate. But why have him keep me prisoner? Why not just kill me and avoid the risk of me returning?"

"You're not my enemy, Elisar. I wanted you to see all that we could achieve by helping Dawn free all of Veil from the exile of this broken realm. I wanted you to see our restoration of the old world and our rightful place in it."

"You held me hostage to prove me wrong," Gordan said with a bitter laugh. "And now what? How is that plan of yours going to work out now with just a small army of rogues? Your partner Venarius doesn't have what he needs to accomplish anything. Your plan requires the fera, and Venarius doesn't have Nicole *or* the journal."

"Yes, I know. There is still time to remedy that."

Nicole and Gordan exchanged glances. He took Nicole's hand discretely between them. She pulled them into the ether—believing they would emerge in the Divale Manor, but they crashed back into solid form, tumbling into the dirt beneath the late afternoon sun.

Nicole lifted her head to see the ruins of the wastelands and a circle of dragons surrounding them. Gordan rose to his feet slowly beside her and took Nicole's hand as she picked herself up.

"What *was* that?" she muttered.

"A redirection spell," Gordan said.

Nicole went rigid at the sight around them and her grip tightened fiercely around his hand. She tried again to pull them into the ether, but it pushed back, throwing them to the ground again.

"Gordan," She looked up at him, fear burning in her eyes.

"They should be afraid of you, remember?"

She pulled her sword free from its sheath on her back. He rolled his head, releasing the tension in his spine as his body unfurled into its true shape. The circle of dragons hissed and beat their wings, stirring the dust at their feet into a cloud that closed in around them.

"Stay close," he growled.

Her body burned with adrenaline and power. She let a wave of it roll off her and through the air, pushing back the dust, but Gordan wasn't there.

"Gordan!" She looked around and a hissing thorny dragon lunged out of the dust. She swung her sword and the momentum sent her power through the blade like a shot from a cannon. It hit the dragon in its front leg and for a moment seemed to do nothing. Then its leg turned to stone and the magic crept through the rest of its body. It shook and struggled and shrieked until it went still and utterly silent.

The dust cleared and she could finally see that at least ten dragons had converged on Gordan and when she ran for them, another dragon lunged out of line to intercept her, then a second one. They didn't want her helping him this time. She knew Venarius wanted her alive, and the last move he made was to eliminate Raiden. *Now Gordan*, she realized—heart dropping into her stomach.

Gordan struggled to catch a glimpse of Nicole. He was trapped, surrounded by more rogues than he could count. Their massive bodies slammed together, crushing in around him. He couldn't duck beneath one without being met by another. When he pushed past one thorny hide, an armored body crashed into him.

Craning his neck and peering through the churning dust in the air, he saw her, doing her best to fend off three dragons. The rogues around him pushed him into the ground, pressing his skull under their weight. Past the underbellies and talons clawing into the dirt, he caught sight of Bein as she conjured a terrible spear from the air, then walked toward Nicole and the three dragons with purpose. His heart dropped. *No!*

He jerked free from the crushing force on his head, but he was still stuck in the mass of them. There was no getting to Nicole like this. She was too distracted by the fight to notice Bein's approach. He knew a way out. As quickly as he ever had in his life, he condensed himself, pulling in his wings and limbs, folding into the form of a man, less powerful but small enough to escape.

The dragons around him crashed together as his size diminished, but they turned into a chaotic tangle of bodies too hindered

by their confusion to catch him as he slipped through their block-
ade, weaving past claws, necks and tails until he was out in the open
and running, a flash across the plain.

Nicole's sword cut halfway into the neck of the largest dragon when
the tail of another swatted her off her feet and sent her sailing
through the air and into the dirt before she could push gravity away.
She tried to jump back onto her feet, stumbling, too out of sorts to
regain her balance, blinking dust from her eyes.

She heard Gordan's voice call her name, loud, hoarse, and unlike
she had ever heard it. She turned blindly toward him, her eyes still
stinging. He collided with her, his hands gripping her shoulders as
he spun her around. He lurched, shaking her in her confusion and
dropped his head against her. A sharp jab over her heart yanked her
attention down, and she saw the spearhead protruding from
Gordan's chest, its tip piercing her chest inches below her collar
bone. She pulled herself back, removing herself from the mere inch
of blade in her flesh. Gordan sagged, slipping from her hands. He
dropped and there stood Bein, a scowl disturbing the emotionless
mask Nicole had come to know.

"What a shame," Bein sneered.

Nicole stood frozen, stricken by pain and disbelief, stuck trembling between the need to cry and scream, between dropping to
Gordan's side and lunging for Bein to tear the vocal cords from her
throat. Bein could have taken advantage of her utter shock, but despite her attempt to do away with Nicole, Bein turned and walked
away. Her fellow dragons followed her and they left Nicole there
shaking.

She crumpled to her knees beside Gordan. He didn't move. He
didn't wince. His eyes were blank—the spear in his heart. He was
gone, no final words or gasping breath, no chance to say farewell.

A wretched cry fell from her lungs and her trembling breaths
turned into panicked gasps as she placed her shaking hands on his
face.

The spear protruding from his chest watched her, dripping

mockingly. In a frenzy of desperate hope, she broke the spearhead off and removed the shaft from his torso with a dreadful yank. She eased him onto his back, pressed her hand into the bloody gaping mouth of the wound to silence its scream of accusation and let her magic rush into him.

"Come on," she whispered. "Come on," she whimpered.

Torn flesh fused. Shattered bones reformed, it was almost like nothing happened, only a star-shaped scar from the spearhead remained, glowing white with her magic like a brand. She could almost believe he was wearing someone else's blood, her blood, but he remained still. She lowered her head to his chest and laid her ear against his sternum. His heart, though whole again, remained silent.

"Please," she said, placing her hands atop each other over his heart, pressing them into his chest. "You can't leave too."

"That's no use. His soul is gone," a cold voice said and she jumped, looking up to see Amarth. His pale presence unnerved her. Why here—why now—was he following her?

"You," she said.

"I told him you would lead him here. He chose death…for *you*." There was a chillingly delicate anger in his voice, but Nicole's thoughts were too heavy to care that his mask of indifference had cracked. Gordan was gone—that alone rang through her mind sharp and grating.

"Can you bring him back?"

"I cannot. It is not within my abilities to resurrect the dead for I myself am no longer connected to this world. There are rules."

"Can you bring him here like you are?" She pleaded. "I need to talk to him."

"I've told you before, it is not so easy as that," Amarth quipped.

"How do I get to him?" She demanded.

"Follow if you wish. You have what you need," Amarth cruelly motioned to the spear on the ground, red with Gordan's blood.

"I don't mean by dying—I just need the chance to say goodbye," she pleaded.

"You are no necromancer," he scoffed. "You cannot leave your body behind and travel into death at will as they do. It is not a place for the Living."

"I *can't* lose someone else like this." Her pain broke her stunned composure. She screamed at him, "Do you understand? Do you *feel* anything?!"

Amarth gave her a smug look. "You would get lost in Death just to speak a few final words? Fine, I can open the door for you to get there if you really want to speak to him." He offered her his hand.

Without hesitation she took it, but her grip passed through him and her fingers went numb. Then he stepped toward her, through her. The world flipped upside down and she was falling—no, sinking, resistance pressing in around her. Something like water gurgled in her ears, but her vision didn't seem blurred by it.

Instinctively she held her breath and her movements slowed with drag. Below her, or was it above her, an eerie glow wobbled through a rippling surface. She was no longer sinking—no, she was rising, kicking and pulling herself through the strange liquid darkness toward the surface and whatever lay beyond it.

When she broke the surface of the unearthly water, she could not keep herself from gasping for air before she could even wonder if it *was* air. Whatever the atmosphere was, it proved breathable and she was startled by an unexpected firmness in the water around her. She pulled her arms out and when she brought them back down, the surface was solid, suddenly more like ground although it still pulsed and rippled like liquid. She dragged herself out of the black water and onto the ambiguous terrain of Death.

Then she felt a bizarre tug at her heart and looked down to see a vivid red glow in the center of her chest and a thick red rope pulsing with the same light was anchored to her. It extended down into the darkness, tethering her to the world she had left behind— to the living world.

She took a resolute breath and looked around, searching the cold fog-choked realm around her, but she was alone. With nothing but her own breathing in her ears and her pounding heartbeat pulsing in every cell of her body, each thud tugged on the chord anchored in her chest.

"I see you made it," Amarth said, his voice coming from the mists. "That must have been difficult. I shouldn't have to tell you that living bodies don't belong here."

"Yeah," she said, looking around for him, uncertain why she was here at all. She knew she had come for something important.

"I do hope you haven't forgotten anything—the waters of Death have a nasty habit of washing memories away. I wouldn't waste time if I were you, that won't last long," he said and she looked down at her glowing red tether. "But, while you're here, do enjoy the music." Amarth's voice didn't return.

She looked down at the rope and watched carefully, it shrank ever so slightly. She gasped. "Why am I here?" She looked around, placing her hand over her anxiously pounding heart. Then she heard it—music. There didn't seem to be any distinct direction of origin; it hovered around her, like it was coming from her. A lamenting brassy melody climbed in an attempt to soar only to sink back down into quiet swells again.

She shook her head. "Come on, why am I here?" She placed her hand over her heart where the tether tugged at her, then her fingertips caught the thickened skin of a scar below her collar bone and she felt a sense of Déjà vu. *Gordan!*

"Gordan?!" She called, horrified to hear her cry smothered into almost nothing in Death's atmosphere. "Gordan!" She tried again, as loud as her voice could muster, but it didn't seem to carry. "He has to be here," she muttered, pained by the logic that he'd only died minutes ago. Surely, he wouldn't be far.

Caught between urgency and uncertainty, she took several timid steps into the fog. The tether to her heart pulled with each step and she winced every time, annoyed. She'd get nowhere this way. An idea struck her—she took the chord and twisted it around her hand with a turn of her wrist. Now with a firm grip on the chord, she took bolder steps into the fog, each pull on the tether endured by her grasp instead of her heart.

She forged onward, baring the pull of her lifeline with her tensed left arm. The fog churned in the dim atmosphere. She watched anxiously for familiar shapes.

"Gordan," she called again. Then she thought she heard something between the rasp of her own breaths in her ears. She held her breath and listened, indistinct whispers in the distance crept out of the fog.

The fog parted and as suddenly as the massive form emerged, the sound of splashing and dissonant chords of off-key strings hit her ears. The hulking shape thrashed in the very water upon which she walked with ease. It was the dragon whose neck she severed almost completely. She was less surprised to see its grim fate as she was to see it floundering in the black waters. Why were they firm beneath her feet but not this dragon? She puzzled over the beast's inability to heave itself free of Death's currents until it occurred to her—she had *wanted* to be here, accepted her arrival to this realm. The dragon pitched and flailed, churning the waters into violent waves, which undulated underfoot. She lurched and fell, but did not crash into the water. *It's resisting*, she thought. *It's fighting Death even though it's already lost.*

This dragon refused to accept its defeat, and so it remained stuck in the waters to spend eternity drowning or as long as it took for it to accept death. Nicole wobbled and stumbled on the barely firm waves as she picked herself back up and moved away from her deceased foe and its disturbance of her sturdy ground. Her lifeline was tight around her hand as she resisted its pull into the darkness below, imploring her to return to the land of the living where she belonged.

The fear that she might be headed in the wrong direction, moving away from where Gordan wandered in the fog rather than toward him, had her heart beating furiously, each thump tugging at the chord.

"Not yet," she said through gritted teeth and pulled on the chord. It dug into her hand and she realized it had gotten much thinner. What had started out thick as her thumb was now half as substantial. The further she went the more she pulled, the thinner her lifeline became. "Damnit," she hissed, looking around more urgently.

A complimentary melody crept into the music around her, a soothing rich tone, a French horn.

"What do you think you're doing?!" Someone demanded behind her.

Nicole whirled around, her heart yanking hard at the chord with a burst of jubilant relief, only to see the figure standing there was not Gordan.

"Mitch," his name fell from her stunned mouth.

She pitched toward him, and threw her arms around him. His arms closed around her hard but only briefly before he stepped back to look her in the eyes.

"Why are we *here*?"

Nicole shivered in the cold. Her stomach twisted into a knot of anxious nausea. She looked down at her tether, having slipped from her grasp in her zeal to embrace her brother; it was just a red string now, as thick as yarn. She wrapped her hand and pulled.

"Gordan," just saying his name was difficult. "I have to find him."

"Oh, you know your way around here? Cause I sure as hell don't."

"Haven't you been here since…?"

"No. I've been with you since Venarius—look, it doesn't matter, I've got to get you back."

"Gordan, he—" her throat constricted, seizing her words.

Mitchell's face crumpled. "I saw it all, but you heard what that creep said. I haven't been here long but there are rules, you can't just—"

"I can't lose you both, Mitch."

"No, you listen to me. Dad, Anthony, Raiden—they can't lose *you*. I know how much this hurts. Trust me, I know how fucked up it all is. I know you want to rip the whole world apart to change it—"

A low lamenting notes upon strings crept around them. Then a voice, "Mitchell…Nicole?"

They looked up to see Gordan. The atmosphere swelled with mournful harmonies between the three of them—brassy chords and deep vibrato tones.

"You're *both* here?" He looked between them, pain in his eyes for Mitchell and shock for Nicole. She understood the horror there in his gaze—he thought he had saved her.

"I'm only visiting," she said, cringing as she raised the tether wrapped around her hand. It was as thin as thread now, biting into her skin.

"She's *leaving*. Now," Mitchell said through his teeth, his jaw clenched in aggravation.

"We're all leaving," she insisted.

"No, I'm not," Mitchell said.

"Excuse me?"

"Isn't it bad enough that Venarius still has my body? You want to bring me back and deliver that kind leverage to him again? He'll kill me a second time, or worse ensure you never find me. I won't do that to you. Now you need to go."

"Nicole, he's right," Gordan said.

She shook her head. She couldn't let him go now that she had him back.

"Mitch, we can figure this out. Please," she begged. "Let me try." Tears rushed hot and burning to her eyes. "What am I supposed to tell Dad?"

Mitchell's face pinched with sorrow. He placed his hands on her face—his touch was ice, "Tell him I kept my promise."

His hands fell from her cheeks. She dropped her gaze to see white cracks spider-webbed around her feet.

A high tenuous note wavered out of the mists, a single mistuned violin—drowning out the soft music around them. "You are full of surprises," a cold voice said from the fog.

Amarth stepped out into the open, a frown on his usually-placid face. In this place he was not pale and insubstantial. He looked as solid and real as a living person, a young man with an olive complexion, brown hair and a Roman nose.

Nicole saw Gordan start beside her.

"I see you recognize me now, Elisar. I was so disappointed when you didn't before. I thought you had forgotten me."

"You know him?" Nicole whispered.

"It's time for you to leave," Gordan hissed.

"Not without you," Nicole insisted, holding her lifeline out to him.

"Are you sure you want to go down this path?" Amarth asked, his mouth curling.

He wants me to let my time run out. "I'll take the risk," she said.

Gordan looked at Mitchell.

"Don't stay here for me," Mitchell said.

Gordan's face crumpled and he took hold of the glowing red thread—Nicole gasped. The thread turned white and her heart went cold. A chill rolled through her as the firm surface beneath them broke like glass. Gordan disappeared into the black waters.

"What?" Amarth spat incredulously. A screeching note cut through the atmosphere and a chilling melody descended upon them.

Nicole fell into the water after Gordan, but something caught her hair and yanked her back up.

"Your lifeline may not have broken but you will still pay a price for what you've done," Amarth said, laughing. "And when you do, you will wish you had let him die."

Her vision was filled with Amarth, clutching a fistful of her hair, *white* hair, and his slight youthful form twisted, growing into something monstrous.

❧

Gordan slammed into his body and gasped, his heart hammering in a frenzied rhythm, burning with an all-too-familiar power—Nicole's. His pulse pounded and the energy lingering in his healed heart coursed through him, waking and moving his congealed blood, flooding his cooling body with heat. Her power thundered in his head, droning loud in his ears as he shook himself out of his corpse-stupor.

How long had he been gone? How long had that reservoir of Nicole's magic kept the rot at bay? He sat up, looking around. The blood on the ground beneath him was cold and congealed not yet soaked into the earth. It couldn't have been more than ten minutes, despite what seemed to him like days searching for Mitchell in the fog of Death.

His heart gave an anxious thud, nudging him. *Nicole.* Where was Nicole? He fought his way to his feet like a newborn foal and turned himself around, searching the plain of ruins for any sign of her.

She was right behind me, he thought anxiously. Any minute, she should be here.

He waited. He stood there until the blue sky darkened into the preliminary purple hue that heralded the night. He *knew* she was coming. She had been right behind him. His path back had been along *her* lifeline. But Bein was headed for the mainland now, and for every hour or even *day* that he waited for Nicole, Bein drew nearer to Venarius who must have a plan to get that journal back. He feared what her army of rogues would bring to the mainland— he doubted they were as interested in Venarius' plans as she was.

He knew he couldn't wait for Nicole any longer. He couldn't allow Bein to go on dragging their kind through the filth of history. For better or worse he was the king of the dragons. Whatever that meant to his kind, he wasn't entirely certain, but to him it meant he had an obligation to stop Bein from adding any more atrocities to the dragons' legacy.

The decision weighed heavily on his shoulders, and he heaved a laborious sigh from his lungs before rising to his feet, consoling himself with the knowledge that Nicole would return and would know where to find them. Even if a hundred years passed before she emerged from Death, he would see her again. He desperately hoped it would not be that long, for Raiden's sake.

❧

Venarius looked at his watch. Bein walked past his apprentice without a cursory glance as he opened the door and invited her into the study.

"You're finally here," Venarius said from his desk, snapping his watch closed and tucking it back into his vest. "How many of them have you brought?"

Bein's pale face never betrayed her emotions if she had any, "Just more than two hundred of the fiercest survivors of the first war." She was a column of red silk.

"That's all? You promised that they would be easily persuaded to this cause. There are almost two-*thousand* of you left and you've had *ten years* to convince them."

"That was when this realm had nothing to offer them but exile," Bein said. "If you had kept up your end of the deal and kept Elisar out of the way, there would be more of us here."

"You should have let me kill him, dear, and he couldn't have come back."

"He was your problem too," Bein retorted. "How many times did he impede your plans?"

Venarius took a deep breath to quell his annoyance.

Bein gave him a smug nod. "Luckily for you he's gotten in the way for the last time."

"So, you killed him then? That can't have been easy with Nicole by his side."

"Easier than you may think," she said with a quiet laugh. "He did all the work. I tried to free her soul for you, and he took the blow instead. If she was broken by her brother's death, she's destroyed now. She should be no problem for you next time you see her."

Venarius scowled. He stood, straightening his suit for a moment, straining for composure. "That was not a part of your instructions," he said, struggling to quiet his anger. "You could have ruined everything if he hadn't stepped in."

"You're a necromancer, Death is no barrier for you."

"No, but it is certainly less trouble to capture a soul in life than it is to hunt it down in Death, you simple-minded fool. Killing her is my last resort. If I am forced into that solution, I will have to *wait* for her soul to return."

"You said yourself that her death would only set us back a few decades at most."

"I'm a patient man, but I grow tired of the incompetence of everyone *else* around me," he said, glaring at her.

Her composure wavered for a moment. "What does it matter? She's alive and her pet Elisar can no longer trouble you."

"It matters because I do not tolerate disobedience. Step beyond your orders again and you will not enjoy the glory you crave so desperately. You can watch in chains as you intended Elisar to do while the rest of us restore the world. Have I made myself clear?"

It took her a moment to answer. "Perfectly," she said, her mouth twitching with the slightest sneer.

"Now, see to it that your sad excuse for an army doesn't step out of line while I see to the rest of the preparations. I can't have them drawing *any* attention to us before its time. Can you do that much?"

"Of course," she said tersely and turned to leave.

⁂

Raiden struggled to focus on the book as he sat in a dusty wing-backed chair in the foyer. The single light bobbing over his lap lit the words, but he couldn't get through a single page without his mind wandering back to Nicole and Gordan. The Divale spirit was seemingly very fond of his shoulders now and curled around his neck to purr while he waited and worried and tried to read.

When a dark shape materialized in the entranceway of the house. Raiden lurched out of the chair and she sprang off his shoulders onto the seat cushion. Raiden waved his hand, throwing light charms into the foyer lamps as Gordan stepped into the light—his hands were large scaled talons, trembling as they shrank back into slender human hands. The front of his flannel shirt torn halfway open and blood staining his chest. Raiden's heart fell into his stomach.

Raiden looked around—no Nicole—and his excited relief

turned to a sickly pallor of anxiety as he rushed across the room.

"Gordan, are you—"

"I'm fine," Gordan said, his voice heavy with pain. The sound of it crushed Raiden with foreboding.

"No," he said, trying to pull his heart back from the precipice of his worst fear.

"She's alive, Raiden."

"Then where is she?" His mind went immediately to Venarius and the deal he had seen her make with him.

"She—she came to get me—"

"What happened?"

Gordan touched his bloodied chest. "I protected her. I kept her alive. She just wouldn't let me go."

"Where is she, Gordan?" His voice shook, his heart going cold.

"I lost her on the way back from Death," Gordan confessed. "She's—she was right behind me."

Raiden's heart sank further, proving it could reach new depths. Nicole was in Death. Days might pass before her return…or years.

"I waited all day—I had to return."

Raiden swallowed back the thick dread in his throat. It was just as likely that she could return after he was dead and gone as it was that she might step out of the ether behind Gordan at any moment. His eyes slid past Gordan and watched the shadows of the entrance way, but that hope could not lift him out of his grief because the gut-wrenching truth of it was that she was gone and until she re-turned—if she returned—she was still gone.

He didn't even have the time to decide if he could allow himself to mourn a future without her. There was urgency in Gordan's voice and eyes. Gordan would see her again. Even if a hundred years passed before she returned, he could outlive that uncertainty. At least she wouldn't come back to a world where she would be alone.

"There's more?" Raiden guessed. What more was there to weigh on his shoulders? What must they face without her now?

"Nicole hoped to enlist the dragon king's support," he said.

"Right," Raiden answered. His stomach clenched, imagining a

new enemy coming for them.

"The truth is, you two always had it," Gordan said and Raiden heard the strain of sadness in his voice. "I won the throne when I killed the dragon king. I just wanted to end the war, that was the only way."

Expecting some terrible news, this revelation jarred him, a tremor that rolled through his memories. If he had told them that when they first met, Raiden would have never believed the righteous tale; but now, after all they'd been through, Raiden didn't doubt it in the slightest.

"What happened in the wastelands, Gordan?"

"Bein, my consort, has been sewing dissent and uniting the rogues. She made a deal with Venarius long ago I was removed from the throne so that she could carry out her part of his plan. He wants the dragons on his side when he destroys the barrier and returns us all to the old world, but with my return and Nicole's arrival, her work to rally the rest of the dragons crumbled. I realized a little too late what was going on and Bein coaxed us into an ambush. They could already be on the mainland by now."

"That is a problem."

"Bein and her rogues are my responsibility and I know it's unfair to ask you to face this, but I could use your help."

Raiden nodded, "If they are aligned with Venarius, then they are both our responsibilities."

Gordan had to take a deep breath to steady himself against the surge of Raiden's sorrow before he could continue. He marveled at Raiden's capacity to endure it—*practice*, he supposed, recalling his early days with him in Yuma. He had recognized then that Raiden was a soul prone to numbness, but he had Nicole. Gordan realized that he had never truly seen what Raiden could become without someone to disturb the anesthetic stillness in his soul.

"What's our plan?" Gordan asked.

"I had a thought," Raiden said. "We know Venarius has some way into the palace, so instead of trying to reclaim the safety of it for our defense, I thought why not turn it into a trap so that next time he sneaks in, he can't get back out."

"That sounds promising, but difficult. That kind of spell work will be complicated contending with the ancient spells at work in the palace," Gordan said, knowing full well that he was useless in this kind of endeavor.

"Yes, it's complicated, but I think it could be done," Raiden insisted. "It might be our best chance if Venarius decides to make his move before any help arrives."

"Help?"

"I've already gotten letters to Belen, Eisen and Cinder. I don't have a lot of hope that Cinder will send assistance, but I think we can count on Eisen, maybe Belen. What we might *not* have is time to wait for them, but if we could seal them inside the castle, that's more than half the battle. Either way, we know he'll come for Nicole and the journal."

Gordan flinched at the pang of remorse from Raiden when he said her name. They stood there in solemn silence until Gordan finally broke it, "What we don't want to do is make it seem like we're preparing for a battle. The moment he catches onto that scent, he'll make his move."

"We'll go back to the palace and act like things are normal—like we think the palace is safe again. We'll keep up the charade and act like Nicole is there while I work on this trap."

Gordan nodded. There didn't seem to be any other options if they wanted to see to the end of Venarius.

"Maybe it's for the best," Raiden said, the weight of his words weighing on Gordan's shoulders. "For once he won't be able to get to her."

❧

They returned to the palace. Everyone was on edge, preparing themselves for Venarius while trying to look like they weren't preparing at all. The collective anxiety of the entire palace manifested in a high-pitched ringing always in Gordan's ears. He couldn't escape it—even up in the tower on the lookout for the dragons —because everyone was living in the same nervous frequency.

They got word that Eisen was on his way with troops disguised as a diplomatic caravan, and Raiden was close to sorting out all he needed to set their trap. The palace settled into a strange calm on the surface, with a near manic vigilance poised beneath it.

"We have to get the staff out of here, I can't set this trap with innocent lives inside," Raiden said, pacing the tower. "But the moment we evacuate the staff, our cover is blown. He'll know we're preparing, and he may make his move."

"We'll have the trap though."

"Hopefully."

"It's been over a week, we can't expect him to keep holding off, Raiden. Sealing them inside this palace will cost less lives than fighting them."

"I'm still worried I won't get it right."

"You will," Gordan insisted.

Raiden looked at Gordan pointedly.

"What?"

Raiden sighed, "I think I should visit the manor, just to check the crystal once."

Gordan shook his head and shrugged, "What can it hurt at this point?"

Raiden nodded, his form jolted but did not slip into the ether. Confusion pinched his face. Dread churned in the air. "Gordan," he said, his voice grave. "I can't leave."

Their eyes met in the same terrible realization. *They're here.*

❧

Gordan matched Raiden's pace as they raced through the palace. The ether barred against Raiden's key and so they had to reach the throne room the hard way, find Loak and Leone, the guards, and Caeruleus—they couldn't possibly have time enough for it all. Raiden's dread rolled through the corridors with a distinct current of sadness beneath it—Gordan understood—Raiden was right that Nicole was safer not being here, that it was better this way, but they both wished she was with them. Her absence was wrong.

Venarius watched with smug satisfaction as the doors to the palace of the keys broke open, the doors no conqueror had been able to force his way through gave way to him. He was used to the taste of victory—he knocked on open door and stepped over the threshold with a smile, his vicious intentions welcome inside the palace now. The old fortress of foolish idealizations could no longer expel him. Freed from the constraints of games, he laughed. He was done with games. It was time to wipe them all off the board—every last fool who had the nerve to stand between him and what belonged to him. Nicole was going to hand him the journal herself, then he'd rip her soul from that troublesome body and be done with it.

Bein followed him up the steps and moved cautiously through the doors behind him, her rogues waiting for her command as she waited for his.

"Let's begin," he said with a nod, turning to see Bein raise her arm. Behind her the dragons hissed, snarled and surged forward up the steps, crowding in through the doorway as he calmly stepped aside and out of their bloodthirsty path.

Loak's voice boomed in the corridor, "We're losing ground!"

Raiden cursed between heaving breaths. Slowly but surely the dragons advanced. *I'm getting them killed.* Several guards had already perished as they fought in retreat. They could not keep this up. Raiden could not move through the ether even within the palace. He was a detriment to this fight. He was anchored and his sword could fight flesh but not fire. Everyone else *did* have the advantage of movement through the ether, through the fray, more nimbly than he could. Venarius had managed to beat him at his own plan, by reversing the magic that barred the ether for everyone but the keys, turning the palace into a trap. Stuck on his feet, Raiden had to fall back from the advancing conflagration, spells against the heat did not last as long against dragon fire as any common flame. He didn't dare bring out his wings, nor did his father with the flurries of flames churning in the halls, singeing the carpets, scorching the walls, catching on the tapestries and climbing up through the woven colors, turning them black until they crumpled to the floors in heaps of smoldering rags. The corridors gradually grew hazy and stifling with smoke. Raiden's eyes watered and his lungs protested.

As they fell back, he kept close to Gordan, a living shield against the dragon fire and the only large, scaled beast on their side fighting against his own kind. A dragon covered in long spines lunged toward them, tackling Gordan and forcing Raiden to throw himself out of the way, scrambling away to escape the crushing force of their tumbling mass. He pushed himself off the floor and heard someone shout his name.

"Ray!"

He turned and caught a glimpse of Caeruleus down the corridor before he shifted through the ether, appearing in a blink to shove him aside. Raiden fell and Caeruleus disappeared into the massive jaws of a dragon snapping shut. Raiden could feel the scream in this throat as he lurched off the ground, but he couldn't hear it over the crackling roar of flames that rolled toward him as he charged mindlessly toward his friend inside the mouth of the largest dragon in the fray. He would have run right through those flames to get to Caeruleus, but a pair of arms plucked him effortlessly off his feet. He shouted, kicked and pulled against Loak's arms uselessly. *No. No! He's not—he can't be gone!* He tried again and again to get into the ether, but he knew he could not get to Caeruleus, not anymore.

"We have to fall back!" Loak implored in Raiden's ear, his baritone words nearly drowned in the cacophony of chaos, the pounding of devastation in Raiden's chest—was there even a heart beating in there anymore or just bursts of agony trying to break him open? What did he even have any more without Nicole or Caeruleus?

"Fall back!" Loak roared again, sounding far away even though he was right above his head. He finally set Raiden down, catching his sleeve in an iron fist to halt his dazed advance back toward the fray, he wasn't registering anything before his eyes anymore. His mind swam somewhere beyond the war-torn corridor. He couldn't feel anything, much like being swept up in the Sight, only now there was nothing, no sensation, no emotion, no future, just numb nothing. Loak pulled on him and he blinked, lost in his blurred vision until it finally focused again and he registered the writhing wall of dragons bearing down on them and Gordan scrambling away from his adversary, nearly overtaken by the coming wave of scaled hides, talons and jaws. They ran—the only way there was to go—up—further into the palace.

Forty-five

Nicole's hair was caught in Amarth's growing fist, and she cried out as he dragged her out of the water, her colorless lifeline pulled taught, a sharp thread slicing into her hand. She almost couldn't see it. She twisted against Amarth's grip and caught a glimpse of Mitchell, his arms locked around Amarth's neck as he wrestled the writhing form off its feet and down into the waters with her.

Then she was free and the line anchored to her heart yanked her forward, face first into the dark waters. The sensation of descending into the depths shifted into her heart-pounding ascent; she could feel the buoyancy of the air in her lungs and the pull on her heart. But strangely, even as she kicked and swam for all she had, her progress slowed. The water around her grew thick, first like loose mud, then wet sand, then damp dirt. Her lungs pulled desperately for air, which she could not provide as the waters of Death turned to the immobilizing embrace of an unmarked grave. She strained to move anything, and the earth finally shifted around her arm.

With as much strength as her arm could muster she pushed against the earth, reaching, hoping the surface was close. The dirt shifted and at last her arm broke free into the air. Her heart gave a spasm of relief and panic as she struggled against the weight of earth around her and clawed at the ground with her free hand until at last, she loosened the dirt enough to drag herself part-way free.

Gasping the clear glorious air, she sagged to the ground. She lay there, her legs still caught in the dirt, half exhumed, exhausted, alive and broken. Mitchell—*he was right there, I could have*—a sob broke through her gasping breaths. She let out a hoarse scream that soared mournfully across the ruins-riddled plain of the wastelands. The rising sun herded long shadows along the ground, chasing the night away. What would happen to Mitchell? Could he die *again* facing…whatever deformed thing Amarth had become?

Nicole dragged herself forward, twisting and pulling her legs until they came free and she was able to crawl away from the hole in the earth. She felt like a wretched thing heaving itself out of its grave where perhaps it should have stayed. Yet here she was again, alive, panting on her hands and knees, caught between the desire to stand and the need to collapse into the dirt and sleep for a thousand years.

Pale spirals hung around her face, swaying in the morning breeze. It took several long seconds for the curtain of white around her face to penetrate the sludge of exhaustion and the agony of grief choking her thoughts. She sat upright, butt on her heels and looked around. She caught a lock of hair. The soft coiled tendril in her grip tugged at her scalp, it was certainly hers. She thought back to when Gordan took hold of her lifeline, how the thread turned white and her heart went cold. Even the hair on her arms and skin had gone pale.

She dragged her fingers through her hair and pulled it over her shoulder, watching the sun glint silver on the strands. Her heart struck her sternum in realization and the air in her lungs fell from her mouth in disbelief. *Raiden. Gordan.*

At last her mind caught up with her. She looked around frantically, but Gordan's body was gone. *Where is he?*

A breeze whispered through the ruins, trying to tell her something. Her eyes glided over the inert shape of the dead dragon, disregarding its shadowy form at first, but then her gaze lingered on it. Morning light struck white bones shedding their rotting shroud after an existence concealed in the darkness of flesh.

"What?" she balked, scrambling to her feet, unsteady on her legs for several steps before her balance returned. The corpse was halfway gone. *No…How long has it been?* The corpse's silence seemed to snicker at her as dread slithered around her bones.

Panic set in and flamed the smoldering embers of magic deep in her core. She had to get back to them. Gordan made it, she knew he had, and if he wasn't here, then he was with Raiden. The corpse before her insisted what she tried not to acknowledge: *it's been too long.* Instinctively, she reached for her sword and grasped only air, realizing the scabbard on her back was empty.

Where is it? She thought back, remembering she last had it in her hands when she killed the dragon lying there in front of her. The rising sun glinted off something, a purple flash from the sword's hilt as though it was waving to her. She held out her hand expectantly. The blade dislodged from bone and leapt into the air to fly back into her hand. She slid it home into the scabbard.

Her body slipped into the ether with Raiden in her thoughts, then she collided with a wall of heat. Her head spun in her surge of magic as her form converged and she hit the ground. Her ears rang. This was painfully familiar, a barrier blocking her path to Raiden. She sat up, her thoughts warbling between her ears. *Where the hell am I*—her vision cleared and standing before her was the towering palace of the keys. *I can't get in? What does that mean?* The ringing in her ears went silent, and she could finally hear the cacophony of battle from within the palace.

She lurched to her feet. Her heart echoed the clamor spilling out from the palace. All she knew for certain was that Raiden was in there. She pulled her sword free from its sheath and marched up the steps to the palace doors. The noise from within swelled as she reached them. They were broken and hanging open.

Her heart surged into a crescendo of fear. Perhaps this was it, all there would ever be, some fight against some enemy—for this life and the next. If they won this time, there would be another someone looking to take all they could just because they wanted it.

Nicole took a deep breath, trying to feel Mitchell beside her, wishing so desperately that he was there. It was like that spear-tip hit her chest again. This was what the fera was—the legacy she had inherited. *We fight*, she thought and felt the fera nod inside her. *The world pushes and we push back*. With a shuddering breath she broke her stillness and plunged into the tumult within the palace.

Raiden and Gordan, she thought, *finding them is all that matters*. She would take the path of least resistance if she could, but she was prepared to forge a path to them through stone—through flesh and bone if she had to.

The first trace of the fight she came upon was several of the palace troops dead on the floor, their uniforms scorched and their faces blackened into unrecognizable masks. Her heart grew heavy, unsure whom she was mourning, but she forced herself past them.

Suddenly the vast open halls of the palace were cramped, choked with the hulking forms of Bein's rogue dragons forcing their way further into the palace, unconcerned with the corridors behind them. Nicole sprinted for the gap between the wall and a dragon, then dropped beneath another, sliding to clear its belly and scrambling back onto her feet.

They finally noticed her. One swiped at her. She brought her sword down on it, severing its talons and leaving a stump. Hot blood sprayed at her, slapping across her chest. Then the dragons converged on her. A surge of fire rolled toward her and Gim bolted down her sleeve, spitting a barrier of fire—avoidance was no longer an option. She needed more than one sword.

Skidding to a stop on the soot-covered floor, she thrust her blade into the stone floor and let her magic surge through it. Dragon's lunged at her. Power pulsed through the floor and walls, then sharp crystal spears erupted from the stone, impaling her adversaries from nearly every direction. The dragons hissed and writhed but could not reach her. She yanked her sword free and pressed on, traversing through the skewered bodies of dying dragons and around the crystal spears as quickly as she could.

The smell of smoke hit her. The air turned into a grey haze, stinging her eyes. She was relieved to run past the first of the fallen dragons although there were more of the palace guards dead among them. She lurched to a stop when a black shape swooped in front of her nose. The raven landed on the head of a dead dragon and cawed at her. Then she thought she saw a human arm move between the jaws of the corpse, a sword blade protruding from the top of its skull from the inside.

With a cry of dismay, she bolted for the survivor. She grabbed the hand and it clamped fiercely back.

"I've got you," she called, giving the hand a hard squeeze of assurance before releasing it so that she could work her hands into the slick mouth of the dragon. Her hands slipped on saliva and blood as she pried at the jaws. Movement in the corner of her eye jerked her attention away as another dragon came creeping down the wall above her and pounced. It was no bigger than a human but knocked her off her feet before she could grab her sword from the floor.

She spit curses as she squirmed away from claws and snapping teeth. Then she managed to catch its head in her arms and trapped it, locking its mouth shut. The thing whipped its body in every direction trying to free itself from her furious embrace. Its tail coiled around her. It pushed and strained to pull its head free. Without her sword her magic had nowhere to go, so she let it flood the dragon's head. It squealed and thrashed until she couldn't hold it any longer. The dragon pitched forward into a frantic escape and veered left, headlong into the wall with a crack. It slumped to the floor.

Nicole lunged back to the dead dragon and the human arm still pawing and grasping to get out. Prying the mouth open wasn't going to work. *Idiot*, she thought and grabbed the hand and shared her magic with them to pull their body through the ether for just a moment. She stumbled back as the person in her grasp slipped momentarily through the air and free from the dragon's jaws. She fell back into the wall with her comrade in tow. He was soaked head to toe in blood, coughing and gasping as he straightened up unsteadily. If not for the eyepatch, she wouldn't have known it was him.

"Caeruleus!"

"Nicole?" He wiped at his eye and blinked.

The stench of dragon saliva and blood made her head swim and she gagged. He looked at her, his eye a blue beacon in a gory red mask.

"Are you okay?" she asked, cringing, placing her hands on his shoulders to keep him steady.

He nodded before he could answer. "I'm fine—not my blood." He swayed a little, and she wondered if it was the smell or some injury that made him dizzy.

"Are you sure? Is Raiden still in there?"

"Yes," he insisted. "We better hurry."

Nicole released him uneasily, but he stood on his own without issue and stooped to grab the sword from the unidentifiable soldier lying beneath the dragon carcass. He had to pry the hilt from the charred grasp.

True to his word, Caeruleus shook off his daze and surged into an impressive pace which Nicole matched gratefully. The smoke grew thicker as they caught up with the fray.

"Back! Fall back!" It was Loak's booming voice.

"They're heading for Raiden's chamber. We'll be locked out," Caeruleus said between heaving breaths.

"Raiden!" she screamed from her gasping lungs.

Raiden stopped and looked back into the smoke.

"What are you doing? Come on!" Andrus said as he ran past him into the room.

"Raiden," Gordan said forcefully.

But Raiden was sure he heard it again. He grabbed Gordan by the shoulders.

"Tell me you heard it," he implored him, fearing that his aching heart might have finally driven him mad.

Gordan listened through the shouts, the pounding of feet as they retreated, then his eyes went wide, confirming what he knew to be true, and Raiden pushed away from him, reeling around and running headlong into the smoke.

"Raiden!" Gordan shouted after him.

"Get inside and close the door," Raiden called back.

He ran into the smoke, the shadowy forms of dragons advancing within their smokescreen, tongues of fire lashing out around him. *I heard her, she's here*, he insisted, his eyes watering as he strained to hear her voice once more and slip by the dragon's unseen. He made it to the bottom of the stairs on the fifth floor, then a swinging tail caught him, slamming him against the wall. He staggered forward, regaining speed, but the dragon hissed and several guttural snarls answered in kind. Long flashes of fire leapt out of the smoke in every direction, they were firing blind, and he was getting nowhere now; in fact, he was falling back.

An eruption of fire barreled toward him, forcing him to fall backwards, and then he heard it.

"Raiden!" She was so close.

His heart clenched. "Here!" he yelled back hoarsely, scrambling to his feet.

Then the smoke parted, receding like a curtain, parting and crawling up the walls revealing the dragons that had him surrounded. A dozen menacing gazes locked on him. He froze with nowhere to go. Then a crystal spear erupted from the floor, piercing the chest of a dragon. One after another, crystals jutted from the walls and floor, impaling some dragons, pinning some and trapping others in cramped cages of crossing crystal bars.

He saw her, sprinting, sword in hand, her face a mask of desperate effort to push her legs faster, and a flurry of silver hair whipping behind her. He slipped on blood creeping across his path, stumbled and ran, dodging crystals and pinned dragons still swiped at him. Neither of them slowed. They collided as hard as the day they first met and held fast to each other. She gasped and a dumbfounded laugh escaped his chest.

"Do that later," a gruff voice snapped as a figure drenched in blood ran past them, already halfway to stairs.

Raiden released her, and they ran past struggling dragons. The sound of crystals cracking pushed them faster, up the stairs to the sixth floor. Outside Raiden's chamber a solitary dragon stood among Leone, Priseil, and Loak, defending the open door.

"Go!" Loak barked as the three ran inside, past Gordan, snarling as his fellow dragons surged toward them from the staircase.

Everyone outside the door broke their defensive stances and rushed into Raiden's room. The door shut with a resonating thud, followed by a bang as dragons slammed against it from the other side.

Raiden gasped and heaved, Nicole bent over her knees beside him. He caught a rancid smell and looked up at the man coated in dragon blood. The gore-cloaked figure looked back at him. Raiden knew that single blue eye.

He seized his friend by the arms reflexively, "Caeruleus!" he said, cringing at the smell.

Gordan collapsed to his belly and transformed into a man on his hands and knees. Panting, he picked himself up and marched across the room. Nicole was bent over, gasping and all he could see was her back and silver-white hair. He caught her shoulder and turned her around.

White curls around her face, white brows pinching over her eyes—the same vivid amber stones—growing wide and watery as she looked at him. He pulled her into his chest and clamped his arms around her. He was angry at her—she was so damn reckless—but his heart strained with relief and dizzying joy. His arms trembled, holding her as tightly as he could.

"You couldn't just let me pay my debt," he muttered.

"I told you," she mumbled into him, her arms tightening around him, "you have to live to pay me back."

"Mitchell," he said, pained by the sound of his name and by

not knowing what became of him.

"I don't know," she said, shaking her head against him. "Amarth grabbed me when you went back and Mitch—he's the reason I got away, but I don't know what happened to him."

Gordan sighed. He released her.

"All those years I knew his heart had grown cold but…I never thought he could become something like that."

Nicole frowned in confusion. She gasped. "*Amarth*? He was the love who chose Death over you?"

"He would tell you I chose Life over *him*. I saw him in Cantis, and I didn't even recognize him. When I first met him, he was… vibrant."

She dropped her gaze.

"Excuse me," Raiden said, stepping between them and wrapping his arms around Nicole, lifting her feet off the floor. He pressed his forehead to hers and sighed, her curtain of hair falling around their faces.

"Please forgive me," Gordan heard Raiden whisper.

Raiden's elation was intoxicating as it collided with Gordan's.

Nicole's heart swelled with joy and agony. She had enough loss aching in her bones to last her a lifetime. She would have no more of it.

"I forgive you."

"This whole time," Raiden said. "It was you."

Nicole laughed incredulously—the sound brought the bitter taste of sadness to her mouth. Her eyes burned, this bliss was salt in a wound without Mitchell. Sobs followed her laughter. She pulled herself closer to Raiden, burying her face in the crook of his neck.

"Mitch was there," she said. "He helped me make it back."

Raiden sighed, holding her tight.

"We can't expect that to hold forever," Priseil said, her wooden arm was blackened, cracking as she flexed the hand. "Can we?"

The pounding against the doors rolled through the room. Raiden set her down.

"Looks like waiting for them to break through is our only option," Loak said.

"That can't be the only option," Nicole said.

"The palace's defensive spells have been reversed," Raiden explained.

Nicole frowned, thinking. That explained why she had been repelled when she tried to get inside, and why the ether—once open only to them—was now closed to them.

"But the palace used to let us come and go, baring everyone else, right?" She looked to him, then Gordan. "Has anyone else tried to get out?"

She was met with blank and dumbfounded expressions. None of them had even thought to leave Raiden.

"Even if we can," Leone said, flustered. "We can't leave you two here."

"Yes, you can," she said. "They think we're all in here, not out there."

Loak's yellow eyes went wide. "And they won't see us coming," he said.

"What will you do, then?" Priseil asked.

"Wait for you," she said. "Here, take Gim, he'll be more help to you than me." She caught the little golden dragon in her fingers and gave him to Priseil. He sniffed her charred wooden hand and Nicole pointed a stern finger at him. "Not food," she warned.

"Well?" Raiden looked around. "Has anyone tried?"

Andrus sighed. "See you in the square?" he said and disappeared. Priseil followed.

Leone frowned. "Caeruleus?"

Caeruleus looked to Raiden, his expression lost in the drying blood on his face.

"There's nothing you can do from in here," Raiden said.

Caeruleus shook his head, but Leone put his hand on Caeruleus' shoulder and Loak placed his hand on Leone's, pulling them both into the ether. The remaining guards slipped into the ether as well. Netti and Sage gave Nicole troubled looks of regret before they escaped the palace. Only Nicole with Raiden and Gordan remained.

"I'll stay," Gordan said.

"They need your help more than we do," Nicole said. "We're fine in here," she said, raising her hand to the door which stood solid despite the pounding.

"For now," Gordan retorted skeptically.

"The more fire power they have, the faster we get out of here," Nicole said.

His expression was stony and unmoved.

"Gordan, come on," she implored.

"I have nearly lost you too many times—I am not leaving you two again."

"Don't you trust me by now?" she snapped at him.

Gordan looked appalled. "I trust you—"

"Then go—help them turn this around. We're useless in here, but you don't have to be."

"So help me, Nicole, you stay in this room and wait for us," Gordan said, practically growling.

He sounded just like Mitchell—her face crumpled. "Where are we going to go?" she laughed bitterly.

Gordan hugged her then turned to Raiden who beat him to the embrace.

"See you soon," Raiden said with weak optimism.

Gordan nodded and disappeared.

Nicole and Raiden stood there in the would-be silence, listening to the pounding of dragons throwing themselves against the door and the occasional roar of flames.

"Do you really think we're safe in here until they can overcome them," Raiden asked her.

"No," she said, staring at the door. "But what else could we do?"

He sighed and turned into her, his arms closing around her heavily.

Nicole turned her cheek to Raiden's chest and looked around the room. What could they do if the dragon's got in—hide maybe, but that would only buy them a few childish minutes at best. They couldn't get rid of the keys, she knew that too well. *My nightmare come true; we can't escape this goddamn palace.*

She sighed, then turned her head to look up at Raiden, an epiphany prying her eyes open wide.

"What?" he asked.

"We can't leave the palace."

"I know."

"What if we don't try to leave?"

"Pardon?"

"Forget trying to go some*where* else—how about *when?*"

"Nicole, I don't know if—"

"It could work."

"Time magic is—those spells are complex."

"It's our only option," she insisted.

"I don't—without any books I—"

"You and your books—just hold on," she said, synching her arms around him and pressing her face into his chest. She closed her eyes. How far back could she go, if she pulled every particle of magic out of herself, if she had to use it all and have nothing left for the rest of her days could she get back to when Mitchell was alive and save him?

Her eyes burned with tears and magic. She could feel the heat pass through her and into Raiden, but he held on tighter despite the fire.

ↄⱦ

When the heat subsided, Raiden thought if he opened his eyes, he would find the room around them blackened and smoking. He lifted his head and blinked. The room looked exactly the same, but it was silent, no pounding at the door. Then Nicole crumpled and nearly slipped through his arms.

"Nicole?"

She didn't answer. He lowered her to the floor gingerly, his heart accelerating as he placed his ear to her chest. A slow tired rhythm answered him. He dropped his head into his hand, relieved. He looked around but the room did not tell him what the outcome of

Nicole's absolute limit had been. He hooked an arm behind her knees and the other beneath her arms, heaving her off the floor, he crossed the room. He had to find out *when* they were, but he couldn't do that with her, so he moved her to the bed. His fingers lingered in her silver hair when he brushed it from her face, studying the pale curl for a moment before he placed a kiss on her forehead and left for the door.

For a moment he listened and heard no hissing, no breathing, nothing. His body tense with apprehension, he opened the door to find the hallway perfectly clear, unsinged, not even the faintest smell of smoke. His heart thundered as he stepped out into the hallway, closing the door behind him so that he knew she was safe—of course if anything happened to him, she'd be left in there until she woke up.

Don't be ridiculous, he thought. There was nothing to fear in the palace until Venarius arrived, except the chance that he could run into himself. He belonged here after all. Still, it was difficult to let go of the urgency from where they had been only minutes ago. He moved down the hall, trying to reign in his anxious compulsion to run like the dragons were coming—they were after all, he just didn't know how soon.

If he and Nicole were going to be help to anyone, he needed to wake her up. He needed to know *when* today was. He knew the best place to get useful information would be Tovar's study. Interfering as little as possible with the goings-on of the past was paramount, but he had five floors between his destination. He looked down the hall outside his room to each staircase that led up from the sixth floor, wondering which one he should take, but he saw the keys' passage across the hall—shortcut to the second floor.

Crossing the hall resolutely, he stepped into the passage. The floor turned to a steep slope sooner than he expected. His heart raced as the passage dropped and he accelerated until finally he slid across the second-floor corridor and into the wall. He picked himself up and practically ran for Tovar's study, panicking for a moment when he bumped into someone who rounded the corner, but it was

Gordan and his relief to see him was twofold.

"Raiden," he said, sounding perplexed. "I thought I just saw you outside the throne room looking for Tovar."

"Ah—yes," he agreed, but that didn't help him with what day it was. He scratched his head, if he was sometime in the last two weeks, then Nicole wouldn't be here. "Have you seen Nicole?"

Gordan's confusion shifted to a pained shock. "No, Raiden— I'm sorry."

Raiden felt guilty for jabbing that wound, but now he knew they were somewhere during the last two weeks. "Have we gotten word from Orodon yet?"

Gordan frowned. "Are you all right?"

"Fine—why do you ask?" Raiden tried to chuckle, but it caught in his throat.

"I just told you about King Eisen's letter not ten minutes ago."

Two days ago, Raiden almost shouted out loud. "Right, sorry," he fumbled for an excuse. "I've just been thinking about Nicole."

"I understand," Gordan said. "I have too."

Raiden's face crumpled. He wanted so badly to tell Gordan she was back, that she was upstairs and safe, but he had to keep these days as unaltered as he could. Changing the past never works out as planned. He wouldn't try, he wouldn't affect anything if he could help it, but perhaps he could sneak a few helpful things out of Tovar's workroom without interacting with anyone.

"I better get back to finding Tovar," Raiden said.

Gordan looked confused again, turning his head as though hearing a faint sound, but he shook his head and said, "Right. I'll be in the tower keeping watch if you need me."

Can he feel her? That chance alone pushed Raiden to move quickly. He knew exactly where his past self was right now—outside with Leone and Loak where they were keeping their discrete perimeter around the palace disguised as training drills. Raiden knew he had a clear shot to Tovar's workroom.

He made good time and knocked just in case, but no answer came. The doorknob turned and Raiden let himself inside, closing the door after him. He ran past the cluttered worktable with several open books scattered across its surface and jars of herbs and powders. His interest was on the cabinet at the back of the room where he crouched down and opened a lower door to find Tovar's shelf of vigil's brew. Raiden looked at the small bottles of sky-blue potion. He didn't know how long Nicole might be out; she might need days of sleep to recover from what she'd done, but he knew they didn't have that kind of time. He would need a way to wake her up.

He took several bottles and slipped them into his pockets—no telling who might need to banish their exhaustion for this fight—then he closed the cabinet and wondered what else might be useful, but his building anxiety had his mind racing, and he didn't want to risk running into Tovar and getting dragged into conversation that might compromise everything. Gordan had already noticed his uncanny appearance elsewhere in the castle. *No time*, he thought and moved toward the door. His eyes slid across the worktable as he went in case there was anything helpful. What caught his eye, however, seized his heart with dread.

Raiden stared down at a letter with a sickeningly familiar insignia pressed into the wax seal. He looked around the table, there were at least three other letters and a book before him, open to a passage on spell reversal, another book providing spells and complex analysis of all potential interference. The pages blurred as his eyes lost focus and his head spun.

He pushed the disturbing epiphany back in his mind and ran for the door, peeked into the hall before letting himself out of the workroom, and raced down corridors and upstairs until he was back at the door to his chamber. He slipped inside, gasping, shut the door and sagged back against it. He slid to the floor in utter disbelief. *Tovar? Tovar reversed the palace spells?*

"But has he done it yet?"

Raiden lurched forward onto his feet and across the room to Nicole, dead asleep on the bed. He gathered her up and hoped as he thought of the Divale manor. Their forms wobbled through the ether and when they arrived in the foyer, Raiden gasped, realizing he'd been holding his breath.

"Okay," he breathed. "All right. We're okay," he said to Nicole, still asleep in his arms.

"Welcome home," the laranimus said, appearing at his feet. She looked up at him, Nicole in his arms, and blinked. "You haven't cursed her again, have you?"

"No," he said, his relief allowing him to let out a breathy laugh. "She's pushed herself too far. She just needs sleep…I hope."

Raiden returned Nicole to her bed upstairs, apprehensive with the prospect of her waking up here again after the last time, but she didn't stir or show any signs of waking up soon; in fact, her slumber looked as heavy as the curse. He removed the vigil's brew bottles from his pockets and placed them on the small bedside table.

"What do we do now? We sent them out there to keep fighting. They think they're coming back for us and we're not there." He sighed, then realized he was forgetting none of it had happened yet.

He stood up. He and Nicole would be there waiting for them all when they abandoned the palace—then what will Venarius have? Just an empty palace, no keys, no fera, no journal. They could end this. He looked to Nicole, her white hair, the branching scar up her arm, the coin-sized star below her collar bone, a replica in miniature of the scar on Gordan's chest—she had been altered, marked and marred inside and out by The Council and Venarius. She'd lost Mitchell, lost Gordan and dragged him back, and seen too-many others lose their lives for what Venarius was after.

They *had* to finish it this time. Their plan to set a trap for Venarius could still work if they could get reinforcements. King Eisen was their only chance. Eisen had been the only one to answer their letters, possibly the only one to receive them, and Raiden wondered if Tovar had intercepted the others. He glowered, sickened by this betrayal trust. Then he enjoyed a respite of smug satisfaction because King Eisen and his best men and women were on their way across Dusor under the guise of a leisurely diplomatic visit, their weapons and armor concealed, warriors dressed as courtiers and subjects. Raiden just had to pay them a visit and get them close to the palace as discretely as possible.

He bent over Nicole, took her hand and pressed it against his face. "We're ending it this time," he promised. "Keep her safe," he said to the laranimus as the cat hopped up onto the bed. As he stood to leave, he tried not to let himself worry that she might never wake up.

❧

Raiden returned to the manor the afternoon of the next day after finding King Eisen still a good three days trek away from Keystone, keeping up their pretense of diplomacy perfectly. Raiden explained everything, and they set to work moving the entire caravan through the ether to Keystone two and three at a time, settling them into the inns and moving their caravans to the hills outside the city.

Raiden was barely on his feet when he fell out of the ether and into the manor. The house was silent. He went upstairs to find Nicole was still utterly asleep. The house spirit was curled up next to the pillow. He sighed and sank down beside her. It seemed absurd to sleep, knowing what was coming for them with the dawn of the next day, but they had no choice but to wait for the worst to happen, nothing to do but sleep. Knowing that King Eisen and his warriors were there waiting to turn the tide allowed his mind the ease he needed to give himself up to the darkness behind his eyelids.

When he opened his eyes to Nicole's sleeping face, he realized she was curled up beside him—she had moved in her sleep. He hoped that meant her slumber was not so heavy as before, and he might be able to wake her.

"Nicole?"

She didn't answer. He got up and checked the clock—still five hours until dawn—there was more time yet. But the hours dwindled swiftly in his anxious wait for Nicole to wake on her own and when the first blush of dawn lit the sky outside, he couldn't wait any longer. He took a bottle of vigil's brew from the table and sat down beside her.

"Is that a good idea?" the Divale spirit asked.

"We need her," he said. "I have to wake her up."

She didn't stir, so he propped her up, uncorked the bottle, and tipped the potion into her mouth a little at a time. She swallowed each sip reflexively until the first bottle was gone, but she remained asleep. He waited a minute, two minutes, hoping it would work. Then, reluctantly, he took a second bottle from the table. *Come on, Nicole.* With the second bottle gone she finally stirred and for a moment he was relieved, but she didn't wake. He sighed and reached for a third bottle.

"I'm sorry to do this," he said. She would be awake for days on end, but at least she'd be awake. He coaxed the third potion down, worried that it just wasn't going to work when finally, her eyes opened wide and she lurched up, her hand pressed against her heart. He knew what she was feeling, her heart racing. Coming out of a deep sleep to that incredible rush had to be startling.

"Raiden?"

"I'm right here," he said.

"We're in the manor?" She said, disappointed. "When—?"

"It's the morning of the attack," he said. "You managed to take us back two days."

"*Two days*? That's all?" Her face contorted, and he realized why. She'd been hoping to get much further—to Mitchell.

"What you did has turned this day around," he said. "King Eisen and his warriors are hiding in the city waiting for us. When everyone gets out of the palace, we'll be there to meet them. We have a fighting chance now thanks to you—we can end this today."

She nodded, her voice solemn but clear and stern, "We will."

∾

Gordan wrenched himself away from his friends and left them under siege in the palace. The ether rattled him violently, his desire to reach his destination was shaky, his heart aching as his feet hit the ground in the city square. He raised his eyes to see Loak, Priseil and Leone with smiles on their faces. His confusion was immediate, their circumstances certainly didn't warrant these expressions—then Leone inclined his head toward Gordan, or past him. He turned.

"Took you long enough," Nicole said, standing beside Raiden and King Eisen with a legion of no less than two hundred behind them.

He shook his head slowly, amazed. "How?"

"She took us back two days," Raiden said.

"I knew something was strange," Gordan said. "I *did* feel you in the palace." He couldn't suppress the grin pulling at his mouth.

"Everyone ready to go back in?" Nicole asked.

A chorus of affirmatives answered her and Caeruleus stood up from the fountain in the center of the square, mostly clean save for subtly red-stained clothes now sopping wet.

"I am now," he said.

"Welcome back," Raiden said to his friend, clapping his wet shirt in a swift embrace.

"Let's take back the palace then," Nicole said. "Eisen?"

"We're with you," Eisen bowed.

Gordan watched Nicole swallow the anxiety in her throat and nod. Then she looked at him with fire in her eyes. She was brimming with adrenaline and venom, her charge saturating the air with an intensity he'd not felt before. His chest swelled with the heat of her ferocity and his admiration of her—that she could have so much love and softness in her and yet stand up time and again after being broken, willing to use her own pieces to fight back, and make them bleed. She was the most dangerous and resilient of anyone here— he wished Mitchell could see her like this.

He walked beside her and glanced over her head at Raiden who wore a hard mask of apprehension and outrage. The swell of adrenaline and anticipation from behind them was intoxicating, overwhelming. He welcomed the bolstering enthusiasm of King Eisen's warriors. He had already been to Death and back with Nicole, what couldn't they face together? They marched from the square to the palace steps where the doors hung open on their hinges. The palace was filled with dragons and somewhere in there Venarius was searching for Nicole.

As Orodon's forces surged into the palace, their boots

drumming a thunderous rhythm, Nicole stood as immovable as great stone in a current, staring ahead. Her heart was racing but her breathing was steady, her focused gaze chillingly calm.

"We go in together, we come out together," she said. "Promise?"

"Promise," they answered her, then their gazes locked over her head. Gordan felt baffled that those blue-green eyes once burned with such distrust for him.

Nicole looked at Raiden, his blue-green eyes betrayed no flicker of doubt as his hand closed around hers. She looked to Gordan and he nodded, his promise bright in his violet gaze. She looked ahead, wondering what would have become of them if they had just accepted the roles this world tried to cast upon them. Perhaps everything would have been easier—to be the last fera groomed for purpose by her maker, to be the vile dragon Veil preferred to hate, to be a seer facing the future alone. But even now, Nicole could not bring herself to wish they had, not even when she supposed Mitchell would be alive in that world. She pulled her sword from the sheath on her back and they strode inside together.

"Watch for Tovar," Raiden said. "If he's still here, he's helping Venarius."

"What?" Nicole and Gordan reacted in unison.

"He reversed the palace spells," he explained.

"Right, as usual, Raiden."

They turned to see Tovar standing in the doorway, his back to them. Splinters floated up from the ground returning to the buckled doors as they straightened, closed, and sealed shut. Nicole tensed, jabbing her sword into the floor.

"I truly regret that it had to turn out this way," Tovar said turning to face them. "But I was a member of Dawn long before we became friends."

"We're clearly not friends."

"No? You're hesitating."

"I'm waiting," Raiden clarified.

A pulse of magic rolled through her sword and into the floor. Crystals shot up from the ground, glistening spikes, where Tovar stood. He lurched to the side, slipping through the ether and emerging a foot one way, two feet another way, narrowly avoiding the spears. And then he appeared right in front of Nicole so suddenly she couldn't react before his flat palm hit her sternum. She fell back, losing her grip on her sword and the crystals ceased sprouting as she slid across the floor. On her back gasping to fill empty lungs, she saw Raiden swing his sword, but Tovar was already gone—reappearing behind Raiden in the blink of an eye.

Gordan transformed and as suddenly as he lunged, his body shrank down into a miniature of himself small enough to be crushed under a shoe. Tovar had Raiden's sword now, holding the blade against Raiden's throat. Nicole ran for her sword still standing in the floor.

"Wrong way, *your highness*," Tovar said.

The corridor spun around her as she ran, and suddenly, she was running the opposite direction right at Mitchell, who stood there with that blank stare. Her heart seized and she lurched to a stop. Mitchell's body turned and walked toward the throne room. Nicole turned back, her sword was out of reach and Tovar looked at her expectantly, holding the sword under Raiden's jaw.

"Go on," Tovar insisted. "I won't hurt him so long as you go to Venarius alone."

"Liar," Raiden choked out. "Don't, Nicole," he strained to speak over the blade.

Her heart hammered as furiously as it could, knowing where Venarius was waiting, pulling on Mitchell's invisible strings. Bile crept up the back of her throat, and she glanced down a split second to see Gordan crawl onto her boot. She refused to let Venarius puppet her brother's body any longer, to dangle his death in front of her again and again. This was personal. She closed her eyes, her body trembled with the effort to stand still, the vigil's brew mixing with her magic into something unbelievable, a hum so loud she couldn't hear her own breathing.

She opened her eyes and glared at Tovar, letting her magic seep into the floor beneath her feet. "Fuck you, traitor."

A crystal spike erupted from the floor behind Tovar, piercing him in the back. The sword clattered to the floor and Raiden staggered away as Tovar gasped, still very much alive. Breathing heavily after holding his breath against the blade, Raiden picked up his sword and turned his bemused expression to her.

But she couldn't share in the victory. Her forehead crumpled. "I've got to," she said. She turned and ran for the throne room.

"Nicole!" Raiden shouted, sprinting after her, his footsteps echoing in the corridor but he was too far behind to catch her before she slipped inside the throne room and the door shut behind her.

Raiden knew he wasn't going to reach her. The door shut, and he threw himself against it, striking the stone with the butt of his fist. He pulled back and swung his sword, the blade glanced off, ringing in a shrill wobbling pitch. Raiden huffed, lowered his sword and stalked back down the corridor to Tovar, his breathing labored as he struggled to hold still on the crystal spear. Gordan was nowhere to be seen.

"We're going to set the palace spells right," Raiden said, his voice shaking with fury. He hadn't thought it possible to hate anyone more than Moira, the Council, or Venarius. But looking into the face of a man he called a friend when his loyalties belonged to Dawn all this time—Raiden's head pounded with vitriol and bile crawled up his throat.

Nicole crossed the throne room with long deliberate strides, her gaze shifting from Venarius to her brother's empty shell, and to another strange form like a blank mannequin without so much as a hint of facial features in its pale pink flesh.

Venarius smiled. "How lovely to see you again."

Nicole clenched her teeth together.

"Bein, dear, if you could do the honors."

Nicole looked around frantically, but a slender white arm reached around her, cold fingers catching her face in a vice, pressing her cheeks into her teeth and forcing her mouth open. Nicole threw her elbow back into Bein's stomach, caught her arm and heaved Bein's weight over her head, throwing her down to the floor. The look of crazed shock on Bein's upside down face as she lay there on her back almost made Nicole smile.

Venarius sighed. "We don't have all day. Surely you can handle this."

Bein picked herself up, furious breaths whistling in and out through her nose.

Nicole smiled. "Oh, I'm sorry, do people not usually treat you like that?"

Bein's face puckered into a scowl. Smug satisfaction curled on Nicole's mouth. Bein lunged at her, transforming in a blink, but Nicole leapt into the air just as quickly and Bein sailed beneath her. Nicole whirled around, but Bein caught her ankle and yanked her down, slamming Nicole into the floor. She felt the stone buckle beneath her. Her head rang. She knew her bones should be shattered, but her body hummed with powerful heat. When something scrambled free from the collar of her sweater. The tiny serpentine body leapt at Bein who shook her head, scratched and swatted at Gordan's diminished form until the spell that shrank him dissipated, and he ballooned to his true size.

He and Bein struggled, snapping and hissing, Bein twisting her long slender body around him until he was caught. Then he shifted into human form, slipping from her coils.

Nicole climbed out of the crater beneath her, her eyes locked on Gordan's match until the moment she straightened up face to face with Mitchell. His arm moved inhumanly fast—his hand clamped on her face, pushing her chin up and her mouth open. A bitter liquid filled her mouth and she coughed, trying to spit it out, but some of it made it down her throat and her stomach churned.

Mitchell released her and walked away. She spit and wiped her mouth, but she knew it wouldn't make much difference, the room around her was already wobbling.

"There, that wasn't so hard," Venarius said. "He's the perfect tool, isn't he?"

Nicole seethed, growing dizzier by the second, unable to keep Venarius steady in her sight. She turned her head and felt like the room was spinning violently as her eyes searched for Gordan. He had Bein's head trapped in his arms and she transformed, trying to pry herself free. They tumbled to the floor together. She transformed back into a dragon and so did he, on it went.

Nicole staggered, her head growing hot and her body heavy.

"Seeing as they're quite busy, you and I will have to get on with our business," Venarius said. "I've decided to make this easy on you."

"Fuck you," she spat, struggling to stay on her feet, feeling like she was on a pitching boat.

"That's precisely what I'm going to free you from. I'm giving your soul a new home, see?" He turned to the blank humanoid body standing beside him. It took a step forward, then another, walking toward her. "It's flesh and bone, but that's about it. You won't have to worry about the world around you anymore, or the people you can't seem to protect, or even who you are."

Her head dropped forward for a split second. She jerked it back up to see the faceless thing getting closer. She lost her balance and toppled to the floor.

"It's so easy to call a detached soul to an empty vessel," Venarius said. "That potion shouldn't take much longer. I believe you're familiar with it. The Council liked to use it—ironic, no? They banned necromancy and used it for themselves when it suited them."

"Gordan?" she called, giving in to the weight of her body and sinking to the floor. She just wanted to hear him.

"Your body doesn't have to go to waste either," he said. She felt his hand on her face. "It will make a nice pair with your brother to protect me from your friends. It's just so hard to destroy something you're fond of, isn't it?"

"No!" Gordan cried, and the sound turned into a roar, but it faded as her ears filled with a low hum. The vigil's brew and her magic buzzed in her head like a swarm of bees. Her heart raced, throbbing in her skull, a storm of rage. She burned, fire in her blood, a cleansing flood of white-hot light tearing through her in the sweetest agony she'd ever felt. She welcomed it. *Fine, let me burn.* She would gladly turn to ash, burn this palace into a hollow black shell if she could take him with her and end it. Heat cascaded through her, poured out of her, she became the fire, she swelled and burst—rolling through the room.

Then she opened her eyes to see the ceiling above her. The room wasn't spinning. She sat up—her head was clear and steady. Every cell in her body still ringing with pain, but the nauseating creep of the potion was gone, her veins scorched clean of it.

Venarius and looked down at the blank body sprawled on the floor—twitch of the arm, tiny jerk of the head. He let out an angry groan through the snarl on his face. Nicole heaved her body off the floor, standing tall and staring him down defiantly.

Venarius breathed heavily, glaring back at her, his clothes disheveled by her outburst.

"Fine—a trade then," he said breathily. "Return the journal to me, and I'll return your brother to you."

Even if she still had the journal, he wasn't the kind to give in so easily. A trade would be a defeat to someone like him; he would bring Mitchell back just to make her suffer again. A bitter smile pulled at her lips.

"I burned the journal—it's *gone.*"

He took several careful breaths, composing himself. "Since it seems you can overcome the Death's Door potion, and ruined any chance of starting over, I suppose I'll just have free your soul the hard way…and wait however long it takes for it to come back." He waved his hand and Mitchell's body picked itself up from the floor.

At the sight of her brother rushing her, her heart clenched and she backed away. The urge to plead with him died in her throat and she choked, trying to find her resolve to destroy this empty shell of her brother so that Venarius couldn't degrade him anymore. *That's not Mitchell*, she reminded herself as he advanced, swinging his arm at her. *That's not my brother,* she ducked and jabbed her knuckles into his ribs to no avail.

He kept coming. She kept hitting, but no hook or uppercut phased him. She knew she had to—she threw both palms into his chest and they burned through his shirt. At the sound of his skin hissing beneath her hands she recoiled, she couldn't reduce her brother to ashes even though he wasn't there in those eyes anymore. His hands caught her head, but someone crashed into Mitchell, and all three hit the ground. Nicole rolled free and looked on in shock to see the faceless human form wrestling Mitchell to the floor.

"Nicole," Gordan cried out and she looked to him, doing all he could to detain Bein.

Venarius stepped into the ether and appeared across the room, catching her throat in his hands. "I'll do it myself," he said through his teeth.

She grabbed his wrists, but when she tried to push her magic through her hands and into him nothing happened.

He laughed, squeezing her neck tighter. "Do you think I'm foolish enough to deal with you unprotected? Magic won't work this time. So much for all that power."

She threw her arms up between his, breaking his hold at the wrists, and shoved the butt of her palm into his face. His nose broken, he staggered back a step, laughing.

"I made you what you are," he said and licked his lips then wiped at the stream of blood flowing over his mouth. "I gave you the power you have. And it's made you arrogant. Did you think you defied Death? Do you think it makes you strong, breaking the rules like a petulant child? Your defiance has only brought pain and hardship to everyone around you."

He motioned around the throne room, to Mitchell's body pulling the faceless form to pieces and to Gordan caught in human form beneath Bein's claws as she pressed him into the floor—he was unable to transform this time—was he too exhausted?

He clicked his tongue at her.

"Let's see how well that arrogance serves you this time."

Raiden appeared out of the ether. "Nicole!"

But a bloody grin spread across Venarius' face, and the throne room pitched. She lurched forward, face first into the dark waters between Life and Death. It wasn't like before—she was being dragged, pulled down so fast she could only hold on to the line anchored in her heart. She knew who was drawing her into the depths, an unfortunate fish on her lifeline.

"Welcome back," Venarius said as he pulled the glowing white tether to her heart hand over fist. She wrapped her hand around the rope of light and tried to pull it back from his hands, but he stood on solid black ground while she kicked and floundered in the water, trying to pull her lifeline free from his grasp.

"Tsk, tsk," he said, shaking his head. "Look what you've done to your lifeline." He released a little slack and smiled as she dropped below the surface, her pounding heart drumming in her head.

She pulled harder on her line, but his grip held firm and her arms felt weak. Splashing crashed around her ears but couldn't drown out Venarius' snide words.

"Defiant as ever. Fight as long as you like, wash away your memories."

She faltered, her heart tripping on the fear of forgetting Raiden or Gordan—

"What could you be forgetting, Nicole—the reason you're fighting, your loved ones? Better yet, forget who you are completely and solve my problem." He sneered.

She pulled on her lifeline, she kicked and clawed at the water—she had to get out, but it refused to solidify. Her body was heavy. She could only think of life, of everyone she was going to lose if she didn't win this fight.

"Hey!" A figure charged out of the mists, tackling Venarius to the ground—her lifeline gaining slack as they fell.

I know him!—she slipped down into the water but lurched to a stop. Her heart clenched painfully at the sight of that familiar face. She dragged herself up to the surface along the jerking white line, still anchored in Venarius' grip as he struggled with the young man.

"You're more trouble dead than you were alive," Venarius growled, producing his knife.

The sight of the black blade ripped through her fears. She remembered—Venarius pulling that knife across his throat—*Mitchell!* Nicole burned—suddenly much lighter—and heaved herself out of the dark water which turned to glass beneath her. She wrapped her lifeline around her forearm and hand.

A rich horn notes clashed with the rattle and moan of ringing brass rods as Venarius and Mitchell grappled she was jerked forward by her lifeline. She landed on her hands and knees. Delicate white cracks sprouted from beneath her hands. *How do I end this?* Her gaze shifted from the spreading web of cracks to her hand and the glowing white tether wrapped around it. *Lifeline*—he had to have one. She picked herself up, searching for a glimpse of red light, but there was no chord linked to his heart. Then she spotted it—Venarius' lifeline—floating behind him, a black chord emitting an eerie light like Life had no sway over him. Venarius slashed at Mitchell's face, leaving a vivid red line across his cheek and jarring Nicole from her mystified stare. Mitchell knocked the knife from his hand. The blade went sliding across the black glass toward the curling mist.

She gasped and pitched forward after the knife.

Then from somewhere in the mists there came a distant wailing that struck her memory like a dissonant chord and sent a chill through her. She lunged for the black knife—a slender double-sided blade set into a carved bone handle—but she was wrenched off course by a hard pull on her lifeline. She yanked back on the white tether, fighting to reach the handle of the blade, her feet slipping on the glass.

Another furious wail warbled through the mists, and a familiar chilling melody crawled through the atmosphere—Amarth was coming.

Venarius pulled on her lifeline, dragging her back, away from the knife. Craning her neck she looked back at him, grappling with Mitchell while straining to keep his eyes on her and deter her from the knife. She dared to let her tether unwind from her hand, giving herself the slack she needed. She dove for the knife and her hand closed around the handle. Then the mists churned and the glass trembled—a shudder that moved through her bones. She scrambled to her feet as the towering twisted form crept—hunched—out of the haze, its eyes scanning the mists. The faint cover she had parted and Amarth's eyes locked onto her.

"Nicole!" Mitchell shouted.

Venarius let out a crazed laugh.

She turned and ran, spotting them ahead of her—so much farther away than she remembered. Mitchell had Venarius' arms locked against his back and leaned hard on him—grinding his face into his own reflection in the black glass.

"You can't run from the monsters you create," Venarius laughed.

The beast shrieked. It surged toward them fracturing the glass under its furious claws. Her thundering heart filled her ears as she ran—racing the spreading cracks back to Mitchell. The floor shattered around them and the level plane beneath them buckled. Mitchell was thrown off his feet and Venarius crawled away. She fell—the knife tumbled from her grasp. The knife slid toward Venarius as Nicole scrambled after it. Churning mists rolled in around them and she felt blindly for the blade—she knew it was just ahead of her as she fumbled over the uneven glass. Her heart reeled as her hand seized the knife, but Venarius' hand clamped around hers and pulled. He dragged her underneath him. The air shivered with the dissonant ringing of metal rods—the sound seemed to come from his gaze, his movement, his smile.

"You see, Nicole," he breathed in her face, pushing her hand and the knife toward her. "You cannot change what you were *made* to be." He yanked hard on her lifeline and she cried out in pain, her heart rending in her chest. "I will keep coming for you," he said, forcing the blade in her own hand toward her taught lifeline as she fought. He leaned over her.

Nicole scowled, contracting her core in a sudden thrust—the crown of her head slammed into Venarius' face. He reeled back with a grunt. Amarth bellowed in the mists—searching—a single high note rang in the air, sharp and thin like a wire about to snap, cutting into her thoughts.

Then Venarius lurched and the snarl on his face turned to flat shock, "Wh—"

Nicole twisted her wrist, breaking her hand from his grip and freeing the knife. She scrambled out from under him, his lifeline straight as a bow-string, pulling him back as he strained against it, dropping her glowing tether to reach futilely for his own. Jumping to her feet she lunged around him, beyond his reach. Her fist trembled angrily around the handle of the knife as she caught it on the glowing black tether behind Venarius. She pulled and the blade down. His lifeline severed with a snap. Venarius fell forward crashing through the broken glass and into the waters.

Her ears rang in the sudden silence. Was he really gone? Nicole wobbled on the crumbling surface under her feet as the waters rose around her ankles. She forced shallow breaths in and out of her lungs through her disbelief. She turned—her steps splashing—searching the mists for any sign of her brother.

"Mitch?" she called into the mists and her heart quickened in fear when a guttural moan answered her. Her lifeline tugged at her, only it didn't pull her down into the water. A vicious shrieking note rang around her, throttling her thoughts.

She screamed—hoisted into the air—swinging—grasping at her lifeline to lessen the force pulling at her heart. Her body swung and she gasped at the massive twisted visage that leaned in close. The knife was still in her right hand and she gripped it fiercely as Amarth's face drew nearer.

"Why would he die for you?" his deep growl rattled in his throat.

Nicole gritted her teeth and plunged the black blade into Amarth's monstrous eye. An ear-splitting screech cut through the mist and she fell—crashing through the crumbling glass, into dark water…and silence.

☧

Nausea struck Raiden when Venarius' head dropped back, but he remained standing while Nicole collapsed to the floor. Raiden dropped to his knees beside her, easing her gingerly onto her back.

"Gordan," he called, helplessly, disturbed by the uncanny statuesque presence of Venarius standing there before them, looking blankly up to the sky.

From over his shoulder he saw Gordan struggling to restrain the porcelain woman, hissing and kicking in her elegant red dress. Her form expanded. Red silk split. Gordan's clasped hands broke and she escaped his arms—her true form whipping through the throne room—flying toward the ceiling.

Bein burst through the crystal pane of the oculus. Raiden

flinched, bending over Nicole, shielding her as the shattered skylight rained down on them. When he looked up, he saw a ribbon of glistening scales undulating into the blue. Gordan staggered to Raiden's side—bent over his knees—gasping beside him for a moment.

"Gordan, she's—" Raiden shook his head and took a steadying breath. "What do we do?"

"There nothing we *can*—"

"No! That's not—There has to be *something* we—" the words caught in his throat as he looked down at her. "I just got her back."

"Raiden," Gordan began solemnly, placing a hand on Raiden's shoulder—then Venarius crumpled to the floor.

Their gazes snapped together, faces mirrored—eyes wide, mouths slack.

Raiden peered back at Venarius, "Is he…?"

Gordan nodded, "Dead."

They both looked down at Nicole. Raiden gathered her into his arms, "Nicole?" If Venarius was dead then surely, she wasn't. She would be back…any second. Raiden swallowed the doubt in his throat.

A hoarse gasp cut through the silence of the throne room, but Nicole remained utterly motionless—it hadn't been her. Raiden and Gordan looked up—eyes searching—and found Mitchell rolling onto his hands and knees, coughing.

"Mitch?" Raiden uttered in disbelief.

Gordan stood frozen, his mouth slack as his breathing quickened.

"Where's Nicole?" Mitchell gasped as he fought his way to his feet only to sink back to the floor.

Gordan's breath shuddered from his lungs and he stumbled forward, sagging down beside Mitchell and taking his face in his hands. Raiden watched—relieved, dumbfounded, and heartbroken—as Gordan studied Mitchell's face—there was a fresh red slice across his cheekbone. Mitchell smiled feebly back at Gordan.

Gordan shook his head, "How are you here?"

"The last thing I remember is grabbing that asshole's lifeline to pull him off Nicole. The next thing I know I'm being dragged through the water—suddenly I'm here, with the worst hangover of a lifetime," Mitchell answered, his voice heavy. "Ugh, my head's killing me, but the rest of me feels numb."

Gordan helped Mitchell onto his feet and into an embrace.

"Where's Nicole?" Mitchell asked again, his view of her blocked by Gordan.

Raiden's face crumpled. "She's right here, but…she hasn't returned."

"What?!" Mitchell stumbled forward, dropping to his knees beside Nicole, cradled in Raiden's lap. He looked around, spotted Venarius, then looked back to Gordan. "They're still there?"

"Venarius is dead," Gordan clarified.

"Then why isn't she here?" Mitchell demanded.

Raiden sighed, "The flow of time in Death fluctuates."

"What does that even mean?"

"Mitchell," Gordan said gently. "Do you remember when Nicole came to get me?"

"Yes."

"To her she was only moments behind me. But she didn't return until almost two weeks after I made it back," Gordan explained.

"Two *weeks*?!"

"There's no telling how much time will pass before she returns," Raiden added. "It could be two days…or—"

Nicole lurched upright, gasping.

Raiden froze. Mitchell fell back in surprise. Gordan lunged to her side.

She blinked and let out a trembling breath, staring ahead in a daze.

"Nicole?" Gordan intoned, crouched beside Mitchell.

Raiden touched her face and she looked at him. "My head's spinning," she said, scrunching her eyes closed. "Are you okay?"

He let out a relieved breath through his smile—she just fought her way back from Death and, of course, she was worried if he was okay. "I am…now that you're back," he said.

"Gordan, are you—" She turned her gaze to find Mitchell there beside her. Her face pinched in confusion. "Mitch?"

"Hey," he answered.

She raised her trembling hands and touched his face. "You're really here?"

"Yeah." He nodded. "I'm here."

She pulled her hands back, covering her mouth as the sobs came. "You promise?" her words shook and she reached for him.

"Promise," he said, closing his arms around her. "I'm here," he repeated softly.

She held her brother fiercely, her arms shaking with effort. Raiden's heart ached for her as she succumbed to everything she'd locked inside so that she could keep going. Gordan's face was knotted, Nicole's pain streaming from his pinched eyes. Her sobs—even muffled in Mitchell's chest—filled the throne room…until, at last, they shrank away into short staccato breaths.

She took a shaky breath. "I thought Amarth caught you back there," she confessed, sniffling.

"No—I almost lost you and Venarius in the mists. I grabbed his lifeline to pull him off you but then I was yanked into the water. What happened back there?" Mitchell asked.

Nicole released him. "I cut his lifeline," she said.

"Then…you're here because you stole a necromancer's lifeline," Gordan mused.

"Wow," Mitchell shook his head. "That's kinda gross. He's not, like…a part of me now, is he?"

Gordan let out a single silent laugh and brushed Mitchell's cheek with the back of his hand, "No. There's not a trace of that man here. You're entirely you."

Raiden saw troubling memories lingering in Nicole's eyes. "What happened after you cut his lifeline?" he wondered.

She shook her head. "Nothing, really. Amarth was close, but my lifeline pulled me back. That's it."

Raiden stood and helped Nicole to her feet. Gordan helped Mitchell to his. When Gordan absently placed his hand on

Mitchell's chest, he winced. Gordan pulled his hand away as Mitchell inhaled through his teeth and dropped his chin to look down. There was a large hole burned in his tunic revealing two pink hand-shaped burns and an array of blooming bruises.

"Guess it takes a while for the body to wake up when you've been dead for a month," he chuckled, cringing. "You sure didn't pull any punches, Nikki."

Nicole's face twisted in mortification. "I'm so sorry!"

"Don't be," he said, reaching for her and hooking one arm around her neck. "I'm so goddamn proud of you," he said softly, letting out an airy laugh.

She huffed with a smile. "At least let me fix it…"

A distant muffled voice yelled from outside the doors of the throne room. "Raiden!?"

The doors moaned open—Loak, Leone and Caeruleus pushed into the room. They stopped, stunned for a moment by what they found. Nicole, Mitchell, Raiden and Gordan gathered in the center of the grand room, Venarius dead behind them, shattered crystal sparkling across the cratered floor.

A bated breath fell from Leone's mouth and he crossed the room to catch his son in his arms. Raiden clapped his arms around his father. Leone released him and Raiden laughed, throwing his arms gratefully around Caeruleus. Then Raiden noticed the people filing in. King Eisen's towering troops, their own palace guards, members of the staff singed and blood-spattered from joining the fight— Gwyn smiling among them.

A gold flash bolted across the room and up Nicole's leg. The little glistening dragon's breath reclaiming its keeper, settling around Nicole's neck. Gazes fell to the body on the floor and the silence in the vast room brimmed with the electricity of triumph.

"It's really over," Mitchell said, placing his hand thoughtfully against his chest.

"Yeah," Nicole breathed and a baffled smile spread across her face.

Raiden took her hand and held it tight, "You're free now." *We're free*—he realized, his heart suddenly racing blissfully. They were at the threshold of everything that had seemed beyond their reach.

She took a deep breath and shook her head. "Not quite," she murmured to him, looking down and pulling the key out from beneath her shirt.

That's right, his heart sank and he felt the weight of every gaze in the room on Nicole and him.

Nicole looked to Gordan. "I know you didn't want the Dragon King's legacy," she said to him as she pulled the key off. In the silence her words filled the room without effort. "You ended the dragon wars, Gordan. This is your legacy, *not* mine." She held out her key.

Gordan's face pinched and he held out his hand. Nicole placed the key on his palm and closed his fingers around it.

"Which do you prefer, 'your *highness*' or 'your *majesty*?'" Mitchell inquired in his ear with a slyly curled mouth.

Nicole glanced at Raiden, half a smile on her face.

Raiden nodded and pulled Nicole close to him, "You know what I think Veil needs?"

Murmurs percolated through the room as Raiden pulled his key off and held it out to Mitchell.

"You're joking," Mitchell accused skeptically.

"Not in the slightest," Raiden assured him.

Mitchell cocked his head, considering the white quartz key in Raiden's hand. He looked to Gordan who pulled the chord of the amethyst key around his neck. "You wanna rule the realm together?"

Gordan smiled.

"I do," Mitchell said, taking the key from Raiden and placing it around his neck.

"Look," Caeruleus nodded toward the thrones and the collective murmur went silent as all eyes fell on the two crystal-hewn seats.

The thrones swelled with light, as did every crystal vein in the floor, the ceiling, the walls, and the pillars around them. Light flooded the room to a chorus of gasps—it filled their eyes and washed the world away for a pure blinding moment before it faded, leaving everyone to blink the stunned stupor from their pupils.

Loak broke the silence with his gravely whisper. "What in the skies was that?"

The silence grew heavy with every set of eyes that echoed Loak's question.

"I think the palace has accepted its new kings," Leone answered.

They exchanged glances and unspoken questions. Nicole and Raiden shared a look of unbelievable relief. Raiden looked to Gordan and Mitchell, their gazes locked and hands clasped.

"Well, then," Caeruleus nodded. "To the kings," he said, raising his voice as much as he could. The silent hall made up for his strained volume, carrying his words up to the ceiling and out the doors.

A roaring chorus cheered back, "To the kings!"

Mitchell grinned and Gordan smiled timidly amid in the boisterous flood of approval. Mitchell raised their joined hands. Raiden pulled Nicole as close as he could, the thought of letting her go an unbelievable concept to him now.

In Keren's cottage in the orchard, Nicole stepped out of the little bathroom, shaking her curls dry with a little magic. She was relieved to have the weight of her long hair gone again after cutting more than half of it away—now it bounced between her jawline and her shoulders. Her fingertips came away pink from her freshly dyed scalp. She had been awake for the last two days—body humming and brimming with magic—the vigil's brew still thrumming in her veins, stoking the euphoria of freedom into a strange, delirious high. Venarius was gone and she could finally go home.

She skipped down the stairs of Keren's house, smiling at the absence of a key bounding against her stomach. Nicole, ruler of Veil was no more.

"Wow," Fen gasped at her arrival to the living room.

"Aw, I liked your pretty silver hair," Asi said.

Nicole smiled. "It will be there when the pink grows out." She knew because she already tried—coaxing her magic into her scalp until her hair grew inch after white inch. The change was lasting and every time she had spotted her reflection, she caught herself wondering if there might be some other effect to her lifeline turning white. Raiden couldn't give her an answer, despite his time reading a necromancer's text on Death when he was back in Atrium. She had shared her lifeline with Gordan, that was all she knew—and that Amarth warned she would regret it. Her white hair in the mirror only reminded her of that nagging uncertainty—thus, she dyed it and the reminder disappeared under the bright prospect of countless possibilities. She could dye her hair any color she wanted, she could be any*body* she wanted because 'fera' and its purpose died with Venarius. *No more fera. No more king. Just Nicole now*, she thought.

She changed the subject eagerly, "Is the door gone yet?"

"Let's see," Fen opened the door that lead to Nicole's—now Gordan's—chamber back in the palace of the keys, but instead of opening to the palace it opened to a wall. "Gone," Fen declared.

"Are you going back today, Nicole?" Asi asked.

"I am," she said. "I'm meeting the guys at the manor. Raiden is setting up the new door to the palace so Mitch and Gordan can come and go."

"What will you do when you get back to the old world?" Fen wondered.

"Figure out how to salvage my senior year of high school," Nicole answered with sigh.

Keren loped down the stairs, her long hair swinging. "Well, the garden sure loves having you here, Nicole—honestly a little too much. The roof might cave in if this keeps up."

"Sorry," Nicole chuckled anxiously, she couldn't keep her magic contained with the vigil's brew in her system—her magic was on overdrive. "I'll get out of your hair."

"Not for too long, I hope," Keren said.

"No, not for long," she agreed, reaching toward the fire place for Gim, who scurried onto her hand, up her arm and around her neck before she stepped into the ether with Raiden on her mind.

She stepped out of the air into the foyer of the manor, her eyes in awe, eager to sweep the room. She took a step back and bumped against Raiden behind her.

"Oh," he turned around as she did. "Hello," he said—eyes widening at the sight of her wild watermelon-pink hair. His stunned mouth curled into a smile before he caught her in his arms.

"Do you like it?"

He pulled her mouth to his eagerly and a laugh passed from her lips to his.

"I'll take that as a 'yes,'" she declared.

He touched one of her pink spirals curiously, and she lost herself for a moment in his blue-green eyes. His glasses made her smile wider.

"What?" he inquired.

"Nothing," she shrugged, pulling him down by the collar of his hoodie to kiss him again.

"Knock knock—who's ready to go home?" Mitchell's voice filled the silence. The drumming of four feet descending the stairs to the foyer pushed her heart into an excited rhythm. The thrill of going home made her a little dizzy—or it was the vigil's brew, she didn't know anymore. She just knew she couldn't wait to go back any longer. She stepped out of the foyer to meet them at the bottom of the stairs—Mitchell and Gordan each wearing their key.

"Whoa," Mitchell spotted her hair. "Where'd my sister go?"

"Who the hell knows," she said with a laugh and a shrug, incapable of sinking into the very real uncertainty beneath her words with the hum of the potion in her head and her veins. She saw the three of them exchange glances and pretended not to notice. "Can we go now?"

"Let's," Gordan said, taking Mitchell's hand. "Take us home." He held out his other hand and she took it to pull them into the ether.

Gordan sighed as they emerged from the ether on to the empty Cantis street. It was a clear day, the air crisp and bright with the scent of life in bloom—Spring at last. Nicole was still buzzing; Gordan could feel the vigil's brew through their clasped hands like a fever. He feared how hard she would crash from this high when the potion finally wore off. Her hand slipped from his and she skipped eagerly toward the gate at the edge of the little yard, there was a buoyancy in her stride like she was barely earthbound at all. Her pink curls swung as she looked back, amber eyes bright, cheeks flushed with enthusiasm.

"How much longer is she going to be the energizer bunny?" Mitchell asked, real worry in his quiet voice.

Gordan squeezed Mitchell's hand to quell his concern. His gaze lingered on the red scar across Mitchell's cheekbone—the mark made in Death by a necromancer's blade, it matched the long scar across his throat.

Raiden sighed as they followed her through the gate. "I had to give her three vigil's brews to wake her after we made it out of the palace. Her own magic could end up prolonging the effects. Maybe in another day or so, it should wear off." He trailed off and Gordan could feel the air around Raiden get heavier.

Gordan understood Raiden's concern. Beneath the potion-intensified elation of her victory and having Mitchell back, the damage that had been done these past few months was still there. Victory didn't erase all she had endured—not even Mitchell's return erased the scars of his loss. Gordan was guiltily grateful that he had not witnessed it himself—he knew Nicole would never forget that day or any of the harrowing trails behind her. For now, at least, she was alive and vibrant again—her joy was contagious. At least she would have a safe place to heal and she would have them.

"What's going on at the palace, *your highnesses?*" she asked, turning to bow to them and turning back to the front door in a fluid pirouette.

"Still cleaning," Gordan confessed. "Dragon blood can be a bit of a challenge."

"We can't have a coronation party with blood on the walls," Mitchell remarked sarcastically as Nicole opened the door.

"Actually...that's precisely how my first coronation was held," Gordan said.

Mitchell choked, "What?"

Gordan smiled. Nicole and Raiden laughed.

Mitchell bit his lip and shook his head, "Marry me."

Gordan could sense only deep sincerity behind the sly smile on Mitchell's face, but all he could do was follow them inside, dumbfounded, his heart reeling.

They all stopped in the dim, dust-shrouded living room, taking in the scene—tattered curtains, peeling wallpaper, and obliterated staircase lying in a pile of debris—the forlorn vestige of a home. Nicole took a deep breath and huffed. She waved her hand at the destruction and her magic rolled through the air. The little house rattled. The mound of broken wood trembled, lifted and twisted back into the staircase it had been long ago. The current of energy mended what was tattered and torn. It swept away the dust and cobwebs of a lonely decade. Nicole didn't hardly miss a beat, her stride surging forward again. She caught Raiden's hand and pulled him up the stairs before he could shake himself from the resurrection of his childhood home.

Gordan could feel her heart rate accelerate, pulsing through the air, as their feet thumped against the steps.

"Hold up, Nikki," Mitchell complained, pulling Gordan up the stairs as he hurried after his sister. "Wait for us."

They reached the landing when Nicole and Raiden stopped at his bedroom door. The hinges whined.

"Dad," she called as Gordan and Mitchell moved down the hall to join them. "We're home."

Thank you!

Thank you so much to my Patreon patrons who have supported my creative endeavors! Sarah Logan, Kristin Marie Gunsch, Zahra Garcia, Eric Schuck, Leticia Villa, and—of course—my mom Susan and my sisters Amanda and Renee. There will be so much more magic to come—thanks to your support.

Find C.C. Rae at

TikTok @chaoticalsea

Instagram @chaoticalsea

patreon.com/chaoticalsea

www.chaoticalsea.com